Reader's Digest

Reader's Digest

VOLUME 3 1997
THE READER'S DIGEST ASSOCIATION, INC.
PLEASANTVILLE, NEW YORK

READER'S DIGEST

Editor-in-Chief, Books & Home Entertainment: Barbara J. Morgan
Editor, U.S. Condensed Books: Tanis H. Erdmann

CONTENTS

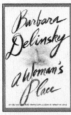

A Woman's Place

Barbara Delinsky

Claire Raphael has managed
everything so well. Marriage, children,
a thriving business—somehow she has
kept it all together. Until now.

For now, out of the blue, Claire's
world has been turned upside down.

And suddenly she is wondering
how she will ever rebuild her life—
find her place as a woman.

Chapter 1

HAD I been a superstitious sort, I would have seen the smell as an omen. I had wanted the morning of our leave-taking to be smooth and was down to the wire. The last thing I needed was Dennis annoyed.

But I was a trusting soul. Entering the kitchen that October Friday, I sensed nothing of the broader picture. All I knew was that something had gone bad. A rank smell sullied what should have been the sweetness of fall—the scent of crisp leaves drifting in from the backyard, a basket of newly picked Macouns.

I checked under the sink, but the air there was fine. Nothing hit me when I opened the refrigerator. Still, I checked the milk, the chicken that was ready for Dennis to eat while we were gone, the cheese bin, where plastic wrap might hide something fuzzy and blue.

Nothing.

But the offensive odor remained, another glitch in a week of glitches. With a husband, two children, and a career to juggle, preparing to go away was always a challenge, but I was going away for eleven days this time, in part on a dreaded mission. My mother was dying. My equilibrium was shaky, well without glitches.

Having ruled out the obvious, I was beginning to wonder if something wasn't rotting under the two-hundred-year-old floorboards of the house, when my son padded in, in his stockinged feet. He looked more sober than any nine-year-old with mussed hair, an authentic Red Sox baseball shirt, and battered jeans should look, but he was a serious child under any conditions, and perceptive. Much as I had tried to minimize the meaning of our trip, I suspected he knew.

He made a face. "*Peewww.* What stinks?"

I slid him a despairing glance. "Good question. Any ideas?"

"Ask Kikit. She's the one always leaving things lying around. Are you sure I'll be home in time for practice Tuesday?"

"The plane lands at one. Football practice isn't until five."

"If I miss practice, I'll be benched."

I took his face in my hands. His cheeks were boy-smooth. "The only way you'll miss practice is if the flight is delayed, in which case Daddy or I will talk with the man—"

"It's a rule," Johnny broke in, and took a step back. "No practice, no play. I can't find my sneakers. Where are they?"

"On the landing in the garage. Want something to eat? Brody will be here in forty-five minutes." Silence. He was through the mudroom and into the garage. I used the pause to shout upstairs for my youngest. "Kikit?"

"She's moving the menagerie from her bedroom to the den," my husband announced, tossing the morning *Globe* onto the table. "Does she really need all those stuffed things?" He sniffed and screwed up his face. "What's that?"

The question was worse coming from Dennis. In the overall scheme of our marriage, the house was my responsibility. But I couldn't hunt more now. I just didn't have the time. "It may be a rat. The exterminator rebaited some of the basement traps."

Johnny ran through with a pithy "Gross."

His sneakers left a trail of dried dirt, but there wasn't time for remopping, either. "Eggs, Dennis?"

"Maybe. I don't know." He sat down and opened the paper.

I said gently, "Eggs, yes or no? I have forty minutes to be cleaned up, packed, and gone."

"What about that smell? I can't live with it for eleven days."

"It may go away on its own," I prayed. "If not, give the exterminator a call. His number is on the board."

"But I won't be here to let him in. I'm leaving right after you do to meet the Ferguson group in the Berkshires. That was the whole problem with driving you to the airport." He shot me a disparaging look. "I can't believe you messed up with the service."

"I didn't. I don't know what happened, Dennis. I booked the airport run two weeks ago and have the confirmation number to prove it. They say I called and canceled last week. But I didn't. If I hadn't called to check a little while ago, we'd be waiting an hour from now for a ride that isn't coming. Lucky thing Brody can take us. And as for the smell"—I tried to keep calm—"have the exterminator come when you get back."

I reached for the egg tray. Just as I took it out, skipping footsteps came from behind, then the voice of seven-year-old Clara Kate. "Mommy, I'm taking Travis, Michael, and Joy, okay?" She gazed up at me with an angel's face framed by a barretted mass of chestnut curls. My own hair was the same color, though the curl had long since fallen prey to scissors and a blow-dryer.

Hooking an arm around her neck, I held her close while I beat eggs. "I thought we agreed you'd only bring two."

Her cheek moved against my arm. "Well, I said I would, but which one can I leave? They're always together, those three. Besides, I want them to see Auntie Rona, and they'll cheer Grandma up. What's her hospital like?"

"I don't know. I haven't seen it."

"Is it all shiny and noisy, like mine?"

"Only the parts that treat little girls who have allergic reactions to things they're not supposed to eat."

"Can Grandma talk?"

"Of course she can." I opened a pack of shredded cheddar and offered it to her.

She took a fistful. "Will she have tubes in her nose?"

"No. I told you that last night."

She put the fist to her mouth and, nibbling cheese, ducked free of my arm. "Daddy, why aren't you coming with us?"

"You know why," he said from behind the paper. "I have to work."

"If you have to work," she asked, "why'd you put your golf clubs in the car?"

I whisked together shredded cheddar and eggs, but softly.

"Because," Dennis said, "I'm playing golf after I work."

"Are you meeting us at the plane on Tuesday?"

"Yes."

"The airport's really big, so how will you know where to go?"

"I'll know where to go," he said.

"He'll be there to meet you," I called as she hopped from the room. I poured the egg mixture into a skillet, pushed the toaster down. "The flight information is on the board," I told Dennis. "The Cleveland numbers are there, too, and, after the kids get back, who's taking who where on what day, with phone numbers."

The newspaper went down; his chair scraped back. He went to the board by the phone and made a grunting sound.

"What?" I asked.

"Same old same old. We need a nanny. I know you say we do better without"—he tossed an impatient hand at the board—"but that list of who's taking who where and when is a joke. Even when you're home, things get hairy. Remember last week?"

How could I forget? I had kept Kikit and her friends waiting an hour after ballet when the store in Essex, where I had been working at the time, lost electricity, and the clocks stopped.

"You're overextended," said the die-hard pessimist.

"I'm not," said the die-hard optimist, "as long as you help."

"It'd be simpler to hire someone to drive the kids around."

"They'd hate it," I said, scrambling the eggs. "They want us. *I* want us. Besides, we have a sitter for emergencies—Mrs. Gimble."

"She doesn't drive."

"She lives two doors away and loves the kids. Dennis"—I waited for him to look up from the paper—"you'll be at Johnny's game Saturday, won't you?"

"If I can."

Oh, he could. The issue was whether he would. "He'll be heart-broken if you aren't there."

"If something comes up and I can't be there, I can't. I'm running a business, too, Claire."

I couldn't forget that either, not with him reminding me so often. Nor could I point out that with his business a shadow of its former self, he had time to parent if he chose, because that would put him on the defensive. This wasn't the time to travel that road again. I simply needed to know that the children would have Dennis's full attention while I was gone.

The toast popped up. I buttered both slices, cornered them on a plate, slid the eggs into the center, and slipped the plate into the gap between the paper and Dennis. Then I set to scrubbing the skillet. "The game is at ten Saturday morning. Plan business around it. Please? Johnny needs one of us to see him play."

"I said I'd try," Dennis warned. "What *is* that smell?" He shoved the paper aside, pushed back his chair, and started banging cabinets open and shut. "Your mind has been everywhere but here lately. You must have put something where it didn't belong."

It was possible. But I didn't expect him to find anything in the cabinets. They had been thoroughly cleaned the week before.

"Here," he said with disgust. "Get rid of this."

A reeking baggy landed in the sink. It contained half of a decaying onion. I had no idea how it had ended up in a cabinet, but when I looked questioningly at Dennis, he was backing away from the stench.

I disposed of the onion. "See?" I said on an up note. "You're good at finding things. Much better than me."

He shot me an irritated look before returning to his breakfast.

BRODY arrived thirty minutes later. He talked business with Dennis while I finished packing, made the beds, and slipped into a suit. It had gray pants, an ivory vest, and an apricot jacket, and would be perfect for my business travel following my stay in Cleveland. More, my mother would love it. She loved fine things, loved the sight of them on her daughters, and understandably so. She had known hard times and was pleased they were past.

Once Dennis had been hugged and kissed and left waving on the front porch of our Cape Cod Georgian, which wasn't on the Cape at all but in a small township just north of Gloucester, we joined the Boston commuters and headed for Logan Airport.

Settling into the seat of Brody's Range Rover, I exhaled.

"Tired?" he asked softly.

I smiled and nodded. Yes, I was tired. And worried. I was also, at that moment, relieved to have Dennis behind me. He hated my traveling, saw it as an imposition on our lives, even in spite of my attempts to minimize the inconvenience. Actually, he hadn't been too difficult this time. Maybe he was mellowing. Or feeling bad about my mother. Whatever, there hadn't been any major explosions.

"You're a peach to drive us to the airport," I said, turning my head against the headrest. Brody, the CEO of my company, was as easy on the eye as he was on the mind—light brown hair, wire-rimmed glasses over deeper brown eyes still soft from sleep. He was loose and laid-back, a welcome balm.

"My pleasure," he said. "By the way, I think Dennis is onto something with the Ferguson deal. The company has solid management and megabrains. It just needs a little money to work with. If Dennis can arrange that, he may have a winner."

I hoped so. He had had too few of them of late, which made my own success with WickerWise more difficult for him.

"I should get the St. Louis franchise contracts back today," Brody went on in his competent way. "Once the franchisee is locked in, I can hire a builder for the renovation work. I'll have that information faxed to your hotel. Do you have the design plans?"

I touched the briefcase by my leg. "Hard to believe this is franchise number twenty-eight."

It had been twelve years since the first WickerWise had opened. That flagship store still operated out of an abandoned fire station in Essex, a short fifteen-minute drive from the house. It had become the model for a chain of stores that stretched from Nantucket to Seattle. We kept a tight rein on our franchises, Brody and I. All were in freestanding buildings—old schoolhouses, abandoned general stores, even a retired church or two. That was part of the charm. The rest came from the internal design, based on our central plan, and the presentation of the wicker furniture we sold. Brody and I controlled that, too. One of us directed the opening of each franchise and revisited twice yearly.

Twenty-eight franchises, another dozen boutiques in upscale deparment stores, a wicker plant in Pennsylvania—it boggled my mind. I had potted a tiny plant, and it was blooming wildly.

"Know where we're going?" Kikit asked Brody.

"Cleveland, I believe," he answered, ever so patient, though we both knew what was to come.

"You ever been there?"

"You know I have, Clara Kate," he dutifully said. "I went to college in Cleveland. That's where I met your dad."

"And my mom."

"And your mom. But first your dad. We were fraternity brothers; then we graduated and went to business school in different places and didn't see each other for a while."

"Six years."

"You know the story better than me."

I smiled. She did indeed.

"You and Daddy went into business together, but not in Cleveland. Did you know my grandma in Cleveland?"

"Nope. Didn't meet her until I was living out here."

"Is she gonna die?"

My eyes flew open. I looked back at Kikit, about to scold her for suggesting such a thing. Then my gaze slid to Johnny's alert face, and I realized that she was only saying what they were both thinking.

"Not today or tomorrow," Brody answered for me. "But her body's getting pretty tired."

"I get tired sometimes."

The final *s* had a faint *th* to it, the remnant of a lisp that only appeared at moments of stress. The mention of sickness would do it.

"Not the same," Brody said. "You get tired like we all get tired. With your grandma it's her age and the sickness she has."

"Cancer." I steeled myself for a deepening of the onslaught, only to hear Kikit continue. "Brody, are we going to the circus this year? You promised me we would."

"I have tickets."

She lit up. "You do? When? Are we sitting in the middle like we did last year? It . . . was . . . so . . . cool. Joy"—Brody's daughter, as distinguished from Kikit's doll—"is coming, too, isn't she? I want another alligator like Hector. Can I get one, Mommy? A purple one this time? Can I, please?"

CONNIE Grant had always been a small woman, but everything about her seemed to have shrunk even more in the few weeks since I had seen her last. Size, color, energy—all less. She was heavily medicated. Her eyes focused only in spurts. The immediate problem, the doctor had explained during one of my calls, wasn't the cancer but her heart. Repair work was out of the question. My mother was too weak.

She must have called on every last bit of strength she had to be alert for the children, because as soon as Johnny and Kikit took off with my sister, she closed her eyes and lay silent.

Heavyhearted, I sat close by her side. After a few minutes I began to hum and was rewarded enough by her weak grin to put words to the tune. Connie loved Streisand. I finished the last few bars of "The Way We Were" and smiled.

Her own smile was brief and wan. "So much idle time," she said in a frail voice. "I'm not able to do much but lie here and think. Ironic." She sighed. "I was always so busy. It's frustrating, all I wanted to do in life and didn't."

"You did tons," I said. "Starting way back when Daddy died. You held two jobs, worked night and day."

"I chased my tail was what I did. Couldn't seem to get ahead. Like now. I get a handle on the pain; then it hits me again."

It frightened me to hear her despair, made me angry, too, because Connie Grant didn't deserve to be dying at sixty-three. She had fought long and hard for a better life, had fought even when things hadn't come easy. "Oh, Mom. There have been positive things. Lots of them."

"You, certainly." She sighed again. "Rona—I don't know. She's thirty-eight going on twelve."

"Well then, for a twelve-year-old she's a whiz. She's been here for you, Mom. Much more than I have. I wish I lived closer."

"Even if you did, you have a family. You have a business. Rona has nothing."

"She has friends."

"They're as lost as she is. Not a one of them has direction, other than to the beauty shop for a manicure. What would Rona do if she didn't have me to hover over? Two husbands have come and gone; she has no children, no career. I worry about her."

"She's just a little lost. She'll find herself."

"Will you watch out for her, Claire?" Connie pleaded, more pale than ever. "Once I'm gone, Rona will have no one but you."

"I'll do what I can."

"Offer her a franchise."

"I have. She won't take it."

"Offer it again. She'll go through Harold's money in no time." Connie sank deeper into the pillows. "Now, tell me everything."

I told her about Johnny singing with the church choir, about Kikit's Brownie troop's flower sale, about the new WickerWise store in St. Louis. I talked until she wilted again, and then I left her to her rest, promising to be back at dinnertime.

RONA was a scant two years my junior, and we should have been close. That we weren't stemmed from the fact that we had to share Connie. Sharing her wasn't hard for me. Connie and I were so much alike that I always came out on top when comparisons were made. Rona was the different one, the one out of sync, the one who wanted Mom's approval and tried so hard that she bombed every time. Still, she came back for more, determined to get it right.

Thinking to rescue us all from poverty, Rona had rushed into marriage at twenty to the richest, most eligible bachelor she could find. Three years and two mistresses later, Jerry became her ex. Not to be discouraged, particularly since I was on the verge of marriage, she found husband number two. Harold was the richest, *oldest* eligible bachelor she could find, and he didn't cheat on her. He died.

My children loved Rona, and she them. While I visited with Mom, she took them to movies, to toy stores, to the science museum, to restaurants. The need to be moving that came across as restlessness when she was with adults came across as stamina when she was with children. And why not? She was a child herself when she was with them—albeit the one with the open wallet. There was defiance in what she did with Kikit and Johnny, as though the goal wasn't so much to do one thing or another, but simply to do what I wouldn't. Rona might live to please Connie, but she loved challenging me. I was the scrooge, the disciplinarian. I was, when all was said and done, the cause of her deepest angst.

The children joined me at the hospital twice each day, short visits designed to be light and cheery, but they were upset by their grandmother's frailty. So Rona, quite happily, took off with them. My arrival was her escape. It was payback time.

Not only was Rona here all those days when I wasn't, but she saw a different, more judgmental side of Connie. I didn't blame her for wanting time off. Given a choice, I'd have been anywhere else, too, because it is painful watching a mother die.

THE children stayed in Cleveland until Tuesday, and then saying good-bye to their grandmother was only the first of our trials. We arrived at the airport to learn that incoming planes had been delayed by hurricane rains whipping up the East Coast. Departure times were moved back, and back, and back. I called Dennis—at work, at home, once, twice, three times—and left messages when he didn't answer.

Johnny started worrying about missing practice.

Kikit started worrying about Dennis missing their plane.

I wasn't any happier than the children. I didn't like their flying alone to begin with, but when I suggested they wait for better weather, perhaps until the next morning, Johnny got so upset about missing practice that I relented. The airline finally rerouted them through Baltimore, and all I could do was leave another message for Dennis and put the children on the plane with lingering hugs and the sworn word of the flight attendant that she would hand-deliver them to Dennis at Logan.

I returned to the hospital with one eye on the clock and continued to try Dennis. It wasn't until shortly before their original flight would have landed that I reached him.

"You'll be there?" I asked, giving him the new information.

"Of course I'll be there," he answered.

But he wasn't. The children landed at Logan at six. Dennis didn't arrive until six forty. He claimed that was the time I had told him.

It wasn't. But arguing was pointless. All I wanted to do was to calm the children as best I could long distance, then fall into bed.

I PUT St. Louis off until Thursday to allow an extra day with my mother. Friday, Brody and I met at the International Home Furnishings Show in North Carolina and put in twelve-hour days through Monday, meeting with sales rep after sales rep.

Attuned to my worry about Connie, Brody did Denver and New Orleans for me. I did Atlanta, and late Tuesday returned to Cleveland. No matter that I was anxious to be home with the kids. Connie Grant was the only mother I would ever have. For too long I had lived too far away. Too soon it wouldn't matter.

The children were disappointed but understanding. Having just seen their grandmother, they knew how ill she was. I wished their father had been half as gracious. He made me swear to be home on the Thursday afternoon flight.

THAT last Wednesday, Mother seemed stronger. She insisted I call the kids so she could talk to them, and was disappointed when we got the answering machine.

"Dennis must have them out doing something good," I said.

Mother's expression grew wistful. "They're wonderful children— articulate, mature. You're a better mother than I was."

"No, I'm not. I've been lucky, that's all."

"Luck has little to do with it. People make their luck."

"Maybe some of it, but not all. Aside from Kikit's allergies, we're healthy. The children have nice friends; they do well in school."

"Well, anyway, I am proud of you, Claire."

I leveled my shoulders. "I'm proud of me, too."

"Is Dennis?"

My shoulders didn't stay quite as level. "Hard to tell. He doesn't say so in as many words."

"How's his work?"

"I wish I knew, but he doesn't say much about that, either." I hesitated. It seemed wrong to be complaining, what with Connie so sick. But she had always been my sounding board. "I don't understand it sometimes. You'd think he would want to toss ideas around. I may not have a business degree like he does, but I do have some sense of what works and what doesn't. But he keeps everything to himself. Like he won't risk my shooting him down. Fat chance of that. For years and years I've held my tongue when I doubted something he did."

"You should have spoken up."

"He would have hated it when I was right and blamed me when I was wrong." I smiled. "Anyway, Brody thinks well of the group Dennis met with last week. With any luck Dennis will convince them he's the man who can gather the backers to keep them afloat."

Connie didn't argue with my reference to luck that time. Nor did she remind me that I was already successful enough in my own right not to need a penny of what Dennis earned. We both took the kind of comfort from that that only people who had once been overboard without a life jacket could feel.

"I'm not ready to die," she said.

"I'm not ready to let you go."

She smiled. The look that followed was adult, woman to woman, startlingly acute, and I felt such a surge of love and grief that my eyes filled and my throat went tight. Beyond love and grief was admiration. Connie Grant was mulish. Hard as life had been, she had always pushed on. Often, now, she was so riddled with pain she could barely think. Still, she refused to die.

"You're a stubborn woman," I said when I could speak.

"Well, what choice do I have?" she countered. "The alternative is—what?—defeatism? You don't put dinner on the table by walking away from the kitchen. Your sister never learned that."

She sank back, momentarily spent, to rest and regroup. When she opened her eyes, she was mellow. "Claire, Claire, you're like my own mother, Kate. She was resourceful. Determined." Her eyes took on a faraway cast. "There was a story. I'd nearly forgotten. Sweet Kate and her pearls."

"Pearls? Grandmother Kate was dirt-poor."

"Poor in things, not thoughts. Her pearls were moments—one beautiful one and another and another strung together on a fine, strong thread. Bits of sand . . . well, she just brushed them aside and forgot them. Some people, she said, couldn't see the pearls through the sand, or only had the strength of character to push away sand from a few pearls and ended up with chokers. Your grandmother Kate's strand was quite long. Yours will be, too. Rona . . . well, Rona won't apply herself long enough to one thing to create a pearl. Me"—she sighed—"I'm still working at it. Seeing the children, seeing you—they're good times, Claire. Better than morphine, you know? You'll come see me again soon, won't you, baby?"

THE story of Grandmother Kate's pearls was one of the more philosophical my mother had shared. I thought about it through the flight home Thursday, thought of my own pearls: wonderful family moments—so many I couldn't count—moments of pleasure and pride at work. Suddenly the dislocation I had been feeling all week intensified. I couldn't get home fast enough.

My plane landed on time. The driver was there to meet me on time. Incredibly, my impatience grew. I had been away too long and needed to be home, needed to touch the children, needed to talk with Dennis. Home was my anchor. I needed to be moored.

When I arrived at the house, it was five thirty, just when I had told the children to expect me. I was surprised that they weren't waiting outside—two beautiful little pearls of my own. Dennis should have had them picked up and home half an hour before.

Sure enough, his car was parked by the garage at the side of the house. I went to the front door with my luggage and had to use my key—another surprise. Whoever arrived home first usually unlocked both doors for the children.

"Hello?" I called.

I waited for the answering shrieks that usually hailed my arrival but got none, and the silence was the least of what unsettled me. Aside from my own bags at the bottom, the stairs leading to the second floor were clean. There were none of the sneakers, backpacks, and other miscellanea that usually gathered while I was gone.

"Hey, you guys, I'm home."

"I hear," Dennis said, materializing in the doorway of the study on my right. He was holding a bourbon on the rocks.

Maternal instinct—personal instinct—no matter, I felt a fast unease. "What's wrong?" I asked into the silence, knowing that something was and fearing, fearing Kikit sick, Johnny injured, Connie gone. "What's wrong?" I repeated. "Is it my mother?"

Dennis put his shoulder to the doorframe and shook his head.

"Where are the kids?"

"At my parents' house."

My in-laws lived just over the New Hampshire line, an easy thirty minutes away. I could understand their helping Dennis with the children while I was gone. "Should I go pick them up?"

"No." His voice was as odd as his expression, colder than usual, firmer than usual. I had a sudden flash to another discussion, one we'd had several months ago. That one had started with spit and fire before reaching the colder-than-usual, firmer-than-usual stage in which Dennis had suggested we separate.

"Why not?" I asked now, but cautiously.

He took a drink.

"Dennis?" I didn't like the things I was thinking or feeling. I had argued against a separation that last time, just as I had other times before that, but he looked more self-assured now.

The doorbell rang. My eyes flew behind me to the door, then back to Dennis. "Who is it?" I asked when he showed no surprise.

He gestured for me to open the door, which I quickly did. A pleasant-looking middle-aged man stood there. "Claire Raphael?"

"Yes."

He handed me an ordinary business envelope. No sooner had I taken it than he turned and started back down the walk.

I closed the door. The envelope had my name on it. The return address read "Office of the Constable of Essex County."

With an uneasy glance at Dennis I opened the envelope.

THE heading proclaimed the paper a temporary order issued by the Probate and Family Court Department of the Commonwealth of Massachusetts, Essex Division. Dennis's name was typed in as plaintiff, my name as defendant.

Bewildered, I glanced up at him; then I read on.

> Pending a hearing on the merits or until further order of the court, it is ordered that:
>
> The plaintiff/father is to have the temporary custody of John and Clara Kate Raphael, the minor children of the parties.
>
> The wife is to vacate the marital premises for the weekend beginning forthwith and up until noon on Monday, October 28, at which time all parties are to appear to show cause why the order for temporary custody and vacate should or should not continue. At said time a hearing will be held to determine temporary child custody and support payment in advance of a final divorce settlement.

The form was dated that day, Thursday, October 24, and signed by E. Warren Selwey, Justice of the Probate and Family Court.

I stared at the paper for the longest time. All I could think was that Dennis was playing a sick joke to drive home the fact that he hated my traveling. But the paper looked real, and Dennis wasn't laughing.

"What is this?" I asked. "It looks like a court order."

"Smart girl," he said. "I've filed for divorce. The court has given me temporary custody of the kids and ordered you out of this house."

Definitely a joke. "You're kidding."

"No. That paper makes it official."

I shook my head. It made no sense. "This isn't the way two rational people who have been married for fifteen good years behave. People like that approach each other and talk."

"I tried. You wouldn't listen. Three times I mentioned divorce. The last time was in August."

He had been upset. A deal he'd been working on had just fallen through. At the same time, compounding his humiliation, the second-quarter figures for WickerWise had come through looking better than ever. So he had threatened to move out. He did that when he was upset or humiliated. It was part of the pattern.

"I didn't think you were serious."

"I was. Very."

"Dennis." My voice rose. I was getting scared.

He looked totally placid. "I want the house. I want alimony. I want sole custody of the kids."

"What?"

"You aren't a responsible mother."

"What?"

"For heaven's sake, Claire, do you want me to spell it out? Between your mother and your work, you're in a state of personal crisis. The children are suffering."

"Suffering how?"

"You're never here, for one thing. For another, when you are here, you're so preoccupied with your work, you forget the kids."

"Kikit's ballet class. We've been over that a dozen times. The store lost electricity. The clocks stopped."

"What about the accident you had last month? The car was totaled. It was a miracle the kids weren't killed."

"Dennis, that accident wasn't my fault. I was hit by a man who was having a heart attack. The police agree."

"The judge doesn't. He agrees with me that if you'd been more alert, you could have swerved out of the way and not risked your kids' lives, speaking of which, Kikit had a whopper of an allergy attack while you were gone."

My insides lurched. "When? To what?"

"Tuesday night. To the casserole you left frozen. What did you put in it, Claire? If anyone is supposed to know what Kikit can and cannot eat, it's you—and that's not the worst of it. There was no Epi-Pen. You must have left it in Cleveland."

"I didn't. I packed it. It was right in her bag."

"No, it wasn't. I looked. There was nothing there and nothing here. By the time we got to the hospital, she was nearly blue."

I pressed my chest. More than anything else this took my breath. Any allergy attack Kikit had was serious. "There was antihistamine and a spare Epi-Pen. I always keep extras in the basement refrigerator. I've told you that. Is she all right?"

"They stabilized her, but it took a while. She was crying for you, only you weren't there."

I felt a swift fury. "Why wasn't I called?"

"I tried to call. You had the cell phone turned off, and your sister's line was busy."

"I used my phone. It was on. And Rona's line couldn't have been busy that whole time. You could have reached me if you'd wanted to. I'd have flown home right away."

"Would you have? You've been gone thirty-four days of the last ninety. You love being on the road. Face it, you do."

"I don't. Especially not when one of the kids is sick. You actually counted how many days I've been gone? How many of those were spent visiting my mother?" I would have counted myself if I hadn't been so upset.

Poor Kikit. I knew how her attacks went. There would have been several hours of panic, followed by a swift physical recovery. The emotional one wouldn't be nearly so swift. Until we identified what had triggered the attack, she'd be afraid to eat. And I hadn't been there. She must have thought I had deserted her.

Furious at Dennis for keeping me in the dark, I ran into the kitchen and lifted the phone to call her at my in-laws. Dennis pressed the disconnect button before the call could go through.

"Don't." I tried to remove his hand. "I need to talk to Kikit."

"You need," he said with deadly slowness, "to leave. That's a court order, Claire. If you resist it, I'll call the cops."

"You wouldn't."

"I would," he said, and I believed him. His face held no warmth, no fondness. He was a stranger to me.

"You're scaring me, Dennis. This is my home. Where am I supposed to go?"

"You'll figure something out," he said with an odd expectancy, as if he knew something I didn't. "You think I don't know about you and Brody."

I drew a blank. "Me and Brody what?"

"Sleeping together."

"Sleeping together? Me and *Brody?*" I couldn't take the charge seriously, it was so absurd. "This is madness, Dennis. What's wrong with you?"

"Did you think I wouldn't notice? You touch him all the time."

"Touch him?"

"A hand here, an arm there. And even aside from touching, there's the way you look at each other, the way you talk to each other. Hell, you all but finish each other's sentences."

"Brody is my CEO."

"A convenient arrangement. Like the office at his house."

"The office is at his house," I argued, "because you didn't want it here. I could have had a perfect office in the attic, but you said no. So we put the office in Brody's garage. Not his house. His garage."

"You're in his house all the time. You use the kitchen. You use the bathroom. I'll bet you know his bedroom soup to nuts."

I nearly screamed, he made the picture so dark and dirty. "You're dead wrong. There is nothing going on between me and Brody. He's my CEO," I repeated. "My business partner." I pushed a hand through my hair, as if that would straighten everything out. "You've known Brody almost twenty-five years. He was your business partner long before he was mine. He was your best man. He's our kids' godfather. What's going on here?"

"This," Dennis said, slapping the paper that hung from my hand. When I took a step back, he swung in front of the phone. I was too stunned to react when he put the receiver to his ear and punched in a call, then befuddled when he gave our address and said, "Get someone here fast." It wasn't until he hung up the phone that I realized what he'd done.

My husband, who had given me a hug and waved me off barely two weeks ago, had just called the police.

"Dennis"—I fought panic—"you're burning bridges here."

"Leave."

"I need the children; they need me."

"They have me now."

"Now? Now? All of a sudden? Where have you been for the last nine years? I *want* my children."

"Tell it to the judge on Monday. I want you out."

"But I'm your wife."

"According to the court, we're formally separated."

I was having trouble breathing. "I don't care about that court order. I care about my kids!" I started to cry, but I didn't care about that either, not even when the doorbell rang. I was on his heels all the way to the front door. "They're terrific kids. They're well adjusted and secure. They're happy. What you're doing—the way you're doing it—is going to screw them up. You're going to ruin them, Dennis!"

"She won't leave," Dennis told the police officer. It was Jack Mulroy. We knew him, and he knew us; ours was a small town.

"I'm their mother," I told Jack through sniffles and swipes at tears that kept coming. "Some judge I've never met can't just—just order me out of my own home, away from my own kids!"

Jack opened a hand for the court order that was crushed in my fist. I uncurled my fingers and gave it to him. He would understand, I reasoned. He had helped me once when Kikit had had a bad allergy attack. He knew I was a decent person. He knew that I loved my children and wouldn't ever do anything to hurt them.

"I'm afraid you do have to leave," he said.

"But it's wrong. I haven't done anything wrong."

"You'll have to say that in court on Monday."

"I can't wait until Monday. If I do, the kids will be hurt." I looked at Dennis. "There has to be a better way."

He folded his arms on his chest.

"Dennis," I begged.

"Please, Mrs. Raphael," said Officer Mulroy. "Are these your bags? Here, I'll carry them to your car."

I was half hysterical. "My car was totaled. I haven't bought a new one yet."

"There's a rental in the garage," Dennis told Jack. "I rented it for her yesterday."

Jack took my arm. "I don't want to have to call for support," he said. The reality of the situation hit me then, good and well.

If I didn't leave, I would be removed.

If I had to be removed, Dennis would tell the judge.

If that happened, the judge might believe I was out of control, and if he believed that, I might lose my kids.

Arms, legs, insides—everything seemed to be shaking. I took a deep breath that was part sob and thought of what my mother had said. "Well, what choice do I have?" she had asked about having to deal with her body's betrayal.

My body wasn't betraying me. My husband was. Well, what choice do I have? I could panic. I could rail against a system that was making me do something I didn't want to do. Or I could seek a remedy.

Ignoring Dennis, I said to Jack in a small voice, "I'm not sure what to do. I've never been in this situation before."

"You need to leave here. That's the first thing."

Kneeling, I picked up my carry-on. Jack took the larger bag. "Is this everything you'll need?" he asked.

I nodded. Having lived out of these two bags for the past thirteen days, I could manage for another three.

I didn't look at Dennis, didn't speak to Dennis, didn't trust myself not to cry or beg or snarl. Concentrating solely on reaching the car without falling apart, I led Jack to the garage.

The rental car was burgundy. Jack stowed the bags in the trunk. I slid behind the wheel, and somehow I managed to back out. I pulled around until I was beside the police cruiser, rolled my window down, and waited for Jack to reach me.

When he did, he said, "You need to see a lawyer as soon as possible." His voice held greater sympathy now that we were out of the house.

A lawyer. I hadn't thought that far. A divorce lawyer. The thought shook me. First, though, I wanted to see my kids.

Jack nixed the idea. "I wouldn't. You're upset. They'll pick up on it. Besides, what'll you tell them?"

I didn't know what I would say. It seemed important, for the children's sake, that Dennis and his parents and I coordinate our stories, but I had no idea what they had already said.

"It might be easier if I call them on the phone." I could fudge it, could say I was delayed in Cleveland or something. "Am I allowed to do that?"

"The court order doesn't forbid it, but if your husband doesn't want it, you may have trouble getting through."

Panic was creeping in again. "I'm a responsible mother. This is crazy. So is talk of a divorce." I looked at the house, my house, the one from which I'd been banned. "This is mind-boggling."

"See a lawyer. You have until Monday to appear in court. There's your chance to change things."

I HEADED north, toward New Hampshire and the children. It wasn't a conscious decision, just where my heart directed the car. My mind was preoccupied, replaying what had happened at the house. It wasn't until I reached the highway that I came to the part where Jack Mulroy asked what I would say to the kids.

I pulled to the side of the road then. I was suddenly sweating, shaking, not knowing where to turn or what to do.

I pulled the cellular phone from my purse. I thought of calling my mother but decided that I couldn't tell her about this. She was too weak. Had Rona and I been close, I might have called her. As things stood, I couldn't risk her delight. I couldn't talk to the kids, either. Not until I knew what to say.

What to do, what to do. "Help," I cried. Then suddenly I knew where I wanted to go. There was only one place where I could be sure of a haven, only one person I knew I could trust.

BRODY'S house was a neat three-bedroom cape built of cedar shakes that had weathered to gray. It sat on the shore, a gentle fifty-foot climb over sand and rocks from the water's edge.

Remarkable, given how upset I was, but turning in off the main road, I felt a sense of peace. Something eased up in my chest and unclenched in my stomach. It was a response triggered by the first crunch of pebbles under my tires. I'd had only positive experiences here, first visiting Brody, later coming daily to work. I loved what I did, and this place represented comfort, challenge, and success.

The office was closed now, but Brody was home. My headlights picked out the Range Rover in the carport. The lights pouring from the house spoke for themselves. Stepping from the car into the moist ocean air, I felt more grounded than I had seconds before.

He didn't answer the bell. I rang a second time. He wasn't expecting me. We hadn't planned on meeting until morning. We had both assumed I'd be busy with the children and Dennis until then.

The thought of that brought pain, the rushing return of reality, disbelief. Quickly, before I started to cry right there on Brody's side steps, I singled out his house key from the others on my ring and let myself into the kitchen. The warmth hit me first. Then I caught the smell of a stew simmering on the stove. If Brody had left something cooking, he was out running.

Praying he was nearly done, I went to the stovetop and gave the stew a hard stir. Bits and pieces of things came and went in the eddy—chicken, carrots, onions, mushrooms, all in a red sauce that smelled decidedly burgundy and surely tasted good. Brody could take a pot, throw in most anything, and make it work.

I had been looking forward to eating with the children tonight. Now I didn't even know when I would see them again. I refused to panic. Still, my stomach started to churn.

But fate was with me. Just when my emotions were threatening a revolt, I heard Brody thumping up the wood steps. He opened the door and entered the kitchen, a tall, slightly winded, very sweaty athlete wearing running shorts, a T-shirt, and a broad smile. "Hey, terrific. I didn't expect you tonight," he said, but the last word was barely out when the smile faded.

I didn't have to wonder why. I was scared. I was worried. I hadn't eaten since breakfast. I must have looked like death warmed over.

Pulling the crumpled court order from my pocket, I gave it to Brody, then stood close while he read. His face was flushed. His breathing remained rapid. I felt his warmth.

Dennis, who worked at looking good, had cause to be wary of Brody. Brody wore glasses, wire-rims, which he took from the counter and put on as soon as I handed him the court order. He had straight hair that was a mild pecan shade and receding at the part. Twice a year he went into Boston's finest men's specialty store, bought a suit or two, a casual outfit or two, but he didn't agonize. On his time off, he wore old jeans and older plaid shirts. He was one of the least vain, most gorgeous men I knew. He was also divorced. But I hadn't slept with him. So help me, I hadn't. Nor had I ever lorded Brody's looks over Dennis.

Brody's face was blank at first. He was mopping sweat from his forehead with his sleeve when a frown appeared. Then he said in the deep voice that was his alone, "This is a joke, isn't it?"

"He wants a divorce," I said, calmer now that I wasn't alone. "He wants the house; he wants alimony; he wants the kids."

Brody looked so stunned that I nearly hugged him. He stared

blankly at the court order. "What judge in his right mind would issue this?"

"One who has been read a list of my sins."

"What sins?"

"Dennis says I'm in a state of personal crisis that is interfering with my parenting, but you haven't heard the best. He says you and I are having an affair."

Brody jerked his head back. I couldn't tell if his cheeks grew redder, what with the color already there, but I could have sworn there was something. Maybe it was in his eyes, an intimate twinge. I felt it myself. Embarrassed, almost.

"He says we're having an affair," he muttered. "That's priceless. What kind of evidence does he have?"

"Stupid stuff. Working together, traveling together."

"He's crazy. Damn it"—he looked stricken—"I know about the pain of divorce. I never wanted it for you. Never wanted it for Johnny and Kikit." He swore softly.

"I want my kids back, Brody. Dennis made me feel like I'm getting what I deserve. Am I? How did I do wrong by trying to do everything right?"

Brody started to put an arm around me but stopped. So I did it myself, slipped my arm around his waist. I didn't care if he was sweaty. I wanted the comfort. And it was innocent.

Pulling me closer, Brody said a vehement "You didn't do anything wrong. You've worn three hats at the same time and worn them well. You deserve a medal. Dennis knows that. What's got into him?"

"I don't know. What I do know is that I need a lawyer fast. I have to be in court on Monday to answer this charge." I looked up at him, feeling a twinge of hysteria.

"You should talk to Carmen Niko."

The hysteria stalled. Here was a name. I had heard it before. "Is that a man or a woman?"

"A woman. She's about your age—thirty-nine, forty—very smart, passionate about her work."

"Have I ever met her? Is she a customer?"

"I dated her."

"Oh, I remember. That was a long time ago." But hot and heavy for a time, though I wasn't sure how I knew that. Not from Brody. His love life was one of the few things that was off-limits between us.

"How do I reach her?" I asked.

Brody pulled free, crossed to the phone, and dialed a number. After a minute he said, "Carmen? It's Brody. I need to talk with you. If you're there, pick up the phone."

I held my breath. It was nearly nine. I had to see someone tomorrow.

"Carmen," Brody chanted, "come on, Carmen. This is a professional call. A great case."

I must have looked like I was dying inside, because he took my hand, brought it to his mouth, and kissed it—all of which made me feel cared for and loved, which was what I desperately needed—but what really helped was when he said, in response to what I assumed was a dry greeting from Carmen, "It's a great case. Right down your alley. Successful woman being sued for divorce by a less successful man, who wants to boost his ego by milking her dry. We're talking money, possessions, and two young kids who love her to bits and, p.s., have spent far more time with her than with him. She got back a few hours ago from Cleveland, where she was visiting her mother, who's dying, and he had her served with an order to vacate. She has until Monday to answer it. I told her you were the best."

He paused, listening, still holding my hand, for which I was grateful. This was foreign ground for me. If someone had told me twenty-four hours ago that I would be embroiled in a custody suit, much less a cold-turkey divorce, I would have laughed.

"Eight thirty tomorrow morning?" Brody asked me.

I nodded vigorously.

"She'll be there," he said into the phone. "Her name is Claire Raphael."

"Can I call the kids?" I whispered.

He related the question, listened to Carmen's answer, nodded to me. "Anything else tonight?" he asked me.

Oh, yes. There certainly was. I reached for the phone.

"Hold on, Carmen. Here's Claire."

"Hi," I said. "I am really really grateful for this."

The voice that came back to me was throaty and amused. "Your case sounds interesting."

"I want it to go away. I wasn't expecting any of this."

"The good guys never are. It's the bad guys who scheme."

"You said I can call the kids, but can I see them, too? My son has a football game on Saturday. I want to watch. My daughter will be there. She had an allergy attack while I was gone that I knew nothing about until just now. I want to talk to her."

"What do your kids know about the situation?"

"I don't know."

"Find out, if you can. You don't want to upset them. Phone calls are easy. The kids don't have to know where you're calling from. But if you show up at a football game and then don't go home with them afterward, there's more to answer for."

"Is there any way to reverse this order before Monday?"

"Only if your husband suddenly does something to put the children in danger. Will he?"

I wanted to say yes. He was a distracted parent, but would he put the children in danger? I sighed. "I don't think so."

"Then be patient. Come see me tomorrow. We'll strategize then."

HOWARD and Elizabeth Raphael were in their late sixties. They liked me. I had often suspected they trusted my career more than Dennis's. Even if they felt guilty for that, even if they felt it was time to be more loyal to their son, they knew what I felt for and meant to my kids. I didn't know what Dennis had told them about our separation, but I refused to believe they would hang up on me.

As it happened, they didn't have a chance. The voice answering the phone belonged to Kikit. "Hello?"

My heart beat up a storm; my eyes filled with tears. The sound of her was heaven. "Hi, sweetie."

"Mommy," she squealed. Then her voice left the mouthpiece to yell, "It's Mommy, Grammy Bess. I told you she'd call. Where are you, Mommy? I had the worst allergy attack the other night, but I don't know what I ate. Daddy said it was something in the casserole, but I always eat that casserole. He had to take me to the hospital. Johnny kept saying we should call you, but Daddy said he wasn't leaving me alone to go do it, and by the time we got home and he tried, he couldn't get through to you, and then I fell asleep. Where was my medicine, Mommy?"

I brushed at tears with the heel of my hand, then took the tissue Brody handed me. "I don't know, baby. I'm sure I put the kit in your bag when I packed you up to leave Cleveland, and there was extra stuff in the basement fridge. I don't know what made you sick, either. There was nothing new in the casserole."

"Daddy was mad when I got sick."

"Not mad. Upset. Are you feeling okay now?"

"Well, I'm not really hungry. Where are you?"

"You have to eat, sweetie. If you're scared, eat pure things, like bananas and eggs. And turkey. I froze packets of it. Tell Daddy to take them out of the freezer."

"Where are you?"

"Where do you think I am?"

"Daddy said you're in Santa Fe, but we told him you didn't have a store there, so he said you were opening one. You didn't tell me about it." I heard Elizabeth's voice in the background, then Kikit's averted "But I want to talk to Mommy. Can't I talk just a little more?"

"Kikit?" I rushed out before Elizabeth could take her away from me. "Does your chest feel okay?"

"Yuh. Daddy stayed with me the whole day I missed school."

That was something, at least. Dennis usually headed in the opposite direction when the children were sick.

"How is school, sweetie?"

"Okay. Johnny wants to talk. He got an A on his math test."

"Hi, Mom," Johnny said, and my throat knotted up again.

I swallowed hard, pressed the tissue to my eyes. "Hey, congratulations. When did Ms. Anders hand back the test?"

"Yesterday. I would have called you last night, only Dad said the cell phone wasn't working and he didn't know your hotel. Why didn't you call us?"

I hated Dennis for making me lie. "It was too late. There's a time difference. Did Grandma cook dinner?"

"No. We went to Bertucci's. Are you okay? You sound like you have a cold."

"No cold. I'm just missing you and Kikit."

"When are you coming home?"

"I'm trying to figure that out."

"Here's Grandma."

"I love you, Johnny," I said before he passed on the phone.

A chipper Elizabeth came on the line. "Well, hello, Claire. How are you? You missed a good supper. Bertucci's is a national chain, I believe. Have you seen one in Santa Fe?"

"Claire?" came Howard's voice. "I'm in my den, Claire. Elizabeth, hang up the phone."

"I will. Oh, dear." There was a ruckus in the background. "Wait."

Kikit came back on. "We were singing last night—'Jeremiah Was a Bullfrog'—and Daddy was so funny when he croaked, only it wasn't the same without you. I miss you, Mommy."

My breath went short again. Singing was a Raphael thing. Dennis and I had shared a year in the same a cappella group in college— his senior year, my freshman year. We had met singing, had dated singing. Some of the kids' earliest memories were of our singing together—bedtime, car time, holidays.

We hadn't done it as much lately as we used to. Either Dennis was away, or I was away, or one of the kids was out doing something else. Still, singing together was special. Sometimes three of us improvised when the fourth wasn't there. But this was different. This time Dennis had sung with the kids, knowing that he was about to boot their mother out of the house.

The pain was excruciating. Fresh tears flowed. It was all I could do not to let Kikit hear them. "I miss you, too, baby."

Elizabeth returned. "You have a good trip now, Claire."

There was a click, then only the faint rattle of Howard's breathing. "Are you all right?" he asked.

"No, I'm not," I wailed, and took a minute to recompose myself. "I'm sick about this. Do you know what's going on?"

"Dennis wants a divorce." There was a pause, then a reluctant "Look, Claire, I don't care for the method he's chosen, but Dennis is like this when he takes up a cause. He dives into it headfirst."

"I know. I've watched him do it and seen him fail. This time the stakes are higher. I'm worried about the kids. Do they know any of what he's doing?"

"No. He's been good about that, I have to say. He's waiting to tell them until after the hearing on Monday. I'm hoping he'll soften some before then, but his lawyer sounds tough."

"Who is the lawyer?"

"Arthur Heuber," he mumbled, then raised his voice. "Dennis will be coming back here soon. I should hang up. He'll be angry if he thinks I'm telling you things."

"Did he tell you the charges against me?"

"Claire."

"They aren't true, Howard. You know I adore my kids."

"It's been hard for you, worrying about your mother and all."

"No. I'm handling it. Dennis is the one who isn't." I took a quick breath. "Did he tell you his thoughts about Brody?"

There was a pause, then a quiet "Yes."

"And you believe it? You *know* Brody," I cried.

"I have to go, Claire."

"I'm just trying to get a handle on this, Howard. I don't know what to do. I don't want the children hurt; they're innocent of wrongdoing."

"Dennis loves them, Claire."

Yeah, well, he was supposed to have loved me, too. Hadn't he said the words just last month on my birthday? He had handed me a gift-wrapped package that contained a pair of earrings made by an artist he knew I admired. And yes, he had said, "I love you."

So what had he meant by the words?

I SPENT THE NIGHT AT BRODY'S, in the room his daughter, Joy, used when she came to visit. He made me eat his burgundy chicken and take a long, hot bath. With Brody I was free to rant and rave or sit quietly. I did both.

In the morning he insisted on driving me into Boston to see Carmen, and I didn't argue with him. A hole gaped inside me where home and family had always been. I felt washed-out and empty, weak, frightened. I'm not sure I could have managed without Brody. I was eternally grateful for his presence.

Chapter 2

CARMEN Niko was warm and straightforward, not naturally beautiful, but put together in a way that belied it. Tall, dark-haired, and olive-skinned, she wore a soft squash-colored suit and no jewelry save gold hoops at her ears.

I watched her face while she read the court order, steeling myself for whatever her response might be. But she simply nodded when she was done, said "This is a standard order," and set it aside. She uncapped her pen and softly, sympathetically, asked me to tell her what had happened the day before. She took notes while I talked, asked questions when I skimmed details, returned to the beginning when I had finished, seeming intent on knowing everything there was to know about my homecoming.

"So your husband knew when to expect you."

"Give or take fifteen minutes."

"Tell me about the police officer who came. How much did Dennis say on the phone?"

" 'Get someone here fast.' That's all I remember him saying."

"But only one officer came—Jack Mulroy. He rang the bell and waited for Dennis to answer. Did he have a gun drawn?"

"Good Lord, no." It was a minute before I saw what she was getting at. "You think Dennis tipped them off beforehand?"

"It's possible. Probable, actually. The normal reaction to a 'Get someone here fast' would have been that either your daughter was having an attack or there was a break-in or an assault. But they didn't send an ambulance or a SWAT team. They sent one guy, one peaceful guy you knew and would listen to."

Feeling humiliated, I rubbed a spot on my chest that burned. "I left here two weeks ago thinking Dennis loved me. Now I find that he talked with the police. Told them about the court order. Told them he thought I would make a scene." But it did make sense, given the police response. "Why would he do that?"

"To make you look bad," Carmen suggested. "We have to find out whether what he really wants is the kids or something else. Most immediately, we need to counter his arguments." Her voice was throaty but soft, her manner calm. "Okay. Tell me again the examples he gives of how you're a neglectful parent."

I went through the list and gave arguments against each. Finishing, I asked, "How can a judge make a decision after hearing only one side?"

"They do it all the time," Carmen said. "My job is to make sure he hears the other side." She flipped her pad back to an earlier page. "What about the allergy medication?"

I had been racking my brain about that. "We don't go anywhere without that medication. It's a ritual that goes with having a child with a severe allergy problem—like reading ingredients, buying baked goods only in certain bakeries. She can't eat shellfish, nuts, or celery. Nuts are the biggest problem. If they're ground up, you can't tell they're there. So we always pack the medicine kit. There's an Epi-Pen for injecting epinephrine, and an oral antihistamine. When she gets sick, it happens quickly. Her throat can be swollen and closing in twenty minutes. I'm positive I packed the medicine, Carmen. I *remember* packing it in Kikit's bag."

"Who would have done the unpacking?"

"Dennis." But that would mean he had knowingly risked Kikit's life. I couldn't even consider it. "Maybe Kikit unpacked. Maybe she inadvertently tossed it somewhere. I keep spares, but Dennis is a where-do-you-keep-the-milk kind of guy. Then there's the whole issue of what she ate. It wasn't the casserole, that's for sure. But, okay. She got sick. So why didn't he call me? I wasn't incommunicado. He could have reached me. Everyone else who wanted to did."

"Which brings us to Brody," Carmen said. "How often did you talk with him while you were away?"

"Every day. Brody is business."

"Do you love him?"

"Brody? Don't we all?"

"But you've never been sexually involved?"

"Never. We've never even kissed on the lips. There's never been anything inappropriate. Dennis is jumping to conclusions."

"Did Dennis ever, at any other time before yesterday, accuse you of being a negligent mother?"

"No."

"Did he ever, before yesterday"—she flipped back several pages—"suggest that you were in 'a state of personal crisis'?"

"No, and I have to tell you, he didn't think up that term himself. Dennis doesn't go in for pop psychology. Someone else fed him that. His lawyer is Arthur Heuber. Would he have done it?"

Carmen frowned. "He could have, I guess."

I pointed at the court order that lay on the near edge of Carmen's desk. "Could Heuber be behind this whole thing? It's such a sudden step. Such an extreme step." A new thought came. "If I wanted to be cynical, I could say Dennis set me up."

I expected her to tell me I was paranoid. Instead, she said, "What makes you suggest it?"

"Little things. Like the smell in the kitchen the morning I left for Cleveland. He made a big deal about it, then produced a rotting half-onion from the wrong cabinet, like he knew where to look. And the mix-up with my ride to Logan. I arranged for it. Someone canceled it"—something else struck me then—"and he conveniently couldn't take us to the airport, knowing Brody would, so he could hold that against me, too. And as for the mess-up with Johnny and Kikit's return from Cleveland, Dennis says I gave him the wrong information. Maybe I gave it to him right, and he got it wrong."

I was close to tears. "I want my kids back. This is a total nightmare. My life was fine. Our lives were fine. Dennis was never a full-time father. He never wanted to be one. So why is he doing this now?"

"Probably for money," Carmen said.

I gawked. "He has plenty of money."

"He does, or you do?"

"*We* do. Our savings are in joint accounts."

"Who earns the most?"

"Me."

"By how much?"

I was about to say twice as much. Then I realized that that was an understatement. "I earned four times what he did last year."

"Will it be the same this year?"

"No. The discrepancy will be greater. He's working less."

"By choice?"

"Partly. He doesn't have to work. WickerWise brings in more than enough for us to live well on."

"What's the other part?"

I hesitated. Bad-mouthing my husband to a stranger seemed wrong. Then I realized the absurdity of that, given what he was doing to me. "He isn't very good at what he does," I stated. "He had a few breaks early in his career, but those breaks stopped coming when the economy soured. He tries, now that the market is improving, but he can't make things work the way he used to. The more desperate he gets, the worse his judgment."

"So," Carmen said, "I repeat. It could be that he wants money. That's what often happens in cases like this. The father uses custody of the kids as a bargaining chip. Dennis might trade custody for higher alimony."

"He can have money," I cried. "All he wants. I don't care. If this is about money, and a phone call will do it, call his lawyer."

"It isn't that simple. The issue in court wasn't money. It was your ability to parent. We have to convince the judge to reverse both the temporary custody order and the order to vacate."

"Call Heuber. Dennis can have however much he wants."

"What if he asks for a lump sum of ten million?"

My laugh was a reedy sound. "I don't do *that* well."

"He may argue there's that and more in WickerWise."

"Whatever is or is not in WickerWise isn't liquid."

"That won't matter if you give him carte blanche. He'll figure out what percentage of your business he's entitled to because he was the one who stood by your side and helped you to build it—"

"He didn't help me build anything," I cried. "WickerWise was always a quiet little aside. Dennis wasn't even aware of it being anything more than a hobby until the profits started to mount. WickerWise was my baby from the start—my time, my hard work. It isn't his. He has no claim on it."

"Give him carte blanche, and that's what he'll take."

I was quiet then. The unfairness of it was too much.

Carmen touched my hand. "I'm sorry for being so blunt, but you should know this won't be simple. Few divorces are."

"Divorce." I swallowed.

"That's where this is headed. Do you want a divorce?"

"He's already filed. I don't have much choice."

"But do you want one?"

Yes, I wanted a divorce. I was furious at Dennis. No, I didn't want a divorce. Dennis was my husband. We had been married for fifteen years. There had been rocky times. But good times, too.

"I remember being pregnant," I said with a sad smile. "Dennis was incredible both times. He was attentive. There were bunches of flowers out of the blue. There were pictures of me and my belly that were just beautiful. Dennis was into photography then, and he was good. He made me feel special."

Dennis could be charming. He could be witty. He could be a wonderful companion. Yes, indeed, there had been good times. More than that, I had wanted for myself and my children what I hadn't had myself. I had *so wanted* this marriage to work.

"Think about it," Carmen said. She rose and turned the date-book around on her desk. "We'll need several hours together to do this affidavit. How about tomorrow, same time?"

"That's fine," I answered quickly. Tomorrow was Saturday, the weekend. I was grateful she was willing to work. "What about my children? What should I do?"

"Nothing until we go to court. Dennis will be watching what you do and reporting it to the judge. Right now, the children think you're in Santa Fe. Call them on the phone. Tell them you'll see them Monday night. But for now, respect the court."

"Like it respects me?" I asked with feeling.

"The courts aren't perfect. I like to think justice prevails in the end, though I've had cases where it hasn't."

I shifted in my seat. "Will it in mine?"

"Eventually," Carmen said, but she was too slow in answering.

"Why not right away?"

She held up three fingers in succession and ticked off, "Dennis Raphael, Art Heuber, and E. Warren Selwey. I don't know about Dennis, but the other two are tough. Art isn't one of those showy divorce lawyers, and he sure isn't talkative, but when he speaks, people listen. As for the judge, well, he's something of a throwback."

"Throwback?"

"He believes in keeping women barefoot and pregnant. As far as he's concerned, the humbler the woman, the better."

Suddenly overwhelmingly uncomfortable, I crossed my legs. "So the fact that I own a successful business was a strike against me even before he heard Dennis's other charges?"

Carmen nodded. "Most likely. Selwey's second wife was a lawyer. She stopped work to have a couple of kids, but when they reached school age, she went back to work. She and E. Warren divorced soon after that. She took him to the cleaners."

"So how can he be in this court? No *way* is he unbiased."

"It was a political appointment."

I uncrossed my legs. "Can we get another judge?"

"Not for Monday. Selwey issued the order. He'll be the one to reconsider it. But we have a strong argument—that your husband manipulated events to make you look irresponsible when you aren't. We'll give it our best shot."

I stood. "And if it doesn't work?" I asked.

She must have sensed that I was starting to lose it, because everything about her grew fierce. She took me by the shoulders. "It'll be all right, Claire. If we don't get satisfaction from Selwey, we'll appeal."

"But that takes time!"

"If so, it's to your benefit. Give Dennis enough rope, and chances are he'll hang himself—tire of the kids, tire of parenting. It's hard work. Let's see him stick with it."

"I want my children Monday."

"Then spend the weekend working. Meet me here tomorrow, and bring files with you. I'll need financial information about your business and Dennis's. Also, think about Dennis as a father. List the negatives. Be detailed. Our argument will be that Dennis set you up and that, in fact, you're the more attentive, more responsible parent."

"What if Dennis and I reach an agreement before Monday?"

"We still go before Selwey, but it'll be a simpler procedure. Where can I reach you?"

I was about to give her my home number, then realized that I couldn't go there. So I opened my purse and fumbled around for a business card. "I'll be at the office. After that, at Brody's."

"To sleep?" She shook her head. "I don't think so."

"I use Joy's bedroom."

"Doesn't matter. Play it safe, Claire. Stay at a hotel."

I wanted to argue. I wanted to rant and rave. I wanted to beg Carmen, positively beg her to get my kids back for me. I wasn't used to putting my fate in someone else's hands. I believed that if you wanted things done right, you did them yourself. Brody was one of the few people I trusted more than I trusted myself.

Did I trust Carmen Niko? She seemed knowledgeable. She seemed experienced. She seemed to understand my situation.

Did I trust her? I guess I had to for now.

AT ITS SIMPLEST, THE WORD "wicker" means woven. Common usage makes it a noun, referring to objects made by weaving pliant twigs and willow branches around a frame. Baskets were the earliest form of wickerwork. According to folklore, the first wicker chair came into being when early Sumerians, returning from market, grew tired, removed empty baskets from their camels' sides, turned them upside down, and sat.

The wicker chair that had inspired my love of the medium was a rocker from my childhood that had sat on the front porch of the house next to ours. The family living in that house was as poor as we were but happier. Laughter came from that porch nearly every summer night. More kisses were thrown from it, more smiles and waves, and in the midst of it all sat the rocker. There was a delicacy to it, and a strength. As an adult looking back, I saw that that family had problems of its own. Still, I clung to the image. That old wicker rocker became synonymous with life's joy.

When I studied interior design in college, my appreciation of wicker took on new dimensions. I knew that wicker had come to America with the Pilgrims and that it was wildly popular in the late 1800s and early 1900s. I also knew that it had fallen out of vogue for a while, and I counted my blessings for that. At the time I was starting in the field, there were wonderful finds to be had for a song in old attics, at flea markets and estate sales.

Refinishing those antiques came naturally to me. I had the patience, and I learned the skill. In time I could recane a chair, replace broken weavers and spokes, and tighten scrollwork. At first I barely charged for the work I did. I might find a matching wicker set—chair, love seat, footstool—at an auction, then repair it and refinish it for the sheer joy of the process.

The joy never dimmed. During the years when I was a furniture buyer for a national chain, I spent my free time buying and refinishing antiques, then selling them on consignment. Working with wicker was therapy for me.

It was still true. WickerWise brought me pleasure, but refinishing antiques brought me joy. So there was a hidden benefit in situating the headquarters of WickerWise in Brody's huge garage. It was large enough for a suite of offices *and* a workroom—and that workroom was a dream. It had exquisite natural light, plenty of wide-open space, and a storage loft, too. I filled it with pieces I picked up in my travels, and refinished them one by one. Sometimes I did it for a client. Other times I did it just for me.

This was one of those times.

Upon my return from Boston I quickly dropped my bags at a hotel. I knew that if I let myself think about what I was doing and why, I'd fall apart. I felt safer when I arrived at the office.

Angela, our receptionist, who was on the phone when I walked in, waved me a big greeting. I mouthed a hello and hurried into the inner office that Brody and I shared. He had gone to meet with the graphic artist who did our ads, so I had the office to myself.

Desperate to do something about the mess I was in, I spent a while gathering financial information on WickerWise, but gathering information on Dennis's work was harder. Most everything was in the den at home—our checkbook, bank statements, paid bills. I did have the tax forms we had filed jointly the April before, so I added those to a large manila envelope.

Turning to WickerWise work, I emptied my briefcase of papers from the trip. There was information to be reviewed on a possible franchisee in Atlanta, notes from my interview with her. But I couldn't concentrate on any of it now. My mind kept returning to Dennis, and to Johnny and Kikit.

So I went into the workroom and changed into the ratty jeans and sweater I kept there. I needed to do something physical, to see progress, to feel in control.

There were two pieces—a matching rocker and table—that were in need of repair and new paint. The very first step would be to comb each piece from top to bottom in search of broken weavers and remove every last one.

I removed piece after piece of broken wicker, picking here, pushing there. I unwove with care, cutting the pieces I removed at staggered spots to make for a more blended repair.

How had I learned to do this? I had read book after book, had located experts and watched them work. There was an order to wicker repair, a pattern: Clean first. Remove the bad. Soak new lengths. Weave in with the pattern. Cut when firm. Dry. Sand. Paint.

I was an orderly person. I liked having rules and respected them, which wasn't to say I was a follower. To the contrary. I thrived on pushing rules to their limits. That was why, among other novel transformations, I had once ended up with a Victorian bassinet whose wicker was threaded with new wooden beads in bright colors and designs that both my client and her baby adored.

It was also why I had ended up with a business that had grossed twenty million dollars last year.

I hadn't broken any rules. I did everything Dennis asked of me as a wife, did everything Johnny and Kikit asked of me as a mother. WickerWise came after that, had always come after that. I had simply pushed my own limits.

Okay, so I was sometimes late, sometimes distracted. All workingwomen were. All workingmen were. My children hadn't suffered for it. They knew they were loved.

So where had I gone wrong?

CARMEN wasn't able to reach Art Heuber until the very end of the day, and then the news wasn't good. "They won't settle. Dennis plans to stick to his claim that you aren't of a mind to be mothering. So we need to advance as strong a case as we can. Are you coming up with countercharges?"

I sighed. "Most show insensitivity, not out-and-out neglect."

"You say he's away a lot. How much is for work?"

"He works fifteen, maybe twenty hours a week. No more."

"Can you document it?"

I could access his calendar on my computer, but I couldn't believe it had come to this.

"Can you do it, Claire?"

"Yes."

"Then do it. And Claire, watch out for Brody."

I glanced at the workroom door. Brody was in our office, having returned a while back. Since Angela had left for the day, he had been the one to tell me that Carmen was on the phone.

"What does that mean, watch out for him?" I asked. "I've already taken a room at the Royal Sonesta. I've checked in. So now I'm at my office, which just happens to be Brody's, too. I can't very well banish him to Siberia for the weekend."

"Maybe you can banish him somewhere else. He called me before. He's angry at Dennis, feels personally betrayed. He wants to call him. He's spoiling for a fight. Don't let him do it, Claire. It'll make things worse."

BRODY was at his desk, and he wasn't happy.

"Don't worry," he grumbled. "I won't do anything stupid. I'm furious at the guy, that's all." He tossed his glasses onto the desk and pinched the bridge of his nose. "Dennis and I have been through a lot together. I would never have done anything to mess up your marriage. So what was it he saw between us?"

"Closeness. Warmth."

"You gave him closeness and warmth."

Maybe. Maybe not. Certainly not the same way. My relationship with Brody was free and easy. He was that kind of guy. Dennis wasn't. "We were married, Brody. There's tension in every marriage."

"I made it worse, I guess. I'm so sorry, Claire. I never meant to do that."

"Oh, Brody. You didn't do anything. It was me." I let the doorframe take my weight and folded my arms close on my chest. "I didn't listen. Those times he talked about moving out, I thought he just wanted to upset me. But I guess he must have meant it." I squeezed my arms. "It's only until Monday. Only until Monday."

There must have been something in my tone, an inkling of doubt that only a person who knew me as well as Brody did could hear, because his feet suddenly hit the floor. He came to me and folded me in his arms.

"Dennis's charges are bogus, every last one," he said. "If he wants a divorce, let him have it. But he's nuts. He won't do better than you, Claire. Not in a million years."

SATURDAY morning I met with Carmen. Our main focus wasn't divorce, but the immediate issue of regaining custody of the kids. To that end she asked question after question about my daily life, details like who made breakfast, what time I went to work, who did the laundry, shopped for clothes, made doctor appointments.

But custodial details were only part of it. "The judge will want to know about your frame of mind," she said. We were in her conference room, seated at a table along with the financial information I had brought and Carmen's ubiquitous yellow pad. "He'll want to know how you're handling your mother's illness, how often you'll be flying out to see her, whether you're so upset that you're upsetting the children."

"Of course I'm upset. She's my mother, and she's terminally ill, but I don't grieve to the point of obsession. When I'm doing things with the kids, my mind is on them. Same with work."

"When will you see your mother again?"

"I was hoping to get to see her every other week."

Carmen spread a calendar on the table. "What business trips have you planned?"

"Nothing immediately. Brody is making a swing through our West Coast stores the week after next. I was hoping to visit our department store boutiques right before Thanksgiving."

"Can it wait?"

"Not really. Our boutiques do a huge amount of business at Christmastime. And there are parties and charity fund-raisers. I like to check out the setup before each one."

"Can't Brody?"

"That isn't really his domain. I'm the artist."

"Send him this time. It's important that you be around."

Something didn't feel right, something she wasn't saying. "But if we go to court on Monday and get the order against me dismissed, it's done, isn't it? At least, the issue of child custody?"

Carmen didn't look as optimistic as I wanted her to be. "Only if Dennis cedes, but I doubt he will. He won't give you sole custody, certainly not before a divorce settlement is reached. He may agree to shared custody, but even then the judge will probably want a study done before he makes his final ruling."

"Study?" My gut clenched. "What kind of study?"

"Of you. Of Dennis. Of the children. It's done by someone appointed by the court to be a guardian ad litum, a neutral party who interviews you and makes a recommendation to the court."

"How long does that take?"

"The judge allows thirty days. Negotiations for a divorce settlement could take longer. If things get acrimonious, if we have to go to trial, we could be talking six months, even a year."

I let out a pained breath. "A year in limbo? I won't survive that. Get me my kids, Carmen. I need my kids."

I HAD to believe that the judge would reverse his order. I could understand that Dennis and his lawyer might have pulled a fast one when I wasn't there to defend myself, but I would be there on Monday, personally presenting my side of the story. The judge had to see the truth then. Nothing else made sense.

That was the major reason why, when I talked with Johnny and Kikit that night, I told them I would be home Monday afternoon.

Chapter 3

JUDGE Selwey's courtroom wasn't exactly chaotic, but it came close. Selwey was a small man who was in and out of his seat, black robe flying as he strode from one end of the bench to the other, grabbing a book here, waving a paper there, as though to make his presence known. The room held several small groups—

two, three, four to a huddle—whispering, murmuring, rustling papers. And over it all, the radiators hissed and knocked.

I didn't see Dennis. I had been looking for him since parking my car—looking nervously, because I wasn't sure what my reaction to seeing him would be. But he hadn't been on the courthouse steps or in the lobby, and he wasn't in here.

Once Carmen and I were seated, she pulled a sheaf of papers from her leather case and leaned close. "Look these over. They're a restatement of everything we discussed Saturday."

There were four pages of numerically ordered items. I read through them, found them truthful, took the pen Carmen offered, and signed my name on the designated line.

Carmen took back both pen and papers. Talking low, she said, "As soon as Dennis and Art get here, we'll notify Missy, the blonde over there. She's the judge's administrative clerk."

I kept my voice as low as hers, whispered actually. "Is every woman who comes before Selwey doomed?" I asked.

"Not every one," Carmen said. "He has to be careful. There have been complaints against him, even an article or two in the paper. So he walks a thin line. When the argument is compelling, his rulings are fine. The trouble comes when things are hazy."

The door at the back of the courtroom opened, and Dennis came through. I felt a sharp thump against my ribs. He was my husband, now my adversary. I was having trouble making the shift.

With him was a man who was unremarkable in every respect but his carriage. He held himself straight and walked slowly, as though he had all the time and confidence in the world.

"Is that Arthur Heuber?" I asked.

"That's Arthur Heuber," Carmen answered. "He's been doing divorce work for better than thirty years." She pursed her lips. "He knew what he was doing when he picked Selwey."

My eyes flew to hers. "Picked him? Can he do that?"

"Three judges sit on the probate court. When a motion is filed, it is given a sequential docket number. The last digit of that number determines which judge will hear the case."

"Then it's random," I said.

"In theory. It's possible for a lawyer to manipulate the judicial assignment by picking when to file. Docketing clerks have been known to notify lawyers when the numbers roll around for a particular judge."

I felt a flurry of fear. "That isn't fair. Can we change judges?"

"Oh, I tried. Believe you me."

Carmen slipped off the bench, carrying the affidavits I had signed. I watched her cross to the far side of the courtroom and talk briefly with Heuber. Then the two approached the clerk. Heuber had his own papers, though I couldn't imagine what they held. More accusations? But what? My eyes went to Dennis, drawn there, I swear, by some force of his, because he was waiting, looking straight at me. I started to shake.

Carmen slid in beside me. "Take a deep breath. You'll do fine."

"The Raphael matter," came the clerk's call.

Calming myself, I followed Carmen to a spot to the right of the judge's bench that had been vacated minutes before. We were a foursome this time—Dennis, Art, Carmen, and I, in that order.

I stayed calm. Calm had worked for me when my father had died so suddenly, though I was only eight at the time. It had worked when the money I had counted on for college had to be used when Rona totaled a neighbor's car. It had worked when, after a year of marriage, some of my husband's past sins came to light.

Had I mentioned those past sins to Carmen Niko? No. They were ancient history, irrelevant to the present.

The judge read one set of affidavits, then the next. Finally, he tossed both down and looked at Carmen. She took her cue.

"Your Honor," she said, "as you've just read, my client was stunned by the order issued against her last Thursday. She's led an exemplary life. She is strong, mentally and physically. As the primary caretaker, she has raised two happy and well-adjusted children, two children who are confident of the love she feels for them and are missing her terribly right now. Her husband has a history of absenteeism. He never before suggested that his wife was an unfit mother. She had no idea he was serious about wanting a divorce—he is that uncommunicative. Mr. Raphael's action on this matter has been so furtive that we have to question his motive. His business is failing. He's never wanted to be a full-time parent before. Our guess is that he's after money. My client is prepared to be generous. We will be quite happy to negotiate a settlement, but only after the current situation is resolved. Mrs. Raphael loves her children, and they love her. She needs to be with them. We request that the order to vacate be nullified and that the children be returned to her care."

The judge took a paper Missy handed him. He signed it and was handing it back when he said, "From what Father says, the children are doing fine without her."

The children didn't know that they *were* without me, I thought on a note of hysteria. They thought I was doing business as usual in Santa Fe and that I would be home tonight.

Carmen picked up where my mind left off. "The children are used to their mother traveling, but as you saw in my client's affidavit, they rely on her being home to do all the things their father doesn't do while she's gone. He doesn't cook. He doesn't buy their clothes. He doesn't help them with homework or meet with their teachers. These children are young. One of them has a medical problem, for which my client is the major caretaker."

"A questionable one"—Selwey thumbed the papers—"according to this."

"There was allergy medicine, Your Honor. Mr. Raphael panicked and didn't know where to find it, though Mrs. Raphael has told him numerous times. In that sense he displayed the very negligence he accuses her of. Mr. Raphael should have known to look in the basement refrigerator. That he didn't suggests something lacking. My client, by contrast, isn't lacking."

"No? She's a busy lady. She has a mother who's sick and a business that keeps her flying around. She's distracted. She's put her children in danger more than once."

"I haven't," I said. I couldn't help it, couldn't just stand there being denigrated by a man who didn't know the first thing about me.

His eyes shot to mine. "Mrs. Raphael. This is a hearing. Nothing you say has any bearing, since you haven't been put under oath. Do you understand? Your lawyer speaks for you."

My heart was beating so loudly that I thought for a minute he might scold me for that, too, but I managed to nod.

"Good. Now." He took up a fresh piece of paper and started writing as he spoke. "Since the parties disagree on who should have custody of the children, I'm naming a guardian ad litum to study the case." He peered over his glasses at Carmen.

My heart fell. We had discussed GALs—Carmen and I. GALs studied things for thirty days, but I wanted this over now.

"I'm appointing Dean Jenovitz," the judge continued, and wrote the name on his sheet. "Psychologist. Ph.D. If you haven't heard from him in a week, give him a call."

A *week? Plus* thirty days for his study?

"Your Honor," Carmen began, "with regard to the order—"

"I'm leaving the children with their father."

I gasped.

He shot me a warning glance. "There are one too many doubts about your ability to behave rationally at this point in your life."

"What doubts?" Carmen asked.

"She appears to have trouble with the truth."

"Everything in her affidavit is the truth."

"Then what is this?" he asked, and unfastened something that had been clipped to Dennis's affidavit. He passed it to Carmen. Looking on from her elbow, I saw a photograph of Brody and me, taken from outside his kitchen window the Thursday before, if the date in the right-hand corner was correct. We had our arms around each other. Brody's head was bent to mine.

"That was right around the time he called you," I told Carmen in a horrified whisper. "I was distraught. He was comforting me, that's all." But it was being made out to be more. Suddenly angry, I looked across at Dennis. "Did you take this? You were supposed to be with the kids, only you weren't there when I called. Was it because you were skulking around with a camera?"

"Your Honor," Carmen said, "I respectfully submit that if you're allowing for evidence like this photograph, my client should be permitted to testify. Her side hasn't been heard."

"Dean Jenovitz will hear it."

"We request that you give custody of the children to my client while the study is being done."

"They'll stay with their father," the judge said, and walked the papers across the bench to his clerk.

Carmen raised her voice to follow him. "Then we request that the order to vacate be nullified. There's no reason why both parents can't live in the home during the study."

"The parents don't get along," he said, strolling back.

"Visitation rights, then," Carmen said quickly. "The children were told that their mother is on a business trip, but they're expecting to see her tonight. They'll be upset if they don't."

"She can see them later today—with Father present. For the duration of the study I'm limiting visits to Wednesdays and Saturdays."

I felt like I'd been hit. "Carmen?"

"That isn't nearly enough," Carmen argued. "The children will be devastated. Two days of visitation a week is too little."

"I'm not comfortable allowing more until the guardian assures me she is a reliable influence. On the matter of temporary support, Father will have the same access to funds that he's had all along." He looked over at me. "Who pays the bills?"

"My client, Your Honor," Carmen said with a composure that, just then, I totally lacked. "But we have reservations about leaving things as they are. Mr. Raphael is a binge spender. Cars, clothes, trips—there's no telling what he'll do now that he knows his days of unlimited access to his wife's funds are numbered."

"Your Honor," drawled Dennis's lawyer in an old-boy tone, if ever there was one, "that was a spiteful potshot."

The judge didn't say yea or nay. All he did was to tell Carmen, "Have your client make note of any unusual spending. It will be taken into consideration when a permanent settlement is discussed." He turned to his clerk. "Who's next, Missy?"

I MADE IT AS FAR AS THE courthouse steps before my legs rebelled. Resting my weight against the stone wall there, I braced my hands on its edge and took breath after shallow breath. I struggled not to cry, though tears were close. "This is wrong, Carmen. Unfair. It is not in the best interests of my children."

She put an arm around my waist. "Damn right it isn't fair. Selwey was way off-base. As soon as I get back to my office, I'll put together a motion for reconsideration. If Selwey denies that, I'll file a motion to recuse, and if he denies that, I'll file an interlocutory appeal. That will be heard by a judge on the appeals court."

"What if it's denied, too?" I asked.

"At that point, we'll have other options. One is to get a temporary restraining order against Selwey's rulings by filing a gender discrimination suit against him in federal court. His remarks today suggested that he discriminated against you largely because you work, so that's one possibility. Another is to sue Dennis."

"For what?"

"Malicious prosecution. Intentional infliction of emotional distress."

I rubbed the flat of my hand on my chest. The ache there was intense. It grew worse when I saw Dennis emerge from between the large granite columns and trot down the steps with his lawyer. With his tread light, he looked to be feeling pretty good, and why not? He'd just pulled off a whopper of a snow job.

I saw him smile, presumably at something Art Heuber said. The smile broadened as the two halted. It was only then that I saw the woman who met them at the foot of the steps.

She was small, blond, young, and strikingly attractive.

"Aaaahh," Carmen murmured. "The missing piece. Phoebe Lowe. She works with Art Heuber."

"Works with?"

"She's a partner. She's thirty-two, though people rarely guess it. Needless to say, Selwey wouldn't care for her much. That may be why Art is here. He may be the point man, while Phoebe's the brains behind the operation."

"She's Dennis's lawyer, then?"

"Officially they'll work as a team." Carmen nodded slowly as she studied them. "Art is tough, but he isn't usually underhanded. Phoebe is. She's a manipulator. It'd be just her style to coach Dennis on the best ways of making you look bad. See how they're talking? I smell familiarity. She and Dennis aren't strangers. Yes, I'd guess she's Dennis's original lawyer."

The threesome seemed pleased with themselves. Their smiles were all the more hurtful, given how devastated I felt. It was something of a relief when they started along the street.

Carmen took my arm and guided me down the steps. "I'm sorry, Claire. I wanted this over today, too. But right after I file the motion for reconsideration, I'll call Dean Jenovitz and get the GAL study going. The sooner we start, the sooner we end."

"Tell me what to expect from Jenovitz," I said.

"He's stodgy. Conservative. More annoying than harmful. He'll ask lots of questions. He'll interview you and Dennis and the kids. He'll ask about your marriage and your homelife. You'll give him the names of people who have dealings with the kids, and he'll check them out, but mostly it'll be talks with the four of you. You and Dennis will go to Dean's office. When the children are involved, Dean will go to your home."

"My home." From which I was now banished. "I don't have my clothes. Don't have my checkbook. I don't have a place to sleep tonight."

"The hotel?"

I gave a sharp shake of my head. I had checked out after three sleepless nights and would rather die than return.

Carmen steered me toward my car. "Take a short-term rental."

I didn't want a short-term rental. I needed history, needed roots. That was what the last fifteen years had been about.

"You know," I said, "I spent months looking for that house. I spent months decorating it. When Dennis's business failed, we took out a second mortgage. I was the one who paid it off. So why am I the one kicked out?"

"Because you're the stronger one," Carmen said.

My bark of laughter held a bitter taste. I started shaking again.

Carmen tightened her grip on my arm. "As much of a temptation as it is, Claire, don't stay with Brody."

I thought of the picture the judge had produced and felt betrayed. "Dennis must have followed me to Brody's on Thursday. If he'd been half as clever in business, we'd never be standing here now. This has to do with his ego. He's jealous of WickerWise, jealous of my relationship with the kids, jealous of my friendship with Brody"—I looked at her—"but I swear, nothing is going on between Brody and me. Nothing ever has."

"I believe you. And the judge had no right to consider that piece of evidence without allowing us to offer others. That'll be one of the things I'll argue in the motion for reconsideration."

"Oh, Carmen," I said with a tired sigh, and came to a stop beside my car. The injustice of it was too much.

"I'll keep busy on my end," Carmen said. "Meanwhile, you keep busy on yours. Find a place to stay. Get back to work. Be available for the times when Dennis calls in a panic because he doesn't know what to do for the kids." She held my arm with reassuring strength. "We will win, Claire. The facts are with us."

I wanted to believe that so badly. I would find a place to stay, and I would buy the car that the insurance company had sent a check for, and I would get back to work. I would do anything and everything I could to advance my legal case.

But there was something more pressing, more challenging. Thrusting my hands deep into the pockets of my coat, I braced myself for the hard part. "So what do I tell the kids?"

Without knowing my children, Carmen couldn't know for sure what approach to take. Still, she thought for a minute, then made suggestions that reflected her experience with other clients.

"Be honest," she said. "Indulge them the inevitable confusion and fear. Admit to sadness, even frustration, but blame the situation rather than Dennis. Leave the children out of your argument with him. You want your options open and your bridges intact."

MONDAY AFTERNOON, WHEN I put the same question to Dennis shortly before the children came home from school, he looked perplexed.

"We have to tell them something," I said.

But he was silent.

I rummaged through the front-hall closet, removing my trench coat and my wool overcoat.

"Why can't we just say you're traveling?" he finally said.

I stared at him in amazement. "They aren't babies. They'll see through that. Besides, I'm done lying to them. It bothered me having to do it last weekend. I won't do it again." I set the coats on a bench by the door and took off up the stairs.

He came right along. "So what will you tell them?"

I rounded the top of the banister and strode down the hall. "I'll tell them we've decided to separate. That may not be the whole truth, but it's the bottom line. If I tell them about the court order, they'll ask why, and if I tell them why"—I shot him a look as I went into the bedroom—"they'll hate you for it. That wouldn't be in their best interests."

"Ahhh, Claire. You're so noble."

I turned on him fast, struggling to keep my tone civil. "All I've ever wanted for them, Dennis, was to see them happy. That's all I've worked for. And now you're going to mess it all up." I wanted to be calm, but rage hovered close. "I am having so much trouble understanding all this. Has our life together been so awful? Have I been such a terrible wife that you have to punish me this way? That you have to punish the kids this way?"

His handsome face turned bored. "Don't get melodramatic. Marriages fall apart all the time."

"Not mine!" I cried. I had wanted us to be different. *Needed* us to be different. "You'll just throw it away, good times and all?"

"What good times?"

"Christmases. We always had great Christmases. And vacations. Remember when we took the kids to Arizona? I dare you to say that wasn't fun."

"Those were family times. What about between you and me?"

By way of answer I glanced at the bedroom wall. It was covered with photographs of me, photographs that Dennis had taken, developed, printed, framed, and hung himself. They captured the ten years between when he and I had become engaged and when his interest in photography had waned. They were beautiful pictures; I had felt beautiful in them.

Still, he said, "It's over, Claire. I've made up my mind."

"Is there someone else?"

He made a face. "Why do you have to ask that?"

I held my ground. "Because there was once."

"Way before you."

"You were with her, knowing she was married to someone else. That's not much different from your cheating on me."

"Look who's pointing a finger."

"Brody and I aren't involved that way. You know it, Dennis."

He settled in against the wall. "Uh-huh."

I stared at him for a minute, then pulled a suitcase from the closet, opened it on the bed, and went to the dresser.

"I'm not changing my mind," he said. "I want my freedom."

I choked out an incredulous laugh. "You want your freedom, with sole custody of two young children? That shows how much you know, Dennis. If that weren't so pathetic, it would be funny."

He had the gall to grin. "So why are you sore? You should be pleased to have a little time off."

The grin did it. I felt a powerful, primitive urge to hit him.

With a conscious effort I relaxed my jaw. I filled my arms with sweaters and dropped them into the suitcase. "Let me tell you"—I straightened and faced him head-on—"this is just the beginning. You want a divorce, I'll give you a divorce. But if you're thinking to use the kids as a bargaining chip to get more money, think again. I'll go from court to court if need be. You can't win, Dennis. Not in the long run. I've been too good a mother."

"You overrate yourself," he said, and turned toward the door. "Johnny has practice at five. Be gone by four."

"I can drop him off."

"No, Claire. You have till four. If there's a problem after that, I'll call Jack Mulroy." With a last warning look he left the room.

NOT wanting the children to suspect anything amiss before I could explain, I put the suitcases I had lived out of for the past two weeks in the back seat of the car. They would know what those were. I filled the trunk with everything I didn't want them to see— older suitcases holding the rest of my clothes, dress bags, and coats. I took as many pictures of the children as I could without leaving gaping holes on dressers and bookshelves. I took a box containing our checkbook, bank records, and the financial information that I hadn't been able to access on the computer.

With fifteen minutes to spare before the school bus passed through, I headed for the kitchen. Within seconds the oven was on and cookie makings covered the counter. The children loved hot, fresh-from-the-oven cookies, and I loved making them. It was such a mommy thing to do, a little way of saying "I love you."

I had the first batch in the oven, had the second on sheets at the ready when I heard the kids charge through the garage. It was panic time. How was I going to keep from crying when I saw them?

Then the door to the mudroom swung back, and I didn't have time to think about tears. I barely had time to wipe my hands and open my arms when Kikit launched herself into them.

"Mommeeee!" She squeezed my neck hard enough to pinch nerves, but I didn't care one bit. When Johnny followed her in, I opened an arm and hugged him, too.

"Hi, Mom." The voice was pushed deep, no doubt to compensate for the way he hugged me back. "When d'ya land?"

"A little while ago," I said. It was only a little white lie. I wasn't ready to tell them what I had to yet.

I held them both, Kikit with her bottom on the counter and her legs around me, Johnny still within the circle of my arm. "You guys look great." I focused on Kikit. She was the image of health. "Feeling okay?"

"Yup." She crinkled up her nose and gave a sniff. Her eyes lit up. "Somethin's in the oven," she sang.

"Chocolate chocolate-chip," Johnny said.

"I want a cookie," Kikit said. "Are they almost done?"

Two more minutes, and they were. Then another two to cool. While we waited, Johnny told me about the boy who had broken an arm at school that day, and Kikit told me about the turkey that had visited her classroom.

Johnny wasn't as chatty as Kikit. He didn't hold my hand or touch my hair or my face, as she did, but he stayed close to my side until I gave the word, then wielded the spatula himself. We were incorrigible—always rushing this part, peeling off the first of the cookies when they were too hot to hold their shape so that they curled around our fingers instead, but we laughed. We licked melted chocolate from our fingers. We drank milk.

Then Kikit said to the doorway, "Hurry up, Daddy. They're nearly gone."

The look Dennis gave me was expectant in a demanding, sharply focused way.

Johnny jumped up from the table and retrieved his backpack from the mudroom. He was passing back through the kitchen en route to the hall when he asked, "What's for supper?"

I wasn't making supper. I was supposed to leave by four. If I didn't, Dennis would have the cops usher me out.

I said, "You'll have to ask your dad what's for supper."

Kikit looked from Dennis to me and back, then said with hushed excitement, "Are we celebrating something?"

I waited for Dennis to answer her, but all he did, the yellow-bellied coward, was to hitch his chin my way.

I let out a breath. "No celebration. Just talk. Come sit, Johnny."

Johnny was frowning at me from the door. He didn't move. "Is it Grandma?"

I gave him a sad smile—such a sweet, sober, intuitive child he was—and shook my head. "Not Grandma. Us." There wasn't an easy way to say it. "Your dad and I are separating."

"What does that mean?" Kikit asked.

I gave Dennis a look that asked him to explain, but he stood with his hands on his hips and seemed as curious to hear what I was going to say as Kikit. Apparently, he wasn't there to help. He was supervising.

"Separating means that we'll be living apart," I said.

Kikit took that in stride. "In separate houses?"

"Yes."

"But you can't," she stated. "You're our parents. You have to be with us."

"We will be. Just in different places. You'll be with Daddy some of the time and me the rest."

"Why?" she demanded.

I turned to Dennis again, hoping he would take a stab at that one, but he was looking blank. So I fell back on the age-old "Because we think it's best."

"Well, I don't," Kikit insisted. "Where'll we live?"

"You'll live here. I'll have another place."

"Where?"

"I don't know yet. But you can be with me there."

"I want you here all the time. Why can't you live in the den?"

It was Johnny who said, "They don't want to live in the same house with each other. They don't like each other anymore."

I left the table and went to him. His body was stiff, his eyes sunken. I slipped my arm around his shoulders and said, "There's more to it than that. It's pretty complicated."

"Tell me. I wanna know!" Kikit cried, but I continued talking to Johnny. "The one thing you have to remember—the only really important thing—is that we both love you and Kikit."

"But you don't love each other," he said.

Four days before, I would have argued. Now? "I don't know. This is kind of a trial period."

"Are you gonna cook, Daddy?" Kikit asked.

"Sometimes."

"What about my medicine? Who'll make sure it's here?"

"I will," he said.

Her little face crumpled then. Tears welled and spilled. "I didn't mean to get thick. I didn't mean to, really I didn't."

"Oh, God," I whispered, and dragged Johnny with me to the table so that I could hold Kikit, too. "You didn't do anything, baby. Shhh. This isn't your fault."

"I got thick—*sick*—so he got mad at you—"

"No, baby, no, it wasn't that. Don't ever think it was that."

"I want you to live here," Kikit said.

"I can't do that now. But you'll see, I'll find someplace to live that you'll just love."

"In Santa Fe?" asked my son, clearly grappling with the puzzle.

"No, sweetie, not in Santa Fe. That's much too far away. I was thinking about something five, maybe ten minutes from here."

"What about Thanksgiving?" he asked.

"Hmm. I haven't given that much thought. What do you think we should do?"

"Have it here, like we always do."

Thanksgiving. Christmas. Johnny's birthday, then Kikit's. They were all family occasions, but they'd no longer be the same.

"Mommy," Kikit whined, "tomorrow is look-see at ballet. Will you bring cupcakes for afterward?"

Tomorrow was Tuesday. Not Wednesday, like the judge had said. If Dennis was willing, we could change days.

But Kikit wasn't done. She was hanging on me now. "And Wednesday is parents' day at the library."

So much for switching days. But I could do both.

No, I couldn't. Dennis told me that in the next instant with the subtlest shake of his head.

"I'll do Wednesday at the library," I said. "Daddy will do look-see at ballet tomorrow."

"But I want you to. The mother sets it all up, you know, on the table in the back room."

"I'll buy the cupcakes, and Daddy can bring them."

"It's not the same," she cried. "And what about Thursday?

Thursday's Halloween. You'll be here for Halloween, won't you?"

Of course I would. I loved Halloween, always made special costumes. This year's were done—Kikit's a mouse, Johnny's a pirate. Of course I would be part of the ritual.

"She may not be able to," Dennis said.

Kikit turned on him. "Why not?"

He hitched his chin my way. Kikit looked up at me. I was trying to decide whether to argue with Dennis, or to tell the children the truth or to lie, when she pulled back. "Is it because you don't want to live here anymore?"

"I do—"

"You don't love us anymore," she wailed.

I reached for her, but she skittered away. Her mouth was turned down, her chin quivering. Releasing Johnny, I came out of my seat, caught her, and pulled her into my arms. I held her there tightly, even when she squirmed to escape.

It was a minute before I cleared the emotion that clogged my throat. Then my voice was hoarse, fierce, as I bent over the top of her head. "I love you dearly. You and your brother mean more to me than anything else in the world."

"So why can't you be here?"

"Because the judge says I can't. He says you'll be with me Wednesdays and Saturdays, just until we get all this worked out."

"But why?"

"I don't know, baby," I crooned against the warmth of her hair. "But that's what we have to do."

It was nearing three forty-five. Time was running out.

"But I'll miss you," she said.

"Bah," I teased. "You'll call me whenever you want, both of you." I looked around to include Johnny, only he wasn't there.

My eyes flew to Dennis. He shot a thumb toward the hall. Furious that he had just let the child go, I scooped Kikit up and deposited her in her father's arms. "Hold tight, baby," I told her in a tone far gentler than the look I gave Dennis.

Johnny was in his room, sitting with his back to the headboard of the bed. The way he stared at me as I crossed to him nearly broke my heart. I sat and took his hand.

"This isn't what I want, Johnny. Things are out of my hands."

"Since when do judges tell parents what to do?"

He was right. "It's a long story, sweetie. Complicated."

He crossed his arms on his chest and wore a look that I suspected I had worn myself more than once, when I wanted an explanation for something I felt was wrong.

"The judge thought," I tried, "that with Grandma being so sick, Daddy would be able to give you and Kikit more attention. It's just for now."

"For how long?"

"I don't know. It could be a few days, or a week, or a month."

"Then what?"

"Then whatever we decide is best for you and Kikit."

I heard a noise and looked back to see Dennis in the doorway. He was still holding Kikit. "Everything okay here?" he asked.

"Everything is fine," I said. But it wasn't. Kikit's face was streaked with tears. Johnny looked like he was crying inside. And I was bleeding, positively bleeding from the soul.

It was three fifty. Dennis started looking at his watch.

I refused to look at him, but concentrated solely on my children during my last few minutes with them. I tried to be reassuring, but I felt as if my insides were being pulled slowly away from my body. When Dennis set Kikit down and came toward me—I think he'd have taken my arm if I hadn't risen on my own—I felt a tearing.

"Say good-bye to your mother now," he told the children.

Fighting tears, I reached for Johnny. He didn't budge.

"Please, John," I whispered. "I need your help."

He let me draw him into a hug. I swallowed against his head and managed a wobbly "I'll talk with you later, okay?"

"Hold me, Mommy," Kikit cried. "Hold me."

I kissed Johnny's forehead, whispered "I love you, sweetie," and turned to Kikit. She was in my arms in an instant, holding me so tightly she trembled. Or was the trembling mine?

"Claire," Dennis said.

I kissed her and whispered, "Gotta go, baby."

Her arms tightened. "No, Mommy, don't."

Dennis scooped her up from behind, breaking her hold of me. The sight of her reaching for me, arms and legs, even while Dennis drew her away, broke my heart.

"Wednesday" was all I could manage, and that, brokenly. I didn't look back again. I ran down the stairs, grabbed my purse and keys, and ran out the front door to the car.

Kikit must have escaped Dennis, because no sooner had I backed out of the driveway than she bolted from the front door. Dennis caught her when she was halfway across the yard, swept her up in his arms, and turned back to the house.

My last view of the house that day was of Dennis's rigid back, Kikit's furious feet kicking over his arm, and, off to the side and alone, Johnny staring at me as I drove away.

I WENT to the office straight from there because I was too upset to go anywhere else. Carmen had said I couldn't live with Brody, so I wouldn't, but this was where I worked. Anyway, Brody wasn't around. He was on Martha's Vineyard negotiating with contractors to work on our store there.

The office was deserted. I let myself in and dropped my coat on the divan by the reception desk. Then I stood in the dimness and looked around. How many other times I had done the same, feeling pride at what WickerWise had become. I felt none of that now. WickerWise seemed a liability, a reason for Dennis to rebel, an excuse for the judge to take away my kids.

I headed for the workroom. The rocker that I had been working on was there, but I didn't feel like doing that. I felt drained of life, beaten down and weak.

Without turning on a light, I made my way up the open staircase that hugged the wall. The storage loft was festooned with skylights that, at their lowest, offered night glitters from boats, houses ashore, even the lighthouse several miles up the coast.

I stepped carefully over and around stacked pieces until I reached a long, enveloping wicker sofa. Its seat was deep, its arms broad, its back tall to the shoulders.

It creaked when I sat—the soft, easy creak of time and heart. There was more creaking when I wedged myself into a corner and kicked off my flats, more creaking when I snagged a bedraggled afghan from a perambulator that stood nearby. Knees bent, heels touching my bottom, I covered myself and closed my eyes.

I must have fallen asleep, because the view from the skylights was different when next I looked. I heard the ocean and something else—a car, probably what had woken me.

I heard the door open in the reception area. Then, "Claire?"

Brody. He was supposed to be on the Vineyard. He wasn't due back until the next day.

"Claire?" Closer now, at the door of the workroom.

"Up here," I said, and tightened the afghan around me.

I heard him cross the workroom floor and start up the stairs. "What are you doing up here?"

"What are you doing *back* here?"

He materialized at the top, shadowed but large. "I got to Woods Hole. There was a problem with the ferry, so I turned around and came back. I didn't want to be there anyway."

So much for relying on Brody. "You had meetings planned."

"They'll hold, Claire," he said, and began picking his way to my sofa. "Why are you up here?"

"Where else should I be? I'm homeless."

I hugged my knees while he drew up a chair that awaited recaning. He slouched into it, crossed his arms and his ankles.

"Do you know how bad that is for the chair?" I asked.

I got no response at first. Then I heard a chuckle.

"You think it's funny? This is my livelihood, Brody. For all I know, Dennis will sock me so hard for alimony that refinishing this stuff will be the only thing standing between me and the local soup kitchen."

Brody snickered.

"And you sit there and laugh," I groused. "Well, what should I have expected? Men have always let me down."

"Not me."

"Yes, you," I shouted. "You hugged me. Right there at the window. Didn't it occur to you someone might be outside watching?"

"Frankly, no."

"Well, it should have. You're a man. You should have *known* what Dennis was capable of."

I heard the creak of Brody's chair.

"Don't come near me," I said. "I want to be alone."

"I don't believe you. I think you want to let off steam, and you have every right, but I'd rather be sitting beside you than opposite you when you do it."

"Don't sit here," I warned as he lowered himself to the sofa. I straightened my legs and pressed the soles of my feet against his thighs to keep him at that distance at least, but with an easy scoop he had my feet in his lap. "Brody," I protested.

"I've never heard you like this, Claire."

It wasn't until he began rubbing my feet that I realized how cold they were, and then something about the warmth of his hands, his presence, got to me. Absurdly, I started to cry.

When he pulled on my legs to draw me closer, I kicked out against him, but with that small movement went the last of my anger. I didn't fight when he pulled a second time—first my legs, then my arms—until he had me turned and drawn to his chest.

I cried for a long time, belly-deep sobs that gradually slowed, lulled by the motion of his hand on my shoulder, my back. In time the tears stopped, but I didn't move away. Within seconds sheer exhaustion combined with his warmth to put me to sleep.

When I awoke, we were sprawled on the sofa with my head on his chest and his heart beating too fast by my ear. I pushed myself up and looked at him. His eyes were wide-open, clear as day. He didn't speak, nor did I. Nor did either us move. Shock, I told myself. Embarrassment, I told myself. But there was intrigue, too.

That was when I knew I was in trouble.

Chapter 4

ARLY Tuesday morning I called the house. Dennis picked up the phone, said he was in the middle of making breakfast, I'd have to call the kids later, and hung up.

Next, I called my mother. She sounded frail and discouraged, but she perked up when I gave her a preview of the sales meeting I would be leading that morning in our Essex store.

Finally, I called Carmen's office and left word where I'd be at roughly what time. She had filed the motion for reconsideration the afternoon before and was expecting Selwey's clerk to notify her about a hearing.

I was off the phone, dressed for work, and at the store with ten minutes to spare. Sales meetings were a weekly ritual in all our stores, and I led the ones in Essex whenever I could. I talked about a new line and showed samples of various finishes and fabrics offered with it. By the time I was done, it was time to open the store.

Ducking out as only the president of the company could do without a twinge of guilt, I drove across town to meet with Cynthia Harris, the real estate broker who had originally helped us buy our house. My order was a big one. I wanted a short-term rental that was equidistant to the kids, the office, and the store. It didn't have to be large, but it had to have charm and appealing outdoor space. It had to lend itself to wicker furniture.

I watched Cynthia browse through her listings. She rejected one after another. "Too far away," she would say, or "No land." She kept returning to study one, frown, move on, then return again a short time later. Finally I asked what it was.

"Not a rental," she said. "The owners moved south. The place has been on the market for a while."

She went to the file cabinet then. Seconds later, when she opened a folder and I caught sight of the color photograph inside, I knew what it was that kept drawing her back.

REAPER Head was a small, egg-shaped island connected to the mainland by a causeway. A newly automated lighthouse stood at its wide end; private homes were strewn among pines through its middle. At its narrow end stood a second lighthouse. This one had been built in the mid-1800s and relieved of service a century later, at which time it had been bought by the adventuresome young couple that, no longer young, had just moved south.

Made of fieldstone, it stood three stories high and was broader than most lighthouses—more a thimble than a needle. Its entrance was through the keeper's cottage, a single-story structure that housed an eat-in kitchen, an open living area, and a bathroom. Through an archway the ground floor of the tower offered a den in the round with a spiral staircase at its heart. Up the staircase the second floor was divided into three arched rooms and a second bathroom. The top floor, originally the lantern room, was narrower than the lower floors but bounded all the way around by windows.

The stuccoed walls needed painting, and the wood floors needed sanding. But the kitchen was state of the art, as were the bathrooms. And the asking price was reasonable. I could afford it.

I walked through the place again, picturing wicker, wood, and rattan, picturing art on the walls and fabric above the windows and nothing, absolutely nothing, blocking that all-around view from the top. Johnny and Kikit would love that room, though I wouldn't give it to them. Their bedrooms would be on the second floor and seafaring in decor. The lantern room would be mine.

"I must be crazy," I said when I rejoined Cynthia in the kitchen, but somehow this seemed the most sane thing that had happened since I had returned from Cleveland five days before. Everything about the lighthouse was right—from the fact that it was a short ten minutes from the children, the office, and the store, to the fact that it was the perfect size, to the fact that it was unoccupied, unfurnished, and in need of little more than cosmetic aid, to its charm.

"What'll you do with the place once things are settled at home?" Cynthia cautioned.

"I'll keep it," I answered, perhaps impractically, but I didn't care. I had spent my life being practical and responsible, and look what had happened, thank you very much. My gut said I wouldn't regret the purchase. That was good enough for me.

THE only condition I put on buying the old Reaper Head light was that I had to have immediate access. I wanted to actually sleep there that night. As fate had it, the attorney for the owners was a local man familiar with my business. He readily vouched for my character— what a balm that was, after the battering I'd taken. I spent the rest of the day finalizing the sale and setting things in motion.

I made several phone calls to Carmen, because no matter how diverting buying the lighthouse was, I couldn't forget why I was doing it. She hadn't heard from Selwey's clerk by noon or by two. She had already talked with Dean Jenovitz and directed me to give him a call. At the advice of his voice mail I left my name, the number of my cell phone, and an offer to meet with him wherever and whenever suited him best.

I called Dennis to remind him to bring cupcakes to Kikit's ballet look-see. I didn't tell him about my new home. Nor did I offer to buy the cupcakes. If I was on my own, so was he.

I would have liked to share my news with Brody, but he was off to the Vineyard again, this time for sure. There had been a faint tension between us that morning, so we had kept our breakfast talk light and business related. I sensed he was as unsettled by what had happened on the sofa in the loft as I was, and as ill prepared to deal with it just then. That was why I planned to sleep in the lighthouse that night.

Carmen called shortly after four to say that Selwey had denied the motion for reconsideration without a hearing.

"I'm preparing a motion to recuse," she said. "We'll ask that he disqualify himself from this case because of bias."

"Is there anything I can do to help?"

"Keep your spirits up, that's all."

THE lighthouse did it. Moving in enough so that I could sleep there that night kept me busy until well past sunset. Then, perched on a stool, eating pad thai from a take-out container, I called the kids. Kikit answered the phone.

"I've been waiting for you to call, Mommy. Where are you?" The sweet sound of her voice was an instant balm.

"I'm in my new place," I said.

"What new place? Where is it? I want to see."

"You can't see it now. It's too late. You'll see it tomorrow."

"Where is it? What's it like? Will I have my own room?"

"Yes, to the last," I said, dipping my chopsticks into the container, "and I'll tell you the rest as soon as you get your brother to pick up so he can hear it, too. Where is he?"

"Upstairs. Want to hear the coolest thing? Know what kind of cupcakes Daddy brought to ballet? Hostess ones."

I returned the chopsticks to the container. "Yuk!"

"I was thinking that, too, but they were really soft and squooshy, and everyone loved 'em. I'm glad for Daddy. He was feeling funny, I think, because it was him and all the moms at the look-see. Mommy, I want to hear about your place."

"Tell your brother to pick up upstairs so I can tell you both." Hostess cupcakes? Had Dennis actually stood there tearing open two-pack after two-pack? I was intrigued.

"Johnny," Kikit screamed. I held the phone away while she yelled, "Pick up. It's Mommy," which was followed quickly by, "You have to. She wants to talk to you!" Then to me, "He says he's busy. What a grouch. He wouldn't talk to Daddy, either."

My heart ached for Johnny, sitting alone in his bedroom, but denying Kikit would only compound the wrong. So I told her about the lighthouse, about her room, about the view from the lantern room. Her excitement was precious. I was sure Johnny would feel it, too, but when I had her call him again, he still refused to talk.

What to do? Short of making a big deal about it to Dennis, which would likely make things worse, I was helpless, which brought back the whole of my predicament. Again I felt the anger, the sorrow, the fear—all made worse by the distance at which I was being kept. After working so hard to make a secure and happy home for my kids, I felt thwarted.

MINUTES later Dennis called. Without so much as a hello he said, "You rented a lighthouse? What is this, a cockamamy scheme to win over the kids? Give them something that's fun and irresponsible and dangerous? Right on the water, with winter nearly here," he sputtered.

"I'm not renting," I said, delighted to feel in control again. "I'm buying."

"Buying. Talk about binge spending—"

"Whoa," I cut in, all nonchalance gone. "I need a place to live because, thanks to you, I've been kicked out of the first place I bought. So I found a place I like and that, yes, the children will like."

"And Brody?"

I took a steadying breath. "Brody is out of town. Brody doesn't know I looked at it, doesn't know I bought it. Brody is not an issue here. He never was." I was trying to contain myself, but I had spent too many long hours since last Thursday asking questions I couldn't answer. "Just out of curiosity," I said, "how did you find out about this alleged affair?"

He paused, then muttered, "It just became obvious."

"Lipstick on his collar? Love notes in my purse? Or was it your lawyer, Dennis? Not Art Heuber. Phoebe Lowe. Did she put a bug in your ear about Brody and me?"

"She's handled cases like ours before," he said, but a mite defensively. "She's seen everything."

So I had hit the nail on the head. The satisfaction of it goaded me on. "What is it between you, anyway? A professional relationship or something more?"

"None of your business. We're separated. I can do what I want."

"She's attractive, Dennis. You make a dynamite couple."

"You're a shrew," he said, and hung up the phone.

WHEN the phone rang again five minutes later, I figured it was Dennis with a second wind and nearly didn't answer it. Then I thought of the kids, and I couldn't let it ring. "Hello?"

"Hey."

Brody. I let out a breath, habit telling me I could relax, then drew it in again, because relaxation wasn't all I felt. Somewhere way deep inside was an illicit little hum. I wondered if he felt it, too. A single "hey" didn't tell me a lot. "Where are you?"

"Home. The Vineyard's taken care of. Where are you?"

I took a deep breath. "I'm at the old Reaper Head lighthouse."

There was silence, then a warm chuckle. "Care to elaborate?"

I did care to elaborate, went on for a good ten minutes describing my surroundings—walked through them as I spoke—because I think I'd been wanting to tell him all day.

I knew he would love the sound of the place, and he did. I knew he would understand why I'd bought it, would see the challenge in it, the artistic possibilities. Maybe he would even understand my need to be near the sea.

By the time I was done with my description, I was in the lantern room, standing in the dark, looking out. The view at night was spectacular, a little frightening, a little awe-inspiring, a little lonely.

"I think something's wrong with me, Brody. My life is a nightmare. I've been evicted and slandered, my mother is dying, my son won't talk to me, my husband is just waiting for me to trip up—and in spite of it all I had fun this afternoon. I went up and down the aisles of our warehouse, pointing at what I wanted. Bill and Tommy loaded the truck up there and unloaded it here."

"Nothing's wrong with you," Brody said. "You needed a break from the mess in your life. You needed to make that place yours. Is it livable?"

"Very. Warm, dry. The view is . . . is . . . How to describe it? I'm up top, in a circular space maybe twenty-five feet in diameter, with windows all around. I'm looking in your direction. Come see me?"

It was the most natural thing to say. But the words were no sooner out than reality returned with a shattering crash, and I felt an awesome emptiness.

"Oh, Brody," I whispered. I wanted him to hug me. I could control that little hum. I didn't have to act on it. Brody was my best friend, and I needed his support. It wasn't fair that I should be deprived of this, too.

Quietly, with a gentle understanding that made me want to cry, he said, "I'll come over in the morning, in daylight. Okay?"

I'M NOT sure that anyone who hasn't ever been granted "visitation rights" to his or her own children can possibly understand what that means. Visiting is the least of it, and there are precious few rights. I had to tell Dennis what time I was picking the children up, where we were going, and what time I would have them home, but that wasn't the worst. The worst was being with them, loving them to pieces, and prizing every second with them, but feeling an awkwardness, trying to pretend things were the same when we all knew they weren't. The very worst was having to drop them back with Dennis and return alone to my own place, which was deadly empty once the kids had been and gone.

Predictably, they liked the lighthouse. Even Johnny was fascinated with it. But when I tried to get him to talk about what he was feeling, he gave me one-word answers and shrugs. I needed time alone with him, but Kikit wouldn't leave my side. Given the paucity of our time together, I couldn't ask her to.

Dropping the children back at the house, I begged Dennis to let me pick Johnny up from school the next day and take him out alone for an hour to talk. He said we had to stick to the schedule.

Carmen filed the motion to recuse late Thursday. So began another wait for a call from Selwey's clerk.

The lighthouse was shaping up well. I wanted the children to see it as home. To that end I felt justified in neglecting other things to finish the decorating.

WickerWise was sturdy enough to bear the neglect without much damage. I dealt with only the most urgent problems. The rest of the work I left for Brody.

I saw him each day when I checked in at the office, talked with him about what had to be done, then left. It was better this way, I told myself. Less tempting. But I missed him. I was going through the worst time of my life, and he was the one person who might have helped.

The court said we were having an affair. We weren't. But something had changed between us. Whether it was the power of suggestion or the fact that I was now separated and theoretically available, or whether there had been an attraction all long, I didn't know. All I knew was that our friendship wasn't as innocent as it had once been. Something did exist, but I couldn't pursue it.

That wasn't to say I didn't think of Brody often. I wanted to call him Thursday night to tell him how dismal Halloween had been. Dennis had opted for having his mother give out candy at the house while he took the kids around the neighborhood, and though I trusted that he would go through every last bit of the candy Kikit received and throw out anything with nuts, I would rather have been there myself.

I wanted to call Brody on Friday night after discouraging talks with my mother and sister. They wanted me in Cleveland, and while I couldn't go, I couldn't tell them why.

I wanted to call him Saturday night, when I was feeling blue after a day with the kids. After Johnny's game I had taken them to lunch and a movie, then brought them to the lighthouse and sat with them in my tower overlooking the waves. Kikit had hogged my lap—not that I didn't want her there, but I wanted Johnny to feel a little warmth, too. When I reached out to him, he eluded my grasp. I wanted to tell Brody that and more, but I didn't dare call. I didn't trust myself that far.

Sunday morning he took things out of my hands. I had been up at dawn feeling lost, so I had driven to the office and set myself up in the workroom removing the rest of the broken weavers from the rocker I had started on the week before. I wasn't more than an hour into the work when Brody showed up with brunch.

How could I resist warm bagels? They were whole grain, my favorite. Smart, smart Brody. And hot black coffee. Chicory blend, my favorite, too. When my best friend said, "It's been a rotten week for you, and you haven't told me a thing, so come on, I want to hear," how could I not answer?

It spilled out—all the frustration and all the heartache.

We were on stools at the worktable with a token corner between us. Brody finished his bagel, wiped his hand on his jeans, and looked me in the eye. "I keep thinking I caused this," he said.

My eyes flew up. "You didn't. Dennis has been dissatisfied with our marriage for a while."

"Have you?"

I didn't answer as quickly. I had only begun to soul-search on that score. Thinking aloud, I said, "Not consciously. I wanted our marriage to work, so I clung to the positives and glossed over the negatives. I should have been more honest, I guess. More realistic. But no marriage is perfect. So where's the cutoff point? At what point is there more bad than good? At what point do you say 'enough'? Dennis clearly reached it before me."

"Clearly," Brody said. He reached into a back pocket, pulled out a piece of newsprint, and handed it over.

I unfolded it and read the short caption beneath the picture. "Dennis Raphael and Phoebe Lowe, dancing at Friday night's Bar Association Gala."

There had been a time when Dennis had smiled at me just the way he was smiling at Phoebe. I studied the clipping. "Why am I not surprised?" Not surprised, but hurt. Very hurt.

"That's from Hillary's column. It could mean anything."

Hillary Howard wrote a column for the local weekly. She had a vivid imagination and a weakness for gossip.

I refolded the paper. "I think they're involved. I mean, seriously involved. When I threw it at him, he didn't deny it."

"And he accuses *you?*"

"He says the rules change once you separate."

"You're right there," Brody said in a pointed way.

Looking at him then, I searched my conscience for germs of infidelity. His features were so very familiar—warm brown eyes behind wire-rimmed glasses, the ghost of freckles across his nose, a jawline that was faintly squared and shadowed, full lower lip. I had never touched those features as a lover would. But there were different ways to love.

I respected Brody, craved his company, relied on his opinion. Was my love for him deeper than my love for Dennis? Was I more attracted to him than I was to Dennis? Why hadn't I seen it before?

"I need time, Brody. If I do something that even hints of wrongdoing, I'll lose my kids."

"There's a double standard here. You know that, don't you?"

I threw a hand in the air. "What else is new? Every woman knows there's a double standard. So what do we do? If we want to succeed within the system, we have to work within it. I'm trying to do that, Brody. I'm trying."

He rose and came toward me. "Maybe more than you have to."

I wasn't sure what he meant, only knew that my insides stirred the closer he came.

He stopped within an arm's length. "Don't sacrifice our friendship," he said. "Don't give Dennis the satisfaction of that. I don't like feeling guilty when I look at you or call you on the phone. I don't like having to think twice before I give you a hug. I don't like having to measure every word I say."

"You? Measure every word?" I tried to laugh, but it came out sounding choked.

He touched my cheek then. "Did you ever wonder what it'd be like if we kissed?" he asked. "Or made love?"

"No. I can't, Brody. I can't now."

"Someday?"

"Maybe. I don't know. Up until two weeks ago I assumed Dennis would be the only man I'd ever sleep with."

"Okay," he said, "but will you start thinking about me that way?"

I tried another laugh. This one was slightly hysterical. "How can I help it?"

He grinned, then wrapped his arms around me and drew me close before I could protest. Once there, I didn't want to. Being held by Brody was being in the safest place that I had ever been in my life. I just might have stayed there forever if he hadn't kissed me on the forehead and released me first.

He was smiling as he backed away. Then, as quietly as he had come, he was gone.

It had been a long time since I'd felt so sexy, but Brody made me feel that way. As distractions from reality went, it wasn't bad.

MONDAY afternoon brought my first meeting with Dean Jenovitz, and Carmen had it right. He was definitely stodgy. I guessed that he had spent the last thirty-five years behind the same desk.

He reached for a pipe, filled it with tobacco, tamped it down. It wasn't until he had a match lit and poised in midair that he paused. "You aren't allergic, are you?"

"No, no. Go ahead." Any kind of smoke bothered me, but I could live with it more easily than I could live without my kids.

He lit the pipe, took a long drag, blew out a thick white stream of smoke, and sat back in his chair. "So how are you?"

"I'm all right. A little shaky, I guess," I said quietly.

"Court orders can be upsetting. But you must have had some inkling of a problem beforehand."

"No. My husband sent me off on a trip without giving me a clue."

"Sent you off? It's my understanding that you were the one who instigated this trip. Wasn't it for your business?"

"What I meant," I explained, "was that he kissed the children, kissed me, stood on the porch, and waved good-bye. He was totally pleasant. I had no idea what he was planning."

"It's my understanding that he wasn't planning anything then. Not then. He gave you slack, what with your mother sick. Then came the mix-ups with the children's flight and your daughter's medicine. What with things that had happened before, he saw a pattern emerging and felt compelled to act."

"I think he had this planned earlier," I said.

"Do you have evidence of it?"

"Phone bills. Dennis has been calling his lawyer since January."

Jenovitz frowned and pushed some papers around. "There's nothing about that in your affidavit."

"No. I only went through the bills last night."

"So you were taken by surprise. Are you acclimated now to divorce?"

"I guess so. Yes."

He studied me for a minute before saying, "That's a fast turn-around. Most women would be mourning."

"I am. I lie in bed at night and feel empty. I wake up in the morning and feel hurt. The intact family I always wanted is no more. The kids will be torn. Pulled in two directions at once."

"They may do just fine."

"I hope so."

"Do you?" he asked.

For an instant I couldn't respond. Then, sharply, I asked, "Why wouldn't I?"

"Well, you are the one who is against this divorce. Some mothers in your situation would make everyone involved miserable."

"I love my children," I protested. "No one, not even my husband, can deny that. I'd have done most anything to have spared them the upset, the pain of a divorce, but now that it seems inevitable, I'll do most anything I can to ease them through it."

He drew on his pipe, exhaled another thick stream of smoke. "Your husband says you're under a great deal of strain."

"Only because of the divorce."

"Your mother's condition has to be stressful."

"Well, it's another thing to think about. To worry about. The stress I'm feeling comes from wanting to fly out to see her but fearing that it'll be held against me."

Jenovitz shrugged. "You're free to go."

"Last time someone said that to me, I came home to chaos."

"But was the chaos of your own doing? You've taken on a great deal, Mrs. Raphael. The question is whether you're up to it. Your husband says no."

"The chaos had nothing to do with my visiting my mother." I pointed at his file. "Those examples my husband uses to show I'm not in control are the kinds of things that happen to people all the time. Good Lord, I could have been the one going to court to show that my husband messed up the kids' arrival times and lost my daughter's medicine or, worse, let her eat something she shouldn't have. Would the court have taken the kids away from him for that?"

Jenovitz gave a smoky sigh. "Your husband's life is simpler. You're the one running every which way, trying to do everything."

My stomach was starting to twist. I was feeling more discouraged by the minute. Quietly I said, "I'm not running every which way. I have my sister to help with my mother, my husband to help with the children, and my CEO to help with the business."

He regarded me speculatively. "Tell me about the CEO."

"His name is Brody Parth," I said. "He was my husband's business partner before he became mine."

Jenovitz nodded. "Are you sexually involved with him?"

"No."

The pipe left his mouth. "That's an unequivocal no?"

"An unequivocal no."

"Your husband showed me pictures."

"That picture was taken from outside Brody's kitchen window the night Dennis had me evicted. I was upset. Brody hugged me. He was a friend offering comfort. That's it."

"There are telephone records. They're pretty suggestive."

"So are the ones between Dennis and his lawyer. He works with Phoebe Lowe far more than with Art Heuber."

"Are you changing the subject?"

"No. I'm making a point."

Jenovitz sat like a rock, staring at me.

"Look," I said, frustrated. "Brody is my CEO. That explains

telephone records. He's also a longtime friend, which explains the hug he gave me." But Jenovitz claimed to have seen pictures, plural. To my knowledge, only one had been presented in court. "Have you already met with Dennis?"

"I saw him last Friday. Does that bother you?"

"No." I looked at the bright side. "I'm glad he came in. I was worried he'd try to hold things up. Thanksgiving is less than a month away. I'm hoping this will be resolved by then."

Jenovitz sucked in on his pipe and studied the ceiling.

"Will it?" I asked nervously. I had to believe there was a limit to what the court was making me endure. Carmen said the guardian ad litum had thirty days. I was counting.

"Is there anything I can do to make it happen faster?" I asked when he didn't speak. "This is very painful for me."

"Understandable. It's a situation that you can't control."

That was quite a statement. It was direct and judgmental. I didn't know whether it came from his own observation or from Dennis. In either case I disagreed. "It isn't about control. It's about being without my children."

"It's about control."

"Excuse me, Dr. Jenovitz, but I'm getting mixed signals here. Isn't it my alleged lack of control that got me into trouble?"

A bell rang. The psychologist's next client was announcing his arrival, just as I had mine an hour before.

Jenovitz flipped through his datebook. "How's your schedule?"

"Wide-open."

"Same time next week, then." He made a notation.

"How many times will we meet, do you think?"

"Three, four, depending on how things progress." He stood. "Next time bring me a list of the children's teachers, coaches, doctors, any other adults who know them well."

"When will you talk with Kikit and Johnny?"

"When I know more about you and your husband." He opened the door and waited beside it.

Gathering my coat, I approached him. "They don't know there's a contest here. I don't want them fearing they have to take sides."

"And you think I'll make them choose one parent or another? Credit me with a little sensitivity, Mrs. Raphael. Please?"

I WANTED to do that, truly I did, but driving home from Boston, I struggled with it. If Dean Jenovitz was sensitive, I hadn't seen evidence of it. He hadn't been warm or understanding. He certainly hadn't tried to put me at ease or hide his opinion of me.

"Take heart," Carmen told me when I called from the car. "He'll get great reports from the people he calls. They know you far more than they know Dennis, and they like you."

"Can I trust him with the children?"

"Yes. The grandfather in him comes out with kids." She paused. "So Jenovitz didn't pick up on Dennis and Phoebe?"

"No. He said I was accusing Dennis of something to justify my affair with Brody. I need proof. How do I get it?"

"We hire Morgan Hauser. He's a private investigator, and he's good. He'll find out if they're currently having an affair. That's easy. It may be harder to prove that they were involved before the separation, though proof of that will help us the most."

It would definitely boost our case. I wasn't sure it would boost my morale. I cringed thinking of Dennis with another woman.

My silence must have tipped Carmen off. She said, "If proof is there, we need it. Selwey agreed to hear the motion to recuse, but his clerk says he isn't happy about it. No judge likes being accused of bias. My guess is that the hearing will be a token one."

Still, it was a hearing. My spirits rose. "When?"

"Thursday morning at ten."

"I'll be there."

"I'm meeting with Art Heuber later that day to talk about what Dennis wants by way of a settlement. We could use a bargaining chip. Proof of Dennis's infidelity would give us that."

Proof like that smacked of blackmail. Yes, Dennis had used much the same against me, but I resented having to stoop to his level. Still, the custody situation was the bottom line.

"Call Morgan Hauser," I told Carmen. "See what he can find."

I would do most anything in a heartbeat when it came to the children.

THAT was a prophetic thought if ever there was one. I had barely bathed and settled into bed that night, worn down by calls to Rona and Connie, when the phone rang. It was Dennis saying that Johnny was sick and that he didn't know what to do.

I knew what to do. I dressed and drove right over.

Chapter 5

MY KEY still worked. I let myself in, dropped my coat on the stairs, and ran right up. Dennis was coming out of Johnny's room when I reached it.

"He threw up after dinner. Can't seem to keep anything down."

I could smell that the minute I entered the room. Johnny was huddled under a blanket on the bare mattress. Mattress pad, sheets, and comforter were wadded up on the floor.

"Hi, sweetie," I said. My throat knotted as I sat down on the bed by his side. Praying that he wouldn't turn away from me as he had done last time I was at the house, I stroked his face. His cheeks were flushed, fever-hot. "Not feeling so good?"

He shook his head. "I couldn't get to the bathroom in time."

"It's okay, sweetie." I fished one of his hands from under the blanket. He was wearing undershorts and nothing more. I assumed his pajamas were in the pile on the floor. "Tell me what hurts."

"Everything. Just aches all over."

"Flu going around school?"

"Mm."

Dennis stood at the door. His hair was mussed and his shirt untucked in a way that might have suggested concern for his child, had it not been for the peeved look on his face.

"Is there anything left in his stomach?" I asked.

"There can't be. Not with all that came up."

I rubbed the back of Johnny's neck. "Know what I think would be good? A nice bath. While you're in it, I can put on fresh sheets. How does that sound?"

"Okay."

While Dennis ran the bath, I sat with Johnny, wiping his face with a damp cloth. When the tub was ready, I helped him into the bathroom, then left Dennis with him so I could see to the rest.

First, though, I looked in on Kikit. The sight of her sleeping brought a swift tightening to my chest. The picture was definitely a pearl in my life's strand. It was all I could do not to go in and touch her, but I didn't want to wake her, lest she be upset.

It was odd moving around the house, so like I had never been gone that I could almost forget the circumstances. Things were organized just the way I had left them—fresh sheets piled neatly in the linen closet, laundry detergent beside the washer in the basement. Granted, the dryer held clothes waiting to be folded, and the detergent bottle was covered with blue drips. Granted, coming back through the kitchen, I found the refrigerator filled with food I hadn't bought. Still, the bulletin board held the very notes I had left there, the wide cranberry candles still stood on the table on either side of the apple bowl, and the answering machine was blinking red to indicate a message waiting to be heard.

Dennis never erased his messages, just left them for me to erase. I pressed the PLAY button.

"Hi," came a clipped female voice. "Selwey gave them a hearing on a motion to recuse. It's for show. He'll never grant it. But we have to be there for the hearing Thursday at ten. Be at my office early, and we'll get breakfast. For the settlement meeting that afternoon, I revised our demands. There's no reason we can't shoot for more, since we're in the driver's seat. I'll give my list to Art. He'll do the talking. Anything else? No. *Ciao*."

I stabbed at the ERASE button, then further vented my fury by chipping ice into small pieces in a bowl. Returning to the bedroom, I closed the window I'd opened. By the time I had the bed freshly made, Johnny was walking bleary-eyed from the bathroom wearing the clean pajamas I had passed in to Dennis.

I helped him into bed and gave him the ice chips to suck. He was ghostly pale but cooler. I rubbed his back and sang softly. He started to doze, caught himself, started to doze again, caught himself again.

He was so obviously fighting it that I coaxed, "You can sleep."

"Are you staying?" he asked so directly that it hit me with a gnawing twist inside that that was why he was fighting sleep. He didn't want to sleep and find me gone when he awoke.

"I'll stay for a while. I like watching you." He seemed pleased enough by that to let himself go. Only when he was sleeping deeply did I slip away.

I was in the laundry room, shifting sheets from washer to dryer, when Dennis came to the door and said, "That was messy."

My first impulse, sheer habit, was to offer sympathy—poor Dennis, swamped in vomit during his watch, I'm so sorry—but it was followed by a swift anger. "It wasn't deliberate."

"I know. But I couldn't ask my mother to come. She's almost seventy."

My hands went still for the space of several stunned breaths. "You could have done it yourself. It doesn't take an advanced degree to clean up after a sick child."

"Well, this worked out fine."

I didn't say anything to that, couldn't think of a comeback that wouldn't be snide.

Leaning back against the washer, I studied Dennis. He was the same man I'd married—same looks, same quick tongue, same ego—but different. A stranger. I had thought it before. Now I wondered when it had happened. For the life of me I didn't know. "Where did we lose it, Dennis?"

"Lose what?"

"Whatever it was that made our marriage work."

"Our marriage never really worked."

"It did. At the beginning, at least. What did you see in me then that you don't see now?" I was still slim and attractive.

"Humility," Dennis said. "You were approachable back then."

"I'm approachable now."

"You're up on a high horse now. You weren't back then. You were there for me. Things changed when the kids were born and later on when you started the business. Your loyalties changed."

"They didn't change. I just had more people to be loyal to."

"They changed."

"You're the one whose loyalties changed," I argued. I was tired, so tired of being unjustly accused. "You turned on me, Dennis. You went to a lawyer, then a judge, with stories of things I'd done that weren't even true. Good Lord, the story I could have told about you, but I didn't, and it *was* true. But I value loyalty. I have never betrayed you, not once. I have never told a soul what you did."

"Brody knows."

"You told him about Adrienne yourself. Brody and I kept your secret even when we wondered if there was more to the story than you let on. Maybe we didn't want to know. Maybe we were protecting you. So who's loyal? Think about it, Dennis." Disgusted, I slammed the dryer door and stabbed at the START button.

"Have you told your lawyer?"

"About Adrienne? No. It's irrelevant. Unless there is more to the story. Is there?"

"I can't believe you're asking that."

With a bark of exasperation I started up the basement stairs, then, in a moment's boldness, turned back and said, "Is it Phoebe? She's young and attractive. Are you in love with her?"

"She's my lawyer."

"Do me a favor? Erase messages once you've listened. And tell her to watch what she says. The kids listen to those messages."

"Her messages are harmless."

"They're telling. It sounds like she's running the show."

He looked bored. There was nothing new in that, either. It was his pet response when he knew I was right.

Then, as though looking bored wasn't enough, he said, "You won't win on the motion to recuse. Judges never grant them. My lawyer is meeting with yours on Thursday afternoon. We need the third-quarter figures on WickerWise."

"We need the third-quarter figures on DGR." Dennis's initials. Short for the DGR Group, the formal name of his company. No matter that it wasn't a group at all, strictly a one-man operation, but it sounded good—group. Chic and successful.

"If you're thinking," he warned, "that the profits of one will cancel out the profits of the other, don't. I'm going for blood, Claire."

"You already have," I said quietly, and let myself out.

If it was money he wanted, he could have it. I had made that clear to Carmen from the start. Me, I defined blood differently.

DENNIS was right about the motion to recuse. Judge Selwey made a show of listening to Carmen argue that he should remove himself from the case, then denied the motion.

Forewarned wasn't forearmed. I was frustrated beyond belief.

"It's part of the process," Carmen remarked as she directed me through the clusters of lawyers gathered on the courthouse steps. "Now we go for an interlocutory appeal."

"How does that work?"

"I write up a petition setting forth the facts of the case and requesting relief from Selwey's ruling. A clerk screens it, then writes a synopsis for the judge, who will read that, then grant us a hearing. I'll file our petition with the appeals court by Monday. We should hear something later next week."

So many steps. Agonizingly slow.

We had stopped at the curb. "Will I get the kids then?"

"I hope so. Interlocutory appeals are hard to win, but at least we'll be dealing with a different judge. Meanwhile," Carmen continued, "I'm meeting with Heuber this afternoon at three."

"What if we have an agreement signed within the week?"

"If we do, we'll notify Selwey. He's just stubborn enough to insist that the divorce agreement has nothing to do with the custody issue and that he wants to let Jenovitz finish his study."

"As things stand, that might be the quickest thing," I said with a discouraged sigh.

FROM the courthouse I drove to the Essex store and spent a few hours working the floor. I did it often, both for the sake of staying in touch with the mood of the clientele and for the sheer pleasure of the work. If anything could distract me from my personal woes, this was it.

Three o'clock arrived. Doubting I would be able to concentrate while Carmen's meeting with Art Heuber was in progress, I drove from the store to the office and took refuge in my workroom. I removed the last of the broken weavers from the antique rocker, put the matching table where the rocker had been, and set about removing its bad weavers, too. I had most of them picked out when Angela poked her head in to say that she was leaving for the day.

That was my sign. I was meeting Carmen in her office at six. I cleaned up and drove back to Boston.

I was in Carmen's reception area, skimming the table of contents of *Forbes,* when she strode down the hall.

"What's the word?" I asked.

She hitched her chin toward her office and waited until we were in it. Then she sat on the edge of her desk and sighed. "He isn't making it easy. He wants half of all assets, including the business."

"Give him *all* of the business. It's his. I don't want it."

"Half of *your* business."

"Half of my business? You mean, half of its worth?"

"No. He wants a part ownership of WickerWise."

"You're kidding." But I could see she wasn't. "Dennis wants to be a partner in WickerWise? What a joke! He doesn't know the first thing about WickerWise. And working with Brody and me? After all he's accused us of doing? No, Carmen. It has to be the money he wants."

"He says it isn't. He says he wants the job. Apparently, he's dissolving his own business. It isn't doing well."

"No surprise there," I scoffed, but the joke was on me if I didn't turn things around. "Is he dissolving DGR for the sake of these negotiations? What about the money he'll take from it?"

The look on Carmen's face should have warned me. She turned, took a paper from her file, and handed it over.

I studied it. The figures were astonishing. "It's worth nothing! What about his other holdings? When he puts together an investment package, he often takes a small piece for himself. Those small pieces must amount to something."

Carmen handed me another sheet. There wasn't much to see.

"This is it?" I was furious. "The sum total of his business worth? What about life insurance? A retirement account? Stocks?"

"The stocks have been sold. And as for the others, he borrowed against them. They aren't worth much."

I was stunned. "He kept talking about a nest egg. Every time he made one of his little investments, he said it was for our future. I felt safe all those years, thinking there was something." Furious? That didn't begin to describe what I was feeling. I shook the paper I held. "Some of these were supposed to provide for the kids' education. Now anything that was there is gone. And this is the man who wants to run my company? I don't want him touching it. He'll run it right into the ground!" I sat back in my chair. In the next breath, dawning realization brought me forward again. "I know what he's up to. He wants a foothold in WickerWise so that he can find a buyer and make me sell. That sleaze!" I grew cautious. "Can he do this, Carmen? Do I have to take him in?"

"We're negotiating a settlement. We don't have to agree to a thing. Will the court make you do it if it comes down to that?" She didn't answer right away, seemed to be thinking. "If the court decides that everything built during the course of the marriage should be considered joint property and split, Dennis has a shot. If we can make a case for his lack of accountability—if we can argue that he shirked his financial responsibility during the marriage—the advantage is ours. Unfortunately, either way involves a trial. A trial could be six months or more down the road."

"I don't care. I can wait. He's the one in the rush, not me. The custody issue is decided separately, isn't it?"

"Theoretically. But if we disagree with Jenovitz's finding, we would go to trial on custody concurrent with the divorce."

Panic was beating its wings right around the corner. "I'll die living apart from the kids for six months. Something else has to give. So what's our next step?"

"For starters, we stall. Let Dennis think that we're considering his demands. If he asks you about it, don't answer. Say that you don't know what your lawyer's latest thought is. In the meantime, Morgan is working on documenting a romantic link between Dennis and Phoebe Lowe. That could give us leverage of our own."

"A little character assassination."

"Uh-huh. He did it to you. What's sauce for the goose."

I hated Dennis a little more for making me stoop so low.

SOME say that love and hate are two extremes of the same emotion. I didn't know about that. I did know that what I felt for Dennis in my anger was stronger than most anything I had felt for him before. If that meant what I thought it did, the overall shape of my marriage had been pretty sad, and if that was true, what was sad was my blind adherence to it.

I might have spent hours brooding on that if Rona hadn't called soon after I returned to the lighthouse to say that Connie had had a heart attack. Rona's panic came over loud and clear. Connie was in intensive care; the next few hours were critical.

I phoned Carmen, phoned Dennis, phoned Brody. Then I took the first plane to Cleveland.

The trip was excruciatingly slow. I bought into Rona's fright hook, line and sinker, and imagined finding Mom unconscious, kept alive by machines. I imagined the doctors shaking their heads in despair.

In fact, Mom wasn't quite that far gone. As heart attacks went, hers had been mild, caught quickly, and treated effectively. Yes, the next few days were crucial, the doctor told me when I arrived, but Mom was conscious and alert, sleeping lightly as we spoke.

"I thought she was gone," I said to Rona in a hushed whisper as we stood in the ICU corridor a short distance from where Connie lay.

"So did I." Rona sounded thoroughly aggrieved. "It's one thing, now that she's stabilized, to look back and say she was never that sick. It's another thing when you're going through it. I'm sorry if I dragged you all the way out here, but she's your mother, too. Was I wrong?"

"No." I sighed. "You weren't wrong." I pushed a weary hand through my hair, put a shoulder to the wall. "A heart attack is a heart attack, and even without it she's sick enough. Believe me, Rona, I wish I could be here more, but things are tense at home."

"Tense, how?" she asked.

"Dennis and I have separated."

She was utterly still for a minute. Then came an elongated "No." Her voice might have held disbelief, even upset, but she was clearly intrigued. "You and Dennis? What happened?"

"Long story. I can't go into it now. The bottom line is that I've bought a smaller place."

"You moved out? Ahh, so that's what the new phone number was about. But why did you move out? You're the woman. You're the one with the kids. He's the one who's supposed to move out."

I rubbed the back of my neck. "Yes, well, that's how things usually happen, but this isn't the usual situation."

"Why not?" she asked, indignant now.

"Because he's the one with the kids."

"Dennis has the kids? *Claire*."

"Look, this isn't how I wanted things, but I didn't have much choice. I travel for work, my career is more demanding than his, and then there's Mom," so Dennis's argument went. Then I rationalized, "I wouldn't have been able to get away as easily as I did tonight if I'd had to start arranging for the kids."

I wasn't ready to tell the whole story. I didn't want her knowing about the court order, didn't want her knowing that a judge had thought me inadequate. I was feeling too vulnerable.

"Does Mom know about this?" Rona asked.

"No. Don't tell her, please? She'll be too upset."

"Disillusioned, you mean. She thought you were the perfect one."

"She knew I wasn't perfect, that my marriage wasn't perfect."

"Funny, she never told me." Rona was looking at me strangely. "Dennis with custody? That's quite a blow to the old image."

"The old image," I said, "was a figment of your imagination."

"A figment of Mom's imagination."

"Maybe. Okay. Probably. And she was wrong if she held you to a cooked-up standard, but maybe she held me to it, too, you know?" It hadn't occurred to me before, but it made sense. "Maybe I felt pressure, too."

Rona didn't respond to that, simply stood there looking gorgeous— more gorgeous than I ever could, though Mom had picked on her for that, too—leaning against a wall within arm's reach of me. Sad, we didn't touch. At a time in our lives when contact might have offered solace, we couldn't give it. Our relationship wasn't defined that way. I wasn't sure why.

But boy, was I sorry. The need to hold and be held was great just then, because no matter that Connie wasn't as sick as I'd feared, the prognosis was poor.

"Is this a trial separation?" Rona asked.

"No," I told her. "This is the real thing."

"That bad, huh?" She smiled. "I'm amazed."

I pushed away from the wall. "For the record, it's been a painful experience. I would have thought you'd understand, having gone through it yourself." I might have said more, might have shared thoughts and fears, had Rona and I been able to communicate. But we couldn't. I had always blamed that on Rona's competitiveness. It struck me now that maybe I was competitive, too. I was embarrassed to confess that my marriage had failed. I had wanted to be better than that.

So now I was humbled, as Rona had been all those times. Again I thought to reach out to her. Again something held me back. I started down the hall. "I'll go sit with Mom for a while," I said.

THOUGH SHE SLEPT MOST OF the weekend, my mother knew I was there. From time to time she opened her eyes, squeezed my hand, whispered my name. We were quiet together, Mom and I, and it was surprisingly peaceful. She seemed comforted enough by my presence that I didn't feel the need to perform. Her heart behaved. By Saturday afternoon she left the ICU and returned to her room.

Rona brought fresh flowers. She brought Mom's favorite cologne, brought a cassette recorder and more books on tape than Mom would be able to listen to in a month.

Was Mom grateful? Hard to tell. There were smiles, nods, and the same sad look I knew well. Even in her dimming view of the world, she thought Rona was hopelessly ditzy.

Did I? No. But I didn't know how to tell Rona that without confirming that Mom felt it, which would have done even more harm. So I praised Rona for the presents she brought and thanked her for being there for Mom, and the part of me that hated being competitive didn't mind that she knew about the demise of my marriage.

I'VE ALWAYS had trouble with partings. This time was truly the pits. I promised to call my mother and be back to see her in another week or two, but we both knew that my words could well prove empty if by the time I returned she was gone.

Walking out of that hospital room on Sunday morning was so hard that had things been different, I would have stayed and said, "To heck with this. The children will understand." But Dennis wouldn't understand. Nor would his lawyer, or the judge, or Jenovitz, with whom I had a Monday appointment. If I had chosen my mother over my children, I would have been called a lousy mother. So I was a lousy daughter instead.

Life was a shopping list of compromises, Connie had once bemoaned. I only wished I could have explained to her why I made this particular compromise. It would have helped to know she agreed.

SOON after the start of our meeting, Dean Jenovitz outlined a game. I couldn't very well refuse to play.

"Consistent," he said.

I considered his scale. If I rated myself low for the sake of modesty, he might buy into that rating. Modesty had a limited role when it came to salesmanship, and salesmanship, it seemed, was what this study was about. Not justice. Salesmanship.

I gave myself a nine.

"Resourceful."

"Nine."

"Competent."

"Eight."

"Why not a nine again?"

"Because competence is relative. What I do, I do well, but there are other things that I don't do well at all. I farm those things out. I know how to delegate. That's half of why I'm good at what I do."

Jenovitz sat staring at me. Finally he said, "Are you angry?"

I blinked. "Maybe," I said.

"Care to say why?"

My head came up. "Because I'm in the middle of a situation that I didn't want and don't like. Whenever I'm with my children, every other word out of the little one's mouth has to do with when I'm coming home, and the big one is subdued, and they both get edgy—for that matter, I do, too—when the end of our time together nears. I don't know what they're feeling after I drop them back with their father, but I know what I am, and it isn't warm and fuzzy. It's lonely. It's afraid. It's worried. This is very very hard for me, Dr. Jenovitz. I'm a mother. I love my kids. Every ounce of maternal instinct I possess is telling me they'll be hurt. So, yes, I'm angry. I have a right to be, don't I?"

"Not if the charges against you are true."

"They aren't," I insisted, and sank into the chair.

"That's what I'm trying to determine," he said. "Anger gets in the way." He paused to lean sideways, open a drawer, and fish inside. I heard the rustle of plastic wrap. When he straightened, he was pushing a sour ball into his mouth.

"Patience. How would you rate yourself?"

"With regard to my children? Nine point five."

He looked skeptical. "Amazing you never thought of teaching, with a patience level like that."

I gave a diffident laugh and said, "Just because I'm patient with my own kids doesn't mean I'm patient with other people's kids."

"Did you always know you wanted only two?"

"Yes."

"Why?"

"Two seemed right. Few enough for individual attention, for individual love. Besides, children cost money. We had no idea back then that we would have what we have now."

"Is that why you put it off?" When I frowned, he said, "You weren't young having your first."

"I was thirty-one. That isn't old."

"But you were married at twenty-five. You told me you resigned your job at that point and freelanced. Plenty of flexibility there, so why the hold on kids?"

I didn't know what he was driving at, but it didn't feel right. Cautiously I said, "I felt we needed time alone, Dennis and I."

"Did he agree?"

"He certainly didn't argue. Is there a point to this, Dr. Jenovitz? I don't see what it has to do with how I mother my kids."

"It has to do with your attitude toward being a mother."

"In what way?" I asked.

"Some women want children but resent their presence."

"I'm not one of those women."

"That isn't what your husband says."

"Excuse me?"

"He says that he wanted a baby but that you were vehement about postponing parenthood."

I was dumbfounded. Sitting erect, I said, "Let's set something straight. It wasn't that I didn't want a baby. We were having personal differences. I wasn't sure the marriage would last."

"Your marriage was shaky?"

"It seemed it at the time. We hadn't been married very long, and there were problems. It wasn't the right time for us to have a child. Dennis agreed with me on that."

"That isn't what he said."

"No, it wouldn't be, would it. The problems we were having stemmed from something very wrong that he did. Did he tell you about that?"

"No."

I hesitated for only a second longer.

"Several years before we were married, Dennis had an affair with a married woman. She was the wife of his boss. When it ended, she blackmailed him with threats of telling what they'd done and having him booted out of the firm and blackballed in the field if he didn't pay up. So he sent her a monthly check. We were married a year when I found out about it. It mightn't have been so bad if he'd been up front about it, but even when I had the canceled checks in my hand, he gave me a story or two before he told me the truth. Adultery and blackmail. It was hard for me to accept."

Jenovitz regarded me patiently.

"Up until then, I had thought Dennis was just about perfect. Suddenly I was disillusioned. I was seeing a side of him that I hadn't known existed. We were arguing a lot—and incidentally, after Kikit was born, he had a vasectomy. What does that say about his desire to parent?"

"A vasectomy after two children doesn't tell me much."

I held up a hand. "What about the affair he had? If it was so serious as to warrant blackmail, it must have really been something. What does that say about Dennis?"

"Good grief, you're belligerent."

"You people have made me belligerent. I wouldn't have mentioned that affair on my own. It was over and done years ago. But there are two sides to every story. Am I supposed to hold mine in? Am I supposed to say nothing while you draw conclusions that aren't true? Am I supposed to do nothing when my husband comes in here and lies? I didn't ask for any of this. Belligerent? Hell, yes. I'm fighting for my kids, Dr. Jenovitz. How else should I be?"

I DIDN'T HAVE AN APPOINTMENT with Carmen, but I was upset enough to go to her office without one. I was shown into a conference room to wait. By the time she joined me, I was as angry with myself as I was with Dennis.

"I blew it," I said after I told her what had happened. "Jenovitz said I was belligerent. But I was furious at Dennis for lying. I'm sorry, Carmen. I've made things worse. But I couldn't just sit there without defending myself. So"—I held my middle—"is it over? Will I lose the kids?"

"No," Carmen said. "We have other irons in the fire. I filed this morning for the interlocutory appeal." But she looked worried.

"Jenovitz doesn't like me," I said. "We got off on the wrong foot, and it's gone downhill." My fears broke free. "He's going to recommend against me. I can feel it. *When* he finally makes his recommendation. Every time I ask when he's planning to talk with the children, he says he isn't ready. If he hasn't even set up a meeting with them, how can he file a report by the end of the month? I've been counting on this all being done by then." I could feel hysteria rising. What Carmen said next didn't help.

"It may take longer. The court will give Jenovitz extra time if he needs it."

"How much extra time?"

"TWO more months?" Brody echoed when I told him what Carmen had said. He was just as disbelieving as I had been, just as incensed. "Ninety days to decide whether you're fit to take care of your kids? That's the craziest thing I've ever heard."

We were in my workroom. I had come here after returning from Boston. I was thinking of working on the wicker rocker and table, but in the end, I'd been too upset to do a thing.

I went to the window and stared out at the night. "Ironic, how things come full circle," I remarked. "At the time I found out about Dennis's affair, I was terrified of having a child. I kept thinking that Dennis and I would divorce and that I'd end up like my mother, with a baby and nothing else. So the divorce part's finally coming true. Wouldn't it be something if I lose my kids now because I didn't want kids then?"

Brody approached. He didn't touch me, but I felt him. His warmth was a lifeline. "You won't lose the kids. Not in the end."

My fingertips gripped the mullion. "I want to believe that, but my hands are tied. I need to do something." I thought of my first talk with Jenovitz. "So maybe I am controlling." I looked up at Brody. "Am I controlling?"

"You've never controlled me, not in any negative way."

"You're strong. You wouldn't allow it. But Dennis isn't strong. I keep thinking back to those times he suggested we separate. He would always say things like, 'The good things aren't there anymore,' and I would say, 'But they can be,' and they were for a little while after each talk. Things were better. We both tried. Maybe me more than him, because I was the one who really didn't want a divorce. So am I a controlling person?"

"No. Dennis could have argued more. He could have moved out. You didn't chain him to the house."

"Well," I sighed, "when he finally acted, he finally acted."

"In more ways than one," Brody said.

My eyes flew to his.

His voice was low, possibly to soften the blow, possibly in anger. "The thing about Dennis wanting into WickerWise? You were right. He wants in so that he can turn around and sell it. He's already negotiated to buy into another business."

My jaw dropped.

"Pittney Communications. It is a telecommunications company in Springfield, small but growing. One of its major players died last July. The widow is looking to sell his share. If we want to make the argument that Dennis launched this divorce when he did for the sake of the money, the timing is right. He met with the surviving partners for the first time late in August."

I had thought myself past the point of being hurt, but I was wrong.

Brody must have sensed it. "Look," he hedged, "maybe he didn't go with the idea of buying into it himself, but was thinking of putting a group together. Telecommunications companies are hot. The market has mushroomed."

But we both knew the truth.

"Pittney Communications is for him," I said. "The timing says so. He had been talking to his lawyers for months by then. He was probably biding his time, waiting for the right business to open." Dennis had been scheming, and I hadn't sensed a thing. Where had I been?

But agonizing over my shortcomings wouldn't help now. "He's barking up the wrong tree," I vowed. "WickerWise isn't his to sell."

"What if he offers a swap—half-ownership for custody of the kids?"

"He can't have it," I insisted, though I was starting to feel cornered. "Carmen will negotiate. What Heuber suggested is only a starting point." But I didn't have much room for maneuvering where the children were concerned. Dennis had me over a barrel. I had to do something.

Brody touched my hair lightly, then went to the loft stairs, sat on a rung, and stretched out his legs. "You had doubts," he said. "Way back when. You were never sure that Adrienne Hadley's blackmail stopped at infidelity. You always suspected something more."

"Did you?"

He shrugged. "I used to hear things. Never firsthand or factual. People wondered, that's all. Dennis hit the big time real quick. His performance since then has been mediocre. There's been nothing to validate that early brilliance."

Old thoughts. Long-buried suspicions set aside for the sake of the marriage. I drew in a deep, shuddering breath. Things were different now from how they were way back when. Now I had the children to consider. Playing dirty wasn't my first choice, but what other leverage did I have?

I approached Brody. Sitting on the loft stairs, he was on eye level with me. I looped my arms around his neck.

"Give me a hug," I whispered. "I need fortification." When his arms went around me, I sighed in relief, nodded in pleasure.

Suddenly he took my face in both hands and kissed me. I had imagined what kissing Brody would be like, but this was something else. It was the kind of thing that cleared my head of any other thought that might have been there. It was sweet. Secret. Special.

So I let it linger, dragged it out until a storm raged inside me. The need was so strong it was frightening. But the ramifications were, too.

I took several breaths and waited for the shakes to ease. Then I rested my chin on Brody's shoulder and just let myself be held, because there was unconditional pleasure in that, too. No strings. Just the feel of Brody's body and the knowledge of his love.

It amazed me that I had been so close to him all these years without having this. "I must have been blind," I whispered.

"No," he whispered back, on my wavelength as always. "Just married."

And still was, which brought me full circle, back to the dilemma I faced. I drew back. "Gotta run. Gotta think."

"Gotta eat, too. Come on over to the house. I'll make you dinner."

"What a line."

"I mean it."

"I know. That's the trouble." But did it ever sound good.

I gave Brody a last kiss, then fled before I forgot what I had to do.

BACK at the lighthouse, sitting cross-legged on the carpeted floor of my bedroom with my face to the sea, I thought back to that first major trauma of our marriage. How I had agonized. I feared there was more to the story, but Dennis swore I knew everything. Maybe I did. Then again, maybe I didn't.

Going downstairs, I dragged a carton from the small storage bin off the living room, opened it, and thumbed through some files, mostly records of my earliest WickerWise days.

But the folder I wanted had nothing to do with WickerWise. It contained canceled checks, a letter, and an obituary notice. I singled it out and tugged it up. The minute that folder cleared the others, I knew something was wrong. It was way too thin. Opening it was a formality. I already knew it was empty.

THE FOLLOWING MORNING Carmen called me to say that Morgan Hauser had hit gold.

"Dennis's calendar says that he attended an investment seminar in Vermont last July. Morgan cross-checked those days with hotel records and credit card receipts. Dennis was in Vermont last July, all right, but at a motel, a small motel. The owner and the desk clerk, both male, identified photos of Dennis and Phoebe."

It was certainly good news for my case, though I couldn't deny the hurt. July. The thought of it made me sick. And angry.

I had already told Carmen about Adrienne. Now I shared my deeper doubts.

TWO days later she and I met Morgan in the no-name coffee shop in Charlestown that was, apparently, as close to an office as Morgan had. We had our own private corner and a steady supply of hot coffee. Morgan, a tall, fair-haired Swede, was neat, clean, observant. For the most part, he listened and took notes while I talked.

"When Dennis graduated from business school, he took a job with an investment firm in Greenwich, Connecticut. It was a mid-level position, with room to move ahead if he proved himself. He hadn't been with the firm long when he met the wife of one of the senior partners. She was much older than he was but sexy and smart."

"Was her marriage on the rocks?" Carmen asked.

"She told Dennis that, but he found out it wasn't. She had no plans to divorce her husband. She just liked playing around."

"Were you and Dennis dating at the time?" It was Carmen again. Morgan just listened.

"Long distance. I was a senior in college. We talked a lot, but we didn't see each other more than once a month. I had no idea what was going on between visits."

"When did you find out?"

"A year into my marriage."

"He married you, and all the while he was having an affair?"

"Oh, no. The affair ended before we got to the altar. Funny, but we waited. We could have gotten married sooner, but something held us back. I always thought it was just Dennis needing time. In hindsight I realized it was Adrienne."

"Adrienne who?" Morgan asked.

"Hadley." I watched him write down the name. "I learned about her by accident—or so I thought. Only later did I realize it wasn't an accident. Dennis left a letter from her right there with the rest of the bills. It seems he'd been paying her hush money to the tune of a thousand a month. She wanted more. That was probably why he wanted me to know. He was feeling squeezed."

"Hush money for what?" Carmen asked.

"He said it was to keep their affair a secret."

"A thousand a month," Morgan said. "Why didn't Dennis just quit and go work somewhere else?"

"I asked him that. More than once. He said that she could hurt his career no matter where he worked and that at the time the payments began, he was doing too well at Hadley and Gray—that was the firm—to rock the boat. And he was doing well. He knew exactly where to point his clients. They made money. So did he. He moved up fast. The firm thought he was brilliant. Then things quieted. By the time I found out about the payments, after we were married, his career had leveled off. I told him that I didn't see why he had to keep paying Adrienne. If Hadley and Gray wasn't magic for him anymore, he could open his own firm."

"Could he?" Carmen asked.

I paused while the waitress topped off our coffees, then said, "I'd have thought so. He did it a few years later, anyway. At the time, though, he argued that Adrienne was threatening to spread a rumor that he was involved in illegal trading. I actually read that in the letter she sent. She said—and this is pretty nearly a quote—that he would be hard put to find clients if they thought he was on the verge of indictment. She said she needed more money, that she was desperate. She hadn't seen her husband in a year, and she was sick. She actually died four months later of lung cancer. I read that in the obituary that was supposed to be in my file, along with the letter and a handful of canceled checks."

"Why did you keep the file?" Morgan asked.

"I'm not sure. I guess I thought that having it was like having insurance, like as long as I had proof of what Dennis had done, he wouldn't dare do it again."

"Did he know the file existed?" Carmen asked.

"I never thought so, but he must have. No one else had either the opportunity or the cause to clean it out."

"Any idea when it was done?"

"None. The file must have been emptied before I took it from the house. For all I know, it's been empty for years. Maybe he found it one day and just threw everything out. Or maybe he did it last month as a precaution."

"A precaution against what?" Carmen asked.

"Precisely," I answered with a pointed look at Morgan. "I have to know if there's more."

Chapter 6

HOW are you, Mom?"

"I'm okay, though sometimes I wonder why I'm still here. Is there a purpose?"

"Yes. Us. Just knowing you're there means a lot."

"Are you happy, Claire?" Out of the blue.

"Happy?" I asked, thinking fast.

"In life. I need to know. I miss seeing you smile."

"I'm smiling now. Johnny, Kikit, Brody, Joy, and I are off in an hour to the circus." The truth was that Dennis had rarely come to the circus, so it being five of us rather than six wasn't a first. "The kids are excited."

"Well, that's good. Memories, you know. Me, I couldn't bear the animal smell."

I laughed. It was an old line, the standard excuse.

"I should have taken you," she said sadly. "I blamed the money, but I had enough. I was just frightened to spend. So there's another regret."

"No regret. Rona and I did fine without the circus."

"Well, I didn't. I lie here thinking maybe I wouldn't have minded the animal smell at all. But I'll never know."

"I'll just have to bring you a whole bunch of souvenirs, then."

"When? I miss you."

"Same here, Mom. I'm hoping to get there next Thursday. As early as the planes fly. Shall I bring breakfast?"

"Oh, I'd like that," she said. "And the latest catalogue? The one with winter cruisewear? Has it come?"

She had said the one thing that could boost my spirits. The day when my mother no longer cared to dream over clothes would be the day the end was truly near.

"I'll bring it if it has," I assured her. "Mom, it may be too late for me to call when we get back tonight. Can I talk with you in the morning?"

"If I'm here."

"You'll be there."

SO MANY of the same things that I loved about Brody, I loved about his teenage daughter, Joy, but it was never more true than that Saturday. I wasn't sure what Brody had told her about the situation between Dennis and me, but she handled herself like a pro. She had lived through her own parents' divorce. Being intelligent and sensitive, she answered Kikit's questions with aplomb.

Many of them had a fearful edge, like, "If parents stop loving each other, can they stop loving their kids?" or "Do Johnny and I get split up if Mommy and Daddy do?" or "What if one of them marries somebody else?"

Johnny listened intently from that side of Joy where Kikit wasn't, which was where he stayed for most of the day. I tried to coax him out so that I could talk with him more, tried talking about innocuous things like football. Occasionally I succeeded, though not for long. Inevitably he gravitated back to Joy.

Things got easier as the day went on. By the time the circus ended and we drove back to the lighthouse, even Johnny seemed to have forgotten anything was amiss.

Since Joy had never seen the lighthouse, Kikit and Johnny showed her around. The instant their footsteps had faded from the second floor, indicating that they had gone up another flight, Brody looked at me. "Hangin' in there?" he asked.

I choked out a laugh. "I need this settled, Brody. Everything about my life—Dennis, my mother, WickerWise—it's all up in the air."

He came close. "What about me?"

"You, too."

He gave me a short, sweet kiss. It was still new, still that little bit shocking. Before I could melt, he took me in his arms and held me, just held me, standing there, swaying as if in a dance.

"What's the song?" I asked against the warmth of his neck.

"No song."

"There has to be one. You're moving in time to it."

"Nope. I'm tone-deaf. Can't hear the tune *or* the beat. But you knew that."

"I didn't. If I'd known, I never would have kissed you. I don't get involved with men who can't sing." I caught myself. "Of course, look where I got with a man who could. You might not be such a bad risk after all."

Our dance was interrupted by the ringing of the phone. I picked up the receiver.

"Claire?" I had heard my sister's voice in every possible emotional state, but this one was new. "You have to come, Claire. She's comatose. They don't know how long she'll last."

RONA hadn't exaggerated this time. I flew out on Sunday morning to find that the doctors shared her pessimism. No dramatic medical twist had brought on the coma. Connie had simply slipped into it and didn't have the strength to pull herself out.

Rona looked devastated. "Thank God," she breathed when I arrived at the hospital. She was standing beside Connie, clutching the bedrail. "Are you all right?"

I paused, swallowed, nodded. "Just shaky." Then I went to the bed and leaned down. "Hi, Mom. I'm here. See, even sooner than I said." My voice broke on the last word. Her face was pale and waxy. "Mom?" She didn't respond.

"The doctors say we should talk to her," Rona said in little more than a whisper. "They say she might be able to hear."

"I'll tell her about the circus," I said.

I paused, then did just that. I told her about the lions, the horses, and the elephants. I told her about cotton candy and the purple alligator that Kikit had bought.

We were silent for a while. When Rona left to get coffee, I kept the vigil alone. I talked softly, calling Connie's name, touching her hand. I had expected that Rona would take her time, what with me there, but she was back within ten minutes with coffee for us both.

We drank it without speaking, kept standing close. Awkwardness had given way to the need for human warmth. We were family, all that was left of the core unit now that Connie was edging away.

"Maybe we're taking the wrong tack," I said. "The doctor said we can tell her it's okay to let go."

Rona looked appalled. "He told me that, too, but I can't tell her to die."

"We wouldn't be doing that. We'd be saying she doesn't have to hang on if she's too tired. It may be the merciful thing."

"But I need her. I need to tell her things."

I put my arm around Rona's shoulder. She and I hadn't seen eye to eye on many things in life. Still, I could relate to this pain.

"Mom thinks I'm shallow, but I really loved Jerry, and I really loved Harold, and they really loved me for a little while, and it felt so good. So safe. Okay, so I didn't work like she did and you do, but does that make me a bad person?"

Safe. I needed that, too. I had married Dennis for it. But Brody provided it. Did that make me a bad person? "No."

"Then why did she make me feel that way?"

"Maybe she was jealous."

"Jealous?"

"You had luxuries she wanted but couldn't have. Either couldn't have or didn't take. She felt like a coward. You had guts. She envied that."

"She did?"

I imagined so.

SUNDAY morning became Sunday afternoon. Doctors and nurses stopped by, but Connie didn't so much as blink.

Rona curled up in a chair and slept for a while, then woke up and returned to her post at the bedrail. I kept expecting her to go home to shower and do herself up in her usual done-up way, but she wasn't budging from the room other than to go for coffee or food. Dressed in a warm-up suit, with her hair in a ponytail, and no makeup, she remained more unadorned than I had seen her in years. I found her more approachable this way, though that might have been my own need for company. I also thought she was even prettier this way and told her so.

She sighed. "Mom always said that, too."

More than once I wished Brody were with me. But this wasn't a time for Brody. It was a time for Connie, Rona, and me. As the hours passed, as afternoon gave way to night and still Connie stayed with us, her face grew almost opalescent. I thought about the story of Grandmother Kate's pearls and couldn't help but imagine that Connie was becoming one herself. It struck me that that was what deathwatches were about—a chance for family to pull together for a few last hours of peaceful communion, the creation of a final memory, a last pearl to add to the strand. In that sense I was grateful Connie lingered.

I MADE Rona go home that Sunday night for a few hours' sleep while I dozed by Connie's bed, but Rona was back well before Monday's dawn. She had showered and changed into jeans and a sweater, but still the ponytail and the naked face remained. She looked about eighteen.

We curled up in side-by-side armchairs by the bed, ate fresh croissants, sipped coffee, and talked—hushed and intimate—as we hadn't done since we were teenagers intrigued with boys. Now, instead of boys, we talked about men—Rona of her husbands, me of Dennis. Whether we felt drawn to confessions because of the quasi-religious nature of the occasion, I didn't know. But there, in the purple light of dawn, Rona confessed to having a nonexistent sex life with Harold, and I confessed to being evicted by Dennis.

"Do you miss him?" she asked when I was done with my tale.

I had asked myself that more than once. "Those first few days were so filled with fury that there wasn't room for missing much besides the kids," I said. "Now? I miss knowing I'm married. Obviously, I miss the kids. That never stops. Do I miss Dennis? The man himself?" I thought for another minute, just to be sure I wasn't being rash. But of all the emotions I had felt in the last few weeks, missing Dennis wasn't one. Those good parts of my marriage were memories now. Pearls. I would never lose them. But there wouldn't be any more that included Dennis.

"No," I said. "We had grown apart emotionally. We aren't the same people we were when we got married. We shaped each other in ways that made us less compatible. Ironic, isn't it?"

"Does he know you're here?"

"I called him yesterday." My eyes drifted back to Connie. "He said he would fly out with the kids . . . if necessary."

CONNIE remained comatose through Monday. Exhausted by evening, Rona and I left the hospital, picked up pizza on the way to Rona's house, scarfed it down in her kitchen, and slept until early morning. Then we returned to the hospital.

That Tuesday we talked about our childhood, tossing memories back and forth across Connie's bed. On occasion we laughed, and laughed hard. We didn't think Connie would mind. She would have liked the idea that Rona and I were communicating after so long.

During those hours I felt oddly relaxed. I was with my mother. I was with my sister. Work, the children, the custody battle—all seemed distant.

Tuesday night the bubble of tranquillity burst with the rattle of Connie's breathing. Rona and I took to looking at each other in alarm with each new sound that Connie made.

The noise ended in abrupt silence just shy of midnight. The doctor came and made the pronouncement, followed by the nurses, who turned off the machines. Rona and I stood holding each other while they did what they needed to do, but when they would have taken Connie from the room, we protested.

"A few more minutes?" I begged. Rona was crying softly by my side.

They backed out and closed the door, leaving the three of us alone a final time.

I drew Rona with me toward the bed. "She looks peaceful," I said. "I hope she is."

"So do I. She wasn't such a bad mother." Rona drew in a shaky breath and said a wry "Something has to explain why I stayed around so long."

My eyes filled. "You loved her. And she loved you. Mothers never give up on their kids. They can't. It isn't in their constitution."

WE BURIED Connie on Thursday morning in a brief graveside ceremony beneath a cold and somber sky. I hugged Kikit throughout the service, passing her to Rona from time to time, while Dennis held Johnny close.

On Friday morning Dennis and the children flew home. I stayed on until Saturday evening to be with Rona.

Our goal was to spend the day at Mom's apartment deciding what to do with its contents, and for a time we did try. First memory distracted us, though, then grief. By the time Rona drove me to the airport, the only decision we had made was that I would take the cat. I boarded the plane with my overnighter on one shoulder and Valentino in his bag on the other.

BRODY MET ME IN BOSTON. HE took my bag and Valentino, threw an arm around me, and guided me to the car. I remember driving over the bridge, but I slept right through a stop at the market for cat food and litter. He woke me when we reached the lighthouse, carried everything inside, and got Valentino set up while I stared out at the sea. Then he poured me a glass of wine and held me close in the huge wicker chair-and-a-half in the dark of my den.

I cried for Mom and for Rona, cried for unfulfilled dreams and regrets that didn't have to be. By the time I ran out of tears, I was sleepy again, but I wouldn't let Brody leave. We fell asleep there in the chair, me burrowing into Brody, he holding me close. I was so overloaded with feeling that the only thing making sense was how much I loved him.

I don't know how long I slept—an hour, maybe two. I awoke restless and moved against him. By the time I realized that he was awake, I was needing him so badly that short of the lighthouse falling into the sea, nothing was pulling us apart.

We kissed, and kissed deeply. We touched. We arched and shifted, pushing clothing aside to feel flesh, and if there was anything unwise in what we did, I couldn't think of it. I loved Brody.

Afterward we curled against each other and slept again, but when I awoke, Brody felt tense. I wrapped my arms around him and said a fast "I know how your mind works, Brody Parth. It's saying you took advantage of me at a time when I was weak, and if not that, it's saying you've single-handedly blown my chances of getting the kids back, but it isn't so. I don't regret what we did for a minute. Not for one minute!" I emphasized the last with squeezes to his rib cage and waited for his response.

He took my hand to his mouth, kissed it. "I have no regrets," he said. "Not a one."

"Good."

"I've wanted you for a long time. A *long* time."

"You never let on."

"How could I? You were married to my best friend."

I was starting to feel differently about certain things. "I'm going to win this case," I said with conviction. "I'll do whatever it takes, Brody. I'm not going to find myself five or ten years from now wishing that I'd done more. My mother died thinking of all she didn't do. I don't want to be like that."

I was silent then, thinking of Connie.

Brody gave me that time, a silent meditation. Then he said, "Is that what our making love was about?"

I took his face in my hands and said in a whisper-soft voice, "Our making love was the most positive thing to happen to me in weeks. It was the most honest. The most real. I've been sitting around feeling helpless for a month now, but I'm tired of it. I need to be proactive, not reactive." I pressed kisses on his eyes and the bridge of his nose. "What time is it?"

He glanced at the clock behind me. "Two."

"Stay with me. In my bed. Until morning. I need to roll over and feel you there. It's been quite a week."

I could see he was pleased. Still, he said, "What if there's someone out there on a boat with an infrared telephoto lens?"

"I'm a separated woman," I said, for the first time feeling the full freedom of that. "I can do what I want."

THAT thought held when Dennis rang my bell the next morning at the ungodly hour of eight. I might have lied when he mentioned Brody's car outside. I might have said Brody had come over for an early breakfast, but I was done with being made out to be the guilty party, and I was proud to be Brody's lover.

So when Dennis asked if Brody was still in bed, I said, "Yes."

He seemed almost sad, then curious. "No more denials?"

Valentino came from nowhere to curl around my leg. Scooping him up, I said, "I never denied what was true. Brody and I weren't romantically involved until you and I separated."

"Aren't you afraid it will hurt your chances to regain custody?"

"How could it? We weren't sexually involved until this weekend. You and Phoebe Lowe were involved last July. I have records from your stay in that motel in Vermont." When he blinked, I rubbed it in. "I'll raise it in court, Dennis. I'll raise that, plus anything else, if there is anything else, about Adrienne."

"What else could there be?"

"You tell me. She threatened to implicate you in illegal trading. At least, that's what you said at the time."

"You won't find proof of anything."

"Do I need it? All you had against me was innuendo, and the courts went for it. You really shouldn't have emptied that file. That's what made me suspicious."

Dennis looked sober. "Innuendo can't hurt me. That business with Adrienne was long ago. Even if there was something more, the statute of limitations has expired. The law can't touch me."

"Maybe not. But Pittney wouldn't be pleased to hear about it."

That shook him. "How did you know about Pittney?"

"It doesn't matter. But if I have to go to them, I will. I want my kids back."

"Boy, you've gotten tough."

"You've made me tough. You were the one who took me to court and took away my kids and my home."

I was thinking clearly, feeling stronger than I had in days. "For the past month you've been playing dirty. Well, I can play dirty, too. I don't want to, but if I have no choice, I will. I'll also take you to court on the divorce settlement. You've piddled away all the money you ever made. You're not going to piddle away mine. So back off," I warned, and was about to slam the door in his face when I frowned. "We agreed that I would come for the kids at noon. Why are you here now?"

"They spent the night with my parents," he said, still sober. "I'm on my way to pick them up. I wanted to talk to you first. We have to tell them about Jenovitz, and I thought we should coordinate our stories."

I stared at him in amazement, wondering what was behind his solicitousness. But he looked perfectly serious, even humble. When I couldn't see the slightest hint of either arrogance or deceit, I stood back. "Come in. I'll make coffee, and we'll talk."

So Dennis intruded on my first morning with Brody. But it was necessary, a precedent-setting of sorts. Dennis and I had to learn to deal civilly with each other where the children were concerned. Dennis also had to learn to see me with Brody.

That didn't mean I lost my resolve. As soon as he left, I called Carmen at home. She reported that Art Heuber had filed his opposition to our petition on Wednesday, that the judge was studying it and would be in touch on Monday. As for the rest, Morgan Hauser was still searching.

First thing that Monday before Thanksgiving, Carmen called with good news and bad news. The good news was that a justice of the appeals court had agreed to a hearing on our petition. The bad news was that the holiday would hold things up. The hearing wouldn't be held until the Monday after.

That afternoon I had my third meeting with Dean Jenovitz. He was back to the pipe this time, filling it with tobacco, tamping it down, scrutinizing the bowl, tasting the stem, and so on. I had the impression that he was bored.

Worse, I had the impression that he had already made his decision and was simply marking time.

"He doesn't react to things he should," I told Carmen on the phone after the meeting. "When I told him about Dennis and Phoebe being at a motel in Vermont last July, he grunted, then asked why I was fixated on their relationship. What's going on?"

"I'm wondering," Carmen said, "if he has a sweet deal with Selwey."

"Sweet deal?"

"Word is, he's tired, that he's thinking of retiring, but money is an issue. By way of compromise, he's cutting back on his private practice and letting court cases like yours support him. He's paid by the hour. It's easy money."

"Easy money?" It was my money, my problems. "Gee, thanks."

"You know what I mean. There isn't any therapy involved. Some cases are cut-and-dried. If one of the parents is abusive or unstable, the children are placed with the other parent. For the other cases, he usually recommends shared custody."

"He hasn't mentioned shared custody to me." I wondered why not and found no comfort in the answer.

"How would you feel about it?"

"I don't want to share my children." The thought of it brought back all the anger. "Dennis had no right doing what he did. I don't want a man like that being a major influence on my kids."

"He is their father. He's doing an okay job of it, isn't he?"

No, I wanted to say. He's doing a lousy job.

But the truth was that he wasn't. The children were clean, well fed, well supervised. Between what I had seen and what they had told me, Dennis was trying. I hated to admit it, but there it was.

"What's with Morgan?" I asked.

"He's getting inklings of things. He won't elaborate until he has proof, and that's hard to come by with something that happened so long ago. Finding witnesses is tough. Dennis was right about the statute of limitations. He isn't at risk."

"Maybe not legally," I said, "but I meant what I told Dennis. If I have to, I'll call people at Pittney. It's not that I want to ruin Dennis. I just want custody of the kids."

Chapter 7

THANKSGIVING was an eye-opener. It was my first major holiday separated from Dennis, my first major holiday without Connie. Technically, little was different. I was still the one cooking the turkey, still the one laying the table.

What was different was Brody, who was either freed by Dennis's absence, so used to doing for himself, or so much in love with me that he did more than his share of the work.

What else was different was the lighthouse, which dressed up so beautifully, with its view of the ocean, that we might have been at an idyllic Plymouth Rock.

What *else* was different was Rona. She was more agreeable than I had ever found her.

And then there were the children. Dennis had suggested I take them on Thanksgiving Day so that he could take them for a weekend of skiing. I was worried that the holiday would be like salt on the wound of their parents' divorce, and yes, I'm sure there were moments that stung. But they were pleased to be spending the night here—"Can we sleep in your bed, Mommy, and turn out all the lights and pretend we're in the middle of the ocean for the whole night and watch the sun come up? Can we, pleeease?" asked Kikit—and they loved being with Joy and with Rona and with Brody.

Yes, even Johnny. It took him a while to warm up, perhaps to forget that Dennis wasn't there, but once it happened, he was more his normal self than he had been since the split.

My only moments of regret in the aftermath of that Thanksgiving had to do with Mom. I missed her.

It was Friday morning. The children had left, Brody had taken Joy into Boston, and Rona and I were braving the winds, bundled up on the rocks not far from the base of my light. We had our feet tucked beneath us and were watching the swirl of the water a mere ten feet away.

"There's good reason," Rona was saying, "why you didn't tell Connie you were getting divorced. She would have been so hung up on the concept that she wouldn't have seen the reality. I can see the reality, and it isn't so bad.

"The reality," Rona went on, "is that there isn't the tension there used to be when Dennis was here. When he was here, you needed to make things perfect."

"Did I?"

"Definitely."

I thought about it. "Maybe I wanted to make him proud."

"Maybe you knew his eye was wandering, and wanted to make

yourself indispensable." Her mouth thinned. "Dennis cheated on you for years, Claire."

"I don't know that."

"He did. Trust me." She tipped up her chin and looked out to sea. "Dennis made a pass at me once."

"What?"

"Touched me in a totally inappropriate way. I mean, *totally* inappropriate way. Nothing innocent intended."

"When?"

"Between Jerry and Harold."

"Why didn't you tell me?"

She gave me an are-you-nuts look. "Because you were married to the guy. Besides, Mom would have blamed me for wearing a tight dress and accused me of making a pass at Dennis." She put her chin on her knees, but not before I saw that her look had turned stricken.

I patted her arm. "How are you doing without Mom?" I asked gently.

"Fine. There's plenty to keep me busy—big sale at Neiman Marcus, huge gala at the country club, incredible special on sculpted nails at the Ten-in-a-Row Emporium."

"I'm serious, Rona."

"So am I."

"I'll rephrase the question, then. How are you during the time when you aren't busy?"

"Lost," she said without pause. "I was thinking of moving. I'm tired of Cleveland. Everyone there thinks I'm as much of a ditz as Mom did." She gave a small sigh and sought the horizon. "But you wouldn't know about that, would you?"

She was wrong. I did know. I had learned what it was to be judged—and judged unfairly, though it hadn't occurred to me to make the connection between Rona's experience and mine. I did now, and the connection was there.

NO AMOUNT of apologizing on my part could change what Rona had experienced in the past, but I could help her in other ways.

The first of those came to me late that afternoon. We were at the office—Rona, reading *USA Today,* and I, reviewing the monthly reports from our franchises in Milwaukee, Kansas City, and Charleston. We were waiting for Brody, who was dropping Joy at the airport and coming back to take us to dinner.

When he finally arrived, he looked distracted. He went to his desk and turned papers around to study them from the front so that he wouldn't have to unseat Rona. Then he straightened and put a hand on the top of his head.

I knew that gesture. "Brody?"

He looked my way, held up his hand, and smiled. "No sweat. I'm cool." He bent over the desk again. "I'll handle it."

I had a feeling I knew what the problem was. "The Christmas boutiques?" I asked. Not only the boutiques but three charity events begging for our attendance.

We had been wrestling with the problem for days. Technically, the boutiques would survive without us. We had already received detailed reports on the Christmas displays, had given our approval or disapproval where it fit. The visits were more for employee morale. But we were big on morale. It set our operation apart from many others and was a powerful incentive for hard work and loyalty. We made our people feel important. Personal visits did that.

Since I couldn't make them this year, Brody had agreed to. But he was also doing double the work here at the office, what with my distractions. He had worked late most nights this week and was planning more of the same for the weekend.

I glanced at Rona. She looked half asleep.

"Rona," I called sharply. "How would you like an all-expense-paid trip across the country?"

Her eyes snapped to mine, and her brows rose.

"We need someone to check out our Christmas boutiques," I said. "There are twelve of them. What do you say?"

She looked confused.

"We'd give you a checklist of things to look for. You'd report back at the end of each stop. It'd actually be kind of fun. You'd take our people out to breakfast or dinner, whichever works out best, be a goodwill ambassador of sorts."

Rona looked from me to Brody and back. Eyebrows still raised, she pointed a questioning finger at herself.

"Yes, you," Brody told Rona. "You'd be perfect at it."

Rona scowled. "Are you sure this isn't just a makeshift dummy's mission to give me something to do with Mom gone?"

Brody's expression was nearly as priceless as his voice. "Makeshift dummy's mission? Rona, I've been pulling overtime all week trying to get ready for this, it's that important. If you don't do it, it's right back in my lap. You'd be doing me a huge favor."

Rona sat back. "What about a salary?"

Brody didn't blink. "Two hundred a day."

She made a face. "I'd make more as a janitor at Cleveland Heights High. Three hundred a day."

"You wouldn't want to be a janitor. Besides, you don't need the money. Two fifty, plus expenses. Take it or leave it."

"You drive a hard bargain, Brody Parth," she said, but there was a smile on her face that made me feel nice.

THREE days later, on the first Monday in December, Carmen and Art faced off before Justice David Wheeler of the Massachusetts Court of Appeals. Since the justice already knew the facts, the purpose of the hearing was to allow him to ask questions, but only as they pertained to the earlier hearings with Selwey. This hearing was simply a review of that court action. No new evidence would be put forward. Carmen's argument, dictated by the nature of the appeal, was that Selwey had abused judicial discretion by making a decision that was beyond the bounds of reason. Heuber argued to the contrary. Neither Dennis nor I was asked to testify.

The hearing lasted for just under an hour. We had been hoping that Justice Wheeler would announce his decision from the bench at the end of that time. In fact, he took the matter under advisement, promising a written opinion within several days.

So we waited. Again. Still.

Tuesday came and went without his decision, then Wednesday. I tried to apply myself to WickerWise, but working was easier said than done. Two hours at a time was as much as I could manage before restlessness set in and I retreated to my workroom.

The dirty work was already done on the antique rocker and its side table. I had cleaned and smoothed every area where broken wickers had come out. Now I cut new reeds to lengths that would allow for comfortable overlap, soaked them to make them pliable, and started to weave them in, one by one.

BY LATE Thursday I was vacillating between hope and despair. Then Carmen called.

My heart began to hammer. "What?" I asked.

"I'm sorry, Claire. I just got the call. A written opinion will follow, but the gist of it is that since Dennis appears to be a capable father, Wheeler didn't think Selwey's decision was irrational."

I let out a heartsick breath and sank into a chair. "What about me?" I cried. "Does he think I'm an incapable mother?"

"No. Simply that leaving the children with their father pending the guardian's study was a reasonable move. That's all the appeal was about."

I closed my eyes and pressed a fist to my heart.

"Are you there?" Carmen asked cautiously.

"I'm here." I sighed. "Then everything rests on Jenovitz?"

"For now. He'll be our fastest source of relief."

My heart dropped. "Assuming he rules in my favor."

"Well, we're working on that, too. If we can get figures to show that his findings are inordinately supportive of Selwey's rulings, we'll have a shot at another motion for reconsideration. It'd help if we could reach an agreement with Dennis on custody. Unfortunately, there's another problem. Heuber called right after the judge's clerk did."

I braced myself. "What?"

"Dennis has a buyer for WickerWise."

"WickerWise isn't for sale."

"Heuber says," Carmen mocked, "that Dennis had been weighing the Pittney option all along and now feels he wants that instead. So from you, by way of a settlement, he wants half the market value of WickerWise. Since you can't—don't have that kind of money lying around, he suggests selling WickerWise and paying him off. Your instincts were right."

That was small solace. "I'm not selling. I'll take this to trial before I do that."

"It won't come to that. We have Dennis on Phoebe and Adrienne and whatever else Morgan is getting. Call this Heuber's last stand. They're posturing. Calling our bluff."

"Hold out," I ordered. "Dennis has a right to a say in what we do with the kids. I accept that. But WickerWise is mine."

It sounded good. It sounded tough. Still, I knew I could lose it.

There was nothing I could do but wait. That was the worst. I waited for Carmen's associates to find dirt on Jenovitz, waited for Morgan Hauser to find dirt on Dennis, waited for Dennis to tire of fathering, waited for Jenovitz to reach his decision.

SEVEN weeks to the day after my children were removed from my care, Jenovitz spent an hour with them. One hour. Since neither Dennis nor I was allowed to listen, we didn't know what was said. We waited in the kitchen, while they took the den.

Carmen had been right. Jenovitz was good with kids. Kikit liked him, but even Johnny, who was naturally wary, emerged from the meeting unscathed.

It was rather comical, those moments after, with Dennis and me hovering close, dying to ask what had been said in that room and not daring to. I don't know how Jenovitz did it, whether he had sworn them to secrecy or what, but not even Kikit revealed much. She was more concerned with showing me the nest she had built for the purple alligator she had bought at the circus.

My heart nearly broke when Johnny asked, with unmasked hope, if I was staying for dinner.

Of course, Jenovitz didn't see that. He was long gone by then.

BRODY'S MEETING WITH Jenovitz was more upsetting.

It was held at six on the Thursday evening of that second week in December. I had taken refuge after hours in our Essex store and was sitting on the floor in the light of a single lamp, surrounded by sketches of spring displays, when Brody came in. Beyond my pool of light the store was dark, so I didn't immediately see his expression, but his footfall on the carpet was emphatic.

He strode to the edge of the light. "You're right, Claire," he said. "Something stinks. He has his mind made up. He knew how he felt about me from the get-go. What's going on?"

"I wish I knew. It's like someone has a personal vendetta against me." I put my sketch pad aside. "What did he say?"

" 'Tell me about yourself' was what he said, and then he just sat there fiddling with the pipe."

Brody's indignation made me smile. He was such a laid-back, easygoing sort on the average that explosions of passion were all the more meaningful. And he was validating every one of the feelings I'd been getting from Jenovitz myself.

"Then, after a string of insulting questions, he asked what my intentions were."

I waited to hear his response, but he wandered off to the shadowed front of the store. His large frame bent when he set his fists on the sales desk.

"Brody?"

His voice was less distinct coming back to me. "He knows your marriage is ending. I figured he'd be thrilled to know I wanted to marry you. I figured he'd be thrilled to know we'd be able to offer the kids a stable two-parent home."

I rose and went to him. "He wasn't?"

"Nope. Said I had gall, wanting your business *and* you. Said I was complicating the custody issue. Said I was confusing the kids. Said I was distracting you at a time when you couldn't afford it." Brody turned his head, almost looking at me but not quite. "Said I'd be doing you more of a favor by leaving town."

"No."

His eyes found mine. "Maybe he's right."

"No." For the briefest moment I imagined what it would be like if he left. The sense of loss was devastating.

"I'd do it, Claire. I lived for years thinking I'd never have you, and I could have survived that way. I know you, Claire. I know what your kids mean to you. If the choice comes down to me or them, I'll give it all up and vanish."

"Without asking me what I want?" I cried in a burst of anger. "Without giving me a say in the choice? You're starting to sound like *them!*"

He hooked an elbow around my neck and dragged me close.

"In the first place," I reasoned, "if Jenovitz has already made up his mind, it won't make one bit of difference whether you're in the picture or not. In the second place, I'm not living without you."

"They'll make you pay."

I drew my head back fast. "Who? Dennis? The judge? Jenovitz? Who are they to tell me how to live my life? Like they're paragons of virtue," I muttered, feeling a great swell of contempt. "Well, I'm tired of being put on the defensive. I'm tired of having to second-guess everything I do for the sake of meeting some standard that isn't anywhere near as good as the standard I've always set for myself. I'm done doing it, Brody," I warned. "If Jenovitz doesn't give me my kids, I'll take Dennis to trial, and I'll go from one court to another if I have to. I'm fighting. I'm fighting for the kids, and I'm fighting for you. I'll even fight *you* for you if I have to."

"But the kids, Claire."

I kissed him. "Help keep this part of my life on track, and I'll take care of the kids. I'll get them. So help me, I will."

OFTEN in the darkest hours of the night I awoke feeling empty inside. Part of it had to do with Connie. The rest had to do with the kids, with the fact that they were surviving without me and the fear that I would never get them back.

During one of those night awakenings, I imagined squirreling them away on a day when they were in my care. I imagined hiding out with them in Argentina, changing their names, and raising them without the interference of Dennis or the court.

Would I do it? Seriously? I wasn't sure. I was a law-abiding citizen. But the law hadn't treated me well recently.

And then the call came from Carmen. "Morgan's on his way over," she said, excitement in her voice. "He found something."

THE wait was worth it this time.

"There was meat behind Adrienne's threat," Morgan said. "There was more between them than sex. Adrienne gave Dennis inside stock tips. She got them eavesdropping on conversations her husband had. Easy enough to pass them to Dennis."

I was torn between wanting to believe and wanting to argue. "Who told you this?"

"Three people, so it's corroborated. That's what took the time. One was an old friend of Adrienne's, another a colleague of Dennis's, the third a cellmate of Adrienne's husband."

I swallowed. "Cellmate?"

"Soon after Dennis's rise, Lee Hadley was indicted for trading irregularities. Dennis was one of many in the firm who were interviewed by the government. He was spared indictment in exchange for testifying against Lee. Lee did time in Allenwood—cushy enough—but his income flow stopped. Adrienne kept herself in the style to which she was accustomed, in part by blackmailing Dennis with the threat of exposure."

Carmen asked, "Then he didn't tell the feds everything?"

"No. He hid the extent of his own use of those tips. So he paid Adrienne."

I let out a long, shaky breath. Oh, yes, we had needed something like this, but the victory was bittersweet. I remembered how I had felt learning about Adrienne. The disillusionment now was nearly as strong. "Then he wasn't a wunderkind at all."

"No."

Carmen touched my hand. "You need to share this information with Jenovitz."

I nodded.

"Claire?"

"I will."

"You're having second thoughts. You're feeling sad, even disloyal. Don't, Claire. This may be the strongest weapon you have in your fight for the kids."

With a conscious effort I shrugged off those feelings. It wouldn't do to think of what I had lost with Morgan's discovery, since so much of that had been illusory. I preferred to think of what I had gained. The more I thought about it, the better I felt.

JENOVITZ didn't want to meet with me. I left message after message on his answering machine, but he didn't return my calls. Finally, after three days of calling, my perseverance paid off. He inadvertently picked up the phone when I was at the other end, and even then it took a whale of convincing. He felt he had already asked me what needed to be asked. Eventually, though, he gave in, but with a marked lack of grace.

That lack of grace carried over to our meeting. He looked awkward and impatient. He was back to popping sour balls, and didn't sit for longer than ten minutes at a stretch before jumping up and leaving the office.

In an effort to be as gracious as I could, I thanked him profusely for giving me his time. Then I told him what Morgan Hauser had learned. I tried to be as detailed as I could with the telling. When I was done, I set a copy of Morgan's report on his desk.

Jenovitz tapped a finger on the report, nodded, stared.

"I'm surprised you aren't shocked," I said. "My husband is guilty of things that could have put him behind bars if they'd come out at the time. But he hid it. He lied. Under oath. Doesn't that bother you? Won't you think twice about giving custody of two young children to a man capable of breaking laws that way?"

"He's older now. More mature. He has more to lose. Back then he didn't have children. Now he does. Having custody of them gives him good reason to walk the straight and narrow."

Jenovitz's defense of Dennis left me dumbfounded. "But—but what about me?" I asked helplessly. "Historically, the mother has been considered the more appropriate parent to have custody. Why is my case any different?"

"You work, but your husband is free. He has the time, desire, and ability to parent the children."

"Did he tell you about his new business prospect? He's hoping to buy a vice presidency in an up-and-coming company. It's in Springfield, halfway across the state. I live ten minutes from my office, ten minutes from the kids—home, school, you name it. I have a second-in-command who runs the company for me when I'm not around, but I'm the boss. I don't have to ask permission to take time off. I have more flexibility than most workingwomen, certainly more than most workingmen."

Jenovitz swiveled in his seat, extracted a file from the pile on the credenza behind him, and tossed it open on the desk. He gestured toward it with a dismissive hand. "It's right there—the number of hours you work, the number of days you travel, the missed rides and canceled appointments."

I didn't protest. Instead, bluntly I asked, "Do you think I'm a bad mother?"

"Do you think your husband is a bad father?"

"Bad?"

I barely had the word out when Jenovitz signaled a break and left the room. By the time he returned, I had given his question some thought.

"Dennis isn't a bad father. I'm sure he loves the children. Do I think he understands what full-time parenting entails? I think he's beginning to, but two months is nothing."

"You think his patience will exhaust itself."

"I think his desire will, once the settlement is decided."

"You make this sound like a game."

"Me?" My laugh was brittle. "I've taken this seriously from the start. It's everyone else who treats it like a game. Believe me, Dr. Jenovitz, the thought that the future of my children depends on bartering makes me sick. Are you aware of what Dennis is asking by way of a divorce settlement?"

"Children are my concern, not things."

"But one goes with the other in this case," I argued. "He's asking that I sell my business. He claims he wants the money, but that's only part of it. He wants me to lose WickerWise. Its success is a thorn in his side. It emasculates him."

"Emasculates?" Jenovitz asked dryly. "You're an angry woman. That kind of anger isn't good for children to see."

He was definitely stonewalling. It was the only explanation for the absurdity of his argument. I tried to let it go but couldn't. "My husband feels anger and more. He feels jealousy; he feels the need for revenge. How healthy is that for the kids—not to mention a history of infidelity and dishonesty, not to mention a new top-management position with new responsibilities and new pressures? If you think I'm gone a lot, how much will he be around?"

"He has his parents to fill in. Who do you have?" Jenovitz asked, but he was out of his chair and slipping out the door again before I could answer.

I fingered my watch. Time was running out. It was only then starting to hit me that I had played my ace and failed. Dean Jenovitz didn't care about Dennis's past misdeeds.

Brody was right. Something was very weird. A sweet deal. That had to be it. A sweet deal between Selwey and Jenovitz.

After several minutes I heard footsteps on the stairs. Soon after, the door opened. Jenovitz returned to his chair.

"Can I talk about anger for a minute?" I asked.

He gave an indifferent wave. "Talk about anything you want."

Softly I pleaded, "Injustice makes me angry. Unfairness infuriates me. You people are the ones who've created those conditions. Correct them, and there's no anger."

Jenovitz frowned. "Give you what you want, let you have your way, and there's no anger. Is that what you mean?"

I sat forward. "It isn't." I held up a hand. "You're a psychologist. So please help me understand what's going on here. Nothing about this case rings true. There's no logic. There's no open-mindedness. I'm being viewed as a stereotype, but I'm not one. I've tried to convey that, but I'm not getting through."

"This case is about choices," he said. "We can't *be* everything at once, but that's what you want. Not only that, but you want us to tell you you're doing a great job. Choices, Claire, choices. Surely that makes sense."

"Actually, no," I reasoned. "My children spend most of the day in school. Afterward they need to be with their peers. I have time to do other things without taking time from them."

"You spread yourself too thin."

"But I don't."

He stood and looked down at me. "If you're thinking to change my mind with arrogance, you're mistaken." He reached for the door.

"Where's the choice here?" I asked. "Nothing I've done or said in this room has mattered. You knew what you thought about me the first day you met me, and it hasn't changed."

He left and closed the door behind him without argument.

I rose from my chair, paced to the side of the office, then back. I looked at my watch. I looked at Morgan's report, unheeded on top of my file. Something was very weird here.

I gave Morgan's report a little push. Beneath it were the children's school records. Curious, I gave them a little push.

I whipped my hand back. I wasn't a snoop.

Then it hit me that that file belonged to me. The court may have put Jenovitz to the task, but I was the one paying him to do it.

Still, I listened. There was no sound on the outer stairs. If Jenovitz's two previous returns were any indication, I could expect to hear his footsteps for five, maybe six seconds before the door opened.

Alert for that sound, I flipped through the file. I didn't know what I was looking for—didn't know why I was looking at all. Curiosity, perhaps. Or defiance. Whatever, I saw Carmen's letterhead and Art Heuber's letterhead. I saw court records and Jenovitz's own typed notes in front of a piece of stationery with the official seal of the Essex County Probate Court at the top.

Something else was at the top, a handwritten note above the letterhead. To this day I don't know what made me look closer. But I did. I pulled it out and had read enough when I heard Jenovitz's footfall on the stairs.

I hesitated for only as long as it took me to realize that I wasn't stealing; that report was rightfully mine. Then I folded the paper, put it in my pocket, and slipped into my seat.

The door opened. I looked at Jenovitz in the same way I had each other time he had returned. I didn't look guilty, didn't feel guilty. If my heart was thudding, it could as easily have been from agitation as from elation or sheer and pervasive relief. Relief was what I felt, all right. I felt as though a band had been removed from my chest, a weight from my shoulders.

"We don't have much time left," Jenovitz advised me. "Is there anything more you want to say?"

I cleared my throat to keep my voice from shaking. "A question, actually. Out of curiosity. Was there anything I might have done differently to have earned your respect?"

He neatened the papers and closed the file. "You might have indicated that you wanted to change. But I never got that from you. You seem to feel that you're doing just fine and that if there are problems in your life, they're caused by others. Sometimes, Claire, we have to take responsibility for our actions."

I couldn't have agreed with him more.

With my elation threatening to show, I mustered my composure, thanked him for his time, and left.

TEN minutes later I unfolded the letter I had filched and spread it flat on Carmen's desk. It was a form letter assigning the Raphael matter to Dean Jenovitz. It gave dates and noted enclosures. There was nothing remotely personal in its body.

The personal note was at the top. It was a scrawl in the same blue ink as the judge's signature at the bottom.

"Dennis Raphael seems sincere," it said. "Let Father win this time."

Chapter 8

SNOW was falling when I returned to Reaper Head, large flakes drifting steadily down to settle in clumps on the needled boughs of the pines. Though this wasn't the first snow of the season, it had that freshness. Dirt disappeared. Dusk sparkled. The artist in me saw things differently when they were reduced to white.

Then again, it could have been the woman in me seeing things differently now that I had found a method to the court's madness.

I parked beside the keeper's cottage, scuffed my way to the door just for the joy of seeing the snow bunch ahead of my feet, let myself in, and set several bags on the kitchen counter. I was making dinner for Brody. We were celebrating, and though I would have liked to have the children with us, it was enough to believe that they would be soon enough.

Brody called at seven to say that we might well be snowed in and could he pick anything up on the way.

I had shrimp-and-scallop risotto, a spinach salad, and a crusty Italian bread all set to eat, and didn't need anything else but him.

When he arrived at seven thirty, I didn't need the food, either. We were kissing by the front door when the phone rang.

"Let it ring," he whispered.

But the mother in me couldn't. I made it, breathless, to the phone seconds before the answering machine clicked on. "Hello?"

"Meet us at the hospital," Dennis said in a voice I barely recognized. "Kikit's sick."

My breath caught. "Allergy sick?"

"Yeah. We're in the car. The driving's lousy, but it was faster than waiting for an ambulance."

I heard him swear; I heard, muted, the awful, awful sound of Kikit's wheezing. "Did you give her epinephrine?" I asked.

"That and antihistamine, but late. She didn't call me right away."

"Put the phone to her ear." The wheezing came louder. "Kikit? Sweetie, it's Mommy. You're going to be fine. Just relax and try to breathe slowly. Don't be scared. I'll be at the hospital soon after you get there, okay?"

Her half-sobbed "Mah—mee" nearly broke my heart.

"You don't have to breathe deeply." I knew she couldn't. "You'll do just fine with shallow breaths, but don't be frightened. You're such a good girl. Can you let me talk to Daddy?"

Dennis's "Yeah?" sounded scared.

"Keep her calm. I'm leaving now. I'll see you there."

Brody had my coat waiting when I hung up the phone. Within minutes we were on the road.

The drive was a nightmare. The Range Rover fishtailed around a corner or two, but Brody was an ace. We pulled up to the emergency-room entrance and parked behind Dennis's car.

Johnny was sitting straight in a chair in the waiting room. The instant he saw us, he bolted up and ran across the room. He took my hand and started pulling me forward. "We were gonna eat supper out, but the lines were awful for Chinese and pizza, so we got takeout from Mad Mel's and brought it home, and Dad took all the nuts off the salad, so we don't know what it was. She just got up when we were done and went to her room."

We had reached a small cubicle. Brody put an arm around Johnny to hold him back while I slipped inside.

Kikit lay on the examining table. Had her face not been swollen, it would have been swallowed up by the oxygen mask. I couldn't tell if the wheezing had begun to ease; the mask muted the sound. I could see large hives on her bare chest and imagined, from the way she was squirming, that they were everywhere. One small hand had already been hooked up to needles. A blood-pressure cuff was in place. Hovering close were two doctors and their stethoscopes, one nurse, two IV bags, and Dennis, who was holding her free hand, leaning in, talking softly. His tone was soothing, in stark contrast to the look of panic he sent me.

"Here's Mommy," he said. He moved aside to make room for me, but he didn't release Kikit's hand.

"Hi, sweetie." I stroked her hair. It was damp. "How do you feel, baby? Any better yet?"

Her eyes were small and frightened in her bloated face, opening to see me, then closing again. My own flew to the doctors.

"It may take a little while," the older of the two doctors said. "She was well into the reaction by the time your husband gave her the first shot."

Dennis looked devastated. His voice was low and hoarse. "It would have been even longer if Johnny hadn't heard her wheezing. There were pine nuts on the salad. I thought I got them all. She'd already eaten her hamburger and didn't eat more than half of the salad when she said she was done. She must have started to feel lousy but not wanted to say anything."

Of course she hadn't wanted to say anything, I thought hysterically. Her last attack had immediately preceded our separation. No doubt she connected the two.

"She must have thought I'd be angry," Dennis went on, "and no wonder, I've done it before"—he leaned in again—"but I'm not, Kikit. I'm not. If anyone was at fault, it was me."

Her eyes remained shut. When a tiny tear escaped from the corner of one, Dennis made an anguished sound. "This isn't your fault, baby. I should have checked up on you sooner. I love you, Kikit." Worriedly he asked me, "Where's Johnny?"

"Outside with Brody."

"He blamed himself for not hearing her sooner."

I brushed the tear from Kikit's eye and kept my hand touching her, so she would feel me. "It wasn't Johnny's fault."

"It was my fault."

Of course it was your fault, a tiny voice inside me said. She was in your custody. It was your job to see she stayed safe!

But that angry voice died a quick death. "It wasn't your fault, either. Allergic reactions happen. You tried to avoid it. At least this time we know its cause."

The doctor pumped up the blood-pressure cuff and released it, listening to Kikit's pulse.

"It was a candy bar last time," Dennis said close by my ear.

I looked at him fast and whispered, "What?"

"A candy bar," he repeated quietly enough that Kikit wouldn't hear. "I found the empty wrapper in her room a few days later."

In a flash I relived the agony of wondering what she had eaten and how we could protect her when we didn't know, not to mention the guilt of fearing that there *had* been something in the casserole I had made. And all the while Dennis had known the truth.

I stared at him in disbelief. "Did she know it was the candy?" I asked.

Dennis's nod was superfluous. Of course she had known. That would explain why she hadn't been freaked out more than usual by the attack. It would also explain the way she had cried and blamed herself that day she had learned we were separating.

"What about the medicine?" I whispered.

He shook his head. "I couldn't find it. I swear."

A sound from Kikit, a small cry, brought my attention back to her, but her eyes remained closed. "I'm here, baby. It's okay. Mommy and Daddy are here. The doctors will make it better."

We continued to talk to her, using the same encouraging tone. Usually the worst was over in an hour or two, and we were on our way home. This time was different. The wheezing went on.

Dennis left to check on Johnny. I glanced at the door when it opened to readmit one of the nurses. On the other side, Dennis had his arms around Johnny. Seconds after that, he returned. I actually felt better with him back, less alone.

The doctors conferred with each other at the far end of the cubicle. Their voices were muted, their faces grave. I knew what worried them. If Kikit didn't start responding to the medication soon, she would be in trouble. Much more swelling in her air passages, and she would suffocate.

Dennis and I exchanged frightened looks.

The doctors returned. One held the oxygen mask more firmly in place. The other monitored Kikit's lungs with his stethoscope. The one holding the oxygen mask adjusted the speed of the drip. With pale faces and anxious eyes they listened and watched and waited while we looked on in horror.

Do something, I wanted to cry, only I knew there wasn't anything more they could do. A tube in her trachea couldn't convey air if her lung capacity was too diminished to hold it.

Her face had a bluish tinge. The doctors had begun to talk to her, too, but while we pleaded, they commanded.

I think I died ten deaths, standing there looking helplessly on while her breathing grew more and more shallow. Tears streamed down my face. I heard Dennis's frantic "Come on, Kikit, come on," then the doctors' more demanding urgings. I prayed silently, desperately, and put a hand to my mouth to stifle an anguished cry when the cutting sound of her breathing suddenly eased.

It was a minute before I heard the doctors' relieved "There you go, sweetheart. That's better," and realized that she wasn't dead at all but over the hump. I held my breath over the next few minutes until her color began to improve. Then I smiled through my tears and cried out sigh after thankful sigh.

It was only then that I noticed Dennis. He was against the back wall of the cubicle, bent from the waist with his hands on his knees, making the same kind of relieved sounds I had, only deeper. I went over to him and touched his shoulder. He hung his head lower, seemed to gather himself, then wiped his face with his palms. His eyes were red when he stood, but he was marginally composed. Still, I didn't object when he put his arms around me. We held each other for a minute of silent, shared relief before returning to Kikit.

The improvement was slow but sure. When I felt certain that she was out of the woods, I went looking for Johnny. He was still with Brody, just outside Kikit's cubicle. Neither of them knew how bad things had been, yet when I appeared, two backs went ruler-straight, two faces asked the same frightened question.

I managed a tired smile. "She's starting to respond. We'll stay here for a while, though. They'll probably want to admit her."

Johnny's eyes were large and dark. "Why?"

"Her blood pressure's low. They're giving her medication to raise it, but it's best given intravenously."

"Is she gonna be all right?"

"She's gonna be fine," I said, feeling weak with the knowledge. I was thinking that I ought to return to her, when Johnny said in a rush, "Dad looked for all the nuts; he looked real hard. You should'a seen him. He was shoving lettuce and tomatoes all over the place looking for them. He had a whole pile on the napkin."

I reached for Johnny. Holding him tightly, I said against his hair, "I don't blame Daddy. Things happen sometimes, even in spite of the care we take so that they won't." I gave him a squeeze. "He's been a super dad tonight. He hasn't left Kikit's side for anything other than to make sure you're okay. He's going to stay here with me to make sure she gets better. You, though, need sleep."

"I don't. I'm not tired."

"You have school tomorrow."

"We won't have school if it keeps snowing. I want to be here with you guys."

"Know what would help most? Our knowing you're safe at home. We'll worry about you if you're just sitting out here. Let Brody take you home now, before the snow gets much worse."

There was a pause. "To the house?"

That was what I had pictured. If a sense of normalcy was what I wanted for him, it seemed the best place. But maybe normalcy wasn't what Johnny needed most just then. "Where would you like?"

Johnny thought for a minute and shrugged. "I dunno." He looked at Brody. "Where are you going?"

"I kind of thought I'd go to the lighthouse," Brody said. "There's good food there. And I don't feel like being alone. Not tonight. Not in the snow. Not after this scare."

There was another pause. Then to me, "Will Dad be mad?"

I smiled. "Dad will be fine."

KIKIT WAS SETTLED IN THE pediatric ward in a double room whose second bed was empty. The doctors and nurses left, promising to be back. As soon as the door closed on them, I climbed onto the bed and carefully resettled Kikit in my arms. After a few minutes of close crooning she fell into a fitful sleep, in effect leaving Dennis and me alone for the first time since the night's ordeal had begun.

"So where's the gloating?" he asked.

I drew a blank.

"She got sick under my care," he prompted. "After all I said about you, you have a right to say a few things back."

I had felt anger earlier. If I delved into my psyche, I could probably conjure it back up, but the effort didn't seem worth it. I had been through a wringer and was feeling drained. It seemed best to concentrate what energy I had left on helping Kikit.

By way of answer I laid my head down on hers and closed my eyes.

DOCTORS and nurses came and went, seeming content with the improvement they saw.

Somewhere around midnight I began to feel light-headed and realized that I hadn't had dinner. I found cookies and juice in a machine at the end of the hall and called Brody along the way to learn that he and Johnny had made it through six inches of snow and were safely ensconced at the lighthouse. I returned to Kikit revived.

That revival was a mixed blessing. While it gave me new strength to watch Kikit, it also cleared my head. Strange, though, I didn't think of the twist my life had taken that day or what Dennis would say when he learned of it. Nor did I think of those awful, awful moments in the emergency room when we thought we might lose Kikit. Rather, I thought of another bedside vigil held less than a month before, of the hours of standing at my mother's bedside.

"Are you all right?" Dennis said. "You're shaking."

I wrapped my arms around myself. "I've seen enough of hospitals lately to last a lifetime."

He was quiet for a time. Then he said, "I'm sorry about Connie. Was it difficult, waiting there?"

"Yes. No. Odd. Rona and I had a good talk. She's on the road for WickerWise as we speak."

"Rona?"

I smiled at his disbelief. "She's doing a pretty good job. I should have thought of it sooner." I shifted my attention when Kikit opened her eyes. "Hi, baby."

"I'm itchy, Mommy."

Grateful for something to do, I got moisturizer from the nurse and began to rub it in. It would have been a perfect time for Dennis to take a break, but he stood right there, holding the bottle while I smoothed the cream on, handing me a towel when I was done. Kikit had fallen back to sleep by then.

As the hours passed, as I came to grips with remembering Connie's last days and separated those from the relative optimism here, I began to think more about Dennis. He looked different. Tired, yes. But older, too. For the first time he looked like he was shouldering his share of the responsibility.

"Where are Elizabeth and Howard?" I asked.

He seemed startled by the question. "In New Hampshire."

"Have they helped out much since we split?" I asked.

"No. That wasn't the point."

"What was?"

He didn't answer right away. His eyes remained on Kikit. Finally he said, "It started out one thing and became another. It started out as a challenge to you and ended up as a challenge to me. I'm not the world's worst father."

"I never said you were."

"You said it in court."

"My lawyer argued that I was in a better position to care for the kids."

"She said I wasn't fit to be a father."

"No, Dennis."

"Well, it felt that way."

"Not a good feeling, was it?" I remarked.

The look he shot me held a flicker of the old annoyance. Then he sighed, and it was gone.

SHORTLY before dawn the snow finally stopped. Soon after that, Dennis went home to shower and change. He returned in less than an hour carrying Kikit's small flight bag stuffed with Travis, Michael, and Joy, a pair of pajamas, and her Barney slippers.

I was touched that he had thought to bring them and that he had done it with a minimum of fanfare. He took out the dolls and arranged them on the bed. I took out the pajamas and slippers and put them on the bedside table. Then I reached back into the bag. Something was still inside. I could feel its weight.

The bag was a lightweight backpack, too large for school use but perfect for travel. I felt around inside but found nothing. I peered inside but saw nothing. I slid my hands over the nylon until I located the weight, unzipped a back pocket, and reached inside.

My heart skipped a beat seconds before my hand brought out the Epi-Pen and antihistamine that "hadn't been packed" when the children had returned from Cleveland in October.

Dennis's gaze was riveted to them. For a second I wondered if his astonishment was a cover for mortification at having been found out. Then his eyes rose to mine, and I saw the kind of horror that said he honestly hadn't known. He closed his eyes, hung his head, ran a hand around the back of his neck.

"Oh, God," he finally said, and raised his head.

I had to ask, had to hear the words. "You didn't know?"

"I didn't know." With a look of disgust he turned his head away. "What a rotten mess."

"Didn't you know it would be?" I cried.

"I didn't," he confessed. "The lawyers made it sound clear. They made it sound simple. The judge was in agreement from day one."

I was grateful that Kikit chose that moment to wake up. If not, I might have told him about Judge Selwey's note to Jenovitz, which wouldn't have been the best thing to do. We were still locked in a legal battle. Carmen had a surefire weapon in her hands. I had faith that she would use it wisely, and owed her that chance.

BY THE time Brody showed up with Johnny and take-out break-fast, I had bathed Kikit and put her in her own pajamas. With the swelling down and the oxygen mask replaced by nasal prongs, she was beginning to look more herself.

Dennis was subdued. He hung back while Johnny and Brody sat on Kikit's bed telling jokes to cheer her up. I hung back myself. I was starting to feel the lack of sleep.

My first impulse when Brody suggested driving me home for a nap was to refuse on the grounds that Kikit needed me. I went with my second impulse, which had to do with Kikit's being out of the woods and needing to know that her father was there for her, too.

So Brody drove me to the lighthouse. I had barely made it out of the shower and into bed when Carmen called to say, with a satis-faction verging on glee, that we'd been granted a hearing on our new motion to recuse. Selwey would see us the following afternoon at two.

Not only that, she said, but we had the figures we needed on Jen-ovitz. In only two of twenty-three cases referred to him by Selwey in the last three years had his recommendation differed from Selwey's ruling. Of the twenty-one remaining, more than half had eventually been reversed.

I hung up the phone, grinned at Brody, and promptly fell into a sound sleep.

BY EARLY afternoon Kikit was back at the house that I had started to think of as Dennis's. I had a feeling Dennis would have let her come to the lighthouse if I had asked, but Kikit needed both of us, and frankly, I didn't want Dennis at my place.

Dennis, on the other hand, had no objection to my being at his. He took an active role in getting Kikit settled on the sofa bed in the den and seeing that she had everything her little heart desired, but he remained subdued. I wasn't sure whether the severity of Kikit's attack had shocked him or he'd had some other epiphany, but he was different. I sensed he was looking back on the last two months through different eyes.

By midafternoon Johnny was out sledding with friends, Brody was at the office, and I had sung Kikit to sleep. I dozed briefly there on the sofa bed beside her and awoke smelling coffee. My nose led me to the kitchen. Dennis was at the window, holding a steaming mug between his hands.

"I'm impressed," I said. When he glanced at me, I gestured toward the coffeemaker. Then my eye caught on a long Pyrex dish nearby, and I was doubly impressed. It contained chicken prepared Kikit's favorite way and ready to bake.

He grunted. "Amazing what a guy can do when he has to."

I filled a mug and leaned against the counter.

"Heuber called a few minutes ago," he said. His eyes held resignation when he raised them to mine. "Are you raising the Adrienne business?"

"If that's the only way I can keep the kids. But that isn't what the hearing's about."

"What is it about?"

"We have evidence of something fishy going on between Selwey and Jenovitz. We want Selwey to leave the case."

Dennis didn't argue. He simply stood at the window, studying the snow. "I fired Phoebe," he said without turning.

"Fired her?"

"Fired, broke up with, whatever."

"Do you love her?"

"Nah. I thought I did at first. We worked everything out so I'd get custody of the kids and a neat divorce settlement after that. Then a funny thing happened. I found that I liked my kids." He looked at me. "Phoebe doesn't like kids."

"Ah. Has she met ours?"

"No. It never got that far."

"Did you fall for Phoebe before or after you talked to her about getting a divorce?"

"After."

I felt an odd relief. After was preferable.

"She was so on my side," he said. "She told me I was right and you were wrong. She told me I was smart. She loved my looks."

"Flattering."

"Yeah. So maybe it was a midlife thing—at least with her. But the other, the stuff about the business, it's been tough for a while. There was a time when I had the magic touch. But it's gone."

I might have reminded him that the magic touch hadn't been magic at all but mere sleight of hand, thanks to the late Adrienne Hadley. But I didn't want to spoil the mood. He seemed to be feeling what I was—tired and mellow, benevolent, what with Kikit on the mend. We desperately needed to talk this way, for ourselves as much as for the kids.

"You never really wanted WickerWise, did you?" I asked.

He snorted. "What would I do with it? I don't know the first thing about wicker."

"Then it's for the money? For Pittney Communications?"

He nodded, drained his coffee, leaned against the window frame facing me. I saw caution on his face.

"Would you make me sell WickerWise?" I asked.

His smile was skewed. "Can't do that now, can I? You know about Hadley."

"But if I didn't, would you do it? Knowing how much the business means to me?"

He frowned, lowered his chin. "Probably not."

Well, that was something.

His expression was gentle when he looked at me. "I was listening when you sang Kikit to sleep. Your voice is as clear as it was twenty years ago. Can you believe it's been that long? Twenty years. I fell in love with that clarity." He lowered his eyes and studied his mug. "It was good when we sang."

"Yes. Singing was one of the good things. There were others. Certainly the kids. I don't regret our marriage, if for no other reason than them."

"So what happened to us?"

I had asked him that same question way back when. His answer then had been accusatory. He had blamed our breakup on me. I had every right to turn the tables now, but I didn't.

"We need different things," I said. "I'm wrong for you. You shouldn't have to compete with a wife. You need someone who's vulnerable and will lean on you and look up to you and devour every word you say. Me"—I gave a wry smile—"I'm an old hand when it comes to self-sufficiency. I've been at it since I was eight. So I needed other things from my marriage."

"Like what?"

"The security of knowing I'd never be left alone."

It was a while before Dennis said, "Guess I blew that."

I didn't respond at first. My mind was sorting things out. "Maybe I'm too self-sufficient. Sometimes I find solutions and impose them. Sometimes I jump in and take charge before others can, even when they want to or need to."

Dennis smiled gently. "I'm not arguing."

"Jenovitz accused me of not wanting to change. He's wrong," I vowed. But I knew I couldn't change with regard to Dennis. I had let him be weak. I had let him lean on me. Now he was too heavy. I no longer had the trust or respect to prop him up. I didn't want to catch him if he fell. "I'm just not sure I can change, where you and I are concerned," I said.

And where Brody was concerned? Overpowering self-sufficiency had never been an issue with him. From the very first I had been able to lean on him. He was a strong man.

Dennis was studying his mug again. When he raised his eyes this time, they held a vulnerability that did something to me. It brought back all the positive parts of our marriage, the feelings of warmth and affection and, yes, love, that had seen us through for years.

"Is there any chance for us?" he asked.

With the passing of that first swift instant came another. This one held all that I hadn't said about our marriage, all that had come into focus only after Dennis himself had broken it up.

I gave him an apologetic smile and a quick headshake. "It may be we'll be better friends than lovers. I'll try that, if you will."

I STAYED at the house until dinner was done and the children were settled in; then I left them in Dennis's care with a new sense of peace. I headed for the lighthouse, changed my mind, and headed for Brody's, changed my mind again, and headed for my workroom. By the time I got there, I was on an adrenaline high.

Setting the rocker and its table side by side on the workbench, I studied them. The reweaving was nearly complete, though I wasn't entirely satisfied with the job I had done. Often, while working during the last few weeks, I had been distracted, and it showed.

I was focused now. With infinite patience I removed those reeds that I hadn't placed well, soaked new lengths, and wove them in. They fit smoothly. With similar ease I wove replacement pieces into those spots previously empty. I had the touch tonight. My hands were magic.

Standing back, I admired my work. As jarring as the two pieces had looked filled with holes, so now they looked mended. They weren't perfect yet. There would be cleaning and sanding, then priming and painting. I was hoping for a particular shade of green, something warm and lime. If I didn't get it right with the first coat, I would get it right with the second.

Had it not been for those still damp reeds, I might have started the priming right then, my energy level was so high. As fate had it, Brody appeared at the door and gave me another outlet.

A BLUSTERY wind blew me along Federal Street the following afternoon, but my shivering was as much emotional as physical. All too well I remembered the first time I was here, when Dennis had held all the cards. Now I held a few. But despite the change in circumstance, too much was at stake for complacency.

The courthouse scene was much as it had been in October. Lawyers and their clients huddled; uniformed court officers chatted; the judge moved up and down his bench.

Carmen and I sat at the back of the courtroom waiting to be called. She had already handed Missy a copy of Selwey's letter and a statistical analysis of Jenovitz's reports, which were affixed to our motion to recuse. Since Dennis and Art Heuber sat ahead of us by several rows, I couldn't see their expressions.

I had talked with Dennis briefly in the lobby, and there was an awkwardness between us here. It didn't matter that we had come to an understanding of sorts at home. Here we were adversaries.

"The Raphael matter," Missy called.

We took the same places we had in October—Dennis, Art, Carmen, and I, in that order. Selwey took Carmen's brief from Missy and stood swaying before us while he read it. I was acutely aware of the moment when the swaying stopped. Lips pursed, he read on a bit, then set the papers down and said to Carmen, "You are aware that your client has committed theft."

"No, Your Honor," Carmen dared say. "Since she is personally paying the guardian to conduct his study, we argue that the contents of that folder are hers. I don't expect that Dr. Jenovitz will press charges. He won't want us arguing our case in open court." She hitched her chin toward the papers Selwey held. "He won't want to risk those figures coming out. *You* may not mind."

Of course Selwey would mind. His manner said it clear as day. Everything about him was small and tight and angry. "What, exactly, do you want?" he asked.

"It's stated in our petition," Carmen said, sparing him a public statement. We had asked Selwey to excuse himself from the case, to reverse his orders against me and dismiss the case.

In a huff he said, "I was brought into this case on behalf of two young children. What about them?"

Art Heuber answered. "Your Honor, my client has agreed to drop the original charges. The parents would like to determine custody of the children themselves."

"If the parents weren't able to do that two months ago, what makes them able to do it now?"

"A dialogue has begun," Heuber said.

Selwey moved his arms, black robes fluttering, feathers ruffled. "Well, what happened to those original charges?"

"There was a misunderstanding."

"A misunderstanding? You've wasted the time of this court and a GAL on a misunderstanding?" With a disdainful flourish he made a notation on the paper he held. "This case is dismissed."

As quickly as that, it was over.

I MADE it as far as the courthouse steps before my legs rebelled, this time from utter relief. I rested my weight against the stone wall and took breath after deep breath of the cold December air. With each one I felt stronger, freer, happier.

When Carmen joined me, her grin was as broad as mine.

"Nice work," I said.

Her lips quirked. "It's always nice when you can stand there like a lady and not say a word while the other guys squirm."

"Not that I'd have minded if you'd accused Selwey in a big loud voice of unethical conduct, the pompous jerk."

"The accusation's coming," Carmen promised. "That letter will make the rounds until Selwey is off the bench. Trust me. He's gone. Jenovitz will have to feed at another trough."

"So he was in it for the money. What did Selwey get from the deal?"

"Ego. Control. Power. He'll lose all that now. As he should."

Dennis emerged from between the stone pillars on the top step. He hesitated when he saw us, then pulled up his collar and started down toward us. His hands were deep in his coat pockets, his expression sober.

"Congratulations," he said to Carmen. Then to me, "I didn't know about the note Selwey wrote. Neither did Art or Phoebe. We knew he had a bias, but we didn't think it went that far." He paused. "So what happens now?"

"We talk," I said. "The way we should have in October."

"I still want the kids."

Calmly I said, "So do I."

Carmen broke in. "I think we should discuss this when Dennis has counsel present. I'll call Art and set a date to meet."

Dennis nodded her way. Then, persistent as ever, he turned to me again. "I won't be kicked out of the house."

"You can have the house," I said, which took the wind from his sails for a minute, but only that.

"So who gets the kids?"

WE OPTED for joint custody. It was the obvious solution. Kikit and Johnny would stay with Dennis while I traveled and stay with me while he traveled, and the rest of the time we would rotate weekly, with the assumption of added flexibility as the children grew older. We agreed to share all major decisions and responsibilities, and to consult with each other on all matters relating to the kids. Child support was never an issue. I was thrilled to be able to give my children a level of financial security that I had never had.

The divorce settlement was more thorny. Dennis held out for a large chunk of money. I simply held out longer. The final deal included my paying monthly alimony in an amount that would enable Dennis to live comfortably, plus a lump sum for the past year and each of the next four, equal to twenty-five percent of the net profit of WickerWise.

For all of Dennis's complaints that I would thwart his ability to earn a decent living, he bought into Pittney Communications even without the larger share of WickerWise that he wanted. The first lump sum that I paid him, plus an advance on the second, plus a deal with Pittney that enabled him to pay for the rest with a portion of his monthly take, and that vice presidency was his.

All things considered, it was more than he deserved.

But I was satisfied. Dennis's ego was a major player in his life. The more satisfied that ego, the more agreeable the man. The more agreeable the man, the greater the well-being of my children. And that was the bottom line. It always had been.

By the middle of January we had our agreement in writing. By the first of February we had a hearing in court. Ninety days later our divorce became final.

WITH the coming of May the sun was high enough and strong enough to counter the chill of the Atlantic and warm Brody's back porch for a late Sunday brunch. It was a private affair, just Brody and me. The children were with Dennis in New Hampshire. Rona was with Valentino at the lighthouse.

Wrapped in a fleece blanket, I sat on my lime-green rocker, and while its runners creaked to and fro on the weathered planks of the porch, I looked lazily out at my kingdom. The air held the salt smell that I loved, along with the sweeter one of the first tiny lilies of the valley to bloom at the foot of the porch. Later there would be morning glories and lilacs, and beach roses in the thickets where grass met rock. I was looking forward to watching the sun rise over them all.

Smiling, I fingered the long strand of pearls that looped around my neck. Connie had been right. My strand was long and ever growing. In the last few months alone, I swear, a dozen new pearls had appeared. There was one with a beaming Kikit posed prettily in her tutu at the dance recital, and one with Johnny's arms raised in victory when his basketball team won the league championship. There was one at the joint birthday party we threw for the children, with thirty of their friends, one magician, Dennis and his parents, and Brody and Rona and me in amiable attendance.

There were pearls on my strand that were still half formed but growing—Rona searching for the place in WickerWise that suited her best, she and I puzzling out a comfortable personal relationship.

I was working on other pearls, brushing at sand that stubbornly resisted my desire for perfection. Though Kikit had gone since December without an allergy attack, the last one had left her skittish about eating anything other than what we had checked and she had checked, and even then she searched for things as she ate. Johnny was still tussling with the divorce, still trying to figure out what the rules were, what position he played, and how he could score.

Divorce is never an ideal situation. As agreeable as Dennis was, I hated making arrangements about who would have whom when. As sensible as shared custody was, I never stopped wanting the children all the time.

On the positive side, Dennis had come to know the children.

And I had Brody. Ahhh, Brody. So many pearls there, I couldn't begin to count them. Smooth and precious—best friend, lover, husband-to-be—my fingertips touched each. As I watched, the sun caught on the diamond he had given me. It was as multifaceted as our lives.

"You look like you're taking root," he mused, drawing up the rocker's matching table and setting down a tray. It held French toast, fresh strawberries, and a carafe of coffee.

I gave him a lazy smile. "I might just."

Hunkering down before me, he slipped his arms around me and gave me a kiss. I felt happier than I would have believed possible a few short months before.

Softly I began to sing. It was a love song. I had sung more than my share of late.

He put his head down, cheek to my thigh. I stroked his hair. A sweet peace filled me as I hummed the rest of the song. Life didn't get much better than this.

Still softly but exuberant now, I shifted songs. This one was about wedding bells, chapels, and champagne, which was where we were headed.

Brody lifted his head and grinned. Laughing, I wrapped myself around him. He might never carry a tune or be able to clap to a beat, but Lord, I did love him so.

THE
UNLIKELY
SPY

DANIEL SILVA

One woman.

One man.

One secret that will

change history . . .

PREFACE

IN APRIL 1944, six weeks before the Allied invasion of France, the Nazi propagandist William Joyce—better known as Lord Haw-Haw—made a chilling radio broadcast directed at Britain.

According to Joyce, Germany knew the Allies were at work on large concrete structures in the south of England. Germany also knew those structures were to be towed across the English Channel during the coming invasion and sunk off the coast of France. Joyce declared, "Well, we are going to help you boys. When you come to get them under way, we're going to sink them for you."

Alarms sounded inside British intelligence and the Allied High Command. The concrete structures were actually components of a giant artificial harbor complex bound for Normandy, code-named Operation Mulberry. If Hitler's spies truly understood Mulberry's purpose, they might well know the most important secret of the war—the landing place of the Allied invasion of France.

Several anxious days later those fears were put to rest when U.S. intelligence intercepted a coded message from Japan's ambassador to Berlin to his superiors in Tokyo. The ambassador received regular briefings from his German allies on preparations for the looming invasion. According to the intercepted message, German intelligence believed the concrete structures were part of a massive antiaircraft complex—not an artificial harbor.

But how did German intelligence make such a crucial miscalculation? Did they simply misread their own intelligence? Or had they been deceived?

CHAPTER ONE

Suffolk, England: November 1938

BEATRICE Pymm died because she missed the last bus to Ipswich.

Twenty minutes before her death she stood at the bus stop and read the timetable in the dim light of the village's single streetlamp. To see better, she stood on tiptoe and ran down the numbers with a paint-smudged finger. "Blast," she muttered.

Normally Beatrice was punctual to a fault. In a life without friends, without financial responsibility, without family, she had erected a rigorous personal schedule. Today she had strayed from it—painted too long, started back too late.

Her home in Ipswich was at least five miles away, too far to walk; perhaps someone would give her a lift. She picked up her things— a rucksack, a canvas, a battered easel—and reluctantly set out. She had spent the day painting along the river Orwell. Painting was her only love and the Suffolk landscape her only subject matter.

Beatrice shivered with the cold and thought of home, a large cottage left to her by her late mother. Behind the cottage, at the end of the garden walk, she had built a studio, where she spent days at a time, often without speaking to another human being.

All this, and more, her killer knew.

After five minutes of walking, Beatrice heard the rattle of an engine behind her. She felt a gust of wind as a van swept by. Then she watched as the vehicle pulled to the side of the road and stopped.

The hand, visible in the moonlight, poked from the driver's side window and beckoned Beatrice forward. A thick leather glove, she noted, the kind used by workmen. A workman's overall. But the wrist was pale and hairless—not like the wrist of any workman Beatrice had ever seen.

Still she felt no alarm. She reached the passenger door, pulled it open, and set her things on the floor in front of the seat. Then she looked up into the van for the first time and noticed the driver was gone. She closed the door and called out. Seconds later she heard the sound of a boot on gravel. She turned her head and saw the driver standing there. She looked to the face and saw only a black woolen mask. Two pools of pale blue stared coldly behind the eyeholes. Feminine lips glistened behind the slit for the mouth.

Beatrice Pymm opened her mouth to scream. She managed only a gasp before the driver rammed the gloved hand into her mouth. The fingers dug into the soft flesh of her throat. Beatrice gagged, then felt the other hand probing at the bottom of her ribs.

Beatrice heard a sharp click. An instant of excruciating pain, a burst of brilliant white light. Then a benevolent darkness.

The killer had trained endlessly for this night, but it was the first time. The killer removed the gloved hand from the victim's mouth, turned, and was violently sick. There was no time for sentiment. The killer was a soldier—a major in the secret service—and Beatrice Pymm soon would be the enemy. Her death, while unfortunate, was necessary.

The killer pulled hard, and the stiletto slipped out. An excellent kill—clean, very little blood. Vogel would be proud.

The killer wiped the blood from the stiletto, snapped the blade back into place, then dragged the body to the rear of the van and lifted it inside. Soon the van was on the move again, flashing through the darkened village and turning onto the deserted roadway.

It was a long drive, four hours at least. During the preparation, prior to stealing the van, the killer had driven the route by motorcycle. That same bike now lay beside Beatrice Pymm in the back of the van, two jerry cans of petrol next to it.

First stop, ten minutes later, the bank of the river Orwell, the same spot where Beatrice Pymm had been painting that day. The killer walked to the passenger side of the van and removed the easel, the canvas, and the rucksack. She erected the easel very near the water and placed the canvas on it. She opened the rucksack, removed the paints and palette, and laid them on the damp ground. Next the killer removed an empty bottle of claret, dropping it at the legs of the easel. Poor Beatrice. Too much wine, a careless step, a plunge into frigid water, a slow journey to the open sea.

Six hours later the van passed through the West Midlands village of Whitchurch and turned onto a rough track at the edge of a barley field. The grave had been dug the previous night—deep enough to conceal a corpse but not so deep that it might never be found.

The killer dragged the body from the back of the van and stripped away the bloody clothing. Then she walked back to the van and removed an iron mallet, a brick, and a spade. When it was over, she could barely look at what was left of Beatrice Pymm's face. Using the mallet, then the brick, she had pounded bone and shattered teeth, rendering the face unrecognizable.

She had done everything they had ordered her to do. She was to be different. She had trained at a special camp for many months, much longer than the other agents. She would be planted deeper. That was why she had to kill Beatrice Pymm. She wouldn't waste her time doing what the other, less gifted agents could do: counting troops, monitoring railways. That was easy. She would be saved for bigger and better things. She would be a time bomb, ticking inside England, waiting to be activated, waiting to go off.

She pushed the corpse into the grave and covered it with earth, then tossed the bloodstained clothing into the van. From the front seat she took a small handbag containing a Dutch passport, an Amsterdam driver's permit, and photographs of a fat, smiling Dutch family, all forged by the Abwehr in Berlin.

She threw the bag into the trees at the edge of the barley field. If everything went according to plan, the badly decomposed and mutilated body would be found in a few months, along with the handbag. The police would believe the dead woman to be Christa

Kunst, a Dutch tourist who entered the country in October 1938 and whose holiday came to an unfortunate and violent end.

The killer had just lost her own identity. For six months she had lived in Holland, because Dutch was one of her languages. She had carefully constructed a past, voted in a local election, even permitted herself a young lover. Now Christa Kunst lay in a shallow grave on the edge of an English barley field. The killer would assume a new identity in the morning. But tonight she was no one.

She refueled the van and drove for twenty minutes to the village of Alderton—a place where a van burning at the roadside in the middle of the night would not be noticed immediately. She pulled the motorbike out of the van. One of the jerry cans still contained some petrol. She doused the inside of the van, dumping most of the petrol on Beatrice Pymm's blood-soaked clothing.

By the time the van went up in a fireball, the killer had kicked the bike into life, turned south, and headed for London.

Oyster Bay, New York: August 1939

DOROTHY Lauterbach considered her fieldstone mansion—with its exquisite gardens, red clay tennis court, and royal blue swimming pool—the most beautiful on the North Shore. Most of her friends agreed because they wanted invitations to the two parties she and Bratton threw each summer—a raucous, drunken affair in June and a more reflective occasion in late August.

The Lauterbachs had two daughters—Margaret and Jane. On that morning—the morning after the final party of the summer—the sun blazed, and a shimmering haze hung over Long Island Sound. Upstairs in her bedroom, Margaret Lauterbach Jordan pulled off her nightgown and looked in the mirror. She had finally lost the last few stubborn pounds she had gained while pregnant with Billy, her first child. She put on a pair of white cotton slacks, a sleeveless blouse, and a pair of sandals. She thought, And soon you're going to be a fat cow again!

Peter stirred, still asleep. Once, she had thought all engineers were men with flattop haircuts and thick black glasses. Peter was not like that—strong cheekbones, a sharp jawline, soft green eyes, nearly black hair. Lying in bed now, his upper body exposed, he looked, Margaret thought, like a tumbled Michelangelo.

She glanced out the window at the hazy sky and frowned. Peter detested August weather like this. He would be irritable all day. There would probably be a thunderstorm to ruin the drive back into the city. She thought, Perhaps I should wait to tell him the news.

"Get up, Peter, or we'll never hear the end of it," Margaret said. Peter didn't move. "Coffee," he pleaded.

The maids had left coffee outside the bedroom door. Margaret poured a cup and handed it to him. Peter rolled onto his elbow and drank some. Then he sat up and looked at Margaret. "How do you manage to look so beautiful two minutes after getting out of bed?"

Margaret was relieved. "You're certainly in a good mood. I was afraid you'd have a hangover and be perfectly beastly all day."

"I do have a hangover. Benny Goodman is playing in my head, and my tongue feels like it could use a shave. But I have no intention of acting—" He paused. "What was the word you used?"

"Beastly." She sat down on the edge of the bed. "There's something we need to discuss."

"Hmm. Sounds serious, Margaret."

"That depends." She held him in her playful gaze. "It's about the phone call yesterday afternoon."

"The one you were so evasive about?"

"Yes. It was from Dr. Shipman. We're going to have another baby. I've been afraid to tell you."

"Why on earth would you be afraid to tell me?"

But Peter knew the answer. He had told Margaret he didn't want more children until he had realized his life's dream: starting his own engineering firm. At just thirty-three he had earned a reputation as one of the top engineers in the country. After graduating first in his class from the Rensselaer Polytechnic Institute, he had gone to work for the Northeast Bridge Company, the largest bridge construction firm on the East Coast. Five years later he was named chief engineer, made partner, and given a staff of one hundred. The American

Society of Civil Engineers named him its engineer of the year for 1938. *Scientific American* described him as "the most promising engineering mind of his generation." But he wanted more—he wanted his own firm. The threat of war had put a damper on that. If the United States was dragged into a war, all money for major public works projects would dry up overnight.

He said, "How far along are you?"

"Almost two months. You're not angry with me?"

Peter's face broke into a smile. "Of course not."

"What about your firm—about waiting to have more children?"

He kissed her. "It doesn't matter. None of it matters."

WALKER Hardegen joined the Lauterbachs for lunch by the pool. They sat beneath an umbrella: Bratton and Dorothy, Margaret and Peter, Jane and Walker. A damp, fickle breeze blew from the Sound. Hardegen was Bratton Lauterbach's top lieutenant at the bank. A Harvard man, he was tall, and thick through the chest, and most women thought he looked like Tyrone Power.

A short time after Hardegen came to the bank, he had asked Margaret out, and they dated several times. Hardegen wanted the relationship to continue, but Margaret did not. She terminated it, but they remained friends. Six months later she met Peter and fell in love. Hardegen was beside himself. One evening at the Copacabana, a little drunk and very jealous, he cornered Margaret and begged her to see him again. When she refused, he grabbed her roughly by the shoulder and shook her. By the icy look on her face Margaret made it clear she would destroy his career if he did not end his behavior. The incident remained their secret. Even Peter didn't know. But Margaret sensed there was an unspoken tension between Hardegen and Peter, a natural competitiveness.

"You really must see the *Tannhäuser* at the Metropolitan. It's marvelous," Hardegen said, pausing to sip his chilled white wine.

"I've heard such good things about it," Dorothy said.

She loved to discuss the opera, theater, and new books and films. Hardegen, who managed to see and read everything despite an immense workload at the bank, indulged her. She adored Hardegen, preferring him to Peter. Hardegen was from a wealthy, conservative family in Maine. Peter came from a lower-middle-class Irish family on the West Side of Manhattan. He would never be "one of us."

The servants brought out lunch—chilled poached salmon—and the conversation shifted to the looming war in Europe.

Bratton said, "Is there any way of stopping Hitler now, or is Poland about to become the easternmost province of the Third Reich?"

Hardegen had been placed in charge of disentangling the bank from its German and other risky European investments. Inside the bank he was affectionately referred to as Our In-house Nazi because of his name, his perfect German, and his frequent trips to Berlin. He also maintained a network of excellent contacts in Washington and served as the bank's chief intelligence officer.

"There's no stopping Hitler," Hardegen said. "The Germans now have sixty divisions along the Polish border."

"So what's Hitler waiting for?" Margaret asked.

"An excuse. Hitler will invent a reason to attack, a provocation that will allow him to invade without a declaration of war."

"What about the British and the French?" Peter asked. "Will they declare war on Germany if Poland is attacked?"

"I believe so," said Hardegen. "Britain and France now realize Hitler must be dealt with."

Dorothy decided the talk of war had gone on long enough. She touched Hardegen's arm. "Walker, I'm so sorry you couldn't come to our party last night. Let me tell you *all* about it."

THE lavish apartment on Fifth Avenue had been a wedding present from Bratton Lauterbach. At seven o'clock that evening Peter Jordan stood in the window. A thunderstorm had moved in over the city, and the wind drove rain against the glass. Peter had driven back into Manhattan alone because Dorothy had insisted that Margaret attend a garden party at Edith Blakemore's. Margaret was being driven in by Wiggins, the Lauterbachs' chauffeur.

Peter glanced at his watch for the fifth time in five minutes. He and Margaret were supposed to meet the head of the Pennsylvania road and bridge commission at the Stork Club for dinner at seven thirty. Pennsylvania was accepting bids for a new bridge over the Allegheny River. Peter's boss wanted him to lock up the deal tonight. Where was Margaret?

He telephoned the Oyster Bay house and spoke to Dorothy.

"I don't know what to say to you, Peter. She left in plenty of time. Perhaps Wiggins was delayed by the weather."

"I'll give her another fifteen minutes. Then I have to leave."

At seven fifteen he took the elevator downstairs and stood in the lobby while the doorman flagged down a taxi.

The dinner went well, despite the fact that Peter left the table three times to telephone Dorothy. By eight thirty he was worried sick. At eight forty-five the headwaiter presented himself at Peter's table. "You have a telephone call at the bar, sir."

Peter excused himself. At the bar he had to raise his voice above the clinking glasses and the din of conversation. It was Margaret's sister, Jane. "Peter," she said, "I'm afraid there's been an accident."

"Where are you?"

"I'm with the Nassau County Police."

"What happened?"

"A car pulled in front of them on the highway. Wiggins couldn't see it in the rain. By the time he did, it was too late."

THE funeral was held at St. James's Church on Madison Avenue, where Peter and Margaret had been married four years earlier. President Roosevelt sent a note of condolence and expressed his disappointment that he could not attend. Germany had invaded Poland, and the world was waiting for the other shoe to drop.

Billy stood next to Peter during the service. He wore short pants and a little blazer and a tie. As the family filed out of the church, he reached up and tugged on the hem of his aunt Jane's black dress. "Will Mommy ever come home?"

"No, Billy, she won't. She's left us."

Edith Blakemore overheard the child's question and burst into tears. "What a tragedy it is," she cried. "What a needless tragedy!"

Margaret was buried under brilliant skies at the family plot on Long Island. During the Reverend Pugh's final words a murmur passed through the graveside mourners, then died away.

When it was over, Peter walked back to the limousines with his best friend, Shepherd Ramsey. "What was everyone talking about?" Peter asked. "It was very rude."

"Someone arrived late, and they'd been listening to a bulletin on the car radio," Shepherd said. "The British and French just declared war on Germany."

London: May 1940

PROFESSOR Alfred Vicary vanished without explanation from University College on the third Friday of May, 1940. A secretary named Lillian Walford was the last member of the staff to see him before his abrupt departure.

Vicary spent his last hours in his cramped, disorderly office putting the final touches on an article on the current crisis for *The Sunday Times*. It was a glorious late spring day, bright sunshine but deceptively chilly. Vicary, an accomplished if reluctant chess player, appreciated deception. He rose, put on a cardigan sweater, and resumed his work.

The fine weather painted a false picture. Britain was a nation under siege—defenseless, frightened, reeling in utter confusion. Vicary, a noted historian, had watched his nation's jittery preparations for war with a mixture of pride and quiet depression. Throughout the '30s he had warned, in periodic newspaper articles and lectures, that Hitler posed a serious threat to England and the rest of the world, but Britain, exhausted from the last war with the Germans, had been in no mood to listen. Now the German army was driving across France with the ease of a weekend motor outing. Soon Adolf Hitler would stand atop an empire stretching from the Arctic Circle to the Mediterranean. And Britain, poorly armed and ill-prepared, stood alone against him.

Vicary finished the article and set down his pencil. The war—it was making him look more fondly upon his countrymen. He marveled at how they made jokes while filing into the underground to escape the Luftwaffe's bombs and at the way they sang in pubs to hide their fear. During his lifetime of study Vicary had concluded that patriotism was the most destructive force on the planet, but now he felt its stirring in his own chest, and he did not feel ashamed. We are good, and they are evil. Our nationalism is justified. He had decided he wanted to contribute.

At six o'clock Lillian Walford entered without knocking. Tall, with shot-putter's legs, she began straightening papers and closing books with the quiet efficiency of a night nurse. For ten years she had overseen the details of Vicary's uncomplicated life. She made certain there was food at his house in Chelsea. She saw to his bills and lectured him regularly about the state of his poorly managed bank account. She hired new maids with seasonal regularity because his fits of bad temper drove away the old ones.

"If you don't mind, Professor Vicary, I'll be going home."

"Of course, Miss Walford." He looked up at her. He was a fussy, bookish little man, bald on top except for a few uncontrollable strands of gray hair. His long-suffering half-moon reading glasses rested on the end of his nose. He wore a weather-beaten tweed coat and a carelessly selected tie stained with tea. A shattered knee during the last war had left him with a stiff-jointed, mechanized limp.

"Miss Simpson telephoned to say she'll be unable to have dinner with you tonight," Miss Walford said. "Her mother has taken ill. She asked me to tell you it's nothing serious."

"Blast," Vicary muttered. He had been looking forward to the date with Alice Simpson. She taught literature at a girls' school and wrote rather good romantic novels under a pseudonym. She was intelligent and witty and a touch irreverent. He supposed he might be in love with her. It was the most serious he had been about a woman in a very long time. "Is that all?"

"No—the prime minister telephoned."

"What! Why on earth didn't you tell me?"

"You left strict instructions not to be disturbed. When I told this to Mr. Churchill, he was quite understanding. He says nothing upsets him more than being interrupted when he's writing."

Vicary frowned. "From now on you have my explicit permission to interrupt me when Mr. Churchill telephones."

"Yes, Professor Vicary," she replied. "You're expected for lunch tomorrow at Chartwell."

Vicary and Churchill had been friends since 1935, when Vicary attended a lecture delivered by Churchill in London. Churchill, confined to the wilderness of the back benches, was one of the few voices in Britain warning of the threat posed by the Nazis. England must rearm at once, he argued that day, or face enslavement by Germany. The audience thought Churchill had lost his mind, and heckled him mercilessly. Returning home after the lecture, Vicary had sat at his desk and jotted Churchill a note: "I attended your lecture in London and agree with every word you uttered." Five days later a note from Churchill arrived at Vicary's home: "I am not alone after all! The great Vicary is at my side. Please do me the honor of coming to Chartwell for lunch this Sunday."

Their first meeting had been a success. Vicary was immediately absorbed into the ring of academics who would give Churchill advice and intelligence on Germany for the rest of the decade.

Vicary knew that this latest summons to Chartwell wasn't just to have a friendly chat.

VICARY'S pulse quickened as the car Churchill had sent for him turned into the drive at Chartwell. Churchill's man Inches stood at the door to greet him.

"Good morning, Professor Vicary. The prime minister has been awaiting your arrival most eagerly."

Vicary handed over his coat and his hat and stepped inside. About a dozen men and a couple of young girls were at work in the drawing room, some in uniform, some in civilian clothes. They spoke in hushed, confessional tones, as though all the news was bad.

"I hope you had a pleasant trip," Inches was saying.

"Marvelous," Vicary replied.

"As usual, Mr. Churchill is running late this morning." Then he added confidingly, "He sets an unattainable schedule, and we all spend the rest of the day trying to catch up with it."

"I understand, Inches. Where would you like me to wait?"

"Actually, the prime minister is quite eager to see you. He asked that you be shown upstairs immediately upon your arrival."

"Upstairs?"

Inches knocked gently and opened the bathroom door. Churchill lay in his tub, a cigar in one hand, a glass of whiskey resting on a small table within easy reach. "Vicary, my dear man," he said. "How good of you to come."

Vicary found it hard not to laugh at the enormous pink man splashing about in his bath like a child. He removed his tweed jacket and, reluctantly, sat down on the toilet.

Churchill pursed his lips. "I wanted a word in private, Vicary. I must admit from the outset that I am angry with you."

Vicary stiffened.

"You never told me that in your Cambridge days you were quite good at chess. Brilliant, ruthless, so I'm told."

Vicary, thoroughly confused, said, "I apologize, Prime Minister, but the subject of chess never arose during our conversations."

"You also served in the Intelligence Corps in the First War."

"I was only a courier in the motorcycle unit," Vicary protested.

Churchill smiled. "You have a nimble mind, Alfred. I've always admired that. I want you to take a job in military intelligence."

"But Prime Minister, I'm not qualified for that sort of—"

"Nobody over there knows what they're doing," Churchill said, cutting Vicary off. "Especially the professional officers."

"But what about my students? My research?"

"Your students will be in the service soon, fighting for their lives. And as for your research, it can wait."

Vicary made a brief show of thought. "I suppose I accept."

"Good." Churchill thumped his fist on the side of the tub. "You're to report first thing Monday to Brigadier Sir Basil Boothby. He is the head of the division to which you will be assigned. He is also the complete English ass. He'd thwart me if he could, but he's too stupid for that."

"Sounds charming."

"He knows that you and I are friends, and therefore he will oppose you. Don't allow yourself to be bullied by him. Understood?"

"Yes, Prime Minister."

"I need someone I can trust inside that department. It's time to put the *intelligence* back in military intelligence. Besides, Alfred, it's time you emerged from your dusty library and rejoined the living."

Vicary was caught off guard by Churchill's sudden intimacy. "Yes, Prime Minister, I believe it *is* time. Just what will I do for military intelligence?"

But Churchill had vanished below the waterline.

Rastenburg, Germany: January 1944

REAR Admiral Wilhelm Franz Canaris was a small, nervous man with white hair and piercing blue eyes. He was seated in the back of a staff Mercedes as it rumbled from the Rastenburg airfield to Hitler's secret bunker nine miles away. Usually the Old Fox, as Canaris was known, shunned martial trappings of any kind, but since he was about to meet with Adolf Hitler and the most senior military officers in Germany, he was reluctantly wearing his Kriegsmarine uniform.

In 1933 Canaris was serving as commander of a naval depot on the Baltic Sea when Hitler unexpectedly chose him to head the Abwehr, the intelligence and counterespionage service. Hitler commanded his new spymaster to create a secret service on the British model, and Canaris formally took control of the spy agency on New Year's Day, 1934. The decision would prove to be one of Hitler's worst. Since taking command of the Abwehr, Wilhelm Canaris had been engaged in an extraordinary high-wire act—providing the German general staff with the intelligence it needed to conquer most of Europe, while at the same time using the service as a tool to rid Germany of Hitler. He was a leader of the resistance movement dubbed the Black Orchestra—Schwarze Kapelle—by the Gestapo.

A tightly knit group of German military officers, government offi-
cials, and civic leaders, the Black Orchestra had tried unsuccessfully
to overthrow the Führer and negotiate a peace settlement with the
Allies. Canaris had engaged in other treasonous activities as well.
In 1939, after learning of Hitler's plans to invade Poland, he warned
the British in a futile attempt to spur them into action. He did the
same in 1940, when Hitler announced plans to invade the Low
Countries and France.

Canaris knew there would be more attempts on the Führer's
life—more brave Germans willing to sacrifice their own lives in order
to rid Germany of Hitler—but he also knew time was running out.
The Anglo-American invasion of Europe was a certainty; Germany
would be destroyed. Canaris also realized his tenuous grip on the
Abwehr was growing weaker by the day. His enemies were plotting
to seize control of the spy agency and put his neck in a noose of
piano wire. His long and dangerous high-wire act was nearing an end.

The staff car passed through a myriad of gates and checkpoints,
then turned into the compound at Hitler's Wolfschanze—the Wolf's
Lair. The conference was to be held in the frigid, airless map room
in the underground bunker. Canaris climbed out of the car and
walked morosely across the compound.

"IN NOVEMBER, I issued Führer Directive Number Fifty-one,"
Hitler began without preamble, pacing the room violently, hands
clasped behind his back. He wore a dove-gray tunic, black trousers,
and resplendent jackboots. "Directive Number Fifty-one stated my
belief that the Anglo-Saxons will attempt to invade northwest
France no later than the spring, perhaps earlier. During the last two
months I have seen nothing to change my opinion."

Canaris, seated at the conference table, watched the Führer
prancing around the room. Hitler's stoop, caused by kyphosis of the
spine, had worsened. Canaris wondered if he was finally feeling the
pressure. He should be. Germany had conquered far more territory
than she could possibly defend.

It was Hitler's own fault, the damned fool! Canaris glanced up at the map. In the east, German troops were fighting along a two-thousand-kilometer front. Any hope of a military victory over the Russians had been crushed. And in the west, Germany was defending six thousand kilometers of territory stretching from the Netherlands to the Bay of Biscay. Hitler's Festung Europa—Fortress Europe—was far-flung and vulnerable.

Canaris looked around the table at the men seated with him: Field Marshal Gerd von Rundstedt, commander in chief in the west; Field Marshal Erwin Rommel, commander in northwest France; Reichsführer Heinrich Himmler, head of the SS.

Hitler stopped his pacing. "If the Anglo-Saxon invasion succeeds, the consequences will be disastrous. So it is here, in northwest France, where the most decisive battle of the war will be fought." Hitler paused, allowing his words to sink in. "The invasion will be met with the full fury of our might and destroyed at the high-water mark. If that is not possible, and if the Anglo-Saxons succeed in securing a temporary beachhead, we must be prepared to stage a massive counterattack and hurl the invaders back into the sea. But to achieve that goal, we must know when the enemy intends to strike. And, more importantly, where. Herr Generalfeldmarschall?"

Gerd von Rundstedt rose and wearily moved to the map. Canaris did not envy his situation. On paper he presided over a large and powerful force in the west: one and a half million men, including three hundred and fifty thousand crack Waffen SS troops and ten panzer divisions. If deployed correctly, Rundstedt's armies were still capable of dealing the Allies a devastating defeat, but if he deployed his forces incorrectly or made tactical blunders, the Allies would establish their precious foothold on the Continent and the war in the west would be lost.

"In my opinion the equation is simple," Rundstedt began. "East of the Seine at the Pas de Calais or west of the Seine at Normandy. If the enemy secures a beachhead at Calais, he can turn to the east and be a few days' march from the Ruhrgebiet, our industrial heartland. The Americans want the war to be over by Christmas. If they succeed in a landing at Calais, they might get their wish." Rundstedt paused to allow his warning to sink in. "There is another reason why Calais makes sense militarily. The Channel is narrowest there. There are three excellent deepwater ports in the Pas de Calais area—Boulogne, Calais, and Dunkirk. The enemy needs ports. Without a major port he cannot supply his troops."

"Impressive, Herr Generalfeldmarschall," Hitler said. "But why not Normandy?"

Rundstedt continued in a monotone. "Normandy presents the enemy with many problems. The distance across the Channel is much greater. At some points high cliffs stand between the beaches and the mainland. The closest harbor is Cherbourg, at the tip of a heavily defended peninsula. But the most logical argument against Normandy is its geographic location. It is too far to the west. Even if the enemy succeeds in landing at Normandy, he must fight us all the way across France before reaching German soil."

"And you, Admiral Canaris?" Hitler snapped. "What is your Abwehr intelligence telling you?"

"Our initial intelligence tends to support the field marshal's assessment—that the Allies intend to strike at Calais. According to our agents, there has been increased activity in southeast England, directly across the Channel from the Pas de Calais. We have monitored wireless transmissions referring to a new force called the First United States Army Group. And one of our agents inside Allied High Command reports that General Eisenhower has secretly arrived in London."

Hitler seemed to be impressed. If only Hitler knew the truth, Canaris thought, that the Abwehr's intelligence networks in England were very likely in tatters. Canaris blamed Hitler. During the preparations for the Führer's aborted invasion of Britain, Canaris and his staff recklessly poured spies into England. Because of the desperate need for intelligence, the agents were hastily recruited, poorly trained, and even more poorly equipped. Canaris suspected most had walked straight into the arms of MI5. He could not admit that now. To do so would be to sign his own death warrant.

Hitler was pacing again. Canaris knew Hitler did not fear the coming invasion. Quite the opposite, he welcomed it. "Let us reverse the roles," Hitler said. "If I were going to invade France from England, what would I do? Would I come by the obvious route, the route my enemy expects me to take? Or would I take another route and surprise my enemy? Would I broadcast false wireless messages and send false reports through spies? The answer is yes. We must expect the British to engage in deception. We must be prepared for the possibility of an invasion at Normandy or Brittany. Therefore our panzers must remain safely back from the coast until the enemy's intentions are clear. Then we will concentrate our armor at the main point of the attack and hurl them back into the sea."

Hitler turned to Rommel. "And you, Herr Generalfeldmarschall, what do you think?"

Rommel made a brief show of thought, then said, "I must admit, my Führer, that all signs point to an invasion at the Pas de Calais."

"So," Hitler said, waving his hand. "My generals think it will be Calais. I'm skeptical." He spun on his heel and glared at Canaris. "Herr Admiral, I want you to settle the argument."

"That may not be possible," Canaris said carefully.

"Does the Abwehr not have spies inside Britain?"

"Of course, my Führer."

"Then I suggest you get to work, Herr Admiral. I want you to bring me the secret of the invasion—and quickly. Let me assure you, you don't have much time."

Berlin

THE Abwehr had two primary kinds of spies operating against Britain. The S-Chain consisted of agents who entered the country, settled under assumed identities, and engaged in espionage. R-Chain agents were mainly third-country nationals who periodically entered Britain legally and collected intelligence. But there was a third, smaller network—a handful of exceptionally trained "sleeper" agents who burrowed deeply into English society and waited, sometimes for years, to be activated. It was named the V-Chain for its creator and single control officer, Kurt Vogel.

Vogel's modest empire consisted of two rooms on the fourth floor of Abwehr headquarters, in a pair of dour town houses at 74-76 Tirpitz Ufer, in the heart of Berlin. The windows overlooked the Tiergarten. Once, it had been a spectacular view, but months of Allied bombing had left panzer-size craters in the park. Vogel's only assistant—a decorated Wehrmacht lieutenant named Werner Ulbricht who had lost a leg fighting the Russians—worked in the anteroom.

Kurt Vogel officially had the rank of captain in the Kriegsmarine, but like his mentor, Canaris, he rarely wore a uniform. He had iron-gray hair that looked as though he had cut it himself, and the intense gaze of a coffeehouse revolutionary. His voice was like a rusty hinge, and after a decade of clandestine conversations it rarely rose above a chapel murmur.

Vogel's office contained only one personal item, a portrait of his wife, Gertrude, and his twin girls. He had banished the three of them to Gertrude's mother's home in Bavaria when the bombing started, and he saw them infrequently. He kept a small flat near the office for those rare nights when he permitted himself to escape.

Vogel had earned a doctorate of law from Leipzig University. He was a brilliant student, and his professors had predicted he would one day sit on the Reichsgericht, Germany's supreme court.

Hitler changed all that. Hitler believed in the rule of men, not the rule of law. Within months of taking power, he turned Germany's entire judicial system upside down. *Führergewalt*—Führer power— became the absolute law of the land. In Vogel's opinion the darkest day in the history of German jurisprudence came in October 1933, when ten thousand lawyers stood on the steps of the Reichsgericht in Leipzig, arms raised in a Nazi salute, and swore to "follow the Führer to the end of our days." Vogel had been among them. That night he went home, burned his lawbooks, and drank himself sick.

Several months later, in the winter of 1934, Wilhelm Canaris asked Vogel if he would be willing to go to work for the Abwehr. Vogel accepted on one condition—that he not be forced to join the Nazi Party—and the following week he vanished into the world of German military intelligence. Officially, he served as Canaris's in-house legal counsel. Unofficially, he was given the task of preparing for the war with Britain that Canaris thought was inevitable.

Now Vogel sat at his desk hunched over a memo written by Paul Müller, who ran the Abwehr's networks in America. It had been given to him by Canaris earlier that day, a few hours after the Old Fox returned from a meeting with Hitler at Rastenburg. "Hitler wants results, Kurt," Canaris had said. "He wants proof. Is it Calais or is it Normandy? Perhaps it's time we brought your little nest of spies into the game."

Vogel reread the memo. It was perfect—the opportunity he had been waiting for. When he finished, he summoned Ulbricht.

"Werner, I want to see Paul Müller first thing in the morning. Make me an appointment."

That night the bombers came at midnight as Vogel dozed fitfully in the office. He rose from his camp bed and walked to the window as the aircraft droned overhead. Berlin shuddered as the first fires erupted. Vogel wondered how much more punishment the city could absorb. Vast sections had already been reduced to rubble.

The memo ran around in his head while he watched the raid.

To: Wilhelm Canaris
From: Paul Müller
Date: 2 Nov 43

On 21 October, Captain Dietrich debriefed American asset Scorpio in Panama City. According to Scorpio, a renowned American engineer, Peter Jordan, was recruited by the U.S. Navy last month and dispatched to London to work on a highly secret construction project. Scorpio knows Jordan personally and spoke with him before his departure. Scorpio says the project is definitely connected to the enemy's plan to invade France.

Jordan is a widower. His wife was killed in an accident in 1939. Scorpio believes Jordan is highly vulnerable to approach by a female asset. He now lives alone in the Kensington section of London. Scorpio has provided the address as well as the combination of the safe inside the study.

Vogel removed his key ring from the desk drawer and went to a locked steel cabinet. The file was inside an unmarked black folder. Returning to his desk, Vogel opened the cover. It was all there: photographs, background material, performance reports. He didn't need to read it. He had written it himself. She was perfect for it, everything he was looking for. She was beautiful, she was intelligent, and her English and her knowledge of British society was faultless.

PAUL Müller was in charge of the Abwehr's intelligence networks in the United States. He was short, tubby, and impeccably dressed in a shiny French suit. His thin hair was combed straight back from his cherubic face. "Imagine this, the great Kurt Vogel, here in my office," Müller said with a smirk. "To what do I owe this privilege?"

Vogel was used to the professional jealousy of the other senior staff. Because of the special status of his V-Chain network he was given more money and assets than the other case officers. He was also allowed to poke into their affairs. He removed his copy of Müller's memo from his pocket. "Tell me about Scorpio," he said.

"So the Old Fox finally circulated my note. Look at the date on the thing. I gave it to him two months ago. It's been sitting on his desk gathering dust. And that information is like gold. But it goes into the Fox's lair and never comes out again." Müller paused. "You know, Kurt, sometimes I wonder whose side Canaris is on."

"Tell me about Scorpio," Vogel repeated.

"I had dinner with him at the home of an American diplomat before the war. The fellow's German was better than mine. Thought the Nazis were doing great things for Germany. Only thing he hated worse than the Jews was the Bolsheviks. It was like an audition. I recruited him the next day. Easiest snare of my career."

"What's his background?"

Müller smiled. "Investment banking. Ivy League, contacts in industry and Washington. His information on war production has been excellent."

"His name?"

"Come on, Kurt. He's one of my best agents."

"I want his name."

"This place is like a sieve, Kurt. I tell you, everybody knows."

"I want a copy of Scorpio's file on my desk in an hour," Vogel said, his voice barely a whisper. "And I want everything you have on the engineer."

"You can have the information on Peter Jordan."

"I want it all, and if I have to go to Canaris, I'll do it."

"All right, Kurt, you win." Müller was digging in a file cabinet. "Here. You don't have to run to the Old Fox. Hell, you're worse than the Nazis sometimes."

VOGEL spent the rest of the morning reading about Peter Jordan. When he finished, he removed a pair of files from one of his cabinets and returned to his desk.

The first file contained information on an Irishman who worked on a small farm on an isolated stretch of Britain's Norfolk coast. The second file contained the dossier of a former Wehrmacht paratrooper who had been barred from jumping by a head wound. The man had all the qualities Vogel liked: perfect English, an eye for detail, a cool intelligence. Vogel pushed the files aside and drafted two messages. He added the ciphers to be used, the frequencies at which the messages were to be sent, and the transmission schedule. Then he called for Ulbricht.

"Yes, Herr Captain," Werner Ulbricht said. He entered the office, limping heavily on his wooden leg.

"I want you to go to Hamburg tomorrow night," Vogel said. He handed Ulbricht the transcripts of the messages. "Stand over the radio operator while he sends these. Make certain there are no mistakes. See that the acknowledgments from the agents are in order."

"Yes, sir."

"Before you go, I want you to track down Horst Neumann. He's in Berlin." Vogel walked to the window. "And contact the staff at the Dahlem farm. Tell them to expect us for a week. We have a lot to go over. And tell them to rig the jump platform. It's been a long time since Neumann jumped from an airplane. He'll need practice."

"Yes, sir."

Ulbricht went out, leaving Vogel standing at the window thinking it through once more, worrying himself to death. The most closely guarded secret of the war, and he planned to steal it with a woman, a grounded paratrooper, and a British traitor.

London: January 1944

THE Imperial Security Intelligence Service—better known by its military intelligence designation MI5—was headquartered in a small, cramped office building at 58 St. James's Street. MI5's task was counterintelligence. In the lexicon of espionage, counter-intelligence means protecting one's secrets—and, when necessary, catching spies. It was MI5 that Professor Alfred Vicary joined in May 1940 and where, on a dismal rainy evening five days after Hitler's secret conference at Rastenburg, he could still be found.

The top floor was the preserve of the senior staff. Brigadier Sir Basil Boothby's office was there, hidden behind a pair of intimidating oak doors. A pair of lights glared down from over the doors, a red one signifying the room was too insecure to permit access, a green one meaning enter at your own risk. Vicary, as always, hesitated before pressing the buzzer.

Vicary had received his summons at nine o'clock, while he was tidying up his hutch, as he referred to his small office. When MI5 exploded in size at the beginning of the war, space had become a precious commodity. Vicary was relegated to a windowless cell the size of a broom closet. He didn't complain. Churchill had been right—it had been time for him to rejoin the living. He thrived on the atmosphere of wartime intelligence: the long hours, the crises, even the dismal tea. He loved being an actor in the theater of the real. He seriously doubted whether he could be satisfied again in the sanctuary of academia.

The light over Boothby's office suddenly shone green. Vicary pressed the buzzer and stepped inside. Boothby's office was big and long, with fine paintings, a gas fireplace, rich Persian carpets, and a magnificent view. Sir Basil kept Vicary waiting the statutory ten minutes before entering the room through a second doorway connecting his office to the director general's secretariat.

Brigadier Sir Basil Boothby had classic English size and scale—tall, angular, still showing signs of the physical agility that made him a star athlete at school. It was there in the easy way his strong hand held his drink, in the square shoulders and thick neck. His gray-blond hair and eyebrows were so lush the department wits referred to him as the bottle brush.

Officially, little was known about Boothby's career—only that he had served in Britain's intelligence and security organizations his entire professional life. In Vicary's opinion Boothby symbolized all that was wrong with British intelligence between the wars—the wellborn Englishman, educated at Eton and Oxford, who believed the secret exercise of power was as much a birthright as his family fortune. Rigid, lazy, orthodox, a cop in handmade shoes and a Savile Row suit, Boothby had been eclipsed intellectually by the new recruits drawn into MI5 at the outset of the war: the top brains from the universities, the best barristers. Now he was in the unenviable position of supervising men who were more clever than he and at the same time attempting to claim credit for their accomplishments.

"Sorry to keep you waiting, Alfred. A meeting in the Underground War Rooms with Churchill, the director general, Menzies, and Ismay. I'm afraid we've got a bit of a crisis on our hands. I'm drinking brandy and soda. What will you have?"

"Whiskey," Vicary said, watching Boothby. Despite the fact that he was one of the most senior officers in MI5, Boothby still took a childlike pride in dropping the names of powerful people. The group of men who had just gathered in the prime minister's underground fortress were the elite of Britain's wartime intelligence community—the director general of MI5, Sir David Petrie; the director general of MI6, Sir Stewart Menzies; and Churchill's personal chief of staff, General Sir Hastings Ismay.

Boothby pressed a button on his desk and asked his secretary to bring Vicary's drink. It came on a silver tray, resting atop a white paper napkin. Boothby sat down next to Vicary and crossed his long legs, pointing the polished toe of his shoe at Vicary's kneecap like a loaded gun. "We have a new assignment for you, Alfred. And in order for you to truly understand its importance, we've decided to lift the veil a little and show you more than you've been allowed to see previously. Do you understand what I'm saying to you?"

"I believe so, Sir Basil."

Boothby rose, went to his desk, and brought back a secure briefcase. It was made of metal and had a set of handcuffs attached to the grip. Boothby opened it and withdrew a beige folder emblazoned with the sword and shield of SHAEF—Supreme Headquarters Allied Expeditionary Force. "You're about to become privy to the most important secret of Overlord—the time and place of the invasion of France," he said. "But first I'd like to ask you a question. Where do you think we're planning to strike?"

"Based on the little I know, I'd say Normandy."

"And how would you assess the chances of success?"

"Amphibious assaults by their nature are the most complicated of all military operations," Vicary said. "Especially when they involve the English Channel. I'd say the chances are no better than fifty-fifty."

Boothby snorted. "If that, Alfred, if that." He looked at Vicary. "You're right, by the way. It *is* Normandy. And it's scheduled for the late spring. And if we are going to have even your fifty-fifty chance of success, Hitler and his generals need to think we're going to attack somewhere else." Boothby sat down and held up the folder. "That's why we've developed Plan Bodyguard."

The code name meant nothing to Vicary. Boothby sailed on with his lecture. "Bodyguard was named out of respect for a rather eloquent remark the prime minister made to Stalin at Tehran. Churchill said, 'Truth, in war, is so important it must always be accompanied by a bodyguard of lies.' The Old Man has a certain way with words, I'll grant him that. Bodyguard is not an operation in itself. It is the code name for all the strategic cover and deception operations, to be carried out on a global scale, designed to mislead Hitler about our intentions on D-day."

Boothby picked up the folder and flipped violently through it.

"The most important component of Bodyguard is Operation Fortitude. The goal of Fortitude is to slowly convince Hitler and his generals that we intend to stage not one invasion of France, but two. The first, according to Fortitude, is to be a diversionary strike at Normandy. The second strike, the main thrust, will take place three days later at Calais." Boothby paused to sip his drink. "Fortitude says that the goal of the first assault is to force Rommel and von Rundstedt to hurl their crack panzer units of the German Fifteenth Army at Normandy, thus leaving Calais undefended when the *real* invasion occurs. Obviously, we want the opposite to take place. We want the panzers to remain at Calais while we come ashore at Normandy."

"Brilliant in its simplicity."

"Quite," Boothby said. "But with one glaring weakness. We don't have enough men to pull it off. By late spring there will be just thirty-seven divisions in Britain—American, British, and Canadian—barely enough to stage one strike against France. If Fortitude is to have any chance of succeeding, we must convince Hitler and his generals that we have the divisions necessary to stage two invasions."

"How in heaven's name are we going to do that?"

"Why, we're simply going to create an army of a million men. Conjure it up, I'm afraid, completely out of thin air."

"You can't be serious."

"Yes, we can, Alfred—we're deadly serious. By the time we're finished, the Germans are going to believe that we have a massive and powerful force coiled behind the cliffs of Dover, waiting to lash out across the Channel at Calais."

"Does this phantom army have a name?" Vicary asked.

"Indeed—the First United States Army Group. FUSAG for short. It even has a commander, Patton himself. The Germans believe General Patton is our finest battlefield commander and think we would be fools to launch any invasion without him. At his disposal Patton will have some one million men, made up primarily of nine divisions from the U.S. Third Army and two divisions of the Canadian First Army. FUSAG even has its own London headquarters in Bryanston Square."

Vicary blinked rapidly, trying to digest the extraordinary information he was being given. Imagine creating an army of a million men completely out of thin air. "Hitler's no fool, and neither are his generals," he said. "They aren't going to believe there's an army of a million men camped in the Kent countryside just because we tell them it's so."

Boothby smiled. "True, Alfred. In the coming weeks, as the phantom forces of FUSAG begin arriving in Britain, we're going to flood the airwaves with wireless traffic—some of it in codes the Germans have already broken, some of it *en clair.* Some of those messages will provide small clues about the location of the forces or their disposition. Obviously, we want the Germans to find those clues and latch onto them."

"Unbelievable," Vicary said beneath his breath.

"Yes, quite. And that's only a small part of it. We also have to take into account what the Germans see *from* the air. We have to make it look as though a massive army is staging a slow and methodical buildup in the southeast corner of the country. Enough tents to house a million men, an armada of aircraft, tanks, landing craft. From the ground they'll look like what they are—plywood and canvas fakes. But from the air they'll look like the real thing."

Vicary was shaking his head. He said, "Wireless signals, aerial photographs—those are two of the ways the Germans can gather intelligence about British intentions. The third way, of course, is through spies."

But were there really any German spies left? In 1939, the day war broke out, MI5 and Scotland Yard engaged in a massive roundup. All suspected spies were jailed, turned into double agents, or hanged. In May 1940, when Vicary arrived, MI5 was in the process of capturing a new wave of spies Canaris was sending to England to collect intelligence for the coming invasion. Those new spies suffered the same fate as the previous wave.

Spycatcher was not an appropriate word to describe what Vicary did at MI5. He was technically a Double Cross officer. It was his job to make sure the Abwehr believed its spies were still in place, still gathering intelligence, and still sending it back to their case officers in Berlin.

"Exactly, Alfred. Hitler's third source of intelligence about the invasion is his spies. Canaris's spies, I should say. And we know how effective they are. The German agents under our control will make a vital contribution to Bodyguard by confirming for Hitler much of what he can see from the skies and hear over the airwaves.

"Eisenhower is in London, by the way," Boothby went on. "Only a select few on our side have been made aware of that. Hitler knows it, however. In fact, the Germans know he is here because we told them he is here. In the coming weeks Canaris's spies will begin to see signs of a massive buildup of men and matériel in southeast England. Your own Double Cross network will play a critical role."

Boothby paused, lit a cigarette. "But you're shaking your head, Alfred. I suspect you've spotted the Achilles' heel of the entire deception plan. All it would take is one decent German spy to walk the south coast of England from Cornwall to Kent. If that happened, the entire deception would come crashing down, and with it the hopes of Europe. Which is why you're here now."

Boothby stood and slowly paced the length of his office. "As of this moment we are acting under the reasonable certitude that we have in fact poisoned all Hitler's sources of intelligence. We are also acting under the reasonable certitude that we have accounted for all of Canaris's spies. We wouldn't be embarking on Fortitude if that weren't the case. I use the words 'reasonable certitude' because there is no way we can ever be truly certain of that fact. Two hundred and sixty spies—all arrested, turned, or hanged."

Boothby vanished into a dark corner of his office. "Last week Hitler staged a conference in Rastenburg. All the heavies were there. The subject was the time and place of the invasion. Hitler ordered Canaris to learn the truth or face some rather distressing consequences. Canaris in turn gave the job to a man on his staff named Vogel—Kurt Vogel. Your job is to make sure Kurt Vogel doesn't learn the truth. I haven't had a chance to read his file. I suspect Registry may have something on him."

"Right," Vicary said.

Boothby had drifted back into the dim light. "Alfred, I want to be perfectly honest with you from the outset. The prime minister insisted you be given the assignment over the strenuous objections of the director general and myself. You have done marvelous work, but both the director general and I feel that a more senior man might be better suited to this case."

"I see," Vicary said. A more senior man meant a career officer.

"But obviously," Boothby resumed, "we were unable to convince the prime minister that you were not the best man for the case. So it's yours. Give me regular updates on your progress. And good luck, Alfred. I suspect you'll need it."

CHAPTER TWO

London

CATHERINE Blake had made one demand at the time of her recruitment—enough money to live comfortably. She had been raised in large town houses and sprawling country estates, and spending the war in some hovel of a boardinghouse was out of the question. Her cover was a middle-class war widow, and her flat matched it to perfection—a modest yet comfortable set of rooms in a Victorian terrace in Earl's Court.

The sitting room was cozily furnished, though a stranger might have been struck by the lack of personal mementos. There was a separate bedroom, a kitchen with all modern appliances, and her own bathroom with a large tub. The flat was on the top floor, where her AFU suitcase radio could receive transmissions from Hamburg with little interference, and the bay window in the sitting room provided a clear view of the street below.

It was eight o'clock in the morning when she let herself into her flat. She had spent a long and busy night as a volunteer nurse at St. Thomas's Hospital, assisting with casualties of the blitz. The work was time-consuming and exhausting, but it was essential for her cover. It wouldn't look right for a young widow with no family to be doing nothing for the war effort.

She went into the kitchen and made tea. Like all Londoners, she had become addicted to tea and cigarettes. She wanted to crawl into bed and sleep, but she had work to do. She would have been home an hour earlier if she had taken the underground straight across London to Earl's Court, but Catherine did not move around like a normal woman. She had taken a train, then a bus, then a taxi, then another bus. She had stepped off the bus before her stop and walked the final quarter mile to her flat, constantly checking to make certain she was not being followed. After more than five years some agents might be tempted to become complacent. Catherine would never become complacent. It was one of the reasons she had survived.

She went into the bathroom and undressed in front of the mirror. She was tall and fit; years of heavy riding and hunting had made her much stronger than most women and many men. She undid the clasp that held her hair in a discreet nurse's bun, and it tumbled about her shoulders. Her eyes were ice-blue—the color of a Prussian lake, her father had always said—and the cheekbones were wide and prominent. The nose was long and graceful, the mouth generous, with sensuous lips.

She climbed into the tub feeling suddenly very alone. Vogel had warned her about the loneliness. Sometimes it was worse than the fear. She had not allowed herself a lover since Holland. She missed men, but she could live without them. Besides, the last thing she needed was a lovesick man looking into her past.

After her bath Catherine put on her robe and went through the kitchen to the pantry. The suitcase radio was on the top shelf. She brought it down and took it into the sitting room, near the window. Each week she switched it on for ten minutes. If Berlin had orders for her, they would send them. For five years there had been nothing.

Catherine slipped on her earphones and poured another cup of tea. She nearly spilled it when, five minutes later, the operator in Hamburg tapped out a burst of code.

Catherine acknowledged and signed off. It took several minutes to find her codebook and several more to decode the message: EXECUTE RENDEZVOUS ALPHA.

Kurt Vogel finally wanted her to meet with another agent.

Hampton Sands, Norfolk

RAIN drifted across the Norfolk coast as Sean Dogherty, done in by five pints of ale, tried to mount his bicycle outside the Hampton Arms pub. He succeeded on his third attempt and set out for home.

Dogherty was a small man of fifty, with green eyes and a derelict gray beard. He wore an oilskin coat and a woolen cap. Cycling steadily, he barely noticed the village: a dreary place, really—a cluster of cottages along the single street, the pub, St. John's Church. Dogherty pedaled over the wooden bridge spanning the sea creek. A moment later the village disappeared behind him.

The curtain of rain parted, and the terrain came into view—broad emerald fields, endless gray mudflats, salt marshes deep with reeds and grass. To his left a wide beach ran down to the water.

Dogherty reached the cottage. It was a smallholder farm on rented land, but it provided an adequate living: a small flock of sheep that gave them wool and meat, chickens, a small plot of root vegetables that fetched good prices these days at the market. Dogherty even owned a dilapidated old van for transporting goods to market. He turned into the drive, climbed off his bicycle, and pushed it along the pitted pathway toward the barn.

Sean Dogherty had been recruited to spy for the Abwehr in 1940. It had not been difficult for them to convince him to betray England and go to work for Nazi Germany. In 1921 his older brother was hanged by the British for leading an Irish Republican Army flying column.

Inside the barn, Dogherty unlocked a tool cabinet and took down his suitcase transceiver. It had been more than three years since the Abwehr had asked him to do anything. Still, he dutifully switched on his radio at the instructed time and waited for ten minutes.

Dogherty was about to shut off the radio when it suddenly came to life. He lunged for his notepad and wrote furiously, then quickly tapped out an acknowledgment and signed off. It took him several minutes to decode the message. When he finished, he couldn't believe his eyes: EXECUTE RECEPTION PROCEDURE ONE.

The Germans wanted him to take in an agent.

IT HAD been fifteen minutes since Mary Dogherty, standing in the kitchen window, had seen her husband enter the barn. She knew what he was doing in there—he was on the radio with the Germans. She hated Sean's spying and feared he would be caught. Everyone was on the lookout for spies; it was a national obsession. One slip, one mistake, and Sean would be arrested and executed. Shuddering, she moved to the fire.

The pounding at the door startled her. It was not like Sean to lock himself out. She pulled back the door, prepared to yell at him for leaving the cottage without his key. Instead, she saw Jenny Colville, a young girl of sixteen who lived on the other side of the village. She stood in the rain, a shiny oilskin coat hanging over bony shoulders. Her shoulder-length hair lay plastered against her head, framing an awkward face that one day might be very pretty.

Mary could tell she had been crying. "What happened, Jenny? Did your father hit you again? Has he been drinking?"

Jenny nodded and burst into tears.

"Come in out of the rain," Mary said. "Take off those clothes. They're soaking wet. I'll get you a robe to wear until they're dry."

Mary disappeared into the bedroom. Jenny did as she was told. Mary came back with the robe and helped Jenny into it, wrapping it around her tightly. "Now, isn't that better?"

"Yes. Thank you, Mary." Jenny started to cry again. "I don't know what I'd do without you."

Mary drew Jenny to her. "You'll never be without me, Jenny."

Jenny climbed into an old chair next to the fire and covered herself with a musty blanket. The shivering stopped. Moments later she was asleep.

Mary was reading next to the fire when Sean Dogherty let himself into the cottage. He pointed to the chair where Jenny slept and said, "Why is she here? Her father hit her again?"

"Shhhh," Mary hissed. "You'll wake her." She rose and led Sean into the kitchen and set a place for him at the table.

He sat down. "What Martin Colville needs is a bit of his own medicine. And I'm just the man to give it to him."

"Please, Sean, the last thing we need is for you to attract the attention of the police by getting in some stupid fight. Now finish your dinner and be quiet. You'll wake the girl."

Dogherty took a spoonful of the stew and pulled a face. "This food is stone-cold."

"If you'd come home at a decent hour, it wouldn't be. Where have you been?"

Dogherty cast Mary an icy glance. "I was in the barn."

"Maybe one day the boys in Berlin will give you a real assignment. Then you can get rid of all the hate that's inside you, and we can get on with what's left of our lives." She rose. "I'm going to bed. Put some wood on the fire so Jenny will be warm enough."

When Mary was gone, Dogherty went to the cupboard, took down a bottle of whiskey, and poured a generous measure. "Maybe the boys in Berlin will do just that, Mary Dogherty," he said, raising his glass in a quiet toast.

London

ALFRED Vicary had actually engaged in deception to get a job with military intelligence during the First War. He was twenty-one, nearing the end of his studies at Cambridge. His best friend, a brilliant philosophy student named Brendan Evans, had heard the army was starting up an Intelligence Corps. The only qualifications were fluent German and French, the ability to ride and repair a motorbike, and perfect eyesight. Brendan had contacted the War Office and made appointments for them.

Vicary was despondent; he did not meet the qualifications. He had fluent German and passable French, but he had no idea how to ride a motorbike, and his eyesight was atrocious.

Brendan Evans was everything Vicary was not—tall, fair, strikingly handsome—but they had one thing in common: flawless memories. Vicary conceived his plan.

That evening Brendan taught him to ride a motorcycle. The following morning they took a train to London and went to the War Office. Brendan went inside while Vicary waited outside. Brendan emerged an hour later, grinning broadly. "I'm in," he said. "Now it's your turn. Listen carefully." He proceeded to recite the entire eye chart used for the vision test.

Vicary passed with flying colors and was commissioned as a second lieutenant in the motorcyclist section of the Intelligence Corps. A week later Brendan Evans and Alfred Vicary, along with their motorbikes, sailed for France.

It was all so simple then. Agents slipped behind enemy lines, counted troops, watched the railways, used carrier pigeons to deliver secret messages. Now it was more complex, a duel of wits over the wireless that required immense attention to detail.

Double Cross. . . . A German spy named Karl Becker was a perfect example. He was sent by Canaris to England during the heady days of 1940, when a German invasion seemed certain. Becker, posing as a Swiss businessman, set himself up in Kensington and began collecting every secret he could lay his hands on. It was his use of counterfeit sterling that set Vicary onto him. Vicary, with the help of watchers, went everywhere Becker went—to the parties where he traded in gossip, to his meetings with live agents, to his dead drops, to his bedroom. After a month Vicary arrested Becker and rolled up an entire network of German agents.

But instead of hanging Becker, Vicary turned him—convinced him to go to work for MI5 as a double agent. Becker's Abwehr controllers were so impressed by his subsequent reports that they asked him to recruit more agents, which he did—actually, which Vicary did. By the end of 1940 Karl Becker had a ring of a dozen agents working for him. All were fictitious, products of Vicary's imagination. Vicary tended to every aspect of their lives. They fell in love; they had affairs; they complained about money; they lost houses and friends in the blitz. Vicary even allowed himself to arrest a couple of them; the Abwehr would never believe none of their agents had been lost. It was mind-bending, tedious work, requiring attention to the most trivial detail, but Vicary found it exhilarating and loved every minute of it.

Vicary took the stairs from Boothby's lair down to the Registry. Opening the door, he was struck by the smell of the place: decaying paper, dust, tangy mildew from the damp cellar walls. There were files on open shelves, files in the file cabinets, files stacked on the cold stone floor. A trio of pretty girls known as Registry Queens moved quietly about amid the paper and the gloom.

The files on Abwehr personnel were stored on open floor-to-ceiling shelves in a small room at the far end of the floor. Vicary peered through his half-moon glasses. Blast! The V's were on the top shelf. One of the Registry Queens brought him a ladder. Vicary climbed it and picked through the files. He found a manila folder with a red tab: VOGEL, KURT—ABWEHR BERLIN. He pulled it down and looked inside. The file was empty.

Nicholas Jago had been the head archivist at University College and was recruited by MI5 the same week as Vicary. He was assigned to Registry and ordered to impose some discipline on the department. Jago, like Registry itself, was irritable and difficult to use. He also knew how to lose a file as well as find one.

Despite the late hour, Vicary found Jago working in his cramped glass-enclosed office. Unlike the file rooms, it was a sanctuary of neatness and order. When Vicary rapped against the windowed door, Jago looked up, smiled, and waved him in.

Vicary sat down and swapped banalities, then cleared his throat. "I'm looking for a file on a rather obscure Abwehr officer. The cover is on the shelf, but the contents are missing."

"What's the name?" Jago asked.

"Kurt Vogel."

Jago's face darkened. "Let me take a look for it. Wait here, Alfred. I'll just be a moment."

"I'll come with you," Vicary said. "Maybe I can help."

"No, no," Jago insisted. "I wouldn't hear of it. Stay here. Make yourself comfortable. I'll just be a moment."

That's the second time you've said that, Vicary thought.

Jago rushed out of the office but was back a moment later. He handed Vicary the file and sat down. "Just as I thought," he said. "It was right there on the shelf. One of the girls must have placed it in the wrong folder. Happens all the time."

Vicary listened to the dubious excuse and frowned. He didn't believe a word of Jago's story. He believed the file had been pulled by someone recently and hadn't made its way back to the shelf. And that someone must have been very important, judging by the look on Jago's face when Vicary had asked for it.

"Who had Vogel's file last?" Vicary asked.

"Come on, Alfred, you know I can't tell you that."

"All I have to do is ask Boothby for a chit to see the access list, and he'll give it to me," Vicary said. "Why don't you save me the time?"

"He might; he might not."

"What do you mean by that, Nicholas?"

"Listen, old man, the last thing I want to do is get between you and Boothby. Talk to him. If he says you can see the access list, it's all yours."

Leaving Jago in his glass chamber, Vicary went back upstairs to his office, the Vogel file under his arm.

SOMETHING about the dossier just wasn't right—that Vicary knew. Better not to force it. Better to set it aside and let his subconscious turn over the pieces.

Vicary set the file on his desk and switched on the lamp. He read it through twice. Then he looked up and said, "Harry, I think we have a problem."

Harry Dalton, Vicary's partner, sat with the other junior men in the common area outside Vicary's office. He got to his feet and came inside. Harry was tall and athletic, with intelligent blue eyes and a ready smile. Before the war he had been a detective inspector of the Metropolitan Police Department's elite murder squad.

"Vogel's got brains, that's for certain," Vicary said. "Look at this: doctorate of law from Leipzig University. Doesn't sound like your typical Nazi to me. The Nazis perverted the laws of Germany. Someone with an education like that couldn't be too thrilled about them. Then in 1935 he suddenly forsakes the law and goes to work for Canaris as a sort of in-house counsel for the Abwehr? I don't believe that. I think he's a spy."

"You have a theory?" Harry asked.

"Three, actually. Number one, Canaris has lost faith in the British networks, and he's asked Vogel to investigate. Theory two, Canaris has commissioned Vogel to construct a new network. And theory three is that Kurt Vogel is the control officer of a network we don't know about."

"An entire network of agents that we haven't uncovered? Then all our doubles would be at risk."

"It's a house of cards, Harry. All it takes is one good agent, and the entire thing comes crashing down." Vicary lit a cigarette. "But Kurt Vogel has to use his radio or send an agent into the country. And when he does, we'll be onto him."

They sat in silence for a moment. Then Vicary told Harry about what had happened in Registry.

"Lots of files go missing now and again, Alfred."

"Yes, but why *this* file? And more importantly, why *now?*"

Harry said, "I know one or two of the Registry Queens. I'll poke around quietly, ask a few questions."

"Jago's lying—he's hiding something."

"Why would he lie?"

"I don't know, Harry," Vicary said, crushing out his cigarette, "but I'm paid to think wicked thoughts."

Bletchley Park, England

OFFICIALLY, it was called the Government Code and Cipher School. A large, ugly Victorian mansion surrounded by a high fence, it was not a school, but most people in the town of Bletchley understood that something portentous was going on there. The staff was an odd collection—the country's brightest mathematicians, chess champions, crossword puzzle wizards—all assembled for one purpose: cracking German codes.

Before the war Denholm Saunders had been a top mathematician at Cambridge. On this January afternoon he was seated at his desk in the mansion, working over a pair of messages sent by the Abwehr in Hamburg to German agents inside Britain. The messages had been intercepted by the Radio Security Service, flagged as suspicious, and forwarded to Bletchley Park for decoding.

The work that afternoon was far from challenging; the messages had been transmitted in a variation of a code Saunders had unbuttoned in 1940. "My goodness, but they are getting a bit boring, aren't they?" Saunders said to no one in particular. Still, an officer at MI5 named Alfred Vicary had put out a red flag for this kind of thing just yesterday.

Selsey, England

"IT WAS the oddest thing I've ever seen, Mabel," Arthur Barnes told his wife over breakfast that dreary January morning. Barnes, as he did every morning, had walked his beloved corgi Fionna along the waterfront. Part of it still was open to civilians; most of it had been sealed off as a restricted military zone.

Fionna spotted the thing first; then Barnes did. "A giant concrete monster, Mabel. Like a block of flats lying on its side."

The concrete monster had a boat attached to it, pushing through the choppy seas. Off its portside Barnes spotted a small vessel with a bunch of military types on deck. "I couldn't believe it, Mabel," he recounted, finishing the last of his toast. "They were clapping and cheering. Imagine that. Our boys getting excited because they can make a giant hunk of concrete float."

The giant floating concrete structure spotted by Arthur Barnes was code-named Phoenix. It was two hundred feet long and fifty feet wide. More than two hundred were scheduled to be built. Its interior—invisible from Barnes's vantage point—was a labyrinth of hollow chambers and scuttling valves, for the Phoenix was not designed to remain on the surface. It was designed to be towed across the English Channel and sunk off the Normandy coast. The Phoenixes were just one component of a massive Allied project to construct an artificial harbor in England and drag it to France on D-day. The code name for the project was Operation Mulberry.

The invasion planners had determined that attempting to capture a port intact was hopeless. The men and supplies, they decided, would come ashore the same way—on the flat, barren Normandy beaches. But weather was a problem. Studies of the French coast showed that fair conditions could be expected to last no more than four consecutive days. The planners had to assume that supplies would have to be brought ashore in a storm. But a storm would create havoc; an artificial harbor would be needed.

The British and Americans had agreed to build two harbors for the Normandy invasion, a task of unimaginable proportions. Hundreds of topflight engineers would be needed, as well as tens of thousands of skilled construction workers.

The only assignment equal to the task of building the Mulberries would be keeping them secret—proven by the fact that Arthur Barnes and his corgi were still standing on the waterfront when the coaster carrying the team of British and American Mulberry engineers nosed against the dock. As the team disembarked, one of the men broke away and walked to a waiting staff car. The driver opened the rear door, and Commander Peter Jordan climbed inside.

New York City: October 1943

THEY had come for him on a Friday—the thick, stubby American and the thin, smooth Englishman. In reality their names were Leamann and Broome, or at least that's what it said on the identification cards they waved past him. Leamann said he was with the War Department; Broome, the angular Englishman, that he was attached to the War Office. Neither man wore a uniform. Leamann wore a shabby brown suit that pulled across his stomach, Broome an elegantly cut suit of charcoal gray, a little too heavy for the American fall weather.

Peter Jordan received them in his magnificent lower Manhattan office with its view of the East River.

Leamann, it seemed, had memorized Jordan's résumé, and he recited it as if Jordan had been nominated for an award. "*Scientific American* says you're the greatest thing since the guy who invented the wheel," he said. "You're hot stuff, Mr. Jordan."

"Do you know a man named Walker Hardegen?" asked Broome, the narrow Englishman.

Jordan had the uncomfortable feeling he had been investigated. "I think you already know the answer to that." Jordan sat down behind his desk. "All right, gentlemen, suppose you tell me what this is all about."

"It has to do with the invasion of Europe," Broome said. "We may need your help."

Jordan smiled. "You want me to build a bridge between England and France?"

"Something like that," Leamann said.

Broome lit a cigarette. He blew an elegant stream of smoke toward the river. "Actually, Mr. Jordan, it's nothing like that at all."

London: January 1944

ALFRED Vicary hurried across Parliament Square toward the Underground War Rooms, Winston Churchill's subterranean headquarters beneath the pavements of Westminster. The prime minister had personally telephoned Vicary and asked to see him straightaway.

MI5 was in a panic. The previous evening a pair of decoded Abwehr signals had arrived from Bletchley Park. They confirmed Vicary's worst suspicions. At least two Abwehr agents were operating inside Britain without MI5's knowledge, and it appeared the Germans were planning to send in another. It was a disaster.

The Royal Marine guard glanced at Vicary's identification and waved him inside. Vicary descended the stairs and crossed the small lobby. Shielded by four feet of concrete reinforced with old London tram rails, the underground labyrinth was regarded as absolutely bombproof. Along with Churchill's personal command post, the most vital and secret arms of the government were housed here.

An aide took Vicary immediately into Churchill's private quarters, located in room 65A. It was a tiny space, much of it consumed by a small bed made up with gray army blankets. At the foot of the bed stood a small desk, with a bottle, two glasses, and a humidor for the prime minister's cigars.

Churchill, cloaked in a green silk robe, the first cigar of the day between his fingers, sat at his desk. He was not the same man Vicary had seen in May 1940. Nor was he the jaunty, confident figure of newsreels. He was obviously a man who had worked too much and slept too little. He managed a smile for his old friend.

"Hello, Alfred. How have you been?"

"Fine, but I should be asking that of you."

"Never better," Churchill said. "Bring me up to date."

"As you know, two German agents we never knew about are operating inside Britain, and the Germans are planning to insert a new agent into the country."

"What are you doing to stop them?"

Vicary briefed Churchill on the steps they had taken thus far. "But unfortunately, Prime Minister, the message to the existing agent was a code phrase only: 'Execute reception procedure one.' It tells us nothing, and unless we're very lucky, the chances of capturing the new agent are slim."

"Damn!" Churchill swore, bringing his hand down on the arm of the chair. He rose and poured brandy for them both. "You've done marvelous work, Alfred, but it will all mean nothing if these spies find what they're looking for."

"I understand the stakes involved, Prime Minister."

"I want them stopped, Alfred. I want them crushed." Churchill's cigar had gone dead in his hand. Relighting it, he indulged in a quiet moment of smoking. "How's Boothby?" he said finally.

Vicary sighed. "As ever, Prime Minister."

"Supportive?"

"He wants to be kept abreast of every move I make."

"I never told you this, Alfred, but I had my doubts about whether you truly had what it took to operate in the world of military intelligence. Oh, I never doubted you had the brains, but I doubted whether you could be ruthless enough."

Churchill's words stunned Vicary.

"Now, why are you looking at me like that, Alfred? You're one of the most decent men I've ever met. The men who usually succeed in your line of work are men like Boothby. He'd arrest his own mother if he thought it would further his career."

"But I have changed, Prime Minister. I've done things I've never thought I was capable of doing."

"You must make a stone of your heart, Alfred," Churchill went on in a hoarse whisper. "You must set aside whatever morals you still have, whatever feelings of human kindness you still possess, and do whatever it takes to win. Is that clear?"

"It is, Prime Minister."

Churchill leaned closer. "There is an unfortunate truth about war, Alfred. While it is virtually impossible for one man to win a war, it is entirely possible for one man to lose one." He paused. "For the sake of our friendship, Alfred, don't be that man."

Shaken, Vicary showed himself to the door. Behind him he heard Winston Churchill muttering to himself. It took Vicary a moment to understand what he was saying. "Blasted English weather," Churchill murmured. "Blasted English weather."

DEAD leaves rattled across Vicary's path as he hurried back to MI5 headquarters. He moved quickly with his stiff-jointed mechanical limp, head down, hands plunged into coat pockets.

The Abwehr had just so many ways of inserting an agent into Britain. Many put ashore in small boats launched from submarines. Vicary already had asked the coastguard and Royal Navy to be especially vigilant, but the English coastline stretches thousands of miles, impossible to cover entirely.

The Abwehr had parachuted spies into Britain. It was impossible to account for every square inch of airspace, but Vicary had asked the RAF to be watchful. The Abwehr had dropped and landed agents in Ireland. To get to England, they had to take the ferry. Vicary had asked the ferry operators to keep an eye out for anyone uncomfortable with the ferry routine, the language, or the currency. He couldn't give them a description; he didn't have one.

It is virtually impossible for one man to win a war. It is entirely possible for one man to lose one.

Vicary thought, Damn the Old Man for laying that on me.

There was something else Churchill had said. The prime minister, safe in his subterranean shelter, complaining about the weather . . .

Back in St. James's street, Vicary rushed past the guard and hurried upstairs to his office.

"Harry, if you needed to get a spy into the country on short notice, which route would you use?"

"I suppose I'd come through the east—Kent, East Anglia."

"My thoughts exactly. Which mode of transportation?"

"I suppose I'd choose an airplane."

"Why not a submarine? Put the spy ashore in a raft?"

"Because it's easier to get a small plane on short notice."

"Exactly, Harry. And what do you need to drop a spy into England by plane?"

"Decent weather, for one thing."

"Right again, Harry." Vicary snatched up the telephone and asked for the RAF meteorological service.

After a brief conversation he turned back to Harry. "If our theory holds, our agent will try to enter the country by parachute tomorrow night."

Hampton Sands, Norfolk

SEAN Dogherty let himself out the back door of the cottage and walked along the footpath to the barn. He wore a heavy sweater and an oilskin coat and carried a kerosene lantern. The last clouds had moved off. The sky was a mat of deep blue, thick with stars. The air was bitterly cold.

Inside the barn, Dogherty switched on his radio and slipped on his earphones. Soon the radio crackled into life. The message was brief. He sent back an acknowledging signal, dashed outside, and rode his bicycle down to the beach.

Dogherty felt an intense excitement rising in his chest. He had not felt anything like this since the first time he met his Abwehr contact in London early in the war.

Dogherty dismounted at the end of the road and pushed the bicycle into a grove of pines at the base of the dunes. He climbed the dunes, scrambled down the other side, and ran across the beach. That afternoon he had laid signal fires and doused them with petrol. The fires were still intact, ready to be lit. In the distance he could hear the low rumble of an airplane. Dogherty thought, Good Lord, he's actually coming! He lit the fires. In seconds the beach was ablaze with light. The plane descended over the beach, and a moment later a black dot leaped from the back. The parachute snapped open as the plane banked and headed out to sea.

The German made a perfect landing, rolled, and was gathering up his black parachute by the time Dogherty reached him. "You must be Sean Dogherty," he said in perfect public school English.

"Right," Sean replied. "And you must be the German spy."

The man frowned. "Something like that. Listen, old sport, I can manage this. Why don't you put out those fires before the whole world knows we're here."

CHAPTER THREE

London

IT HAD been six days since Catherine Blake received the message from Hamburg. During that time she had thought long and hard about ignoring it.

Alpha was the code name of a rendezvous point in Hyde Park, a footpath through a grove of trees. She couldn't help but feel jittery about going forward with the meeting. The smallest mistake might get her arrested or killed. Like the rendezvous site, for example. It was a bitterly cold night; anyone loitering in the park would automatically come under suspicion. It was a silly mistake, so unlike Vogel. He must be under enormous pressure.

Catherine turned into Hyde Park. Although she was reluctant to make the rendezvous, she was going ahead with it because of her father's safety. Catherine had not volunteered to work for the Abwehr as a spy; she had been forced to do it. Vogel's instrument of coercion was her father. Vogel had made it clear that her father would be harmed—arrested, thrown into a concentration camp, even killed—if she did not agree to go to Britain. If she refused to take an assignment now, her father's life would surely be in danger.

She entered the grove and waited for Vogel's agent to show.

THE afternoon train from Hunstanton arrived at Liverpool Street Station a half hour late. Horst Neumann collected his small leather grip from the luggage rack and joined the line of passengers spilling onto the platform. The station was chaos. Knots of weary travelers waited for hopelessly delayed trains. Soldiers slept where they liked, heads pillowed on kit bags. Small, agile, bright-eyed, Neumann sliced his way through the crowd.

The two men at the exit had "authority" written all over them. Instinctively Neumann reached inside his jacket and felt for the butt of his pistol before brushing past the two men and joining the crowd on Bishopsgate Road.

The street was pitch-dark, the only light provided by the shaded headlamps of the evening traffic and the pale blackout torches carried by many of the pedestrians. Twice Neumann smashed straight into a pedestrian. Once he collided with a lamppost. London certainly had changed since his last visit.

He was born Nigel Fox in London in 1919 to a German mother and an English father. When his father died, in 1927, his mother returned to Germany and a year later remarried. Erich Neumann wasn't about to have a stepson named Nigel who spoke German with an English accent. He changed the boy's name to Horst, allowed him to take his family name, and enrolled him in military school.

Miserable at first, Horst quickly distinguished himself as one of the best junior track athletes in Germany. He joined the Hitler Jugend—the Hitler Youth. In 1936 he was invited to attend the Olympic Games in Berlin. Sitting in the grandstand, Horst dreamed of 1944, when he would be old enough to compete for Germany. But the war would change all that.

Early in 1939 he joined the Fallschirmjäger, the paratroopers. He jumped into Poland on the first day of the war, and later into France, Crete, and Russia. Then he sustained a head wound in a bar fight in Paris when he tried to fend off a group of SS officers who were brutalizing a French girl. That ended his jumping days. Because of his fluent English he was assigned to an army intelligence listening post in northern France, monitoring wireless communications originating in England. It was drudgery. Then came the man from the Abwehr—Kurt Vogel. He said he was looking for qualified men willing to go to Britain and conduct espionage. Neumann accepted on the spot and returned to Berlin that night with Vogel.

Before coming to Britain, Neumann was taken to a farmhouse in Dahlem, just outside Berlin, for a week of intense preparation. Mornings were spent in the barn, where Vogel had rigged a jump platform for Neumann to practice. He also brushed up his skills with a handgun, impressive to begin with, and silent killing. Afternoons were spent on dead drops, rendezvous procedures, and radio. Neumann was allowed forty-five minutes for running. For three days he was permitted to go alone, but on the fourth day, his head filling with Vogel's secrets, a jeep shadowed him from a distance.

Evenings were Vogel's private preserve. After a group supper in the farmhouse kitchen Vogel would lead Neumann into the study and lecture him by the fire. He told him of Sean Dogherty and Catherine Blake and an American officer named Peter Jordan.

Enter Hyde Park from the north, Vogel had told him. From Bayswater Road. Which Neumann did now. Follow the pathway to the trees overlooking the lake. Make one pass to make certain the place is clean. Make your approach on the second pass. Let her decide whether it is safe to continue. She is very good.

THE SMALL MAN APPEARED ON the pathway. He wore a wool overcoat and a brimmed hat. He walked past without looking at her.

She stood in the trees, waiting. She heard the footsteps. It was the same man who had passed her a moment earlier.

"I say, I seem to be a bit lost," he said. "Can you point me in the direction of Park Lane?"

Catherine pointed east. "Park Lane? It's in that direction."

He smiled and said, "Catherine Blake, as I live and breathe. Why don't we go somewhere warm where we can talk."

NOTHING in Harry Dalton's professional experience had been as frustrating as this. He was looking for a German agent, but he didn't have a single clue or lead. His only recourse was to telephone local police forces in the countryside and ask for reports of anything out of the ordinary. He couldn't tell them he was looking for a spy. That would be a breach of security. Through the afternoon he had fielded dozens of calls, one more bizarre than the next.

It was now four o'clock, shift change in Registry. Grace Clarendon would be coming on duty. Harry thought, Maybe I can make something out of this day. He took the lift down to Registry and found Grace pushing a metal cart brimming with files. She had a shock of short white-blond hair, and her cheap blood-red wartime lipstick made her look as if she were tarted up for a man. She wore a schoolboy's gray woolen sweater and a black skirt that was a little too short. Her heavy stockings could not hide the shape of her long, athletic legs.

She spotted Harry and smiled warmly, then, with only a sideways glance of her bright green eyes, told him to meet her in one of the small side rooms. She joined him a moment later, closed the door, and kissed him on the cheek. "Hello, darling."

It had started in 1940 during a night raid, when they sheltered together in the underground. In the morning Grace had taken him to her flat and to her bed.

"I need a favor, Grace," Harry said, voice low.

She kissed him again. "All right, Harry, what do you need?"

"I need to see the access list on a file."

Her face darkened. "Come on. You know I can't do that."

"An Abwehr man named Kurt Vogel. When Vicary came down to pull Vogel's file, it was missing. He went to see Jago, and two minutes later he had the darn thing in his hand. Jago spun some yarn about it being mislaid."

She was angrily digging through the cart and placing files on the shelves. "I know all about it, Harry. Jago blamed it on me. He wrote a letter of reprimand and put it in my file."

"Why?"

"To cover himself, that's why."

Harry took her hand. "Grace, I need to see that list."

"The access list won't tell you anything. The person who had that file before Vicary doesn't leave a trail."

"Grace, please. I'm begging."

Grace picked up another handful of files, then looked up at him. With her blood-red lips she mouthed the initials B.B.

"HOW is it possible you don't have a single lead?" Basil Boothby said as Vicary sank down into the deep overstuffed couch. Sir Basil had demanded nightly updates on the progress of the investigation. Tonight Boothby sipped a gin and bitters while pacing the length of the room. "We have three German agents loose in the country," he said. "If one of them tries to contact one of our doubles, we're going to be in trouble. The whole Double Cross apparatus will be in jeopardy."

"My guess is they won't try to contact any other agents."

"Why not?" Boothby asked.

"Because I think Vogel is running his own show. I think we're dealing with a separate network of agents we never knew about."

"That's just a hunch, Alfred. We need to deal with the facts."

"Ever read Vogel's file?" Vicary said as carelessly as possible.

"No."

And you're a liar, Vicary thought. "Judging by the way this affair has unfolded, I'd say Vogel has kept a network of sleeper agents inside Britain since before the war. If I had to guess, the primary agent is operating in London, the subagent somewhere in the countryside, where he could take in an agent on short notice. The agent who arrived last night is almost certainly here to brief the lead agent on his assignment." Vicary hesitated, aware of the response his next suggestion was likely to generate. "I think we should schedule a meeting with General Betts to brief him on developments."

Brigadier General Thomas Betts was the deputy chief of intelligence at SHAEF. He had the unenviable job of making certain that none of the several hundred American and British officers who knew the secret of Overlord gave that secret, intentionally or unintentionally, to the enemy.

"That's premature, Alfred." Boothby sipped his gin and bitters.

"Premature? We have three German spies on the loose!"

Boothby snorted. "I will not permit you to tarnish the reputation of this department, Alfred. I won't have it."

"Perhaps there's something else you should consider besides the reputation of this department, Sir Basil." Vicary struggled out of the soft, deep couch. "If the spies succeed, we may well lose the war."

CATHERINE Blake watched Horst Neumann as he led himself on a tour of her flat. He went to the drawing-room window, parted the curtains, and gazed down into the street.

"Even if they're out there, you'll never spot them," she said.

"I know—but it makes me feel better to look."

"You're a soldier. At least you used to be. What's your rank?"

"I'm a lieutenant."

She smiled. "I outrank you, by the way."

"Yes, I know—*Major*."

"What's your cover name?"

"James Porter. I was wounded at Dunkirk and invalided out of the army. I'm a traveling pharmaceutical salesman now."

"Where are you staying?"

"The Norfolk coast—a village called Hampton Sands. Vogel has an agent there, an IRA sympathizer named Sean Dogherty."

Neumann told her his story, ending with his recruitment.

"Our Kurt is good at finding work for the restless," Catherine said. "So what does Vogel have in mind for *me?*"

"One assignment, then out. Back to Germany."

One assignment, then out. And with a highly capable former paratrooper to help her make her escape. She was impressed. She had always assumed she would be forced to fend for herself. "And when it's all over? How are we supposed to get out of Britain?"

"Vogel has arranged passage aboard a U-boat off the coast. He has a boat waiting to take us out to the submarine."

As Neumann was about to explain, the air-raid sirens wailed.

"Do we need to take this seriously?" he asked.

She smiled. "Welcome back to London, Lieutenant."

Gloucestershire, England

"CONGRATULATIONS, Alfred. Come inside. I'm sorry it had to happen this way, but you've just become a rather wealthy man." Edward Kenton thrust out his hand. Vicary shook it, then walked past Kenton into the drawing room of his aunt's cottage. "Bitterly cold outside," Kenton was saying as Vicary removed his coat. "I hope you don't mind, but I've made a fire. There's tea as well. I'll see to it." He went into the kitchen.

It wasn't really a cottage. That was what Aunt Matilda had insisted on calling it. It was a rather large home, with spectacular gardens. She had died of a stroke the night Boothby assigned him the case. Vicary had planned to attend the funeral, but he was summoned by Churchill that morning, after Bletchley Park decoded the German radio signals. He felt horrible about missing the service. Matilda had virtually raised him after his own mother died when he was just twelve. They had remained the best of friends.

Just this morning Bletchley Park had forwarded Vicary a decoded message from a German agent in Britain. It said the rendezvous had been successful and the agent had accepted the assignment. Vicary was growing discouraged about his chances of catching the spies.

Kenton came in, set a tray down on the table in front of the couch, and poured tea. Then he sat down opposite Vicary and fished a batch of papers from his briefcase. "She left you the house and a large amount of money," he said.

Vicary was stunned. "I had no idea." He spent the next few minutes signing his name to a pile of legal and financial documents.

At the last one Kenton looked up and said, "Done."

"Is the telephone still working?" Vicary asked.

"Yes. I used it myself before you arrived."

The telephone was on Matilda's writing table. Vicary picked up the receiver. "Edward, if you wouldn't mind, it's official."

Kenton smiled. "Say no more. I'll clear away the tea things."

The operator came on the line, and Vicary gave her the number. It took a few moments to connect him to Harry Dalton.

"Any news?" Vicary asked.

"I think so, actually."

Vicary's heart leaped.

"I've been going over the immigration lists one more time, just to see if we missed anything." The immigration lists were the meat and potatoes of MI5's contest with Germany's spies. In September 1939, while Vicary was still on the faculty at University College, MI5 had used immigration and passport records as the primary tool in a massive roundup of spies and Nazi sympathizers. Anyone who had entered the country before the war and could not be accounted for was assumed to be a spy and hunted down. Germany's espionage networks were rolled up and smashed, virtually overnight. "A Dutch woman named Christa Kunst entered the country in October 1938 at Dover. A year later her body was discovered in a shallow grave in a field near Whitchurch. The face and skull had been crushed. They used the passport found nearby to make the identification. It sounds too neat to me."

"Where's the passport now?"

"The Home Office has it. I've sent a courier to collect it. The photograph got roughed up a bit, but it's worth a look."

"Good, Harry. At least it's a lead. I should be back in the office late this afternoon. I'm leaving now."

THE BACK OF THE ROVER WAS cold as a meat locker. Vicary sat on the big leather seat, legs covered in a traveling rug. Harry's news intrigued him. Now, as he watched the Gloucestershire countryside sweep past his window, he thought about his rival in Berlin, Kurt Vogel. Vogel would have to assume immigration and passport control records would be used to find his agents. But what if the person who entered the country was dead? There would be no search. It was brilliant. But there was one problem. It required a body. Was it possible they actually murdered someone to trade places with Christa Kunst? Could one of Vogel's agents be a woman?

"Stop in the next village," Vicary said to the Wren driving the car. "I need to use the telephone."

The next village was called Moreton. Vicary made his call at a bakery while munching on a cheese sandwich.

"I don't think that was Christa Kunst they dug out of that grave in Whitchurch," he said when Harry came on the line.

"Then who was it?"

"That's your job, Harry. Get on the phone with Scotland Yard. See if a woman went missing about the same time. Start within a two-hour radius of Whitchurch, then go wider if you have to. When I get back to the office, I'll brief Boothby."

"What are you going to tell him?"

"That we're looking for a dead Dutch woman. He'll love that."

East London

CATHERINE Blake knew that finding Peter Jordan would not be a problem. Finding him the right way would. Berlin had put together an extraordinary amount of information on Jordan. She knew that he worked at Grosvenor Square at the Supreme Headquarters Allied Expeditionary Force. She had the address of his house in Kensington. What was missing was a minute-by-minute account of his daily routine in London. Without it Catherine could only guess at how best to make her approach.

Following Peter Jordan herself was out of the question; it would be too dangerous. She could be spotted by military policemen or by

Jordan himself. She needed nondescript vehicles and nondescript men to tail him. She needed help. She needed Vernon Pope.

Vernon Pope was one of London's most successful underworld figures. Along with his brother Robert, he ran protection rackets, illegal gambling parlors, prostitution rings, and a thriving black market operation. Early in the war Vernon Pope had brought Robert to the emergency room at St. Thomas's Hospital with a serious head wound suffered in the blitz. Catherine made certain he was seen by a doctor straightaway. A grateful Vernon Pope had left a note for her: "If there's ever anything I can do to repay you, don't hesitate to ask." The note was in Catherine's handbag.

Somehow Vernon Pope's warehouse had survived the bombing. It stood intact, an arrogant island surrounded by seas of destruction. Catherine had not ventured to the East End in nearly four years. The devastation was shocking. It was difficult to make certain she was not being followed. There were few doorways left for shelter, no boxes for false telephone calls, no shops for a small purchase, just endless mountains of debris.

She watched the warehouse from across the street, a light cold rain falling. She wore trousers, sweater, and a leather coat. The doors of the warehouse were pulled back, and three heavy lorries rumbled out into the street. A pair of well-dressed men pulled the doors shut quickly, but not before Catherine caught a glimpse inside. It was a beehive of activity.

A knot of dockworkers walked past her, coming off the day shift. She dropped in a few paces behind them and walked toward the Pope warehouse.

There was a small gate with an electric buzzer. Catherine pressed it, received no answer, and pressed it again. She felt she was being watched. Finally the gate drew back.

"What can we to for you, luv?" The pleasant cockney voice did not match the figure before her. He stood well over six feet tall, with close-cropped black hair. The muscles of his upper arms filled out the sleeves of his expensive gray suit.

"I'd like to speak to Mr. Pope, please." She handed him the note.

He read quickly, as though he had seen many of them before. "I'll ask the boss if he has a minute. Come inside."

Catherine stepped through the gate, and it closed behind her.

Pope's man led her into the warehouse. Men in overalls were loading crates of goods into half a dozen vans. Boxes stood floor to ceiling on pallets—coffee, cigarettes, sugar. Barrels of petrol. Vernon Pope was obviously doing a brisk business.

"This way, luv," the man said. "Name's Dicky, by the way." He led her into a freight lift and pulled shut the doors.

"THAT'S some favor," Vernon Pope said. He rose from his comfortable leather sofa and poured himself another whiskey. He was tall and handsome, with pale skin, fair brilliantined hair, wintry gray eyes. His suit might have been worn by a successful executive.

"Can you imagine that, Robert? A volunteer nurse wanting to mount a surveillance operation on an Allied officer?"

Robert Pope knew he was not expected to answer. Vernon Pope moved to the window, drink cupped in his hand. "You're not working for the Germans, are you, Catherine?"

"Of course not," she said calmly. "My reasons are strictly personal. And frankly, they're none of your business."

Pope turned around and faced her. "Very good, Catherine. You've got guts. I like that. Besides, you'd be a fool to tell me."

There was a long silence while Pope paced the room. "I'm into a lot of shady things, Catherine, but I don't like this. No, I don't like it one little bit. But I made you a promise, and I'm a man of my word." He paused, looking her up and down. "Besides, there's something about *you* I like. Very much."

"I'm glad we can do business together, Mr. Pope."

"It's going to cost you, luv."

Catherine reached inside her purse and withdrew an envelope. "How does two hundred pounds sound? One hundred now, one hundred on delivery of the information. I want Commander Jordan followed for seventy-two hours. I want a minute-by-minute accounting of his movements. I want to know where he eats, who he meets with, and what they talk about. Can you manage that, Mr. Pope?"

"Of course."

"Good. Then I'll contact you Saturday." Catherine laid the envelope on the table and got to her feet. "You can't contact me."

"I thought you would say that." Vernon Pope smiled pleasantly. "Dicky, show Catherine the way out."

Catherine spotted the tail two minutes after leaving. She had expected it. Stupid of them to put Dicky on the street to follow her. After all, she knew his face. Losing him would be easy.

She ducked into an underground station, melting into the evening crowds. She crossed through the tunnel and emerged on the other side of the street. A bus was waiting. She boarded it and found a seat. Through the fogged window she watched Dicky charge up the stairs into the street, panic on his face.

She felt a little sorry for him; Vernon Pope would be furious. She would take no chances—a taxi ride, two or three more buses, a stroll through the West End before returning to her flat.

THE surveillance of Commander Peter Jordan began early the following morning when Robert Pope and Dicky Dobbs arrived outside Jordan's house in Kensington in a black paneled grocer's van. They waited there until seven fifty-five, when an American military staff car drew up and blew its horn. The door of the house opened, and a man of medium height and build emerged. He wore a U.S. Navy uniform and a dark overcoat. A thin leather briefcase hung from his arm. As he vanished into the car and closed the door, Dicky started the van.

Grosvenor Square presented them with their first challenge. It was crowded with taxis, staff cars, and Allied officers rushing in every direction. Jordan's car passed through the square, entered an adjacent side street, and stopped outside a small unmarked building. Robert Pope hopped out of the van and walked back and forth along the street while Dicky circled. Ten minutes later Jordan emerged from the building, a heavy briefcase chained to his wrist.

Dicky collected Pope and headed back to Grosvenor Square,

arriving in time to spot Jordan walking into SHAEF headquarters. Dicky found a parking space in Grosvenor Street with a clear view, turned off the engine, and waited.

At midday the grocer's van was replaced by a laundry service van. At two o'clock they were brought tea and sandwiches. An hour later Robert Pope was growing nervous. If Jordan left in the gloom of the blackout, it would be nearly impossible to spot him. But at four o'clock, the light almost gone, Jordan left the building by the main door on Grosvenor Square.

He walked across the square to the smaller building, the same heavy briefcase chained to his wrist. He emerged a few moments later, carrying the smaller briefcase he had had earlier. Jordan apparently decided a walk would do him good. He headed west, then turned south in Park Lane. Following him in the van would be impossible. Pope hopped out and shadowed him on foot, but lost him in a crowd of soldiers at Hyde Park Corner and ran back to the van.

After further chase through the buzzing evening traffic, Dicky and Pope found Peter Jordan in Kensingon.

THE Vandyke Club was a club for American officers in Kensington, off-limits to British civilians. Jordan went inside.

Forty-five minutes later he came out and flagged down a taxi.

Dicky eased the van out into traffic and followed the cab to the Savoy Hotel. He and Pope watched as Jordan paid off his taxi and stepped inside the hotel.

Minutes later Jordan stood alone among the throng in the crowded Grill bar, trying vainly to get the bartender's attention. Pope stood near him. He caught the bartender's eye and ordered a neat whiskey. When he turned around, Jordan had been joined by a tall American naval officer with a good-natured smile.

The tall man said, "What do you have to do to get a drink around this place?"

"Yell louder than anyone else," Jordan said.

"Two martinis, please, William."

The bartender looked up, grinned, and reached for a bottle of Beefeaters. "Hello, Mr. Ramsey."

"Well done, Shepherd."

Pope thought, Shepherd Ramsey.

"It helps to be a foot taller than anyone else."

"Did you make a dinner reservation?" Jordan asked.

"Of course I did, old sport. Where have you been anyway? I tried calling you all last week. Rang your office. They said you couldn't come to the phone. Same story the next day. What were you doing? When are you going to tell me what you're working on?"

"When the war is over."

"That important, huh?" Shepherd Ramsey downed his drink. "William, two more, please."

"Are we getting drunk before dinner tonight, Shepherd?"

"I just want you to loosen up, that's all. I've invited a couple of people to join us. Girls, actually. In fact, they've just arrived."

Pope followed Jordan's gaze to the front of the bar. There were two women, both young, both very attractive. The women spotted Shepherd Ramsey and Jordan and joined them at the bar.

"Peter, this is Barbara. But most people call her Baby."

"That's understandable. Pleasure to meet you, Barbara."

Barbara looked at Shepherd. "He *is* a doll." She spoke with a working-class London accent. "Are we eating in the Grill?"

"Yes. In fact, our table should be ready."

The maître d'hôtel showed them to a table.

Pope, gazing through the entrance of the Grill, could see the table beside them was empty. He quickly went out into the street and waved Dicky inside. "We're having dinner," he said.

A moment later Dicky and Robert were being seated at the table next to Peter Jordan and Shepherd Ramsey. They were close enough to hear what the Americans and their dates were saying.

IT WAS Dicky who followed them outside after dinner. He watched as they placed the two women in a taxi.

"You might have at least been civil, Peter."

"I'm sorry, Shepherd. I just wasn't interested."

"Well, when are you going to get interested? Six months ago you promised me you were going to start dating."

"I would like to meet an intelligent, interesting grown-up, Shepherd. I don't need you to go out and find me a girl."

"No. You're right. It's just that my mother died when my father was forty. He never remarried. As a result he died a lonely, bitter old man. I don't want that to happen to you."

"Thanks, Shepherd, it won't. How about a lift home?" Jordan flagged down a taxi, and they both climbed in.

The taxi drove off. Pope and Dicky followed in the van.

IT HAD been Alfred Vicary's inability to repair a motorbike that led to his shattered knee. It happened on a glorious autumn day in France, and without a doubt it was the worst day of his life.

Vicary had just finished a meeting with a spy who had gone behind enemy lines in a sector where the British planned to attack at dawn the next morning. The spy had discovered a large bivouac of German soldiers. He gave Vicary a note on the strength of the German troops and a map showing where they were camped. Vicary placed the papers in his saddlebag and set out back to headquarters.

Vicary knew he was carrying intelligence of vital importance; lives were at stake. He opened the throttle full and drove perilously fast. The engine rattle began ten miles from headquarters. Over the next mile it progressed to a loud clatter. A mile later he heard the sound of snapping metal, and the engine lost power and died.

Vicary bent down and looked at the motor, but the hot, greasy metal and twisting cables meant nothing to him. He took hold of the bike by the handlebars, and as the afternoon light diminished to a frail pink dusk, he began pushing at a brisk pace. It was not until the twilight had died away that the shelling began.

Vicary never heard the shell that wounded him. He regained consciousness in the early evening and nearly fainted at the sight of his knee—a mess of splintered bone and blood. He forced himself to crawl to his bike and blacked out beside it.

Vicary came to in a field hospital the next morning. He knew the attack had gone forward, because the hospital was overflowing. He lay in his bed all day, head swimming in a drowsy morphine haze, listening to the moaning of the wounded and dying.

Brendan Evans—his friend from Cambridge who had helped Vicary deceive his way into the Intelligence Corps—came to see him the next morning. The war had changed him. His boyish good looks were gone. He looked like a hardened, somewhat cruel man. Brendan pulled up a chair and sat down next to the bed.

"It's all my fault," Vicary told him. "I knew the Germans were waiting. But my motorbike broke down, and I couldn't fix the damned thing. Then the shelling started."

"I know. They found the papers in your saddlebag. No one's blaming you. It was just awful luck, that's all."

Sometimes Vicary still heard the screams of the dying in his sleep—even now, almost thirty years later. In recent days his dream had taken a new twist. He dreamed it was Basil Boothby who had sabotaged his motorbike.

Vicary had tried to refrain from the inevitable comparisons between then and now, but it was unavoidable. He did not believe in fate, but someone or something had given him another chance—a chance to redeem himself for his failure on that autumn day in 1916.

Tonight he thought the party in the pub across the street from MI5 headquarters would help him take his mind off the case. It had not. He had lingered at the fringes, thinking about France, gazing into his beer. He was jolted out of his trance when Harry Dalton walked in. He walked over to Vicary and said, "We need to talk. Let's head back to the office."

THEY arrived in Vicary's office and sat down. "Her name was Beatrice Pymm," Harry began. "She lived alone in a cottage outside Ipswich." Harry had spent several hours in Ipswich that morning, delving into Beatrice Pymm's past. "No friends, no family, no boyfriends, not even a cat. The only thing she did was paint."

"Paint?" Vicary asked.

"Yeah, paint. The people I spoke to said she painted almost every day. She left the cottage early in the morning, went into the surrounding countryside, and spent all day painting. She didn't own a car. She either rode her bicycle or walked or took the bus."

"What do they think happened to her?" Vicary asked.

"The official version of the story—accidental drowning. Her belongings, including an empty bottle of wine, were found on the banks of the Orwell. The police think she may have had a little too much to drink, lost her footing, slipped into the water, and drowned. No body was found. Case closed."

"Sounds like a very plausible story."

"Sure, but I doubt it happened that way," Harry said. "Beatrice Pymm was very familiar with the area. Why on that particular day did she have too much to drink and fall into the river?"

"Theory number two?"

"She was picked up by our spy after dark, stabbed in the heart, and her body loaded into a van. Her things were left on the riverbank. The corpse was driven across the country, mutilated, and buried outside Whitchurch."

"Is this all supposition, Harry, or do you have facts to support it?" Vicary asked.

"Half and half, but it all fits your guess that someone was murdered in order to conceal the spy's entry into the country."

"Let's hear it."

"The body was discovered in August 1939. The Home Office pathologist estimated it had been in the ground six to nine months, which is consistent with Beatrice Pymm's disappearance. He was unable to fix a cause of death. He did find one interesting clue, though, a nick on the bottom left rib. That nick is consistent with being stabbed in the chest."

"You say the killer used a van? What's your evidence?"

"I asked the local police for reports on any crimes or disturbances around Whitchurch the night of Beatrice Pymm's murder. Coincidentally, a van was deserted and set ablaze outside a village called Alderton. It had been stolen in London two days earlier."

Vicary rose and began pacing. "So our spy is in the middle of nowhere with a van blazing on the roadside. What does she do?"

"How about a motorbike in the back of the van?"

"Good idea. See if any motorbikes were stolen about that time."

"She rides back to London and ditches the bike."

"That's right," Vicary said. "And when the war breaks out, we don't look for a Dutch woman named Christa Kunst, because we assume incorrectly that she's dead."

"I'VE drafted this memorandum to General Eisenhower, General Betts, and the prime minister," Vicary said when he finished briefing Boothby on Harry Dalton's discoveries that day. He handed the memo to Boothby, who remained standing, in a hurry to leave for the country. "To keep quiet about this any longer, Sir Basil, would in my opinion be a dereliction of duty."

Boothby was still reading; Vicary knew this because his lips were moving. Sir Basil liked to pretend he still had perfect vision.

"I thought we'd discussed this once already, Alfred," he said, waving the sheet of paper. A problem, once dealt with, should never resurface—it was one of Sir Basil's many maxims. Careful deliberation was the province of weaker minds.

"We *have* discussed this, Sir Basil," Vicary said patiently, "but the situation has changed. It appears they've managed to insert an agent who has met with an agent in place. It appears that an operation is now under way. To sit on this information instead of passing it on is to court disaster."

"Nonsense," Boothby snapped. "This department is not going to officially inform the Americans and the prime minister that it is incapable of performing its job."

"That's not a valid reason for concealing this information."

"It is a valid reason, Alfred, if I say it is a valid reason."

Conversations with Boothby often assumed the characteristics of a cat chasing its own tail. "Are you prepared to forward my memorandum to the director general?" Vicary asked. He pretended to study the pattern of Boothby's costly rug.

"Absolutely not."

"Then I'm prepared to go directly to the D.G. myself."

Boothby bent and put his face close to Vicary's. "And I'm prepared to squash you, Alfred. Let me remind you how the system works. You report to me, and I report to the director general. I have determined it would be inappropriate to forward this matter to the D.G. at this time."

"That's completely unfair."

"Is it? Since you've taken charge of this case, it's been one disaster after another. My heavens, Alfred—a few more German spies running loose in this country and they could form a rugby club."

Vicary refused to be baited. "If you're not going to present my report to the director general, I want the official record to reflect that I made the suggestion at this time and you turned it down."

The corners of Boothby's mouth lifted into a terse smile. Protecting one's flank was something he understood and appreciated. "Already thinking of your place in history, are you, Alfred?"

"You're a complete bastard, Sir Basil. And an incompetent one."

"You have a great deal to learn, Alfred."

"I suppose I could learn it from you."

"And what is that supposed to mean?"

Vicary got to his feet. "It means you should start thinking more about the security of this country and less about your personal advancement through Whitehall."

Boothby smiled easily. "But my dear Alfred," he said, "I've always considered the two to be completely intertwined."

CATHERINE Blake had a stiletto hidden in her handbag. She had demanded a meeting alone with Vernon Pope. As she approached the warehouse, she saw no sign of Pope's men. The gate was unlocked, just as Pope said it would be. She stepped inside, then took the freight lift up to his office.

Catherine knocked and heard Pope's voice tell her to enter. He was standing at a drinks trolley, a bottle of champagne in one hand, two glasses in the other. He held one out to her.

"No, thank you," she said. "I'm just staying for a minute."

"I insist," he said.

"You had me followed. Why?" She accepted the wine.

"I have everyone followed, darling. That's how I stay in business. My boys are good at it, as you'll see when you read this." He held out an envelope, then pulled it away as Catherine reached for it. "That's why I was so surprised when you managed to give Dicky the slip. That was smooth—ducking into the underground and then jumping on a bus."

"I changed my mind." She drank some champagne. It was ice-cold and excellent. Pope held out the envelope, allowing Catherine to take it. She set down her glass and opened it.

It was exactly what she needed—the hours Peter Jordan kept, the places he did his eating and drinking, even the name of a friend. Catherine slipped the report inside her handbag, took out the money, and dropped it on the table. "Here's the rest," she said. "Thank you very much. I think that concludes our business."

Pope stepped forward. "Actually, Catherine darling, our business together has just begun."

"If it's more money you want—"

"Oh, I want more money. And if you don't want me to make a call to the police, you're going to give it to me." He took another step closer, pressed his body against hers. "But there's something else I want from you." He started to undo the buttons of her sweater.

Catherine thought, This can't really be happening. Once she submitted to blackmail, it would never end. Her financial resources were not unlimited. Vernon Pope could bleed her dry. With no money she would be rendered useless. She had to play his game. Better still, she had to control it.

Pope led her toward the couch. Catherine kissed him, fighting an impulse to gag. Then she slammed her knee into his groin.

Pope doubled over, gasping for breath. Catherine reached inside her handbag. The stiletto was there. She pressed the release, and the blade snapped into place.

CHAPTER FOUR

ATHERINE assumed that Allied officers who knew the most important secret of the war had been warned about approaches by women. Peter Jordan was also a successful, intelligent, and attractive man. He would be discriminating in the women he chose to spend time with. The scene at the Savoy the other night—described in Vernon Pope's report— was evidence of that. Catherine would have to approach carefully.

Which explained why she was standing on a corner near the Vandyke Club with a bag of groceries in her arms. It was shortly before six o'clock, and London was shrouded in the blackout.

When they collided, there was the sound of paper splitting and tins of food tumbling to the pavement.

"I'm sorry. I didn't see you there. Please, let me help you up."

"It's my fault," said Catherine. "I've misplaced my blackout torch, and I've been wandering around out here lost. I feel like a fool."

"No, it's my fault. I was trying to prove that I could find my way home in the dark. Here, I have a torch. Let me turn it on."

"Do you mind turning the beam away from my face and toward the pavement? I believe my rations are rolling toward Hyde Park."

"I'm sorry, you're— I don't think that sack of flour survived."

"That's all right."

"Here, let me help you pick these things up. And let me replace the flour. I have plenty of food at my house. My problem is I don't know what to do with it."

"Doesn't the navy feed you?"

"How did—"

"I'm afraid the uniform and the accent gave you away."

"Please, let me replace the things you've lost."

"That's a kind offer, but it's not necessary. It was a pleasure bumping into you." She turned and started to walk away.

"Hold on a minute. I have another suggestion. I wonder if you might have a drink with me sometime."

She turned around, hesitated, then said, "I suppose you look harmless enough. The answer is yes." She walked away again.

"Wait, come back. I don't even know your name."

"It's Catherine," she called. "Catherine Blake."

"I need your telephone number," Jordan said helplessly.

But she had melted into the darkness and was gone.

When Peter Jordan arrived home, he went into his study, picked up the telephone, and dialed. He identified himself. A pleasant female voice instructed him to remain on the line. A moment later he heard the English accent of the man he knew only as Broome.

Ham Commons, Surrey

THE large, rather ugly three-story Victorian mansion was surrounded by a pair of perimeter fences to shield it from the outside world. Once it had been an asylum, but in 1939 it was converted into MI5's main interrogation and incarceration center.

The room into which Alfred Vicary was shown smelled of mildew, disinfectant, and vaguely of boiled cabbage, but it had one feature that made it highly functional—a tiny slit of a window, through which an aerial had been strung.

Vicary was being stretched to the breaking point. He had considered asking to be relieved of the Becker network but had quickly rejected the idea. He was the genius behind the network; it was his masterpiece. He would keep control of it and try to capture the spies at the same time. It was a brutal assignment.

Now Vicary opened the lid on the Abwehr-issue suitcase radio— the very one he had seized from Karl Becker in 1940—and attached the aerial. He yawned and stretched. It was eleven forty-five p.m. Becker was scheduled to send his message at midnight.

Becker came into the room sandwiched between a pair of hulking guards. He smiled and stuck out his hand. Vicary shook it. They sat down on opposite sides of a small scarred table, as if facing off for a game of chess. Vicary handed Becker a package, and like a small child, he opened it right away. In it were a half-dozen packets of cigarettes and a box of Swiss chocolates.

Becker looked at the things. "Cigarettes and chocolate. You're not here to seduce me, are you, Alfred?" He opened a packet of cigarettes and tapped out two, giving one to Vicary. He struck a match and lit both cigarettes. They sat in silence for a while.

"How's brother Boothby?" Becker finally asked.

Vicary let out a long breath. "As ever."

"We all have our Nazis, Alfred."

"We're thinking of sending him over to the other side."

Becker chuckled. "I see you've brought my radio," he said. "What heroic deed have I done for the Third Reich now?"

"You've broken into Number Ten and stolen all the prime minister's private papers."

Becker threw back his head and laughed. "It's terrible to be a spy, Alfred. But it's better than the Wehrmacht. I'd be sent off to the east to fight the blasted Ivans. No, thank you. I'll wait out the war right here in my pleasant little English sanitarium."

"Of course." Vicary reached inside his pocket and withdrew the coded message Becker was to send assessing the new activity in Kent detected by the Luftwaffe. Then he took out the photograph from the passport of the woman named Christa Kunst. A look of distant recollection flashed across Becker's face.

"You know who she is, don't you, Karl?"

"You've found Anna," he said, smiling. "Well done, Alfred. Bravo." He paused to open the box of chocolates.

Vicary sat like a man straining to hear distant music, hands folded on the table, making no notes. He knew it was best to ask as few questions as possible, best to allow Becker to lead him where he wanted.

Becker popped a chocolate into his mouth and held the box out to Vicary. "People like me, they get almost no training," he said. "Oh, sure, a few lectures by some idiots in Berlin who've never seen England except on a map. Then they send you off in a rubber raft to win the war for the Führer."

"But there were others they took more care with," Vicary said.

"Yes, there were others. Absolutely." Becker dug out another chocolate. "These are delicious. Are you sure you won't have one?"

VICARY listened on a spare pair of headphones as Becker tapped out the message, waited for Hamburg to confirm, then signed off. Becker would sulk for a while—he always did after sending a Double Cross message. Vicary suspected Becker was ashamed of betraying his own service. Not that he had much of a choice.

Vicary slowly packed away the radio. Becker smoked, and he ate a few more chocolates. Vicary feared he had lost him.

"I saw her once in Berlin," Becker said suddenly. "She was immediately separated from the rest of us mere mortals. I don't want you to quote me on this, Alfred—I'm just going to tell you what I heard. If it doesn't turn out to be accurate, I don't want the boys to come in here and start throwing me off the walls."

"You have my word, Karl," Vicary said.

"They said her name was Anna von Steiner—that her father was an aristocrat. Prussian, rich, dabbled in diplomacy—you know the type. She was beautiful, tall as hell. Spoke perfect British English. The rumors said she had an English mother. That the Abwehr spotted her, put the screws to her, telling her that if she didn't cooperate, Papa von Steiner would be shipped off to a concentration camp."

"Her control officer—was his name Vogel?"

"I don't know—could be. Sour-looking bastard."

"So what happened to her?"

"We heard there was a camp somewhere in the mountains south of Munich. A place where they sent a few special agents—the ones they planned to bury deep. It was an English village in the middle of Bavaria. There was a pub, even an Anglican church. They read London newspapers, did their shopping in English, and listened to the BBC. They were given special codes, special rendezvous procedures, and more weapons training—silent killing, stuff like that."

"This Anna—did you ever meet her in Britain?"

"No. I never saw her again."

"Do you know her cover name? I want the truth, Karl."

"I'm telling you the truth."

"Do you know if she's operating in London?"

"She could be operating on the moon for all I know, Alfred."

Vicary exhaled loudly in frustration. "Why haven't you told us this before—the business about the special agents?"

"But I have, Alfred old man. I told Boothby."

Vicary felt his heart begin to beat furiously. Boothby? Why in the world would Boothby be interrogating Karl Becker? Becker was Vicary's agent. Vicary arrested him. Vicary turned him. Vicary ran him.

His face calm, he said, "When did you tell Boothby?"

"I don't know. Months ago. September, maybe. No, October."

"What did you tell him, exactly?"

"I told him about the agents. I told him about the camp."

"Did you tell him about the woman?"

"Yes, Alfred, I told him everything. He's a vicious bastard. I don't like him. I'd watch out for him if I were you."

"Was there anyone with him?"

"Yes. Tall fellow. Handsome, like a film star. Blond, blue eyes. A real German superman. Thin, though—skinny as a stick."

"Did the stick have a name?"

Becker made a show of searching his memory. "It was a funny name. Something you use in the house. Mop? Bucket? No, Broome! Imagine that—the guy looks like a stick, and he calls himself Broome. You English have a marvelous sense of humor."

London

THE murder of a prominent underworld figure like Vernon Pope was big news in all the London newspapers. The police had misled the newspapermen, though—they said that the victim had been found with his throat slit, not stabbed through the heart. They were obviously trying to filter out crank leads from real ones. According to the papers, the police wanted to question Robert Pope but had been unable to find him.

Pope was sitting twenty feet from Catherine Blake in the Savoy bar, angrily nursing a whiskey. He was there because he suspected Catherine was involved in his brother's murder. Finding her had not been difficult. All he had to do was go to the places frequented by Peter Jordan, and there was a good chance she would appear.

Catherine turned her back to him. She was not afraid of Robert Pope. He was more a nuisance than a threat. Still, as a precaution, she had started carrying her silenced Mauser at all times.

Deciding whether to kill Robert Pope was not Catherine Blake's biggest worry, for at that moment Peter Jordan walked into the bar of the Savoy along with Shepherd Ramsey.

She wondered which man would make the first move. Things were about to get interesting.

As PETER Jordan crossed the bar toward her, Catherine thought she had never seen a man look quite so handsome as he did in his dark blue American naval uniform. His hair was dark, nearly black, and in striking contrast to his pale complexion. His eyes were a distracting shade of green—pale green, like a cat's—his mouth soft and sensuous. It broke into an easy smile.

"I believe I bumped into you in the blackout last night," he said, and held out his hand. "My name is Peter Jordan."

She took his hand. "Catherine Blake," she said.

"Yes, I remember. You're waiting for someone?"

"I am, but it appears he's stood me up."

"He's a fool. But can I buy you that drink now?"

Catherine glanced across the bar at Robert Pope, who was watching them intently. "Actually, I would love to go somewhere a little quieter. Do you still have all that food at your house?"

"Let me get my coat."

DURING the taxi ride Catherine realized quite suddenly that she was nervous. It was not because a man who possessed the most important secret of the war was sitting next to her. She was just not very good at this—the rituals of courtship. She knew she was an attractive woman, a beautiful woman. She knew most men desired her. But during her time in Britain she had gone to great lengths to adopt the look of an aggrieved war widow: heavy dark stockings, chunky sweaters. Tonight she was dressed in a striking gown. Even so, for the first time in her life Catherine worried about whether she was pretty enough.

The taxi drew up in front of Peter Jordan's house. He unlocked the front door and showed her inside. "My goodness," she said. "How did you get a billet like this? I thought all American officers were packed into hotels and boardinghouses."

"My father-in-law bought the house years ago. He spent a great deal of time in London and wanted a pied-à-terre here."

He helped her off with her coat and went to hang it in the closet. Catherine surveyed the drawing room. It was handsomely furnished with deep leather couches and chairs. The walls were covered with photographs of bridges.

"You're married, then," Catherine said.

"I beg your pardon?" he said, returning to the room.

"You said your father-in-law owns this house."

"My wife was killed in an automobile accident before the war."

"I'm sorry, Peter. I didn't mean to—"

"Please, it's fine. It was a long time ago."

She nodded toward the wall and said, "You like bridges."

"You might say that, yes. I build them."

"I didn't know the navy needed bridges."

Jordan hesitated. "I'm sorry, I can't discuss my—"

"Please. Believe me, I understand the rules."

"I could do the cooking, but I couldn't guarantee that the food would be edible."

"Just show me where the kitchen is," Catherine said.

"Through that door. If you don't mind, I'd like to change. I still can't get used to wearing a uniform."

"Certainly." She watched his next movements carefully. He removed his keys from his trouser pocket and unlocked a door. That would be his study. He was inside for less than a minute. When he emerged, he was no longer carrying his briefcase. He probably locked it inside his safe. He climbed the stairs. His bedroom was on the second floor. It was perfect.

While Peter was changing, Catherine set the table in the dining room and made an omelette.

They ate quickly, before the omelette could go cold, washing it down with wine. The meal was surprisingly good. By its end Catherine felt pleasant and relaxed. Jordan seemed that way too. He appeared to accept that their meeting was wholly coincidental.

"Have you ever been to the States?" he asked as they cleared away the dishes and carried them into the kitchen.

"Actually, I lived in Washington when I was a little girl."

"Really?"

"Yes. My father was a diplomat. He was posted in Washington in the early '20s. I liked it very much, except for the heat."

"Is your father still a diplomat?"

"No. He died before the war."

"And your mother?"

"My mother died when I was a little girl." Catherine stacked the dirty dishes in the sink. "I'll wash if you dry."

"Forget it. I have a woman who comes a couple of times a week. She'll be here in the morning. How about a glass of brandy?"

"That would be nice."

There were photographs in silver frames over the fireplace, and Catherine looked at them while Jordan poured the brandy. "Your wife was very beautiful."

"Yes, she was. Her death was very hard on me."

"And your son—he's the image of you. Who's caring for him now?"

"Margaret's sister." Jordan smiled. "Please, sit down."

They sat down next to each other on the large leather couch.

Jordan said, "So tell me how it is that an incredibly beautiful woman like you isn't married."

Catherine felt her face flush. She sipped her brandy.

"My goodness, you're actually blushing. Don't tell me no one has ever told you that you're beautiful."

She smiled and said, "No. It's just been a very long time."

"That makes two of us. I never thought I'd find another woman beautiful after Margaret died. Until I crashed into you in the blackout last night. You took my breath away, Catherine."

"Thank you. I can assure you the attraction was mutual."

"Are you going to tell me why you aren't married?"

Catherine stared into the fire for a moment. "I *was* married. My husband, Michael, was shot down over the Channel the first week of the Battle of Britain. He was my entire world."

There was a long moment of silence. Catherine realized she could stay like this for quite a while, sitting next to the fire with her brandy and this kind and gentle man. She tried for a moment to make herself hate him, but she could not. She hoped he never did anything that would force her to kill him.

"I realize you can't talk about your work, but I'm going to ask you one question, and I want you to tell me the truth."

"Cross my heart."

"You're not going to get yourself killed, are you?"

"No, I'm not going to get myself killed. I promise."

She leaned over and kissed him on the mouth. He pulled her close to him, and she kissed him again.

After a moment she drew away. "If I don't leave now, I don't think I ever will."

"I'm not sure I want you to leave."

"When am I going to see you again?"

"Will you let me take you to dinner tomorrow night? A proper dinner, that is? Somewhere we can dance."

"I'd love that."

"How about the Savoy again. Eight o'clock."

Hampton Sands, Norfolk

A GRAY dawn was leaking through thick clouds as Horst Neumann scrambled down the dunes. He wore a gray tracksuit and a pair of running shoes. The tide was out, and there was a wide swath of hard sand—perfect for running. He set out at an easy pace.

He had received a message from Hamburg earlier that morning instructing him to begin regular pickups of material from Catherine Blake. It was to be done on the schedule Kurt Vogel had given him at the farm outside Berlin. The material was to be placed through a doorway in Cavendish Square, where it would be collected by a man from the Portuguese embassy and sent to Lisbon inside the diplomatic pouch. It sounded simple, but Neumann understood that courier work on the streets of London could take him straight into the teeth of British security forces.

The running worked its magic. He was taken with a pleasant floating sensation, almost flight. He picked out an imaginary finish line half a mile down the beach and increased his pace, pounding his feet savagely against the sand until he leaned across the finish line and stumbled to a halt. It was then that he noticed Jenny Colville watching him from atop the dunes.

"Very impressive, Mr. Porter," she said as she approached.

"You should try it sometime. It's good for the body and the soul." Neumann stamped his feet. "I need to walk. Otherwise I'm going to be stiff as a board."

"Would you like some company?"

He nodded. It was not the truth, but he saw no harm in it. Jenny Colville had a terrible schoolgirl crush on him; it was obvious. She made up some excuse to drop by the Dogherty cottage every·day. Neumann had carefully avoided being alone with her. Until now. He would try to turn the conversation to his advantage—to take stock of how well his cover story was holding up in the village.

Jenny said, "Do you mind talking about the war?"

"Of course not."

"Your wounds— Were they bad?"

"Bad enough to give me a one-way ticket home."

"But what are you doing in Hampton Sands?"

"I needed a place to rest and get well. The Doghertys offered to let me come here and stay with them, and I took them up on it."

"My father thinks you're a criminal or a terrorist. He says Sean used to be a member of the IRA."

"Jenny, can you really picture Sean Dogherty as a member of the IRA? Besides, your father has serious problems of his own."

Jenny's face darkened. "And what's that supposed to mean?"

"It means he drinks far too much." Neumann reached out and touched her face gently. "And it means he mistreats a beautiful, intelligent young girl who's done absolutely nothing to deserve it. Now, I'm going to finish my run. I suggest you go on home."

She turned to leave, then stopped. "James, do you really mean that I'm beautiful and intelligent? No one's ever said that to me before."

"Of course I mean it."

She stepped forward and kissed him on the mouth very briefly before turning and running across the sand.

London

ALFRED Vicary felt he was sinking in quicksand. The more he struggled, the deeper he descended.

The source of his despair was a pair of decoded German messages that had arrived from Bletchley Park that morning. The first was from a German agent in Britain asking Berlin to begin making regular pickups. The second was from Hamburg to a German agent in Britain asking the agent to do just that. It was a disaster. Vicary feared that if he ever *did* catch the spies, he might be too late.

The red light shone over Boothby's door. So like Boothby to demand an urgent meeting, then keep his victim waiting.

Why haven't you told us about this before?

But I have, Alfred old man. I told Boothby.

Was it really possible Boothby had known of the Vogel network and kept it from him? It made absolutely no sense. Vicary could think of only one possible explanation. Boothby had vehemently opposed Vicary's being assigned to the case. But would Boothby's opposition include actively trying to sabotage Vicary's efforts? Quite possible. If Vicary displayed no momentum in solving it, Boothby might have grounds to sack him.

The light shone green. Vicary, slipping through the grand double doors, vowed not to leave without clearing the air.

Boothby was seated behind his desk. "Let's have it, Alfred."

Vicary briefed him on the two messages and what background he had pieced together on Anna von Steiner.

"In 1937 Anna vanished. We can only speculate after that. She undergoes Abwehr training, is sent to the Netherlands to establish her identity as Christa Kunst, then enters England. By the way, Anna Steiner was allegedly killed in an auto accident outside Berlin in March 1938. Obviously, Vogel fabricated that."

Boothby rose and paced his office. "It's all very interesting, Alfred, but there's one fatal flaw. It's based on information given to you by Karl Becker. Becker would say anything to ingratiate himself. I very much doubt the veracity of anything the man says."

"So why did you spend so much time with him last October?"

Sir Basil was standing in the window. He turned slowly to face Vicary. "The reason I spoke to Becker is none of your affair."

"Becker is my agent," Vicary said, anger creeping into his voice. "I arrested him, I turned him, I run him. He gave you information that might have proved useful to this case, yet you kept it from me. I'd like to know why."

"Becker told me the same story he told you: special agents, a secret camp. To be honest, Alfred, I didn't believe him at the time. We had no evidence to support his story. Now we do."

It was a perfectly logical explanation—on the surface at least.

"Why didn't you tell me about it?" Vicary asked.

"It was a long time ago."

"Who's Broome?"

"Sorry, Alfred."

"I want to know who Broome is."

"And I'm trying to tell you as politely as I can that you're not entitled to know who Broome is." Boothby shook his head. "This department is in the business of counterintelligence. And it operates on a very simple concept: need to know."

"Is 'need to know' a license to deceive other officers?"

"I wouldn't use to the word deceive," Boothby said.

"How about the word lie? Would you use that word? I was just wondering why you lied to me about reading Kurt Vogel's file."

The blood seemed to drain from Boothby's face. It was a risky strategy, and Grace Clarendon's neck was on the block. When Vicary was gone, Boothby would call Nicholas Jago in Registry and demand answers. Half the War Office knew Grace Clarendon was involved with Harry. Jago would surely realize Grace was the source of the leak. It was no small matter. She could be sacked immediately. But Vicary was betting they wouldn't touch Grace, because it would only prove her information had been correct. He hoped he was right.

"Looking for a scapegoat, Alfred? Someone or something to blame for your inability to solve this case?"

Vicary thought, And you're not answering my question. He rose to his feet. "Good night, Sir Basil." He walked to the door.

As THEY entered the Savoy Grill, the band began playing "And a Nightingale Sang in Berkeley Square." Jordan took Catherine's hand, and they walked onto the dance floor. He was an excellent dancer, smooth and confident, and he held her very close. Catherine looked stunning. She was wearing a black crepe dress with a deep plunge in the back. She wore her hair down, held back by a smart jeweled clasp, and a double strand of pearls at her throat. Everyone in the room seemed to be staring at them.

Jordan drew away a few inches so he could look at her face. "Can I make a confession?"

"Of course you can."

"I didn't get much sleep after you left last night."

She smiled and drew him near. "I didn't sleep at all."

"What were you thinking about?"

"You tell me first."

"I was thinking how much I wished you hadn't left. I don't want you to leave tonight."

"I think you would have to throw me out bodily if you wanted me to leave."

"I don't think you need to worry about that."

IT WAS LATE, AT LEAST FOUR o'clock, though Catherine couldn't be sure, because it was too dark to see the clock on the bedstand. It didn't matter. All that mattered was that Peter Jordan was sleeping soundly next to her. They had eaten a large meal, had a lot to drink, and made love. Unless he was a very light sleeper, he would probably sleep through a Luftwaffe raid right now. She slipped out of bed, put on the silk robe he had given her, and padded quietly out of the room and closed the door behind her.

The silence rang in her ears. She could feel her heart pounding, but she forced herself to be calm. One silly mistake and it would destroy all she had done. She walked quickly down the stairs and along the hall. She found his keys on a small table in the hall, next to her handbag, and went to work.

Catherine had limited objectives tonight: She needed her own copies of the keys to the front door, to the study door, and to Jordan's briefcase. His key ring held a number of keys. The key to the front door was larger than the rest. She reached into her purse and removed a block of soft brown clay. She pressed the key into the clay, making a neat imprint. The key to the briefcase was the smallest. She repeated the same process. The study door was more difficult, but the fourth key she tried fit the lock. She pressed it into the clay.

By her estimate she had been out of the bed less than two minutes. She could afford two more. She went into the study and switched on the light. There was a large desk and a leather chair and a drafting table with a tall stool in front of it. Catherine reached inside her handbag, withdrew her camera, and clicked off two photographs of the room. Next she unlocked Jordan's briefcase. It was virtually empty—just a billfold and a small appointment book.

Three minutes. Work quickly now, Catherine. She opened the notebook, adjusted the desk lamp so that the light shone directly onto the page, and started snapping photographs. Names, dates, short notes written in Jordan's scrawling hand. Crude sketches of a boxlike figure with numbers.

Four minutes. One more item tonight: the safe. It was next to the desk. Vogel had given Horst Neumann a combination that was supposed to unlock it. Catherine knelt and turned the dial. Six digits. She pulled open the door and looked inside: two binders filled with papers, several loose-leaf notebooks. It would take hours to photograph everything. She would wait. She aimed the camera at the inside of the safe and took a photograph.

Five minutes. She closed the safe door and spun the dial. She returned Jordan's appointment book to his briefcase and locked it. She shut off the lights and locked the study door.

Six minutes. Too long. She carried everything into the hall and placed the keys and her handbag on the table. Done! She went into the kitchen and filled a glass with cold water. She drank it down, refilled it, and carried the glass upstairs to the bedroom.

Peter Jordan was sitting up in bed in the moonlight. "Where have you been? I was worried about you."

"I was dying of thirst." She couldn't believe the calm, collected voice was really hers.

"I hope you brought me some too," he said.

"Of course." She handed him the glass. "What time is it?"

"Five o'clock. I have to be up for an eight-o'clock meeting."

She kissed him. "So we have an hour left."

"Catherine, I couldn't possibly—"

"Oh, I bet you could."

CATHERINE Blake, later that morning, strode along the Chelsea Embankment as a light, bitterly cold rain drifted across the river. Vogel had provided her with twenty different rendezvous locations in London and forced her to commit them to memory.

Neumann was walking toward her, hands plunged into the pockets of his reefer coat, collar up against the rain, slouch hat pulled down. "You look like you could use a cup of coffee," he said. "There's a nice warm café not too far from here."

Neumann held out his arm to her. She took it, and they strolled along the Embankment. She gave him the film, and he carelessly dropped it into his pocket. Vogel had trained him well.

Catherine gave him the clay imprints of the keys. "Find someone who can be persuaded to make copies of these for a price. Drop them in my letter box today. Tomorrow, when Jordan goes to work, I'm going to go back inside his house and photograph everything in that study."

Neumann pocketed the block of clay. "Impressive. Anything else?"

"Yes. From now on, no more conversations like this. We bump into each other, I give you the film, you walk away. If you have a message for me, write it down and give it to me. Understood?"

"Understood."

She kissed his cheek, then turned and walked away.

CHAPTER FIVE

Berlin: February 1944

IT'S called Operation Mulberry," Admiral Canaris began, "and as of now we don't have the slightest idea what it's about."

A smile flickered across Brigadeführer Walter Schellenberg's lips and evaporated as quickly as summer rain. As head of section VI of the Sicherheitsdienst—better known as the SD—the intelligence and security service of the SS, Schellenberg was responsible for gathering intelligence on the Reich's enemies in foreign countries, an assignment very similar to that of the Abwehr. As a result he and Canaris were locked in a desperate competition, and they often withheld information from each other.

Walter Schellenberg had just two goals: destroy Canaris and the Abwehr, and bring Adolf Hitler the most important secret of the war—the time and place of the Anglo-American invasion of France. Schellenberg had nothing but disdain for the Abwehr and the cluster of old officers surrounding Canaris.

"A few days ago the Luftwaffe shot these surveillance photographs." Canaris laid two enlargements on the low, ornate coffee table around which they were seated. "This is Selsey Bill in the south of England. We are almost certain these work sites are connected to the project." Canaris used a silver pen as a pointer. "Obviously, something very large is being hastily constructed at these sites. There are huge stockpiles of cement and steel girding. In this photograph a scaffolding is visible."

"Impressive, Admiral Canaris," Hitler said. "What else do you know?"

"We know that several topflight British and American engineers are working on the project. We also know that General Eisenhower is intimately involved. Unfortunately, we are missing one very important piece of the puzzle—the purpose of the giant concrete structures." Canaris paused. "Find the missing piece, and we may very well solve the puzzle of the Allied invasion."

"I have just one more question, Herr Admiral," Hitler said. "The source of your information—what is it?"

Canaris hesitated.

Himmler's face twitched. "Surely, Admiral Canaris, you don't think anything said here this morning would go beyond this room."

"Of course not, Herr Reichsführer. One of our agents in London is getting the information directly from a senior member of the Mulberry team. The source of the leak does not know he has been compromised. According to Brigadeführer Schellenberg's sources, British intelligence knows about our operation but has been unable to stop it."

"This is true," Schellenberg said. "I have it from an excellent source that MI Five is operating in crisis mode."

"Well, well. Isn't this refreshing—the SD and the Abwehr working together for a change instead of clawing at each other's throats." Hitler turned to Canaris. "Perhaps Brigadeführer Schellenberg can help you unlock the riddle of those concrete boxes."

Schellenberg smiled and said, "My thoughts precisely."

London

CATHERINE Blake tossed stale bread to the pigeons in Trafalgar Square, at the same time watching Neumann's approach to be sure he wasn't being followed.

She was especially anxious to deliver this film. Jordan had brought home a different notebook last night. This morning, after he left for his office, she had returned to the house. When the cleaning lady left, Catherine slipped inside, using her keys, and photographed the entire book.

Neumann was a few feet away. Catherine had placed the rolls in a small envelope. She withdrew the envelope and prepared to slip it into Neumann's hand. He took it, handed her a slip of paper, and kept walking.

It was a message from Vogel, and she read it while drinking weak coffee in a café in Leicester Square. It began with a commendation for her work so far, but Vogel said more specific information was required. He also wanted a written report on how she had made her approach, how she gained entry to Jordan's papers, everything he had said to her. Catherine thought she knew what that meant. She was delivering high-grade intelligence, and Vogel wanted to make certain the source was not compromised.

She walked up Charing Cross Road. She paused now and again to gaze into shopwindows and see if she was being followed. She turned into Oxford Street and joined a bus queue. When the bus came, she got on and took a seat upstairs near the rear.

She had suspected the material Jordan brought home would not paint a complete picture of his work. It made sense. Based on the report given to her by the Popes, Jordan moved between a pair of offices, one at the SHAEF headquarters on Grosvenor Square and another, smaller office nearby. Whenever he carried material between them, it was handcuffed to his wrist.

Catherine needed to see that material. But how? She decided she would be patient and wait. If she continued to enjoy Peter Jordan's trust, eventually the secret of his work would appear in his briefcase. She would give Vogel his written report, but she would not change her tactics for now.

The bus was crossing Oxford Circus. It was then that Catherine noticed the woman watching her. She was seated across the aisle, and she was staring directly at her. Catherine thought, Why is she looking at me like that? She glanced at the woman's face. Something about it was distantly familiar.

The bus was nearing the next stop. Catherine gathered up her things. She would take no chances. She would get off right away. The bus slowed, and Catherine got to her feet. Then the woman reached across the aisle and said, "Anna, darling. Is it really you?"

Catherine rushed off the bus. She took a taxi to Marble Arch. Badly shaken, she chastised herself for not handling the episode better. After the woman called her by her real name, she should have stayed on the bus and calmly explained to the woman that she was mistaken. It was a dreadful miscalculation. Several people on the bus had seen her face.

She had lived in London for two years after her mother's death, when her father was assigned to the German embassy here, and she knew it was always a remote possibility that she might run into someone who recognized her. Vogel had decided it was an acceptable risk—that the chances of actually bumping into someone she knew were remote. For six years it did not happen. She had grown careless. When it did happen, she panicked.

She finally remembered who the woman was. Her name was Rose Morely, and she had been the cook at her father's house in London. Catherine had two choices: pretend it never happened or investigate and try to determine the extent of the damage. She chose the second option.

She paid off the driver at Marble Arch and got out. Dusk was fading quickly into the blackout. A number of bus routes converged on Marble Arch, including the bus she had just fled. With luck Rose Morely would get off here and change for another bus.

The bus stopped, and Rose disembarked. Catherine stepped forward and said, "You're Rose Morely, aren't you?"

The woman's mouth dropped open. "Yes—and you *are* Anna. I knew it was you. You haven't changed a bit since you were a little girl."

Catherine took Rose Morely's arm and headed for Hyde Park. "Let's walk for a while," she said. "It's been *so* long, Rose."

ALFRED VICARY FELT AN evening at home might do him some good. He wanted to walk, so he left the office an hour before sunset, enough time for him to make it home before becoming stranded in the blackout. London was alive. He watched the crowds in Parliament Square, marveled at the antiaircraft guns on Birdcage Walk. He crossed Belgrave Square and walked toward Sloane Square. Crossed Sloane Square and drifted into Chelsea.

As he walked, he thought about the latest message forwarded to him by the code breakers at Bletchley Park. It had been sent to an agent operating inside Britain. It said the information received thus far had been good, but more was needed. It asked how the agent had contacted the source. Vicary looked for a silver lining. If Berlin needed more intelligence, it did not have a complete picture, which meant there still was time for Vicary to plug the leak.

He arrived at his home, pushed back the door, and waded through several days of unanswered post. He considered inviting Alice Simpson to dinner but decided he didn't have the strength for polite conversation. Their relationship had lapsed with the war. They still spoke at least once a week, but only saw each other occasionally for dinner.

Vicary drank a glass of whiskey and read the newspapers. Since his induction into the secret world he no longer believed a word in them. Then the telephone started ringing. It had to be the office. No one else ever bothered to call him any longer. He picked up the receiver and said, "Yes, Harry?"

"Your conversation with Karl Becker gave me an idea," Harry said without preamble. "Anna Steiner lived in London with her diplomat father for two years in the early '20s. Rich foreign diplomats have servants—cooks, butlers, maids."

"All true, Harry. I hope this is leading somewhere."

"For three days I've been checking with every agency in town, trying to find the names of the people who worked in that household. I've got a few. Most are dead, or old as the hills. There was one promising name, though: Rose Morely. As a young woman, she worked as a cook in the Steiner house. Today I discovered she works here in London for a Commander Higgins of the Admiralty."

"Good work. Set up an appointment first thing in the morning."

"I planned to, but someone just shot Rose Morely through the eye and left her body in the middle of Hyde Park."

"I'll be ready in five minutes."

"There's a car waiting outside your house."

The driver was an attractive young Wren who took him as close to the murder scene as she could. The rain had started up again, and he borrowed her umbrella. He climbed out and softly closed the door, as though arriving at a cemetery for a burial. A searchlight beam caught his approach, and he had to shade his eyes from the glare. A detective chief superintendent walked him the rest of the way.

A tarpaulin had been hastily erected over the body. The rain pooled in the center and spilled over one edge of the tarp like a tiny waterfall. Harry was squatting nearby. Rose Morely had fallen backward. The contents of her handbag and a cloth shopping bag were strewn about her feet.

Harry noticed Vicary standing there next to the superintendent and came over to them.

"It could be a coincidence," Harry said, "but I really don't believe in them. Especially when it involves a dead woman with a bullet through the eye." He paused. "Street thugs don't shoot people in the face. Only professionals do."

"How long has she been dead?" Vicary asked.

"Just a few hours. Since late afternoon or early evening."

Vicary said, "I'm declaring this a security matter as of now. I want Harry to coordinate the investigation, Superintendent. He will draft a statement in your name. I want this described as a robbery that went wrong, but the wound described accurately. I want the statement to say the police are searching for a pair of refugees of undetermined origin seen in the park around the time of the murder. And I want your men to proceed with discretion. Thank you, Superintendent. Harry, I'll see you first thing in the morning."

Harry and the superintendent watched Vicary limp away toward his car. The superintendent turned to Harry. "What's his problem?"

By MIDAFTERNOON OF THE following day Harry Dalton and a team of police officers had pieced together the final hours of Rose Morely's life. Now Harry was in Vicary's office, his long legs propped up on the desk.

"The receipt we found in Rose's bag was for a shop in Oxford Street," Harry said. "We interviewed the shopkeeper. He remembered her. He said she bumped into another woman that she knew, a domestic like herself. They took tea at a café across the street. We spoke to the waitress there. She confirmed it."

Vicary was listening intently, studying his hands.

"The waitress says Rose crossed Oxford Street and queued for a westbound bus. About a half hour ago we found the ticket collector who was on Rose's bus. He remembered her. Said she had a brief conversation with a tall, very attractive woman who jumped off the bus in a hurry. Said that when the bus arrived at Marble Arch, the same woman was waiting there."

A typist poked her head in the door. "Sorry to interrupt, but you have a call, Harry. A Detective Sergeant Colin Meadows from the Metropolitan Police. Says it's urgent."

Harry took the call at his desk.

"It's concerning the Hyde Park shooting. I think I have something for you," Meadows said. "I hear the suspect is a woman. Tall, attractive, thirty to thirty-five years old."

"Could be. What do you know?"

"I've been working the Vernon Pope murder."

"I read about it," Harry said. "Someone slit his throat."

"Actually, Pope was stabbed in the heart. We changed the description of the wound to weed out the crazies. You'd be surprised how many people wanted to take credit for the killing."

Harry remembered what the pathologist had said about the body of Beatrice Pymm. The knicked rib on her left side. Possible stab wound. "Keep going, Detective Sergeant."

"A woman matching your girl's description was seen entering the Popes' warehouse the night Vernon Pope was killed. I have two witnesses. And there's one other thing."

"Spill it, Detective Sergeant."

"I questioned Robert Pope last week. I want to question him again, but we haven't been able to locate him."

CATHERINE Blake packed her handbag for the evening—a stiletto, her Mauser pistol, her camera. She was meeting Jordan for dinner. She assumed they would go back to his house afterward to make love. They always did. She made tea and read the afternoon newspapers. The murder of Rose Morely was the big news of the day. The police believed the murder was a robbery that spun out of control. They even had a pair of suspects. Just as she thought. It was perfect. She undressed and took a long bath. She was toweling her wet hair when the telephone rang. Only one person in all of London knew her number—Peter Jordan.

"I'm afraid I'm going to have to cancel dinner tonight. I apologize, Catherine. Something very important has come up."

"I understand."

"I have to leave London very early tomorrow morning, and I have to work very late tonight. I'm still at the office."

"I'm not going to pretend I wasn't looking forward to being with you, Peter. I haven't seen you for two days."

"It seems like a month. I wanted to see you too."

"Is it completely out of the question?"

"I'm not going to be home until at least eleven o'clock."

"That's fine. Here's my suggestion. I'll meet you in front of your house at eleven. I'll make us something to eat. You can relax and get ready for your trip. I'll let you sleep, I promise."

"I'll see you at eleven."

"Wonderful."

THE red light shone over Boothby's door for a very long time. Vicary reached out to press the buzzer a second time, but stopped himself. From the other side of the heavy doors he heard two voices elevated in argument, one female, the other Boothby's. "You can't do this to me!" It was Grace Clarendon's voice, loud and slightly hysterical. Boothby's voice was calmer, a parent lecturing an errant child. Vicary, feeling like an idiot, leaned his ear against the seam in the doors. "Bastard!" It was Grace again. Then the sound of Sir Basil's private door slamming. The light suddenly shone green.

The office was dark except for the single lamp burning on the desk. Boothby was working in his shirtsleeves. Without looking up, he commanded Vicary to sit. "I'm listening," he said.

Vicary told him about the results of the investigation into the murder of Rose Morely. He told him about the possible link between the German agent and the murder of Vernon Pope. He explained that finding and questioning Robert Pope was imperative, and requested men to assist in the search.

"Well," Boothby said. "This is the first piece of good news we've had on this case. I'll telephone the head of the watchers—order him to give you as many men as he can spare."

"Thank you, Sir Basil," Vicary said, standing up to leave.

"I *do* hope you're right about all this, Alfred." Boothby hesitated. "I spoke with the director general a few minutes ago. He's given you twenty-four hours. If all this doesn't produce a break, I'm afraid you're going to be removed from the case."

The moment Vicary left, Boothby picked up his secure telephone. He dialed the four-digit number and waited.

"Yes?" said the man at the other end of the line.

Boothby did not identify himself. "Our friend is closing in on his prey," Boothby said. "The second act is about to begin."

HER taxi stopped outside Peter Jordan's house at five minutes after eleven. Catherine could see him standing outside his front door, blackout torch in hand. She climbed out and paid the driver. The taxi drove off. She took a step toward Jordan and heard the roar of an engine, the sound of tires spinning. She turned and saw Dicky Dobbs in the van bearing down on her. It was just a few feet off, too close to get out of the way. She closed her eyes and waited to die.

A sharp pain laced the back of her head, and a great weight pressed down on her body. Her lungs cried out for oxygen. She saw bright lights, like comets, shooting across a vast black emptiness. Someone was shaking her, calling her name. She opened her eyes and saw Peter Jordan's face. "Catherine, can you hear me, darling? Are you all right? Oh, my God, I think he was trying to kill you!"

NEITHER of them felt much like eating. Both of them wanted a drink. Jordan had his briefcase chained to his wrist—it was the first time he had brought it home like that. He went to the study. Catherine heard him open the safe, then close it again. Then he went into the drawing room and poured two very large glasses of brandy and carried them upstairs.

Catherine had trouble holding on to her glass. Her hands shook. Her heart was pounding inside her chest, but she forced herself to drink. The warmth of the brandy took hold, and she began to relax. She undressed and lay down on the bed. She should have killed Robert Pope and Dicky Dobbs when she had the chance.

Jordan sat down next to her. "I don't know how you can be so calm about this," he said. "After all, you were almost killed just now."

"It's called English reserve," she said. "We're not allowed to show our emotions, even when we're nearly run over in the blackout. You could have been killed too. Why did you do it?"

"Because when I saw that idiot bearing down on you, I realized that I was desperately, madly, completely in love with you. I never thought anyone would ever make me happy again. But you have, Catherine. And I'm terrified of its all going away."

"Peter," she said softly. She reached up, took hold of his shoulder. "Do you mean that, Peter?"

"I mean it with all my heart."

Catherine pulled him toward her. She kissed him again and again and said, "Peter, I love you so much." She was surprised by how easily the lie came to her lips.

MUCH much later Catherine unlocked the study door, went inside, and closed it softly behind her. She switched on the desk lamp. From her handbag she removed her camera and her Mauser.

She laid the pistol on the desk, the butt facing her, so she could grab it if necessary. She knelt in front of the safe, rotated the dial, and turned the latch. Inside was the briefcase—locked. She unlocked it and looked inside.

A black bound book with the words TOP SECRET on the cover. Catherine opened it and read the first page:

PHOENIX PROJECT
1) design specifications
2) construction schedule
3) deployment

Catherine thought, I've done it. I've actually done it! She photographed that page and turned another. Page after page of designs. A page labeled CREW REQUIREMENTS, another labeled TOWING REQUIREMENTS. She photographed all of them.

Then she heard the noise upstairs—Jordan getting out of bed.

She turned another page and photographed it.

Catherine heard him walking across the floor.

She photographed another page. Two more pages.

She heard water running in the bathroom. She would never have access to this document again; that she knew. If it truly contained the secret of the invasion, she had to keep working.

She heard the sound of the toilet flushing. Just a few more pages. She photographed them quickly. She returned the binder to the briefcase and placed the briefcase back in the safe. She spun the lock. She picked up the Mauser, turned out the light, and crept into the hall. Jordan was still upstairs.

Think quickly, Catherine! She walked down the hallway and into the drawing room. She put the Mauser in her handbag and the handbag on the floor. She turned on the light and was pouring herself a glass of brandy when Peter Jordan walked in.

HARRY Dalton was waiting outside the Popes' warehouse in a department surveillance van. He had two men with him—Detective Sergeant Meadows and a watcher named Clive Roach. Harry was in the front passenger seat, Roach behind the wheel. Meadows was getting a few minutes of sleep in the back.

It was dawn, after a long and dreadfully boring night, when the silence was broken by the sound of another van drawing up in front of the warehouse. A tall, thick man climbed out.

"Know him?" Clive Roach asked.

Harry said, "Yeah. His name is Dicky Dobbs. He's Pope's main enforcer. Wake up Sleeping Beauty back there."

Dobbs unlocked the gate and went inside the warehouse. A moment later the main door was pulled upward. Dobbs emerged, climbed back inside his van, and drove it into the warehouse.

Roach gunned the motor of the police van, nosing it inside before Dobbs could close the door again. Harry jumped out of the van.

Dobbs yelled, "What do you think you're doing?"

Sergeant Meadows said, "Turn around and put your hands up."

Harry stepped forward and threw open the rear door of Dobbs's van. Robert Pope was sitting on the floor.

CATHERINE Blake took a taxi to her flat. It was early, just after dawn, the sky a flat mother-of-pearl gray. She had six hours until she was to meet Horst Neumann on Hampstead Heath. She desperately needed a few hours of sleep, but she had something to do first.

It had been too close tonight. If Jordan had come downstairs a few seconds earlier, she would have been forced to kill him. She had told him she'd been unable to sleep and thought a glass of brandy would help to calm her nerves. He seemed to accept her excuse, but she doubted he would buy it twice.

She sat down at her writing table, took a sheet of paper, and wrote four words: "Get me out now!" She adjusted the lamp and held her camera to her eye. She placed her left hand next to the paper. Vogel would recognize it. There was a scar across the thumb where she had been cut during one of his silent killing classes. She photographed her hand and the note twice, then burned the note in the bathroom sink.

CHAPTER SIX

THEY were in a small glass-enclosed office on the warehouse floor, Robert Pope seated in a wooden chair, Harry pacing like a caged jungle cat, Vicary sitting quietly in the shadows. Harry and Vicary had not revealed their true affiliation; to Pope they were just a pair of Metropolitan Police officers. For one hour Pope had denied any knowledge of the woman whose photograph Harry kept waving in front of him.

Harry said, "I've got a witness who says this woman entered your warehouse the day your brother was murdered."

"Then your witness is wrong."

"Why have you been avoiding the police, Pope?"

"I haven't been avoiding the police. You blokes managed to find me." Pope looked over at Vicary. "That one ever speak?"

"Shut up and look at me, Pope. You *have* been avoiding the police because you know who killed Vernon and you want to pay them back your own way."

"You're talking nonsense, Harry."

"You've been looking for her for days."

"I don't know what you mean."

Harry noticed a sheen of perspiration on Pope's face. He thought, I'm finally getting to him.

Vicary must have noticed it too. "You're not being honest with us, Mr. Pope," he said politely. "But then we haven't been exactly honest with you, have we, Harry?"

Harry thought, Perfect timing, Alfred. Well done. He said, "No, Alfred, we haven't been completely honest with Mr. Pope here."

Pope said, "What the devil are you two talking about?"

"We're connected with the War Office. We deal in security."

A shadow passed over Pope's face. "What does my brother's murder have to do with the war?" His voice had lost conviction.

"I'm going to be honest with you," Vicary said. "We know this woman is a German spy. And we know she came to you for help. And if you don't start talking, we're going to be forced to place you under arrest for espionage." Vicary's voice had taken on a menacing edge. "So I suggest you start talking *now*."

Robert Pope blinked rapidly. He was defeated. "I begged Vernon not to take the job, but he wouldn't listen," Pope said. "I knew there was something wrong with her."

Vicary said, "What did she want from you?"

"She wanted us to follow an American officer. She wanted a complete report on his movements around London."

"What does she call herself?"

"Catherine. No last name."

"And what was the officer's name?"

"Commander Peter Jordan, U.S. Navy."

VICARY immediately made arrangements to have Robert Pope and Dicky Dobbs stored on ice at an MI5 lockup outside London.

For a while no one at headquarters could find Boothby. It was still early, and he had not arrived at the office. Finally, shortly after nine o'clock, he arrived looking inordinately pleased with himself. Vicary—who hadn't bathed, slept, or changed his clothes in nearly two days—followed him into his office and broke the news.

Boothby walked to his desk and picked up the receiver of his secure telephone. He dialed a number and waited. "Hello, General Betts? This is Boothby calling from Five. I need to run a check on an American naval officer named Peter Jordan." A pause. Boothby said, "He is? Oh, blast! You'd better find General Eisenhower. I need to see him straightaway. I'll contact the prime minister's office myself. I'm afraid we have a serious problem." Boothby slowly replaced the receiver and looked up at Vicary, his face the color of ash.

FROZEN fog hung like gun smoke over Hampstead Heath, but Catherine Blake, sitting on a bench surrounded by beech trees, could see for several hundred yards in every direction. She was confident she was alone. When Neumann appeared out of the fog, she said, "I want to talk to you. It's all right; we're alone." He sat down next to her, and she handed him an envelope containing the film. "I'm fairly certain this is what they were looking for," she said.

Neumann pocketed the envelope. "I'll make sure it gets safely into the hands of our friend from the Portuguese embassy."

"There's something else," she said. "I wrote Vogel a note, which I photographed, then destroyed. I've asked him to pull us out. Things have gone wrong. I don't think my cover will hold up much longer."

"COME in and sit down, Alfred," Boothby said. "I'm afraid we have a force twelve disaster on our hands." Boothby had just walked in the door, and his cashmere overcoat still hung like a cape from his shoulders. He shed the coat and handed it to his secretary. "Coffee, please. And no interruptions. Thank you."

Vicary lowered himself into a chair. He was feeling peeved. Sir Basil had been gone three hours, having rushed out the door muttering something about mulberries. The code word meant nothing to Vicary. And there was something else that bothered him. The case had been his from the beginning, and yet it was Boothby who was briefing Eisenhower and Churchill.

The secretary came in bearing a tray with a silver pot of coffee and dainty china cups. She placed it carefully on Boothby's desk and went out again. Boothby poured. "Milk, Alfred? It's real."

"Yes, thank you."

"What I am about to tell you is highly classified," Boothby began. He reached inside his briefcase, withdrew a chart, and spread it on the desk. "Here are the beaches of Normandy," he said, using his gold pen as a pointer. "The invasion planners have concluded that the only way to bring men and supplies ashore quickly enough to sustain the operation is through a large, fully functioning harbor. Without one, the invasion would be a complete fiasco."

Vicary, listening intently, nodded.

"There is just one problem with a harbor. We aren't planning on capturing one," Boothby said. "The result is this." He pointed to a series of markings depicting a structure along the French shoreline. "It's called Operation Mulberry. We're constructing two complete *artificial* harbors here in Britain and towing them across the Channel on D-day."

"Remarkable," Vicary said.

"The backbone of the entire project is here, here, and here," Boothby said. "Their code name is Phoenix. They do not rise, however. They sink. They're giant concrete-and-steel caissons that will be towed across the Channel and sunk in a row to create a breakwater. They are *the* most critical component of Operation Mulberry." Boothby hesitated. "Peter Jordan is assigned to that operation."

"Good Lord," Vicary muttered.

"It gets worse, I'm afraid. The Phoenix project is in trouble. The structures are huge—sixty feet high. Some have their own crew quarters and antiaircraft batteries. The project has been hampered with shortages of raw materials and construction delays. Last night Commander Jordan was ordered to tour the construction sites in the south and make a realistic assessment of whether the Phoenix units can be completed on time. He walked out of Forty-seven Grosvenor Square with a briefcase chained to his wrist. Inside that briefcase were the plans for the Phoenixes."

Vicary thought, None of this would have happened if Boothby had passed on my security alert. He said, "So if Commander Jordan has been compromised, a major portion of the plans for Mulberry may have fallen into German hands."

"I'm afraid so. And if they discover we are building an artificial harbor—some means of circumventing the heavily fortified ports of Calais—they may very well conclude we're coming at Normandy."

"Where is Commander Jordan now?"

"Still in the south inspecting the sites. He's due back at Grosvenor Square at seven o'clock. He was supposed to meet with Eisenhower and Ismay at eight o'clock to brief them on his findings. I want you and Harry to pick him up at Grosvenor Square—very quietly—and take him to the house at Richmond. We'll question him there. I want you to handle the interrogation, Alfred."

Richmond upon Thames, England

MI5 had purchased the red brick Victorian mansion before the war to use for clandestine meetings and interrogations and as lodgings for sensitive guests. Vicary was alone in the back of a freezing Rover. Peter Jordan and Harry were in a second car. During the drive from Grosvenor Square, Vicary had read the contents of Jordan's briefcase. His eyes burned, and his head was throbbing. If this document was in German hands, the Abwehr could use it to unlock the secret of the invasion. They could use it to win the war. And it's all because I couldn't find a way to catch that damned spy!

Vicary's Rover approached the house. A Royal Marine guard appeared out of the darkness and opened the car door. He led Vicary through the cold, timeworn hall and into a large room containing a heavy oak banquet table. A fire burned in the huge fireplace. A pair of Americans from SHAEF intelligence sat as quietly as altar boys in the chairs nearest the flames. Basil Boothby paced in the shadows.

Vicary found his spot at the table. He looked up, caught Boothby's eye, and nodded. Then he looked down again and began unpacking his briefcase. He heard footsteps crossing the floor.

A moment later Vicary heard Jordan's weight settle into the chair directly across the table. Vicary did not look up. Then, finally, he lifted his head and looked Peter Jordan in the eye for the first time.

"How did you meet her?"
"I bumped into her in the blackout—outside the Vandyke Club."
"When?"
"About two weeks ago."
"What did she call herself?"
"Catherine Blake."
"Had you ever seen her before that night?"
"No."
"And how long were you with her that first night?"
"Less than a minute."
"Did you make arrangements to see her again?"

"Not exactly. I asked her to have a drink sometime. She said she'd like that, and then she walked away."

"She gave you her telephone number?"

"No."

"So how were you supposed to contact her?"

"I assumed she didn't want to see me again."

"When *did* you see her again?"

"The next night."

"Where?"

"The bar of the Savoy. I was having a drink with a friend."

"The friend's name?"

"Shepherd Ramsey."

"And she came to your table?"

"No, I went to her. She said she'd been stood up. I asked if I could buy her a drink. She said she would rather leave. So I left with her."

"Where did you go?"

"To my house. She cooked dinner, and we ate. We talked for a while, and she went home."

"Did you make love to her that night?"

"Listen, I'm not going to—"

"Yes, you bloody well are, Commander Jordan. Now answer the question. Did you make love to her that night?"

"No!"

"Are you telling me the truth?"

"Of course I am."

"You don't intend to lie to me, do you, Commander Jordan?"

"No, I don't."

"Good, because I wouldn't advise it. You're in enough trouble as it is. Now let's continue."

For the next hour Vicary walked Peter Jordan through his personal history, scribbling as if his notebook, not hidden microphones, would chronicle the evening's proceedings. Finally he turned to a fresh page in the notebook.

"Her name isn't really Catherine Blake," Vicary said. "And she isn't really English. Her real name is Anna von Steiner. She was born in London before the First War to an English mother and a German father. She returned to England in October 1938 using this false Dutch passport. Do you recognize the photograph?"

"It's her. She looks different now, but that's her."

"We assume she came to the attention of German intelligence because of her background and her language ability. In order to conceal her entry into the country, she brutally murdered a woman in Suffolk. We think she's murdered two other people as well."

"That's very difficult to believe."

"Well, believe it."

"Why did she choose me?"

"Did she choose you? Or did you choose her?"

"What are you talking about?"

"It's simple, really. I want to know why you're acting as an agent of German intelligence."

"That's ridiculous."

"Is it? What are we supposed to think? You've been carrying on an affair with Germany's top agent in Britain. You bring home a briefcase full of classified material. Did she ask you to bring home the documents so she could photograph them?"

"No!"

"Why were you walking around with them in your briefcase?"

"Because I was leaving early in the morning to inspect the construction sites in the south. Under certain circumstances I am allowed to bring classified documents home if they are locked in the safe."

"Have you knowingly or willingly supplied Allied secrets to the woman known to you as Catherine Blake?"

"No!"

"Are you in love with Catherine Blake, Commander?"

"Until a couple of hours ago I was in love with the woman I *thought* was Catherine Blake. I didn't know she was a German agent. You must believe me."

"I'm not sure I do, Commander Jordan. But let's move on. You enlisted in the navy last October."

"That's correct. I was *asked* to join the navy."

"Tell me how it was done."

"Two men came to my office in Manhattan. It was clear they had already checked out my background. They said my services were required for a project connected with the invasion. They didn't tell me what that project was. I never saw them again."

"What were their names?"

"One was called Leamann. I don't recall the other name."

"Were they both American?"

"Leamann was an American. The other one was British."

"How did he look?"

"He was tall and thin."

"Well, that narrows it to about half the country." Vicary opened Jordan's file. "Tell me about the house you're living in."

"My father-in-law purchased it before the war. He wanted a comfortable place to stay when he was in London."

"Did your father-in-law's bank have German investments?"

"Yes, many. But he liquidated most of them before the war."

"Did he oversee that liquidation personally?"

"Most of the work was done by a man named Walker Hardegen. He's the number two man at the bank. He also speaks fluent German and knows Germany inside and out."

"Did Walker Hardegen use the house in London?"

"He may have. I'm not certain."

"How well do you know Walker Hardegen?"

"I know him very well."

"Then I suppose you're good friends?"

"No, not really."

"You know him well, but you're not friends?"

"I think he was always in love with my wife."

"How much does Walker Hardegen know about your work?"

"Nothing."

"He knows you were sent here to work on a secret project?"

"He could probably deduce that, yes."

"Did you ever tell anyone about Operation Mulberry?"

"No."

"Did you have plans to see Catherine Blake again?"

"I don't have plans to see her. I never want to see her again."

"Well, that may not be possible, Commander Jordan."

"What are you talking about?"

"In due time. It's late. I think we could all use some sleep. We'll continue in the morning."

VICARY rose and walked to where Boothby was sitting. He leaned down and said, "I think we should talk."

"Yes," Boothby said, rising. "Let's go in the next room." He took Vicary by the elbow. "You did a marvelous job," he said. "My Lord, Alfred, when did you become such a bastard?"

Boothby pulled open a door and held it for Vicary to enter. Vicary stepped inside and couldn't believe his eyes.

Winston Churchill said, "Hello, Alfred. So good to see you again. I'd like to introduce you to a friend of mine. Professor Alfred Vicary, meet General Eisenhower."

Dwight Eisenhower rose from his seat and stuck out his hand.

The room had been a study once. There were bookshelves built into the walls and a pair of wing chairs where Churchill and Eisenhower sat now. On the table between them was the small speaker they had used to monitor the interrogation. The door opened, and a fifth man entered the room—Brigadier General Thomas Betts, the man charged with safeguarding the secret of the invasion.

"Is Peter Jordan telling the truth, Alfred?" Churchill asked.

"I'm not sure," Vicary said. "I want to believe him, but something is bothering me, and I'm not sure what it is."

Boothby said, "Nothing in his background would suggest he's a German agent or that he's willingly betrayed us. After all, he was *recruited* to work on Mulberry; he didn't volunteer. You saw his file. His FBI background check didn't turn up a thing."

"All true," Vicary said. "But what about this man Walker Hardegen? Was he checked out before Jordan came to Mulberry?"

"Thoroughly," General Betts said. "The FBI looked into Hardegen's background with a microscope. He is as clean as a whistle."

"Well, I'd feel better if they took another look," Vicary said. "How on earth did she know to go after Jordan? And how's she getting the material? It's possible she's getting into his papers without his knowledge, but it would be very dangerous. And what about Shepherd Ramsey? I'd like to put him under surveillance."

Eisenhower said, "I want you gentlemen to take whatever steps you feel are necessary."

Churchill cleared his throat. "This debate is very interesting, but it doesn't address our most pressing problem. This fellow—intentionally or not—has delivered a very significant portion of the plans for Operation Mulberry into the hands of a German spy. Now what are we going to do about it? Basil?"

Boothby turned to General Betts. "How much can the Germans discern about Mulberry from that one document?"

"It's difficult to say," Betts said. "The document Jordan had in his briefcase just tells them about the Phoenixes. But if the Germans are able to determine the purpose of the Phoenixes, it won't be difficult for them to unlock the secret of the artificial harbor project."

"My suggestion is that we use Jordan to lure Catherine Blake into the open," Boothby said. "We arrest her and turn her. We use her to convince the Germans that Mulberry is anything but an artificial harbor meant for Normandy."

Vicary said, "I fully agree with the second half of that proposal, Sir Basil, but everything we know about this woman suggests she is highly trained and thoroughly ruthless. I doubt we'd succeed in convincing her to cooperate with us. I suggest that Jordan continue to see her, but from now on we control what's inside that briefcase and what goes home into that safe. We let her run, and we watch her. We discover how she's getting the material back to Berlin. We discover the other agents in the network. Then we arrest her. If we roll up the network cleanly, we'll be able to feed Double Cross material directly to the highest levels of the Abwehr—right up to the invasion. Until then we keep Jordan under round-the-clock surveillance."

Churchill said, "Basil, what do you think of Alfred's plan?"

"It's brilliant," Boothby said, "but do you think Jordan can pull it off? After all, he just told us he was in love with this woman. She betrayed him. I don't think he's going to be in any condition to continue carrying on a romantic relationship with her."

"Well, he simply has to," Vicary said. "He's the one that got us into this mess. And he's the only one who can get us out."

Churchill looked at Eisenhower. "General?"

Eisenhower thought for a moment, then said, "I support the professor's plan. General Betts and I will make certain you have the necessary support from SHAEF to make it work."

"Then it's done," Churchill said. "God help us if it doesn't work."

"MY NAME is Vicary, by the way. Alfred Vicary." It was early the next morning, an hour after dawn. Vicary and Peter Jordan were walking a narrow footpath through the trees. The air smelled of woodsmoke from the fires burning inside the house.

Vicary explained to Jordan what they wanted him to do.

When Vicary finished, Jordan said, "I'm not up to it. You'd be a fool to use me."

"Believe me, Commander Jordan, if there were some other way to reverse the damage that's been done, I'd do it. But there isn't. You *must* do this. You owe it to us. You owe it to all the men who will risk their lives trying to storm the beaches of Normandy."

"How long will it last?"

"As long as necessary. It could be six days or six months. I will end it as soon as I can. On that you have my word."

"I didn't think truth counted for much in your line of work."

"Not usually. But it will in this case."

"What about my work on Operation Mulberry?"

"You'll go through the motions of being an active member of the team, but the truth is, you're finished." Vicary stopped walking. "We should get back to the house, Commander. We have a few papers for you to sign before we leave."

"What sort of papers?"

"Oh, just something that binds you to never breathe a word of this for the rest of your life."

"Believe me, you don't need to worry about that."

Rastenburg, Germany

KURT Vogel and Wilhelm Canaris were the first to arrive at Hitler's Wolfschanze. Vogel watched as the most powerful men of the Third Reich filed into the room: Reichsführer SS Heinrich Himmler, Brigadeführer Walter Schellenberg, Field Marshal Gerd von Rundstedt, Field Marshal Erwin Rommel, and Hermann Göring.

They all rose when Hitler entered. He wore slate-gray trousers and a black tunic. He remained standing after everyone else sat. Vogel had never met the Führer, and he watched him, fascinated. The hair was graying, the skin sallow, the eyes red-rimmed, with dark circles like bruises beneath them. Yet there was a daunting energy about the man. For two hours he led the discussion on preparations for the coming invasion. His attention to detail was astonishing. Finally he turned to Canaris and said, "So, I'm told the Abwehr has uncovered another piece of information that might shed some light on the enemy's intentions."

"Actually, my Führer, the operation was conceived and executed by Captain Vogel. I'll allow him to brief you on his findings."

"Fine," Hitler said. "Captain Vogel?"

"My Führer, two days ago in London one of our agents took possession of a document that brings us closer to learning exactly what Operation Mulberry is. We now know much more about the giant concrete-and-steel structures being built in England. They are code-named Phoenix. When the invasion comes, they will be towed across the Channel and sunk off the coast of France."

"Sunk? For what possible purpose, Captain Vogel?"

"Each of the submersible units contains quarters for a crew and a large antiaircraft gun. It is possible the enemy is planning to create a huge coastal antiaircraft complex to provide additional cover for their troops during the invasion."

"Possible," Hitler said. "But why waste precious supplies on an antiaircraft facility? Do you have a second theory, Captain Vogel?"

"We do, my Führer. It is a minority opinion, very preliminary, but one of our analysts believes the submersible units might actually be components of some sort of artificial harbor."

Himmler cleared his throat gently. "An artificial harbor sounds a little far-fetched to me."

"No, Herr Reichsführer," Hitler said. "I think Captain Vogel may be onto something here. Let's take it to the next level. If the enemy is actually engaged in an attempt to build something as elaborate as an artificial harbor, where would he put it? Von Rundstedt?"

The old field marshal rose. "The enemy knows we will deny him the use of ports for as long as possible and that we will cripple those ports before surrendering them. I suppose he might be constructing facilities in Britain that would allow him to reopen the ports more quickly. *If* that is the case, I still believe it is Calais. Calais still makes the most sense militarily and strategically."

Hitler listened carefully, then turned to Vogel. "What do you think of the field marshal's analysis, Captain Vogel?"

Vogel knew he had to proceed carefully. "Field Marshal von Rundstedt's argument is extremely sound. But for the sake of discussion, may I offer a second interpretation?"

"Do so," Hitler said.

"My Führer, what if it were possible for the enemy to build up his supplies on open beaches rather than through a port? If that were indeed possible, the enemy could avoid our strongest defenses, land on the beaches of Normandy, and attempt to supply an invasion force through the use of an artificial harbor."

Hitler's eyes flickered. He was intrigued by Vogel's analysis.

Field Marshal Rommel was shaking his head. "Even in spring the weather along the Channel coast can be extremely hazardous—rain, high winds, heavy seas. My staff has studied the patterns. And no portable device, no matter how ingenious, would survive."

Hitler stepped in. "Obviously, Captain Vogel, your agent must discover more about the project."

"There *is* a problem, my Führer," Vogel said. "The agent feels the

British security forces may be closing in—that it may not be safe to remain in England much longer."

Walter Schellenberg spoke. "Our own source in London says quite the opposite—that the British know there is a leak but have been unable to plug it. Your agent is imagining the danger."

Vogel thought, Arrogant fool! He said, "My agent is exceptionally intelligent. I think—"

Himmler cut Vogel off. "Clearly your agent should remain in place until we know the truth about these concrete objects, wouldn't you agree, Captain Vogel?"

Vogel was trapped. To disagree with Himmler would be like signing his own death warrant. He trusted Anna's instincts, but to pull her out now would be suicide. He had no choice. She would remain in place. He said, "Yes. I agree, Herr Reichsführer."

London

THE operation was hastily code-named Kettledrum. It was too complex and too sensitive to be run from his cramped quarters at MI5, so for his command post Vicary procured a stately Georgian house in West Halkin Street. The drawing room was converted into a situation room, with telephones, a wireless set, and a map of London tacked to the wall. The upstairs library was turned into an office for Vicary and Harry. There was a rear entrance for the watchers and a pantry stocked with food.

A watcher led Vicary upstairs to the library. A coal fire burned in the fireplace; the air was dry and warm. Vicary was exhausted. He had slept poorly after interrogating Jordan, and his hope of catching a little sleep on the ride back to London had been dashed by Boothby, who used the time to talk.

Overall control of Kettledrum was Boothby's. Vicary would run Jordan and keep Catherine Blake under surveillance while trying to discover the rest of the agents in the network and their means of communication with Berlin. Boothby would be the liaison to the Twenty Committee, the interdepartmental group that supervised the entire Double Cross apparatus, so named because the symbol of

Double Cross and the Roman numeral for twenty are the same: XX. Boothby and the Twenty Committee would produce the misleading documents for Jordan's briefcase and use other Double Cross assets to help bolster Kettledrum's credibility in Berlin.

"Nice digs," Harry said as he entered the library. He warmed his back against the fire. "Where's Jordan?"

"Upstairs, sleeping," said Vicary. "What have you got?"

"Fingerprints from someone other than Jordan, all over that study. We can assume they were left by Catherine Blake."

Vicary shook his head slowly.

"Jordan's house is ready to go," Harry continued. "We put so many microphones in that place you can hear a mouse fart. We evicted the family across the street and established a static post. Anyone goes near that house gets their picture taken."

"What about Catherine Blake?"

"We traced her telephone number to a flat in Earl's Court. We took over a flat in the building opposite."

"Good work, Harry. I'm going to have a bite to eat, then try to get some sleep. What about you?"

"Actually, I had plans for the evening."

"Grace Clarendon?"

"She asked me to dinner. I thought I'd take the opportunity. I don't think we'll have much free time the next few weeks."

"Harry, I don't want to take advantage of your relationship with Grace, but I wonder if she could quietly run a couple of names through Registry and see if anything comes up."

"I'll ask her. What are the names?"

"Peter Jordan, Walker Hardegen, and someone called Broome."

IT BEGAN the following morning when Peter Jordan, standing in the upstairs library of the house in West Halkin Street, dialed the number for Catherine Blake's flat.

"Listen, I'm sorry I haven't had a chance to call sooner. I was out of town a day longer than I expected, and there was no way to call."

Silence while she tells him there's no need to apologize.

"I thought about you the entire time I was away."

Silence while she tells him she can't wait to see him again.

"I want to see you too. In fact, that's why I'm calling. I booked us a table at the Mirabelle. I hope you're free for lunch."

Silence while she tells him that sounds wonderful.

"Good. I'll meet you there at one o'clock."

Silence while she says she loves him very much.

"I love you too, darling."

Jordan was quiet when it was over. At noon he went to his room and dressed in his uniform. At twelve thirty-five he walked out the rear door of the house. He was quietly shadowed by three of the department's best watchers, Clive Roach, Tony Blair, and Leonard Reeves. None of them saw any signs that Jordan was under surveillance by the opposition.

At twelve fifty-five Jordan arrived at the Mirabelle. He waited outside, as instructed. At precisely one o'clock a taxi braked to a halt in front of the restaurant, and a tall, attractive woman stepped into view. Ginger Bradshaw, the department's best surveillance photographer, was crouched in the back of a van across the street. As Catherine Blake kissed Peter Jordan's cheek, Ginger quickly shot six photographs. The film was rushed back to West Halkin Street, and the prints were sitting in front of Vicary by the time Catherine and Jordan had finished lunch.

"CLIVE Roach has never lost a German agent before," Boothby said, glaring at the watch report that evening in his office. "The man could follow a gnat through Hampstead Heath."

"He's the best," Vicary said. "Catherine Blake is just darned good and extremely careful. That's why we've never caught on to her. That's why three of our best watchers just lost her."

"There's another explanation, Alfred. It's possible she spotted the tail." Boothby tapped the thin metal attaché case containing the first batch of Kettledrum material. "If she knows she's under surveillance and we give her this, we might as well publish the secret of the invasion in the *Daily Mail* under a banner headline. If they know they're being deceived, they'll know the opposite is true."

"Roach is convinced she didn't spot him."

"Where is she now?"

"She's in her flat."

"What time is she supposed to meet Jordan?"

"Ten o'clock at his house. He told her he was working late."

"What were Jordan's impressions?"

"He detected no change in her demeanor, no sign of nerves or tension." Vicary paused. "He's good, our Commander Jordan. If he weren't such an excellent engineer, he'd make a marvelous spy."

Boothby tapped the metal attaché case with his thick forefinger. "If she spotted the tail, why is she sitting in her flat? Why isn't she making a run for it?"

"Perhaps she wants to see what's inside that briefcase."

"It's not too late, Alfred. We can arrest her right now and think of some other way to repair the damage."

"I think that would be a mistake. We don't know the other agents in the network, and we don't know how they're communicating with Berlin."

Boothby rapped his knuckle against the attaché case. "You haven't asked what's inside this briefcase, Alfred."

"I didn't want another lecture about need to know."

Boothby chuckled and said, "Very good. You're learning. You don't *need* to know this, but since it's your brilliant idea, I'm going to tell you. The Twenty Committee wants to convince them that Mulberry is actually a giant offshore antiaircraft complex bound for Calais. The Phoenix units already have crew quarters and anti-aircraft guns, so it's a neat fit. They've just altered the drawings a bit."

"Perfect," Vicary said.

They sat in silence for a time. "It's your call, Alfred," Boothby said finally. "You control this part of the operation. Whatever you recommend, I'll back you up on it."

Vicary did not take comfort from Boothby's offer of support. The first sign of trouble, and Boothby would be diving for the nearest foxhole. The easiest thing would be to do it Boothby's way: arrest

Catherine Blake, try to turn her, and force her to cooperate with them. But Vicary remained convinced it would not work—that the only way to funnel the Double Cross material directly through her was to do it without her knowledge.

"I say we let her run," Sir Basil said.

VICARY nervously paced the situation room at West Halkin Street. Through the microphones he could hear Jordan prowling the inside of his house, waiting for Catherine Blake. Finally Vicary heard the door buzzer.

He closed his eyes and listened. Their voices rose and fell as they moved from room to room. "Can I top up your drink?" "No, it's fine." "How about something to eat?" "No, I had a little something earlier. But there is something I want desperately right now."

Vicary listened to the sound of their kissing. He searched her voice for false notes as she told Jordan how much she loved him. Clinking glass. Running water. Footsteps ascending the stairs. The sound of Jordan's bed creaking. Vicary had heard enough. He turned to Harry and said, "I'm going upstairs. Come get me when she makes her move on the documents."

It happened at two forty-five a.m. Harry bounded upstairs and nearly broke down the door to the library. Vicary had brought his camp bed from the War Office. He came awake and followed Harry down to the situation room. Vicary recognized the sound immediately. Catherine Blake was photographing the first batch of Kettledrum material.

CATHERINE was especially anxious to make today's rendezvous. She wanted to know Vogel's response to her demand to be taken out of England. Part of her wished she had never sent it. She felt certain MI5 was closing in on her. She had made terrible mistakes, but at the same time she was gathering remarkable intelligence from Peter Jordan's safe. She found she wanted to continue, but why? It was illogical, of course. She had never wanted to be a spy; she had been blackmailed into it by Vogel. She never felt any great allegiance to Germany. In fact, Catherine felt no allegiance to anything or anyone—she supposed that's what made her a good agent. There was something else. Vogel had always called it a game. Well, she was hooked on the game. She liked the challenge of the game. And she wanted to win the game. She didn't want to steal the secret of the invasion so Germany could win the war and the Nazis could rule Europe for a thousand years. She wanted to steal the secret of the invasion to prove she was the best, better than all the bumbling idiots the Abwehr sent to England. She wanted to show Vogel that she could play his game better than he could.

HORST Neumann, standing in a doorway near Leicester Square, ate fish-and-chips from the newspaper wrapping. He spotted Catherine entering the square amid a small knot of pedestrians. He crushed the oily newspaper, dropped it into a rubbish bin, and followed her. After a minute he pulled alongside her. Catherine looked straight ahead, reached out her hand, and placed the film in his hand. He wordlessly gave her a small slip of paper, and they separated.

ALFRED Vicary said, "Then what happened?"

"She went into Stockwell underground station," Harry said. "We sent a man in, but she had boarded a train and left. We put a man on the train at Waterloo and picked up her trail again."

"How long was she alone?"

"About five minutes."

"Plenty of time to meet another agent. Then what?"

"Usual routine. Ran the watchers all over the West End for about an hour; then she made one pass across Leicester Square and headed back to Earl's Court."

"No contact with anyone?"

"The watchers didn't see anything."

Vicary made a church steeple of his fingers. "I don't believe she's out running around because she likes fresh air, Harry. She either made a dead drop somewhere or met an agent."

"We just have to keep following her. She'll make a mistake."

"I wouldn't count on that, Harry. Did you talk to Grace?"

"Yeah. She ran the names every way she could think of. She came up with nothing."

"What about Broome?"

"Same thing. It's not a code name for any operation or agent."

Berchtesgaden

THE sweeping view from the living room of Hitler's mountain lodge nearly took Kurt Vogel's breath away. The snow-covered peaks glistened in the sun. Vogel thought, Now I know why he dragged us all the way up here from Berlin. Vogel moved to the seating area next to the fire, where Canaris, Himmler, and Schellenberg were already sitting on overstuffed couches. Classic statuary was scattered about. A steward poured coffee for the four of them. The doors flew open a moment later, and Adolf Hitler pounded into the room. Canaris, as usual, was the last one on his feet. The Führer gestured for them to return to their seats, then remained standing so he could pace.

"Captain Vogel," Hitler said without preamble, "I understand your agent in London has scored another coup."

"We believe so, my Führer. Our agent has stolen another remarkable document." Vogel hesitated. "Based on this new document, we believe Operation Mulberry is a giant antiaircraft complex. It will be deployed along the French coastline in an effort to provide protection from the Luftwaffe during the critical first hours of the invasion."

Vogel reached into his briefcase. "Our analysts have used the designs in the document to render a sketch of the complex." Vogel laid the drawing on the table. Schellenberg and Himmler both looked at it with interest.

"The plans do not specify where Mulberry will be deployed, but based on the rest of the intelligence collected by the Abwehr, it would be logical to conclude it is destined for Calais."

Hitler had walked away and was staring out the windows toward his mountains. "And your old theory about an artificial harbor at Normandy?"

"It was premature, my Führer. The evidence was not in."

"No, Captain Vogel, I believe you were right the first time. I believe Mulberry *is* an artificial harbor. And I believe it is destined for Normandy." Hitler turned and faced his audience. "I know this—here." Hitler thumped his chest.

Walter Schellenberg cleared his throat. "My Führer, we do have other evidence to support Captain Vogel's intelligence. Two days ago I debriefed one of *our* agents in England." Schellenberg dug a document out of his briefcase. "This is a memorandum written by an MI Five case officer named Alfred Vicary. It was approved by someone with the initials B.B. and forwarded to Churchill and Eisenhower. In it Vicary warns that there is a new threat to security and that extra precautions should be taken. Vicary also warns that all Allied officers should be especially careful of approaches by women. Your agent in London—it's a woman, is it not, Captain Vogel?"

Vogel said, "May I see that?"

Schellenberg handed it to him.

Hitler said, "Who is B.B.?"

"Basil Boothby," Canaris said. "He heads a division within MI Five. Alfred Vicary is a friend of Churchill's."

Hitler was pacing again, but slowly. "Vogel, Schellenberg, and Canaris all are convinced. Well, I'm not." He turned around. "I'm telling you it's going to be Normandy. Normandy!"

"AN INTERESTING turn of events, wouldn't you say, Herr Reichsführer?" Hitler was watching the sun vanishing in the west, the mountain peaks purple and pink with the Alpine dusk. Everyone had gone except Himmler. "First Captain Vogel tells me Operation Mulberry is an artificial harbor; then it is an antiaircraft complex for Calais."

"Quite interesting, my Führer. I have my theories."

Hitler turned from the window. "So let me hear them."

"Number one, Vogel is telling the truth and has received new information. Number two, the intelligence he has just presented is totally fabricated, and Kurt Vogel, like his superior Wilhelm Canaris, is a traitor."

Hitler looked at Himmler carefully. "I see by that look on your face that you have another theory, Herr Reichsführer."

"Yes, my Führer. Vogel believes the information he is presenting is true, but he has been drinking from a poisoned well."

Hitler seemed intrigued. "Go on, Herr Reichsführer."

"My Führer, I have always been frank with you about my feelings for Admiral Canaris. I believe he is a traitor. I know he has had contact with British and American agents. If my fears are correct, wouldn't it be logical to assume he has compromised the German networks in Britain? Wouldn't it also be logical to assume that the information from Canaris's spies in England is also compromised?"

Hitler was pacing restlessly again. "You have a plan, I can see it."

"Yes, my Führer. And Kurt Vogel is the key. He can bring us the secret of the invasion and Canaris's head on a platter at the same time. He will have to be handled very carefully."

CHAPTER SEVEN

London: February 1944

SAME thing as before, Alfred. She led the watchers on a merry chase for three hours, then headed back to her flat."

"Blast!" Vicary said. The operation had entered its third week. He had allowed Catherine Blake to photograph four batches of documents. And four times the watchers had failed to detect how she was getting the material out of England. Vicary was edgy. The watchers were exhausted, and Peter Jordan was ready to revolt. "Perhaps we're going about this the wrong way, Harry. What if we started looking for the agent who's making the pickup?"

"But how? We don't know who he is or what he looks like."

"Actually, we might. Ginger's taken dozens and dozens of photographs of Catherine. Our man is bound to be in a couple."

"It's possible. Certainly worth a try."

Harry returned with a stack of photographs. Vicary sat down at his desk and scanned the faces for suspicious looks—anything.

Two hours later Vicary thought he had a match. "Look, Harry, here he is in Trafalgar Square. And here he is again outside Euston station. Could be coincidence, but I doubt it."

"Well, I'll be!" Harry studied the figure: small, dark-haired, with conventional clothing. Perfect for pavement work.

"He needs a code name," Vicary said.

"He looks like a Rudolf."

"All right," Vicary said. "Rudolf it is."

Hampton Sands, Norfolk

AT THAT moment Horst Neumann was pedaling his bicycle from Sean Dogherty's cottage toward the village. It was a bright, clear day, the last such day they would see for a while. Heavy weather was forecast for the entire east coast, beginning midday the following day. Neumann wanted to get out of the cottage for a few hours while he had the chance. He needed to think. The wind gusted, making it nearly impossible to keep the bicycle upright on the pitted track. He turned and looked over his shoulder. Dogherty had given up. He had climbed off his bicycle and was pushing it morosely along the path.

Neumann pretended not to notice. He cycled up a small hill, then coasted down to the bridge over the sea creek. He laid the bicycle at the edge of the track, sat in the grass, and stared out at the sea.

The message he had received from Vogel early that morning troubled him. He was to conduct countersurveillance on Catherine Blake—follow her to make certain she wasn't being followed by the opposition. The request could mean that Vogel just wanted to make certain the information Catherine was receiving was good, or it could mean he suspected she was being manipulated by the other side. In that case Neumann might be walking right into a trap. He thought, Damn you, Vogel. What are you playing at?

And what if she *was* being followed by the other side? Neumann had two choices. If possible he was to contact Vogel by wireless and request authorization to extract her from England. If there was no time, he had Vogel's permission to act on his own.

Dogherty coasted across the bridge and stopped next to Neumann. A large cloud passed before the sun. Neumann shivered in the cold. He stood up and walked with Dogherty into the village, each man pushing his bicycle.

"Listen, Sean, I may need to leave soon, in a hurry."

Dogherty looked at Neumann, his face blank.

Neumann said, "Tell me about the boat."

"Early in the war I was instructed by Berlin to create an escape route along the Lincolnshire coast, a way for an agent to get to a U-boat ten miles offshore. I found a man named Jack Kincaid. He has a small fishing boat in the town of Cleethorpes, at the mouth of the river Humber. He thinks I'm involved in the black market. I paid him a hundred pounds and told him to be ready to do the job on short notice—anytime, day or night."

"Contact him today," Neumann said.

Dogherty nodded.

Neumann said, "I'm not supposed to make you this offer, but I'm going to anyway. I want you and Mary to consider coming out with me when I leave."

Dogherty laughed. "And what am I supposed to do in Berlin?"

"You'll be alive, for one thing," Neumann said. "We've left too many footprints, and the British aren't stupid. They'll find you. And when they do, they'll march you straight to the gallows."

"I'm not afraid to give my life for the cause."

"That's a lovely speech, Sean. But don't be a fool. You wouldn't be dying for the cause, you'd be dying because you engaged in espionage on behalf of Nazi Germany. And there's something else. You may be willing to sacrifice your own life, but what about Mary's? She was an accessory to your espionage."

They walked in silence to the Hampton Arms pub. "Let me think about it tonight," Dogherty said. "I'll talk to Mary and give you an answer in the morning."

THAT NIGHT NEUMANN LAY awake in his bed, listening to the wind beating against the side of the cottage and wondering whether the entire operation was doomed. He thought of Catherine's warning on Hampstead Heath: *Some things have gone wrong. I don't think my cover will hold up much longer.* He thought of Vogel's order to conduct countersurveillance. He wondered whether all of them—Vogel, Catherine, himself—had already made fatal mistakes.

Neumann closed his eyes and tried to sleep. He was beginning to drift off to sleep when he heard a footfall outside his door. Instinctively he reached for his Mauser. He heard another footfall; then the floor creaked. He leveled the Mauser at the door. He heard the door latch turning. He thought, If MI5 were coming for me, they certainly wouldn't be trying to sneak into my bedroom at night. But if it wasn't MI5 or the police, then who was it?

The door pushed back, and Jenny Colville stood there in the open space. Neumann laid the Mauser on the floor and whispered, "Jenny, what do you think you're doing?"

She reached out in the darkness and touched his face, but she did not answer him. Instead, she pulled her sweater over her head.

"You can't stay here."

"Shhh. It's after midnight. You wouldn't send me out into a night like this, would you?"

Jenny had removed her Wellington boots and her trousers before he could answer the question. She climbed into bed and curled up next to him, beneath his arm.

Neumann said, "If Mary finds you here, she'll kill me."

She kissed him on the cheek and said, "Good night." After a few minutes her breathing assumed the rhythm of sleep. Neumann leaned his head against hers, and after a few moments he slept too.

Berlin

THE Lancaster bombers came at two o'clock in the morning. Vogel, sleeping fitfully on the army cot in his office, rose and went to the window. That afternoon he'd had a visit from Himmler. Now, as Berlin shuddered beneath the impact of the bombs, Vogel thought about their conversation. He had to admit Himmler's theory made a certain amount of sense. The fact that most of the German intelligence networks in Britain were still operational was not proof of Canaris's loyalty to the Führer. It was proof of the opposite—his treachery. If the head of the Abwehr is a traitor, why bother to publicly arrest and hang his spies? Why not use those spies and, together with Canaris, try to fool the Führer with false and misleading intelligence?

The concept was brilliant, but Vogel recognized one glaring weakness. It required total manipulation of the German networks in Britain. If there was a single agent outside MI5's web of control, that one agent could file a contradictory report, and the Abwehr might smell a rat. It could use the reports from the one genuine agent to conclude that all the other intelligence it was receiving was bogus. And if all the other intelligence was pointing toward Calais as the invasion point, the Abwehr could conclude that in fact the opposite was true—that the enemy was coming at Normandy.

Vogel would have his answer soon. If Neumann discovered that Catherine Blake was under surveillance, Vogel could dismiss her information as smoke concocted by British intelligence.

And what if Neumann did uncover proof of a deception? The Wehrmacht would be waiting for the enemy with their panzers at the invasion point. The enemy would be slaughtered. The Nazis would win the war and rule Germany and Europe for decades.

Vogel returned to his cot, closed his eyes, and tried to sleep, but he was tantalized by the prospect of uncovering a massive British deception, of outwitting his British opponents, of destroying their little game. At the same time he was terrified by what that victory would bring. Prove a British deception, destroy his old friend Canaris, win the war for Germany, secure the Nazis in power forever.

London

ALFRED Vicary rode over to the West Halkin Street command post in a War Department Rover. Night had fallen, and with it had come a drenching downpour.

The car stopped outside the house, and Vicary hurried inside. He had come to enjoy the atmosphere of the place—the noisy chatter of the watchers as they dressed in their foul-weather gear for a night on the streets, the technician checking to make sure he was receiving a good signal from the microphones inside Jordan's house, the smell of cooking drifting up from the kitchen.

Vicary climbed the stairs to the library. He hung his mackintosh behind the door and placed his briefcase on the desk. Then he walked across the hall and found Peter Jordan standing in front of a mirror, dressing in his naval uniform.

Jordan turned his head and said, "When is it going to end?"

It had become part of their evening ritual. Each night before Vicary sent Jordan off to meet Catherine Blake, Jordan asked the same question. Vicary always deflected it. But now he said, "Actually, it may be over very soon."

Jordan looked up sharply, then said, "Sit down. You look exhausted. When's the last time you slept?"

"I believe it was a night in May 1940," Vicary said, and lowered himself into a chair.

Jordan finished dressing and sat down opposite Vicary. "Am I allowed to ask you any questions?"

"That depends entirely on the question."

Jordan smiled pleasantly. "Do you enjoy your work?"

"Sometimes. And then there are times when I detest it."

"Like when?"

"Like now," Vicary said flatly.

Jordan had no reaction. It was as if he understood that no intelligence officer could actually enjoy an operation like this.

"Married?" Jordan asked.

"No."

"Ever been?"

"Never."

"Why not?"

"I suppose I never found the right woman."

Jordan was studying him. Vicary didn't quite like it. He was used to the relationship being the other way around. With Jordan and with the German spies he had handled, it was Vicary who did the prying, Vicary who probed for the weak spots and thrust in the dagger. He supposed it was one of the reasons he was a good Double Cross officer; he liked being the one in total control, the one doing the manipulating and the deceiving, the one pulling the strings.

"Any regrets?"

"Yes, I have a regret," Vicary said, surprised at himself. "I regret my failure to marry has deprived me of children. I always thought it must be wonderful to be a father."

A smile flickered across Jordan's face. "My son is my entire world. He's all that I have left. The only thing that's real. Margaret's gone. Catherine was a lie. I can't wait for this to end so I can go home to him." He paused. "What am I supposed to tell him when he asks me, 'Daddy, what did you do in the war?' "

"The truth. Tell him you were a gifted engineer and you built a contraption that helped us win the war."

"But that's *not* the truth."

Something about the tone of Jordan's voice made Vicary look up sharply. He thought, Which part isn't the truth?

Vicary stood and led Jordan across the hall into the library. He handed him a sheaf of papers and said, "I'm sorry. If there was some other way to do this, I would. But there isn't. Not yet at least."

Jordan placed the papers inside his briefcase.

Vicary said, "There's one thing that always bothered me about your interrogation: why you couldn't remember the name of the Englishman who first approached you about working on Mulberry."

"I met dozens of people that week. Can't remember half of them."

"Was his name Broome, by any chance?"

"No, it wasn't Broome," Jordan said without hesitation. "I think I'd remember that. I probably should be going."

CLIVE Roach was sitting at a window table in the café across the street from Catherine Blake's flat. It was raining, and he was drinking tea and halfheartedly leafing through a morning newspaper, but he was more interested in the doorway across the street. Roach liked watching. He had a flare for names and faces.

He drank the last of his tea. He looked up from his table and saw her coming out of her block of flats. He marveled at her tradecraft. She always stood still for a moment, doing something prosaic while scanning the street for surveillance. Today she was fumbling with her umbrella as if it were broken. Roach thought, You're very good, Miss Blake, but I'm better.

He watched as she finally snapped up her umbrella and started walking. Roach got up, pulled on his coat, and walked out the door after her. His assignment was simple—tail Catherine Blake until she handed her material to the agent Professor Vicary had code-named Rudolf, then follow him.

HORST Neumann came awake as the train clattered through London's northeastern suburbs. He yawned, stretched, and sat up in his seat. He had not slept well the previous night. It was the presence of Jenny Colville in his bed. She had risen with him before dawn, slipped out of the cottage, and pedaled home. Neumann hoped her father wasn't waiting for her. It was a stupid thing to do—letting her spend the night with him. He worried about how she would feel when he was gone, when she discovered that he was not James Porter, a wounded British soldier looking for peace and quiet in a Norfolk village. That he was Horst Neumann, a decorated German paratrooper who came to England to spy and who had deceived her in the worst way. He had not deceived her about one thing. He cared for her. Not in the way she would like, but he did care about what happened to her.

The train slowed as it approached Liverpool Street. Neumann stood, pulled on his reefer coat, and shuffled amid the other passengers toward the door.

CATHERINE Blake took a taxi to Charing Cross. The rendezvous point was a short distance away, in front of a shop on the Strand. She started walking, stopped at a phone box, and pretended to place a call. She looked behind her. The heavy rain had reduced visibility, but she could see no sign of a tail. She replaced the receiver and continued eastward along the Strand.

CLIVE Roach slipped from the back of a surveillance van and followed her along the Strand. During the brief ride he had shed his mackintosh and brimmed hat and changed into an oilskin coat and woolen cap. The transformation was remarkable—from a clerk to a laborer. Roach watched as Catherine Blake stopped to place the ersatz telephone call. Roach paused at a newspaper vendor, then melted into the pedestrians and followed her.

NEUMANN spotted Catherine walking toward him. He paused at a shop, eyes scanning the faces of the pedestrians behind her. As she drew closer, he turned from the window and walked toward her. The contact was brief, a second or two. But when it was over, Neumann had a canister of film in his pocket. She moved quickly on, disappearing into the crowd. Neumann continued in the opposite direction for a few feet, then turned and followed softly after her.

CLIVE Roach spotted Rudolf and saw the exchange. He watched as Rudolf turned and walked in the same direction as Catherine Blake. Roach had witnessed many meetings by German agents, but never had he seen one agent turn and follow the other. Roach turned up the collar of his oilskin coat and floated carefully behind them.

CATHERINE walked east along the Strand, then down to Victoria Embankment. It was then she spotted Neumann behind her.

Vogel must have ordered him to follow her. But why? She could think of two possible explanations: He had lost faith in her and wanted to see where she was going, or he wanted to determine whether she was under MI5 surveillance.

She could feel her heart pounding in her chest. She walked to Blackfriars underground station, went inside, and purchased a ticket for South Kensington. Neumann followed her and did the same.

FOR TWO HOURS NEUMANN followed her as she moved through the West End—from Kensington to Chelsea, from Chelsea to Belgravia, from Belgravia to Mayfair. By the time they reached Berkeley Square, he was convinced. It was the man in the mackintosh walking fifty feet behind him. Five minutes earlier Neumann had been able to get a good look at his face. It was the same face he had seen on the Strand three hours earlier—when he had taken the film from Catherine—only then the man had been wearing an oilskin coat. Neumann thought, They've been following us for hours. Why haven't they arrested us both? But he knew the answer. They obviously wanted to know more. Where was the film to be dropped? Where was Neumann staying? As long as he didn't give them the answers to those questions, he and Catherine were safe.

Neumann quickened his pace. He called out, "Catherine! It's been ages. How have you been?"

She glanced up, alarm on her face. Neumann took her by the arm. "We need to talk," he said. "Let's find a place to have tea."

NEUMANN'S sudden move landed on the command post in West Halkin Street with the impact of a thousand-pound bomb. Basil Boothby was pacing and talking tensely to the director general by telephone. Boothby slammed down the receiver and said, "The Twenty Committee says let them run."

"I don't like it," Vicary said. "They've obviously spotted the tail. What's more, I think Rudolf was looking for it. They're sitting there now trying to figure out what to do."

"You don't know that for certain."

Vicary stared at the wall. "We've never observed her meeting with another agent before. And now she's suddenly sitting in a Mayfair café having tea and toast with Rudolf?"

"What do you suggest?" Boothby asked.

"Move in now. Arrest them the moment they leave that café."

Boothby looked at Vicary as though he had uttered heresy. "Getting cold feet now, are you, Alfred? This was your idea—you conceived it, you sold it to the prime minister. For weeks a group of officers has toiled night and day to provide the material for that briefcase, and now you want to shut it all down, just like that, because you have a hunch."

"It's more than a hunch, Sir Basil. Read the watch reports."

Boothby was pacing again, hands clasped behind his back. "They'll say he was good at the wireless game but he didn't have the nerve to play with live agents. Is that what you want them to say about you when this is over, Alfred? Because if it is, pick up the telephone and tell the D.G. you think we should roll this up now."

Vicary stared at Boothby. "It's over," he said in a dull monotone. "They've spotted the surveillance. Catherine Blake knows she's been deceived, and she's going to tell Kurt Vogel about it. Vogel will conclude that Mulberry is exactly the opposite of what we told him. And then we're dead."

"THEY'RE everywhere," Neumann said. "The man in the mackintosh, the girl waiting for the bus, the man walking into the chemist's shop. They've used different faces, different clothing, but they've been following us from the moment we left the Strand."

Catherine picked up her cup of tea, her hand trembling. "Why haven't they arrested us?"

"Any number of reasons. They've probably known about you for a very long time. If that's true, then all the information you've been receiving from Commander Jordan is false. And we've been funneling it back to Berlin for them."

She put down her cup. "If Jordan is working with British intelligence, we can assume everything in his briefcase is false—designed to mislead the Abwehr about Allied plans for the invasion. Vogel needs to know this." She managed a smile. "It's possible those bastards have just handed us the secret of the invasion."

"I suspect you're right, but there's just one problem. We need to tell Vogel in person. We have to assume the Portuguese embassy route is now compromised. We also have to assume we cannot tell him by radio. Vogel thinks all the old codes have been broken. If we broadcast what we know, the British will know it too."

"How in the world are we going to get out of London?"

"We have a couple of things we can use to our advantage. Number one, this." Neumann tapped his pocket containing the film. "I don't think they know how I deliver the film. Also, I'm certain I've not been followed to Hampton Sands. Standard procedure is to find out all the components of a network and then roll it up all at once. Are you supposed to see Jordan tonight?"

"Yes. At seven o'clock for dinner."

"Perfect," Neumann said. "Here's what I want you to do." He spent the next five minutes explaining his plan. "Whatever you do, you must do nothing out of the ordinary. Nothing that would make them suspect that you know you're under surveillance. Shop, go to a cinema, stay in the open. As long as I don't drop this film, you'll be safe. At five o'clock go to your flat and get your radio. I'll meet you there."

Catherine nodded.

"One more problem. Do you have any idea where I can lay my hands on a car and some extra petrol?"

Catherine laughed in spite of herself. "Actually, I know just the place. But I wouldn't suggest using my name."

HORST Neumann drifted in Mayfair until the last light was gone, then walked north to the Baker Street underground station. He was being followed by at least two people on foot as well as by a black van. He took a train to Charing Cross. At Charing Cross he changed trains and headed for Euston station. With two men in pursuit, he walked through the tunnel connecting the underground station to the railway terminus, where he purchased a ticket for Liverpool. The train was already crowded by the time he reached the platform. He searched for a compartment with one free seat, went inside, and sat down.

He looked at his watch: three minutes until departure. Outside his compartment the corridor was filled with passengers. Neumann stood and squeezed out of the compartment, muttering about an upset stomach. He walked to the lavatory at the end of the carriage and knocked on the door. There was no answer. Knocking a second time, he glanced over his shoulder. The man who had followed him onto the train was cut off from view by the other passengers.

Perfect. The train started to move. He waited outside the lavatory as the train gathered speed, then stepped toward the door to the carriage, threw it open, and leaped down onto the platform.

He landed smoothly, trotting a few steps before settling into a brisk walk. He reached the exit and headed out into the blackout. Hailing a taxi, he gave the driver an address in the East End.

Hampton Sands, Norfolk

MARY Dogherty waited alone at the cottage. Outside, the big storm that had been forecast had finally moved in over the Norfolk coast. Rain lashed against the windows, rattling the panes.

Sean was away, gone to Hunstanton to collect Neumann from the train. Mary paced restlessly. Snatches of their conversation of that morning played over and over in her head: *submarine . . . stay in Berlin for a while . . . make my way back to Ireland . . . join me there when the war is over. . . .*

Sean was going to flee and leave her behind to face the consequences. *Just tell them you knew nothing, Mary.* And what if the authorities didn't believe her? What would they do then?

She began to weep. She thought, Damn you, Sean Dogherty! How could you have been such a fool?

Mary heard a knock at the door. It was Jenny Colville. Mary pulled her inside and helped her out of her wet coat and hat.

"Jenny, what in the world are you doing out in weather like this? Sit down by the fire. I'll make you some hot tea."

"Where's James?" Jenny asked.

"He's not here," Mary said. "He's with Sean somewhere."

"Oh," Jenny said. "Will he be back soon?"

Mary looked at her. "Why are you so concerned, Jenny?"

"I like James—very much, Mary. And he likes me."

"You like him, and he likes you?" Mary took hold of Jenny by the shoulders. "Stay away from him. Forget about him."

Jenny began to cry. "I can't forget about him, Mary. I love him. And he loves me. I know he does."

"Jenny, he doesn't love you. Don't ask me to explain it all, because I can't. He's a kind man, but he's not what he appears to be. Let go of it. He's not for you."

Jenny tore herself from Mary's grasp, stood back, and wiped the tears from her face. "He *is* for me, Mary. I love him. You've been trapped here with Sean so long you've forgotten what love is." She picked up her coat and dashed out the door, slamming it behind her.

London

NEUMANN paid off the taxi a short distance from the Pope warehouse and walked the rest of the way in the driving rain.

The warehouse appeared deserted. Neumann rang the bell. No response. He rang again and this time heard footsteps. The door was opened by a black-haired giant in a leather coat.

"What do you want?"

"I'd like to see Mr. Pope, please," Neumann said politely. "I need a few items, and I was told this was the place to come."

"Mr. Pope is gone, and we're out of business." The giant started to close the door.

Neumann put his foot in the way. "I'm sorry. It's really rather urgent. Perhaps you could help."

The giant looked at Neumann. "I suppose you didn't hear me the first time," he said. "We're out of business. Now beat it."

Neumann punched the giant in the Adam's apple, then pulled out his Mauser and shot him in the foot. The man collapsed, howling in pain. Neumann leaned down. "If you make a move, I'll shoot you again, and it won't be in the foot."

Neumann stepped inside the warehouse and closed the gate. It was just the way Catherine described it: vans, cars, motorbikes, stacks of black market food, and several jerry cans of petrol.

He grabbed four cans of petrol and put them in the back of a black van. Then he hauled open the main door of the warehouse, climbed into the van, and sped away.

HARRY DALTON TORE THE blackout shades from the headlamps and drove dangerously fast across London, one hand on the horn. Vicary sat next to him, nervously clutching the dash. The wipers struggled to beat away the rain. Harry sliced and snaked his way through the traffic, eventually turning into Earl's Court Road. He raced down a narrow alley and slammed on the brakes behind a block of flats.

Harry and Vicary entered the building through the rear service door and pounded upstairs to the fifth floor. Vicary ignored the pain shooting through his knee. He thought, If only Boothby had let me arrest them hours ago, we wouldn't be in this mess.

It was nothing short of a disaster. Rudolf had just jumped from a train at Euston station and melted into the city. Vicary had to assume he was now attempting to flee the country. He had no choice but to arrest Catherine Blake; he needed her in custody and scared out of her wits. Then she might tell them where Rudolf was headed. But Vicary was not optimistic. Everything he felt about this woman told him she would not cooperate, even when faced with execution.

Harry pushed open the door to the surveillance flat. The curtains were open to the street, the room in darkness. Vicary struggled to make out the figures standing all around the room: a pair of bleary-eyed watchers frozen in the window, a half-dozen tense Special Branch men leaning against one wall. The senior Special Branch officer was a man called Carter. He led Vicary to the window.

"She just got back," Carter said. "We'll go in through the front door, and two men will cover the back. She'll have nowhere to go."

"It's extremely important that you take her alive," Vicary said. "She's absolutely useless to us dead."

"We'll take her so fast she won't know what hit her."

HORST Neumann parked the van in a quiet side street around the corner from Catherine's flat. The street was in pitch-darkness. He climbed out and groped his way across a pile of rubble that once was the terrace behind the flat. The rubble ended at a wall about six feet high. On the other side of the wall was the garden at the back of the house. He tried the gate; it was locked. He would have to open it from the other side.

He pulled himself to the top of the wall, turned his body, and jumped through the dark. A thorny shrub clawed at his face and his coat. Tearing himself free, he unlatched the gate. He crossed the garden to the back door. The door was locked, but it had a window. He used his Mauser to smash a pane, then unlocked the door and ascended the stairs.

He reached Catherine's door and knocked softly.

He heard her voice from the other side. "Who's there?"

"It's me."

She opened the door. Her face was ashen. "I think something is going on," she said. "I saw men on the street and in parked cars."

Neumann turned off the light. He crossed to the window in a few quick steps and lifted the edge of the blackout shade. The evening traffic was moving below, throwing off just enough light for him to see four men charging across the street.

Neumann turned and ripped his Mauser from his pocket. "They're coming for us. Grab your radio and follow me down. Now."

HARRY Dalton threw open the front door and went inside, the Special Branch men behind him. He switched on the hall light in time to see Catherine Blake stepping out the back door, her suitcase radio swinging from her arm.

HORST Neumann had kicked open the back door and was running across the garden when he heard the shout from within the house. He rushed through the gloom, the Mauser in his hand. The gate flew open, and a figure appeared there, silhouetted in the frame, gun raised, shouting for Neumann to stop. Neumann fired, killing him instantly. A second man stepped into his place, and Neumann squeezed the trigger. The man's head exploded.

Neumann raced through the gate, stepped over the two bodies, and peered into the blackout. There was no one else behind the house. He turned and saw Catherine behind him, three men chasing her. Neumann raised his gun and fired into the dark. He heard two men scream. Catherine kept running. He turned and started across the rubble toward the van.

HARRY felt the rounds whiz past his head, heard the screams of both men behind him. She was right in front of him. He realized he was at a disadvantage; he was unarmed and alone. He could go back inside the house and signal the surveillance flat, but by then Catherine and Rudolf would be long gone and would use their radio to tell Berlin what they had discovered.

The radio! He thought, I may not be able to stop Catherine and Rudolf now, but I can cut them off from Berlin for a while.

Harry leaped through the darkness and grabbed hold of the suitcase with both hands. He tried to tear it from Catherine's grasp, but she turned and pulled with surprising strength. He looked up and saw her face for the first time: red, contorted with fear, ugly with rage. Then Harry heard clicking—the sound of a stiletto blade snapping into place. He saw her arm rise, then swing in a vicious arc toward his throat. He tried to avoid the blade by twisting his head, but the tip of the stiletto struck the side of his face. He could feel his flesh tearing, then searing pain, as though molten metal had been thrown against his face. She raised her arm again, plunging the stiletto into his forearm. Harry yelled with pain, but his hands would not let go of the suitcase. Nothing could make them let go.

She let go of the bag and said, "You're a brave man to die for a radio." Then she turned and disappeared into the darkness.

Harry lay on the wet ground, the rain beating against his face. He was losing consciousness; the pain was fading. He heard the wounded Special Branch men groaning nearby. He felt someone pressing something against his face. When he opened his eyes, he saw Alfred Vicary leaning over him.

"Did they get away?" Harry asked.

"Yes. But you kept her from taking the radio."

Then pain raced up on Harry very suddenly. He started to tremble. Vicary's face turned to water, and Harry blacked out.

WITHIN ONE HOUR OF THE disaster in Earl's Court, Alfred Vicary had orchestrated the biggest manhunt in the history of the United Kingdom. Every police station in the country was given a description of Vicary's fugitive spies. Vicary dispatched photographs by courier to the towns and villages close to London. Most officers were told the fugitives were suspects in four murders dating back to 1938. A handful were discreetly informed it was a security matter of the utmost importance.

London's Metropolitan Police responded with extraordinary speed, and within fifteen minutes of Vicary's call, roadblocks had been thrown up along all major arteries leading from the city. MI5 and railway police prowled the main stations.

Next Vicary turned his attention to the escape routes only a spy would use. He contacted the RAF, the Admiralty, the coastguard service, and the operators of the Irish ferries. He also telephoned the Y Service radio monitors and asked them to listen for suspect wireless transmissions.

Vicary stood up from his desk and stepped outside his office for the first time in two hours. The command post in West Halkin Street had been deserted, and Vicary's team had slowly streamed back to MI5 headquarters in St. James's Street. They sat in the common area outside his office like dazed survivors of a disaster.

The silence was broken at nine o'clock, when Harry Dalton, his face and arm bandaged, walked into the room. Everyone crowded around him. "Well done, Harry, old boy." "Deserve a medal . . ." "Be all over if not for you."

Vicary pulled him into his office. "Shouldn't you be resting?"

"Yeah, but I wanted to be here instead. They gave me something for the pain."

Vicary brought Harry up to date.

"Bold move, Rudolf coming back for her like that," Harry said. "He's got guts, I'll say that for him. How's Boothby taking it?"

"As well as can be expected. He's upstairs with the director general now. Probably planning my execution. We have an open line to the Underground War Rooms and the prime minister."

"You've covered every possible option. They have to make a move somewhere. And when they do, we'll be onto them."

"I wish I could share your optimism, Harry."

The telephone rang. It was Boothby. "Come upstairs, Alfred."

Vicary found Sir Basil pacing and chain-smoking. He angrily waved Vicary toward a chair and said, "Well, the lights are burning all over London tonight: Grosvenor Square, Eisenhower's headquarters at Hayes Lodge, the Underground War Rooms. And they all want to know one thing. Does Hitler know it's Normandy? Is the invasion dead even before we begin?"

"We obviously have no way of knowing yet."

"Two men dead and three wounded! Two spies running loose, possessing the knowledge to unravel our entire deception plan. Needless to say, this is the worst disaster in the history of this department."

"Special Branch went in with the force they deemed necessary to arrest her. Obviously, they made a miscalculation."

Boothby stopped pacing and fixed a gunman's gaze on Vicary. "Don't attempt to blame Special Branch for what happened, Alfred. You were the senior man on the scene. That aspect of Kettledrum was your responsibility."

"I realize that, Sir Basil."

"Good, because when this is all over, an internal review will be convened, and I doubt your performance will be viewed in a favorable light."

THE distant wail of the air-raid sirens started up while Vicary was taking the stairs down to Registry. The rooms were in half darkness, just a couple of lights burning. The light was out in Jago's office. Vicary heard the sharp smack of women's shoes and saw Grace Clarendon's shock of blond hair flash past the stacks. He followed her into one of the side rooms and called her name. She stared at him with hostile eyes, then turned away and resumed her filing.

"Is this official, Professor?" she said. "If it's not, I'll have to ask you to leave. You've caused me enough problems."

"I need to see a file, Grace."

"You know the procedure. Fill out a request slip."

"I won't be given approval to see the file I need to see."

"Then you can't see it," she said coldly. "Those are the rules."

The first bombs fell. Then the antiaircraft batteries opened up. Vicary said, "I know Boothby is making you do things against your will. I heard you quarreling in his office."

Vicary noticed the shine of moisture in her green eyes.

"It's all your fault!" she snapped. "If you hadn't told him about the Vogel file, I wouldn't be in this mess."

"What is he making you do?"

She hesitated. "Please leave, Professor. Please."

"Tell me what Boothby wanted you to do."

"Very well, Professor Vicary, he wanted me to spy on you. And on Harry. Anything Harry told me, I was supposed to tell him."

"What did you tell him?"

"Anything Harry mentioned to me about the case and the progress of the investigation. I also told him about the Registry search you requested." She resumed her filing. "I heard Harry was involved in that mess at Earl's Court. Was he hurt?"

Vicary nodded. "He's upstairs. The doctors couldn't keep him in bed. Grace, I need to see a file. Boothby's going to sack me when this business is over, and I need to know why."

She stared at him. "You're serious, aren't you, Professor?"

"Unfortunately, yes."

She looked at him wordlessly for a moment while the building shuddered with the shock waves of the bombing. "What's the file?"

"An operation called Kettledrum."

Grace furrowed her eyebrows in confusion. "You want me to risk my neck to show you the file on your own case?"

"Something like that. Except I want you to cross-reference it with a different case officer. Basil Boothby."

FIVE minutes later Grace came back with an empty file sleeve in her hand. "Operation Kettledrum," she said. "Terminated."

"Where are the contents?"

"Either destroyed or with the case officer."

"When was the file opened?" Vicary asked.

Grace looked at the tab on the file, then at Vicary.

"That's funny," she said. "According to this, Operation Kettledrum was initiated in October 1943."

CHAPTER EIGHT

Cambridgeshire, England

BY THE time Scotland Yard responded to Alfred Vicary's demand for roadblocks, Horst Neumann and Catherine Blake had left London and were racing northward along the A10. The stolen black van flashed through villages with funny names—Puckeridge, Buntingford—dark, not a light burning, no one moving about. Neumann hunched forward, peering into the little pool of light thrown off by the shrouded headlamps.

During his preparation at Vogel's farmhouse outside Berlin, Neumann had spent hours studying maps of Britain. He suspected he knew the roads better than most Englishmen.

Melbourne, Foxton, Newton, Hauxton. He was approaching Cambridge. The Cambridge police force had enough men to mount a roadblock on a large route like the A10. They had cars to engage in pursuit. Neumann turned into a small side road, skirted the base of the Gog Magog Hills, and headed north along the eastern edge of the city. He rejoined the A10 and continued north toward the Norfolk coast.

The weather worsened the closer they moved to the coast. At times they seemed to be traveling at a walking pace. After more than an hour of difficult driving, they reached Hampton Sands.

The Dogherty cottage appeared in the distance. Neumann turned into the drive. He saw the door open and the glow of a kerosene lamp moving toward them. It was Sean Dogherty, dressed in his oilskin and sou'wester, a shotgun over his arm.

Dogherty had not been worried when Neumann did not arrive in Hunstanton on the afternoon train. Neumann had warned him he might be in London longer than usual. But when Neumann was not on the evening train, Dogherty had become alarmed.

He drove back to the cottage and let himself in. Mary, sitting next to the fire, glared at him, then went upstairs. Dogherty switched on the wireless. The news bulletin caught his attention. A nationwide search was under way for two suspected killers who had taken part in a gun battle with police in the Earl's Court section of London. The newsreader gave a description of the suspects. The first, surprisingly, was a woman. The second was a man who matched Horst Neumann's description perfectly.

Dogherty went upstairs, threw a change of clothes into a small canvas bag, and came downstairs again. He found his shotgun, loaded a pair of cartridges into the barrel, and sat in the window, waiting. He had almost given up hope when he spotted the shaded headlights moving along the road toward the cottage.

Martin Colville went into the kitchen and poured the last precious drops of whiskey from a bottle. He drank the whiskey in one swallow, then placed the empty bottle and the glass in the sink. He heard the grumble of a motor outside. He went to the door and looked out. A van swept past. Colville could see James Porter behind the wheel and a woman in the passenger seat.

Every instinct in Colville's body told him there was something wrong about James Porter. He didn't believe he was a wounded British soldier. He didn't believe he was an old acquaintance of Sean Dogherty's. He didn't believe he had come to Hampton Sands for the ocean air. And if he knew what was good for him, James Porter would stay away from Jenny.

Colville closed the door, thinking, What on earth is Porter doing out driving this time of night? And where did he get the van? Colville decided he would find out. He went into the sitting room, took down an old 12-bore shotgun from over the mantel, and found a box of cartridges. He went outside and climbed onto his bicycle.

Jenny, upstairs in her bedroom, heard the front door open and close once. Then she heard the sound of a passing vehicle, unusual at this time of night. When she heard the door open and close a second time, she became alarmed. She rose from her bed and parted the curtain in time to see her father pedaling away through the darkness. She pounded on the window, but it was in vain.

Jenny dressed and went downstairs. Her Wellington boots were by the door. Pulling them on, she noticed the shotgun that usually hung over the fireplace was gone. Quickly she put on her coat and went outside. She climbed onto her bicycle and pedaled after her father toward the Dogherty cottage, thinking, Please God, let me stop him before someone ends up dead tonight.

SEAN Dogherty opened the door of the barn and led Neumann and the woman inside behind the light of the kerosene lantern.

Neumann said, "Sean Dogherty, meet Catherine Blake. Catherine works for Kurt Vogel too. She's been living in England under deep cover since 1938."

Dogherty looked at them. "The BBC's running bulletins about a gun battle at Earl's Court. I suppose you were involved in that?"

Neumann nodded. "What's the radio saying?"

"They've mounted a nationwide search for you and asked for help from the general public. I'm surprised you made it this far."

Neumann looked at his watch—a few minutes after midnight. He picked up Sean's lantern and carried it to the worktable, then took the radio from the cabinet. "The submarine is on patrol in the North Sea. After receiving our signal, it will move ten miles due east of Spurn Head and remain there until six a.m. If we don't appear, it turns from the coast and waits to hear from us."

Dogherty dug out an old Ordnance Survey map. "Jack Kincaid's boat is here," he said, jabbing at the map. "In a town called Cleethorpes, a hundred miles up the coast. It will be hard driving on a dirty night like this. Kincaid has a flat over a garage on the waterfront. I spoke to him yesterday. He knows we might be coming."

Neumann slipped on the earphones, tuned the radio to the proper frequency, and tapped out an identification signal. A few seconds later the radio operator aboard the U-boat asked Neumann to proceed. Neumann carefully tapped out the message, then signed off.

He turned to Dogherty. "Are you coming with us?"

Dogherty nodded. "I've talked it over with Mary. I'll come back to Germany with you; then Vogel and his friends can help me make my way back to Ireland. Mary will come across when I'm there."

"Then let's go," Neumann said, reaching for the kerosene lamp.

MARTIN Colville left his bicycle next to the road, quietly crossed the meadow, and crouched outside Dogherty's barn. He struggled to understand the conversation taking place inside over the smack of the falling rain. It was unbelievable.

Sean Dogherty—working for the Nazis. The man called James Porter—a German agent! A nest of spies operating in Hampton Sands. Colville felt his heart careening inside his chest. If he left for help, Dogherty and the spies would probably be gone by the time he returned. If he went in alone, he would be outnumbered.

He broke open the box of cartridges, snapped two into the barrel of the 12-bore. Then he stepped toward the door.

JENNY pedaled until her legs burned—through the village, over the sea creek. The air was filled with the sound of the storm and the rush of the sea. The wind nearly blew her over.

She spotted her father's bicycle in the grass along the track and thought, Why not ride it all the way to the cottage? She thought she knew the answer. He was trying to sneak up without being seen.

It was then she heard the shotgun blast from Sean's barn. She leaped from her bicycle and ran across the meadow, thinking, Please God, don't let him be dead. Don't let him be dead.

Scarborough, England

APPROXIMATELY one hundred miles north of Hampton Sands, Charlotte Endicott pedaled her bicycle into the compound outside the Y Service listening station at Scarborough. The ride from town had been brutal, wind and rain the entire way. Chilled to the bone, she dismounted, leaned her bicycle next to several others in the stand, and walked toward the operations room.

She flashed her identification badge at the guard, entered, sat down at her RCA AR-88 superheterodyne communications receiver, and slipped on her earphones. The RCA's special interference-cutting crystals allowed her to monitor German Morse senders all across northern Europe. She tuned her receiver to the band of frequencies she had been assigned that night and settled in.

A few minutes after midnight she heard a burst of Morse in a keying style she did not recognize. The cadence was poor, the pace slow and uncertain. An amateur, she thought. Certainly not one of the professionals at BdU, the Kriegsmarine headquarters. Acting quickly, she made a recording of the transmission on the oscillograph—in effect creating a radio fingerprint of the signal—and furiously scribbled the message onto paper. When the amateur finished, Charlotte heard another burst of code on the same frequency. This was no amateur; she and the other Wrens had heard him before. They had nicknamed him Fritz. He was a radio operator aboard a U-boat. Charlotte transcribed this message as well.

Fritz's transmission was followed by another burst of sloppy Morse by the amateur, and then the communication went dead. Charlotte tore off the printout of the oscillograph, marched across to the night supervisor—a Commander Lowe—and dropped the transcripts and the oscillograph on his desk. "Sir," she said, "I think I just overheard a German spy signaling a U-boat."

Earlier that evening a Major Vicary from MI5 had sent out an alert to look for this very sort of thing.

The radio fingerprint created by the oscillograph could be used to identify the type of transmitter and its power supply. Within ten minutes Commander Lowe concluded the transmitter was probably an AFU suitcase radio commonly used by German spies in Britain. He then contacted his counterparts at the Y Service stations at Flowerdown and Iceland to ask whether they had run oscillographs on the transmission. Both stations had.

Using the three recordings, Lowe attempted to plot a fix on the transmitter. Unfortunately, the communication was short, the fix not terribly precise. In fact, Lowe could narrow it only to a rather large portion of eastern England—all of Norfolk and much of Suffolk, Cambridgeshire, and Lincolnshire.

STANDING on the bridge of *U-509*, Kapitänleutnant Max Hoffman could feel the throb of its electric motors beneath his feet as they wheeled in a circle twenty miles from the British coastline. It was a tedious assignment, sitting off the coast of Britain for weeks on end, waiting for Canaris's spies.

The first officer came onto the bridge. "Our man in Britain has finally surfaced. He'd like a lift home tonight."

Hoffman smiled. "What's the latest weather?"

"Not good, Herr Kaleu," the first officer said, using the customary diminutive for Kapitänleutnant. "Heavy rains, winds thirty miles per hour from the northwest, seas ten to twelve."

"And he'll probably be coming in a rowboat! Organize a reception party and have the radio operator inform BdU of our plans. Set a course for the rendezvous point."

"Yes, Herr Kaleu." The first officer shouted a series of commands, echoed among the crew.

FIVE minutes after *U-509*'s radio operator transmitted his message to BdU in northern France, the duty officer at BdU flashed a brief message to the Abwehr's radio center at Hamburg. Captain Schmidt, the duty officer there, recorded the message, then placed a priority call to Abwehr headquarters in Berlin and informed Kurt Vogel that Horst Neumann had contacted the submarine and was coming out. Schmidt then walked down the street to a nearby hotel, where he booked a second call to Berlin. He did not want to use the thoroughly bugged lines of the Abwehr post, for this call was to Brigadeführer Walter Schellenberg. As soon as Schellenberg was told of the developments, he telephoned Reichsführer Heinrich Himmler and briefed him. They all settled in for the wait.

The location of the Allied invasion of France.

The life of Admiral Canaris.

And it all depended on the word of a couple of spies on the run from MI5.

Hampton Sands, Norfolk

MARTIN Colville pushed back the door of Dogherty's barn. Neumann, still standing next to the radio, heard the noise and reached for his Mauser. Colville spotted Neumann going for the gun. He leveled his shotgun and fired. Neumann leaped out of the way, hit the floor, and rolled. The radio disintegrated.

Colville aimed the gun at Neumann a second time. Neumann rolled up onto his elbows, the Mauser in his outstretched hands. Sean Dogherty stepped forward, screaming at Colville to stop. Colville turned the gun on Dogherty and squeezed the trigger. The blast struck Dogherty in the chest. He died within seconds.

Neumann fired, hitting Colville in his shoulder and spinning him around. Catherine had by now drawn her own Mauser and, using both hands, leveled it at Colville's head. She fired twice rapidly, the silencer dampening the blasts to a dull thud. Martin Colville was dead before his body hit the floor.

WHEN Mary Dogherty heard the shotgun blasts, she sat bolt upright in her bed, threw off her blanket, and raced downstairs. She went outside in the rain wearing only her flannel nightgown, turned toward the barn, and saw light burning there. She called out, "Sean!" and ran to the barn.

Stepping inside, she gasped. As she saw Martin Colville's body, a scream caught in her throat and would not come out. And then she saw Sean lying there dead, and the scream that had been trapped in her throat came out.

Horst Neumann was standing over Sean's body, a gun in his hand. A few feet from Neumann stood a woman holding a pistol aimed at Mary's head. Mary looked back at Neumann and screamed, "Did you do this? Did you?"

"It was Colville," Neumann said. "He came in here, guns blazing. Sean got in the way. I'm sorry, Mary."

"No, Horst. Martin may have pulled the trigger, but you did this to him. Make no mistake about it. You and your friends in Berlin."

Neumann said nothing. He stepped over to Catherine, took hold of the Mauser, and gently lowered it to the ground.

JENNY Colville crouched against the outside wall of the barn and listened to the conversation taking place inside. She heard the voice of the man she knew as James Porter. Then she heard Mary's voice, rising in pitch and quivering with anger and grief.

Jenny waited to hear her father's voice; she waited to hear Sean's voice. Nothing. She knew then they both were dead.

You and your friends in Berlin . . .

It all came together in her mind like pieces of a puzzle: the sudden appearance of the man called James Porter, Mary's warning to her that afternoon. *He's not what he appears to be. . . .*

The man she knew as James Porter was a German spy. And that meant Sean was one too. Her father must have discovered the truth and confronted them. And now he was dead.

Jenny felt hot tears pour down her cheeks. She raised her hands to her mouth to cover the sound of her crying. She had fallen in love with James, but he had lied to her and used her, and he was a German spy, and he had probably just killed her father.

There was movement inside the barn. She heard the German spy's voice and a woman's voice that was not Mary's. Then the spy emerged from the barn and walked down the drive, torch in hand. If he found the bicycles, he would realize she was here too.

More than anything else now she wanted them caught and punished. But what to do? They had to be leaving soon. They had just killed two people, after all. She would hide until they left, and then she would contact the police.

Jenny watched the spy move close to the road. She saw the beam of his torch play over the ground. She saw it settle on something, then flash in her direction. She rose and started to run.

HORST NEUMANN WENT INSIDE the barn. Catherine had covered the bodies with some old sacking. Mary was sitting in a chair, shaking violently. Neumann avoided her gaze.

"We have a problem," he said, gesturing at the covered body of Martin Colville. "I found his daughter's bicycle. I saw her running off. We have to assume she knows what happened. We also have to assume she'll try to get help."

"Then go after her," Catherine said.

Neumann nodded. "Take Mary in the house. Tie her up; gag her. I have an idea where Jenny might be going."

London

AT THAT moment a taxi braked to a halt in the driving rain outside a stubby, ivy-covered blockhouse beneath Admiralty Arch. Commander Arthur Braithwaite emerged and hurried into the Citadel. He made his way down a warren of narrow, winding staircases and entered the submarine tracking room through a guarded door. Several dozen officers and typists worked at tables around the edges of the room. In the center stood the main North Atlantic plotting table, where colored pins depicted the location of every warship, freighter, and submarine from the Baltic Sea to Cape Cod.

Braithwaite pushed back the door of his glass cubicle and sat down at his desk. He reached for the stack of decodes that awaited him each night. The first items were conventional stuff—intercepts of routine communications between U-boats and BdU. The fifth caught his attention. It was an alert issued by a Major Alfred Vicary of MI5. After a few more routine items Braithwaite came upon something else that caught his attention. A Wren at the Scarborough Y Service station had intercepted what she believed was a communication between a U-boat and a wireless onshore. The transmitter was somewhere along the east coast—somewhere from Lincolnshire to Suffolk. Braithwaite rose and walked into the main room, stopping at the North Atlantic plotting table. He fixed his gaze on the waters off Britain's east coast. After a moment he turned to his aide and said quietly, "Patrick, bring me the file on *U-509*."

Hampton Sands, Norfolk

JENNY Colville reached the grove of pines at the base of the dunes and collapsed with exhaustion. She had run there by instinct, like a frightened animal. Neumann found her there and drove her back to the Doghertys' cottage. The door opened, and Catherine came outside. She walked to the van and looked inside at Jenny. Then she looked at Neumann and said in German, "Tie her up and put her in the back. You never know when a hostage might come in handy."

Neumann shook his head and replied in the same language. "Just leave her here. She's no use to us, and she might get hurt."

"Are you forgetting I outrank you, Lieutenant?"

"No, Major," Neumann said, his voice tinged with sarcasm.

"Good. Now tie her up. Let's get out of this place."

Jenny did not resist as Neumann bound her hands in front of her. Then he bound her feet, making sure the knot was not too tight. When he finished, he carried her to the van and lifted her inside.

There was no sign of life on the track to the village. Obviously the gunshots had gone unnoticed in Hampton Sands. They crossed the bridge and drove along the darkened street. Catherine sat next to Neumann, silent, reloading her Mauser.

London

THE submarine's movements had been puzzling Arthur Braithwaite for weeks. *U-509* seemed to be on an aimless patrol of the North Sea, sailing nowhere in particular, going for long periods of time without contacting BdU. When it did check in, it reported a position off the British coastline near Spurn Head.

Braithwaite's aide returned with the file. "Here we are, sir."

Equipped with near-perfect recall, Braithwaite had memorized the biography of every Kapitänleutnant of the U-bootewaffe. Now, instead of taking the file, he began to recite the contents. "Captain's name is Max Hoffman, if I remember correctly. Knight's Cross in 1942, oak leaves a year later."

"Right, sir. Pinned on by the Führer himself."

"Served on Canaris's staff in Berlin before the war."

The aide thumbed through the file. "Yes, here it is, sir. Assigned to Abwehr headquarters, '38 to '39."

Braithwaite was staring at the map table again. "Patrick, if you had an important spy that needed a lift out of Britain, wouldn't you prefer to have an old friend doing the driving?"

"Indeed, sir."

"Ring Vicary at MI Five. I think we'd better have a chat."

CHAPTER NINE

London

ALFRED Vicary was standing before an eight-foot-high map of the British Isles, chain-smoking and drinking wretched tea. "The tracking room says *U-509* has been moving in and out of the waters off Lincolnshire for a couple of weeks now," he said to Boothby, who had come downstairs to join him. "If we pour our men and resources into Lincolnshire, we stand a good chance of stopping them. What's the largest town up there?"

"Grimsby, I'd say."

"How long do you think it would take me to get up there?"

"I'm sure the RAF could have you up there in an hour or so. There's a small base outside Grimsby you could use as your command post. But it's an awful night for flying."

"I realize that, but I'm certain I could do a better job if I were there." Vicary turned from the map and looked at Boothby. "And there's something else. They haven't used their radio to tell Berlin what happened in London today. If we're able to stop them before they send a message, perhaps I can send it for them."

"Devise some explanation for their decision to flee London that bolsters the belief in Kettledrum?"

"Exactly. I'd like to take a couple of men with me—Clive Roach, Harry Dalton if he's up to it."

Boothby hesitated. "And I think you should take Peter Jordan."

"Jordan!"

"Look at it from the other side of the looking glass. If Jordan has been deceived and betrayed, wouldn't he want to be there to watch Catherine Blake's demise? I know I certainly would. I'd want to pull the trigger myself. And the Germans have to think that too. We have to do anything we can to make them believe in the illusion of Kettledrum."

Vicary thought of the empty file in Registry.

The telephone rang. It was one of the department operators. "Professor Vicary, I have a trunk call from a Chief Superintendent Perkin in Norfolk. He says it's quite urgent."

"Put him through."

Moments later Perkin was explaining that one of his constables—a man by the name of Thomasson who supervised a handful of small villages along the Norfolk coast—had just found two bodies in a barn outside a place called Hampton Sands. "The victims are both local men, Martin Colville and Sean Dogherty," said Perkin. "Thomasson found Dogherty's wife, Mary, bound and gagged in the cottage. She was hysterical. She told Thomasson quite a tale."

"Nothing will surprise me, Superintendent. Please continue."

"Mrs. Dogherty says her husband had been spying for the Germans. She says a couple of weeks ago the Germans dropped an agent named Horst Neumann onto the beach. He had been living with them and traveling regularly to London."

"What happened tonight?"

"Mrs. Dogherty's not sure exactly. She heard gunshots, ran out to the barn, and found the bodies. The German told her that Colville burst in on them, and that's when the shooting started."

"Was there a woman with Neumann?"

"Yes. Also, Colville's daughter, Jenny, is missing. Mrs. Dogherty is afraid the Germans found the girl and took her with them."

"Does Mrs. Dogherty know where they were headed?"

"No, but she says they're driving a van—black perhaps."

"Where's Constable Thomasson?"

"He's still on the line from a public house in Hampton Sands."

"Was there any sign of a radio in the cottage or the barn?"

"Hold on. Let me ask him."

Vicary could hear Perkin's muffled voice asking the question.

"He says there's a suitcase filled with something that looked like a wireless. It was destroyed by a shotgun blast."

"Superintendent, I want you to tell absolutely no one about what happened tonight. There is to be no mention of German agents in any report on this affair. Is that clear?"

"Yes, sir."

"I'm going to send a team of my men to Norfolk to assist you. For now, leave Mary Dogherty and those bodies where they are." Vicary looked at the map again. "We suspect those fugitives are heading directly your way. We believe their ultimate destination is the Lincolnshire coast."

"I've called in all my men. We're blocking all the major roads."

"Keep this office informed of every development. And good luck."

Vicary rang off and turned to Boothby. "They've killed two people, they probably have a hostage, and they're making a run for the Lincolnshire coast." Vicary smiled wolfishly. "And it looks as if they've lost their second radio."

Lincolnshire

TWO hours after leaving Hampton Sands, Horst Neumann and Catherine Blake were beginning to have serious doubts about their chances of making the rendezvous with the submarine in time. To escape the Norfolk coast, Neumann retraced his course, climbing into the hills in the heart of Norfolk, then following thin ribbons of road through the heathland and the darkened villages. The journey across the southern edge of the Wash was a nightmare. Wind poured in from the North Sea and whipped over the marshes and the dikes. The rain increased. Neumann hunched forward mile after mile, gripping the wheel. Catherine sat next to him reading Dogherty's old map by the light of her torch. They spoke in German.

Cleethorpes, where their boat was waiting for them, lay next to the port of Grimsby, at the mouth of the Humber. Neumann assumed there would be roadblocks on all major roads near the coastline. He decided to take the A16 halfway to Cleethorpes, then switch to a smaller road. He pushed the van hard through the rain.

Catherine switched off the blackout torch, sat back, and closed her eyes. The rocking of the van lulled her; then fatigue overtook her and she was asleep. She began to dream. And then someone was calling her name. "Catherine. . . . Catherine . . . wake up."

Horst Neumann shook her once more, violently, and shouted, "Catherine. Wake up. We're in trouble!"

IT WAS three a.m. when the Lysander broke through the thick clouds and bumped to a landing at the small RAF base outside Grimsby. A crewman opened the cabin door, and Alfred Vicary, Harry Dalton, Clive Roach, and Peter Jordan climbed down. Two men were waiting for them—a young, square-shouldered RAF officer and a bluff, pockmarked man in a raincoat.

The RAF man stuck out his hand. "Squadron leader Edmund Hughes. This is Chief Superintendent Roger Lockwood of the Lincolnshire County Constabulary. Come inside the operations hut. We've set up a makeshift command post for you."

They went inside. It was a small room with a desk, a wireless, and two battered telephones. "It will do just fine," Vicary said.

Chief Superintendent Lockwood stepped forward. "We've got men on every major road between here and the Wash," he said. "Roadblocks at four junctions. My best men, patrol cars, vans, and weapons."

"Very good. What about the coastline itself?"

"I've got a man on every quay along the Lincolnshire coast and the Humber. If they try to steal a boat, I'll know about it. The open beaches are another story. I don't have unlimited resources. I lost a lot of lads to the army, same as everybody else. But I know these waters, and I wouldn't want to head out to sea tonight in any boat I could launch from a beach."

"This weather may be the best friend we've got."

"Aye. One other thing, Major Vicary. Do we still need to pretend these are just a pair of ordinary criminals you're after?"

"Actually, Chief Superintendent, we do indeed."

NEUMANN had planned to leave the A16 just outside the town of Louth to take a smaller B road to the coast. There was just one problem. Half the police in Louth were standing in the junction. Neumann could see at least four men. As he approached, they waved their torches for him to stop.

Catherine was awake now, startled. "What's going on?"

"End of the line, I'm afraid," Neumann said, bringing the van to a halt. "No talking our way out of this."

Catherine picked up her Mauser. "Who said anything about talking?" she said.

One of the constables stepped forward, carrying a shotgun, and pulled open Neumann's door, leveling the shotgun at his face. "All right. Put your hands up and get out of the van. Nice and slow."

Jenny Colville sat in the back of the van, hands and feet bound, mouth gagged. Her wrists hurt. So did her neck and her back. She had been sitting on the floor for hours.

She could see two policemen in front of the van, and outside, near the back, she could hear the voices of at least two more. She knew that Neumann and the woman would kill the policemen, just like they had killed her father and Sean.

She had to warn the policemen. But how? She couldn't speak. She could do only one thing. She raised her legs and kicked the side of the van as hard as she could.

The officer standing near Catherine's door turned his head toward the sound. Catherine raised her Mauser and shot him through the window. Neumann knocked the shotgun away from the second constable with a sweep of his hand. Catherine turned and fired through the open door. The bullet struck the constable in the center of the forehead.

Neumann tumbled from the door and landed in the road. One of the officers at the rear of the van fired over his head. Neumann shot him in the heart. The fourth constable turned and started running into the darkness. Neumann took careful aim and fired twice.

Catherine opened the rear doors of the van. Jenny, eyes wide with terror, raised her hands to cover her head. Catherine lifted the gun into the air and struck Jenny's face. A deep gash opened over her eye. Catherine said, "Unless you want to end up like them, don't ever try anything like that again."

The police van was parked a few yards away. Neumann lifted Jenny and laid her in the back. Then, together with Catherine, he placed the bodies of the dead constables in the van he'd been driving. The idea had come to him immediately. He would hide the bodies and the stolen van out of sight and drive the police van to the coast. According to the map, it was another thirty miles to Cleethorpes. For the first time since spotting the MI5 men in London, Neumann allowed himself to imagine they just might make it after all.

ALFRED Vicary paced in the hut at the RAF base outside Grimsby. Harry Dalton, Peter Jordan, Clive Roach, and Superintendent Lockwood sat around smoking.

Desperate to do something, Vicary picked up the telephone and asked to be connected to the submarine tracking room in London. Arthur Braithwaite came on the line.

Vicary asked, "Anything, Commander?"

"The navy is moving a corvette—number 745—into the area as we speak. It'll be off Spurn Head within the hour to commence search operations. The coastguard is handling things closer to shore. The RAF is putting up planes at first light."

"Instruct the navy and the RAF to conduct the search as discreetly as possible. Try to make it all look routine."

"I'll pass it up the line. Try to relax, Major Vicary. If your spies try to reach that submarine tonight, we'll stop them."

A STIFF wind drove rain across the Cleethorpes waterfront as Neumann climbed out of the police van. In the faint predawn light he could see a quay and several fishing boats tied up there. They had made excellent time up the coast. Twice they were waved through roadblocks with no question, thanks to the police van.

There was a wooden exterior staircase to Jack Kincaid's flat over the garage. Neumann walked up the stairs and rapped softly. There was no answer. He tried the latch; it was unlocked. He opened the door and was struck by the smell of alcohol. He tried the light switch, but nothing happened. He switched on his torch. The beam caught the figure of a large man sleeping on a bare mattress. Neumann nudged the man with his boot. "You Jack Kincaid?"

"Yeah. Who are you?"

"James Porter. You're supposed to give me a lift in your boat."

"Oh, yes, yes." Kincaid tried to sit up, but couldn't.

"Which boat is yours, Jack?" Neumann asked.

"The *Camilla*." Kincaid was passing out again.

"You don't mind if I just borrow her for a bit, do you, Jack?" Kincaid didn't answer, just started snoring heavily.

Neumann went out and got back inside the van. "Our captain is in no condition to drive," he told Catherine. "Drunk out of his mind. His boat is the *Camilla*. It must be down there on the quay."

"There's something else down there. You'll see in a minute."

Neumann watched as a constable stepped into view. "They must be watching the entire coast," he said.

"It's a shame. Another needless casualty."

"Let's get it over with. What about Jenny? I want to leave her here. She's no use to us now."

"She comes with us. If they find her, she can tell them a great deal. And if we have a hostage, they'll think twice." Catherine turned around and, in English, said to Jenny, "No more heroics. If you make one move, I'll shoot you."

Neumann shook his head, said nothing. He started the motor and drove down to the quay.

"I THINK you need to hear this for yourself, Major Vicary."

Vicary took the telephone receiver Lockwood handed to him. A fisherman named Ian McMann was on the line from Cleethorpes.

"Two people just stole Jack Kincaid's fishing boat and are making for open water," Ian McMann said.

Vicary snapped, "My Lord! Didn't we have a man there?"

"You did," McMann said. "He's floating in the water right now with a bullet through his heart."

Vicary swore softly, then said, "How many were there?"

"At least two that I saw, a man and a woman."

"Tell me about the boat they stole."

"The *Camilla*. She's in bad shape. And no radio. I wouldn't want to be aboard her heading out in a blow like this."

Vicary rang off. Lockwood said, "Well, the good news is we know exactly where they are now. They have to slip through the mouth of the Humber before they can reach open water. Get that corvette in position off Spurn Head, and they'll never make it through."

"I'd feel better if we had our own boat in the water."

"Actually, that can be arranged. The constabulary keeps a small police boat on the river—the *Rebecca*. She's in Grimsby now. If we get under way immediately, we should be able to overtake them."

"Does the *Rebecca* have a radio?"

"Aye. We'll be able to talk to you right here."

"How about weapons?"

"I can pick up a couple of old rifles from the lockup in the Grimsby police station. They'll do the trick."

"Now all you need is a crew," said Vicary. "Take my men with you. I'll stay here so I can remain in contact with London."

Lockwood clapped Vicary on the back and went out. Clive Roach, Harry Dalton, and Peter Jordan followed him.

NEUMANN stayed between the channel markers as the *Camilla* sliced through the choppy waters at the mouth of the Humber. Catherine stood next to him in the wheelhouse. The boat was about forty feet, with a small cabin aft, where Neumann had left Jenny. Off the portside he could see waves breaking over Spurn Head. Spurn Light was blacked out. Neumann put the boat on a heading due east, opened the throttle full, and headed out to sea.

CHAPTER TEN

The North Sea, off Spurn Head

THE *Rebecca* was about thirty feet in length, with a small open wheelhouse amidships, barely big enough for two men to stand shoulder to shoulder. The four men clambered on board, and Lockwood guided the craft into the channel, then opened the throttle. The slender prow sliced through the wind-driven chop. The silhouette of Spurn Light was visible off the portside. The sea was empty before them.

Five miles due east, corvette Number 745 was maneuvering through rough seas. The captain stood on the bridge, glasses raised to his eyes. It was useless. Along with the dark and the curtain of rain, a fog had rolled in. They could pass within a hundred yards of a U-boat and never see it.

THE *Camilla,* though Horst Neumann did not realize it, was seven miles due east of Spurn Head. But the wind and the current, both beating down from the north, kept nudging the boat off course. Neumann struggled to keep them on an easterly heading.

Miraculously, he thought they might actually make it. It was five thirty a.m. They still had thirty minutes left before the window closed and the U-boat turned away.

They had just one problem: The *Camilla* had no radio. Which left them no means of signaling the U-boat. Neumann had only one option—to switch on the boat's running lights. Of course, if the U-boat could see them, so could any British ships in the vicinity.

Neumann threw a switch, and the *Camilla* came alive with light.

JENNY Colville was paralyzed with seasickness. She wanted to die. She was desperate for fresh air. And then there was the noise—the constant deafening rumble of the boat's engine just beneath her.

HORST NEUMANN THOUGHT it might be a hallucination. The glimpse had been brief—just an instant before the *Camilla* plunged downward into yet another trough of seawater. It was then that he spotted the unmistakable silhouette of a German U-boat.

IT WAS Peter Jordan, on the pitching aft deck of the *Rebecca,* who spotted the U-boat first. Lockwood saw it a few seconds later and then spotted the running lights of the *Camilla,* about four hundred yards off the U-boat's starboard side and closing quickly. Lockwood set the *Rebecca* on a collision course with the *Camilla* and picked up the handset to raise Alfred Vicary.

VICARY snatched up the receiver of the open phone line to the tracking room. "Commander Braithwaite, are you there?"

"Yes. And I could hear the entire thing over the line. I'm afraid we've got a problem. Corvette 745 is a mile due south of the U-boat's position. I've radioed the captain, and he's making for the scene now. But if the *Camilla* is really only four hundred yards away from the submarine, they'll get there first."

"Blast!"

"You do have one other asset, Mr. Vicary—the *Rebecca.* Your men have to slow the *Camilla* down until 745 can intervene."

Vicary set down the telephone and picked up the radio handset. "Superintendent Lockwood, listen carefully. Help is on the way, but in the meantime, I want you to ram that fishing boat."

ALL of them heard it—Lockwood, Harry, Roach, and Jordan— for they were all pressed around the cabin, sheltering from the weather. They looked at each other, saying nothing. Finally Lockwood said, "There are life jackets in that locker behind you. And bring out the rifles. I have a feeling we may need them."

KAPITÄNLEUTNANT Max Hoffman, standing on the bridge of *U-509,* spotted the *Rebecca* approaching fast. "We've got company," he said to the first officer. "Civilian craft, four men on board."

"I see them, Herr Kaleu."

"I'd say they're the opposition. Give them a warning shot across their bow. I don't want needless bloodshed. If they persist, fire directly on the craft. But at the waterline, not the cabin."

THE first shot from *U-509* sailed well off the *Rebecca*'s prow. The second, fired ten seconds later, came much closer.

Lockwood turned to Harry and shouted, "I'd say that's the last warning we get. The next one is going to blow us right out of the water. It's your call, but we're no help to anyone if we're dead."

Harry shouted, "Turn away!"

Lockwood turned the *Rebecca* hard to port and circled around. Harry looked back at the U-boat. The *Camilla* was a hundred yards away and closing. Dammit! he thought. Where's that corvette?

As SHE peered through the starboard porthole, Jenny heard the boom of the U-boat's deck gun and saw a splash off the bow of a second boat. She thought, Thank God! I'm not alone after all. But the U-boat fired again, and a few seconds later she saw the little boat turn away, and her spirits sank.

Then she steeled herself and thought, They're German agents. They've killed my father and five other people tonight, and they're about to get away with it. I have to do something to stop them.

But what could she do? She was alone, and her hands and feet were tied. And then she thought, Yes, that's it!

She pushed away the coiled lines and tarpaulins she had been sitting on. And there it was—a door built into the floor of the hold. She managed to open it and was immediately overwhelmed by the thunderous noise and heat of the *Camilla*'s engine.

Jenny knew nothing of engines. Once, Sean tried to explain to her the repairs he was making on his rattletrap van. Something to do with fuel lines and fuel pump. Surely this engine needed fuel to run. Cut the fuel supply, and it would die.

She looked closely at the motor. Several metal lines ran across the top and converged on the side. Could those be fuel lines?

She needed tools. She looked around and spotted a metal toolbox at the end of the cabin. She crawled forward. She opened the box, removed a pair of bladed pliers and a hammer, and crawled back. Turning the pliers toward her wrists, she started hacking through the rope. It took about a minute to free her hands. Then she cut the rope around her ankles.

She picked up the hammer and smashed the first of the fuel lines. It severed, leaking diesel. Quickly she brought the hammer down several more times until the last fuel line was ruptured and the engine died.

Jenny had just closed the hatch over the crippled engine when the door flew open and Neumann stormed down the companionway, his face wild. He saw that Jenny's hands and feet were no longer tied. He shouted, "Jenny, what have you done?"

The boat, now powerless, skidded down the side of a wave.

Neumann leaned down and opened the engine hatch. Jenny raised the hammer and hit him in the back of the head as hard as she could. Neumann fell to the floor, blood pouring from his scalp.

Jenny was afraid she had killed him. He lay very still for a moment, then stirred and forced himself to stand. He was very unsteady, holding on to the side of the cabin. Blood poured from the wound into his face. He said, "Stay down here. If you come up onto the deck, she'll kill you. Do as I say, Jenny."

Neumann struggled up the companionway. Catherine looked at him, alarm on her face.

"I hit my head when the boat pitched. The motor's dead."

His torch was next to the wheel. He picked it up and walked out onto the deck. He aimed the light at the conning tower of the U-boat and flashed a distress signal. The submarine was coming toward them with agonizing slowness.

Catherine joined him on the deck. She couldn't quite believe it. They were about to step onto the deck of a U-boat and sail away. Six long, painfully lonely years—over at last. The emotion of the moment overtook her. She let out a joyous, childlike scream and turned her face to the rain, waving her arms at the U-boat.

The nose of the submarine nudged against the *Camilla*'s prow. A boarding party scrambled down the U-boat's deck toward them. She put her arms around Neumann and held him tightly.

"We made it," she said. "We're going home."

At that moment the captain of corvette 745 gave the order to fire. Seconds later the corvette's deck cannon opened up.

Neumann heard the shots. The first rounds sailed overhead. The second burst clattered against the side of the U-boat. The rescue party fell flat on the deck to avoid the fire as the rounds moved from the U-boat to the *Camilla*. There was nowhere on the foredeck of the fishing boat to take cover. The gunfire found Catherine, instantly shredding her body.

Neumann scrambled forward and tried to reach the U-boat. A round hit him in the head, and there was darkness.

Within a matter of seconds *U-509* was racing from the scene. Two minutes later it submerged beneath the surface of the North Sea and was gone. The *Camilla,* alone on the sea, foundered.

The mood aboard the *Rebecca* was euphoric. The four men embraced as they watched the U-boat roar away. Harry Dalton raised Vicary and told him the news. Vicary made two calls, the first to the submarine tracking room to thank Arthur Braithwaite, the second to Sir Basil Boothby to tell him that it was finally over.

JENNY Colville felt the *Camilla* pitch about wildly. Climbing the companionway was nearly impossible. Finally she reached the deck. Jenny looked toward the prow and saw the mangled bodies. She retched and looked away. She saw the U-boat diving in the distance, disappearing below the surface of the sea. On the other side of the boat she saw a small gray warship coming toward her. A second boat—the one she had seen earlier—was approaching fast.

She waved and yelled and started to cry. She wanted to tell them that *she* had done it. *She* was the one who disabled the motor so the spies couldn't make it to the U-boat. She was filled with an enormous, fierce pride.

The *Camilla* rose on a gigantic roller. As the wave passed beneath the boat, it pitched wildly to the portside. Then it fell downward into the trough and rolled over onto its starboard side, throwing Jenny across the deck and into the sea.

THE *Rebecca* arrived first. Harry threw a life ring overboard. They had seen Jenny twice fight her way up for air and disappear below the surface. Now there was nothing. Jordan leaned over the prow, looking for any sign of the girl. Then he stood and, with no warning, dived into the water.

Jordan surfaced and removed his life vest. He filled his lungs with air and was gone for what seemed to Harry like a minute. The sea was beating against the *Camilla,* driving her toward the *Rebecca.* Harry waved his arms at Lockwood in the wheelhouse, calling, "Back off a few feet! The *Camilla's* right on top of us."

Jordan finally surfaced, Jenny in his arms. She was unconscious, her head to one side. Jordan untied the line from the life ring and tied it around Jenny beneath her arms. He gave Harry a thumbs-up sign, and Harry pulled her through the waves to the *Rebecca.* Clive Roach helped him lift her onto the deck.

Jordan was furiously treading water, waves washing over his face, and he looked exhausted from the cold. Harry quickly untied the line from Jenny and threw it overboard toward him—just as the *Camilla* finally capsized and dragged Peter Jordan under the sea.

CHAPTER ELEVEN

Berlin: April 1944

KURT Vogel was cooling his heels in Walter Schellenberg's luxuriously appointed anteroom. It had been three hours since Schellenberg had summoned Vogel to his office for an urgent consultation about "that unfortunate business in Britain," as he habitually referred to Vogel's blown operation. Vogel didn't mind the wait; he didn't really have anything better to do. Since Canaris had been sacked and the Abwehr absorbed by the SS, German military intelligence had become a ship without a rudder, just when Hitler needed it most. Morale was so low, many officers were volunteering for the Russian front.

Vogel had other plans.

One of Schellenberg's aides came out and waved him inside. The office was as big as a Gothic cathedral, with magnificent paintings and tapestries hanging on the walls. Schellenberg smiled warmly, pumped Vogel's hand, and gestured for him to sit down.

Though Schellenberg and Himmler had been plotting against Canaris for years, it was the disastrous conclusion of Vogel's operation in London that had finally done in the Old Fox. Two Abwehr agents—Horst Neumann and Catherine Blake—had been killed within sight of the U-boat. They had been unable to transmit a final message explaining why they had decided to flee England, leaving Vogel with no way to judge the authenticity of the information Catherine Blake had stolen on Operation Mulberry. Hitler exploded when he heard the news. He immediately fired Canaris and placed the Abwehr in the hands of Walter Schellenberg.

Somehow Vogel survived. Schellenberg and Himmler suspected the operation had been compromised by Canaris. Vogel—like Catherine Blake and Horst Neumann—was an innocent victim of the Old Fox's treachery.

Vogel had another theory. He suspected all the information stolen by Catherine Blake had been planted by British intelligence. He suspected Mulberry was not an antiaircraft complex destined for the Pas de Calais, but an artificial harbor bound for the beaches of Normandy. He also suspected all the other agents sent to Britain were bad—that they had been captured and forced to cooperate with British intelligence, probably from the outset of the war.

Vogel, however, lacked the evidence to substantiate any of this, and he did not intend to bring charges he could not prove. Besides, even if he had the proof, he wasn't sure he would have given it to the likes of Schellenberg and Himmler.

Remaining at the Abwehr and cooperating with the new regime

had its advantages. Vogel had quietly slipped his wife and daughters into Switzerland. He had also moved enough money out of Germany to enable them to live comfortably for a couple of years after the war. He had another asset—the information he possessed in his mind. The British and Americans, he felt certain, would pay handsomely in money and protection.

"So," Schellenberg said. "The reason I asked you to come today, Captain Vogel. Some exciting news from our source inside MI Five." He produced a signal flimsy with a flourish. Reading it, Vogel thought, Remarkable, the subtlety of the manipulation. He finished and handed the flimsy across the desk to Schellenberg.

Schellenberg said, "For MI Five to take disciplinary action against a man who is a personal friend and confidant of Winston Churchill is extraordinary. And the source is impeccable. I recruited him. It proves the information stolen by your agent was genuine."

"Yes, I believe you're right, Herr Brigadeführer."

"The Führer needs to be told of this right away. He's meeting with the Japanese ambassador at Berchtesgaden tonight to brief him on preparations for the invasion. I'm sure he'll want to pass this along."

Vogel nodded.

"I'd like you to come with me and personally brief the Führer. After all, it was your operation to begin with. And besides, he's taken a liking to you. You have a very bright future, Captain Vogel."

"Thank you for the offer, Herr Brigadeführer, but I think *you* should tell the Führer about the news."

"Are you certain, Captain Vogel?"

"Yes, Herr Brigadeführer, I'm quite certain."

Oyster Bay, Long Island

IT WAS the first fine day of spring—warm sunshine, a soft wind from the Sound. The day before had been cold and damp. Dorothy Lauterbach had worried that the memorial service would be ruined by the cold, but by midmorning the sun had burned away the last of the clouds, and the North Shore sparkled.

Shepherd Ramsey had brought Peter Jordan's things from London: his clothes, his books, his letters, the personal papers that the security men had not seized. Ramsey had leafed through the letters to make certain there was no mention of the woman Peter was seeing in London before his death.

The graveside ceremony was packed. There was no body to bury, but they laid a small headstone next to Margaret's. Billy stood next to Jane, and Jane leaned against Walker Hardegen. Bratton Lauterbach accepted the American flag from a representative of the navy.

One man stood slightly apart from the rest, head bowed respectfully. He was tall and thin, and his double-breasted suit was a little too heavy for warm spring weather. Walker Hardegen was the only person present who recognized him. He was Hardegen's control officer, and the name he used was Broome.

SHEPHERD Ramsey carried the letter from the man in London. Dorothy and Bratton slipped into the library and read it during the reception. Dorothy read it first, hands trembling. Her eyes were damp when she finished reading, but she did not cry. She handed the letter to Bratton, who wept as he read.

Dear Billy,

It is with great sadness that I write this letter. I had the pleasure of working with your father for only a very brief period, but I found him to be one of the most remarkable men I have ever met. He was involved in one of the most vital projects of the war. Because of the requirements of security, however, you may never be told what he did. But I can tell you this—it will save countless lives and make it possible for the people of Europe to be rid of the Nazis once and for all. Your father truly gave his life so that others may live. He was a hero. But nothing he accomplished gave him as much satisfaction as you. I was never fortunate enough to be blessed with a son. Listening to your father talk about you, I realized the depth of my misfortune.

Sincerely,
Alfred Vicary

Dorothy went to the window. Beyond the crowd she could see Billy, Jane, and Walker sitting on the grass down by the dock. Jane and Walker had become more than friends, and Jane was actually talking about marriage. Dorothy thought, Wouldn't it be perfect. Billy would have a real family again. There was a neatness to it, a closure that Dorothy found comforting. Life goes on, she told herself. Margaret and Peter are gone, but life most definitely goes on.

Gloucestershire, England

TECHNICALLY, it was an administrative leave pending the findings of the internal inquiry. Alfred Vicary understood that was gobbledygook for a sacking.

Perversely, he took Basil Boothby's advice and fled to his aunt Matilda's house—he could never get used to the notion it was his—to sort himself out. The first days of his exile were appalling. He missed the camaraderie of MI5. He missed his wretched little office. He even found himself missing his camp bed, for he had lost the gift of sound sleep.

He endured a long, blue period of inactivity. But in the spring he focused his energy on his new home. The watchers who paid the occasional visit looked on in horror as Vicary attacked his garden with pruning sheers and a sickle.

The head of his department at University College sent him a letter wondering when he might be coming back. Vicary tore the letter in half and burned it in the fireplace. He went to London just once, in the first week of June, when Sir Basil summoned him to hear the results of the internal review.

"Hello, Alfred!" Sir Basil called out as Vicary was shown into his office. Boothby was standing at the precise center of the floor, as though he wanted room to maneuver in all directions. The director general was sitting on the handsome couch. Boothby shook Vicary's hand a little too affectionately and laid a big paw on his shoulder. Then, with considerable ceremony, he put the review board's final report on the table. Vicary refused to look at it directly.

Boothby took too much pleasure in explaining to Vicary that he was not permitted to read a review of his own operation. Instead, Boothby showed Vicary a sanitized letter purporting to "summarize" the report. Vicary held it in both hands so it would not shake while he read it. It was a vile, obscene document, but challenging it now would do no good. He handed it back to Boothby, shook his hand and then the director general's, and went out.

Vicary spent the night at his house in Chelsea. He awakened at dawn, rain rattling against the windows. It was June 6. He switched on the BBC to listen to the news and heard that the invasion was on. He caught the first train back to Gloucestershire.

Gradually, by summer, his days took on a careful routine. He rose early and read until lunch, which he took each day in the village at the Eight Bells. Then he would set off for his daily forced march over the breezy footpaths around the village. By August he was walking ten miles each afternoon.

He was not aware of the exact day it happened—the day it all faded from his conscious thoughts. His cramped office, the clatter of the teleprinters, the crazy lexicon of the place: Double Cross, Mulberry, Phoenix, Kettledrum . . . Alice Simpson started coming at the weekend and stayed for an entire week in early August.

On the last day of summer he was overcome by the gentle melancholia that afflicts country people when the warm weather is ending. It was a glorious dusk, the horizon streaked in purple and orange, the first bite of autumn in the air. He remembered an evening like this half a lifetime ago, when Brendan Evans taught him to ride a motorcycle. It was not quite cold enough for fires, but from his hilltop perch he could see the chimneys of the village gently smoking and taste the sharp scent of green wood on the air.

He saw it then, played out on the hillsides like the solution of a chess problem. He could see the lines of attack, the preparation, the deception. Nothing had been as it seemed.

Vicary rushed back to the cottage, called the office, and asked for Boothby. By some miracle Boothby answered his own telephone.

Vicary identified himself. Boothby expressed genuine pleasure at hearing his voice. Vicary assured him he was fine.

"I want to talk to you," Vicary said, "about Kettledrum."

There was silence on the line; then Boothby said, "You can't come here any longer, Alfred. You're *persona non grata*. So I suppose I'll have to come to you."

"Fine. And don't pretend you don't know how to find me, because I see your watchers stalking me."

"Tomorrow midday," Boothby said, and rang off.

Boothby arrived promptly at noon in an official Humber, dressed for the country in tweeds. It had rained overnight. Vicary dug out a pair of Wellingtons from the cellar for Boothby, and they walked like old chums around a meadow dotted with shorn sheep. After a while Vicary said, "None of it was real, was it? Jordan, Catherine Blake—it was all bad right from the beginning."

Boothby smiled seductively. "Not quite, Alfred. But something like that. It was the nature of Operation Mulberry that presented us with the problem. Tens of thousands of people were involved. Of course, the vast majority had no idea what they were working on. Still, the potential for security leaks was tremendous. The components were so large they had to be built right out in the open. We knew the Germans would be able to photograph them from the air. We knew one decent spy poking around could probably figure out what we were up to."

Vicary watched Boothby as he spoke. All the bombast, all the fidgeting, was gone. Sir Basil was calm and collected. Vicary had the sickening realization he had underestimated Boothby's intelligence from the beginning. He was also struck by his use of the words *we* and *us*. Boothby was a member of the club; Vicary had only been allowed to press his nose against the glass for a brief interval.

"We had to assume that the Germans would eventually find out what we were up to," Boothby resumed. "Our solution was to steal the secret of Mulberry for them and try to control the game." Boothby looked at Vicary. "All right, Alfred, let's hear it. I want to know how much of it you've really figured out."

"Walker Hardegen—I'd say it all started with Hardegen."

"Very good, Alfred. But how?"

"Walker Hardegen was a wealthy banker and businessman, ultraconservative, anticommunist, and probably a little anti-Semitic. He was Ivy League, and he knew half the people in Washington. His business regularly took him to Berlin. He spoke perfect German—probably admired some things the Nazis were doing. I'd say during one of his visits he came to the attention of the Abwehr."

"Bravo, Alfred."

"Okay. I suppose they soft-pedaled it. Said he would really be helping in the struggle against international communism. I have a question. Was he already an American agent at this point?"

"No." Boothby smiled. "Remember, this was early in the game, 1937. The Americans weren't terribly sophisticated then. They *did* know, however, that the Abwehr was active in the United States. Roosevelt had ordered Hoover to crack down. In 1939 Hardegen was photographed meeting in New York with an Abwehr agent. Two months later they saw him with an agent in Panama. Hoover wanted to arrest him and put him on trial. Luckily, MI Six had set up its office in New York by then. They convinced Hoover that Hardegen was more use to us still in the game than sitting in prison."

"So who ran him, us or the Americans?"

"It was a joint project, really. We fed the Germans a steady stream of excellent material through Hardegen, top-grade stuff. Hardegen's stock soared in Berlin. In the meantime, every aspect of his life was placed under a microscope, including his relationship with the Lauterbach family and a brilliant engineer named Peter Jordan."

"So in 1943," Vicary said, "when the decision was made to invade at Normandy with the help of an artificial harbor, British and American intelligence approached Peter Jordan and asked him to go to work for us."

"Yes. October 1943, to be precise."

"He was perfect," Vicary said. "He was exactly the type of engineer needed for the project, and he was well known in his field. The death of his wife also made him personally vulnerable. So late in 1943 you had Hardegen meet with his Abwehr control officer and tell him all about Peter Jordan. How much did you tell them then?"

"Only that Jordan was working on a large construction project connected with the invasion. We also hinted about his vulnerability, as you put it. The Abwehr bit."

"So the entire thing was an elaborate ruse to foist false documents on the Abwehr. And Jordan was the proverbial goat."

"Exactly. The first documents were ambiguous by design. They were open to interpretation and debate. The Phoenix units could be components of an artificial harbor or they could be an antiaircraft complex. We wanted the Germans to fight, to squabble. We also didn't want to make it too easy for them. Gradually, the Kettledrum documents painted a clear picture, and that picture was passed directly to Hitler."

"But why go to so much trouble? Why not just use one of the agents that had been turned? Or one of the fictitious agents?"

"Two reasons," Boothby said. "Number one, that's too easy. We wanted to make them work for it. We wanted to influence their thinking subtly. We wanted them to think *they* were the ones making the decision to target Jordan."

"Impressive," Vicary said. "The second reason?"

"The second reason is that we became aware late in 1943 that we had not accounted for all the German spies operating in Britain. We learned about Kurt Vogel and his network. But Vogel had taken such care in burying his agents that we couldn't locate them unless we brought them into the open. Remember, Bodyguard was about to go into full gear. We were going to bombard the Germans with a blizzard of false intelligence, but we knew there were live, active agents operating in the country. All of them had to be accounted for. Otherwise we could never be certain the Germans weren't receiving intelligence that contradicted Bodyguard."

"How did you know about Vogel's network?"

"We were told about it."

"By whom?"

Boothby walked a few paces in silence, contemplating the muddy toes of his Wellington boots. "We were told about the network by Wilhelm Canaris," he said finally.

"Canaris?"

"Through one of his emissaries, actually. In 1943, late summer. This probably will come as a shock to you, but Canaris was a leader of the Schwarze Kapelle. He wanted support from Menzies and the Intelligence Service to help him overthrow Hitler and end the war. In a gesture of goodwill he told Menzies about the existence of Vogel's network. Menzies informed the Security Service, and together we concocted a scheme called Kettledrum."

"Hitler's chief spy, a traitor. Remarkable. And you knew all this. You knew it the night I was assigned the case. That briefing on the invasion and deception plans . . . It was designed to ensure my blind loyalty. To motivate me, to manipulate me."

"I'm afraid so, yes."

"So the operation had two goals: deceive them about Mulberry and at the same time draw Vogel's agents into the open."

"Yes," Boothby said.

"So why didn't Double Cross and Bodyguard collapse with the fall of Canaris?"

"Oh, Schellenberg was more interested in consolidating his empire than running a new crop of agents into England. In the meantime, the case officers at Abwehr headquarters went to great lengths to prove the agents operating inside Britain were genuine and productive. Quite simply, it was a matter of life and death for those case officers. If they admitted their agents were under British control, they would have been on the first train east. Or worse."

A cloud passed in front of the sun, and it became cold. "Did it all work?" Vicary asked, setting aside his seething emotions.

"Yes, it worked brilliantly."

"What about the Lord Haw-Haw broadcast?" Vicary had heard it himself, and it had sent a shiver through him. *We know exactly what you intend to do with those concrete units. . . .*

"It sent panic through the Supreme Allied Command. At least on the surface," Boothby added smugly. "A very small group of officers knew of the Kettledrum deception and realized this was just the last act. Eisenhower cabled Washington and requested fifty picket ships to rescue the crews in case the Mulberries were sunk during the journey across the Channel. We made sure the Germans knew this. Our double with a fictitious source inside SHAEF transmitted a report of Eisenhower's request to his Abwehr controller. Several days later the Japanese ambassador toured the coastal defenses and was briefed by Rundstedt. Rundstedt told him about the existence of the Mulberries and explained that an Abwehr agent had discovered they were antiaircraft gun towers. The ambassador cabled this information to his masters in Tokyo. That message, like all his other communications, was intercepted and decoded. At that moment we knew Kettledrum had worked."

"Who was the control officer?"

Boothby looked at Vicary. "Broome, of course."

"Who's Broome?"

"Broome is *Broome,* Alfred."

"Why was it necessary to deceive the case officer?"

Boothby smiled weakly. He stopped walking and stared at the clouds. "Looks like rain," he said. "Perhaps we should start heading back." They turned around and started walking. "We deceived you, Alfred, because we wanted it all to feel real to the other side. We wanted you to take the same steps you might take in a normal case."

"You *ran* me," Vicary snapped. "You ran me, just like any other agent. And when you sacked me, you told the Germans about it because you hoped that the sacrifice of a personal friend of Winston Churchill would bolster their belief in the Kettledrum material."

"Exactly. It was all part of the script. And it worked."

"Manipulative bastards," Vicary muttered. "But then I suppose I should consider myself lucky. I could be dead like the others. My Lord! Do you realize how many people died for the sake of your little game? Pope, Rose Morely, the Special Branch men at Earl's Court, the police officers at Louth and at Cleethorpes—"

"You're forgetting Peter Jordan."

"For heaven's sake, you killed your own agent."

"No, Alfred, *you* killed him. You're the one who sent him out on that boat. I rather liked it, I must admit. The man whose personal carelessness almost cost us the war dies saving the life of a young girl and atones for his sins. That's how Hollywood would have done it. And that's what the Germans think really happened. Besides, the number of lives lost pales in comparison to the slaughter that would have taken place if Rommel had been waiting for us at Normandy."

"I'm glad I'm out! I don't want any part of it. Not if it means doing things like that!"

They crested a last hill. Vicary's house appeared before them in the distance. He wanted to be rid of Boothby. He quickened his pace, pounding down the hill. Boothby, with his long body and athletic legs, struggled to keep pace.

"You don't really feel that way, Alfred. You liked it. You were seduced by it. You liked the manipulation and the deception. I know you miss it all desperately."

They passed through the gate into the drive, stopping at Boothby's Humber. The car's engine fired as Boothby opened the door.

"Who's Broome?" Vicary asked one last time.

Boothby's face darkened, as though a cloud had passed over it. "Broome is Brendan Evans, your old friend from Cambridge. He told us about that stunt you pulled to get into the Intelligence Corps in the First War. He also told us what happened in France. We knew what drove you and what motivated you. We had to— We were running you, after all."

Vicary felt his head beginning to throb. Then Boothby disappeared into his car and was gone.

London: May 1945

AT SIX o'clock that evening, Lillian Walford knocked gently on the office door and let herself inside without waiting for an answer. The professor was there, sitting in the window, his little body folded over an old manuscript.

"I'll be leaving now, Professor, if you've nothing else for me," she said, beginning the straightening of papers that always accompanied their Friday evening conversations.

"No. I'll be fine, thank you."

"You'd better be leaving soon, Professor, if you want to make your train." She removed his mackintosh from the hook on the back of the door, placed it on the chair next to his desk, then turned and walked toward the door. "Good night, Professor Vicary. Have a pleasant weekend."

"I intend to, thank you, Miss Walford. Good night."

Vicary telephoned Alice Simpson, and she agreed to come to the country the next morning. He looked at his watch; there was still time to make his train. He took a taxi to Paddington Station.

The train was crowded, but he found a seat next to the window in a compartment with a boyish-faced soldier clutching a cane.

He looked at the soldier and noticed he was wearing the insignia of the 2nd East York Regiment. Vicary knew the boy had been at Normandy—Sword Beach, to be precise—and he was lucky to be alive. The East Yorks had suffered heavy casualties during the first minutes of the invasion.

The soldier noticed Vicary looking at him, and he managed a brief smile. "Happened at Normandy. Barely made it out of the landing craft." He held up the cane. "Doctors say I'll need this for the rest of my life. How'd you get yours—the limp, that is?"

"The First War, France," Vicary said distantly.

"They bring you back for this lot?"

Vicary nodded. "A desk job in a very dull department of the War Office. Nothing important, really."

After a while the soldier slept. Once, in the passing fields, Vicary saw Boothby's face smiling at him, just for an instant. Then, as the darkness gathered, he saw his own reflection, riding silently next to him in the glass.

THE
CAT WHO
TAILED A
THIEF

LILIAN JACKSON BRAUN

Purloined money and pilfered keepsakes. What's next in the Far North town of Pickax? Is someone about to get away with the perfect crime?

Not likely.

Not when Pickax's famous sleuth, James Qwilleran, is on the case. And certainly not when Jim's purr-ceptive pussycats, Koko and Yum Yum, are ready to lend a helping paw.

ONE

IT WAS a strange winter in Moose County, four hundred miles north of everywhere. First, there was disagreement about the long-range weather forecast. The weatherman at the local radio station predicted a winter of zero temperature, daily snow, minus-sixty wind chill, and paralyzing blizzards—in other words, normal. On the other hand, farmers and woodsmen who observed the behavior of the fuzzy caterpillars insisted the winter would be mild. Bad news!

No one wanted a mild winter. Merchants had invested in large inventories of snowblowers, antifreeze, and long johns. The farmers themselves needed a heavy snow cover to ensure a good summer crop. Dogsledders and ice fishermen stood to lose a whole season of outdoor sport. As for the first annual Ice Festival, it would be doomed.

Throughout November, traditionally a month of natural disasters, the weather was disappointingly good, and the natives cursed the fuzzy caterpillars. Then, suddenly, in mid-December, temperatures plummeted and snow started to fall every day. In downtown Pickax, the county seat, the plows threw up the usual eight-foot walls of snow along curbs and around parking lots. Young people did their Christmas shopping on cross-country skis, and sleigh bells could be heard on Main Street.

The weather was only the first strange happening of the winter, however. In late December an outbreak of petty larceny dampened the holiday spirit in Pickax. Trivial items began to disappear from cars and public places, prompting the local newspaper to run an editorial advising residents to lock their cars, keep an eye on belongings, and stay alert.

Natives of Moose County were a stubborn, independent breed descended from early pioneers, and it would take more than an editorial in the *Moose County Something* to change their ways. Yet there was one prominent citizen who applauded the newspaper's warning.

Jim Qwilleran was not a native, but a transplant from Down Below, as the locals called the metropolitan cities to the south. Surprising circumstances had brought him to Pickax—population 3000—and he was surprisingly content with small-town life.

Qwilleran was a tall, well-built middle-aged man, with a luxuriant pepper-and-salt mustache and hair graying at the temples. If asked, he would say that he perceived himself as a former crime reporter and author of a book on urban crime; a writer of a twice-weekly column for the *Something;* a devoted friend of Polly Duncan, head of the Pickax Public Library; a protector and slave of two Siamese cats; and a fairly agreeable person blessed with many friends.

All of that would be true. He would not perceive himself, however, as the richest man in the northeast central United States, but that, too, would be true.

An enormous inheritance—the Klingenschoen fortune—had brought Qwilleran to this remote region. Yet he was uncomfortable with money, and he immediately consigned his billions to philanthropic purposes. For several years the Klingenschoen Foundation had been managed by a Chicago think tank, with little or no attention from James Mackintosh Qwilleran.

It was not only this generous gesture that caused him to be esteemed in Moose County. Admirers cited his entertaining column, Straight from the Qwill Pen, his amiable disposition and sense of humor, his sympathetic way of listening, and of course, his magnificent mustache with its drooping contours. Actually, there was more to that mustache than met the eye.

ON THE morning of December 23 Qwilleran said good-bye to the Siamese and gave instructions for their deportment in his absence. Their deep blue eyes gazed at him soberly. Did they know what he was saying? Or were they waiting patiently for him to leave so they could start their morning nap?

He was setting out to do his Christmas shopping, but first he had to hand in his copy at the newspaper office—a thousand words on Santa Claus for the Qwill Pen.

Arch Riker, his lifelong friend and fellow journalist, had followed him to Pickax to be publisher and editor in chief of the local paper. A paunchy, ruddy-faced man with thinning hair, he had realized his dream of running his own paper. And he had married the plump and congenial woman who wrote the food page.

"Mildred and I are expecting you and Polly to have Christmas dinner with us," he reminded Qwilleran.

"Turkey, I hope," Qwilleran replied on his way out, thinking of leftovers for his housemates.

Qwilleran then drove to Lois's Luncheonette, a hole-in-the-wall that had been serving comfort food to downtown workers for thirty years. Lois Inchpot was an imposing woman.

When Qwilleran entered, she was banging the old-fashioned cash register. "Hi, Mr. Q! Come on in. Sit anywhere that ain't sticky. My customers got bad aim with the syrup bottle."

"How's Lenny?" Qwilleran asked.

"That boy of mine!" she said proudly. "Nothin' stops him! He has mornin' classes at the college, and then he's found himself a swell part-time job, managin' the clubhouse at Indian Village."

"He's going to be a workaholic like his mother."

"Better'n takin' after his father. Done your Christmas shoppin', Mr. Q?"

"Don't rush me, Lois. It's only the twenty-third."

THE FIRST GIFT HE PURCHASED was a bottle of Scotch. He carried it in a brown paper bag under his folded jacket when he climbed the stairs to police headquarters at city hall. He was a frequent visitor, and the sergeant at the desk jerked his head toward the inner office, saying, "He's in."

Chief Andrew Brodie was a tough cop who resented civilian interference, and yet he had learned to appreciate the newsman's tips and opinions that sometimes helped crack a case. On the job he had a gruff manner. Off duty he was a genial Scot who played the bagpipes and strutted in a kilt at civic functions.

Qwilleran, placing his jacket carefully on a chair seat and sliding into another, asked, "Any suspects in the pilfering?"

The chief leaned back in his chair and folded his arms. "Could be punks from Chipmunk. Could be the kids that hang around George Breze's dump. There's no two incidents alike."

Qwilleran said, "I've been thinking it could be a game, like a treasure hunt—perhaps initiation rites for a juvenile cult."

"We've talked to school principals. They say there's no sign of suspicious activity."

"They'd be the last to know," Qwilleran muttered.

Brodie threw up his hands. "The whole thing's crazy." Then he grinned. "Why don't you assign your smart cat to the case?" The chief was the only person in the north country who knew about the remarkable talents of Qwilleran's male Siamese.

"Koko doesn't accept assignments," Qwilleran said with a straight face. Then he added in a serious tone, "But last night, Andy, he jumped on my bookshelf and knocked down a Russian novel titled *The Thief.* Was that a coincidence or what?"

The chief grunted and changed the subject. "I hear you and your smart cat aren't living in the barn this winter. How come?" He often visited the converted apple barn after hours, dropping in for a nightcap and some shoptalk. Qwilleran, though not a drinker himself, stocked the best brands for his guests.

"It's impossible to heat evenly, Andy. So I bought a condo in Indian Village for the cold months. I can rent it to vacationers in the summer. By the way, I had it furnished by your talented daughter."

The chief nodded a grudging acknowledgment of the compliment. In spite of Fran Brodie's success as an interior designer, her father considered it a frivolous career.

Standing up and presenting the brown paper bag, Qwilleran said, "Here's a wee dram of Christmas cheer, Andy. See you after the holidays."

IN EARLIER days Qwilleran had been frugal by nature and by necessity, while growing up with a single parent and earning his way through college. His new financial status had introduced him to the luxury of giving presents, buying drinks, sending flowers, treating companions to dinner, and tipping generously.

His Christmas shopping list was a long one. He parked his car and trudged around downtown in snow boots. A wintry sun made the mica flecks sparkle in the stone façades of Main Street buildings, and garlands of greens looped across the street between light poles. The babble of voices and rumble of slow-moving vehicles were hushed by the snow piled everywhere. Yet, strangely, the acoustical phenomenon emphasized the bursts of Christmas music and the clang of Santa's bell on the corner.

First Qwilleran went to Lanspeak's Department Store to buy something for Polly. Carol Lanspeak herself waited on him. She and her husband, Larry, were an admirable pair: good business heads, civic leaders, and major talents in the theater club.

Carol said to him with a touch of fond rebuke, "I knew you'd pop in at the last minute, so I set aside a suit in Polly's size, a lovely suede in terra-cotta."

Qwilleran gave the suit a single glance and said, "I'll take it."

"Polly will swoon over it," Carol promised.

"Polly doesn't swoon easily," he said. Polly was a charming woman of his own age, with a soft and musical voice, but there was an iron hand in the velvet glove that ran the public library.

"Where are you two spending Christmas Day, Qwill?"

"With the Rikers. Do you and Larry have plans?"

"We've invited the Carmichaels and their houseguest. Do you see much of Willard and Danielle?"

Not if I can help it, Qwilleran thought. Politely he said, "Our paths don't seem to cross very often." It was the Lanspeaks who had introduced him to the new president of the Pickax People's Bank and his flashy young wife. Her frank flirtiness, raucous voice, and breathy stares at his mustache annoyed him.

"I'm afraid," Carol said regretfully, "that Danielle isn't adjusting well to small-town life. Willard says she's homesick. That's why they invited her cousin from New York to spend the holidays." She lowered her voice. "Step into my office, Qwill."

He followed her to the cluttered cubicle adjoining the women's department, and they sat down.

"I feel sorry for Danielle," Carol said. "People are saying unkind things, but she's asking for it. Skirts too short, heels too high, everything too tight, pounds of makeup, hair like a rat's nest."

"Couldn't Fran Brodie drop a few hints? She's glamorous and yet has class, and she's helping Danielle with her house."

"Fran's been dropping hints, but . . ." Carol shrugged. "You'd think her husband would say something. Willard's an intelligent man, and he's fitting right into the community. He has joined the Boosters Club and is helping to organize a gourmet club. Yet when Larry submitted his name to the country club for membership, nothing happened. We all know why. Danielle's flamboyant manner raises eyebrows. They call her voice cheap. It *is* rather strident."

"Rather," Qwilleran said. It was unusual for Carol to be so critical and so candid.

"Well, let me know if you think of something we can do. Shall I gift wrap Polly's suit?"

"Please. I'll pick it up later."

He next went to Amanda's Design Studio, hoping to find a decorative object for the Rikers and hoping that Fran Brodie would be in. But she was out, unfortunately, and her cantankerous boss was in charge. Amanda Goodwinter was a successful businesswoman and a perennial member of the Pickax City Council.

Her greeting was characteristically blunt. "If you're looking for a free cup of coffee, you're out of luck. The coffeemaker's on the blink."

To tease her, Qwilleran said he wanted to buy a knickknack as a gift for Arch and Mildred Riker.

She bristled. "We don't sell knickknacks!"

"Semantics, semantics. Then how about a bibelot?"

She scowled and suggested a colorful ceramic coffeepot, its surface a mass of sculptured grapes, apples, and pears.

"Isn't it a trifle gaudy?" Qwilleran complained.

"Gaudy!" Amanda shouted. "It's majolica! It's hand-painted! It's old! It's expensive! The Rikers will be crazy about it!"

"I'll take it. And I'd like it gift wrapped, but don't fuss."

"I never fuss!"

FOR the other names on his list he relied on the new Sip 'n' Nibble shop. They would make up gift baskets of wine, cheese, and other treats and deliver them anywhere in the county by Christmas Eve.

On a whim he also went into the men's store to buy a waggish tie for the conservative Riker. It was bright blue, with life-size baseballs, white stitched with red. He hoped it would get a laugh.

His final stop was the Pickax People's Bank to cash a check.

A man came striding out from an inner office. "Qwill! You're the exact person I want to see. Come into my office." The new banker had the suave manner, expensive suit, and styled hair of a newcomer from Down Below.

Qwilleran followed Willard Carmichael into the presidential suite and noted a few changes: a younger secretary, more colorful furnishings, and art on the walls.

"I hear you're living in Indian Village now," Carmichael said.

"Only for the winter. How about you? Have you moved into your house?"

"No, we're still camping out in an apartment at the Village. Danielle has ordered a lot of stuff for the house, but it takes forever to get delivery. Say, are you free for dinner? I'm baching it tonight. Danielle is taking our houseguest to Otto's Tasty Eats—a vile restaurant, if you ask me—so I told her I had to work. Her cousin is spending the holidays with us."

The googly-eyed Danielle made Qwill uncomfortable, but Willard, he decided, was okay.

"I could manage to be free. Where would you like to go?"

"Where could we get pasties? I've never had a pasty. I don't even know what it is."

"It's the official specialty of Moose County, dating back to mining days. And it rhymes with *nasty,* by the way. It's an enormous meat-and-potato turnover—okay for a picnic but not for a civilized dinner. Have you been to Onoosh's Café?"

"No, Danielle doesn't like Mediterranean. When I was in Detroit, though, I used to haunt Greektown for shish kebab."

"Suppose we meet at Onoosh's whenever you're free. I have to go home and feed the cats." He was wearing knockabout clothes, but if he had said, "I want to go home and change," Willard would have said, "Don't bother. I'll just take off my tie."

Feeding the cats was an excuse that was never challenged.

QWILLERAN drove home to Indian Village in his four-wheel-drive van, considered advisable for winter in the country. It was almost new, and he'd got a good trade-in allowance on his compact.

Indian Village, on Ittibittiwassee Road, was outside the Pickax city limits. Along the way was the bridge over the Ittibittiwassee River, which then veered and paralleled the highway to Indian Village. At the entrance, a gate gave an air of exclusivity, but it was always open, giving an air of hospitality. The buildings were rustic board-and-batten compatible with the wooded site, starting with the gatehouse and the clubhouse. Apartments were clustered in small buildings randomly situated on Woodland Trail. Condominiums in strips of four contiguous units extended along River Lane, close to the water that rushed over rocks or swirled in pools. Even in winter a trickle could be heard underneath the snow and ice.

When Qwilleran unlocked his condo in building 5, his Siamese were sitting contentedly in the window overlooking the riverbank. The wintry sun bounced off the white landscape, making a giant reflector that illuminated their silky fawn-colored coats and accentuated their seal-brown points.

"Hello, you guys," Qwilleran said. "How's everything? Any excitement around here? What's the rabbit count today?"

Languorously both cats stood up, humped their backs and then stretched two forelegs and one hind leg. The male was Kao K'o Kung—Koko, for short—the "smart cat" in Chief Brodie's book. He was sleek and muscular, with a commanding set of whiskers and intense blue eyes that hinted at cosmic secrets. Yum Yum, the female, was delicate and affectionate. Her large, limpid blue eyes were violet-tinged. They were both highly vocal, Koko yowling a chesty baritone and Yum Yum uttering a soprano shriek when it was least expected.

Qwilleran brought in the packages from his van, made some calls, fed the cats, and changed into a tweed coat over a turtleneck. Polly had told him he looked particularly good in turtlenecks; their simplicity was a foil for his handsome mustache. He was half pleased and half annoyed by everyone's preoccupation with his unique facial adornment. Fran Brodie called it Second Empire, as if it were a piece of furniture.

What no one knew, of course, was its functional significance to its owner. Whenever Qwilleran suspected that something was out of order in any way, he felt a tingling sensation on his upper lip. Sometimes he would tamp his mustache, pound it with his fist, comb it with his knuckles, or merely stroke it thoughtfully, depending on the nature of the hunch.

When Qwilleran arrived at Onoosh's Mediterranean Café, he felt transported halfway around the globe by exotic oil lamps, the aroma of strange spices, and the twang of ethnic music.

Carmichael was in a corner booth, sipping a Rob Roy. "You're my guest tonight," he said. "What would you like to drink?"

Qwilleran ordered his usual Squunk water on the rocks with a twist, explaining that it was a local mineral water, said to be the fountain of youth.

"It must be true," Carmichael said, "because you certainly look fit."

"How's your lovely wife?" Qwilleran asked politely.

"Oh, she's all involved in decorating the new house."

"You bought the Fitches' contemporary house, as I recall."

"I'm afraid I did. It's ugly as sin, but Danielle likes anything that's modern and *different,* so I acquiesced."

Qwilleran thought, She's spoiled. "How long have you two been married?"

"Not quite a year. My first wife died three years ago, and I was living alone in a big house in Detroit. Then I went to Baltimore on business and met Danielle in a club where she was singing. It was love at first sight. So I brought her back to Michigan."

"What made you move up here?"

"I'd been wanting to get away from the fast track and the pollution and the street crime. I'd been mugged twice. But then I had my car hijacked. That was the clincher. But look here, I'm gassing too much. Let's order some appetizers and another drink." He ordered hummus, and Qwilleran ordered baba ghanouj.

The banker asked, "Do you think a Mediterranean restaurant will go over in a town like this?"

"I hope so. Polly Duncan tells me that Middle Eastern cuisine is on-target healthwise."

"I've met your Polly Duncan, and she's a charming woman," Willard said with a note of envy. "You're a lucky man. She's attractive, intelligent, and has a beautiful speaking voice."

"It was her voice that first appealed to me," Qwilleran said. "*Soft, gentle, and low,* to quote Shakespeare. And it's the first time in my life that I've had a friend who shared my literary interests. Also, I'm constantly learning. Jazz used to be the extent of my music appreciation, but Polly's introduced me to opera." He stopped to chuckle. "She hasn't converted me to bird watching, though, and I haven't sold her on baseball."

"I understand you've bought separate condos in the Village. Have you ever thought of—"

"No," Qwilleran interrupted. "We like our singlehood."

For dinner both men chose the lentil soup, followed by shish kebab for Willard and stuffed grape leaves for Qwill.

The conversation switched to the gourmet society that was being organized. "Cooking is my chief pleasure," the banker said. "It's relaxing to come home and bang pots and pans around. Danielle hates the kitchen, bless her heart. By the way, have you ever been to Mardi Gras? She talked me into making reservations, although I'd rather take a cruise." He shrugged in resignation. "Fran Brodie wants Danielle to join the theater club."

After the entrées were served, Willard said, "I'd like to get your opinion, Qwill, on an idea that Danielle's cousin had. He thinks those old houses on Pleasant Street could and should be restored. He's a restoration consultant, and he's amazed at the possibilities here. Do you know the Duncan property on Pleasant Street?"

"Very well. Lynette Duncan is Polly's sister-in-law. Polly is the widow of Lynette's brother, William. Lynette recently inherited the house."

"Right. We met Lynette at a card party in the Village, and she invited us to Sunday brunch. She has a fabulous Victorian house. In fact, the entire street is a throwback to the late 1880s." Carmichael put down his knife and fork and warmed to his subject. "The way we see it, Pleasant Street could become a mecca for preservation buffs, with houses operating as living museums or bed-and-breakfasts. My bank would offer good deals on restoration loans."

"Exactly what does a restoration consultant do, and what is his name?" Qwilleran asked.

"Carter Lee James. Perhaps you've heard of him or seen his work in magazines. He appraises the possibilities, supervises the restoration, and helps get the houses registered as historic landmarks. He knows the techniques, sources, and—most important—what not to do. It would be a unique attraction, not for hordes of noisy tourists, but for serious admirers of nineteenth-century Americana."

They ordered spicy walnut cake and dark-roast coffee, and the banker continued. "Lynette has a fortune in antiques." He gazed thoughtfully into his coffee. "I imagine she doesn't have to work. Yet she tells me she holds down a nine-to-five job."

Qwilleran tried to find something upbeat to say. "Lynette is the last of the Duncans-by-blood. It's a respected name around here. She likes to keep busy. She's also active in volunteer work. Volunteerism is big in Pickax. You should get Danielle involved."

With a humorous grimace her husband said, "If it means visiting the sick, I don't think my dear wife would qualify." He occupied himself with the check and a credit card, then said, "We'll have to get together during the holidays. You should meet Carter Lee. You'll be impressed. Personable guy. Fine arts degree. Graduate study in architecture. Do you play bridge?"

"No, but Lynette has told me about the Village bridge club and the big glass jar."

It was an antique apothecary jar about a foot high, with a wide mouth and a domelike stopper. At Village card parties each player dropped a ten-dollar bill into the jar and rubbed the stopper for luck. The players also contributed their winnings, and the total was donated to the Moose County Youth Center. He remarked to Willard, "I hope you've contributed generously to the jar."

"I've had a little luck," he admitted. "Lynette is a consistent winner, though. And Carter Lee's pretty good. Danielle should stay home and watch TV."

It was time to say good night. Qwilleran had genuinely enjoyed the conversation and the food. He thanked his host and added, "It's my turn to treat—the next time you're baching it." The qualifying clause was tacked on casually, but he hoped it registered.

On his way home, he recalled the banker's remarks about his "dear wife" and feared the marriage was doomed. Too bad.

Qwilleran tuned in the hourly newsbreak on WPKX. First he heard the high school basketball scores. Then came Wetherby Goode with his forecast and usual silliness: "Boots—boots—boots—boots sloggin' through the snow again." He always had a parody of a song or nursery rhyme or literary work to fit the occasion.

After Wetherby's prediction of more snow the newscaster came in with a bulletin: "A disturbing incident has just been reported in Indian Village. A sum of money estimated at two thousand dollars has been stolen from an unlocked cabinet in the clubhouse. It was being collected in a glass jar by members of the bridge club, for donation to the Moose County Youth Center. Police are investigating."

Qwill huffed into his mustache, thinking, The editorial was right. It's time to lock up.

TWO

ON DECEMBER 24 Qwilleran went downtown at noon to celebrate with the staff of the *Moose County Something.* Arch Riker was beaming as he handed out the year-end bonuses.

Qwilleran said to him, "This is a far cry from the wild office parties we had Down Below. They were all booze, no bonuses."

"Don't remind me!"

Then Hixie Rice, the promotion director and a resident of Indian Village, pulled Qwilleran aside. "Did you hear about the theft?"

"The Pickax Picaroon strikes again! When was the money last seen?"

"The night before last. We put the jar away in the manager's office as usual, camouflaged with a shopping bag."

"But all the players know where it's kept, right? Someone was waiting for it to fill up. Who are these players?"

"Mostly residents of the Village, but a few guest players as well, who drive out from Pickax or wherever."

"Let's get some food before the city-room vultures eat it all."

AFTER the camaraderie of the office party, Qwilleran picked up a few extra gifts, including some small cans of smoked turkey pâté and gourmet sardines for the cats he knew. The first can went to the longhair at the used-book store. The bookseller was overwhelmed.

Slyly he said to Qwilleran, "I know what Santa's bringing you!"

"Don't tell me. I want to be surprised. Just show me what's come in lately."

The bookseller puttered among opened and unopened cartons until he found a box from the estate of a professor of Celtic literature, who had spent his last years in neighboring Lockmaster. "Beautiful bindings," he said. "Some very old, but the leather is well cared for. Here's one published in 1899."

Qwilleran looked at it. The title was *Ossian and the Ossianic Literature,* and it was written by A. Nutt. "I'll take it," he said, thinking he might give it to Arch Riker for a gag. As he left the store, he called out, "Merry Christmas."

HE WENT to Polly Duncan's place for their traditional Christmas Eve together, though this time Polly served a low-fat supper. She had had a heart attack, and after bypass surgery she was on a new regimen of diet and exercise.

"I bought a book on Ossian today," Qwill told her. "The author was someone by the name of Nutt. Wasn't there a scandal concerning Ossian in Samuel Johnson's time?"

"Yes. An eighteenth-century poet claimed to have found the third-century poems of Ossian. Dr. Johnson said it was a hoax."

Polly offered Qwilleran a choice of pumpkin pie or fruitcake.

"Is there any law against having both?" he asked.

"Qwill, dear, I knew you'd say that. By the way, Lynette has been chiding me for calling you dear. She says it's old-fashioned."

"You're the only one in my whole life who's ever called me that, and I like it. You can quote me to your sister-in-law. For someone who hasn't had a love affair for twenty years, she hardly qualifies as an authority on affectionate appellations."

They listened to carols by Swiss bell ringers and French choirs. He read Dickens's account of the Cratchits' Christmas dinner. She read Whittier's "Snow-Bound." In every way it was an enjoyable evening, unmarred by any hostility from Bootsie. The male Siamese, who considered Qwilleran a rival for Polly's affection, had been sequestered in the basement. The blissful occasion ended only when the banging on the basement door became insufferable.

ON CHRISTMAS morning Qwilleran's telephone rang frequently as friends called to thank him for their gift baskets. One of them was a fun-loving, gray-haired grandmother, Celia Robinson.

"Guess what, Chief!" She called him Chief for reasons that only they understood. "My grandson is here for the holidays."

"Clayton?" He knew about the fourteen-year-old science and math whiz who lived on a farm in Illinois. He had never met Clayton, who had helped solve the Euphonia Gage case in Florida, and he felt obliged to extend some hospitality, although he was not fond of the underage bracket. He said, "Would your grandson like to go along with me on an assignment for the paper?"

"Oh, Chief! He'd love it."

"Does he have a camera?"

"Yes. And he has a little tape recorder."

"Good. He can pose as my photographer. Tell him to pick up a roll of film, and I'll pay for it. Meanwhile, I'll set up an interview and call you back."

"Shall I cut his hair?" Celia asked.

"Not necessary. Photographers aren't expected to look too civilized," Qwilleran said as he hung up.

Later Polly called. "Do you know who's just moved into the unit next to you, Qwill?"

"A husky man. Drives a large van."

"That's Wetherby Goode."

"No! What did I do to deserve that clown for a neighbor?"

"Do I detect inter-media jealousy?" she said, teasing gently. "Most radio listeners think he's entertaining. After an ice storm he quoted from 'The Rime of the Ancient Mariner.' One of his listeners had sent it in: *The ice was here, the ice was there/ The ice was all around.*"

"Well, if you have to have a gimmick, I guess that's as good as any," Qwilleran acknowledged.

AT ONE O'CLOCK QWILLERAN and Polly started out for the Riker condo in building 2. They walked hand in hand, muffled in down jackets, scarves, woolly hats, mittens, and boots.

Arriving at their destination, they were greeted at the door by a committee of three—the beaming host in a red wool shirt, the plump and pretty hostess in a chef's apron, and their cat, Toulouse, in his usual tuxedo with white shirtfront and spats.

There was a Scotch pine tree in the living room, trimmed like the one at Arch and Mildred's wedding the previous Christmas: white pearlescent ornaments, white doves, white streamers. The festively wrapped packages under the tree included those sent over by Polly and Qwilleran.

Mildred removed her apron and joined the others around a low party table loaded with hot and cold hors d'oeuvres.

As the four busied themselves with the hors d'oeuvres, conversation came in short bites.

About the theft: "An inside job. An outsider could have stolen it only if an insider talked on the outside."

About Lynette: "Suddenly she's looking ten years younger! Is she in love? . . . She was jilted twenty years ago and hasn't dated since. . . . Maybe it's Wetherby Goode. She thinks he's cute."

About George Breze: "What's he doing in Indian Village? . . . His house is up for sale. . . . His wife left him."

Toulouse rubbed against the cook's ankles as a reminder that the turkey was ready. Mildred served it with a brown rice and walnut stuffing, twice-baked sweet potatoes with orange glaze, sesame-sauced broccoli, and two kinds of cranberry relish.

After dinner the presents were opened. The first—to Qwilleran from the Rikers—was an odd-shaped package about four feet long. "A short stepladder," he guessed. "A croquet set." It proved to be a pair of snowshoes. "Great!" he said. "It's just what I need to get some exercise this winter."

Polly was thrilled with her suede suit, and the Rikers whooped in unison over the majolica coffeepot. Then Arch unwrapped his baseball tie and exploded with laughter, while Mildred screamed in glee.

Qwilleran said, "It was supposed to be a joke, but I didn't know it was that funny!" He understood their reaction a few minutes later, when he opened a long, narrow box from Arch. It was a baseball tie.

The largest box under the tree—to Qwilleran from Polly—was a set of leather-bound books by Herman Melville, a 1924 printing in mint condition. Qwilleran dug into the box excitedly, announcing title after title, and reading aloud some of the opening lines.

"Okay," Arch said, "you've got all winter to read those books. Let's open some more presents."

Also for Qwilleran was an opera recording from Polly: *Adriana Lecouvreur* with Renata Tebaldi. Arch gave Mildred an onyx necklace accented with gold-veined lapis lazuli.

The last gift under the tree was tagged to Qwilleran from Bootsie. "It's a package bomb," he guessed. After unwrapping it with exaggerated care, he exclaimed, "It's a sporran!"

"It looks like something for cleaning the windshield," said Arch.

"A sporran, for your information, Arch, is a pouch worn with a kilt by men in the Scottish Highlands." He turned to Polly. "How did Bootsie find out I'd bought a kilt?"

"Everyone in town knows it, dear."

WHEN Qwilleran finally got home, the Siamese, dozing on the sofa, raised their heads expectantly. He piled all the Christmas gifts in the foyer. Koko and Yum Yum came running, and Koko did his best to open the carton containing the set of Melville's works.

Was he attracted to the leather bindings? Or could he sense that the box contained a novel about a whale? He was a smart cat, but was he that smart? Koko did indeed have a baffling gift of extrasensory perception. He could tell time, read Qwilleran's mind, and put thoughts in Qwilleran's head. He sensed misdeeds, and he could identify misdoers in an oblique sort of way. Melville's novels were concerned with good and evil to a large degree. Was Kao K'o Kung getting the message?

Was it coincidence that he pushed *The Thief* off the bookshelf when Pickax was plagued with larceny?

AFTER CHRISTMAS, QWILLERAN took Celia Robinson's grandson out to interview a dowser in Pickax. The interview could be conducted during Clayton's visit, and then, after spring thaw, Qwilleran could return for a demonstration of the mysterious art.

When he drove into Celia's driveway, he saw Clayton on the snowblower, spraying his grandmother with plumes of white flakes, while she pelted him with snowballs in gleeful retaliation. Brushing snow from their outerwear, they approached Qwilleran's car, and Celia made the introductions. "Mr. Qwilleran, this is my grandson. Clayton, this is Mr. Q. I call him Chief."

"Hi, Chief," the young man said, thrusting his hand forward. His grip had the confidence of a young teen who is expecting a scholarship from M.I.T.

"Hi, Doc," Qwilleran replied, referring to his role in the Florida investigation. Qwilleran sized him up as a healthy farm-bred youth with an intelligent face and freshly cut hair. "Got your camera? Let's go!"

"Where are we off to, Chief?" Clayton asked as they turned into Park Circle.

"We're going to Pleasant Street to interview Gil MacMurchie. Mr. MacMurchie is retired from the plumbing-and-hardware business, but he's still active as a dowser. Know anything about dowsing? It's also known as water witching."

"Sure, I know about that. When our well ran dry, my dad hired a water witch. He walked around our farm with a branch of a tree and found underground water. I don't know how it works."

"No one knows exactly, but proponents of dowsing say it works."

Pleasant Street was an old neighborhood of Victorian frame houses ornamented with quantities of jigsaw trim around windows, porches, rooflines, and gables. The large residences had been built by successful families like the MacMurchies and Duncans in the heyday of Moose County.

"This street looks like Disneyland," said Clayton. "It doesn't look real."

"There may be no other street in the United States with so much gingerbread trim. Right now there's a proposal to restore all the houses and have it recognized as a historic neighborhood."

Qwilleran parked in front of a neat two-tone gray house that still had a stone carriage step at the curb.

"What kind of pictures shall I take?" Clayton asked.

"Close-ups of Mr. MacMurchie and his dowsing stick, plus anything else that looks interesting. But do it unobtrusively."

Clayton had never seen a doorbell in the middle of the door, and he snapped a picture of it. He had never heard the raucous clang it made either.

The man who responded to the bell was a leathery-faced Scot whose red hair was turning sandy with age. "Come in! Come in, Qwill" was his hearty welcome.

"Gil, this is my photographer, Clayton Robinson."

"Hiya, there! Let's go right back to the kitchen. There's some folks from the bank working in the front rooms. All my dowsing gear is laid out on the kitchen table."

As the trio walked down the hall, Qwilleran glimpsed antique weapons in a glass-topped curio table, a small black dog asleep on the carpeted stairs, and a man and a woman examining one of the parlors and making notes.

"Excuse the mess," the dowser apologized when they reached the kitchen. "My wife passed away last year. I'm getting ready to move into a retirement complex, and I'm selling the house and most of my goods. Willard Carmichael at the bank said I can get more for the house if I fix it up so that it's historic. You know Willard, don't you? He sent this out-of-town expert over here today to figure out what needs to be done and what it'll cost. Sounds pretty good to me. Pull up a chair."

Laid out on the table was an array of forked twigs, L-shaped rods, barbed wire, and string. Qwilleran set up his tape recorder.

"How long have you been dowsing, Gil?"

"Ever since I was a kid and my granddad showed me how to hold the forked stick. He found good water for folks, and also veins of iron ore and copper."

Qwilleran asked, "Considering new technology, is water witching a dying art?"

"No way. My grandson's been finding water since he was twelve. It's a gift, and you pass it on, but it skips a generation."

Occasionally there was the soft click of a camera and a flash.

"Are you always successful?"

"If the water's down there, by golly I'll find it. I never charge for my services, and I've made a lot of friends. Of course, I've made enemies, too. There's a well driller in Mooseville who hates my guts." MacMurchie stopped to enjoy a chuckle.

"How about the scientists? The geologists?"

"Oh, them! Just because they can't explain it, they think it's all superstition. How about you, Qwill? What's your opinion?"

"I'll reserve my opinion until next spring, when you give a demonstration. Meanwhile, what are these gadgets?" He waved his hand at the odd assortment on the kitchen table.

"Okay. Here's the famous forked twig. Should be fresh, with the sap in it. You hold it in front of you, stem pointing up. The forks are in your hands, palms up—like this." The camera clicked. "You walk across the ground, concentrating, back and forth. Suddenly the stick quivers, and the stem swings down and points to the ground. There's a vein of water under your feet."

Qwilleran heard voices in the next room—the rumble of a man's voice and a woman's shrill laughter. Catching Clayton's eye, he jerked his head in that direction, and the young photographer quietly left the room.

"Explain these other gadgets, Gil."

"They'll all find water, but mostly it depends on the dowser." MacMurchie looked up suddenly, over Qwilleran's shoulder, and said, "Yes, Mr. James. Want to see me?"

A deep, pleasant voice said, "We'll be back tomorrow to appraise the upstairs. I think you have a gold mine here. Don't let me disturb you. We can find our way out."

"Nice fella," the dowser said as footsteps retreated and a woman's laughter drifted back to them.

Qwilleran stood up and pocketed his recorder. "This has been very enlightening. I'll look forward to the demonstration in the spring. Where's my photographer? Let's go, Clayton."

"Here I am—in the dining room. I've found a friend." He was sitting cross-legged on the floor, and a black schnauzer was curled on his lap, looking up at him with a shameless expression of devotion.

"That's Cody," said MacMurchie. "She was my wife's. You can have her if you want. I can't have a pet where I'm going."

Clayton said, "I live on a farm. She'd like it there. Can I take her on the plane, Chief?"

"Better discuss it with your grandmother."

While Clayton took a few pictures of Cody, the two men walked toward the front door, and Qwilleran asked about the weapons in the curio table.

"They're Scottish dirks—longer than daggers, shorter than swords." He lifted the glass top and removed a dirk from its scabbard. "See these grooves in the blade? They're for blood. Those Highlanders thought of everything." There were also two silver pins three inches in diameter, set with quartz stones as big as egg yolks. "Those are brooches to anchor a man's plaid on his shoulder. We call them poached eggs. Sorry to say, I've got to unload all this stuff. No room in my new place. I'll only keep the dirk with the silver lion. It was a gift from my wife."

"How much do you want for all the others?" Qwilleran asked.

MacMurchie rolled his eyes toward the ceiling. "Well, four dirks with brass hilts and leather scabbards . . . and two silver brooches. . . . You could have 'em for a thousand."

"I'll think about it and let you know," Qwilleran said.

"Are you going to Scottish Night at the lodge?"

"They've invited me to be guest of honor, and I've bought a kilt, but so far I haven't had the nerve to wear it."

"Wear it to Scottish Night, Qwill. There'll be twenty or thirty fellas in kilts there. I'll lend you a knife to wear in your sock. You have to have a knife in your sock to be proper."

MacMurchie disappeared and returned with a staghorn-handled

knife in a scabbard. "Borrow this. It's lucky to wear something borrowed. It's called a dubh, pronounced thoob."

Qwilleran accepted. They said good-bye. Qwilleran and his photographer drove away from Pleasant Street.

"That was cool," Clayton said.

"Did you shoot the whole roll?" Qwilleran asked.

"No, I've got a few exposures left. I'm leaving tomorrow, so I'll
send you the prints."

"Did you get a look at the people from the bank?"

"Yeah. He was okay, but she was weird."

"In what way?"

"I don't know. Her voice—it sounded kind of electronic."

An apt description of Danielle Carmichael, Qwilleran thought.
"What were they doing?"

"He was measuring things and talking, and she was writing down
what he said. I turned on my pocket tape recorder. Want me to
send a transcript when I get home?"

"Good idea. Did you enjoy your holiday?"

"Yeah. Lotsa fun, lotsa food. Grandma made all my favorites."

Then Qwilleran questioned him about life on the farm. It was a
poultry factory. There were no farm animals—just watchdogs
and barn cats, but no indoor pets. Clayton had a stepmother who
wouldn't allow animals in the house.

"I'd like to come up here and live with Grandma and go to
Pickax High School," Clayton said. As they pulled into Celia's
driveway, he said, "Thanks a lot, Chief. It was cool."

WHEN Qwilleran returned home, he noticed heavy vehicle tracks
and large footprints in the snow around his condo. It meant that
some long-awaited furniture had been delivered.

Qwilleran's unit had a lofty living room with large windows overlooking the river. On the opposite wall was a balcony with two bedrooms, and below it were the kitchen and dining alcove. The alcove
would be his office, and he needed a table or desk large enough for
typewriter, lamp, papers, books, files, and two supervisory cats.

On this day, as soon as he unlocked the door, Koko notified him that something had been added, yowling and running back and forth to the office alcove. The writing table was indeed large, and it had character. There was also a huge stripped-pine cupboard with open shelves above and cabinet below.

Qwilleran lost no time in loading the shelves with books recently purchased or brought from the barn. One shelf he reserved for the Melville set, volumes one to twelve, numbered in chronological order: *Typee; Omoo; Mardi; Redburn; White-Jacket; Moby-Dick; Pierre; The Piazza Tales; Israel Potter; The Confidence-Man; Billy Budd;* and *Weeds and Wildings.*

Koko was impressed. He curled up on the shelf with the leather-bound volumes. Had he become a literary critic?

THREE

ON THE last day of the year it snowed as usual, and high winds were predicted. In Indian Village it was customary for neighbors to celebrate with neighbors, and there were numerous at-home parties. For those who liked elbow-to-elbow conviviality, there was a late-night get-together at the clubhouse.

There was much conversation about the theft of the bridge club's money. The new clubhouse manager, Lenny Inchpot, had been questioned by police because the money jar was kept in a cabinet in his office. All agreed there was too much casual traffic in and out. Locking the doors and issuing keys to members would be the first move.

When the time came to ring in the New Year, scores of residents converged on the clubhouse. The main hall had the air of a ski lodge, with a lofty wood-paneled ceiling, exposed beams, and a big stone fireplace.

Since formal dress was optional, clothing ranged from jeans to black tie. Polly was wearing her terra-cotta suit, and Qwilleran was in a suit and tie. A husky man in a double-breasted suit wore a large lapel button inscribed HIT ME! I'M THE WEATHER GUY!

Willard Carmichael and his houseguest wore dinner jackets. Danielle was spectacular in a low-cut, high-cut cocktail sheath, leading Arch Riker to mumble, "You'd think a banker could afford to buy his wife something longer."

"She makes Lynette look like a prison matron," Qwilleran said.

Lynette, wearing a navy-blue taffeta shirtdress and her grandmother's jewelry, had dined with the Carmichaels. She reported that Danielle's cousin was adorable; his deep voice gave her goose bumps; even his name was romantic: Carter Lee James.

When Lynette pointed him out, Qwilleran realized he was the man who had been measuring the MacMurchie house. His voice was indeed pleasant. He had blond hair, medium good looks, and a relaxed way with both men and women.

Polly said, "He has a frank, boyish way of looking at one that's quite disarming."

Lynette said, "All his shirts and sweaters are monogrammed."

"How do you know?" Qwilleran asked.

"He's been playing bridge with us, and I had the three of them to Sunday brunch once. Carter Lee is crazy about my house!"

Wetherby Goode surprised the crowd by sitting down at the piano and playing cocktail music, while Danielle surprised them further by singing ballads.

Lynette said, "I didn't know Wetherby could play."

Polly said, "I didn't know Danielle could sing."

"She can't," Qwilleran muttered as he turned to the buffet table.

Later Willard Carmichael approached him. "Qwill, have you met Danielle's cousin yet? Come with me."

The visiting celebrity stood with his back to the fireplace, answering questions calmly and modestly.

"Excuse me," Willard said loudly. "Carter Lee's visit won't be complete until he shakes hands with the hand that writes the Qwill Pen column."

The group moved aside, and the two men gripped hands heartily. "Welcome to Moose County," Qwilleran said.

"I'm glad to be here," the visitor said with sincerity. "I've been reading your column. Let me compliment you."

"Thank you. Perhaps we could arrange an interview. I understand you have some interesting proposals."

"Well, I have to be in Detroit for a few days on business, but then I'll return, and we'll see what happens."

Willard said, "I'll be down there at the same time, and I'll make sure he comes back. We need him."

Mildred Riker, overhearing them, said, "Willard, how can you miss the first dinner of the gourmet society? It was all your idea."

"I feel worse than you do, but I have to attend a seminar."

Danielle said, "He wanted me to go with him, but it would be so boring!"

The conversation subsided as everyone waited for the magic hour. Champagne corks were popping. The hands of the clock over the bar reached twelve, and the crowd shouted, "Happy New Year!"

Wetherby Goode played "Auld Lang Syne."

As the guests started bundling into their storm wear and trooping out into the snow, everyone was happy, except Carter Lee James. He discovered his lambskin car coat had been taken.

THE New Year's Eve incident was reported to the police, and the residents of Indian Village were in a furor. Qwilleran tried to discuss the matter with Chief Brodie but was brushed off—a sure indication that the police were on the trail of a suspect.

Qwilleran had his own suspicions. George Breze, with his red cap, overalls, and noisy pickup truck, was an incongruous figure in the white-collar community. A few years before, he had had the gall to run for mayor. The locals called him Old Gallbladder. He polled only two votes.

On Sandpit Road outside Pickax, Breze had an empire of marginal commercial ventures behind a chain-link fence. The "office"— a shack with a potbellied stove—was a hangout for kids. On the same property was a large Federal-style house where Breze had lived with his wife until recently, when she went off with a hoedown fiddle player from Squunk Corners. That was when George moved to Indian Village.

Qwilleran had a strong desire to investigate this lead, considering Breze a latter-day Fagin, but he had to work on the Qwill Pen. Finding subject matter in winter was a greater problem than in summer. In a quandary, Qwilleran paced back and forth.

Suddenly there was a crash near the front door, and two cats fled from the foyer. He had hung his snowshoes on the wall, and the Siamese had ventured to investigate something new. Instead of hanging them back up, he decided to give the sport a try. He was clumsy. He tripped. His right shoe stepped on his left shoe. But after he got the hang of it, he enjoyed tramping through the silent woods. He wrote his column on the joys of snowshoeing.

QWILLERAN was invited to join the Nouvelle Dining Club. The prospectus—signed by Mildred Riker, Hixie Rice, and Willard Carmichael—stated, "We are committed to quality, to pleasing the palate with the natural flavors of fresh ingredients."

For each monthly dinner one member would host the event and serve the entrée. Others would bring the appetizer, soup, salad, and dessert courses.

Qwilleran and Polly attended the first dinner one evening in January. It was held at the Lanspeaks' picturesque farmhouse in West Middle Hummock. Twelve members assembled in the country-style living room and talked about food as they sipped aperitifs.

Danielle Carmichael looked mostly puzzled. Foodwise she was age eleven, according to Willard. Since he and Carter Lee had left for Detroit, she had driven to the dinner with Fran Brodie.

For the sit-down courses Qwilleran found himself seated between Mildred and Hixie. Mildred said, "The menu is built around local products: lamb, whitefish, beans, squash, goat cheese, pears, and apples. It's such a pity that Willard couldn't be here. I wonder what he's having for dinner tonight."

"If he's in Detroit," Qwilleran said, "he'll be headed for Greek-town."

Hixie asked, "Do you think Carter Lee will ever come back?"

"I hope so," Mildred said. "He's such a gentleman."

"He has personality plus, and he's not married."

"If you're staking out a claim, Hixie, I think you'll have to stand in line."

Qwilleran said, "He's like some actors I've known: laid back but fired with an inner energy that produces a great performance. I'm looking forward to interviewing him when he returns."

Larry Lanspeak stood and proposed a toast to Willard Car-michael. "To our absent friend and mentor! May he live all the days of his life!"

The entrée was a taste sensation, especially the puree of Hubbard squash and leeks. "I'll never eat mixed peas and carrots again," said Qwilleran.

Just as dessert was being served, the telephone rang, and Carol went to the kitchen to answer it. She returned immediately and whispered anxiously to Fran Brodie, who jumped up and left the room.

Qwilleran stroked his mustache. There was something about this pantomime that worried him. Glancing toward the kitchen door, he saw Fran beckoning him to the phone.

In the family room the baked apples with peppercorn sauce were untouched. There was a murmur of concern. Qwilleran returned and touched Larry's shoulder, and the two of them went to the foyer. Carol joined them, and then the Lanspeaks together went to Danielle and led her to the library.

"What's the trouble, Qwill?" Mildred asked when he sat down.

"Andy Brodie called. He knew Fran was here with Danielle. It's bad news. Very bad. The Detroit police got in touch with him. Apparently Willard was walking to a restaurant when he was mugged. And shot . . ."

"Fatally?" Hixie asked under her breath.

"Fatally."

"Oh, my God!" Mildred said in a horrified whisper.

"They're trying to break the news to her gently."

At that moment there was a shriek from the library.

THE WPKX bulletin about the homicide sent the entire county into shock and rage, and individuals wanted to share their feelings with others. When thwarted by busy signals on the phone, they went out to gather in public places and bemoan the loss of Willard Carmichael in such an unthinkable way. Qwilleran, with his usual compulsion to take the public pulse, joined them and listened to their comments.

"Those cities Down Below are jungles!"

"We've lost a good man. He would have been an asset to the community. He attended our church."

"I feel sorry for his wife. We shoulda been nicer to her, even though she didn't fit in."

"If she moves back Down Below, she's nuts!"

"The church'll send their Home Visitors to call on her and try to give her some comforting thoughts."

With grim amusement Qwilleran visualized Danielle receiving these well-intentioned visitors with their "comforting thoughts." That alone would drive her back Down Below.

Qwilleran went to the department store for details and found Carol Lanspeak still distraught. "Fran took Danielle home last night and stayed with her, and my daughter went over and gave her a sedative. Danielle's a good customer of Fran's and feels comfortable with her, so we thought Fran should be the one to take her to Detroit. Carter Lee James is meeting them at the airport there and taking care of everything. Fran will come home tomorrow."

"I predict Danielle won't return," said Qwilleran, influenced by wishful thinking.

"Well, maybe not, but if she does, we want to have a quiet little dinner for her, and we want you and Polly to be there. Danielle likes you, Qwill."

He hoped the day would never come. He feared he would have

a merry widow on his trail, winking and pouting and remarking about his mustache. Danielle was not one to wear black for very long, if at all.

His next stop was the newspaper office. Qwilleran found the publisher at his massive executive desk, juggling two phones. "What's the latest?" he asked when Riker had a breathing space.

"I talked to Brodie. He's in touch with the Detroit police, but I'm afraid Willard is just another statistic. Thousands of homicides go unsolved Down Below."

On his way out of the executive suite, Qwilleran was hailed by Hixie Rice. He went into the promotion office and sat down.

"What a shocker. Willard was a nice guy. He worked with Mildred and me on the organization of the club and the dinner menu. What did you think of it?"

"Everything was excellent. I don't know about the dessert. No one felt like eating dessert."

"How about lunch, Qwill? I'll put it on my expense account."

"Those are the words I love to hear."

"We'll drive to Mooseville and eat at the Northern Lights Hotel. That's headquarters for the Ice Festival, and I want to fill you in on the plans. You might get a slant for your column."

THEY turned onto the lakeshore drive, where beach houses were boarded up, snowed in, bleak and forbidding. Mooseville, a teeming fishing village in summer, was chillingly quiet in January and relentlessly white.

They parked at the hotel overlooking the expanse of ice that extended to the horizon. The dining room had one waiter and a limited menu: fried-fish sandwich with fries and coleslaw.

Hixie said, "The Ice Festival will be a shot in the arm for the shoreline. All of the activities will take place on the ice: races, fishing tournaments, hospitality, and entertainment."

"What kind of races?"

"Dogsled, snowmobile, motorcycle, cross-country ski, snowshoe, and ice skate. Colleges all over are sending artists to the ice sculpture competition. And there'll be a torchlight parade on Friday night to kick off the whole exciting weekend."

Qwilleran listened dumbly to her exuberant recital, finally asking, "How many people do you expect?"

"As many as ten thousand. Most will be day-trippers, but we have lodging lined up all over Moose County."

The fish sandwiches were not bad, and Qwilleran was contemplating a piece of apple pie when Hixie said, "Could I ask you a favor, Qwill?"

"I thought so," he said. "There's no such thing as a free lunch. What do you want me to do?"

"Would you act as grand marshal of the torchlight parade?"

"What does that entail? If it means wearing a polar bear costume—"

"Nothing like that. You simply ride in a horse-drawn sleigh with the cheering multitude lining the route."

"Let's say I'll take it under advisement."

THE day Fran Brodie was due back from Detroit, Qwilleran left a message on her answering machine: "Fran, you must be bushed. Would you like dinner at the Old Stone Mill?"

Around seven in the evening she called back. "You're right, Qwill. I'm even too exhausted to go out to dinner, but if you want to come over in half an hour, I'll give you a report."

"I'll be there."

Meanwhile, he fed the cats and made his own dinner.

When it was time to visit Fran, he bundled in layers of warm clothing and walked the length of the Village to her apartment. The young woman who opened the door looked pale and frazzled.

"Rough day?" he asked sympathetically.

"Danielle was hysterical," she said, flopping onto the sofa. "When we got home, Dr. Diane was waiting with a hypo, so that helped. In fact, she slept fine, and in the morning we took off. She was groggy until we boarded the jet in Minneapolis. Then she had a drink and started to talk." Dr. Diane was Carol and Larry Lanspeak's daughter.

"Did she feel any guilt?"

"No," said Fran. "After another drink she started putting him down. He called her Danny-girl, which she hates. He was critical of the way she acted, the clothes she wore, and the food she ate."

"They hadn't known each other long before they married," Qwilleran observed.

"She didn't mention how he lavished money on her. He paid cash for the Fitch house and gave her an unlimited budget to do it over. She ordered custom furniture and carpets. Now I'm worried, Qwill. Suppose she never comes back and the studio is stuck for the order!"

"What kind of deposit did they give you?"

Fran looked sheepish. "None, actually. So when we were on the plane and she was jabbering away, I was dying to know her plans. I took a deep breath and said, 'Danielle, this is going to be a rough time for you, but it would help if you'd really get involved in the theater club. You have talent. You should be in our next production.' You can see I was desperate, Qwill."

"People have been struck by lightning for lesser lies."

Fran ignored the gibe. "We're scheduled to do *Hedda Gabler,* and I'm to do the title role, but I'd gladly step aside if it would convince her to stay and finish the house."

"*And let her do Hedda?* You're losing it, Fran."

"No, I mean it! I'd coach her every step of the way."

"Do you want to turn a tragedy into a farce?"

Fran said, "Anything to keep a good customer, as Amanda says. By the time Danny-girl had tossed off her third drink, she wanted to finish the house and add a swimming pool. By the time we landed at Metro, she was feeling no pain. Carter Lee was waiting, and as soon as possible I said good-bye and told them we looked forward to seeing them both in Pickax—soon."

QWILLERAN walked home through the snow and cold, pondering Fran's problem and her dubious solution. Then he called Polly with the news.

She was equally aghast. "That tinny voice? In the role of Hedda?"

"I'm afraid so."

"And what about Carter Lee? Is he coming back? Lynette will be disappointed if he doesn't. By the way, have you heard? The police have arrested a suspect in the string of robberies."

"Who?"

"The name won't be released until the arraignment."

"If I were a betting man, I'd put my money on George Breze."

"LATE to bed and late to rise" was Qwilleran's motto, and he was remarkably healthy, certainly wealthy, and—if not exactly wise—he was witty. On that particular January morning at seven o'clock he was sleeping peacefully when he was jolted awake by the crashing drums and brasses of the *Washington Post March,* as if the entire U.S. Marine Band were bursting through his bedroom wall. He required a few seconds to realize where he was: in a poorly built condominium in Indian Village, and his next-door neighbor was playing John Philip Sousa.

Before he could find Wetherby's phone number, the volume was toned down and the music was replaced by the sound of gushing, pelting water. Wetherby Goode was taking a shower.

Only then did Qwilleran recall the news of the night before—the arrest of a robbery suspect, name withheld. He knew Brodie would confide the name if he went down to headquarters, so he dressed, fed the cats, and left the house without coffee.

His neighbor was shoveling snow instead of waiting for the Village sidewalk blower. "Good exercise!" he shouted, puffing clouds of vapor.

"I can see that. Good concert this morning, too, but rather short."

Wetherby paused and leaned on his shovel. "Sorry about that. I have a new Sousabox, and my cat must've rubbed her jaw against the controls."

"That's all right. What's a Sousabox?"

"It plays fifty Sousa marches. I can get you one wholesale if you're interested."

"I'll give it some serious thought," Qwilleran said.

He went on his way, thinking that Wetherby was friendly and well intentioned, even though he overdid the quotations and had strange taste in music.

There was a coffeepot at the police station, and Qwilleran helped himself before barging into Brodie's office and dropping into a chair.

The chief scowled and said, "Who invited you?"

"I won't stay long. I just came for coffee. Tell me who was arrested, and I'll leave."

Brodie shook his head. "You'll never believe it, Qwill. I didn't myself, but the evidence was there."

"Who? Who?" Qwilleran insisted with some irritation.

"Lenny Inchpot."

"No! What led you to Lenny?"

"Anonymous tip, telling us to search the manager's locker at the clubhouse. We went out there with a warrant and had to cut the padlock. And there they were, all the items reported stolen—well, not all of the stuff. No money. And no lambskin car coat. There was even a rare doll that the Kemple family reported stolen not too long ago. He's being arraigned this morning, with a public defender."

"Can you imagine a young man like Lenny stealing a doll?"

"He's a friend of the Kemples' daughter. Do you know about the family's doll collection?"

"I've heard about it." For two years or more Qwilleran's readers had been urging him to "write up" the Kemple collection. He had written about teddy bears, but that was under duress.

Qwilleran smoothed his mustache. "I get a fishy feeling about this case, Andy."

On his way out he called his attorney, G. Allen Barter.

THE youngest partner in the Hasselrich, Bennett & Barter law firm, G. Allen Barter, was Qwilleran's representative in all dealings with the Klingenschoen Foundation. He was fortyish—a quiet, effective professional whose clients called him Bart.

When Qwilleran turned up in his office, Barter said, "We'll have someone get Lenny released to the custody of his mother."

Qwilleran patted his mustache. "Something tells me it's a frame-up, Bart. I don't know anything about Lenny's personal life except that his girlfriend was killed in that bomb explosion at the Pickax Hotel last fall. But he could have an enemy—a rival who wants his job. It's only part-time, but it's interesting work, good pay, flexible hours. Now, have there been any developments in the Limburger file?"

"Yes. The estate is willing to sell the hotel and the family mansion, and the K Fund is willing to buy, restoring the hotel and converting the mansion into a country inn."

"In that case they might consider Carter Lee James for the restoration work. He's the cousin of Willard Carmichael's widow. He was here for the holidays and had a sensational idea for Pleasant Street. Willard recommended him, and the property owners are impressed. At any rate, the K Fund should check him out."

TWO days later Danielle returned to town. Qwilleran checked in at Amanda's Design Studio to get an update from Fran Brodie.

"Yes, Danny-girl is back. I've only talked to her on the phone. The things I ordered for her house are trickling in."

"How soon can she move into her house?" he asked, hoping for her early departure from Indian Village.

"Her lease at the Village has a few months to run. Besides, the drifts are too deep. Meanwhile, she intends to work with Carter Lee. He'll be back at the end of the week."

"And what news about *Hedda Gabler?* Are you going ahead with your insane idea?"

Fran threw him an expressive scowl she had learned from her father. "Frankly, that's why Danielle returned so soon. She attended rehearsal last night and read lines."

"And?"

Fran's scowl changed to involuntary laughter. "When the snooty Hedda says 'She's left her old hat on the chair' in Danielle's rusty-gate voice, it's hard to keep a straight face."

"I warned you it would turn into a farce," Qwilleran said.

"Don't panic. We'll work it out. Unfortunately, she doesn't like the man who's playing Judge Brack. She'd rather play opposite you, Qwill."

"But I'm the drama critic for the paper, remember?"

"But she's right. You'd be a perfect Brack, and your presence in the cast would sell tickets."

"If you're chiefly interested in the box office, the K Fund will buy out the house for all performances."

"Forget I mentioned it," Fran said.

THE four-o'clock lull at Lois's Luncheonette would be an auspicious time to visit the suspect's mother, Qwilleran thought. Would she be fighting mad or pained beyond words? To his surprise Lenny himself was the only one in sight. He was mopping the floor.

"Mom's in the kitchen," Lenny said. Though in work clothes, he looked more like a club manager than a mop pusher.

Qwilleran said, "Actually, it's you I want to see. Did G. Allen Barter contact you?"

"Yeah. Do you think I need him?"

"You certainly do. Don't worry. The K Fund will cover the expense. Bart will see that you're exonerated."

"But what if I'm guilty?" the young man said with a mischievous grin.

"We'll take that chance, smart ape! Notice they didn't ask you to post bond. Now, would you tell me what you know? I'd like to find the real culprit, not that it's any of my business. How long have you been working at the clubhouse?"

"About six weeks. Don Exbridge is a good boss. All the members are fun. It's better than desk clerk at the hotel."

"Where was the money jar kept?"

"In my office, in a cabinet with pencils, nut dishes, and stuff."

"Who else had access to your office?"

"Anybody who wanted to pay their dues or see the schedule of events—plus there were maintenance guys, cleaning crew, caterers. But nobody knew the jar was there except the bridge club."

"Where was your locker?" Qwilleran asked.

"In the back hall with all the other employee lockers."

"Do they have locks?"

"Padlocks are supplied, but nobody uses them."

"Is your name on your locker?"

"Sure. They all have names."

A loud voice from the kitchen interrupted. "Lenny! Who's that you're gabbin' with? Get off your duff and mop that floor."

Lenny yelled back, "It's Mr. Q, Mom. He wants to talk about the case."

"Oh. Okay. Give him the other mop and put him to work. He can talk at the same time."

"I'm leaving," Qwilleran shouted.

BACK in Indian Village, the Siamese were sleeping in Qwilleran's reading chair. They had cushioned perches everywhere. Yet with feline perversity they preferred his lounge chair.

While they were yawning and stretching, Qwilleran phoned Don Exbridge, Lenny's boss, at home.

"Something's screwy somewhere," Don said. "If Lenny's guilty, I'm a donkey's uncle."

"I just want you to know G. Allen Barter is representing him."

"Great! And his job will be waiting for him when it's all over."

"Well, you know, there's no telling how long Lenny will have to wait for a hearing, and I could recommend a temporary substitute—an older woman, very responsible, cheerful."

"Who is she?"

"Celia Robinson. You wouldn't be disappointed. Why don't I tell her to apply for the job?"

"She's got it. She's got it already."

Feeling smug, Qwilleran hung up the phone and called Celia at her apartment in town.

"Hi, Chief," she greeted him.

"Celia, have you heard about Lenny Inchpot?"

"Have I? It's all over town."

"We're all concerned, and I personally suspect dirty work."

"Do I smell something cooking, Chief?" she asked eagerly.

"Just this: Lenny's position at Indian Village needs to be filled quickly by a temporary substitute. I suggest you apply. Don Exbridge is expecting your call. *It's your kind of job,* Celia."

"Gotcha, Chief," she said knowingly, and hung up.

ONCE a week Polly invited Qwilleran to what she laughingly called a chicken dinner. After Polly's heart attack the dietitian at the hospital had given her seventeen low-cholesterol recipes for glamorizing a flattened chicken breast.

"Think of it as *pollo scallopini appetito,*" Polly suggested. This week's special was FCB with mushrooms and walnuts.

They had much to talk about. Qwilleran described his forthcoming book of Moose County legends, to be titled *Short and Tall Tales.* Homer Tibbitt would kick off with the story of the Dimsdale jinx. Suggestions would be welcome.

"Try Wetherby Goode," she said. "Do you ever see him?"

"Only when he's shoveling his sidewalk. He has a cat, so he can't be too bad." Then Qwilleran changed the subject. "Have you and Lynette made your annual pilgrimage to the hill?" he asked.

Lynette had a driving desire to visit the Hilltop Cemetery once every winter. Her ancestors were buried there, and one gravesite was reserved for "the last of the Duncans-by-blood."

Polly said, "I don't mind going with her. On a good day it's a beautiful sight. Incidentally, Lynette is on cloud nine. Carter Lee phoned her from Detroit. He's coming back and wants her to be cheerleader for the Pleasant Street project."

"Is this a paid position?"

"I don't think so, but she's very enthusiastic about the project. He took her to dinner several times before he left, and she was the first property owner to sign a contract. By the way, her birthday will be soon, and I'd like to give a party. Would you join us?"

"If you'll let me provide the champagne."

"That would be nice. It's her fortieth. I'd invite Carter Lee, of course, and that would mean inviting Danielle, and that would mean inviting another man."

"How about John Bushland?" Qwilleran said. "He'll bring his camera." It occurred to him that the presence of a professional photographer might distract the photogenic young widow.

FOUR

HOMER Tibbitt, the first contributor to *Short and Tall Tales,* was official historian of Moose County. The retired educator was now in his late nineties, and his fantastic memory made him a treasure. He lived with his sweet eighty-five-year-old wife in a retirement village.

Qwilleran turned on the tape recorder. "So, what brought about the Dimsdale jinx?"

"It started about a hundred years ago, when the mines were going full blast. This isn't a tall tale, mind you. It's true."

The old man's account was later transcribed as follows:

There was a miner named Roebuck Magley, a husky man in his late forties, who worked in Seth Dimsdale's mine. He had a wife and three sons, and they lived in one of the cottages provided for workers.

Roebuck worked hard, and the boys went to work in the mines as soon as they finished eighth grade. Betty Magley worked hard, too, feeding her men, scrubbing their clothes, but somehow she always stayed pretty.

Suddenly Roebuck fell sick and died. He'd been complaining about stomach pains, and one day he came home from work, ate his supper, and dropped dead.

Roebuck's death certificate, signed by Dr. Penfield, said

"Heart failure." Seth Dimsdale paid Mrs. Magley a generous sum from the insurance policy he carried on his workers, and she was grateful. She'd been ailing herself, and the doctor was at a loss to diagnose her symptoms.

Well, about a month later her eldest son, Robert, died in the mine shaft of "respiratory failure," according to the death certificate, and it wasn't long before the second son, Amos, died under the same circumstances. The miners' wives flocked around Betty Magley, and Seth Dimsdale authorized a private investigation.

Both Robert and Amos had died, he learned, after eating their lunch underground; Roebuck's last meal had been a pasty in his kitchen. The community was alarmed. "Bad meat!" they said.

Then something curious happened to Alfred, the youngest son. While underground, he shared his pasty with another miner whose lunch had fallen out of his pocket. Soon both men were complaining of pains, nausea, and numb hands and feet.

When word reached Seth Dimsdale, he notified the prosecuting attorney in Pickax, and the court issued an order to exhume the bodies of Roebuck, Robert, and Amos. Their internal organs were found to contain lethal quantities of arsenic, and Mrs. Magley was questioned by the police.

Then the neighbors remembered the doctor's daily visits to treat Mrs. Magley's mysterious ailment. When Penfield was arrested, the mining community was bowled over. He was much admired.

It turned out, however, that he was in debt and his visits to treat the pretty Betty Magley were more personal than professional. He was the first defendant placed on trial. Mrs. Magley sat in jail and awaited her turn.

The miners, convinced of the integrity of the doctor, rose to his support, and it was difficult to seat an unbiased jury. The trial itself lasted longer than any in local history, and when it was over, the county was broke.

The trial revealed that Dr. Penfield had supplied the arsenic— for medical purposes, he said, and any overdose was caused by human error. Mrs. Magley had baked the pasties and collected the insurance money, giving half to the doctor. He was found guilty on three counts of murder and sentenced to life in prison.

Mrs. Magley was never tried for the crime, because the county couldn't afford a second trial. She just left town quietly.

So she disappeared, along with her youngest son, the only one to survive. Seth Dimsdale retired to Ohio and also disappeared. The Dimsdale mine disappeared. The whole town of Dimsdale disappeared. It was called the Dimsdale jinx.

When Homer finished telling his tale, Qwilleran clicked off the tape recorder and said, "Great story!"

It had been a strenuous recital, and the old man's energy was flagging. It was time for him to take a nap. Qwilleran thanked him and left shortly after.

IT WAS January 25, and Qwilleran phoned the public library.

"Polly Duncan here," the chief librarian answered pleasantly.

"What's today's date?" he asked, knowing she would recognize his voice.

"January twenty-fifth. Is it significant?"

"Birthday of Robert Burns. Tonight's the night!"

Gleefully she exclaimed, "It's Scottish Night! You're going to wear your kilt! I wish I could see you before you leave. What time is the dinner?"

"I leave at six thirty, with trepidation," he admitted.

Polly said she would stop on her way home to bolster his courage.

Qwilleran fed the cats early, then disappeared into his bedroom and closed the door. There he faced the unfamiliar trappings: the pleated kilt, the sporran, the flashes, the bonnet, the dubh.

The trick was to develop an attitude of pride in one's hereditary Scottish attire. After all, Qwilleran's mother had been a Mackintosh, and the kilt was worn by brave men skilled with the broadsword.

With this attitude firmly in place, Qwilleran strapped himself into his kilt of fine worsted red Mackintosh dress tartan. On this occasion it would be worn with a white turtleneck and bottle-green tweed jacket, plus matching green kilt hose and red flashes. These were tabs attached to the garters that held up the kilt hose—a vital detail. The sporran hung from a leather belt.

Qwilleran's bonnet was a bottle-green balmoral—a round flat cap worn squarely on the forehead, with a slouchy crown pulled down to the right. It had a ribbon cockade, a pompon on top, and two ribbons hanging down the back.

Studying his reflection in the full-length mirror, Qwilleran thought, Not bad. Not bad at all. He opened the door abruptly. Both cats levitated in fright and streaked down the stairs with bushy tails.

When Polly arrived, she was overwhelmed with delight. "Qwill!" she cried. "You look magnificent. So jaunty. So virile."

DOWNTOWN Pickax was deserted except for men in kilts or tartan trews ducking into the back door of the lodge. Qwilleran was greeted by Whannell MacWhannell, who had invited him.

"Let's go downstairs and look at the new exhibit," MacWhannell said.

The walls of the lower lounge were covered with maps, photographs of Scotland, and swatches of clan tartans. The majority of men were in kilts, and Qwilleran felt comfortable among them.

Gil MacMurchie, the dowser, was wearing a lively Buchanan tartan. Qwilleran said to him, "I'm ready to buy your dirks."

"They're still there." MacMurchie paused and looked down sadly. "But the one I was saving for myself was stolen."

"No! When?"

"While I was running those ads to sell my furniture. Strangers were traipsing through the house, and I couldn't keep an eye on all of them."

"Did you report it to the police?"

"Oh, sure. And after Lois's boy was arrested, I went to the station to see if my dirk turned up in his locker, but it wasn't there."

"How ironic," Qwilleran said, "that the thief should take the one your wife gave you."

The wail of a bagpipe summoned them to the dining hall. As soon as everyone was seated, the doors were flung open, and in came the police chief in kilt, red doublet, towering feather bonnet, and white spats. A veritable giant, he walked with a slow swagger as he piped the inspiring air, "Scotland the Brave." He was followed by a snare drummer and seven young men in kilts and white shirts, each carrying a tray. On the first was the celebrated haggis; on each of the other six was a bottle of Scotch.

A bottle was placed on each table, and toasts were drunk to the legendary pudding, which was sliced and served.

The emcee rapped for attention. The evening would include the reading of Robert Burns's poems and the serious business of drinking toasts to Scottish heroes. First there was a moment of silence, however, in memory of Willard Carmichael. Brodie piped "The Flowers of the Forest" as a dirge.

Then Whannell MacWhannell stood up and announced, "Tonight we honor someone who came to Pickax from Down Below and made a difference. Because of him we have better schools, better health care, a better airport, and a column to read twice a week for entertainment and enlightenment. If you pay him a compliment, he'll give credit to his mother, who was a Mackintosh. It gives us great pleasure to add a name to our roll of distinguished Scots: the son of Anne Mackintosh Qwilleran!"

Qwilleran walked to the platform amid cheers in English and Gaelic. Photographer John Bushland from the *Something* was taking pictures.

"Officers, members, and guests," Qwilleran began. "I confess it has taken some heavy persuasion to get me into a kilt, but here I am, wearing the Mackintosh tartan as a tribute to Anne Mackintosh Qwilleran, a single parent who struggled heroically to raise an obstreperous male offspring. In her name I accept this honor."

Brodie piped "Auld Lang Syne," and the audience stood up and sang, *"We'll take a cup o' kindness yet."*

Later in the evening, after circulating in the lounge and accepting congratulations, Qwilleran said to Gil MacMurchie, "If you're going home from here, I'll meet you there and write a check." In a short while he was on Pleasant Street, and Gil was admitting him to a house that was emptier than before.

The four dirks with scabbards and brass hilts were under the glass in the curio table, along with the two brooches.

"Was the table not locked?" Qwilleran asked.

"Hasn't been for years." He wrapped the dirks and brooches in newspaper while Qwilleran wrote a check for a thousand.

THE Siamese recognized the sound of the car when he drove into the attached garage, and they knew the sound of his key in the lock. They had forgotten their original scare of the kilt. Their greeting was positive without being effusive.

When he unwrapped his purchases on the kitchen counter, both cats jumped up to investigate the large round stones in the brooches, as well as the brass hilts and the scabbards. Qwilleran withdrew one dirk from its scabbard, and Koko went into paroxysms of excitement over the blade, baring his fangs and flattening his ears as he moved his nose up and down the blood grooves.

There were messages on the answering machine from friends who had heard about his honor on the eleven-o'clock newscast, and there were phone calls the next morning. John Bushland was one who called with congratulations.

Qwilleran said, "I saw you taking pictures at the dinner. Was that for the newspaper or the lodge?"

"Both. I'm doing a video for lodge members."

"Did Polly call you about Lynette's birthday party?"

"Yes, and I've got an idea for a gift. On New Year's Eve, I got a great shot of her talking with two guys—eyes sparkling, nice smile. The light was right, and she looked young and happy."

"Who were the guys?"

"Wetherby Goode and Carter Lee James. I could blow it up and put it in a neat frame. Do you think she'd like it?"

"She'd be thrilled. Do it!" Qwilleran said.

QWILLERAN had some errands to do downtown. While there, he stopped at the office of the *Moose County Something* to pick up a free newspaper. On the front page was a full-length photo of him in Scottish Highland attire. He groaned. Did they have to print it four columns wide and eighteen inches high? Then he said to himself, Obviously it was a slow day on the newsbeat. He picked up an extra copy for Polly and left the building, briefly considering a week's vacation in Iceland.

Next he stopped at Amanda's Design Studio, carrying a news-paper-wrapped package.

Fran greeted him. "What do you have wrapped in newspaper?" she asked. "Fresh fish?"

He showed her the four dirks and asked how to display them on the wall. "I don't want them under glass."

She unwrapped the dirks, then vanished into the stockroom, and returned carrying an antique pine picture frame. She said, "We can put a backing in it for mounting the dirks."

"Perfect. You're so clever, Fran."

"The bill will go out in the mail tomorrow."

He started out, then returned. "Do you happen to know the family with the famous doll collection?"

"Of course. The Kemples. I worked with Vivian Kemple on their house on Pleasant Street. They're both involved in rare dolls."

"May I use your phone?" he asked.

A man with a particularly loud voice answered, and Qwilleran identified himself.

"Sure! We've met at the Boosters Club, Qwill. I'm Ernie Kemple." He was the Boosters' official glad-hander, greeting members at every meeting.

"I'm calling about your doll collection, Ernie, as a possibility for the Qwill Pen column."

"Well now, we don't like publicity. We had a doll stolen recently—not worth a lot in dollars but highly collectible. Tell you what. Come and see the collection for your own enjoyment."

"Thank you. I'll accept the invitation." It was a break for Qwilleran. He could satisfy his curiosity without having to write about dolls.

"How about now? My wife's out of town, and I'm waiting for three o'clock so I can pick up my grandson from school."

"I'll be right there," Qwilleran said.

PLEASANT Street looked particularly pleasant that afternoon. A new fall of snow had frosted the lacy wood trim on the houses, and the whole street was an avenue of white ruffles. The Kemple house was painted in two shades of taupe, reflecting Fran Brodie's educated taste.

"A most attractive house," Qwilleran said to Ernie Kemple when he was admitted. Like the exterior, the rooms showed the hand of a professional designer. Traditional furniture was arranged in a friendly, contemporary manner; colors dared to depart from the historically correct.

Kemple replied in a booming voice that would make crystal chandeliers quiver. "You like it? I think it's pretty good. But now my wife thinks maybe we should let Carter Lee James restore it to nineteenth-century authenticity. He and his assistant went through the house, making notes. Vivian says everybody on the street is going along with James. It's supposed to increase the property value, maybe give us a tax break. This James fellow presents a convincing case. What's your opinion?"

"I haven't heard his pitch firsthand, but Lynette Duncan is sold on him," Qwilleran said.

"The question is, Suppose we stick to our guns. Would we want to be the only holdout in the neighborhood? Well, let's go in the kitchen and have some cake and coffee."

Qwilleran sat at the table and looked at a group of framed photos on a wall. "Is the curly-haired blond boy your grandson?"

"Yes, that's my little Bobbie. My daughter's divorced and living with us, and she works part-time, so Vivian and I get pressed into service as baby-sitters. I tell you, it's the greatest thing that ever happened to a retired insurance agent! I have granddaughters, too, but they're in Arizona. That's where Vivian is now, visiting our son."

The kitchen's high ceiling and slick surfaces made Kemple's great voice reverberate and made Qwilleran wince. "Have you ever been on the stage, Ernie?"

"Sure. I belonged to the theater club for years. I left the club when we started doing a lot of traveling."

"The club is casting a play right now that has a perfect role for you. Are you familiar with Judge Brack in *Hedda Gabler?*"

"Sure. I could handle that role. Who's directing?"

"Carol Lanspeak."

"Oh, she's good! I think I'll take your suggestion and surprise Vivian when she comes home. She's always telling me I could play Madison Square Garden without a mike."

The two men applied themselves almost reverently to some Queen Mum's cake, and there was little conversation for a while.

"How did you get interested in dolls?" Qwilleran asked then.

"I needed a hobby. History was my minor in college, and Vivian was getting into classic dolls, so I started researching historic doll makers. It's good for a couple to have a hobby they can share."

"What did Vivian collect before classic dolls?"

"Primitives. Old Moose County dolls that pioneers made. Carved and painted wood, stuffed flour sacks—that type of thing."

Qwilleran remarked that he had yet to see a doll.

"All upstairs. In glass cases."

"Under lock and key?"

"Never thought it necessary, but now . . ." Kemple shrugged.

Qwilleran pointed to another photo in the wall grouping: a pretty young blond woman. "Your daughter?"

"Yes, that's Tracy, around the time she was married."

"She looks familiar."

"You've probably seen her at the Old Stone Mill. She works

lunches there, dinners at the Boulder House Inn. She's a waitress."

Upstairs, there were three rooms outfitted with museum-type cases. The first room contained primitives made between 1850 and 1912. And dazzling was the word for the two rooms displaying the china, porcelain, wax, bisque, and papier-mâché beauties.

Qwilleran asked about the stolen doll. It was carved and painted wood and very old. It was thought to have come from a Native American village on the Ittibittiwassee River.

"It was the first that ever disappeared from our collection," Kemple said. "It was found in Lenny Inchpot's possession."

"In his locker," Qwilleran corrected him. "Police had to cut the padlock, yet Lenny says he never locked it, and I believe him. I've asked my own attorney to take the case. It's my opinion that he was framed."

Kemple looked relieved. "Glad to hear that. Tell your attorney I'll go as a character witness at the hearing if he wants me to. Lenny was Tracy's boyfriend when they were in high school. Vivian and I considered him a future son-in-law."

"What happened?"

"Tracy eloped with a football player from Sawdust City. She's impulsive. It didn't last, and she and Bobbie came home to live with us. Then Lenny's girlfriend was killed, and he started coming to the house again."

"How did Tracy react to his arrest?"

"She was troubled, I could tell, but she wouldn't talk to me. She'll talk to her mother, though. I'll be glad when Vivian gets home. You see, Tracy's always one to go for the main chance, and now she's set her sights on Carter Lee James. My fatherly instinct is flashing red. I don't want her to be disappointed again. It seems to me that all the women are flipping over him."

"Understandably," Qwilleran said. "He has a likable personality, good looks, and a glamorous profession."

"That's for sure, and my daughter is a beautiful young woman. James has wined and dined her a few times, and her hopes are up. What can I say? She's a grown woman."

"Not to digress, but how does she feel about the Pleasant Street project?"

"Oh, she's all for it. She says it'll make our neighborhood world-famous. I'm not sure that prospect appeals to me. But look, why am I burdening you with my problems?"

"No burden at all. I can put myself in your shoes."

Driving home from Pleasant Street, Qwilleran was glad he had no parental responsibilities.

WHEN he arrived in Indian Village, there was a message on the answering machine from Celia Robinson, requesting him to call her at the clubhouse before five thirty, her quitting time. She had a little treat for him and the cats and would drop it off on the way home.

He phoned Celia immediately. "Visitors bearing treats are always welcome."

At five thirty-three her bright red car pulled in. She greeted Qwilleran in a flurry of contagious happiness. "Here's some goat cheese, a thank-you for steering me to this wonderful job!"

She walked into the living room and flopped onto the sofa, facing the frozen riverbank. "Well, I've found a home for the little black dog that Clayton liked. His stepmother wouldn't let him take it home."

"Who wants to adopt the dog?" Qwilleran asked.

"A nice young man from the Split Rail Goat Farm. He came to the clubhouse today to give a talk to the garden club."

"That's Mitch Ogilvie. I know him very well," Qwilleran said. "I'll pick up Cody myself and deliver her. Now tell me, has there been any talk about Lenny at the clubhouse?"

"Plenty! Nobody thinks he's guilty, except for one man who thinks Lenny cracked up after his girlfriend was killed in the explosion. Is there anything I can do about the Lenny case, Chief?"

"Just keep your eyes and ears open," Qwilleran suggested. "Bear in mind that Lenny may have been framed. Who's the man who said he'd cracked up?"

"I don't know. He's around a lot. Want me to find out?"

"Yes. Do that. As soon as possible."

"Okay, Chief."

WHEN Qwilleran went to the MacMurchie house the next morning, he was met at the door by a smiling Scot and a bouncing schnauzer. A carton in the foyer contained Cody's brush, leashes, dishes, a supply of dried food, and some old socks. MacMurchie said, "The food is a combination of rice and lamb that she seems to prefer. The socks are her toys."

Cody was listening, pancaked on the floor.

"On your feet, young lady," Qwilleran ordered. "We're going for a ride."

Cody rode up front in the passenger seat, standing on her hind legs and watching the snowy landscape whiz past. The Split Rail Farm was in the Hummocks, where drifts made familiar landmarks unrecognizable.

Mitch Ogilvie, looking bucolic in his rough beard and heavy storm wear, came from a low sprawling barn to meet them. "What's his name?" he asked.

"Cody is a she. You'll like her," Qwilleran said. He carried her into the house, saying, "Here we are!"

Mitch put the carton in the kitchen. "Let her explore," he said. "We'll have some cheese and crackers while she decides if she wants to live here."

They drank coffee and sampled several cheeses and listened to canine noises as Cody made discoveries. Then Qwilleran asked about the procedure Mitch followed in getting his Victorian farmhouse on the National Register of Historic Places. Built by a Civil War hero, it was the only edifice in Moose County to have official historic recognition.

"There was a lot of red tape," Mitch replied. "There was one government printout *six yards long* that really threw me for a loop. To me it was all gobbledygook. Why do you ask, Qwill?"

"There's a whole neighborhood in Pickax that hopes to be registered, and I wondered about the procedure. Do you still have the six-yard printout? I wouldn't mind reading it."

"Sure. I'll dig it out for you. With your sense of humor you might have some fun with it in the Qwill Pen column."

Cody, having okayed the premises, returned to the kitchen. Mitch found her dishes and put out water and food for her.

"She'll be happy here," Qwilleran said as he put on jacket, hat, and gloves, and put the printout in his pocket. "Take care of her."

LYNETTE'S birthday party lacked effervescence, despite the bubbles in the champagne that Qwilleran poured. The hostess worried about the prime rib she was roasting in a new oven. The bereaved widow was resolutely glum. The guest of honor seemed nervous; did she fear her age would be revealed?

According to Moose County custom, the right-hand end of the sofa was reserved for the guest of honor. Carter Lee sat at the other end, wearing one of his monogrammed shirts.

They said all that could be said about the weather. Carter Lee had no desire to talk shop. Qwilleran's skill as an interviewer failed him; his questions produced no interesting answers. To fill the silences, John Bushland hopped around taking candids.

When Qwilleran suggested that Lynette open her gifts, she said firmly, "No! After dinner." Fortunately, the roast beef was superb; the Yorkshire pudding was properly puffy.

For coffee and cordials the diners moved back into the living room, and Lynette opened her gifts: violet sachets from Polly, a silver "poached egg" from Qwilleran, Bushy's framed photo, a bottle of wine from Danielle, and the smallest of small boxes from Carter Lee.

It was obviously a ring. Was that why Lynette had been self-conscious and Carter Lee had seemed unnaturally shy? When he slipped the ring on her left hand, Polly gasped audibly at the size of the diamond. Danielle merely tapped the floor with her uncommonly high-heeled shoe.

Then the couple answered questions. Yes, the marriage would be soon, because they were honeymooning in New Orleans and wanted to be there for Mardi Gras. No, it would not be a church wedding—just a small affair at the clubhouse. Yes, that's where they had met, across a bridge table.

After the guests had left, Qwilleran's first question to Polly was, "Did you know anything about this little bombshell?"

"Not an inkling! They haven't known each other very long. I hope she knows what she's doing," Polly said. "Danielle seemed less than happy about her cousin's engagement."

FIVE

THE morning after Lynette's party Qwilleran was wakened by what he feared was a pounding heartbeat, but it was the thrum-thrum-thrum of Wetherby Goode's wake-up music on the Sousabox.

The Siamese, too, were awake and could hear and feel the thrum-thrum-thrum. Koko, waiting for his breakfast, sat on his haunches and slapped his tail in time with the percussion.

Qwilleran fed them, brushed them, and joined them in a little active recreation. The sun was streaming in the living-room window and reviving the lone housefly that had come with the condo. Qwilleran stood with folded newspaper, ready to swat; the cats leaped and made passes and crashed into each other as the fly swooped playfully around the two-story living room. He had been living with them long enough to have a name, Mosca, and none of his pursuers really wanted to catch him.

After breakfast the telephone rang, and Qwilleran heard Celia Robinson's voice saying with unusual crispness, "Mr. Qwilleran, this is your accountant's office. The numbers you requested are two, eighteen, five, twenty-six, five."

"Thank you for your prompt assistance," he said.

It was exactly as he had guessed. The code spelled b-r-e-z-e. It was the scoundrelly George Breze who suggested that Lenny Inchpot had "cracked up."

According to conventional wisdom in Moose County, it was Old Gallbladder himself who was cracked—or crooked. He was suspected of everything, yet was never charged with anything.

Qwilleran sat down at his typewriter to start on his next column for the *Something*. Both cats were on his writing table—Yum Yum sitting on her brisket, and Koko, the more cerebral of the two, watching the type bars jump. Suddenly his ears alerted, and he looked toward the phone. A few moments later it rang.

It was Lynette. "I had a wonderful time last night. Thank you again for that lovely brooch. I'll wear it on my wedding day."

"I'm glad you like it," he murmured.

"Now Carter Lee and I have a big favor to ask. Would you mind if we dropped by for a few minutes?"

"Not at all. Come at five o'clock and have a glass of wine."

After that, Qwilleran drove to Pickax to hand in his copy. From the newspaper he went to the design studio to pick up his dirks. "Superb job of framing," he told Fran.

"Don't hang them too high," she cautioned. "Men of your height tend to hang wall decorations too high. It's the giraffe syndrome." Then her manner changed from flip to confidential. "I heard a fantastic rumor this morning. Lynette is getting married at long last! And to Carter Lee James. I'm surprised Danielle didn't tell me—if it's true."

"So how's the play going?" Qwilleran asked, smoothly changing the subject.

"Good news! We were able to get Ernie Kemple for Judge Brack, and it's perfect casting, although his booming voice and Danielle's tinny one sound like a duet for tuba and piccolo. You should come to rehearsal some night and have a few laughs."

ON THE way home Qwilleran thought about Lenny Inchpot and George Breze. He needed to confer with Celia Robinson—but how and where? Her bright red car parked in front of his condo twice in quick succession would arouse the curiosity of neighbors, Polly included. Qwilleran decided to brief Celia by mail. As soon as he arrived home, he typed the following communication:

> TO: Agent 0013½
> FROM: Q
> MISSION: Operation Winter Breeze
> ASSIGNMENT: To tail the subject identified in your report. Code name: Red Cap. Introduce yourself as Lenny's replacement. Find out why Red Cap spends so much time in the TV lounge. Bear in mind that Red Cap may be the Pickax Pilferer, and he *may* be covering up by falsely accusing Lenny. When mission is accomplished, phone headquarters to set up a rendezvous in the fresh produce department at Toodle's Market.

To deliver the briefing to Celia's mailbox at the gatehouse, Qwilleran strapped on his snowshoes and trekked through the woods over a fresh fall of snow. He found it tranquilizing. At the gatehouse he found a certain aesthetic satisfaction in unstrapping the snowshoes and sticking their tails in the snowbank.

AS FIVE o'clock approached, Qwilleran gave the Siamese an early dinner and instructions on how to behave during the visit of the happy couple. "No flying around. No domestic quarrels." They acted as if they understood, regarding him soberly, although actually they were just digesting their food.

The guests arrived promptly at five, Carter Lee driving Willard's Land Rover. In the foyer, they hung their coats on the art deco clothes tree and their hats on the top hook: one angora knit and one black fur toque. They walked into the living room and remarked about the fine wintry view and the beautiful cats.

"This one is Koko, and that one is Yum Yum," said Lynette, who had fed them one weekend in Qwilleran's absence. With typical feline perversity they ignored her and went to Carter Lee.

"Don't take it personally," the host explained to her. "They always consider it their duty to check out a newcomer."

The newcomer said, "My mother, who lives in Paris, has a Siamese called Theoria Dominys du Manoir des Ombreuses. Dodo, for short."

Lynette said, "We're going to France in May."

"Then how about a glass of merlot?" Qwilleran suggested.

While he was pouring, they sat on the sofa in full command of the view. The waning daylight was prolonged by the brilliant whiteness of the riverbank and the frozen river below.

Amiable small talk continued for a while. The couple held hands across the center cushion and exchanged fond glances occasionally. Then Lynette said, "We'd be grateful, Qwill, if you and Polly would stand up for us at our wedding. Polly is willing."

"Of course! I'm honored. What's the date?"

"A week from Tuesday."

Carter Lee added, "We have a reservation in New Orleans that starts Wednesday, at an inn near the French Quarter. After the ceremony we'd like you and Polly to be our guests for dinner at the Boulder House Inn. We're staying there overnight."

"It'll be a Scottish wedding, Qwill," Lynette said. "I'll wear a clan sash over a white dress. Polly will wear her floor-length kilt and a clan sash. Then there are several Scottish customs, like a silver coin in my shoe—for luck. At the reception Polly will break the traditional oatcake over my head. Carter Lee has to leave his left shoelace untied during the ceremony."

"I'll be in dinner clothes," Carter Lee said.

"Yes," Lynette said, "but we're counting on you, Qwill, to wear full Highland dress."

He nodded his agreement, having received innumerable compliments on his Scottish Night debut.

"Since I'm marrying out of my clan, I'm supposed to keep my maiden name. Once a Duncan, always a Duncan. But you don't mind, do you, honey?"

Her fiancé squeezed her hand and smiled indulgently. They were so coyly sentimental that Qwilleran shuddered inwardly. "Carter Lee, how is your cousin?" he said somberly. "Is she— Is she—"

"She's holding up," he replied. "She'd like to marry again, and that's a healthy sign. She should go on with her life. She has so much to give. I hate to see it go to waste, don't you, Qwill?"

Before Qwilleran could formulate an appropriate reply to a debatable question, all three of them were unnerved by a sudden fracas in the foyer—snarling, thumping, hissing, growling. They jumped up and rushed to the scene. The two cats were fighting over the black fur hat, rolling in it and kicking it.

"Stop that!" Qwilleran thundered, and the two culprits streaked away. "My apologies," he said to Carter Lee.

"No problem. I'll just give it a good shake."

They drove away in the Land Rover, and Qwilleran went to dinner at Polly's, but not before giving the Siamese a treat and saying, "You rascals!"

EVERY week Qwilleran spent a predictable weekend with Polly Duncan. He could count on contentment and stimulation in equal quantities. The weekend following Lynette's birthday party, they had Sunday dinner at the Palomino Paddock, a five-star restaurant in Lockmaster County.

Over the whitefish Qwilleran said, "I've decided why Danielle was so moody at Lynette's party. Willard had arranged to take her to Mardi Gras, and it's his hotel reservation that's now being used by Carter Lee for his honeymoon, so Danielle is left out. Unless Lynette jilts him, in which case he can take Danielle."

"It's not a matter for levity," Polly said in gentle rebuke. "Lynette's intensely committed to this marriage. She's resigned from her job at the clinic, and she's transferring her property to joint ownership."

"So it's safe to go ahead and buy a wedding gift?"

"It's a problem, deciding what to give them. She has a houseful of heirloom silver and art."

Qwilleran said, "We could commission a portrait artist to paint the two of them together in front of their gingerbread house. There's a guy in Lockmaster who's quite good."

Polly liked the idea enormously.

THERE WERE TWO CALLS THAT evening when he got home, one in a grating voice that made his blood curdle. "Hi, Qwill. This is Danielle. I've seen you out hiking on your snowshoes."

"It's cheap transportation," he said.

"How would you like to hike over here some afternoon?"

"Thank you for the invitation, but my days are fully scheduled," he said. "I wish I had time to chat, Danielle, but I have a houseful of guests here. Will you excuse me?"

"Dammit!" he said to Koko after hanging up. The cat was sitting on the table, slapping it with his tail—right, left, right, left.

The next call was more welcome, being in the brisk voice that Celia Robinson used for undercover communication: "Mr. Qwilleran, this is Mrs. Robinson. I'm going to Toodle's Market tomorrow. They have a good buy on *apples*. I'll pick up a bagful for you if you want me to. I'm going at ten o'clock before they're all picked over."

"I'll appreciate that. Very thoughtful of you," he said.

At ten o'clock the next morning he found her in the fresh produce department at Toodle's Market, eating cheese spread on a cracker from the deli counter.

Carrying a plastic shopping basket, he sidled up to her and said loudly, "Do you think these are good eating apples?"

"They're Jonathans, a nice all-purpose apple." Then she added under her breath, "Had a long talk with Red Cap. I've got the tape in my handbag." She slipped him something in a paper napkin and then disappeared into the crowd. It was the tape.

WHAT he heard when he played Celia's recording impressed him as a boy-meets-girl script for over-sixties. Her friendly voice alternated with a hoarse male twang:

"Are you Mr. Breze? Hi! I'm Celia Robinson from the manager's office."

"Howdy. Sit down. Have a drink."

"That's a nice-looking shirt you're wearing. I like to see a man in a plaid shirt."

"Wife give it to me eight years ago. 'Bout ready to be washed."

(Female laughter) "Oh, Mr. Breze! You're so funny."

"Call me George. You're a nice-lookin' woman. Are you married?"

"I'm a widow and a grandmother."

"Have a slug o' whiskey. I'm divorced."

"Is that why you're living in the Village?"

"Yep. Gotta house on Sandpit Road—too big for just me. Know anybody with ninety thou to throw away?"

"Ninety thousand! It must be quite a fine house."

"Well, the roof don't leak. If I find me another woman, I'll keep the house and fix it up. There's a feller what says I can get money from the guv'ment to fix it up. Showed me some pitchers, what it'd look like. Mighty purty pitchers. Young feller. Lives here in the Village. What's yer name again?"

"Celia Robinson. I'm substituting for Lenny Inchpot while he's away. Do you know him?"

"Sure. He got thrown in jail for stealin'."

"But people tell me he's a very honest young man."

"They found the goods on 'im, di'n't they?"

"I wonder who tipped off the police to look in Lenny's locker."

"Warn't me!"

"Do you know what kinds of things were stolen?"

"Nope. Di'n't say on the radio. Maybe it said in the paper. Don't read the paper."

"Why not, Mr. Breze? It's a very good one."

"Call me George. It's a waste o' time readin' the paper. I'm a successful businessman. I don't need to read."

"Are you telling me you can't read, Mr. Breze? . . . George?"

"Could if I felt like learnin'. Never took the time. Too busy makin' money."

"What kind of business are you in, George?"

"Any goldurned thing that'll make money."

(Click)

When the tape clicked off, Qwilleran huffed into his mustache.

It was the old duffer he had tried to interview during the mayoralty campaign—the candidate who made news by polling only two votes. His house was an ugly, square two-story barracks. A sad piece of real estate, it had no trees, no grass, no window shutters, not even any paint. Breze himself was either pathetically naïve or arrogantly ignorant.

Koko had been listening and making gurgling noises that sounded sympathetic, and Qwilleran suddenly felt sorry for Old Gallbladder. He had suspected the despised fellow on the basis of prejudice, not evidence. So if Breze didn't do it, who did?

THE Tuesday night wedding took place in the social hall of the clubhouse. A white runner on the red carpet led to the fireplace, which blazed festively. Before it a white-draped table held red and white carnations in a brass bowl and red candles in tall brass holders. A Valentine wedding, the guests said. So romantic! They stood on either side of the runner. Many of the men were in kilts; the women wore clan sashes draped from shoulder to hip.

Lynette's clan sash was brilliant green, cascading down the front and back of her long white dress. The same green tartan figured in Polly's evening skirt and clan sash, worn with a white silk blouse. Qwilleran was resplendent in full Highland kit. Against the Duncan green and Mackintosh red, the groom's black dinner clothes looked ominously somber.

The ceremony was brief and flawless. There were no sentimental tears—only happiness—as the words were said. Then, in the dining hall, an oatcake was broken over the bride's head, and she cut the wedding cake with a dirk.

Champagne was poured and toasts were said and guests kissed the bride. Danielle was the first to kiss her cousin.

"Did you see how the Carmichael woman bussed her cousin?" Amanda Goodwinter muttered to Qwilleran. "I hope Lynette knows what she's doing."

Carter Lee was his usual charming self, flashing his winning smile at the guests in between fond glances at his bride. She was brimming with the joy she had lost when she was jilted twenty years before.

En route to Boulder House Inn, Qwilleran's mustache was giving him some uneasiness. Champagne had flowed freely at the reception, and he was probably the only one who was totally sober. He kept thinking about the kiss that Danielle had bestowed on the groom. And about the hints that they were not really cousins. And about the hasty marriage that was a topic of local gossip.

The Boulder House Inn perched on a cliff overlooking a frozen lake. Snow accented every ledge. Indoors, four-foot split logs blazed in the cavernous fireplace, around which guests gathered after dinner to listen to the innkeeper's stories.

Silas Dingwall, the innkeeper, ushered the wedding party to the best table in the dining room. A wine cooler stood ready, chilling a bottle of champagne, courtesy of the house.

"I'll be your wine steward tonight, and Tracy will be your server."

Involuntarily Qwilleran's hand went to his upper lip as he saw the innkeeper speak to a pretty young blond woman. He saw Dingwall gesture toward their table. He saw her nod.

Lynette and Carter Lee were drinking an intimate toast to each other, with arms linked and eyes shining, when the blond server approached the table. She took a few brisk steps, wearing a hospitable smile, then slowed to a sleepwalker's pace as her smile turned to shock. "Oh, no!" she cried and ran blindly from the dining room, lurching through the swinging doors to the kitchen. There was silence among the diners.

"Well!" Polly said. "What was that all about?"

Lynette was bewildered. Carter Lee seemed poised. Qwilleran looked wise. He thought he knew what it was all about.

The innkeeper, red-faced, bustled up to the table. "I'm sorry," he said. "Tracy is not well. Barbara will be your server."

Before leaving, Qwilleran told Silas Dingwall about *Short and Tall Tales* and made an appointment for the next day to record "something hair-raising." The innkeeper promised him a good one.

On the way home no mention was made of the waitress's outburst. Polly told him he was the handsomest man at the wedding; he told her she looked younger than the bride. Both agreed that Lynette looked beatific.

AS QWILLERAN drove to Boulder House Inn the next day, he reviewed the incident of the previous evening. The server's name was Tracy; she was obviously Ernie Kemple's daughter, who had been wined and dined by Carter Lee James. Now Qwilleran was wondering what kind of husband Lynette had acquired.

Arriving at the inn, Qwilleran was greeted effusively by Silas Dingwall, who said, "We'll go in the office, where it's quiet."

The innkeeper said he had been fascinated all his life by tales handed down through the generations. "My favorite is the 'Mystery of Dank Hollow,' a true story about a young fisherman who was also a new bridegroom. It happened, maybe, a hundred and thirty years ago."

As eventually transcribed, the story went like this:

> A young fisherman by the name of Wallace Reekie, who lived in the village here, went to his brother's funeral in a town twenty miles away. He set out on foot at daybreak and told his new bride he'd be home at nightfall. Folks didn't like to travel that road after dark, because there was a dangerous dip in it. Mists rose up and hid the path, and it was easy to make a wrong turn and walk into the bog. They called it Dank Hollow.
>
> At the funeral Wallace helped carry his brother's casket to the burial place in the woods, and on the way he tripped over a tree root. There was an old Scottish superstition: Stumble while carrying a corpse, and you'll be the next to go into the grave. It must have troubled Wallace, because he drank too much after the funeral and was late in leaving for home.
>
> When he didn't show up by nightfall, like he'd said, his wife sat up all night, praying. It was just turning daylight when she was horrified to see her husband staggering into the dooryard. Before he could say a word, he collapsed on the ground. She

screamed for help, and a neighbor's boy ran for the pastor. He put his ear to the dying man's lips and listened to his last babbling words, but for some reason he never told what he heard.

From then on, folks dreaded the Dank Hollow after dark. By 1930, when a paved road bypassed the Hollow, the incident was mostly forgotten. And then, in 1970, the pastor's descendants gave his diary to the Trawnto Historical Society. That's when the whole story came to light.

Wallace had reached Dank Hollow after dark, and he was terrified to see a line of shadowy beings coming toward him out of the bog. One of them was his brother who had just been buried. They beckoned Wallace to join their ghostly procession, and that was the last thing the poor man remembered. How he had found his way home in his delirium was hard to explain.

The pastor had written in his diary, "Only the prayers of his wife and his great love for her could have guided him." And then he added a strange thing, "When Wallace collapsed in his dooryard, all his clothes were inside out."

"Whew!" Qwilleran said when the story ended. "Is Dank Hollow still there?"

"No, they filled it in a few years ago and built condominiums. I'm not superstitious, but I'd sure think twice before buying one."

While drinking his second cup of coffee, Qwilleran asked, "What happened to the server who was supposed to wait on our table last night?"

"Tracy? Well, she's a good worker, but she's an impulsive type. She suddenly rushed into the kitchen as if she'd seen a ghost. She was hysterical, and my wife took her into our private quarters so the guests wouldn't be disturbed. We called her home, and her father came and got her. It turned out that the gentleman who just got married was supposed to be her boyfriend. She has a little boy, you know. That might be why she lost out."

Especially, Qwilleran thought, when the alternative is a woman with property and inherited wealth.

FROM BOULDER HOUSE INN, Qwilleran drove to the Pickax community hall, where the Boosters Club was having its weekly luncheon business meeting. Ernie Kemple would be there as official greeter, and Qwilleran wanted to have a few words with him.

Kemple was welcoming members at the door, but Qwilleran detected an undertone of anxiety. He said, "Ernie, let's talk afterwards."

During the business session of the meeting Hixie Rice gave the update on the Ice Festival:

- Contestants coming from eight states, including Alaska.
- Donated prizes valued at a quarter million.
- Seven colleges sending student artists to the ice sculpture competition.
- Fifteen thousand polar bear buttons already delivered.
- Jim Qwilleran to be grand marshal of the torchlight parade.
- Volunteers needed for hospitality tents and traffic control.

After the grand rush for the exit, Qwilleran and Ernie stayed behind. "How goes it?" Qwilleran asked in a sympathetic tone.

"Tracy's in the hospital. She had a breakdown. Vivian's flying home from Arizona. That Carter Lee James is a heel! He's been trying to use Tracy to get us to sign up for his project. Last night she found out in the cruelest way."

"I know," Qwilleran said. "I was there, and I just want to tip you off. There'll be a big spread on the wedding in today's paper."

"Well, I'll be glad when Vivian gets home. She's coming in on the five-o'clock shuttle. Tracy won't talk to me. I'd warned her, but she wouldn't listen, so now she hates me because I was right."

"They have to make their own mistakes," Qwilleran murmured as if he were an expert on parenting.

"You don't know how hard it is," Kemple said, "to stand by and see them go over the cliff. This is her second disappointment. She should've stayed with Lenny. She'll never get him back now. But here I am, dumping my woes on you again."

"Don't apologize," Qwilleran said. "I'm really concerned."

There were increasing tremors on his upper lip.

SIX

QWILLERAN bought a copy of the *Something* and took it with him to Lois's Luncheonette.

When the last customer had left, Qwilleran went to the kitchen and shouted at Lois, "Permission requested to speak to the mop jockey."

"Go ahead," she yelled back, "but make it snappy."

"Park the mop, Lenny, and sit down for a few minutes," Qwilleran said. "Did you hear that Tracy's in the hospital?"

"No! What happened?"

"Nervous breakdown. Have you seen today's paper?" He opened it to the wedding page. "The bridegroom is Carter Lee James."

"Oh-oh," Lenny said with a gulp. "Tracy thought she was on the inside track with that guy. I guess it was wishful thinking."

Or, Qwilleran thought, deliberate misrepresentation. "Do you know how she met him?"

"Sure. He was trying to sell the Kemples on signing up for his big project. It meant paying a lot of money up front, and Ernie wasn't keen on the deal. But Tracy was impressed by the houses Carter Lee had had published in magazines. I told her I thought he was a phony. That was a dumb thing to do. All it did was make her mad, and she told me to get lost. That's the story. Now what?"

"It's for you to decide. For starters, you might call Ernie and sympathize with him. He's feeling down."

"Yeah, I could do that. I always got along with Ernie."

"He's willing to appear at your hearing as a character witness. So am I."

"Honest? That's great, Mr. Q! And thanks for lining up Mr. Barter. He's a super guy."

"Okay. See you in court."

Late that same afternoon, Qwilleran was pulling into his drive-way and Wetherby Goode was pulling out. The weatherman low-ered the window. "Got a minute, Qwill?"

There was an element of anxiety in the question that made Qwilleran say, "Sure. Want to come in?"

When Wetherby saw the Siamese, he said, "You've got two top-of-the-line cats here. Mine's an orange tiger called Jet Stream. He answers to Jet-boy."

"Care for a drink, Wetherby?"

"No, thanks. I'm on my way to the station. Call me Joe. That's my real name."

"Well, sit down, Joe, and tell me what's eating you."

He sat on the edge of a chair. "About the Ice Festival . . . I hate to say this, Qwill, but there's a warming trend in the offing. A *real* warming trend."

"It can't last more than a couple of days. This is February."

"The weather's been weird all over the globe. An unseasonable and prolonged warm spell is inevitable. Do you realize what it'll do to the Ice Festival? After I give the long-range forecast tonight, I may have to leave town. . . . Well, anyway, I felt like unloading the bad news on somebody. Thanks for listening."

When Wetherby left, Qwilleran went to his office alcove to read the day's mail and have another look at the wedding photos in the *Something,* only to find that someone had thrown up a hair ball on the newspaper. Both cats crouched nearby, waiting for him to make the discovery.

"I don't know which of you did this, but I consider it a new low! A breach of etiquette."

Yum Yum squeezed her eyes, and Koko acted as if he'd lost his hearing.

THAT evening, while dressing to have dinner at Polly's, Qwilleran received another annoying phone call from Danielle. Impudently she said, "Hi, snookums! Wanna come out to play tonight?"

Stiffly he replied, "Whom are you calling? We have no small dogs by that name at this number."

"Oh, you're a big kidder, Qwill. This is Danielle. Why don't you come on over for drinks and dinner?"

"The invitation is almost irresistible," he said, "but I have a previous engagement."

The brief but irritating exchange made the prospect of flattened chicken breast a gustatory delight. He left his hat and gloves at home. The temperature was incredibly mild, and the sidewalk, instead of being dusted with white, was black with wetness.

"You're not wearing your hat," Polly greeted him.

"It seems to be a little warmer tonight," he said, without revealing his privileged information. "Have you heard from Lynette?"

"No. I'm sure she has other things on her mind," Polly said. "Have you heard how Danielle is doing in the play?"

"Only that tickets for all performances are selling fast. It's my theory that Pickax audiences will eagerly pay money to see the widow of a murdered man."

"How ghoulish!" Polly said with a shudder.

After dinner they listened to Qwilleran's recorded tapes for *Tall Tales*. He said, "Koko has heard them twice, and each time he yowls at 'The Dimsdale Jinx.' Either he's uncomfortable with Homer Tibbitt's high-pitched voice, or he knows what pasties are all about."

The telephone rang, and Polly went to answer it. "Lynette! We were just talking about you. Qwill's here. Wait a minute. . . . Qwill, would you take this phone? I'll pick up the one on the balcony."

"How's New Orleans?" he said to the caller.

"Warm and wonderful!" Lynette talked fast and excitedly. "We're staying at a charming old inn. You should see the French Quarter. So romantic! The parades start Saturday. I can't wait!"

"I get the impression you like New Orleans," Qwilleran said.

"I'm so happy," she said almost tearfully. "Carter Lee is just wonderful. Everything is perfect!"

"Well!" said Polly when the conversation ended. "I'm so happy for her."

AT THE END OF THE EVENING, as he sloshed home through the deepening puddles, Qwilleran thought about the portfolio of Carter Lee's work that everyone praised so highly. Even George Breze had referred to the "mighty purty pitchers." Breze was no arbiter of historic design, but he might afford a way to borrow the portfolio in Carter Lee's absence.

When Qwilleran arrived home, he typed a briefing for Celia:

MISSION: Operation Winter Breeze
ASSIGNMENT: To lay hands on the book of "mighty purty pitchers" belonging to Carter Lee James. Let Red Cap know that you've seen his house and think it would be worth a lot of money if fixed up. Say you're interested in decorating and would like to see the book of pictures. Then contact Danielle Carmichael on Woodland Trail and ask to borrow it for Mr. Breze, who is extremely eager to have his house restored. When mission is completed, signal headquarters.

The next morning Qwilleran deposited Celia's briefing in her mailbox at the gatehouse. Snowshoeing was out of the question. The temperature was in the unbelievable fifties, and a steady rain was turning the white landscape into a porous gray blanket. In the mailroom the sudden thaw was the sole topic of conversation.

"What does this do to the Ice Festival?"

"The fuzzy caterpillars were right after all."

"Yeah, but their timing was off—by about ten weeks."

Qwilleran took his mail home to open, throwing most of the communications into his procrastination file—a small drawer in the hutch cabinet. One was a letter from Celia's grandson, enclosing snapshots of the dowser and a transcript of the tape recording.

When the telephone rang, Qwilleran was pleased to hear the good radio voice of his next-door neighbor.

"Qwill, things are getting pretty sloppy out there, but we have to eat. Are you free? Would you like to go to Kennebeck and eat at Tipsy's?"

"I always like to go to Tipsy's, rain or shine, with friend or foe," said Qwilleran. "Apparently no one has shot the messenger as yet."

"Not yet. But the promoters of the Ice Festival are monitoring the ice from hour to hour."

The two men splashed down River Lane in Wetherby's van.

"How did the landscape liquefy so fast?" Qwilleran asked.

"Warm rain. Like pouring hot tea on ice cubes."

"Is the Ice Festival doomed?"

"I'm not even opening my mouth. All I can say is, the fuzzy caterpillars knew something we didn't know. The parking lot at the Dimsdale Diner is underwater, and the people in Shantytown are being evacuated. They're afraid the old mine may cave in."

"Perhaps we should lay in a supply of emergency foods. I should buy for Polly, too."

The town of Kennebeck was situated on a hummock, and Tipsy's Tavern was high and dry on the summit. The food was simple and hearty; rustic informality prevailed.

After a Squunk water and a bourbon had been brought to the table, Wetherby started talking about Lynette. "She shocked the whole bridge club by marrying so fast."

"Do you know she's one of your greatest fans, Joe? She goes around quoting your daily quips. She's impressed."

"Too bad I didn't know that." Wetherby puffed out his chest. "What do you know about her husband?"

"Not much. I was invited to be best man because I own a kilt."

"Were you surprised at the match between Lynette and Carter Lee? Was Polly surprised?"

"I won't presume to answer for Polly. They're sisters-in-law, and she was glad to see Lynette so happy. But yes, I was surprised."

"The reason I ask: I observed Carter Lee at the bridge club, and the way he buttered her up was marvelous to behold. I'm inclined to think of him as a fortune hunter. Although Lynette has a job and never puts on airs, we all know she inherited the whole Duncan estate. In case you don't know, Qwill, there's another fortune hunter, and she's got her sights on you!"

"Danielle?" Qwilleran dismissed her with a shrug. "Believe me,

I've learned how to deal with Lorelei Lee types. I appreciate your concern, though."

Qwilleran found Wetherby to be good company. He liked his enthusiasm and candor. It occurred to Qwilleran that a weatherman from Pickax might have been a more suitable match for Lynette than a restoration consultant from New York.

ON SATURDAY morning another businesslike call from the "accountant's office" informed him that the "documents" he had requested were being delivered to the gatehouse at Indian Village. To pick them up, he drove his van carefully through flooded lanes, between shrinking snowbanks, under gray skies that were dumping even more water on the soggy terrain.

The clerk in the mailroom handed him a large, flat package wrapped in white tissue and tied with red ribbon.

At home, the Siamese played with the ribbons while Qwilleran read the accompanying note from Celia:

> Dear Chief,
> Red Cap said okay, so I called the lady and she let me pick it up. Just had a letter from Clayton. He wants to know how you liked his snapshots.
>
> Celia

Qwilleran had not even glanced at Clayton's photos. They were in the procrastination file. As for the famous Carter Lee James portfolio, it was a leather-bound scrapbook of color photographs under plastic—interiors and exteriors of old houses. Before he could peruse them critically, the phone rang again, and he heard the booming voice of the retired insurance agent.

"Qwill, this is Ernie Kemple. Is your condo still high and dry?"

"So far, so good. How's Tracy?"

Kemple lowered his voice to a gruff rumble. "Do you happen to be coming downtown? I don't want to talk on the phone."

Qwilleran said, "I could be lured downtown if someone wanted to have lunch at Onoosh's."

"I can meet you there anytime."

"I'll leave right away."

Ittibittiwassee Road was passable. Crossing the bridge, Qwilleran stopped to observe the water level. It was higher than usual but still well below the bridge bed.

He tuned in the hourly newsbreak: "Six inches of rain fell in one hour at the official checkpoint in Brrr. Many paved secondary roads are under five inches of water, and the sheriff's department warns motorists to stay on main highways whenever possible. In the Black Creek valley, volunteer firefighters are going from door to door, warning families to move to higher ground. Emergency shelters are being set up in schools and churches."

Traffic was sparse for a Saturday, and Qwilleran and Kemple were the only customers at Onoosh's. Qwilleran ordered tabbouleh. Kemple decided on falafel in a pita pocket.

"You asked about Tracy," he said. "Her mother's home now. Tracy's calmed down, but now she feels guilty."

"How do you explain that?"

"You remember the little doll of ours that was found in Lenny's locker—we'd reported it stolen? Well, the drama unfolds! Scene one: Tracy had given it as a good luck token to Carter Lee, without our knowledge. Scene two: She and Lenny had a falling-out, and in the heat of battle he said Carter Lee was a phony. Scene three: She's just confessed to my wife that she repeated Lenny's slur to Carter Lee."

"Why?" Qwilleran asked.

"It was on one of her glamorous dates with the big-city dude. They were drinking margaritas at the Palomino Paddock. She was high. She didn't know what she was doing. When the doll turned up in Lenny's locker, she was afraid to come forward. It would spoil her chances with Carter Lee. But now she hates him, and she's filled with remorse for what happened to Lenny. She wants to go to his hearing and tell the judge the truth."

"But in coming to the defense of the one, she's accusing the other. If he planted the doll, one can assume he also planted the rest. And that implies he stole them. Before Tracy does anything, she should consult G. Allen Barter."

Kemple drew a deep breath. "I appreciate your advice, Qwill." He reached for the check. "This lunch is on me, and I'll even throw in a little carved and painted wooden doll for good luck."

"Keep it," Qwilleran said. "I've got all the luck I can use."

As HE drove out Ittibittiwassee Road, Qwilleran was plagued by other questions: Was Carter Lee indeed the petty thief who had annoyed townfolk in December? If so, what was his motivation? Was the petty larceny a rehearsal for the grand larceny in the Village clubhouse?

Nothing made much sense until Qwilleran arrived home. The Siamese met him at the door, prowling restlessly. It was too early for their dinner. They were bored. No birds, no leaves, no snowflakes.

In one drawer of the hutch cabinet there were cat toys galore. Yum Yum could entertain herself for hours with one of these. Koko, on the other hand, preferred the stimulation of the chase, and he sat on his haunches gazing speculatively into the upper reaches of the living room.

"Okay, where's Mosca?" Qwilleran said, folding a newspaper and whacking his left palm.

They waited. Koko gazed upward hopefully; the man whacked his palm. Their pet housefly was conspicuously absent, and a sickening thought occurred to Qwilleran that Koko had caught him and eaten him. "Disgusting!" he said.

Yum Yum was on the hutch cabinet, scratching at the wrong drawer. He rapped on the front of the toy drawer. "No, no! Over here." But with catly persistence she pawed the wrong drawer.

"Cats!" he said, rolling his eyes in exasperation. To convince her, he jerked open the drawer and showed her the procrastination file. In her nearsighted way she studied the letters, brochures, and clippings, then jumped down and went to the kitchen.

It was a reminder to Qwilleran, however, to look at Clayton's photos—candids of the dowser, close-ups of the forked stick, shots of Cody the schnauzer, and one of Carter Lee measuring the mantel and Danielle making notes. In the transcript of Clayton's tape recording, there was an unexpected interlude:

MAN: Refinish floor. Strip and refinish five-foot varnished mantel. Replace two panes in breakfront with crown glass. . . . Hello there! Who are you?

CLAYTON: I'm visiting my grandma. Mind if I take some pictures to show my mom when I get home?

MAN: On the double! We're working here. . . . Danny, where were we?

WOMAN (*shrilly*): With crown glass.

MAN: Replace chandelier with gaslight fixture.

WOMAN: Chuck, did you see those daggers in the hall? One has a lion on the handle.

MAN: Do you like it?

WOMAN: It's my sign. Leo.

MAN: Well . . .

WOMAN: Do you think I could?

MAN: He'll never miss it. . . .

Qwilleran read no further. The stolen dirk had not turned up in Lenny's locker, but Danielle had given one like it to Lynette as a wedding gift. Now he thought he had figured it out: Danielle was a kleptomaniac, stealing at random all over town when she first moved to Pickax. Did Carter Lee know her weakness and humor her? The theft of his lambskin coat on New Year's Eve may have been a prank. Did she steal his good luck doll and plant it in Lenny's locker?

BY SATURDAY evening the pretty, bubbling brooks and picturesque gurgling streams of Moose County had become raging torrents, inundating farmlands and forests.

As Qwilleran dressed for dinner with Polly, he tuned in the WPKX news update: "The sheriff's helicopter rescued a family of five in Plumley Mill an hour ago."

Polly called to see if driving would be too bad. They had a reservation at the Old Stone Mill.

Qwilleran said, "I called the restaurant about their parking lot. No problem. And I called the sheriff about the highways. The road to the Mill is accessible."

The restaurant had been converted from an old gristmill. The waterwheel, almost twenty feet high, was still there, although the millstream had long since run dry. They were ushered to a table by their favorite server, Derek Cuttlebrink.

"Hi! Guess what," he said even before announcing the evening specials. "We may get our millstream back. It was a branch of the Rocky Burn. Now the Rocky Burn is running so high, it could start the mill wheel turning again."

After they ordered drinks, he said, "I'm not supposed to talk about this, but the Ice Festival biggies are having a secret emergency meeting in a private dining room downstairs. It doesn't look good."

Over poached salmon with leek sauce for her and pork tenderloin with black currants for him, Polly said, "I have a feeling Lynette will phone again tonight. She'll have been to the parades. Have you heard if Carter Lee is getting the commission to restore the hotel and the Limburger mansion?"

"The K Fund hasn't decided." He couldn't talk about his disturbing suspicions. He avoided mention of Danielle and the dirk, the doll found in Lenny's locker, Wetherby's opinion of Carter Lee, and his own devious scheme to get a look at Carter Lee's portfolio. Polly would only worry.

They returned to Indian Village in time to receive Lynette's phone call.

"We were wondering about you," Polly said, signaling Qwilleran to pick up the balcony phone. "What have you been doing today?"

Lynette sounded tired. "We went to the parades on Canal Street. You'd never believe the floats, music, costumes, and masks. They throw strings of beads from the floats into the crowd. Then there's the partying in the streets—jostling, screaming, drinking, and goodness knows what else!"

Qwilleran asked, "Are you still doing justice to the food?"

"Oh, hello, Qwill. Well, my tummy doesn't feel too good today; that Cajun stuff is awfully spicy. Carter Lee's gone out to buy some kind of remedy."

"Be careful with shellfish," Polly admonished. "You know how you sometimes react."

With a noticeable sigh Lynette said, "Three more days of Mardi Gras and we go home. I'll be glad to see Pickax again."

It was late afternoon when Qwilleran returned from Sunday at Polly's. Yum Yum was happily engaged with a crocheted mouse from the toy drawer, but Koko was nervous and unfocused.

Whatever was bothering the cat was bothering Qwilleran as well. All the concerns suppressed during the last twenty-four hours were resurfacing. Dejectedly he sprawled in his big chair and listened to the rain. Now Koko was on the coffee table, examining the leather-bound scrapbook. He was a fiend for leather!

On an impulse Qwilleran leaped out of his chair and went to the telephone to look up a number. She lived in the Village. She was not afraid to speak her mind. She was perfect.

The throaty voice that answered had an added note of impatience. "Yes? Now what, dammit."

In his most mellifluous tone he said, "Amanda, this is one of your admiring constituents."

"Oh! It's you!" she said. "What's your complaint?"

"No complaint. Only a request for three minutes of your valuable time."

A FEW minutes later Amanda admitted Qwilleran to her condo. "Sit down. Care for a drink?"

"No, thanks. I just want you to look at this scrapbook."

She accepted it questioningly and scowled at the color photos. "Is this your new hobby? Cutting out pictures from magazines?"

"This," he replied, "is the portfolio Carter Lee James shows to prospective clients. I borrowed it without his knowledge."

"Does he pretend he did all these restoration jobs?"

"Clients get the impression that he did."

"Well, I get the impression he's a royal fakeroo! You notice they're not identified—who or where—and look at this one. A Queen Anne Victorian. It was done by a friend of mine down south, and her name isn't Carter Lee James! I've been in this house!"

Qwilleran was aware she had resented Carter Lee from the beginning.

"Have you done any business as a result of his recommendations, Amanda?"

"Not a penny. I notice there hasn't been any publicity on Pleasant Street in your paper. How d'you explain that?"

"He doesn't want publicity until the whole neighborhood is signed up. Lynette Duncan will be promoting it for him when they return from their honeymoon."

"Poor girl! She should have stayed single."

SEVEN

SUNDAY evening, when Qwilleran drove into his own driveway, his neighbor rushed out, waving an envelope. Qwilleran lowered the car window.

"This letter belongs to you," Wetherby said. "It was in my mailbox. I just picked up my Saturday delivery. Sorry it's a day late."

"Thanks. No problem." It was a manila envelope from Hasselrich, Bennett & Barter, often bad news and always a nuisance. "Would you like to come in for a drink—and a long talk about precipitation and warm fronts?"

"I'll take the drink. Wait till I feed the cat."

When Wetherby arrived and was pulling off his boots, Qwilleran asked, "Bourbon?"

They carried their drinks into the living room and discussed the latest news: After an all-night crisis meeting the promoters of the Ice Festival were forced to cancel the event.

"Has anyone heard from the honeymooners?" Wetherby asked.

"Lynette called Polly last night and is eager to come home. She's going to work with Carter Lee, promoting restoration jobs around the county."

Wetherby said, "I hope, for her sake, his project is on the up-and-up."

"You have doubts?"

"Plenty of suckers in Pickax seem to have twenty thousand to gamble, but what do they get for their investment?"

"Expert advice, supervision of the work, and access to the National Register."

After Wetherby had left, Qwilleran pulled out Mitch Ogilvie's government printout. Unfolded and spread on the floor, it did indeed measure six yards. He read it all, frequently tapping his mustache and sometimes shooing Koko away.

Next he opened the manila envelope from the law office, saw papers to be signed, and tossed them into the procrastination file. He was in no mood for tedious work. He fed the cats, made a sandwich for himself, and determined to spend the evening on his Melville project. It would take his mind off the can of worms that had been opened when Willard Carmichael came to town. Tomorrow he would go to see Brodie and lay it all out: weird incidents, suspicious developments, hearsay, his own qualms, and even Koko's recent idiosyncrasies. Meanwhile, he would read.

Qwilleran was reading the Melville novels in chronological order, hoping to trace the author's development. Koko was equally fascinated by the books, but the cat had his own ideas about the reading sequence. Qwilleran was ready to start volume seven, a story about a writer, titled *Pierre;* Koko wanted him to read volume ten, pushing it off the shelf with his nose. "Thanks, but no thanks," Qwilleran told him as he opened volume seven. The cat lashed his tail like a bad loser.

At eleven o'clock the Siamese had their bedtime treat. Then the three of them trooped up to the balcony, and Qwilleran continued reading in his bedroom. It was about one thirty when his phone rang—an ungodly hour for anyone to call in Moose County.

His apprehension turned to anger when he heard the voice that he loathed. "Qwill, this is Danielle. I just got a call from Carter Lee. He's terribly worried, and—"

"What's wrong?" Qwilleran interrupted gruffly as he felt the unwelcome sensation on his upper lip.

"It's about Lynette. She's real sick. He thought it was too late to call Polly, so—"

"How ill is she?" he demanded.

"She's in the hospital. He took her to emergency."

"Which hospital? Do you know?"

"He didn't tell me. If he calls back—"

"Did he tell you the nature of the illness?"

"It's her stomach."

"Do you have a phone number for your cousin?"

"Well, he was calling from the hospital, and I guess he's still there. If he calls back—"

"How about the inn where they've been staying?" Qwilleran asked impatiently.

"He never told me the name of it."

"Great!" he said with edgy sarcasm. "Let me know if you hear anything further."

Qwilleran sat with his hand on the cradled receiver as he planned his next call. He would not disturb Polly; it would only keep her awake all night.

He phoned the night desk of the New Orleans newspaper and identified himself as a reporter. He said his editor wanted him to track down an emergency case—a local citizen attending Mardi Gras. He said he needed names and phone numbers of hospitals. A minute later a night-desk man was reading off the information.

"Thanks. Sorry to bother you," Qwilleran said.

Then Qwilleran called Dr. Diane Lanspeak and told her the story. He said, "If I call the hospital, they won't even talk to me. As the personal physician, you can ask the right questions. I have the phone numbers of all the medical facilities. Can you do it? Can you locate her and find out her condition?"

"Of course. I'll be glad to do it." Diane had the neighborliness of a Lanspeak. "I'll call you when I have something definite."

Qwilleran stretched out on his bed and waited. He may have dozed, because he suddenly found himself catapulted out of bed by a roar and clatter overhead. Enormous hailstones were pounding the roof and bouncing off the deck. They bothered the Siamese, too, who complained until they were admitted to his own bedroom. They were quiet then, except for one violent outburst from Koko for no apparent reason.

It was four thirty before the phone rang. Dr. Diane's voice was ominously solemn. "I found her, Qwill. She was in critical condition. I called the hospital several times, at intervals, and . . ."

"She's gone?" Qwilleran gasped.

"She died an hour ago."

"What was given as the cause?"

"Gastrointestinal complications, aggravated by alcohol abuse."

"No!" he said. It was impossible, he thought. She never touched hard liquor. Then he remembered Koko's anguished howling about an hour before.

"Qwill! Are you still there?"

"I'm here, Diane. I don't know what to say. How am I going to break the news to Polly?"

"Would you like me to do it?"

"Thanks, but I think I should handle it—but not until her normal wake-up hour. I'll go to her house and tell her in person. . . . Yes, that's the best way."

After hanging up, he called Danielle's number. The line was busy. Shocked, saddened, overcome with sympathy for Polly, he paced the floor and tried to sort out his reactions. Koko watched with the anxious look that can widen a cat's eyes. Qwilleran was angry, too. Who but Carter Lee could be calling Danielle at this hour? After a few minutes he tried her number again and heard another busy signal.

He went downstairs to start the coffeemaker and then called again.

When she answered in her ridiculous voice, he said calmly, "Danielle, I've just heard the terrible news. We've lost Lynette. Did Carter Lee call and tell you?"

"Yes, just now. How did you find out?"

"Our local doctor was in touch with the New Orleans hospital."

"Isn't it awful? My cousin's a basket case."

"I'd like to call him and express my sympathy. Did you get his phone number at the inn?"

"He's checked out already. I told him to get here before the airport shuts down. He's flying in today as soon as he can make all the arrangements."

"I'd be glad to meet the five-o'clock shuttle—"

"He wants me to pick him up. There are some things he wants to tell me. Before she died, Lynette told him to carry on the work. He wants to make Pleasant Street kind of a memorial to her."

"Did he say anything about funeral arrangements? There's a beautiful place where generations of Duncans have been laid to rest, and the last gravesite has been waiting for the last Duncan."

"He didn't say anything about that."

"I see. Well, call me if there's anything I can do."

"He told me to break the news to Polly, but I don't know how."

"That's all been taken care of," Qwilleran said hastily and untruthfully. "You don't need to worry about it."

Fortified by this assortment of half-truths, Qwilleran squared his shoulders, planned his day, and drank his coffee.

At seven o'clock he called the Riker residence. Arch came on the line, grumbling but curious.

Qwilleran said, "Save today's front page for a major newsbreak. We've just heard from New Orleans. Lynette was rushed to the hospital last night, and she died this morning."

"What! What did you say? What happened to her?"

"Gastrointestinal complications."

"In other words, food poisoning," Riker said cynically. "Do you have any details?"

"Only that she phoned Polly a couple of times and said the food was too rich and spicy for her."

"How can we reach Carter Lee?"

"He's flying back on the five-o'clock shuttle."

"I hope WPKX doesn't get wind of it. I'd like to have a clean newsbreak for once."

So far it had been easy. Breaking the news to Polly would be tough.

"OKAY if I come over for a few minutes?" Qwilleran asked Polly on the phone. "I have something to discuss."

"Would you like breakfast?" she offered.

"No, thanks. I have a column to finish."

On the way there he considered his approach: how to lead up to the bad news in some nonfrightening way. She met him at the door, looking keenly interested but not anxious.

"Let's sit on the sofa," he said. "I have a confession to make."

They went into the living room, and he took her hand fondly. "I've been guilty of trying to save you from worry and loss of sleep, and in doing so, I've not kept you fully informed. When Lynette called Saturday night, she complained of a stomach upset. It was worse than she thought. Carter Lee had to take her to the hospital."

"Oh dear!" she said in alarm. "How did you find out?"

"He called Danielle and asked her to notify us. It was after one a.m.—too late to bother you—so I called Dr. Diane. She called the hospital and found Lynette in critical condition with gastrointestinal complications. Diane kept calling for updates during the night, and the last time she was given the bad news."

"Oh, Qwill! What are you telling me?" Polly cried, raising her hands to her cheeks.

"She died about three thirty this morning."

Polly groaned. "She was only forty! She was healthy! Is there something else they're not telling us?"

"I don't know." He had no intention of mentioning alcohol abuse now; that would come later. "You can lose your mind trying to figure it out," he said gently, hoping to steer her away from his own growing suspicions.

"You're right." Polly's voice wavered. "But I can't talk about it now, Qwill. I need to be left alone for a while."

THERE was a call from Dr. Diane on his answering machine when he returned. He phoned her at her office.

"I had a suspicion about something," she said, "so I came to the office early to pull Lynette's file. She had signed a living will, bequeathing her eyes and body tissues for transplant. I called the hospital, and they'd not been advised that she was an organ donor. The body had been released to a mortuary as authorized by the next of kin. I called the mortuary. It was too late even for an autopsy. They said the next of kin had signed for cremation."

Qwilleran said, "That's not what Lynette wanted at all! Even I know that she wanted to be buried at Hilltop in the Duncan plot—with a full funeral, like her brother's."

"Apparently her husband wasn't aware of any of this," Diane said. "Where is her husband? I wonder."

"Flying home today. I plan to call him this evening. Perhaps I can get his explanation."

QWILLERAN needed sleep. Two or three hours would tide him over, with his answering machine fielding calls. By ten thirty he was awake and ready to go. He phoned Polly.

"How are you feeling?" he asked kindly.

She replied wearily, like one who has survived a crying jag. "I feel more in control now. Is there something I should be doing? I'm no longer next of kin, am I? Diane phoned me. None of Lynette's last wishes has been respected. Perhaps he didn't know."

"There is something you could do, Polly, that would be very useful. Help me write a column about the Lynette that everyone remembers: dancing the Highland fling, visiting patients at the hospital, winning bridge tournaments, hostessing at the church bazaar."

"I could do that," she said.

He knew it would do Polly good to participate in something constructive. As it evolved, her reminiscences were so interesting, and she was so well-spoken, that he had nothing to do but transcribe them on his typewriter.

While he was transcribing, there was action on the hutch cabinet, Yum Yum scratching at the toy drawer, Koko pawing the other. It was the first time he had taken an interest in that particular part of the cabinet, and Qwilleran felt a twinge on his upper lip that led him to investigate. On top of the procrastination file lay the manila envelope from the attorneys. Taking time out from his typing to examine the contents, he found what he expected—papers to be signed and mailed in the enclosed envelope. It could be done later, and he tossed everything back into the drawer.

"Yow-ow-ow!" came a scolding command from Koko.

Qwilleran was prompted to take a closer look at the documents and G. Allen Barter's hand-scribbled instructions.

Qwill—Don't neglect to initial paragraphs G, K, and M. Mail soon as possible. . . . Leaving for St. Paul while airport still open. Back Wednesday to discuss CLJ's credentials. K Fund investigators find no connection whatever with restoration field.

Qwilleran phoned the Pickax police station and asked Chief Brodie, "When do you quit today?"

"Four o'clock."

"Don't leave. I'll be there. It's important."

WHEN Qwilleran went to the newspaper office that afternoon to hand in his copy, he picked up the Monday edition with the front-page news story:

LAST DUNCAN DIES AT 40

Lynette Duncan of Pickax, the county's last Duncan-by-blood, died this morning at the age of 40, less than a week after her marriage to Carter Lee James. The couple were honeymooning in New Orleans when she succumbed to "gastrointestinal complications," according to the death certificate. She is survived by her husband, and by her sister-in-law, Polly Duncan, widow of William Wallace Duncan.

Funeral arrangements have not been announced.

As Qwilleran finished reading the news account, he wondered, How will Ernie Kemple's daughter react when she finds Carter Lee is back in the running as a bachelor? Will she still come forward in Lenny Inchpot's defense? To be continued, he told himself, as he sloshed through the puddles to city hall.

Brodie was waiting for him, with the *Moose County Something* on his desk. "Terrible news," he said, tapping the front page. "How must her new husband feel?"

"We'll soon find out," Qwilleran said. "He'll be here when the shuttle splashes down at five o'clock."

"Is the body being shipped in today?"

"Her husband opted for cremation."

"What! Did I hear you right?" Brodie said. "When her brother died, Lynette told me there was one more gravesite waiting for her. She said she'd be proud to join her ancestors on the hill."

"She can still have her funeral," Qwilleran said, "and interment of her ashes on the hill with the traditional ceremony." He could tell by the chief's silence that he was not quite sold on the idea.

Finally Brodie said, "You must know the James fellow pretty well. You were his best man. Why wouldn't he comply with her wishes?"

"Do you think it's something that's discussed in the first week of marriage?" So far Qwilleran had been going with the flow; now he changed course. "I don't know Carter Lee James at all. Willard Carmichael first invited him up here for the holidays because his wife was homesick. They claimed to be cousins. The three of them met Lynette at the bridge club, and she invited them to see her house. That was the beginning of the Pleasant Street project."

The chief nodded. "I talked to Carter Lee about it at the wedding. Seemed like a decent fellow."

"I even suggested that the K Fund hire him to restore the hotel and the Limburger mansion . . . and that's when the wings fell off! They checked his credentials and came up with zilch. I've seen the portfolio he shows to prospective clients, and I doubt whether it's legitimate. I also know the procedures for getting on the National Register, and no restoration consultant can guarantee his clients anything. He can only raise their hopes."

Brodie's scowl intensified as he listened. "Sounds like a scam, all right. The prosecutor should get in on this."

"Not too fast, Andy. On Wednesday, Bart Barter comes home and can tell us more about the K Fund's investigation. And tomorrow afternoon I want to set a little trap for Carter Lee, just to see how he reacts. I'll get back to you with the results."

"Good luck," Brodie growled. Then he allowed himself a chuckle. "What does your smart cat think about this guy?"

"Well, Koko got hold of his fur hat once and was trying to kill it, if that means anything. To a cat it's always open season on fur and feathers."

AFTER his conference with Brodie, Qwilleran waited until a suitable hour to phone the Carmichael apartment. Danielle answered, saying that her cousin was sleeping and couldn't be disturbed.

"That's all right," Qwilleran said. "I wanted only to express my sympathy and invite the two of you for a business discussion tomorrow—and some refreshment. He might find it heartening to hear about two major restoration projects that could use his expertise. Do you think he's willing to take on something big—at a time like this?"

"He is! I know he is! What time tomorrow?"

"How about two thirty? I'm in the last unit in building five. And what do you both like to drink?"

"Margaritas," she said promptly.

After that masquerade of goodwill and hospitality, Qwilleran planned—with an element of elation—how to snare his prey. For bait he would use a few drinks, a lot of sympathy, and a spurious business deal. Then he would spring the trap!

It might or might not be a coincidence that volume ten on the Melville shelf—the one that riveted Koko's attention—was *The Confidence-Man*. The cat was also greatly attracted to A. Nutt's scholarly disquisition on the Ossian hoax! Qwilleran realized now that he should have taken the cat's eccentricities more seriously.

His immediate task was to prepare the trap. His idea was to tell his listeners about *Short and Tall Tales* and play "The Dank Hollow" for them. After that, he would play a tall tale of his own—about a scam that victimized Pickax a hundred years ago. It would be so transparently analogous to the Pleasant Street project that the listeners would be uneasy. Now all Qwilleran had to do was to compose this tricky bit of fiction.

When he sat down at his typewriter, however, the events of the last twenty-four hours crowded his mind. To clear it, he needed a drastic change of thought. What would it be? He looked at Koko; the cat looked at him. Opera, the man thought. *Adriana Lecouvreur.*

"Yow!" said Koko.

It was the compact disc album that Polly had given him for Christmas; he had never played it. Somewhat guiltily he slipped the first disc into the player and stretched out in his lounge chair. Koko sat nearby, comfortable on his brisket.

The music was lush; the voices were stirring. Qwilleran was following the libretto in English, but the cat was hearing it in Italian. As if he knew what it was all about, he made sounds of disapproval as the tension mounted. In the last act, as Adriana was dying in the arms of her lover, Koko howled as if his body would turn inside out.

"You spoiled the finale," Qwilleran chided him afterward.

Yet it was not an ordinary howl; it was a hollow, tortured wail. Qwilleran replayed the death scene: Adriana receiving the box of dead violets, thinking them a cruel message from a lost lover, burying her face sorrowfully in the wilted flowers, not knowing they came from her rival, the princess, not knowing they were poisoned. Koko howled again. He had made the same anguished response to "The Dimsdale Jinx" when the pasties were mentioned—the poisoned pasties.

EIGHT

QWILLERAN sat down at his typewriter with grim purpose. Gone
was his prankish cat-and-mouse approach to setting a trap for a con
man. This was a different ball game, he told himself.

In the local coffeehouses, jokers liked to say, "If you want to murder your wife, do it Down Below, and you can get away with it."
With hindsight Qwilleran now found recent events painfully obvious: the hurried wedding, the transfer of property to joint ownership, the swift cremation without autopsy, the secrecy about Carter
Lee's whereabouts after the death, precluding interference from
anyone in Pickax.

At one point the flash of headlights turning into the adjoining
driveway prompted him to telephone Wetherby. Solemnly he said,
"Did you hear the news from New Orleans?"

"I did. And I'm mad as hell. I feel like kicking a door down!"

"Well, I'm going to kick that door down, and I need your help."

"What can I do?"

"Give me fifteen minutes more at my typewriter, then come over
here."

Qwilleran finished writing his tall tale and had a bourbon ready
for Wetherby when he arrived. "Sit down, Joe, and I'll explain." He
waited until his guest had taken a sip. "Both you and I had suspicions about Carter Lee, and I've been led to believe they weren't far
off base. I intend to confront him in a devious way just to see how
he reacts."

"Where is he?"

"He's at Danielle's apartment." Qwilleran described his scheme
and ripped the tall tale out of the typewriter. "Read this."

Wetherby read it with astonishment. "Is any of this true?"

"Not a word."

"That last line is pretty strong stuff. How do you plan to present it?"

"It'll be on tape, like the other yarns I've collected, and I'd like it to be read by a voice other than my own."

"Want me to do it?" Wetherby asked.

After the recording was completed and played back, Wetherby said he wouldn't mind witnessing the confrontation. "I could hide in a closet."

"Better to be concealed in the bedroom upstairs, with the door ajar. They'll be here at two thirty."

"I'll be here at two."

LATE that evening WPKX broadcast a flash-flood warning. The dam on the Rocky Burn had been breached by rushing water and constant battering by tree trunks, boulders, and other debris, and the Rocky Burn was now pouring billions of gallons into the old riverbed. The giant waterwheel at the Old Stone Mill, dry and weakened after years of disuse, had been wrecked and the timbers swept downstream.

It was the roar of the water that caused Qwilleran to wake the next morning. The river was turbulent but not dangerously high—as yet. Now and then a tree sailed past like a galleon with sails furled. Over his morning coffee Qwilleran recalled how convincingly Carter Lee had postponed publicity on his endeavors and how artfully he had introduced their post-honeymoon plans. They would sit for their portraits, work together on restoration projects, visit his mother in France. And Lynette innocently anticipated all of it.

WETHERBY Goode arrived at the promised time and was sequestered in the bedroom, with the door ajar. "Try not to sneeze," Qwilleran told him. The Siamese were shut up in their own apartment with the television on, minus audio.

Shortly after two thirty the Land Rover pulled up in front of the condo, and Qwilleran greeted his guests with the right mix of solemnity and hospitality. Carter Lee was subdued, but Danielle was her usual giddy self.

"Ooh! Look," she said, pointing at the display of weaponry on the foyer wall. Her cousin turned away in a silent rebuke.

The cordial host took advantage of the situation. Craftily he said, "Those are Scottish dirks from Gil MacMurchie's collection. He had five, but the best one was stolen during that epidemic of thievery a couple of months ago." He unhooked one from the frame and continued his lecture while ushering them into the living room. "The dirk is longer than a dagger and shorter than a sword—a very useful weapon, I'm sure. It's interesting to know that the grooves in the blade are called blood grooves. This hilt has a thistle design, which is an emblem of Scotland, but the most desirable is a lion rampant." He placed the dirk on the coffee table in its scabbard, hoping that its presence would arouse their guilt. Then he asked, "May I offer you a margarita? I've been told I make a good one."

Both faces brightened. They were sitting on the sofa, facing the windows, and Qwilleran would be able to study their countenances. He proposed a toast to Lynette's memory, causing the bereaved husband to nod and look down woefully.

"You're wise to come home and plunge into your commitments," Qwilleran said in his avuncular style.

Carter Lee agreed. "It's painful, but I know Lynette would want me to carry on."

"I hope you're aware," Qwilleran continued, "that this county has enough historic property to keep you busy for a lifetime. There are two projects in which I have a personal interest. First is the historic Pickax Hotel downtown, boarded up since an explosion last year."

"I've seen it," Carter Lee said. "What are the interior spaces?"

"Twenty guest rooms and many public areas, including a ballroom. The other project is the Limburger mansion in Black Creek, slated to operate as a country inn. May I freshen your drinks?"

So far, so good, Qwilleran thought as he mixed two more margaritas. The guests were relaxing. They talked easily about the flooding, Danielle's acting role, and the gourmet club. They listened receptively to the plans for *Short and Tall Tales* and said yes, they would like to hear one.

"I like ghost stories," said Danielle, wriggling in anticipation.

They listened to "The Dank Hollow" and called it sensational. As Qwilleran served another round of drinks, he said, "And now I'm going to play one that no one else has heard. I want your opinion."

A hundred years ago, when Moose County was booming, the wealthy mineowners built mansions in Pickax and lived in grand style on Goodwinter Boulevard. But they had an annoying problem. Their houses were haunted by the restless spirits of dead miners killed underground. A newspaper Down Below went so far as to send a reporter to Pickax by stagecoach; after investigating, he wrote about the moaning and coughing and constant chip-chip-chipping of invisible pickaxes.

Shortly after the story was published, a man by the name of Charles Louis Jones drove into Pickax in a covered wagon, accompanied by a pretty young woman in a sunbonnet, his sister Dora. He said he could rid the neighborhood of ghosts. There was a sizable fee, but the harassed mineowners were willing to give him anything. To do the job, he asked for a pickax, a miner's hat, and several burlap bags filled with sand.

The contracts were signed, and he and his sister went to work—at night, after the families had retired. She carried the pickax and chanted spells, while her brother wore the miner's hat and scattered sand in attics and cellars.

All the while, the two strangers were treated royally, being a friendly and attractive pair. Charles Louis was particularly charming. No one wanted to see them leave, least of all Lucy Honeycutt. Her father owned Honey Hill mine. Though not the prettiest girl on the boulevard, she had the largest dowry. When Charles Louis asked for her hand in marriage, Mr. Honeycutt was flattered and Lucy was thrilled. So the marriage took place—rather hurriedly, the gossips said.

As the tape unreeled, with only the sound of the rushing river to distract, Qwilleran observed the visitors. Danielle was enjoying it; her cousin was listening more critically. At the mention of Charles Louis Jones, his eyelids flickered. As the story went on—Lucy's dowry, the hasty marriage—he uncrossed his knees, set down his glass, glanced at Danielle. He was gradually getting the point, Qwilleran thought. There was more to the tale:

> After the wedding the nightly sand rituals continued; so did the payments. Then, one night, after eating a mullet stew prepared by her sister-in-law, Lucy became ill. The same night, Charles Louis and Dora disappeared in the covered wagon, along with Lucy's dowry and certain silver plate and jewelry from the haunted houses.
>
> It would be easy to chuckle about this tale of haunted houses, gullible countryfolk, and a clever swindle—if it were not for the tragic ending. Lucy died, and the cause of death, according to the postmortem, was not mullet stew but arsenic.

Carter Lee's jaw clenched, and he stared wordlessly at Qwilleran, who said amiably, "Did you enjoy that? Would you like to hear it again?"

The man on the sofa turned to his companion and thundered, "Go to the car!"

"Why?" she whined, pouting at her unfinished drink.

"Go and get in the car. Do as I say!"

Reluctantly she went to the foyer to put on her boots.

"Forget the boots! Get out of here!" Then, as the door slammed, he said to Qwilleran, "Very funny. What kind of game are you playing?"

There was a click overhead as the levered door handle of the cats' apartment unlatched. The other door squeaked.

"An old Moose County game known as Call the Prosecutor."

With one swift movement Carter Lee was on his feet and reaching for the dirk.

Qwilleran jumped out of his chair. "Hold it! There's a witness up there." He pointed to the balcony. Koko was teetering on the railing. Wetherby was coming out of the bedroom.

In the split second that Carter Lee hesitated, a flying object dropped down on him, like an eagle on a rabbit. He screamed as claws gripped his head. Half blinded by trickles of blood, he staggered toward the foyer, falling over furniture, groping for the front door, with Koko still riding on his head and howling. Qwilleran was yelling at him to get down; Yum Yum was shrieking in alarm; Wetherby was bellowing as he pounded down the stairs. It was one minute of chaos until Koko swooped to the floor and Carter Lee made it out the front door.

"Let's follow him!" Qwilleran shouted.

"We'll take my van. It's in the drive."

They grabbed their jackets and left Koko licking his claws.

The Land Rover splashed down River Lane and turned left to the gatehouse, then left again on Ittibittiwassee, with Wetherby's vehicle not far behind.

"Where do they think they're going?" Qwilleran said as he reached for the car phone.

"She's driving. Look at that van weaving. She's drunk too much."

On the phone he said, "Qwilleran reporting. Suspected murderer and accomplice headed west on Ittibittiwassee in white-and-red Land Rover. Now three miles east of bridge. This report from pursuit car. Over."

The reply was inaudible as their tires whined through floods. Plumes of spray from the car ahead hit their windshield, and the wipers worked frantically to maintain visibility.

Qwilleran shouted above the racket, "If they get across the bridge, they'll run right into the police!"

"I'm gonna hang back a bit, Qwill. This is suicide!"

They covered the next two miles without talking. Then Qwilleran shouted, "It worked! The trick worked."

"I heard every word."

"Let's hear it for Koko!"

"The bridge is around the next curve," Wetherby said.

"Stop on the hill."

On the crest they pulled over and parked on a muddy shoulder. From there they could see the fugitive vehicle approaching a bridge, submerged except for the guardrails. The river was churning and roaring.

"They'll never make it."

"They're gonna try."

As the two men watched, a surge came downstream—a huge wave bringing tree trunks and a chunk of concrete from a culvert. The surge hit the bridge like a battering ram as the Land Rover put on speed.

The bridge bed cracked and heaved and pitched the white-and-red van over the guardrail, to be swept along in the turbulent water until it snagged on a fallen oak.

"Can you see them, Joe?"

"No sign of life. I hope their seat belts were fastened."

The flashing lights of police vehicles came into view across the river, and the far-off sirens of rescue equipment wailed above the crashing tumult. Qwilleran called his newspaper to send a reporter and photographer. Wetherby said it would take a crane to release the trapped van, but the rescue squad could probably reach the passengers with a cherry picker.

Qwilleran said, "Let's go home and see if the surge is doing any damage."

"Yeah. And I could use one of those margaritas."

The water was running high past the condos, but there was still no threat to the buildings.

While Wetherby mixed himself a drink, Qwilleran checked in with Polly.

"Qwill! Where have you been?" she asked anxiously. "I've been trying to reach you."

"I had to go out for a while."

"They just announced that a surge coming downstream from the Rocky Burn was diverted by a cave-in at the Buckshot mine, at least temporarily. That's why we're not flooding."

"Stay tuned," he said. "You may hear some more surprising news."

Wetherby called to him, "Shall I pour you a Squunk water?"

"No, thanks. I need something stronger," Qwilleran said. "Open a ginger ale."

MOOSE County's last snow melted in February, an all-time record. The rain stopped falling; the floodwaters receded, and on the air the weatherman said, *"Come, gentle Spring! ethereal mildness, come!"*

"Lynette would have loved that quotation," Polly said to Qwilleran.

"It sounds familiar. Who wrote it?"

"Coleridge . . . I believe."

Since meeting Wetherby Goode, Qwilleran had stopped making needling remarks about his literary allusions. The two men now shared a secret. They had agreed not to reveal their role in the entrapment and flight of Carter Lee James. When Brodie questioned Qwilleran, he shrugged it off. "I simply confronted Carter Lee with what I thought was the truth. He threatened me, and Koko chased him out of the house."

Miraculously the fugitives had survived the rough tumble in the raging river but were still hospitalized under police arrest. The man would be charged with murder and twenty counts of fraud; the woman, an admitted kleptomaniac, would turn state's witness against him in exchange for immunity.

ONE evening Qwilleran and Polly met for their weekly dinner of flattened chicken breast. This time the recipe called for shallots, lemon zest, chopped spinach, and blue cheese.

After dinner he asked, "Do you know anything about the dirk that Lynette used to cut her wedding cake?"

"Yes, it was a gift from Danielle. It had the lion rampant of Scotland on the hilt."

"Well, I happen to know that the light-fingered Danielle stole it from the MacMurchie house. Gil was very much upset. It was the last gift he'd received from his late wife."

"That's terrible!" Polly said. "Lynette would have been mortified if she had known. The MacMurchies were such good neighbors. In a plumbing emergency she could call Gil and he'd rush over with a wrench."

They both fell into silence. Qwilleran was thinking, Was Danielle a genuine neurotic with a compulsion to steal? Or was her pilfering intended to focus public attention on minor crimes while Carter Lee committed a major swindle?

Polly broke the silence. "I never suspected either of them. Did you, Qwill?"

"Well, Carter Lee's talk about the official registration of historic buildings aroused my curiosity. Yet twenty families were convinced, and when I discovered he was a fraud, it was too late."

Polly sighed deeply. "For Lynette's sake I wish we could return the dirk to Gil MacMurchie. She would want it that way. You know, Qwill, I have a key to her house. Do you suppose . . . it would be all right if . . . I went over there and simply—"

"No, it would not be all right," he interrupted sternly. "That would be stealing. However, if you went over there to check up . . . and discovered a leak, you could call Gil, and he'd rush over there with his pipe wrench. It's not stealing if he takes something that belongs to him."

ANOTHER evening, Qwilleran was at home with Wetherby Goode. Koko made an appearance, looking regal, and Yum Yum rippled into the room in the flirty way she had.

"Do they ever catch mice?" Wetherby asked.

"It's Yum Yum's dream, but Koko is more of a thinking cat. He specializes in thought transference. He's telling me he'd like to move back to the barn. Is this weather going to hold?"

"Ask the fuzzy caterpillars. I'm only a meteorologist."

Qwilleran said, "Polly tells me your listeners send you suggestions for your daily quotes."

"They sure do, and I appreciate it. Polly sends me weather quotes all the time—from Shakespeare and all those other old guys."

"She knows the Bard forward and backward," Qwilleran re-marked casually, but it came as a surprise that Polly would conceal anything from him.

The garrulous weatherman rambled on. "Fran Brodie is taking over the lead in *Hedda Gabler,* we're all glad to know. The bad news is that Danielle didn't pay her decorating bill before all this hap-pened. Have you been to Lois's since Lenny was cleared and got his job back?"

"I have. She was so happy she was handing out free apple pie."

"Everyone in the bridge club thinks it was Danielle who framed Lenny. Did you know Willard very well? I've been wondering if he was in on the scam. He brought Carter Lee up here and was push-ing his project."

"That's because his bank wanted to make restoration loans. It's my belief that he didn't know the score. He met Danielle in a night-club and hadn't known her long before they married. I'd guess that she and Carter Lee had been longtime partners in the con game and everything else, and they thought a rich husband would be a big plus."

Wetherby was watching Koko slap the floor with his tail. "What's he doing?"

"Communicating," Qwilleran said. "I've been trying to read that tail for years."

After Wetherby had gone home, Qwilleran watched Koko lashing his tail—right, left, right, left. He was trying to convey something.

"What's bothering you, old boy?" he asked.

Koko stopped the tail business and walked across the room with Siamese poise, stopping on the way to give Qwilleran a stare that could only be described as scornful. He walked to the spot where Yum Yum was sitting contentedly on her brisket and hit her on the head with his paw.

"Stop that!" Qwilleran shouted. "Stop tormenting her."

Koko looked at him impudently and hit her again, adding a con-temptuous "Yow-ow-ow" in Qwilleran's direction.

Qwilleran went immediately to the phone and called Andrew

Brodie at home. "Andy, I have information. Remember when Willard Carmichael attended that banking seminar in Detroit? Carter Lee was down there at the same time, on business of his own." Qwilleran pounded his mustache with his fist. "His business, I'd say, was hiring a hit man to eliminate Willard!"

THE successful prosecution of Carter Lee James would last all spring as preliminary arguments addressed change of venue, conflict of interest, selection of jurors, and TV cameras from Down Below. News media everywhere called it a bizarre case. Only Qwilleran knew how bizarre it really was, and he took pains to conceal Koko's input.

One sunny afternoon he was lounging in his big chair and fantasizing about the "smart cat" in the witness-box, biting the defense attorney, yowling in spite of the judge's gavel, flying around the courtroom in a catfit, swinging from the chandelier.

As a matter of fact, both Siamese were busy being ordinary cats—Yum Yum lounging in the sun and Koko prowling, sniffing invisible spots, scratching an ear, grooming a shoulder blade. He was restless. He had lost interest in Herman Melville. He looked at everything and nothing, jerking his head without reason, racing madly, staring into space.

Qwilleran thought, Koko has more whiskers than the average cat and more senses than the average human, but basically he's just a cat. At that moment Koko leaped four feet in the air, and Qwilleran looked up. He saw a tiny black speck darting around the room in wild swoops and circles.

"Mosca!" he shouted.

BEYOND
RECOGNI

The fires were hot.

Too hot.

A sudden flash of white heat that left nothing behind. Nothing but a mass of concrete and ash. No bodies. No clues.

And for the next victim, no way out . . .

Unless Detective Lou Boldt can find the arsonist before he strikes again. And stop him.

And not get burned himself.

CHAPTER ONE

THE fire began at sunset.

It filled the house like a hot, putrid breath, alive. It ran like a liquid through the place, stopping at nothing, feeding on everything in its path, irreverent and unforgiving. It raced like a phantom, room to room, eating the drapes, the rugs, the towels and linens, the clothes, the shoes, and the blankets in the closets, consuming all evidence of things human. This was no simple fire.

It vaporized the small furniture—chairs, tables, dressers. It devoured the desk she had bought at a weekend flea market, a desk she had stripped of its ugly green paint and lovingly resurfaced with a transparent plastic coating guaranteed by the manufacturer to last thirty years.

Longer than she lasted.

For Dorothy Enwright it was like a camera's flash popping in the dark. It began as a strange growling sound deep within the walls. At first she imagined an earthquake. This was dispelled by the quick, surprisingly chilling spark on the far side of her eyelids. To her it began not as heat, but as a flash of bone-numbing cold.

It burned off her hair and the skin on her face, and she went over backward, her throat seared, unable to scream. Her bones exploded, brittle and fast, like pine needles dumped on a fire.

The toilets and sinks melted, a sudden flow of bubbling porcelain, running like lava.

Dorothy Enwright was dead within the first twenty seconds of the burn. But before she died, she visited hell, a place that Dorothy Enwright did not belong. She had no business there, this woman. No business, given that a member of the fire department had received a threat eleven hours earlier and the person receiving that threat had failed to act upon it.

By the time the fire hoses were through, little existed for Seattle's Marshal Five fire inspector to collect as evidence. Little existed of the truth. The truth, like the home of Dorothy Enwright and Dorothy herself, had been destroyed beyond recognition.

THE Boldts' home phone rang at six forty in the evening on September 10, a Tuesday. Elizabeth passed her husband the receiver and released a huge sigh to make a point of her disgust at the way his police work interfered with their lives.

Lou Boldt croaked out a hello. He felt bone tired. They had seen their precious beauty Sarah to sleep only moments before and had stretched out on their bed to take a fifteen-minute break. Three-year-old Miles was occupied by a set of blocks in the corner.

Boldt wished the phone hadn't rung, because he hated to see Liz angry. He reached over to touch her shoulder but caught himself. No sense in making things worse.

Cupping the phone, he explained to her, "A fire." Boldt was homicide, so it had to be a serious fire.

Liz sighed again. "Keep your voice down," she cautioned. Eight-month-old Sarah was a light sleeper, and the crib was only a few feet away. The baby's crying began immediately, as if on Liz's cue.

Boldt took down the address and hung up.

Liz walked over to the crib, and Boldt admired her. She kept herself trim and fit. She looked ten years younger than her almost forty years. As the cradled baby came eagerly to her mother's breast, Lou Boldt felt his throat tighten with love. There were unexpected moments in his life that would remain with him forever, seared into his consciousness like photographs, and this was one of them. He nearly forgot about the phone call.

Liz talked quietly to the baby. She glanced over at her husband. "Sorry I snapped at you," she said.

They grinned at each other, and Lou Boldt thought himself lucky to share his life with her, and he told her so. She blushed and lay back on the bed with the child. Miles was into creating the second story of his block fort. Maybe he'd grow up to be an architect, Boldt thought. Anything but a cop.

Lou Boldt smelled the fire before he ever reached it. Its ghost, spilled out like entrails, blanketed most of Wallingford in a thin, wispy fog. If, as a sergeant of crimes against persons, Boldt was being called to a fire, it was because a person had perished and Marshal Five had already made a call of suspicious origin.

There were a lot of fires in Seattle in any given year. Not so many homicides—not by national standards. The two seldom mixed, and when they did, it was always firefighters. The Pang fire had been the most recent and the worst: four firemen had died. Boldt had worked that case as well. He didn't want another one.

Boldt had been off duty at the time of the call. Yet there he was, overweight, gray at the temples, feeling anxious, speeding the beat-up department-issue Chevy toward the address. As the department's "most veteran" homicide cop—a pleasant way of saying he was a little too old for the job—Boldt was assigned more than his fair share of tough cases. Many times he had considered the thought that Lieutenant Phil Shoswitz assigned him those cases in an effort to persuade him to apply for a lieutenant's desk. But Boldt preferred people to paperwork.

Fire scenes instilled fear in him, even from a distance. It wasn't the flashing lights, the tangle of hoses, or the wet, glistening pavement. It was the damp, musty smell, the smudged filth that accompanied any fire, and Boldt's own active imagination that too easily invented a claustrophobic room engulfed in flames. To die in fire had to be the worst.

Battalion Chief Witt, clad in his turnout gear, met Boldt as the sergeant approached one of the pumpers, where the crew was busy packing up the rig. Witt shook hands firmly. "Marshal Five's in there," he said, indicating what little remained of the house.

The September air was a pleasant temperature, even without the heat still radiating from the site. Boldt wore a khaki windbreaker, a cotton sweater, and khaki pants. His jaw muscles flexed, reflecting his tension.

"It was called in to our arson boys," Boldt informed Witt. "Must have been mention of a body, because they called me."

"No body found so far," Witt explained. "A neighbor says he saw her in there, though. Just a couple minutes before the flash." He repeated, "Flash, *not* explosion," as if this should hold significance to the sergeant.

"That's your department," Boldt said. "My concern is the body."

"If we ever find her."

Boldt asked, "What's that mean? Is there a body or not?"

"This baby was one hot sucker, Sergeant. Ya know?" Witt shouted above the sound of the trucks and the bark of the radios. "If she's in there, there's not much left. Hot," he repeated. "Like nothing I ever want to see again." Witt's eyes darted to and from the site. He seemed to be keeping something to himself.

"Something bothering you?" Boldt asked bluntly.

"It flashed; it didn't blow," said Witt. "It burned real hot. We shoot for a four- to six-minute response time. We were six, maybe eight on this baby. But she was ripping long before we got here. Ripping mean, right up through the center of the structure. A weird burn. You check air-traffic control, Sergeant. My guess is six, seven hundred, maybe a thousand feet in the first thirty seconds. Something big. Bigger than stink. It scares you, that's all." He walked off, leaving Boldt with the taste of charcoal in his mouth.

It was the taste that confirmed it. A taste that wouldn't go away completely for two or three days. He knew as it rolled over his tongue. As foul a taste as a person could experience.

A dead body. No question about it.

"GET OUT OF HERE. GO UPSTAIRS." Ben had never seen the man with this particular girl before, but she wasn't much different from any of the others. A waitress, maybe, or a girl from the bar— smeared lipstick, tight jeans.

The guy, who called himself Ben's father but wasn't, drew closer. "You listening to me, kid?" He smelled of cigarettes and beer. His name was Jack Santori, and Ben hated him.

"You told me to clean up the kitchen," Ben protested. He wished he were eighteen instead of twelve. He wished he could walk right out the door and never come back, the same way his mother had. He missed his mother something fierce.

"Upstairs," Jack ordered, walking unsteadily toward the fridge and rummaging for beers. The girl cast a sympathetic look in Ben's direction, but it wouldn't help, because she was new around here. She didn't know Jack. If she lasted more than one or two nights, it would be a record. Ben knew what went on down there at night. Jack was rough with them. Same way he was rough with Ben. Best thing about seeing him this drunk was he'd sleep until noon.

Jack had married Ben's mother when Ben was five and she was out of money. She cut hair for a living, but she had been fired. She had explained it all to Ben. "Jack's a pretty nice guy, and he can provide for us." She was proved wrong on both counts, but she was gone, so what did it matter? Ben was stuck with the guy.

"Upstairs. Now!" Jack shouted. The girl stiffened with that tone of voice. Ben turned off the water and dried his hands. Jack liked to pretend how he was so tough, but Ben occasionally heard him crying down there when he was alone. Sobbing like a baby. If Ben hadn't feared him so much, he might have found room to pity him.

That night Ben was unable to sleep for all the noise. He was just drifting off when the girl cried out like Jack was killing her, and then it stopped, and Ben wondered if maybe he *had* killed her. There wasn't much that Ben would put past Jack.

When the morning finally showed its mercy by allowing the sun to rise, Ben got dressed and got out of there before the trouble began. Trouble came with pain in that house.

The southeast neighborhood where he lived was mostly poor. The houses showed chipped paint and carried roofs half rotten from the long, wet winters. He and his mom had lived better before Jack came along, though Ben didn't remember much about those days. He'd never met his real father.

Ben climbed up the hill toward Emily's house, hearing the traffic from Martin Luther King Boulevard. He kept to himself and walked fast. He knew which streets to avoid, which hangouts to circumvent. The neighborhood gangs were about the only thing Ben feared, other than Jack. Once a kid had tried to recruit him to be a drug runner, and it was only through clever thinking that Ben had avoided the job without getting beat up for refusing. He had pulled out his glass eye—his left eye—and, holding it in the palm of his hand, had explained that he couldn't see who was coming from his left, so he made an easy target. A real gross-out, the eye trick worked every time.

The glass eye was the result of a birth defect, and though Ben wished he had two eyes like everyone else, the trick of popping out his glass eye came in handy every now and then. Like with girls. They screamed and ran the other way, which was fine with him. Who needed girls?

Except Emily. She lived in a small purple house with dark blue trim. There was a six-foot-high metal globe on her lawn along with a plastic pink flamingo holding a sign that read FORTUNES $10—TAROT-ASTROLOGY. There was also a blue neon sign in the window that read YOUR FUTURE, YOUR PAST—AT LAST! There were white stars and pale blue moons painted on the purple siding. Ben followed a flagstone path to the front door. He knocked twice. There was no car parked in the drive, so he assumed she didn't have a customer.

"Come in, Ben." Emily always knew it was him. Just how, he wasn't sure. People doubted her powers, but Ben knew better. Emily possessed a gift, and the gift was real.

Emily had rich brown hair, kind blue eyes, and was probably about the same age as his mother, which was old—somewhere around thirty. She wore a flowered dress with a red plastic belt, pink stockings, and red high-top sneakers. She led the way to the kitchen, the pair of them moving with a comfortable familiarity, like mother and son, which was how Ben liked to think of it.

On the way to the kitchen they passed through the room in which she told fortunes. The ceiling was draped in parachute cloth dyed sky blue, the fabric gathered around a white globe ceiling fixture that was on a dimmer, set low. Below the light was a round table with a black tablecloth and two chairs. On the table was a single red candle. A deck of tarot cards was set to the left of Emily's place, and below the lip of the table were three switches that allowed her to control the mood of the room. The small gray box taped alongside these switches controlled the radio-transmitter earpiece that Emily wore.

"How was he last night?" she asked Ben once they were in the kitchen.

"The same. A new girl."

"Drunk?"

"Both of them."

"He hit you?"

"No, not with a new girl, he wouldn't do that. Though he hit *her,* I think. Sounded like he did, the way she was screaming."

"I'm working on it," she said as she fixed tea. "I'm trying."

"I know," Ben said. He knew what she was up to. She wanted them to be together, but she needed evidence against Jack if she was to have any chance of breaking Ben free of him. And Ben didn't feel like giving evidence. He didn't feel like talking to a social worker. He wouldn't allow Emily to take pictures of his bruises. If he offered evidence, if Jack was questioned by the police and for some reason Emily failed, the guy would beat him senseless, maybe even kill him. Better not to try at all than to try and fail. Yet he loved Emily and didn't want to let her down.

He heard himself say, "I'm not ready."

"They can protect you," she said.

"No," he answered. "You don't know him."

Ben was saved from further discussion by the sound of a car in the gravel drive. He smiled at her. They had work to do.

Ben grabbed the handheld device as Emily tucked the plastic earpiece under her hair and into her ear. "Check," he said into the device, and Emily nodded. He slipped out the back door as Emily went to answer the doorbell. He moved over to the corner of the house, just far enough to see the beat-up yellow Ford.

"They're paying me to tell them what they want to hear," Emily had explained to him a long time ago. "The more we learn about them, the closer we come to telling them what they want to hear, the more they keep coming back." It made sense to Ben. He had no problem with spying on them. To him it was a game. He was good at it, and it pleased him to be really good at something.

He heard the front door shut. He walked briskly to the car and began his assessment. The sticker on the windshield was an employee parking permit for Seattle University. Looking through the side window, he spotted a Victoria's Secret catalogue addressed to a Wendy Davis at a street address about a mile north of Green Lake. In the back seat a baby's safety seat was strapped in.

He lifted the walkie-talkie, carefully checking the volume knob. Bringing his lips close, he spoke the woman's name clearly—Wendy Davis—followed by a description of the cluttered condition of the car's interior, the fact that it was an old Ford, the presence of a child's seat. "Hold it," he said, noticing the newspaper wedged beside the driver's seat. It was open to the want ads. A number of apartment rentals were circled. "She's house hunting. It's yesterday's paper." He wouldn't open the car door, no matter how tempted. That was against the law and could get Emily into serious trouble.

Bingo, he thought as he caught sight of the two passport-size color photos stuck into the plastic by the car's speedometer. One was of a baby boy, the other of an older boy, perhaps five years old. He reported this, as well as the fact that the woman smoked Marlboro Lights and drank Diet Coke.

He returned by the back door into the kitchen. Soft New Age music—xylophone, flute, and guitar—purred from the other room, played in part to cover any chance of a customer's hearing the earpiece. He heard Emily's voice cut through the soft patter of the music as she told her customer, "I'm getting an image of a problem . . . a worry . . . a decision, perhaps. And one . . . no, two boys. Children."

"Oh, my gosh!" the unseen woman exclaimed.

"Your children?"

"Yeah! I can't believe—"

"An infant . . ."

"Charles. Charlie," Wendy Davis said.

"And the other is older—what?—four or five?"

"Harry. Just turned five."

"You're concerned for them," the fortune-teller said. "I see suitcases . . . boxes. . . . Moving, are we?"

The customer released an audible gasp. "Oh, my gosh. You're for real." She chuckled, sounding giddy. "I'm sorry. I only meant—" She laughed again. "I mean, a psychic and all."

"Looking for a new place to live," Emily said patiently. "Concerned for the children. You live near a lake—"

"Green Lake!" the woman shouted. "I can't believe this."

Ben felt proud that he had done such a good job. This one would be back. He felt certain of it. Emily would be thrilled, and he lived for her praise.

Judging by her expression as she left, Ben believed Wendy Davis was happier, which made him feel good. This was Emily's goal. She only added her ominous warnings at the end of the session to keep the customer returning. "I see something darker in the future" was her typical line. And Emily kept an appointment book. She could "fit you in" if you were lucky. Every one of her customers was lucky.

"You need something to eat," Emily announced as she entered the kitchen. "You're far too skinny." One of her passions was food. She seemed to him to always be around the refrigerator, inspecting its contents. "I've got some pork loin for you—my aunt's recipe. Marinated in lemon juice, oregano, salt, and pepper."

An hour later they were eating lunch at her kitchen table. He liked the mashed potatoes most of all. "We can have the leftovers for dinner," she said. "It's even better as a leftover."

He was glad she mentioned dinner, because it meant he didn't have to think about going *there*. If he was lucky, Emily would ask him to sleep over. She let him do this about twice a week. Not once had Jack asked him about where he went. His only complaint would be if a chore didn't get done, and those complaints were often of the physical variety, so Ben kept up on the chores.

They did the dishes together. Then Emily made Ben read to her as she sat in her favorite chair. After about twenty minutes Ben heard a car pull into the driveway.

"Another one," he said.

She came out of the chair, stroking the wrinkles out of her clothes. She patted Ben on the head affectionately. "Your reading's getting better," she teased. "You might work out after all."

Ben waited for the car to pull up and the engine to go quiet. Then he slipped out back to do his job.

CHAPTER TWO

Would you like a cup of coffee?"

"No," Lou Boldt told the young patrolman. "Thanks anyway."

Boldt felt sorry for this rookie. He remembered what it was like to be in uniform and on the Public Safety Building's fifth floor for the first time: the pounding heart, the prickling skin. Homicide was viewed by most rookies as the top—the pinnacle of a career. It was true that homicide dealt with life and death as opposed to traffic tickets or jaywalkers, but it came with a price of insomnia, guilt, and frustration. Homicide was no cakewalk.

The forty-two-year-old man sitting in the chair today—graying hair cut close to his scalp, his rounding face reflecting the thirty pounds he couldn't shake, the fingers of his thick hands gnarled from broken knuckles of decades past—was a far cry from the fit, bright-eyed, enthusiastic kid he had once been. He was feeling tired. Miles and Sarah had taken turns complaining through the night, leaving both him and Liz exhausted and in foul moods. A morning encounter in the kitchen—something to do with the yoke of a soft-boiled egg not being right—had erupted into her tirade about how Boldt was allowing himself to be absorbed by the job again, an unfair charge in his opinion, given that he had beaten her home four of the last five nights. Her commercial-banking career was definitely more time-consuming than police work. He had said that to her, which did not score big points except on the Richter scale. At the moment he was suffering through a dull headache.

He carried that headache with him to the medical examiner's office in the basement of Harborview Medical Center, where Dr. Ronald Dixon awaited him. He was one of Boldt's closest friends and a fellow jazz enthusiast.

There was a look of intelligence in Dixon's wide-set eyes. Just looking at the man, one sensed a formidable mind. Dixon came out from behind his desk and winced a smile at Boldt. He indicated a plastic evidence bag on his small conference table.

Boldt examined the contents, a blackened bone three inches by three inches. "From that Enwright fire the other night," Dixon said.

"Is this all?" Boldt asked.

"All that's worth anything," Dixon replied. "It's fairly common in burns for the spine and pelvis to go last. That's a piece of the pelvic bone. Pelvis gives us sex. Spine gives us age. Do you see the calcification on the inside edge? That indicates some aging. This wasn't a teenager. Probably wasn't even in her twenties."

"Her?" Boldt inquired, his own spine tingling.

"What we can tell you is that it was probably a female. Beyond that, I'm afraid . . ." His voice trailed off. "We sifted the site thoroughly. I would have expected to see more than this," he admitted.

"The femur, the spine. . . . Depending on how she fell, they take a while to reduce to ash."

"Time or heat?" Boldt asked.

"The rate of destruction is a product of both."

"This was hot," Boldt informed him. As suggested, he had spoken with air-traffic control. The initial spike of flame had stretched eleven hundred feet into the night sky. No house fire had ever caused such a phenomenon.

"We're hoping for some bone frags to come out of the lab work. We sent off a garbage can of ash and debris." Dixon paused. " 'Circumstances of discovery raise a suspicion that this was a violent death.' That's how I'll write it up."

The medical examiner's determination of a body present in the rubble threw the investigation into high gear. Boldt assigned two of his squad's detectives to the investigation, John LaMoia and Bobbie Gaynes. They would be joined by two probationary firemen, Sidney Fidler and Neil Bahan, loaned to the Seattle Police Department as arson investigators. Boldt would act as case supervisor, reporting directly to Lieutenant Phil Shoswitz.

A coordinating meeting, arranged for the SPD fifth-floor conference room, came off at ten a.m., six days after the fire. It included Boldt's team and four Marshal Five fire inspectors representing various fire districts within King County. Boldt, LaMoia, and Gaynes participated primarily as onlookers while the technical details of the fire were discussed. A burn pattern on wood known as alligatoring had steered the inspectors toward the center of the structure, where destruction was so severe that there was literally no evidence to be gathered. The area of origin—an essential starting point for any arson investigation—was therefore impossible to pinpoint. The longer the meeting went, the more anxious Boldt became. Reading between the spoken words, he experienced a sinking feeling that the fire's intense heat had destroyed all indication of its origin. Worse, all the experts seemed both intimidated and surprised by the severity of the heat.

Neil Bahan summed up the discussion for Boldt and his detectives. "It goes like this, Sergeant. We have the initial plume reported as a flash, *not* an explosion. That's worrisome because it excludes a lot of known accelerants. Add to that the height of the plume and the flame itself being a distinct purple in color, and we figure we're looking at liquid accelerants. The prudent thing to do is send our samples off to the state crime lab and test for hydrocarbons. That will point us to the specific fuel used, which may give us a retail or wholesale source to check out. Meanwhile, we try to make sense of the rest of the evidence."

"Which is?" Boldt questioned.

"We've got some popcorn in the foundation's concrete, some spalling," Bahan said. "The concrete gets so hot so fast that the moisture that's trapped inside boils and explodes the surface. Looks like bad acne. What we don't have is slag or heavy metals, both of which we would expect to see with liquid accelerants. But added to that we have some blue concrete right beneath the center of the house. Blue concrete. That means this thing went off above two thousand degrees. That lops off another load of known accelerants and, quite frankly, gets out of our area of expertise."

"ATF maybe," one of the fire inspectors suggested.

Bahan agreed. "Yeah, maybe we bring in the feds, or send some of the stuff down to their Sacramento lab."

"So what you're saying," Boldt suggested, "is that the origin of the fire is unusual."

Two of the Marshal Fives laughed aloud.

Bahan said, "You could say that, yes. This guy is good."

Boldt bristled at the idea of an arsonist being considered talented. "She was a mom. Did you know? Seven-year-old boy."

"He was in the fire?" another of the fire inspectors gasped. It wasn't difficult to spot the parents in this group.

"Home with her ex-husband, thank God." Boldt imagined his own son, Miles, in a fire like that. "Thank God," he muttered again.

Bahan said, "We turn it over to the lab, and we see what we see. It's really too early to make a decent appraisal. For the time being, it's in the hands of the chemists."

A feeling of impending dread accompanied Boldt on his return to his office, where a blanket of telephone messages had collected like the falling leaves outside.

"Sergeant Boldt?" a deep male voice asked at Boldt's cubicle.

It was one of the four Marshal Fives from the meeting. He was a tall, handsome man with wide shoulders, dark brown eyes, and a full beard. His hair was cut short. Boldt came out of his chair, and the two shook hands. The other's right hand was hard and callused. He introduced himself as Steven Garman.

"What district are you with?" Boldt asked.

"Battalion Four: Ballard, Greenwood."

"I thought the meeting went well," Boldt said.

"Yeah, I suppose," Garman replied anxiously.

The sergeant borrowed a chair from a nearby cubicle and pulled it up to his desk. He offered it to Garman, who viewed it suspiciously and said, "Maybe someplace a little more private."

"Come on," Boldt said. He led him into a small room next to the box—the interrogation room. Boldt closed the acoustically insulated door. They took seats at a bare Formica table.

"Everyone says you're the go-to guy around here," Garman began. "I'm told you're willing to play hunches now and then."

"My own, yeah," Boldt said. "But I'm pretty careful about playing hunches."

From his shirt pocket Garman withdrew an opened envelope. He placed it before Boldt, who elected not to touch it. The address, in blue ballpoint ink, was printed in poorly formed block letters.

"Anyone else handle this?" Boldt asked.

"No. I haven't shown it to anyone."

Boldt found a pencil and expertly maneuvered the envelope to face him, curious but reluctant. "Why me? Why now?" he asked.

The question clearly troubled Garman, and Boldt sensed he had prepared the answer ahead of time. "How many of these do we all get? You get them. I get them. Quacks. Freaks." Garman wiped some perspiration off his upper lip. "But this one arrived the day of the Enwright fire—addressed to my home, not my office."

"You brought it with you today to the meeting but chose not to show it to your colleagues," Boldt reminded him. "Why?"

Garman had naturally red cheeks and a big smile when he allowed it. "Those guys? I'm *one* of those guys. I know how they think. We investigate fires, Sergeant. They would have laughed me out of that room. This," he said, indicating the envelope, "maybe it's something; maybe it's not. Some plastic and a poem. So what? But then I'm thinking maybe it means something. It occurred to me the dates were the same."

Using a pencil's eraser, Boldt carefully opened the back flap. He lifted the envelope with the pencil and dumped out its contents. A blob of what appeared to be melted green plastic slid out. It was about the size of a poker chip.

Using a second pencil, Boldt unfolded the note. His eyes fell to the crude drawing of a small headless man climbing a ladder. Boldt could imagine the figure was a fireman. The fact that it lacked a head would require the interpretation of the department's psychologist, Daphne Matthews. Alongside, in the same undeveloped handwriting as on the envelope, was written, *"He has half the deed done, who has made a beginning."*

After an excruciating silence Boldt looked up at the big man next to him and said dryly, "I don't like this."

"No," said the other. "I know what you mean."

THE psych profile was ready on Friday. Daphne Matthews had notified Boldt by leaving a message on a piece of notepaper.

Sight of her still stopped Boldt's breath. He wondered if it was because of her thick chestnut-brown hair or the narrow face with the sharp features. Perhaps the slender body, the dark skin, and long fingers. She was a woman who could play a set of tennis, talk a suicide out of a window, or hold a press conference where no one shouted. She wore smart clothes, not high fashion. On the morning of September 20 it was khakis and a hunter-green plaid shirt that she filled out deliciously.

On her desk a teapot sat next to a pile of folders. Her office was the only one in the building that didn't smell of commercial disinfectant. She had real curtains covering her window, and the poster art on the walls reflected her love of English landscapes. Vivaldi played from a small boom box on the shelf behind her. She turned down the music, pivoting in her chair, and smiled.

Daphne Matthews was referred to as the staff shrink. She pasted together the cops who fell apart. She also created psychological profiles of suspects based on whatever she could find.

She poured Boldt tea without asking and handed it across the desk. She didn't ask why he was here—there were too many years between them for such formalities. "The green plastic in the envelope mailed to Steven Garman? I don't know what it means."

"The verse?" Boldt asked.

"*He has half the deed done, who has made a beginning.* It's from a poem by Horace. Born in the first century B.C. One of the greatest lyric poets. Heady stuff. Our boy knows his literature."

"Our boy?" Boldt asked. "The killer? You think so?"

"We play it that way, don't we?" she said. "At least until you hand me someone different. The sketch is of a headless fireman going up a ladder. It talks about a deed being done."

"A confession?" Boldt asked, his heart beating strongly.

"More of a warning, I think. He warned Steven Garman. It allows him to dissociate from the consequences of the fire."

"It's Garman's fault," he proposed.

"Exactly. Perhaps Garman is the headless fireman in the sketch—the guy up the ladder." She explained, "I have to caution you that the handwriting—the block letters, the inconsistent spacing—contradicts the notion of a well-educated individual. I'm not sure how to interpret that. He may be young, Lou. Let me run some numbers by you." She picked up a sheet of paper on her desk. "Sixty-six percent of arson arrests are people under twenty-five years old. Juveniles account for forty-nine percent of those." Her face tightened. "Nationally the clearance rate is only fifteen percent."

Boldt sagged, literally and emotionally. Eighty-five percent of arsonists got away with it. "What about a fireman?" he asked.

"Certainly near the top of our list," Daphne answered. "A disenchanted fireman. Someone turned down by the department. Discharged." She clarified this. "It works for the sending of the note, but why kill an innocent woman if you're venting anger? You'd kill a fireman or fire inspector, wouldn't you?"

Boldt nodded. He heard it in her voice, her words. This was bigger than Dorothy Enwright, bigger than anyone had foreseen. The question had to be asked. "It isn't over, is it?"

She met his eyes. "The note tells us that: *He has half the deed done, who has made a beginning.* So what comes next?"

BEN had *Monday Night Football* to thank for keeping Jack Santori away. His stepfather wouldn't come home from work but would head directly to the bar for the game. Sometime around midnight he would stumble in downstairs, bang around, and find his way to bed. By that time Ben would be safe, locked behind his bedroom door, having spent the evening with Emily.

The neon sign in Emily's window was lighted, which meant she was home and open for business. She greeted him as if she hadn't seen him in months, when, in fact, it had been only a couple of days. She gave him a huge hug and immediately insisted that he eat something. She was warming up some lasagna in the microwave when the doorbell sounded.

"Go ahead and eat," she said. "You don't need to help tonight."

"I want to," he protested, jumping up and pulling open the drawer that contained their wireless radio system.

She didn't stop him. He tested the system by speaking softly into the walkie-talkie. She nodded that it was working. Then she checked her appearance in a mirror and headed out to answer the door. Ben slipped out the back.

The vehicle in the driveway was a beat-up blue pickup truck with a dented and chipped white camper shell. Ben went around to the driver's window because from here he couldn't be seen from the front door. Light from the street penetrated the cab, but he couldn't see much of the floor. The ashtray was filled with butts.

"He smokes," Ben said into the walkie-talkie. "Parking sticker on the windshield for Chief Joseph Air Force Base. Nice music system. He's into music." Ben saw a pair of aviator sunglasses on the dash. How badly he wanted to open the door, but Emily had her rules.

Ben stepped back, studying the camper shell. He noticed the rooftop skylight was partially open, and he could picture himself slipping down inside and finding out everything there was to know about the guy. He wanted to give Emily something worthwhile. One of the lower limbs of the cedar tree alongside the driveway went out just above the camper, and he debated climbing out to see down into the shell, but everything was too dark.

He circled the vehicle once more, then crept quietly into the kitchen, taking up his spot at a peephole that Emily had put in the wall. She liked to leave the room now and then and spy on her customers to see what they did when she was gone. She claimed this could tell her a lot about a person. Ben placed his one good eye to the wall, watched, and listened.

The guy was built solid, with wide shoulders, hard features, and pinpoint eyes. His hair was buzz cut, and his jaw was square. Ben looked first to the man's face and then at his right hand, which was hard not to look at. His last three fingers were fused together with pink, shiny skin, so they looked like a small flipper. Because of his glass eye Ben knew what it was like to be a freak, and rather than wince at this hand, he felt empathy toward the man. That hand would be a tough thing to live with.

"Are you sure?" Emily asked her customer.

"Yes, ma'am. Just October second. That's all. Just whether that's a good day for me—you know, as far as the astrology stuff goes. Whether it's a good day for me to do some business."

"I'll need to do a chart and then make a reading. Four or five days. You'll have to come back."

"That's okay. I can get up to the city."

"It's fifty dollars for a chart." She added quickly, "It's just ten dollars a reading from then on—if you wanted more readings."

"I might." He added, "The money's all right. The fifty bucks."

Ben thought the man looked nervous, and he wondered if it had to do with that hand, if this guy always felt uncomfortable, always thought people were staring at it. Ben knew that feeling. He wondered what was so important about October 2. He learned things hanging around Emily. Watching her work. People wanted someone to tell them what to do and when to do it. They would gladly shell out ten or twenty dollars just to hear it.

"Fifty for the chart, ten for the reading," Emily clarified, ever the businesswoman. "I need your birth date, time of day—"

"Time of day?" he asked, interrupting. "I don't know what time of day I was born. Who knows that?"

"Could you call your mother?"

"No!" he said sharply. "There's no one."

Ben felt a chill run to his toes. The words swirled in his head. They might have been his words if he hadn't had Emily. *No one.*

"I have my birth certificate," the man said. "I can get it for you."

"That would work."

Suddenly irritable, he said, "Shouldn't you know these things?"

"You think I don't know about you? You're a military man," she informed him. "Air force. You're considerate of others, the type of man to help someone out who needs a hand. Money is a little tight right now, but there's a deal on the horizon. . . ."

His eyes tried to contain his shock. He rubbed his hands together briskly, although the flipper stayed out of it, as if the knuckles didn't bend. He said, "Okay, so I'm impressed. So what?" He paused. "How could you know any of that?"

"It's my gift," she said.

A warm feeling of goodness surged through Ben. She often called him her little gift. They were a team. He felt ecstatic.

BOLDT was scheduled to meet with Dorothy Enwright's mother and sister. He wanted to know what kind of life the dead woman had lived, her friends, her enemies. He needed to crawl inside and live with her for a while. Something, somewhere in Dorothy Enwright's past, had ensured her untimely death.

Arson investigator Sidney Fidler showed up at Boldt's office cubicle just in time to delay the sergeant's departure for the interview with Enwright's relatives. Fidler was in his early thirties, anxiously thin and prematurely bald. He wore clothes that didn't match, and he always looked half asleep, though he had one of the finest minds of anyone Boldt had worked with. It was too bad that Fidler was a fireman on rotation to SPD rather than a permanent member of Boldt's homicide squad.

"I thought I might interpret this for you, Sergeant." Fidler passed Boldt the lab report. "It's a preliminary memo, to give us an idea of what we'll receive." Such memos, a courtesy of the Washington State Patrol Crime Lab, were typically offered only on cases where the findings were hot enough to expect a leak to the press. Not good news, Boldt mused.

"Go on," he said.

"Bahan and I had a parley with a couple of the task force boys. As you know, the Enwright fire area of origin was nearly entirely destroyed. The thing is, the lab report is going to come back negative for hydrocarbons. In your area of expertise it would be like finding a drowned body with no water in the lungs. It's baffling."

"What's it mean?" Boldt asked.

"It won't look good to the press. But we *did* locate the spalling and the blue concrete, and that sure as hell should test positive for accelerant." Fidler paused, training his rich brown eyes on the sergeant. "You asked what it means," he said. "There had to be one powerful accelerant in that fire. You don't go to eleven hundred feet and turn concrete blue with only a match set to the two-by-fours. We could have missed it for any number of reasons. Best bet is to send samples to the feds and try again. They'll scare up hydrocarbons."

"And if they don't?" Boldt inquired.

"Let's take it one square at a time."

Boldt didn't like the sound of that. "Blue concrete and negative lab reports." He paused. "Next question. Tell me, Sid, what do you think of the stuff that Garman received? Related or not?"

"The timing's good. Weird note. Don't know about the plastic."

"I sent it all downstairs for analysis."

"What's your opinion?" Fidler asked.

"Garman's on the arson task force. But Enwright's home isn't in his district. So if it's legitimate, if the torch knows so much about fire investigations, why send the note to the wrong guy?"

Fidler's face screwed up into a knot. "Hadn't thought about it."

"It bothers me," Boldt said. "Why Garman? You see? It may narrow down the search for us. Someone Garman put away? Someone he knows, works with?"

"Yeah. But that takes us away from the woman—"

"First things first," Boldt replied, interrupting. "I start with getting to know Dorothy Enwright, post facto. Why don't you get to know Steven Garman? Just in case."

THE two Enwright women, mother and sister, had agreed to meet Boldt at four o'clock in the Garden Court of the Four Seasons Olympic Hotel. He had asked them to bring photographs.

Located on Seattle's fashionable Fifth Avenue, the Olympic was one of the country's few remaining grand hotels—ornate, opulent, and spacious. Boldt's love of a formal tea brought him there several times a year in spite of the fourteen-dollar price tag. He welcomed the soothing ambience of the ficus trees, the running water, the thirty-foot ceilings, and the classical piano. The room was open, in three tiers, and smelled of a garden.

Boldt gave the name Magpeace, Dorothy Enwright's maiden name, to the receptionist. She seated him on the second level, near the waterfall, at a table with starched linen and bone china.

Mrs. Harriet Magpeace and her thirty-year-old daughter, Claudia, entered ten minutes later, wearing grim faces. They shook hands all around. It seemed odd to order tea and cucumber sandwiches on the edge of discussing a young woman's brutal murder, but he knew that people seek comfort in extremely individual ways at such times.

Harriet Magpeace kept her graying hair short. She had Irish coloring and a long, elegant neck. Her daughter, who had inherited her mother's green eyes, was wonderful to look at. If Dorothy had looked anything like her sister, she had been a beauty.

The mother removed a small group of photos from her purse and slid them disdainfully across the linen toward Boldt, as if not wanting to see them herself. "Obviously it's a shock," she said. She tensed, and Boldt worried that she wouldn't hold up.

Boldt explained, "This is a lousy job at times. I have to ask questions that imply I don't trust the quality of Dorothy's character. I want you to know right off that that is not the case. I do this only for the sake of getting to the truth."

"We understand," the dark beauty said. Her mother nodded.

Boldt said, "If she was murdered"—at which point Harriet Magpeace twitched violently—"then we start first with looking at people close to her: a husband, a lover, a co-worker. What I need from you is a snapshot of Dorothy's life."

The older woman stared at Boldt sadly. "Yours is a morbid life, isn't it, Sergeant?"

Boldt winced. He didn't appreciate his work, his life, being reduced to such a statement, hated it all the more for the truth of it. Death was a way of life for him, true, but Boldt saw his work as a means to an end, the only acceptable end being justice.

"I'm sure my mother means that sympathetically," Claudia interjected, attempting to lessen the blow. "We certainly appreciate all you're doing to find Doro's killer—if that's actually what happened. I have to tell you, the whole thing is a little fantastic."

Boldt was prepared for disbelief. No one—no one—ever anticipated murder. "Can you tell me a little about Dorothy?"

The mother blinked rapidly. Claudia filled in. "Doro was divorced two years ago. Bob's an architect. Doro writes—wrote— for garden magazines and a few food magazines as well. She . . . it was Doro's fault—the divorce."

"It wasn't her fault!" the mother snapped.

"She fell in love with another man, Mother." To Boldt, Claudia said, "The boyfriend died of cancer a few months after the separation. It was awful." She added, "Dorothy lost the child in the divorce. She only got visitation rights. But there was no hostility on her part. She understood the judge's ruling, much as she hated it."

"She was a lovely girl," the mother mumbled.

Boldt nodded. This too he had heard a hundred times.

Claudia said, "I know what you're looking for, Sergeant. At least I think I do. But Bob would never, ever, do such a thing." She hesitated and then rattled off Bob Enwright's office and home phone numbers, knowing Boldt would want to talk with him.

Boldt asked, "Did she own the house?"

"A rental," the sister replied. The mother looked lost. Claudia said, "You were thinking insurance, weren't you? She burned it for the insurance and got caught in the fire? No chance."

"We consider every possibility," Boldt said.

The mother said, "Someone murder Dorothy? It's absurd."

If given half a chance, if at all average, they would lie to get custody of the child. They would be eager to conspire against the former husband. Boldt had come prepared to see through this. When they failed to make any such attempt, Boldt felt somewhat disappointed.

Wanting this over, Boldt asked Claudia, "Any boyfriends out of her past? Anybody you think I might want to speak with?"

"I know you're only doing your job, Sergeant. I respect that. I just don't think there's anything to tell you. Doro was a wonderful, loving person. She laughed a lot, Doro did. Used to," she added. "The last two years took a lot out of her."

"Was she depressed, drinking—anything like that?"

Claudia cautioned, "She did *not* kill herself, Detective."

"Is that a yes or no to the depression?" Boldt asked, irritated. If there was one thing he had learned early as a homicide investigator, it was how fragile life was, how easily lost. One day here, the next day gone. And if the death came with questions attached, it was Lou Boldt's job to answer them. Of chief concern was why Dorothy Enwright had not run from the house when it caught fire. It had not exploded. She had been seen inside moments before the blaze. She must have had an opportunity to escape, given the way the fire had burned from a central core outward. It had not trapped her by seal-ing the doors. Why, then, had she not escaped?

"Dorothy was having problems," her mother told him, "but she was surprisingly cheerful, wouldn't you say, dear?"

"Absolutely," Claudia agreed. "She was a remarkable woman."

"Who would want to kill her?" the mother blurted out, too loudly for the soft buzz of conversation in the Garden Court. Heads turned. Fortunately, only Boldt saw this.

The two women did not see. Their eyes were filled with tears.

CHAPTER THREE

OCTOBER 2 came and nearly went without Ben's taking any notice of it. But when he arrived at Emily's on the afternoon of the third, she sent him to Steven's Broadway News to buy copies of the Seattle *Times* and the Tacoma *News Tribune*.

Back at her purple house, the two of them read headlines and lead paragraphs, until Ben asked, "What are we doing?"

"The military man," she said. "Do you remember him? May thir-teenth, 1968. The bad hand."

Ben remembered the hand.

"He came back a week later. I told him that the stars looked good for a business deal on October second. He was real nervous, and I got the feeling his business wasn't exactly legitimate."

"So we're looking for something he might have done."

"Yes," she said. "And he'll be back. Very superstitious."

"And you think we may find something in the papers. You think he's a criminal!" Ben felt a pang of excitement in his chest.

"He had something going on the second. I tested if it had anything to do with love and got nothing back from him. I tested money and got a definite reaction—lots of body language, discomfort. He's selling or buying something. If I identify it and he walks back in here and I can tell him about it, I'll have a customer for life. You give people what they want, Ben, and they're yours forever."

Ben read more carefully. The papers were full of various crimes. He said, "Nothing much good."

"No. Nothing very good." She pushed the papers aside and said, "Tell me what you remember about him, Ben."

This was a test. She did this now and then—made him exercise his memory skills. He reeled off all that he could recall about the beat-up truck, the camper shell. He gave her a detailed description of what he had seen through the peephole: buzz-cut hair, pinpoint eyes, the fingers on his right hand.

"How old did he look?" she asked.

It took him a moment to subtract the numbers. "Twenty-eight," he answered, using the birth date she had already supplied.

She reached over and messed his hair, which was her way of saying how much she cared about him.

She said, "He wore black military boots. When he paid me, he pulled out his wallet. He carried a pass to the PX, a discount shopping center on the base, which means he's either active or works there. His driver's license was from Kansas. He had a ticket to the Seahawks in with his money."

"He wore a big silver buckle," Ben added. "Like a rodeo guy."

"Very good!" she exclaimed. "That caught my eye as well. And did you catch it when he turned to leave? His belt had a first name stamped into the leather. Nick."

"The guy's name is Nick?"

"Yes. He's a long way from home, working on the base, a football fan. He's got business dealings that worry him to the point he's having his chart read. The deal is worth a lot more than sixty bucks, or he wouldn't shell out that kind of money."

"We know a lot about him," Ben said, impressed.

"Yes, we do," she answered. "But not what he's up to."

THE BRUNETTE WITH THE TIGHT skirt was in the kitchen cleaning up, and Ben knew that she had to come through the living room to reach Jack, who was waiting in the bedroom. She was a new one, hair pulled back with a hair band, less makeup than the others, thinner than most of the women he dragged home with him. Ben thought what better way to welcome her than to share his cherished death pose with her.

He positioned himself in Jack's favorite lounge chair. He hung his head over the arm, so that the blood ran to his face, turning it a bright red. Then he popped out his glass eye, cupped it in his hand, and opened both his eyes in a dead man's stare.

A minute later he heard the water stop and her footsteps approaching. He spread his arms out so they were floppy, and he held his breath so that his chest stopped moving.

Her scream was loud enough that a neighbor called the police. Before Ben could settle her down, Jack had hold of him.

Jack's belt came out of the loops, and Ben felt it connecting with his butt. The belt kept coming like a whip, and Ben thought he'd be sick to his stomach. The girl screamed even louder for Jack to stop. Somewhere in the ensuing nightmare, Ben threw up on Jack's chair, which only brought the belt down harder.

Maybe the cops saved his life, he thought later, because the knock on the door, followed by the strong voices announcing themselves, forced Jack to send Ben to his room.

Ben could barely move, his butt was so raw, but he flew up those stairs nonetheless. He heard one of the cops say something about a complaint from a neighbor. The cops wanted a look around.

Ben understood his situation clear as day. One, in his condition he couldn't let himself be discovered by the cops. Jack could get in big trouble, which would mean more beatings. Two, the guy was sure to kill him once the cops were gone.

He opened his window and went out the familiar route, along the roof, over to the tree, and down through the limbs. His butt was a source of blinding pain. With a deep inhale of the cool night air he felt free—the most amazing, most welcome feeling of all.

He walked to Emily's, slow on his feet, sticking to back streets. Her house was dark, the neon sign switched off. He was loath to roust her, loath to admit that his existence with Jack was untenable. His fear was not of pain or reprimand, but of being alone. Emily had told him that for a time he would be in the care of the state, and nothing scared him more. She had told him she would rescue him from their care and provide for him, and though he trusted her intentions, he remained skeptical of the system. He feared desertion. His mother had run away without a word.

Briefly the truth clanged inside his chest, as it did on occasion: His mother would never have left him behind.

He climbed the cedar tree beside Emily's driveway, up to the platform—six boards nailed between two old boughs, each capable of supporting a car. He had a more complete tree fort behind his own house, but this platform at Emily's was a safer refuge given the trouble he'd caused. He lay down on the platform, keenly aware of his wounds, and curled himself into a ball, where he hugged himself until he fell fast asleep, pulled down into the drowsiness of a body and mind in need of repair. Of escape.

WHEN Liz voluntarily took the kids with her to the cabin for the weekend, Boldt knew he had trouble. Typically she found the cabin too remote, too far from the city. She had not called him at work, but had left a note he couldn't possibly receive until she and the kids were well on their way, the decision beyond discussion. That struck him as unlike her, until he reached the part in the note where she suggested he "come up if you can get free." Then he realized it was a test. He had a choice: his family or his job.

Liz knew that when he sank his teeth into something like this arson case, there was no letting go. And she resented it. What really hurt was that he was going to fail the test. There was no way he could get up to the cabin for the weekend. Sunday night was going to be pins and needles on the home front.

On the plus side, he had the house to himself. It didn't happen often, and when it did, he felt as if she had handed him the greatest gift of all. Perhaps she had gone to the cabin in sacrifice, know-ing how he valued quiet time during a difficult investigation. He reread her note, hoping to find clarity there, but to no avail. Mar-riage was many things; easy was not one of them.

He switched off the front porch light and put on an Oscar Peterson album. Twenty minutes later a car pulled past his drive, slowed, and stopped. He went to the curtain and peered out: Daphne's red Honda sports car. She climbed out carrying her briefcase—not a good sign. A moment later he heard her footsteps on the back porch and opened the door.

"You not answering your phone?"

"We turn the ringers off—Sarah's a light sleeper. Sorry," he apol-ogized. "Come on in."

"Liz?" She seemed hesitant to enter.

"Took the kids to the cabin. It's all right."

"It's *not* all right." She stepped inside, already down to business. "Today's press conference was a disaster. Shoswitz talks too much. And then there's this." She reached into her briefcase and handed him a photocopy. "The original's with the lab."

Minutes later, sipping from a glass of red wine at the kitchen table, Boldt read the note silently before finally speaking. "*Suddenly a flash of understanding, a spark that leaps across to the soul.* Sent to Garman?" he asked.

Daphne nodded gravely. "It's Plato. Our boy is something of a scholar. Garman delivered it unopened. He knew what it was."

Boldt said, "I really hate this, you know?"

In her eyes he saw a deep-seated sympathy. They both under-stood perfectly well what the note meant. His imagination fixed on the thought of another Dorothy Enwright out there, at home, mind-ing her own business, about to face the gates of hell. Daphne looked tired all of a sudden, and under the same relentless pressure as Boldt. Investigating a violent crime was one thing; anticipating and stopping such a crime another thing entirely.

She continued. "The first note could have been a poorly timed coincidence. This note changes all that. He's going to strike for a second time. He dated both notes, don't forget. If I'm right, that means the fire is today or tonight. He warns; he strikes. By the time the card arrives, he has already targeted his victim, perhaps even rigged the house to burn."

"Oh, Lord!" Boldt expelled his breath.

"It's premeditated, and he's enjoying it. The pressure may be intended for Garman. He's a fire inspector, Lou. His evidence puts arsonists in jail. Revenge is potent motivation."

"Fidler is checking out Garman."

"That will help," she said, knowing Fidler's reputation for detail.

"I've got Bahan working the technical end, the chemistry of the arson." Boldt sensed her unease. "What's up?"

"Firemen," she answered. "Fidler, Bahan, Garman—all of them. Putting out a fire is only one step away from setting it. In fact, firemen set structure fires all the time to train the new boys. They love torching places." She met his skeptical expression. "I'm generalizing, admittedly, but if we're looking for an arsonist, we might not have to look very far."

Boldt said, "Who better than a fire inspector to go torching places and sending himself notes? Is that what you're saying?"

"Anyone in turnouts, Lou. They all have the bug."

"Prior convictions and current firemen. Quite a list." Boldt felt an impending urgency. The second note was like a fuse burning inside him. "How do we stop a second death?"

"How do we stop potential copycat fires?" Daphne asked, avoiding an answer. Arsons were notorious for spawning copycats. "It's your case, Lou," she added. "Everyone should be grateful for that."

Pep talks and compliments—they traded them often. But just the fact that she would attempt to pump him up troubled him. It meant she was as scared as he was.

She offered, "We've had a few calls from psychics wanting to sell us information. I haven't followed up, but I'd like to."

Boldt winced. He had no room for psychics. "Not for me," he reminded her. "Your stuff, not mine."

"Don't start with me," she cautioned. "We take tips from junkies, Lou! Is a psychic less believable than a junkie?"

"You handle the psychics," he quipped. "I'll take the junkies."

She turned, exhaling heavily. She changed the subject, asking, "Did you catch the news? Shoswitz threatening the arsonist?"

"I caught it." Phil Shoswitz, the lieutenant, was terrible with the press, but there was no stopping him.

"Shoswitz may have baited him, Lou. 'Madman, nut case.' He even mentioned you by name. I wish he wouldn't do that."

"Lead detectives are often mentioned," he reminded her.

Boldt's pager sounded. He and Daphne met eyes. They both knew what this was about before Boldt made the phone call.

BEHIND the incessant pulse of emergency-vehicle lights, Boldt and arson investigator Neil Bahan waited for the site to cool enough for them to walk it. They had been waiting four hours by the time the Marshal Five inspector entered the remains of 876 Fifty-seventh Street North. Accompanying the inspector was Steven Garman.

The ground was soggy beneath Boldt's waterproof hiking boots. The air smelled bitter, a mixture of the wet, smoldering materials. Neil Bahan led Boldt through a gaping hole in the side of the building, saying, "Keep a close eye on your footing."

Both Bahan and Boldt carried strong flashlights, illuminating the wreckage. "There's not much left to look at," Boldt commented, pointing down into the basement area, where Garman and the other Marshal Fives were already at work.

"It was overhauled," Bahan explained, sounding disappointed. "The firefighters basically tear the structure apart to be sure all the fire is caught. It's good fire fighting, but it hurts the investigation. Investigators have to look at everything before it moves, to stand much of a chance."

The structure was a tangle of smoldering lumber, bent aluminum window frames, broken glass. Bahan and Boldt carefully dodged through the maze. Well over half the house was missing, a gaping round hole open to the sky above and the basement below. The fire had run like a pillar through this center section and had chewed toward the back of the building. Bahan mumbled, "Never seen anything like this. Except in the Enwright pictures."

"What exactly should I look for?" Boldt asked.

"Most of it will probably be down in the basement," Bahan answered. He shone his flashlight into the hole. "The cellar catches the debris—lumber, glass, tile, insulation. You see what's missing?" Bahan asked Boldt. "Sinks. Toilets. Where are they? Same as Enwright. They're down there, melted flat, which means we're looking at temperature in excess of two or three thousand degrees Fahrenheit. Most everything in this center core was vaporized."

A news helicopter flew overhead, training a blinding spotlight on the structure. Bahan's face was dirt-smudged, and his eyes were bloodshot. The air smelled suddenly different yet familiar, and Boldt glanced around anxiously.

"What is it?" Bahan asked, sensing Boldt's agitation.

"It's a body," Boldt answered solemnly.

"You sure about that?"

"I'm sure," Boldt answered. Panic gripped him. "Maybe a pet. Maybe not a human." Though he suspected it was. Did only homicide cops know that smell? he wondered.

He reached for Bahan's arm, saying, "Someone should conduct a perimeter search before we lose it to contamination. Gum wrappers, toothpicks, Popsicle sticks, pieces of clothing—"

"I'm with you," Bahan said. "But anything this close to the structure went up with the fire. Not gonna be any gum wrappers around."

Boldt appealed to the man. "Humor me."

"Hey, gladly," Bahan replied.

The grass surrounding the structure's foundation was charred black, and the ground beneath it soaked to a spongy mud by water from the fire hoses. Boldt looked for bottle caps, cigarette butts—anything at all that might tie in to a suspect.

As he moved around the concrete foundation, scanning his surroundings, he suddenly stopped. At his feet were two rectangular indentations in the black mud. Next to the right-hand dent were some blue flecks. He crouched and studied the area, disappointed as he identified them as ladder impressions. Firemen, he thought. The legs of the ladder had sunk about two inches into the turf, leaving a distinctive imprint of chevrons.

He looked up to see Bahan standing alongside.

"Got something?" Bahan asked.

Boldt pointed. "I take it the fire crew used ladders fighting this?"

"No way. Too hot. Besides," Bahan said, "there was no wall here to lean a ladder against. The fire destroyed it."

Boldt marked the area with police tape before continuing around the foundation. Only the ladder impressions were found. He telephoned Bernie Lofgrin, the senior identification technician, to send someone out to cast and photograph the impressions and take samples of the colored flecks alongside. Excitement welled inside him. Any evidence at all is paramount in a case.

Boldt stayed on-site for hours, overseeing the collection of the ladder evidence, and was on hand for the grotesque discovery of the charred partial remains of a body in the basement, trapped underneath an overturned bathtub. The sex and age of the victim would be revealed in autopsy the following day.

But it was back at his house that Boldt stumbled—literally stumbled—onto additional evidence, for his boots stuck to the kitchen floor as he stepped inside. He pulled them off and almost touched the melting rubber sole before thinking better of it. Whatever could disintegrate a Vibram sole was nothing to mess with.

He called Bernie Lofgrin again and described the soles of his boots. "What's it mean, Bernie?" Boldt asked his friend.

"A strong base or acid," Lofgrin replied, his voice puzzled. "But what that's doing in a fire is anybody's guess."

BEHIND his Coke-bottle glasses Bernie Lofgrin's eyes looked like hard-boiled eggs cut in half. Lofgrin stood five feet five inches. He was balding and overweight. There weren't many stars in any city department, but as senior identification technician, Lofgrin knew his stuff. He had two decades of experience and a nose for evidence collection and analysis. When Lofgrin was definite about an opinion, Boldt ran with it.

There were only a few people in the department who would travel across town on a Saturday morning to sit around a kitchen table and talk shop. Bernie Lofgrin was one of them. Boldt fixed a pot of coffee, put on a Scott Hamilton album, and cut open a cantaloupe. "Have you been up all night?" he asked.

"I went in at five and worked these impressions, and not because I love you. Your obsequious lieutenant put me up to it. Now that there's a second victim, the media is blaming a serial arsonist, dubbed the Scholar." He grimaced. "You know how many ladders are sold in this city in any given year?"

"No idea," Boldt replied, thinking, Too many.

"Me neither." Lofgrin laughed, then continued. "The width between the pads on the ladder's feet is significant. Extension ladders come in a variety of widths. Some manufacturers use twenty-four inches, some twenty-five, depending on the strength of the materials used—commonly aluminum. All retail extension ladders have small pads that grip the ground. Each company goes with a slightly different grip pattern, like tire treads in tire companies. What we're looking at is a Werner ladder. And that's significant because it's not your weekend chores kind of ladder. The imprints are from the high end of their fiberglass line, a professional line: electricians, painters, that sort of work."

"Firemen?" Boldt asked.

"Not fiberglass. It's flammable. Aluminum is the ladder for fire fighting, steel alloy for the hook and ladders."

"And do we have a particular model we're looking at?"

"It's a Werner twenty-four-foot fiberglass extension ladder," Lofgrin said proudly. "Manufactured between July '93 and August '94. Sold, probably, into '95. And in '94–'95 they only had one wholesaler in western Washington."

"Good stuff, Bernie," Boldt said.

Training his bulging eyes on the sergeant, Lofgrin said, "What? You think that's all I've got? O ye of little faith."

He passed Boldt a black-and-white Polaroid of the cast impressions made at the fire site.

"Impressions are anything but an exact science," he explained, "but we can make certain educated assumptions, given soil-compression ratios and water content. It takes a specific weight to effect a specific depth of impression."

"Are you telling me you can guess the weight of the person who climbed the ladder?"

"Estimate," Lofgrin corrected sternly. "*You* guess; *I* estimate. We measure, we test, we analyze. Give me a few days, and I'll have a minimum and maximum weight for your ladder climber. For the cloth fibers give me a week."

"Can you memo me the Werner ladder info?" Boldt asked. "I want to get Detective LaMoia on it."

Lofgrin passed Boldt a handwritten note. "Consider it done."

Boldt held the memo in his hand. Hard evidence at last.

CHAPTER FOUR

BEN awakened in Emily's cedar tree to the sound of a car pulling into her driveway below. As he sat up, he winced with pain and recalled the whipping that sleep had blotted out.

He looked down to see not a car but a blue truck with a white camper shell, and his heart raced as the man with the buzz-cut hair climbed out and headed for Emily's door. The man with the fused fingers. His name was Nick, and she thought he was a criminal.

The camper's skylight window was open. Ben moved around the trunk of the tree and lowered himself to the next branch. He wanted a look inside that camper shell.

His excitement grew as he worked his way down through the branches, for as he paused and looked into the camper, he saw a dark steel tube that just had to be the barrel of a gun.

His decision was made.

Ben moved through the tree fluidly, lowering himself as effortlessly as a monkey. Easing out on a limb, he inched his way over the camper shell. The farther out he went, the more the branch bowed under him, pointing down toward the camper like an invitation. He slid his hands out on the limb, held his breath, and jumped.

Ben's sneakers caught and grabbed the edge of the camper. He timed it perfectly, coming down quietly on the aluminum roof—toes, knees, palms—as if bending in prayer. The limb whipped back up over his head.

He crawled carefully toward the open skylight, slipped his head into the gap, and peered down inside. It *was* a gun, lying on the padded bench. And next to it, on top of an open sleeping bag, was a green army duffel bag.

Ben heard voices to his right. "You're sure today is okay?" the deep voice asked. "It's sudden, is all."

"It's fine," Emily answered.

The guy, Nick, was at the door. He was *leaving*.

In a second or two he would turn and face his truck. He would see Ben spread out on the roof, his head half inside the skylight.

Ben's reactions were entirely instinctual. He pointed his head down, grabbed the lip of the skylight, and slithered inside. He swung down into the camper space, his toes nearly touching a folding table, and let go, dropping to the floor. Moments later he heard the door on the driver's side of the cab open with a loud complaint. The two spaces, cab and camper, communicated by a small sliding window hidden on the other side of a curtain that was, thankfully, closed.

The truck's engine came to life. Ben glanced up at the skylight. It seemed so small, so out of reach. The truck rumbled and backed up.

Ben scrambled on hands and knees for the half-sized back door. He reached up and turned the handle, preparing for the moment when the driver paused to shift into first. He twisted the doorknob, and to his joy it moved. It wasn't locked.

The truck braked, and the gears made a sound as the driver shifted. Ben pushed on the door. It stopped abruptly, only open an inch—padlocked from the outside.

The truck roared off. Ben was trapped inside.

Panic seized every muscle in his body. For the first few minutes of the drive he couldn't help but focus on how much trouble he was going to be in. He had violated Emily's one rule, and now here he was, locked in the back of a pickup truck with a suspected criminal behind the wheel. The truck was moving quickly, not stopping at lights. They were on a highway, and the logical candidate was I-5, north or south. North was Canada; south, Oregon and California. What if the truck never stopped? Fear ran his blood cold.

The side windows were tiny; there was no way he could go out through one. It might be possible to jump to the skylight from the folding table and pull himself up and out, but only if the skylight was open, and it had fallen shut behind his less-than-graceful entrance. He felt on the edge of tears, afraid for his life.

He crawled around the soiled carpet searching out a broom handle or some other device to help him push the skylight open. As the truck changed lanes, he was thrown onto his stomach. He struggled back to his hands and knees. It was a tiny space, and he quickly realized there was nothing in plain sight to help him.

He lost his balance again and was tossed up against the duffel bag, and he couldn't resist looking inside, hoping something might prove itself useful. What he found scared him half to death: large clear-plastic containers filled with milky fluid. A chemical formula was written on the nearest container in black marker.

Drugs! He had seen a police raid of a meth lab on TV. The thought that he was trapped in a pickup being driven by an armed drug dealer sent his head dizzy, and he nearly swooned, brought back to reality by the truck's sudden slowing. He looked up in time to see the green flash of a highway sign outside the window: SEA-TAC AIR TERMINAL. EXIT ONLY.

He glanced at the duffel bag. Nick was taking a trip. He would be coming into the back after his bag in a matter of minutes! Panic-stricken, he glanced around. Where to hide?

The truck took a right turn at the entrance to the airport.

Ben thought about hiding inside the sleeping bag, but it seemed far too risky. Then he saw it.

The bench that supported the cushion where the gun was resting was a big wooden box, shaped like a coffin. A storage area with a lifting lid. Ben pushed the cushion up, and the gun slid against the back. Cluttered with tools, extension cords, rags, and boxes of ammunition, there was still room for a boy his size. He crawled in and lowered the lid. The truck came to a stop. Ben faintly heard a mechanical voice say, "Take ticket, please."

The truck began spiraling up the airport's corkscrew ramps to the elevated parking. Ben had never been to the airport, but he had seen this very parking ramp in a cop movie. He felt relief that the truck was certain to park and the driver would, hopefully, leave, offering him the chance to escape. The truck slowed, made two more sharp turns, and stopped abruptly. The engine died, and Ben heard the driver's door slam shut. He tried to think what he would do if Nick suddenly opened the bench. He searched blindly in the dark and found a bag of small nails and quietly gripped a fistful of them.

He heard the padlock snap open. Nick was coming inside. It felt about a thousand degrees in the box. Ben was suddenly overcome with claustrophobia. He *had* to get out of there. Now!

A loud noise caused his whole body to stiffen. The driver had sat down on the bench. It sounded like he was strapping on the gun. This discovery sent another electric bolt shooting through Ben. If the man was taking a gun with him, he wasn't getting on any plane but had come to the airport garage to do a deal.

Ben did not want to be a witness to any drug deal. All he wanted was to be back in his own room, the door closed and locked. He didn't care if his drunken stepfather lifted a hand to him every now and then. He just wanted to be home.

The bench creaked as the man stood up. Ben heard the duffel

bag dragging heavily on the floor, and the guy let out a grunt as he struggled with it. The back door slammed shut. There was no sound of the padlock. Ben pushed the bench top up a crack and ventured a look. The camper was empty.

Terrified, exhilarated, he climbed out of the storage bench, his one good eye trained on the camper's back door. Cautiously Ben looked out into the parking garage, then ducked quickly, glad he had not charged out the back as he had been tempted to do. Nick stood waiting for the elevator with the duffel bag at his side. It was stenciled in bold capital letters: USAF. Ben impatiently waited him out.

It was strange how with just the one eye Ben could see so much, or perhaps it was his lack of peripheral vision that sharpened the importance of those objects he *could* see. He was a terrible judge of distance, but if something did enter his visual field, it registered fully, taking on an immediate importance.

It was just a shape. Dark. About as tall as his stepfather. Standing between two parked cars. Watching. The presence of this man caused Ben to fear leaving the back of the truck. He would be seen, and something warned him to avoid this at all costs.

The elevator arrived. Nick, the driver, stepped into the elevator, hauling the duffel bag with him. The doors slid shut. At that same instant the dark figure moved out from between the parked cars and headed straight for the truck.

The man approached quickly, taking long strides. Patches of light flashed across his face, but even so, Ben had trouble actually seeing that face. It was as if the man were wearing a mask.

Ben lifted the bench and dove back into hiding amid the tools and oily rags. The camper door made a noise as it opened. Ben felt his insides go watery. Where the driver had seemed a threat, this dark figure was the one to fear.

As quickly as the door opened, it shut. Ben waited, blood pounding in his ears and chest. He swallowed his fear and ventured to lift the bench a crack and peer out.

Empty. He wanted to shout for joy. He hoisted the bench, climbed out, and hurried to the smudged glass of the back door.

The parking garage appeared empty. Ben twisted the doorknob and pushed. With his luck the door would be . . . locked!

The second man had padlocked the door. A wave of nausea coursed through Ben. He dropped to his knees to study the clasp. As his knee touched the filthy carpeting, he felt an unexpected lump below his kneecap and glanced down to see the corner of an envelope protruding. It was thick and bulging but lightweight. He lifted the flap and saw money. Lots of it. Fifties and twenties and some tens. Old bills.

To him it seemed like a million dollars. He would need money to get home. He reached in and fished out a twenty. And then another. With each bill the temptation grew. Who would know if he took the whole thing? So many times, as Emily slipped her ten-dollar payment into the cigar box she kept in the freezer, she had spoken the words to Ben, "Money is freedom." And here was this envelope, and no one around to see. He could give the money to Emily; he could pay for his food; he could live with her.

He folded the envelope and shoved it into his front pants pocket. A chance at a new life. He felt giddy.

He moved quickly, as if he had done all this before. He checked a tiny closet and found an aluminum baseball bat. Hurriedly he climbed atop the camper's tabletop and pushed open the skylight with the bat. He squatted back down on the table, aimed his single eye above him, and jumped, fingers outstretched.

The wood edge of the skylight slapped his palms, but he gripped the lip and held himself dangling, suspended in midair. He pulled, hooked one elbow, then the other, and pulled higher, worming his torso through the skylight. Kicking his legs, he wiggled and clambered over to a narrow ladder fixed to the back of the shell. When his feet touched pavement, he was off at a run.

He wasn't going on that elevator no matter what. Instead, he took the stairs two at a time, his legs rubbery. He leaped onto the landing, grabbed hold of the railing, and pulled up short.

Nick, the buzz-cut driver of the truck, was standing on the stairs, his full attention riveted on Ben.

Ben stood there, chest heaving, recalling that the slight bulge on the man's right side was a handgun. He thought about the fold of money in his own pocket. Surely the man saw the outline of the envelope there. Surely he knew.

Nick smiled and said, "Slow down there, buddy. Good way to knock some teeth out."

Ben heard very little except something about getting his teeth knocked out. Nick climbed the stairs. Ben was directly in his path and so terrified that the man looked blurry. Their eyes met, and Ben felt a sick, hollow spot where his stomach should have been.

"Excuse me," the smiling man said, and Ben stepped aside. Nick headed on up the stairs.

Ben sneaked onto a downtown hotel courtesy van, pretending to be with a pair of parents who didn't notice what he was up to. He spent the twenty-minute drive into the city debating exactly what he had seen take place. Nick had left with a duffel bag; he had returned without it. The dark, faceless man had left an envelope of money and then locked the camper. A drop. A drug deal.

From downtown Ben rode a city bus home. Exhausted, he headed to his room and locked the door, well ahead of his step-father but not taking any chances. A few minutes later he went downstairs to the kitchen phone. It was something that had to be done—he knew this in his heart. He dialed 911. A woman's voice answered.

Ben said, "I want to report a drug deal. I saw a drug deal—" He caught himself. He could just see explaining this to his stepfather. His butt hurt enough already. He slammed down the phone and sprinted back upstairs.

Down a drab hallway in the Public Safety Building, the Seattle Communications Center, equipped with Enhanced 911 communications software, identified and recorded Ben's telephone number and address. Every moment of the call was recorded, every nuance of his slightly hysterical voice. The call would be logged both by computer and by hand. The operator classified Ben's call as a juvenile prank, which meant that if another two offenses were attributed to the same phone number, an officer of the juvenile court would pay that home a visit.

As Ben headed up to his room, he felt a little dizzy, a little sick. He shut his door and sat down heavily on the bed. At first he didn't believe the empty feeling under his butt. An even deeper fear wormed into his stomach. He reached back to the seat of his pants.

His wallet was gone.

DAPHNE Matthews caught him out of the corner of her eye. Lou Boldt didn't hush a crowd when he entered a room. He was an observer. He noticed things that no one else noticed.

He wasn't particularly good-looking, although to her he was. Couldn't dress himself no matter how hard he tried. Missed buttons. Stains. Scuffed shoes. Hair uncombed. Disheveled didn't do him service. Marriage didn't help. No one could change him. She envied Liz her chance at times.

"Interrupting?" he asked.

"No," Daphne answered, looking up from her desk.

"What's up?" She had asked for his time.

"You're aware that Shoswitz is hanging you out to dry for this?" she inquired. "He uses your name in every press conference, spouts fire and brimstone about how this killer will be caught and brought to justice. How you're the one to do it. Truthfully, I don't like it. It makes you a potential target."

"Now, Daffy—"

"It *does*, I'm telling you. This is *my* field, not yours. You don't taunt a person like that. Shoswitz is wrong to build you into a gun-slinging bounty hunter. These guys operate on hair triggers. He could switch targets like that," she said, snapping her fingers.

"What's done is done," Boldt replied.

"I'm going to speak with Shoswitz," Daphne declared. "Tell him to stop it." She knew that Boldt wouldn't argue with her.

"The body found was the house owner's, Melissa Heifitz," Boldt said. "Dixon confirmed it this morning. Dental records. They found five teeth in the ashes. Two are confirmed as Melissa's. Twenty-nine years old. Divorced mother of one, a bookkeeper for a professional building up on Eighty-fifth. No connection that we can see to Dorothy Enwright. A nice-looking woman," he said, passing her the driver's license photo. She could hear the knot in his throat. He took every homicide victim on as a member of his own family.

"Do you see it?" she asked him, the driver's license photograph still in hand. "The coloring? Even the shape of her head?"

"What are we talking about?" Boldt inquired, sitting forward.

Daphne passed Boldt a snapshot of Dorothy Enwright. "How about now?" she asked.

"Oh, damn," said the man who rarely cursed.

"There's a specific look to his victims: dark hair cut short, thin face. He's chosen death by fire. The fire holds some kind of symbolism for him, or he wouldn't go to all that trouble. It's important to him that they burn. Why? Because of the image of hell? Because his mother intentionally burned him as a child? Because she's unclean and he's attempting to purify her?"

"You're giving me the creeps here," Boldt said.

"I'm giving you motives, the psychological side of what fire may mean to him: religion, revenge, purification. They're all relevant."

"Some guy tapping brunettes because he's screwed up about his mother? I don't need this."

"You do if you're going to catch him," Daphne cautioned. "You better know what makes him tick, Lou, or you're operating on blind luck."

"Is this what you called me for?" he asked, annoyed. "To tell me how to conduct the investigation?"

"I wanted to forewarn you that I intend to speak to Shoswitz. I also wanted to tell you that I'm going to make an appointment with Emily Richland."

"Emily Richland," Boldt muttered.

"The psychic. I called her. She mentioned a man with a burned hand. A badly deformed hand." Daphne could feel his resistance. She snapped, "Why don't you like it, Lou? Because she actually helped us solve a case once?"

Emily Richland, who ran a ten-dollar-a-throw tarot card operation, had helped lead police to a kidnap suspect. At the time, Daphne had been recovering from injuries sustained in another case and had missed the kidnapping. She had never had personal contact with Emily Richland.

"You're saying because it's Richland we should listen?" he asked.

"Is that so wrong? Test the source? What if she's a part of it? I'm not saying she's psychic. I'm saying we listen. A burned hand? Come on!"

Boldt conceded. "You're right. We investigate every lead."

"Try to think of her as a snitch, not a psychic," she suggested. "Define it in terms that are acceptable to you."

"A snitch," he said, testing it.

"Leave it to me," she recommended.

Lou Boldt nodded. "Good idea."

DAPHNE knocked loudly on the door to the purple house. Hearing just how loudly and impatiently she knocked, she questioned whether or not she had the open mind necessary for the ruse she intended. A majority of psychics were nothing more than clever con artists. Though she was loath to admit it to Boldt, she didn't trust psychics. Emily Richland made her living telling lies.

Daphne's mission was multilayered: to reverse roles, tell lies of her own, and subtly interview Emily Richland in an effort to test the woman's authenticity—to attempt to trap her into admitting some connection with the arsons.

Richland had not answered her phone that morning, but the recorded message said she was open for readings. Daphne had written down the address given and headed to Emily's without telling her that she was coming.

The door opened. Emily's long, dark hair was pulled back, stretching the skin of a freckled face that took ten years off her forty. Her eyes were a haunting blue under too much mascara. She wore a thrift-store black velvet gown that was cinched tightly around her narrow waist by a beaded Indian belt. Her earrings featured black-and-white photographs of Elvis. Her smile was radiant yet mysterious, her eyes probing and curious.

"Welcome," Emily said, gesturing inside. "I'm Emily." She led Daphne to a small table with a pack of thumb-worn tarot cards waiting in one corner and a giant stump of a candle.

Daphne saw the woman's hand gently brush the edge of the table as she took her seat. It was a clever, practiced move. The lights dimmed. The room smelled faintly of incense.

"You have a question that needs answering," the woman stated. She studied her. "You're having trouble with a man."

Daphne felt her heart in her throat all of a sudden. How on earth could she know about the problems with Owen Adler, her fiancé? Then she realized that she had spun her engagement ring around so that Owen's absurdly sized diamond was hidden under her finger. The good ones can read body language, she reminded herself.

She felt her face flush. "Yes, but that's not why I've come."

"Something to do with work," Emily said, her hypnotic eyes searching Daphne's. "You're a doctor," the woman speculated, then shook her head. "A paramedic maybe. . . . Something medical. Am I close?"

Daphne shifted uncomfortably in the chair. The woman was good. Calm voice. Penetrating eyes.

"My fiancé's a doctor," Daphne lied convincingly. "But it's not about work, not about him." She had prepared her fiction carefully. "Have you ever dealt with a person's dreams?"

"Dreams can be windows, my dear. Into the past, the future. Do you want to tell me about the dream, or should I tell you a little about you first? You're not a believer, are you? It's all right, you know. I mean, not trusting in the power. But I do *see*—the past, the future. I'll tell you what I see." Her voice was musical and lilting, her eyes warm. "You're someone who's well prepared. You think out potential problems in advance. You're neat. You keep a clean house. You're angry at your fiancé, but it's not about another woman—a young girl, perhaps."

Daphne felt a chill all the way to her toes. How could she know about Owen's daughter, Corky? A lucky guess, Daphne decided.

"It's my dream I'm concerned with." Daphne closed her eyes. "The dream is always the same: a man . . . I can't see his face. He never looks directly at me. He's a strong man. Imposing. And I see people burning," she said in a hoarse, frightened whisper. "White-hot flames. Women burning." She saved the best for last. "Never his face. Just his : . ." She squinted tightly and shook her head. "His hand. A burned hand. Fingers burned . . ."

Emily gasped.

Daphne opened her eyes. Touché! "What is it? Do you know this man?"

Emily's eyes remained enlarged. "Who are you?" she choked out. "You're his girlfriend? You're checking up on me?"

"You *have* seen him."

The psychic's face took on a look of terror. "Yes. I know the man. He has sat in that chair." She stared. "Tell me about the dream."

"I never see his face, just that hand. There's fire, a woman screaming. I've thought about going to the police. After reading about the fires. You can see the connection, can't you? A man with a badly burned hand, the newspaper articles. I've never believed in this kind of thing—psychic phenomena—but now . . . Maybe *you* could call the police."

Emily swallowed dryly. "I can't help you."

"But you *can*," Daphne emphasized. "You've met him; he's been here. You could call the police and tell them that."

"I think we're all done here. There's nothing I can do."

Daphne allowed a long silence to settle over them. Still maintaining eye contact, she said, "It's the car, isn't it?"

Her lips trembling, Emily gasped hoarsely, "What?"

"My car? You see, I remember that I had left mail in the front seat. That's how you knew I belonged to the Northwest Medical Society, which is why you were guessing doctor." The words hit Emily as small bombs. "You know I'm neat, because that's the way I keep my car. That's what gave you away. The comments about my fiancé—the ring, of course—and mention of the young girl threw me off for a moment. But Corky's notebook is in the back of the car, and her name is on it. Whoever you're working with told you the name, but you elected not to use it." Daphne stood from the chair.

"Sit down!"

Daphne took two quick steps toward the door behind Emily and pushed it open in time to see the kitchen screen door thump shut. Whoever had been there was gone. Fast, she thought. Spinning on her heels, she took a step toward Emily. "I make one phone call, and we bring you in on fraud charges. You're out of business."

"You're a *cop?*" It was a question, but also a realization.

They stood only inches apart, Daphne a full head taller. She asked, "Are you part of the arsons? Straight answer. Yes or no?"

"No," Emily gasped, eyes averted, head lowered in submission. Exactly where Daphne wanted her.

Emily glanced back into Daphne's eyes. "It was some kind of business deal. Drugs, maybe, not these arsons. A deal out at the airport. A decent amount of scratch involved—he was willing to pay the sixty for the chart and the reading. It was the date he was worried about, why he came to see me. People consult you for dates, you know, weddings mostly." Emily appeared nervous and scared. "I do charts. And I do have the power."

"The sixty bucks. Cash or check?"

"Honey, do I look like I'd take a check? Gimme a little credit."

Daphne's hope for a quick solution slipped away. Then a thought occurred to her. "The car. His car."

"A truck. Light blue. Old model. White camper shell."

"The dates?"

"October second the first time."

The Enwright fire had occurred September 10; Heifitz, October 4. "The second? You're sure?" He might have set the accelerant for a future fire, she thought.

"Positive. And then again last weekend," Emily answered.

Daphne's pounding heart occupied her chest painfully. The timing seemed off—too rushed—unless October 2 had accounted for Heifitz. What was the significance of the weekend just past?

Another victim to come? She said, "I need everything you have on the man with the burned hand."

"Why should I?"

"Two hundred dollars in your pocket, and I walk away."

"You—people like you—never just walk away. You'll be back."

"Will *he?*" Daphne asked. "The man with the hand? Be back?"

Emily nodded slowly. "Probably." And then she added caustically, "But, honey, that one's gonna cost big."

LIVING in Seattle had taught Ben about rain. On that day it began as a mist, light and delicate, but it evolved quickly into a pelting and unforgiving downpour. When Ben arrived at the purple house after running through pouring rain, running as if he could outrun the guilt for his crime, Emily had immediately seen the worry in his face, or perhaps she read his mind, he thought. She'd led him around back to the porch overlooking the garden. Rain splashed only inches from them, and the wind swirled.

She wrapped a warm arm around him. "So, young man, you have something to tell me."

How would she react if he told her what he had done? His eye stung, and he felt himself begin to shudder and then to cry.

"Ben? You mustn't let Jack do this to you, Ben."

He shook his head, the tears falling harder. "It's not that."

"Your mother," she whispered.

He shook his head again. His memory of his mother was only a face, a smell, something too long ago to remember. "If I lost my wallet in his truck, he'll know where to find me. My address is in the wallet." It just kind of tumbled out.

"Who, Ben? What truck?" He heard concern in her voice.

He looked up at her, his vision blurred by tears. She looked back with sympathy and love, and he knew he was about to tell her everything. He was about to offer her the money—the whole five hundred dollars—and ask if he could stay with her. The truth poured out.

Emily never stopped holding him. She listened to every word, nodding, her own eyes filled with tears, and the two spent over an hour there on the back porch, right through the rainsquall and into a patch of blue sky, welcoming the sun's penetrating warmth that flowed through it, like the intense love that Ben felt for this woman.

CHAPTER FIVE

WHEN his pager sounded, Lou Boldt cringed. At that very moment he had been wondering what to do about his suspicions about Liz, because if he was right, it started a series of unthinkable choices that questioned the survival of their family.

Liz was taking a bath. This was no big deal except that Liz, ever in a hurry, always took showers. But three times this week she had come home from work and immediately drawn herself a bath. And Boldt realized she had taken baths on the same days the week before: Monday, Tuesday, and Thursday. All three days she had come home an hour and a half late. His imagination raced. As a detective he was trained to see patterns. He regretted this ability, resented it. He was maintaining a thoughtful surveillance on his own wife, based on distrust and fear. He heard Sarah crying and felt on the verge himself.

He scooped up his infant daughter from the crib, nuzzled her, and inhaled the sweet milk fragrance of her skin. She reached out, her tiny fingers locking onto his hair.

"Knock, knock," he said, toeing open the bathroom door. Liz, stretched in the tub, looked so incredibly appealing he felt a pang of protective jealousy. She had betrayed his faith once before. Was it so impossible again? Many of the same elements were in place: Both of them working too hard, ignoring the other's needs. The two kids placed burdens on their attentions. Their marriage was all about the family now. It was different.

The mother beckoned with outstretched arms, and the child stopped crying and wiggled to be free. Boldt envied Liz this biological connection and for a moment felt himself a visitor in his own home. Liz sat up in the tub and, cradling the child, offered her breast. She smiled slightly and leaned back against the tub. Boldt studied his wife. He didn't want anyone else having this.

"Didn't I hear your pager?" she questioned.

Did she want him out of the house? He felt a flood of anger surge through him. He stood taller and drew his stomach a little tighter. Was he aging too quickly for her? "Yeah," he answered.

"You going to call it in?"

"Yeah." He was a slave to his work.

"You okay?" she asked, her brow knitted sharply.

"Fine," he lied.

Her eyes widened. She cradled the baby tighter to her. "Honey?"

"Maybe we should talk at some point," he said. He sounded defeated, and he knew she picked up on it.

"I'm all yours," she said.

I wonder, Lou Boldt thought. He nodded, though insincerely. She took the baths to clean herself, to keep him from knowing. He ached, wondering what drove such thoughts.

"Go to work, Lou. I'm not going to get mad about it. I'll wait up," she told him, acknowledging with more certainty than he wished that the page was going to take him from their home. It nearly always did. The pager was a giant stage hook, designed, it seemed, to steal him from his home life. He had come to hate the thing.

"You two are beautiful," he said. He felt his throat choke and turned toward the phone to prevent her from seeing his tears.

GREEN Lake, picturesque and charming, was several acres of black water surrounded by a running path. At eight p.m. the path still saw a great deal of use, men and women running or walking.

Boldt joined Daphne Matthews, and they started walking, holding to the right side of the path, allowing the joggers to pass. The lake was convenient to both their houses, and Daphne had recommended they meet there.

"Emily Richland uses a shill who checks the cars of her clients. Information about the cars is passed to her, and she can make some darn good educated guesses as to who is sitting in front of her."

"Am I supposed to be surprised?" he asked, his mind elsewhere.

"The guy with the burned hand came to her place looking to check a date: October second, two days before Heifitz. Lou, I think it's the arsonist." Before he could speak, she said, "His right hand— the last three fingers are fused in a kind of paddle. He's military. Air force, maybe. I think she's holding out on me. I think she has more."

Boldt's mind raced away from him, removing his concern about Liz's affair and focusing solely on the suspect. "His car?"

"A truck." She gave Boldt the description that Emily had given her. "She thinks this guy is involved in drugs, not arson. And maybe that's right. Maybe he's dealing lab chemicals. Maybe that's how he got the burned hand, but it's one hell of a lead."

"Maybe he's just a middleman." Boldt was thinking aloud. "Maybe he's selling some chemicals to our boy."

"I paid her two hundred. I think another two and we'll get more," Daphne said. "She thinks he'll return."

Boldt stopped walking. "Return?"

"He's already been there twice," Daphne said proudly.

"Military? Maybe Garman was military, maybe air force. Maybe they served together. Maybe that's the connection."

"A woman was involved," she said, reminding him of the connection between the two victims. "A divorced woman. Divorced single moms, Lou. That's what we're looking at. Count on it." They started walking again.

Boldt was a cop who based his investigations on the information a victim could reveal. Thoughts sparked in his head; he could barely contain them. "We can link the victims!" he said.

"Why do you think I paged you? Link? I don't know. But we've got some obvious common denominators."

"Divorced single mothers," Boldt repeated. "Age of the kids?"

"Didn't check."

"We need to." Searching for a way the two women might have been targeted by the killer, Boldt listed, "Group therapy—you know, coping-with-divorce classes, church groups. What else?"

"Book clubs," she suggested.

"Cooking classes, gyms."

"Plumbers, electricians—"

"Ladders!" he barked, stopping again. "We're close! Plumbers, electricians . . ."

"Roofers, masons, chimney sweeps . . ."

"A house painter!" he exclaimed. "We found cotton fibers at the base of the ladder. What do you want to bet they come up positive for petroleum products?"

"Slow down," she said.

"Both of them divorced," Boldt repeated. He grabbed Daphne by the shoulders, overwhelmed with a feeling of accomplishment. "You're a genius!"

NEXT morning Boldt paid a visit to the offices of the Bureau of Alcohol, Tobacco, and Firearms in the Federal Building. An ATF lab chemist, Howard Casterstein, had requested a videoconference, and Boldt brought along the police lab's Bernie Lofgrin, detectives LaMoia and Gaynes, as well as arson investigators Bahan and Fidler.

In the videoconference room Boldt and the others took seats. At ten o'clock sharp the projection television screen sparkled, and the face of Howard Casterstein appeared.

Boldt introduced the face on the wall to his squad, at which point Casterstein began the discussion. "We've been looking at your reports of the fire debris, hoping to support a cause and origin. The first item of significance is the purple flame associated with these fires. That, along with the spalling and bluish color of the concrete, suggests a flammable liquid accelerant. The lack of hydrocarbons in your testing has been confirmed here in Sacramento. Highly unusual for a residential structural arson."

At this point Bernie Lofgrin asked, "Metals?"

Casterstein answered, "Mr. Lofgrin is asking about residual metals found on-site, because magnesium and a number of other metals are often associated with high-temperature fires. Unfortunately, we have found no trace of such metals in our samples." To Lofgrin he said, "We used the EDAX—X-ray fluorescence analysis—along with chemical spot tests, and are showing some inorganics, though the actual accelerant initially proved elusive."

"Initially?" Boldt asked, sensing a breakthrough that Casterstein wasn't revealing. He might have complained about Casterstein's college professor approach, but he had come to accept that labbies gave elaborate explanations, but only once. For this reason Boldt took meticulous notes.

"We have some interesting clues in these burns," Casterstein suggested. "An accelerant, somehow ignited, most likely by timer, or radio-controlled from a distance. What I find of particular interest is this." Casterstein put on a pair of latex gloves. He held up a black blob, and the camera zoomed in on it. "Found by you, Mr. Bahan, according to our documentation."

Those at the conference table looked over at Neil Bahan. His thin brown hair and big build reminded Boldt of the kids in school who never joined in, always standing on the edges and watching. Boldt was reminded of Daphne's warning that a fire inspector is dangerously close in mind-set to an arsonist—two sides of the same fence. He paid particular attention to both Bahan and Fidler for this reason. If they were investigating fires they themselves had set, Boldt might never find the truth.

Bahan said, "I found it up the street from the Heifitz place. It was still warm to the touch."

"We think it significant," Casterstein said, spinning it in his fingers. It was a hard piece of plastic the size of a golf ball. "We've x-rayed it, and there is a piece of a wire melted into it."

"The detonation device," Bernie Lofgrin said quickly.

"Or part thereof," Casterstein agreed. "Further tests are needed, of course. Our principal concern is the identification of the accelerant. If we can give you the accelerant and you can trace its components to their sources, you may be able to end-run this guy."

Bobbie Gaynes said, "I'm still confused as to why both women were unable to get out of their houses in time. These fires were late afternoon, early evening. It's not as if they were asleep."

All eyes turned to Casterstein. "We can't answer that at this time. It might be explained by accelerant in every room," he suggested. "If the device was of multiple origin with simultaneous detonation . . ."

"He rigged the whole place to blow at the same time," LaMoia commented. He glanced at the others, then at the screen. "What is it you aren't telling us? I'm feeling a gaping hole here, and the wind blowing through it stinks kinda bad."

Casterstein allowed a slight smile. "I appreciate your honesty, Detective. I asked Sergeant Boldt here because I wanted to show him this." Casterstein nodded to someone off-camera. The screen went blue. His voice said, "Stand by. What you're about to see is a test conducted by the Fort Worth Fire Department."

The image was of a large deserted supermarket in a sea of empty blacktop. Surrounding the structure were twenty or more fire vehicles, parked at a distance. Crews stood by with hoses. A digital clock counted down in the lower right-hand corner.

Casterstein said, "Pay particular attention to the speed of the burn and the color."

The clock counted down to zero, at which point a bright purple flash rose into the sky like the flame from a wick. The roof of the building melted away. Everything seemed to burn at once. Water shot from ladder trucks exploded into flames as it arrived at the burning core. Boldt had never seen a fire so ferocious.

The video stopped, and Casterstein's image reappeared. "This burn went off at temperatures that caused water to separate into its elements, hydrogen and oxygen, literally exploding the attempts to suppress it. The fire was an attempt to discover the accelerant used in a series of arsons that swept the country from '89 to '94."

Boldt could picture a person inside such a structure. He shuddered from head to toe. All of a sudden he understood the inability of Enwright and Heifitz to flee their homes. "What the hell did we just look at?" Boldt inquired, uncharacteristically brash.

Casterstein pursed his lips and leaned into the camera. "Rocket fuel," he said. "The accelerant in that test was liquid rocket fuel."

THE grounds of Owen Adler's estate overlooking Puget Sound intimidated Boldt. Adler's kind of wealth was measured by the size of his private jet. It was a Gulfstream 3. He was on the Seattle A-list. Adler's marriage to Daphne Matthews had been postponed twice. No invitations had ever been sent. Daphne claimed it was because, in putting his food empire back together, Adler had encountered repeated scheduling problems. But Boldt noticed Daphne was back to volunteering at a shelter for runaway teens, a commitment she had dropped during the infatuation days with Adler. For his part, Adler had twice been photographed in the company of other women for the society pages. Boldt had not asked any questions. Any man who could lift a multimillion-dollar company out of ashes the way Adler had deserved some kind of medal. There was no doubting the man's power to overcome financial obstacles. On the other hand, Boldt thought, Daphne Matthews might be a kind of challenge he had never faced.

Using the front door's intercom, Daphne asked Boldt to go around the house and wait out on the patio. The French doors opened and she ducked through chintz drapes wearing a pink robe and a towel wrapped around her head. "Sorry," she said. "I wanted a shower. I was just getting out—"

"Then it's me who's sorry for interrupting."

"Corky's asleep," she said, referring to Adler's teenage daughter. "I didn't want to wake her."

"Are you living here now?" Boldt asked.

"Owen's in South America this week. Another deal. I didn't want Corky to be with a nanny. Not as long as I'm around."

She sat down and crossed her legs. A plane flew overhead, its wing lights flashing.

"Rocket fuel."

Her head snapped up. "Emily Richland mentioned the air force." Her eyes were wide.

Boldt said, "There's more. Bernie says the ladder impressions put his—or her—weight at one forty tops. That's light."

"A juvenile?" she asked. "The second poem is Plato. Big stuff for a juvenile."

"Messed-up kid, ugly divorce. It's possible, I suppose." He added, "You're the judge of that."

"I'm thinking mid to late twenties, college educated. He could be thin, even gaunt. I could buy that." She leaned forward. "I've talked with other forensic psychiatrists. Our guy could be twenty-five to thirty, sexually inadequate. He hates his mother, girlfriend, whatever. Maybe all of the above. He is judge and executioner. He's intelligent, quiet, and lives alone. If we put this information from the ladder into the mix, then he's slight of build."

"Fidler gave me a report on Garman. Steven Garman, the Marshal Five, the fire inspector—"

"I know who Garman is," she reminded him. "The one receiving the threats is always the first one to look at."

He met and held her eyes. "I don't know that I'm up to this," he confessed. "Another woman is going to burn."

"Not necessarily."

"Sure she is. And I'm at the helm, and I don't want the wheel."

"Understandable. But you've got it."

"Garman lives alone," Boldt went on. "Went through an ugly marriage. He's been with the Seattle Fire Department for twelve years. Highly regarded but keeps to himself. At constant war with his superiors. He's a stickler for details. Meticulous. Demanding. No one can remember his having even dated a woman."

The color of Daphne's eyes changed, and her brow tightened.

"I wouldn't mind if you could find a way to chat him up," Boldt informed her. "Open him up."

"I'll figure a way to get to see Garman so he won't think anything of it," Daphne promised. "Now go home and try for some sleep."

TO CONFRONT A POSSIBLE murderer face to face was the moment Daphne Matthews lived for.

She walked a little lighter, stood a little taller, as she hurried down the street toward SFD's Battalion 4 and its Marshal Five, Steven Garman. As Daphne climbed the stone staircase to the firehouse's second floor, she focused on preparing herself. She intended to establish a rapport with Garman, whatever this required of her: professional psychologist, sexual flirt, attentive listener. Such interviews required her to be an actress, and she loved the challenge.

Daphne knocked lightly on Garman's door and entered.

Garman was ensconced in a large leather chair in an immaculately kept office. He was a big, handsome man with soft brown eyes and a bushy mustache, younger than she had expected. There was a picture of Einstein on the wall and another of Picasso. What were his tastes in poetry? she wondered. There was a color shot of the space shuttle *Challenger* at the moment of its explosion, entrails of white fumes, debris frozen forever in a sky of blue. Garman caught Daphne staring.

"I worked on that," he explained. "The debris reconstruction."

"You were air force?"

"Does it show?" He introduced himself with a handshake.

Maybe it did, she thought as she looked more closely. Maybe it helped explain the hard handshake and the riveting grip of those eyes. At the forefront of her thoughts was Boldt's information that the accelerant might be rocket fuel. Steven Garman, ex–air force, had to be considered carefully.

She said, "Sergeant Boldt wanted to thank you for not opening the most recent note."

"Listen, I wish I could tell you why he's sending this stuff to me. I really don't want any part of it." He motioned Daphne into a chair. "Are you on Boldt's squad?"

"I'm part of the task force." She felt compelled to skirt the truth. Garman might freeze up if he knew she was a psychologist.

"Can I ask you a couple of personal questions?" she said.

"Shoot."

"Did you know either Dorothy Enwright or Melissa Heifitz?"

"Certainly not," he said defensively, his voice strained. "I never knew either of them, never had so much as heard their names."

"You've worked over two hundred arson investigations," she said without consulting any notes. She wanted him to know she had researched his record, wanted to judge any reaction.

"Suspicious fires," he corrected. "Some we call arsons. Some not."

"Twenty-two arrests, nine convictions," she added.

"Listen, I don't keep notches on my gun or anything. It's a job. You quote those numbers, and it depresses me. We only clear fifteen percent of our cases. You guys, it's what? Seventy or eighty? Maybe half my stuff is vehicles. Most of the rest, abandoned structures. Every now and then, revenge or a vanity fire.

"First thing I did," he continued, "when I connected the Enwright fire to that note, was go back through my files. I can't place a single one of those arrests in something like this. A couple are locked up; a couple more moved on. And every one of them was an obvious pour. Gasoline. I'll be damned if I can make any one of my convictions stick for this thing."

"But why are you receiving these notes?" she asked. Garman's neck went florid, and his soft eyes went cold; he nervously rolled a pen between his fingers. It was not what she expected. She registered that look, not wanting to forget it.

"Marshal Five, I suppose. There are only seven of us in this city. Could have mailed it to any one of us. I got lucky, I guess."

"Enemies?" she asked. "Anything in your past that might—"

"No," he interrupted. The pen began to spin again.

"How about your air force serv—"

"Listen!" he interrupted again. "What is it with all the questions about *me*? It's this torch we're after, okay?"

"He's chosen you for some reason, Mr. Garman. There's an explanation, no matter how obscure." Again a red flush crept into Garman's neck, and Daphne knew she had a live one. Like every other living human being, the man had secrets. "I'm asking myself if it doesn't go back to your air force days."

Garman swallowed heavily. His eyes were soft again but scared. "Nothing I can think of," he said. His voice cracked and belied his words. "It isn't relevant. It was nine, ten years ago."

"You were married then," she said, tugging the hook a little.

Garman's eyes went to glass. If the pen had been a pencil, it might have snapped between his powerful fingers. He glanced away, then back at her. There was anger within him. Rage. "Exactly what is the purpose of this meeting?" he inquired tightly.

Instinctively she switched off the role of interrogator. She had more than enough to present to Boldt. "To get to know each other, that's all. Sorry if it came off as the third degree. Product of the profession, I'm afraid." She had saved one last gem. As she rose for the door, she told him, "The ATF lab believes the accelerant was some kind of rocket fuel."

For a split second Steven Garman appeared chiseled in stone. Daphne wished she had a camera. She knew that look. She had seen it a dozen times. She had touched his most sensitive nerve.

She looked over at the photograph of the *Challenger* explosion. Rocket fuel, she thought. He must be something of an expert.

CHAPTER SIX

LOOKING good, Detective," a female voice cooed.

Boldt turned to see the target of the comment.

John LaMoia was style: creased jeans, a crisp polo shirt, ostrich cowboy boots. He had a thin face, large brown eyes, and a prominent nose. Exactly what women saw in LaMoia was a mystery to his senior in rank, but they flocked to him.

LaMoia began as he so often did, without any greeting. He rolled a chair into Boldt's cubicle and straddled it backward. "Needless to say, you have no idea where any of this came from." LaMoia had enviable connections to the private sector: credit unions, insurance companies, banks. Shoswitz said it had to do with his military service, though Boldt thought it was nothing more than the man's undeniable charm and his incredible ability to network. LaMoia knew people, how they thought. He knew the streets. He had the knack.

LaMoia placed a folder in front of Boldt. "Enwright and Heifitz—their financials: credit cards, banking. Nothing there to connect one to the other. Nothing I could see."

Boldt said, "Nothing at all? It doesn't have to jump out at you. A department store they both shopped? A gas station?"

"The wheels."

"What?" Boldt asked.

"Has anyone worked the wheels? The houses were torched, right? Toast. So what was left behind?"

"Their cars." Boldt had not given the victims' cars a thought. "Check them out," he said.

"And here I thought you'd be more interested in the ladders."

Caught by surprise, Boldt asked, "The ladders?"

LaMoia grinned, full of arrogance. "Werner ladders are sold through a single distributor here. The model with this particular tread pattern had a manufacturing problem with the shoes—the little things bolted to the bottom—which meant that this model only stayed in stores for two weeks. The distributor can account for his retail customers: hardware stores, building supply, a couple rental shops. Seventeen in western Washington, but only *four* in King County. It's a high-end ladder, meaning that when some Joe buys one, he pays by check or credit card. Not one of these ladders went out the door for cash. We've gotten that far already."

"You've talked to the retailers?" Boldt felt a surge of optimism.

"You bet," LaMoia continued. "We've asked for sales records. By tomorrow, day after, we'll have every ladder accounted for. We'll have a checking account or credit card number we can trace back to the buyer."

It was good work, and Boldt told him so. They needed a decent break; perhaps the ladder was one of them.

"Mind you," LaMoia interjected, "the ladder was probably ripped off. But from what neighborhood? When? We might get something out of it yet, Sarge. I'm telling you, I can smell it."

"Good work," Boldt repeated. "And get someone to look at the cars. Maybe they shopped the same convenience store, ate a burger at the same place. Maybe that's how the guy spotted them. Maybe there's a wrapper on the floor, a receipt or something."

At that moment Daphne burst through the door, her face flushed. She marched over to Boldt and LaMoia and said, "Steven Garman is hiding something. He knows a lot more than he's letting on."

BEN had been late getting home. He'd locked the door from the inside before he ever smelled the guy. He wasn't exactly thinking about it, but his mind was registering that a house, a home, is a place of familiar sounds and familiar smells.

That smell did not belong: sharp, salty. Not at all the sour smell of booze he had come to live with, not the smell of a girl. It was . . . the smell inside the back of the camper.

At that moment of realization a hand clutched at his shoulder, and Ben screamed and took off for the stairs. The low, angry voice said something behind him, but Ben missed it. His reaction was born of instinct: make it to his room, lock the door, get out the window, run like the devil for Emily's.

He glanced over his shoulder. Nick, the driver of the pickup truck, was faster than Ben's stepfather when he was sober. "My money, you little . . ." A flood of fear ran like a hot liquid over Ben. He slipped on the stairs. Nick grunted, precariously close behind.

With his one good hand the man grabbed Ben's left ankle, tripping him. Ben's chin banged on the stairs as he was dragged downward, and the metallic taste of blood filled his mouth. Ben reared back with his right leg and drove the sole of his sneaker into the center of his attacker's forehead. The man let go.

Ben recaptured the stairs and once again began his ascent. As he cleared the top of the stairs, he heard the man right behind him. Ben didn't look back. He didn't scream. He hurried.

The entire house shook as the back door slammed shut. "Kid?" the familiar drunken voice called out.

Ben couldn't remember a time when that voice had sounded so good. The footsteps behind him paused. "Help!" Ben shouted.

"Who the hell are you?" Jack had reached the bottom of the stairs. "Get out of my house!"

"Your kid took my money!" the intruder shouted.

He was standing on the stairs, looking down at Ben's stepfather. A gun was tucked into the small of his back.

"Dad!" Ben shouted, wondering where that word had come from. Overcome by an unexpected protective instinct, he began to slide feetfirst down the stairs, knocking Nick off his feet and propelling him toward Jack, who gazed drunkenly at the spectacle.

A fight erupted between the two men, but it was nothing like television. They rolled around on the floor in a tangle of limbs. Ben clawed for purchase as he continued to slide down the stairs, grabbing for the handrail. Nick was pummeling his stepfather. "I . . . want . . . my . . . money!" he said with each hard hit.

Nick glanced hotly over his shoulder and met the boy's eyes. Ben felt his stomach go to jelly. Nick sprang like a cat, blocking a chance at the front door. Ben threw a lamp at him and reached for the door of the downstairs closet, the only escape available to him. He grabbed the doorknob and turned.

Nick lunged for him. Ben kicked out, slipped into the darkness, yanked the door shut, and held the doorknob tight. It rotated despite Ben's efforts. The door opened a crack. That burned hand, with its shiny pink skin, slipped through.

At the same moment there was a huge crash. The flipper was smashed in the door, and Nick let out a ferocious cry and withdrew it. Ben reeled backward onto the trapdoor that led to the basement crawl space.

How many times had his stepfather cautioned him not to go down there? He had put the fear of God into him, which had done nothing to convince Ben to stay out. Even nailing the trapdoor shut had not prevented Ben from prying it open, but his subsequent expedition, his encounter with thick spiderwebs and a terrible smell, had finished off his curiosity. That had been over a year ago, and yet he still remembered that disgusting smell.

The enormous crash was followed by total silence. Someone's dead, Ben thought. He pulled hard on the trapdoor, shaking it left and right to wiggle free the loosened nails. It opened. He slipped down inside, the door closing above him.

The crawl space was perhaps three feet high. He had to crouch in order to move. At the far end, dusty gray light seeped through. It smelled damp and foul. Ben crab-walked toward the darkest corner, immediately caught in a sticky tangle of spiderweb.

He froze as he heard slow footsteps overhead. The next sound was the closet door coming open. "Kid," the muffled voice cautioned, "you're making me real mad." The trapdoor squeaked as the man stepped on it. Nick was in the closet!

Ben dragged himself deeper into the darkness, convinced that his stepfather was dead and his own death was imminent. Light flashed behind him as the trapdoor came open. "Don't mess with me, kid."

Slowly, carefully, Ben laid himself down on the dusty gravel. He would hide. It was all that was left.

The ground was disturbed there, humped, the gravel mixed with dried mud. He tried to make himself as thin, as low as possible. The man was coming down after him. He peered toward the open hatch and the flood of light.

Ben's one good eye shifted focus, the resulting perspective out of proportion. It was not gravel or mud that he saw. Nor was it the pair of legs groping for where to land. All this remained within his field of vision, yet the entire focal point of his attention was an arc of dull yellow metal in front of his face. A gold ring.

At once he knew. His mother's wedding ring. He knew this absolutely. His mother's grave.

Impelled by anger, rage, and grief, Ben sprang to his feet, crouched low, and flew through the crawl space, fingers clutching the ring. He charged wildly, knocking Nick over. He then leaped through the trapdoor access and hurried out of the closet.

His stepfather was just coming to, dazed and badly beaten. Ben stopped abruptly and stared down at him. Disappointment drained him: The man was *alive*. Ben held up the ring for him to see. He reared back and kicked with all the force he possessed. Jack's head snapped back sharply and thudded onto the floor.

Ben was out the door at a full sprint. The call to 911 would come, but not until he reached a pay phone several blocks later. "I want to report a murder," the terrified voice was recorded as saying. "He killed my mother! She's under the house!"

For the second time that same youthful voice was recorded by the Seattle Communications Center. The computer-aided dispatch system assigned the call to a patrol car near Seattle University. At the address given by the boy, the driver of that car would find an unconscious man on the living-room floor, the victim of an assault. He would hold this man for questioning and pursue evidence of a possible body in the crawl space.

Far away, a small boy sped through the night.

SERGEANT Lou Boldt was one of many who saw the paperwork on the decomposed female corpse discovered in a crawl space. Boldt felt convinced all they needed was a few hours with the suspect to win a confession. It was the kind of case that attracted Boldt, though due to the arsons, all he could do was manage it from a distance. Based on neighbors' statements, city services was looking for the suspect's young stepson, more than likely the source of the 911 call that had led to the corpse.

Boldt left the office and headed to the police lab, where he met up with Bernie Lofgrin. Lofgrin had run an analysis of the melted green plastic pieces sent by mail. The results offered progress. The torch was sending melted Monopoly houses as part of his threats. The small green plastic cube in the shape of a building. Boldt tried to reach Daphne, hoping to connect some kind of psychological significance to the find, but she didn't answer.

DAPHNE KNOCKED ON THE door of the purple house and then hurried off the front porch to get a look down the driveway.

He was small and he was fast. A boy, ten or twelve years old. He dodged around the corner of the house, froze as he saw Daphne, and then took off like a shot.

The front door opened, and Emily Richland stood there in a black pants dress and an embroidered yellow robe.

"Is he your son?" Daphne asked.

"No. Leave him out of this," Emily protested.

Daphne approached the woman, who stepped back inside. "I haven't heard from you," Daphne told her.

"I haven't heard from *him*."

"How do I know that?" Daphne asked.

"I would call you."

"Would you? I don't think so." Daphne forced her way inside. "Who's the boy?" she asked. "And don't play with me, or you and the boy will end up downtown."

"You're pathetic, you know that? He hasn't been back. I would've called."

"You con people for a living. How am I supposed to trust you? The boy is part of it." The boy was clearly the wild card, the way to get at the woman. "Is he a runaway?"

Emily looked hateful. "You leave him out of this."

"City services would be interested in talking to the boy."

"Don't do this."

"You're going to have to help me." She removed a photograph of Steven Garman from her pocket and handed it to the psychic. "Is that the man?" she asked.

Emily shook her head. "Absolutely not."

"You're sure? You would swear to that in a court of law?" Daphne studied the woman's face. What she saw there was discouraging. The psychic had never seen the man before. Daphne felt crushed. She had convinced herself that it was Garman.

"It's not him. Not even close."

Daphne produced a hundred-dollar bill. "I need an *exact*

description. You withheld some details last time, didn't you?" Emily regarded the money carefully but seemed reluctant to accept it. Daphne said, "Or maybe the boy can fill in some of the blanks."

Emily bristled, took the money, and began a thoughtful and exacting description of her client. An image formed in Daphne's mind—the close-cut hair, the strong build, the rodeo background. The more she heard, the less she liked it. The man did not make the most likely suspect for a person quoting Plato. *Two* suspects? she wondered. A conspiracy?

ANOTHER poem. Garman had delivered it downtown. Boldt drove home to tell Liz that it was going to be a long night. The claw-foot tub was the first place he checked, placing his hands against the side wall, searching for lingering warmth. Stone-cold. He felt an immediate pang of regret. Trust had been the cornerstone of their marriage, and here he was, creeping around and feeling bathtubs.

He found her in the study, and together they put the kids to bed. Then Boldt sat down to a reheated dinner at a kitchen table cluttered with mail—bills mostly.

"You know," she said, absentmindedly opening mail, "I was thinking that I might leave Miles with you and spend this weekend up at the cabin."

The announcement stunned him. "By yourself?" he blurted out.

"No, with my lover," she snapped. Was she using sarcasm to hide the truth? "I'm whipped, Lou. I could use a weekend by myself. I'll take Sarah, of course. A good book." She added, "Not away from you, just this." She motioned around the room. He knew she meant him. And she meant Miles, who at three and a half was a handful.

"It's not the best time," he answered honestly. He had worked three seven-day weeks in a row. "This case—"

"Oh, come on," she complained. "Marina can help you." Marina looked after the kids. "You can't work *every* weekend."

Boldt went over to the sink to pour himself a glass of water and noticed immediately that the window was remarkably cleaner. He noticed because cleaning the windows was his responsibility. He had let this duty slip, and it seemed inconceivable that Liz had washed them. That meant she had paid to have them washed, which in turn helped explain her mood. If he slacked off on his jobs around the house, she hired them done, and it annoyed her to no end. He asked, "Is it the windows? Is that it? Listen, I meant to."

"No, it's not the windows. It was a mistake. The point is—"

"Getting the windows washed was a mistake? I don't think so. They look great to me." He hoped he might be able to press this toward humor and deflect her anger.

She told him, "A mistake. The wrong house. I didn't hire a window washer. The guy was off by one street. He made a mistake."

Boldt smelled a scam. "Did he try and charge you for—"

"No. We cleared it up. He packed up his ladder and took off. He was perfectly nice about it. In fact, he did a good job."

"Better than that other guy you've got." He meant himself.

She came out of the chair then and, suppressing a slight grin, approached her husband and threw her arms around his neck. "Why is it I can't stay mad at you?"

He felt better than he had in ages. He didn't want to let go. He clasped his arms around her waist and squeezed, and he could feel her breath beneath his ear. "I miss you," he said.

"I *need* this weekend, Lou. I wouldn't ask if I didn't. Please."

He felt himself nod, although it was born of great trepidation. He knew this woman well enough to understand that a change was coming—a decision. He leaned back and looked at her. She looked tired. Troubled. A pit of concern burned inside him.

"I'll take Miles," he conceded.

She kissed him on the lips. "We'll talk," she said. "It's going to be okay." He forced a smile. They released their hug.

Boldt was headed to the refrigerator when he heard Miles calling from the nearby room. "Da-a-ddy." It was a cry of longing, not alarm, and it caused a warm stirring in Boldt's heart. He stopped at the kitchen doorway and turned toward his wife, the first nibble of concern beginning inside his chest. "How old?" he asked.

Liz filled the teakettle with water and headed for the stove. "What are you talking about?"

"How old?" he repeated more strongly. "The window washer." By then his body had seized on the idea. He felt a flood of heat like a sudden fever. "A *ladder?*" he barked at his wife.

Her hand trembling, she placed the teakettle on the stovetop. "Mid-twenties. Early thirties? Thin."

"His face?"

"He was up the ladder. I don't know. I was over by the garage. He wore a sweatshirt up over his head. We said about five words. I went inside, and he was gone. Lou?" She reached down to turn the knob on the front of the gas stove. That knob was suddenly all that Boldt could see—it loomed huge in front of him, a trigger.

"Don't touch it!" Boldt shouted loudly.

Liz jumped back. Terror filled her face. Miles cried out, the fright contagious. "Daddy!"

"Don't touch anything!" he cautioned. "Don't *move.*" His mind racing, Boldt hurried outside. A window washer. A ladder.

It was dark out, so he headed to his car and retrieved his police-issue flashlight. He went around the side of the house, the glaring white light fanning out across the grass and throwing moving shadows. In all his years of service no physical threat or trouble had found its way across the threshold of his home. There had been phone calls, but these had been quickly handled. Never this close.

He inspected the grass alongside the house. He could picture a stopwatch running inside his head. He imagined flames sucking the life out of everything within.

The flashlight illuminated two parallel rectangles pressed down into the grass. Recognizing the telltale chevron pattern, he cursed and ran toward the back of the house, Liz staring coldly at him through the freshly cleaned kitchen window.

"Get the kids!" Boldt ordered frantically once inside. He hurried toward their bedroom, where Sarah was in her crib. "You get Miles," he shouted as a panicked Liz sprinted past him.

Sarah, startled by her father's voice, began to cry. Liz stopped at the doorway to their room, held by the sound. Boldt turned around in time to see Liz reaching for the light switch.

"No!" he hollered. "Touch *nothing*. Watch for wires."

"A bomb?" she gasped, suddenly catching on.

"Get Miles, Liz. We'll go out the back door, not the front. We've both used the back door, so it's okay. Just hurry."

Boldt snagged his daughter, drawing her into his arms and pressing her sweetly perfumed baby skin close to him. He met Liz at the door into the kitchen, each bearing a child. Liz was panting from fear. "Let's get out," she said hoarsely.

They cut straight across the kitchen, out the door, down the steps. "No," he called out as Liz headed for her car. He stepped closer to her. "We're out for a walk. Leisurely. Easy does it. Okay?"

Tears ran down her cheeks. She nodded, glancing around.

They walked to a corner convenience store. Boldt dialed the pay phone mounted outside, with Liz and Miles at his side and Sarah in his arms. His wife stayed close, her elbow pressed against him. That simple touch was enough to tighten his throat.

Boldt called Lieutenant Shoswitz at home. He explained his suspicions, requesting the bomb squad, a backup fire truck, and evidence technicians. He suggested the adjacent homes be evacuated, but Shoswitz refused this request, wanting more proof before attracting "that kind of attention."

The comment reminded Boldt of a conversation with Daphne that the majority of convicted arsonists admitted to watching the burn. Witnessing the burn was itself a major motivation for committing the crime. Boldt decided to ask a friend to come pick them up at the convenience store. A plan was forming in his head. He was a cop again, the father's panic subsiding.

The ladder had been in their side yard that same afternoon. If the house had been rigged, the arsonist could be watching the house at that very moment. Depending on what vantage point he took, he might or might not have seen the family leave. It seemed possible he was still in the neighborhood. Boldt suggested this to Shoswitz. Listening in, Liz went pale.

It was agreed that the various squads—lab, fire, bomb—would be placed on call but would not arrive at the residence until a police net had been put in place around the area. The net would be tightened in hopes of squeezing the arsonist into its center.

Twenty minutes later Liz and the kids were headed to a neighbor's house for the night. Boldt and Liz kissed through the open window of the neighbor's Explorer, a loving kiss that meant the world to him. As the red taillights receded, Boldt knew in his heart that if there had been an affair, it was over now. His family was whole again, reunited by this incident.

By nine fifteen p.m. unmarked police cars had taken up positions along the corners and side points of an area roughly a half-mile square, with Boldt's house at its center. A black van belonging to the Emergency Response Team deposited nine highly trained field operatives onto the southwest corner of the Woodland Park Zoo, which was believed to be the suspect's most likely route of escape. Each of the ERT officers was armed and wore a handsfree radio headset and night-vision equipment.

Boldt climbed into the back of a maroon van marked TWO HOUR MARTINIZING. The van was a field communications command center. It was parked on a hill, a block and a half from Boldt's house. Shoswitz occupied an office chair bolted to the floor, as did the communications dispatcher and a field operations officer.

Boldt checked his watch. Even secured radio frequencies could be monitored by the more creative members of the press assigned to the police beat. He estimated the operation had about fifteen minutes in the clear. Boldt made specific note of the time: nine twenty-three.

"All set?" the field operations officer asked Shoswitz.

Phil glanced over at Boldt through the dim red light of the van's interior. The sergeant nodded.

The dispatcher said, "Attention, all units."

Boldt closed his eyes and, listening to the continuous stream of radio traffic, envisioned the events unfolding in the dark outside.

As residents in the neighborhood watched TVs, ERT and uniformed police stole through their lawns, down the alleys behind their homes, and around their garages, with almost no one the wiser. One child of nine announced from his bedroom that outside his window he had just seen a Ninja in the backyard. The father hollered up the stairs for the kid to go to sleep.

A human net constricted toward its center: Lou Boldt's home.

ERT officer Cole Robbie was one of the voices Boldt heard speaking across the nearly constant radio traffic. He was a tall man, six feet one, and on that night he wore all black. Sneaking through people's backyards, aware that many in these neighborhoods armed themselves, aware that his job was to apprehend some unknown assailant, quite possibly a murderer, his heartbeat was clocking a hundred and ten.

He crept over a low fence and into an alley. In his ear the radio traffic became a din, and though he listened for words that might have relevance to his own situation, mostly he tuned it out.

His wrist vibrated silently under his watch face. He stepped out of shadow and looked once left, then right. He saw his fellow squad members, one on each side, twenty to thirty yards away. There was no attempt made at hand signals. Conserve movement.

In four more minutes his wrist would vibrate again, and he would wait for visual contact with his team members. Robbie stepped quietly forward. Just ahead lay the section of park believed to be this perp's most likely escape route. It was pitch-dark beneath those trees. Visual contact was out of the question once they were inside there. His heart rate climbed. He loved this stuff.

BOLDT craned forward in the odd red light to see what the field operations officer, Tito Lee, was attempting to show him.

Pointing to a map, Lee said, "We got ERT in a line right through here. They should be in position within five, maybe ten minutes. At that point we got a human wall between Phinney Way and the zoo. Perimeter patrol cars are in place."

"Who was that woman I just heard?" Boldt asked.

"We got an undercover officer working the streets in an animal control vehicle up to the west side. She's driving around real slow, like she's after something, which of course she is." He grinned. "It gives us an operative on the specific street; she's headed for your place. She'll get out of the vehicle and go door to door asking about a Doberman reported wandering loose."

"She's alone?" Boldt asked apprehensively.

"Who's alone?" Shoswitz interjected, suddenly interested.

Lee answered. "Branslonovich. She's undercover as a dogcatcher."

"No one goes unpartnered on an operation like this." Shoswitz was suddenly concerned. "I want her out of there. Now."

But Lee could not raise her on the radio. Clearly she was not in her vehicle.

The operations officer asked the radio dispatcher, "Can we raise her in the field?"

The dispatcher looked distressed. "She's carrying a unicom, but she's not authorized," he explained.

Boldt understood that she was not in possession of a walkie-talkie capable of transmitting on secured frequencies. This technical restriction isolated her.

Boldt rarely felt prescient about a situation, but Branslonovich was in danger. He was certain of it. Boldt slipped out of the van to go after her himself.

COLE Robbie found the darkness of the trees comforting. A moment earlier he had been ordered to adopt his night-vision goggles, which meant the world was now a green-and-black place, with few shades of gray. Tree trunks rose like black cornstalks from the forest floor. Three dimensions were reduced to two. Inside these goggles motion blurred; fast motion sometimes vanished completely.

A hand signal from his right. Robbie caught it, returned it, and then passed it along to the officer twenty-five yards to his left. He noticed that the line was stretching thin. Pretty soon they would be too far apart for hand signals. It was just such mistakes that hurt operations. Just the kind of thing that got someone killed.

Up ahead to the north the park fed into a hillside neighborhood falling toward Green Lake. Occasionally Robbie glimpsed light from houses, which momentarily blinded the night-vision goggles, burning a bright white hole in the dense green and black. Robbie shifted the goggles to his forehead and avoided their use. Previous experience with "golf balls"—the ERT name for the blinding flashes and burnouts in the light-sensitive goggles—had educated him to avoid the goggles in the presence of *any* artificial light. He would need them every four minutes for hand signals, but in the meantime he preferred the uniformity of the darkness.

A slight glint of yellow light high up in a distant tree caught his attention and provoked him to stop. An airplane light? A person? He hadn't seen exactly where . . . Another glint of light, thirty or forty feet up, perhaps fifty yards directly ahead.

He depressed a small button on the radio device clipped to his belt. "Operative Three." He announced himself at a whisper. "Eye contact with possible suspicious object. Five zero yards. Eleven o'clock. Elevation, four zero feet. Advise."

"All stop," came the ERT commander's voice through Robbie's earpiece. The line hissed static as the commander checked in with the command van. Robbie stood, eyes fixed on that elusive spot.

As it turned out, because of his disdain for the night-vision device, when the firestorm occurred, Cole Robbie was the sole ERT officer not wearing goggles and so not blinded, the only operative able to see a spinning body burning as clearly as if it were a Christmas tree afire. As he began to run toward the animated orange puppet that spun like an unpracticed dancer, he heard it screaming like a woman—worse, in a voice familiar to him. It was, in fact, a woman, a woman consumed by pain and fear. By fire. The closer he drew, the more convinced he was that it was the voice of Officer Connie Branslonovich.

BOLDT found the animal control truck parked well up the hill from his house, two blocks from Woodland Park and the anticipated escape route of the arsonist.

He glanced up and down the road, hoping for a glimpse of Branslonovich. He stopped and looked back at his own house. The arsonist would want a good view, and that seemed most clearly offered from up the hill, which explained the location of the parked animal control truck. Branslonovich had quickly discerned the importance of the elevation.

Boldt chugged up the hill, shoulders hunched. He had a bad feeling about this. Just across Greenwood the park seemed dark, inviting, full of places to hide. Branslonovich might have felt this same thing. Furthermore, an animal control officer had every excuse to roam a wooded area.

Boldt dodged traffic, cutting across Greenwood, suddenly more hurried. He entered the park at a run.

He heard her before he saw the sweep of her flashlight breaking through the stand of tree trunks. She was moving through the park, perhaps thirty yards ahead of him. She was on the arsonist like a bloodhound; Boldt could feel this.

"Hey! Are you the dogcatcher?" Boldt shouted, attempting to maintain her undercover status. "You looking for a Doberman?" She didn't seem to hear him, but before another breath escaped his lips, the ground immediately to her right erupted in a billowing column of purple flame. She had tripped a wire, perhaps, or stepped on a detonator.

The figure ahead of him ignited instantaneously, as did a nearby tree trunk. She spun once, crying—a searing, painful cry. As the bark on the tree trunk exploded, sap combusting like fuel, the concussion of the erupting flames lifted Boldt off his feet and deposited him on his back, ten feet behind where he had been standing. He felt blinded, immobilized, his ears filled with the haunting wail of the detective's final moment on earth.

In the distance, sirens.

Boldt managed to get his hand on his weapon. He aimed straight up toward where the stars should have been and let off three rounds. With any luck at all, someone would hear it and find him before the whole forest burned and he along with it.

COLE ROBBIE SAW HER SPIN IN a complete circle, an all-consuming plume of light. Robbie heard three live rounds and broke into a run, thinking, Someone else is out there.

At that same moment he caught a flicker of a shadow to the left of the inferno—a human form moving away from the fire. The image was there and then gone, the light of the fire so intense that one glance induced temporary blindness, like a camera's flash, and the resulting collage of shifting, slanting shadows turned the landscape into an eerie tangle of sharp black forms.

He moved to his left. He picked up sight of the human form once again, heading right at him. Robbie found the small button on his radio transmitter. "Operative Three," he said breathlessly. "Suspect sighted. Foot pursuit. Identify before weapons fire."

The suspect was closing fast. Robbie dropped to one knee and reached for his handgun, but the sudden appearance of flashlight beams in the darkness alerted him to the reality that he could not fire except in warning, since his teammates were now directly ahead. Robbie came to his feet and continued the chase. A fast runner, he initially gained on the suspect. Then all at once the suspect was gone. He had ducked behind a tree somewhere up ahead. Robbie instinctively dove to the forest floor, anticipating weapons fire. He tripped the radio transmitter and said quietly, "Operative Three. Kill the flashlights. Go to infrared, but do not fire. Copy?"

"Copy, Three," said the commander.

The ERT weapons were equipped with heat-responsive sighting devices that alerted the shooter to a warm-body fix. The infrared devices allowed for nighttime "blind" precision targeting. What Robbie intended, and what the commander ordered, was that the sighting devices be swept through the forest to locate a warm-blooded body in the hope of identifying the suspect. If Robbie saw any red pinpoints of light strike his person, he would alert the ERT to a "bad hit."

All senses alert, Robbie rose to his feet and began to creep ahead.

The suspect came from above, completely unexpectedly, falling out of the darkness and onto Robbie. A pair of hands found Robbie's head. One gripped his chin; the other pressed tightly against the back of his neck. Robbie lay on the ground facedown, still reeling from the impact. He knew this grip. The intention was to break his neck with a single spine-twisting snap. Robbie could defeat the move with a simple anticipation of which direction the suspect would choose. God help me, he thought, and forced his chin left, just as the suspect made an identical move with his hands.

The devastating crack the suspect heard, before abandoning the cop for paralyzed or dead, was not Robbie's neck but his jaw. Robbie would drink from a straw for the next eight weeks, but he would live; he would walk. And he would know for the rest of his days that his moment of decision was born of those words he voiced internally before the deed was done.

The suspect cut through the woods, heading back toward the fire, perhaps aware that heat-seeking devices were useless when aimed in the direction of such an inferno, perhaps only lucky to have made such a choice.

AFTER firing those three shots, Boldt rolled and came to his knees. To the sound of approaching sirens he struggled to his feet, tested out various limbs, and pronounced himself sound. He'd be badly bruised, but he wasn't going to any emergency room.

The fire crews contained what remained of the fire. Strangely, what had begun as a white-hot inferno had quickly petered out into smoldering underbrush. No detonator and no can or jar that might have contained the accelerant was found at the scene.

The bomb squad, the scientific identification unit, and the Marshal Five arson task force, including Steven Garman, gathered at the Boldt home at eleven forty-five p.m., thirty minutes after the fire trucks had departed Woodland Park. The bomb squad and their dogs searched doors, windows, switches, and flooring for triggers. Nothing indicating attempted arson was discovered.

At one a.m. Bernie Lofgrin's identification unit went to work, beginning with the lawn, and plaster casts were made of the ladder impressions. At the end of three hours of intense scrutiny Lofgrin pulled Boldt aside and pronounced his home clean, which after that invasion it was anything but. A more thorough examination was scheduled for daylight, and Boldt was ordered to sleep elsewhere, though nothing suspicious had been found.

Garman, who joined the huddle, said, "Your wife's arrival at the house probably put the guy off his mission."

Lofgrin said, typically technical, "That would explain the discovery of the impressions and the absence of any accelerant."

"It doesn't explain what happened in the woods," Boldt said.

Arson detective Neil Bahan said, "Ah, but it might. The arsonist may have been awaiting a chance at a return visit. To finish the job."

Boldt didn't like any of it.

Thirty minutes later the last of them was out the front door. Boldt locked up tight and called Liz at the neighbors' and woke them all. He spoke to his wife for nearly half an hour, explaining everything as best he could. He said, "I think the cabin is a good idea for you."

"You're scaring me."

"Sorry."

"You want to come over?" she asked. "Sleep with me?"

His wife asking him to sleep with her, to hold her, to comfort her. He wanted nothing more. He said so.

"But you're staying," she said.

"I couldn't sleep if I tried. I'll go downtown, try to sort some of this out," he told her.

"I'd rather just lose the house, you know. I wish he'd gotten the house and left us alone."

Boldt was silent for a long time.

"I know that silence. You're saying he doesn't want the house, he wants *you*." She gasped. "Is that it?"

"We don't know what he wants. We don't know much."

"I hate this. What do we do?" she cried into the phone.

"Can you get a leave?"

"I'm owed *weeks*. But I wish you'd join us."

"The sheriff's department will watch the road. The cabin too."

"I love you," she blurted out. "Always and forever."

"We'll get through this," Boldt said, "and we'll reevaluate, and we'll make sense of the last few months."

"We need to talk," she said, and to him it rang as something of a confession, and his heart wanted to tear from his chest.

"Yeah." If tears made noise, she would have heard them.

"You amaze me. . . ." Liz's voice trailed off. "Have I told you lately how much you amaze me? What an incredible man you are?"

"I love you, Elizabeth."

"Sleep if you can."

They hung up.

Boldt ignored orders and took a long, hot bath in the old clawfoot tub. When he got out, he pulled the drain plug. Ten minutes later the tub was only half empty. He searched the house for a plunger but couldn't find one. Not one plunger in the entire house!

The kitchen sink still filled with dishes hadn't drained either, but Boldt didn't notice it. He was already on his way downtown.

CHAPTER SEVEN

B Y SUNRISE the morning after the botched attempt to net the arsonist, all the crews had left the park. Only a ribbon of yellow-and-black police tape remained. Identification technicians were scheduled to return at first light.

Boldt beat them to it as he ducked under the police tape unseen. Overhead the stark limbs of trees captured the orange-ruby glow of a spectacular sunrise. Boldt walked among the weeds and shrubs, avoiding the path created hours earlier by anxious firemen and patrol officers.

The burned section of trees stuck out like a charred cancer. Boldt steered his way toward it, eyes alert for any stray piece of evidence. Circling the area, he worked his way in toward the center, roughly twelve feet of ground blanketed in white ash, only two tall trees remaining intact, their bark badly burned. Keeping the arsonist's intentions in mind, Boldt shifted left and right in an attempt to provide himself with a view of his home. Then he glanced up.

With that one simple movement Boldt confirmed to his own satisfaction that the arsonist had been up in a tree. Branslonovich had appeared below, and he had bombed her. Boldt studied both trees carefully. The branches of the one nearer him began lower to the ground, and Boldt began to climb. Ten feet . . . fifteen. He pulled himself higher, his attention on the view. There. Nearly a quarter mile away he spotted the roof of his own house. He shifted focus, looking for the next limb to climb, and came face to face with letters and numbers freshly carved into the bark: d A n 3:27.

He stared at it for several minutes. A surge of adrenaline coursed through him. The arsonist had sat in this very spot.

By the time he reached the bottom of the tree, Boldt already had his cellular phone in hand. He called LaMoia. "Meet me at Dorothy Enwright's and bring some running shoes."

"Running shoes?" the vain detective protested.

"Yeah. You can't climb trees in ostrich cowboy boots."

"Two different biblical quotations," Daphne said. "Daniel three, twenty-seven:

> *And the princes, governors, and captains, and the King's counselors, being gathered together, saw these men, upon whose bodies the fire had no power, nor was a hair of their head singed . . ."*

She continued. "This is clearly aimed at police, firemen, *governors and captains.* The other is aimed at retribution. At Dorothy Enwright's it was Ezekiel twenty-four, twelve:

> *She hath wearied herself with lies, and her great scum went not forth out of her: her scum shall be in the fire."*

"This guy has fried his circuits," LaMoia said.

Both he and Boldt had pinesap smeared on their clothing and hands. Locating the carved quotations had been easier than expected. They had isolated the highest ground near the homes of Enwright and Heifitz and had looked for the tallest trees, and the easiest to climb. LaMoia had found both quotes.

"What's of interest to me," Daphne said, "is the confirmation that this individual watched his fires, as we'd expect. What comes as a surprise are these biblical references. The earlier poetry suggested an intellectual, well read; the use of biblical references is typical of a different psychology, a pathologically disturbed individual."

"A fruitcake," LaMoia said, well aware of Daphne's aversion to such terms. He smiled thinly at the psychologist, mocking her.

"Where's it leave us?" Boldt asked, ignoring LaMoia.

"The poem received yesterday was accompanied not by melted plastic, but melted metal," Daphne said carefully. "Remember, as a kid, the pieces you moved on a Monopoly board? The hat—"

"The car!" LaMoia exclaimed.

"Metal," Daphne answered. "The metal pieces were the players." To Boldt she said, "You're a *player* in the investigation. The arsonist sought a means to differentiate between one of his victims in a *house* and a *player*—namely you. Shoswitz spread your name all over every press conference."

"Damn," LaMoia gasped.

Daphne said, "What's of significance here is the decision to take out the lead investigator. This indicates a man with a bigger plan, someone who needs more time. Why?" she asked rhetorically. "To complete some larger goal? Kill more women? Who knows? But more. Something more."

Boldt got up and paced the room. A monster, he thought.

"My advice," Daphne added, "is that we get cranking on every aspect of this case we can."

"I've been putting in sixteen-hour days," LaMoia complained. "I've got all this stuff to go over. I've got sap in my hair and pine needles down my pants. Don't tell me to get cranking."

Daphne bristled at the detective.

"Cool it, John," Boldt said. "What's all this 'stuff' you have for me? Anything useful?"

"Yeah." He held up his detective's notebook. "First thing is these ladder receipts. We culled over eighty hits: eighty transactions of a Werner ladder being bought, complete with credit card or checking account number. Tomorrow or the next day I should have the names that belong to those account numbers." He waited for Boldt to say something, and when he didn't, LaMoia continued. "Cars is next," he said, changing papers. "Nothing worth your time. The Mazda belonging to Heifitz was impounded. Enwright's Ford found its way over to her ex-husband's."

"That's it?"

"Best for last," LaMoia explained. "This possible air force connection—Matthews and her snitch saying this guy was air force. An ATF guy says that if it's rocket fuel, it's clean stuff, military quality. If it's military, it's probably air force. And the ATF guy is as baffled as I am on how a person scores air force quality rocket fuel. I mention McChord," he said, referring to a base south of Tacoma, "and I don't get much of a rise out of him. But McChord is a major airlift center, Sarge. Stuff is coming and going constantly. And I get to thinking, What if some of what they're shipping is rocket fuel? It's possible, isn't it? It's worth looking into."

"Do it," Boldt said.

BOLDT had not stopped thinking about the runaway boy who had called in the homicide. He had been distracted, first by the discovery of the Monopoly pieces, then by the arsonist's targeting of his home. But each time he climbed into his car and drove the streets, he thought of the boy.

Boldt was reminded of him again when Dixon's preliminary report arrived on his desk. A body discovered in a crawl space was not an everyday occurrence. The papers had run the story; a radio show had somehow gotten hold of the boy's 911 call and played it. There was an outcry from a domestic abuse group that too many women disappeared and too few of the disappearances were investigated thoroughly. A press conference was anticipated; Dixon wanted a senior cop present.

When Tina Zyslanski, a community service officer, showed up at the door to homicide, Boldt agreed to an impromptu meeting despite his schedule because the woman she was with, Susan Prescott, worked for human services. Prescott wanted to discuss the "crawl-space murder." The boy, Boldt thought.

He walked them down to the conference room.

Susan Prescott thanked him and said, "It's my job to find this boy, the one who called in the nine eleven. My hope is that maybe crime scene evidence will point to where we might find him. He's likely to be traumatized, alone, and scared. Every day he is outside of adult supervision is another chance he'll be swallowed by this city. The homeless. The child pornography rings. Drugs."

"I have a son, Ms. Prescott. I'm anxious about this too."

"Then perhaps you will allow me into the home," she said.

Zyslanski explained, "The crime scene is sealed with police tape. Human services is requesting access."

"You are aware, are you not," asked Prescott, "that your primary suspect required hospital attention prior to his detention?"

Boldt had not studied the case carefully. He had left it to the lead detective. He didn't dare explain that.

Prescott said, "Your suspect was certainly not beat up by a child. That implies the presence of a third party, and we at HS are concerned about the child's safety."

"I have no problem with you entering that house," said Boldt. "The lead detective on the case will want to join you, just to—"

"Keep an eye on me," Prescott answered, interrupting. "That's fine. It's the drug connection that has us most concerned. You are aware of the earlier nine-eleven call, aren't you?"

"I don't believe I am," Boldt admitted.

"That first call came on October fifth," Prescott explained. "The report was made by a young boy who remained anonymous. The address is the address where the body was found. The boy is the same boy. It wasn't a hoax, as the dispatcher thought. The boy was trying to report a drug deal he had witnessed at the airport."

"Airport?" Alarms sounded inside Boldt's head. *"A drug deal at the airport?"* he shouted. Daphne's psychic had reported a drug deal involving the man with the burned hand. "Ms. Prescott," Boldt said, "I think you may have found your runaway."

DAPHNE'S car was parked across from the purple house. At exactly seven minutes past three a small boy came down the sidewalk and walked around to the back of the house and was not seen again, presumably having gone inside. Daphne glanced over at Susan Prescott, sitting alongside her. "Ready?"

"As ready as I'll ever be," answered the woman.

Daphne climbed out of the car. She was still searching for alternatives. She hated the idea of separating the boy from Emily only to put him in the custody of a public agency. But Boldt needed a witness. She felt heavy and sad.

Susan went to the front door and knocked loudly while Daphne climbed the back porch, placing herself immediately before the door. She heard the muted sounds of a conversation between Susan and Emily. It started low but quickly grew to shouting, with Emily objecting, raising her decibel level to the point that Daphne clearly distinguished the words, "You cannot take him!"

Daphne spread her feet apart a little wider, like a boxer in a stance, braced for the collision that seemed imminent.

"SO THERE I was," Daphne said. "He came through the back door like a train running downhill, head down and hell-bent."

In Boldt's hotel room, Daphne was into her second beer. The room wasn't much—paid for by the city until Boldt was allowed to return to his house.

"I caught him and he fought like crazy. Poor kid. And now it has backfired. We know who he is, but he won't say one word to us. His name is Benjamin Santori. Nice name, isn't it?"

"It's a start," he said, trying to be upbeat.

"A start for us, an end for him," she fired back. "Twelve years old, Lou. His mother murdered. Some kind of exchange at the airport. Emily was protecting him from us, from the courts. Can you blame her?"

"Don't beat yourself up over it," he advised.

"He was crying. Emily was too. It was awful." She was beginning to sound a little drunk. "What are those?" she asked.

Boldt was in the room's studio kitchen. "Dorothy Enwright bought all of this from a hardware store the day of the fire. LaMoia pieced it together." It was a roll of silver tape, a can of Drano, and a pair of rubber gloves.

"Susan's letting him stay with me—the boy," she stated.

"A hardware store," Boldt said. "Might be a connection."

"It's that or some halfway house, and I just can't do that to him. He won't run away, because we've told him that if he does, Emily Richland goes out of business, maybe to jail. He won't do that to her. See how good I am at my job? It's down to threatening twelve-year-olds."

"It's never easy," he answered. "Especially where kids are involved. But the thing is," he said, "the boy may break this open."

Boldt's cellular phone rang. He answered, then listened intently. Boldt disconnected the call with a heart in his chest that couldn't find the beat.

"What was that?" she said, seeing his reaction.

Boldt took a deep breath, then met her eyes. "LaMoia got back the information on the ladders, the credit card names. Steven Garman bought a Werner ladder two years ago."

DAPHNE insisted on tagging along during the hurried drive to Garman's apartment. LaMoia arrived only two minutes behind. As they approached the front door, a patrol car idled at the curb.

Garman wore reading glasses, a cotton sweater, and blue jeans. His pager was clipped to his belt. "Gentlemen," he said, not a trace of concern in his voice.

There were times when Boldt liked to make small talk, establish a rapport, but that evening he went straight for the jugular. "You bought a twenty-four-foot extension ladder manufactured by Werner Ladders."

"Summer before last," Garman informed him, nodding. "You boys are thorough. I'll say that."

Boldt and LaMoia engaged in a quick eye check, both surprised by Garman's forthcoming nature. "We'd like to see that ladder," LaMoia told the fire inspector.

"You're welcome to come inside," Garman offered, opening his door wide. The detectives stepped in. "But you won't find a Werner ladder. It was stolen. Six, maybe seven months ago. Listen, you want to do this downtown, or can we do it here?"

Boldt felt out of sync, the fireman anticipating his every move. He wanted to take Garman downtown, use the box, intimidate the man. But he wondered if it would work with a man accustomed to conducting his own investigations, his own interrogations.

"Here will do," Boldt said.

LaMoia recited the Miranda. Garman just smiled, miming the words along with him. Boldt wanted to pop the guy. Garman was too smug, too prepared. Boldt knew before they started that they weren't going anywhere with this one. He and Daphne sat on a couch that had seen better days. Garman took the recliner. And LaMoia brought out a kitchen chair.

They talked in circles for the next hour, attempting to catch Garman in a misspeak, but the Marshal Five's performance seemed utterly convincing. Then Daphne scored the first big points. "Tell us again about your service in the air force."

He nodded. "I was stationed two years at Grand Forks Air Force Base and six at Minot. I was married then. Young. Good times."

LaMoia said, "Those are missile bases, aren't they?"

Garman smirked. "Look it up. It'll give you something to do."

LaMoia bristled and brought his chair around to face Garman. The lines were drawn—and by Garman himself. He would work with Daphne, respect Boldt at a distance, and spar with LaMoia.

"Your marriage?" Daphne asked.

"Out of bounds, Counselor," Garman replied.

"I'm not a lawyer."

Garman stared at her. "We never did establish your exact role in this, did we? As I recall, you kind of skirted the question."

LaMoia said, "Look it up. It'll give you something to do."

That caused a brief crack in Garman's armor.

Boldt felt a little more optimistic. He said, "So the ladder was stolen."

"I'll answer again if you want," Garman replied. He looked each of them directly in the eye. "It was my truck that was stolen. A white pickup. Damn nice one too. Ford. Bucket seats. Electric windows. The ladder, some turnout gear, my clipboard." He looked at LaMoia. "Of course, maybe I stole it myself and stashed it somewhere to use later in these arsons."

They did the dance for the next forty minutes, but nothing worthwhile surfaced. That particular session was won by Garman, but there would be others. He was the closest thing they had to a suspect, and Boldt was not about to let him go.

Twenty-four-hour surveillance began thirty minutes before their departure. Steve Garman was suspect number one.

BEN'S world had gone down in flames. First the guy trying to kill him, then the discovery of the body. It all had a dreamlike quality, distant yet present at the same time.

The days immediately after the incident had been among the best in his life. Emily had given him his own room. She had cooked his meals and even made him a sandwich for school lunch. He didn't tell her that he didn't go to school for those days—he was too terrified the blue truck might return. He didn't even have the five hundred bucks. It was at the house, hidden in his room, and he sure wasn't going back there.

At night he and Emily played cards together or worked on a jigsaw puzzle. Before bed she would read to him.

Being caught by the police had scared him to death. Convinced that they knew about the five hundred dollars, he had refused to speak at first. But when Daphne Matthews had given him the choice of a juvenile detention center or going home to her houseboat, Ben had spoken up loud and clear. Speaking had broken the ice. Daphne proved to be a nice woman and easy to talk to.

Even so, he missed Emily with an ache in his heart unmatched since he discovered his mother's ring in the crawl space.

He sat on a couch in Daphne's houseboat, the television tuned to Nickelodeon. For the past two days he had never been alone except in the bathroom. Daphne picked him up every afternoon from "school," a place surrounded by wire fence, for juveniles in detention. They went for snacks. They drove around.

The houseboat was small, but he liked it okay. The walls were thin. After dinner, when she thought he was reading, he was actually listening to her on the phone. She spoke to someone named Owen, and he knew that things weren't great between them. Twice she had hung up and started crying. It had never occurred to him that police ever cried.

BOLDT was caught in a mad, frantic race. The psychic's military man with the burned hand, the ATF lab's suggestion of rocket fuel as the accelerant, Garman's purchase of a Werner ladder. It was Boldt's job to shape the investigation into something manageable. That task was made more difficult by two occurrences.

The first was the arrival the day after Garman's interrogation of another poem and piece of green plastic. Was Garman brazenly taunting the police, Boldt wondered, or was he an innocent go-between?

The second was a phone call Daphne received on that same day. She hurried into Boldt's office. "Emily called! Nick, the guy with the burned hand, just made an appointment for five o'clock today. That's only two hours from now. Can we handle it?"

Boldt felt a knot of tension in his stomach. Two hours. Surveillance, ERT, bomb squad—a repeat of the team assembled less than a week earlier. Branslonovich was not seven days in her grave. That spectral vision haunted him. "We'll try."

At four forty-nine p.m. a bald man wearing khakis and deck shoes came out the front door of the purple house on Twenty-first Avenue East. He carried a small brown leather briefcase as he walked briskly to a nondescript station wagon and drove off. The briefcase had contained a lavalier condenser microphone and a radio transmitter, presently taped to the bottom of Emily's "reading" table. The maroon operations van was parked a block away.

Two undercover members of the bomb squad ran a tow truck that was busy—albeit slowly—hoisting an illegally parked car up onto a flatbed. Their location, outside of the driveway to the purple house, allowed them quick access to the light blue truck and white camper shell that was expected any minute.

Boldt, Bobbie Gaynes, and Daphne occupied fuzzy padded seats that faced a large Mylar-covered window in a cream customized recreational van parked across the street. Boldt had his cellular phone in hand. At his feet were two portable radio systems: one that allowed them to communicate with the secured channel of radio traffic, the second a live feed from the transmitter inside the house. On the floor lay two shotguns.

A motorcycle rider and two unmarked cars were spread between the surrounding streets to follow the truck when it left the area.

At four fifty-seven p.m. the motorcycle rider's voice came over the radio.

RIDER: Suspect's vehicle, Washington tag 124 B76, just passed checkpoint Bravo, headed in a westerly direction.

"Right on time," Boldt said, checking his watch.

DISPATCH: 124 B76 is registered to Nicholas Trenton Hall, twenty-six, 232nd Street South, Parkland.

Daphne said, "Is he air force? Can we confirm that?"

Boldt repeated this question into his phone. Dispatch replied that a "full query" was under way. Not thirty seconds passed before Boldt relayed to Daphne, "He was air force for eight years, a civilian employee at Chief Joseph for the last three."

"His discharge coincides with the hand injury. Bet on it."

Boldt glanced out the window and watched the suspect's arrival. Nicholas Hall left his truck and followed the path, his face reflecting the colors in the neon sign. He pushed the doorbell, then glanced around cautiously, suspiciously. His attention focused on the two men hoisting a car up onto the tow truck.

The hand. Even from a distance it was noticeable. Boldt snagged a pair of binoculars. A single piece of red flesh with three fingernails growing out of the end. A moment of panic surged through Boldt. Could such a person climb trees? Could he carve biblical references into a tree trunk?

At the front door, Hall continued to watch the tow truck.

"Welcome," the three in the van faintly heard Emily say as she greeted Hall. The microphone was some fifteen feet behind her, yet it still grabbed some sound. "Come in."

"You seen 'em tow cars around here before?" he asked her.

"All the time," she lied. "But you're okay in my drive."

"One cool woman," Daphne said under her breath.

Hall stepped inside. Emily's voice grew louder as she led him into the room toward the microphone.

Daphne pointed to the radios. "Here we go," she said.

> HALL: I want to check a date with you. It's next Thursday. You can check that, right?

Daphne spoke softly into a walkie-talkie. "Check the charts and tell him it's a bad day. Something sooner would work better."

Over the radio Boldt heard a rustling of paper.

> EMILY: You have a descending moon next week. It's not a fortuitous time for a business deal. You said this was business, not pleasure, isn't that right?
> HALL: Does it make a difference?
> EMILY: Very much so.

Daphne announced to her colleagues, "This is interesting. How can someone quoting Plato believe this stuff?"

Boldt had no comment. The interview with the psychic was only the beginning. They needed hard evidence against Hall. Probable cause to raid the truck and his residence. He felt impatient and edgy. He wanted this clean. They had to follow Hall, make something happen. Justify a raid.

HALL: Business, yeah.

"Bingo," said Daphne. Into the walkie-talkie she said, "Try to draw it out of him."

EMILY: The kind of business can influence the way the charts are read. Sales, for instance, are particularly bad in a descending moon. Negotiations, however, don't suffer so much. But if it's sales, I would suggest you advance the date. (Paper rustling) The next two to three days would be far superior.

HALL: How come you didn't mention this moon thing before?

EMILY: There was no descending moon involved. Your chart was good last time. (Pause) Is it sales, then?

HALL: Sales. Yeah. You could say that.

Daphne said into the walkie-talkie, "Number of people involved. Location."

EMILY: (Clears voice) You have a good Mars and Venus. But Pluto is way off. That says something about numbers. There are not a lot of people involved in this sale, are there? (Pause) One other. Am I right?

HALL: This stuff amazes me.

EMILY: Cars. Darkness. Lots of parked cars. Loud noises. What's that noise? Roaring, like animals.

HALL: Jets.

EMILY: Of course, the airport. (Pause) There's another man involved, isn't there? Not a group of people.

HALL: Not a group.

Boldt sat forward. "The airport drug deal the boy called in."

EMILY: The next day or two. Three at the outside.

HALL: You missed something last time. I nearly didn't come back to you because of that.

EMILY: (Long pause) I'm seeing something outside of your business arrangement. Something missing. You lost something?

HALL: It was stolen. A lot of money. A boy stole it. Right out of my truck. (Pause) I want that money.

Daphne met Boldt's eyes. "Ben," she said.

Boldt nodded. "No wonder he's scared of us. He's worried we're after *him*."

"She knows the whole story. Ben told her," Daphne said.

Boldt, thinking aloud, said, "Hall's air force. It wasn't drugs. It was rocket fuel." The silence in the van was shattered by the speaker.

HALL: I thought you could see this stuff! Why didn't you warn me?

EMILY: You asked me about a particular date. That was all.

HALL: Well, now I'm asking about complications.

EMILY: And I'm warning you that the longer you allow the descending moon—

HALL: To hell with the moon! What about complications?

Daphne said, "I don't like the mood swing here." Into the walkie-talkie she said, "Placate him. Go easy. Be vague."

HALL: What about if I pull it off in the next few days?

EMILY: The stars support success. (Pause) No complications if you act quickly. This boy, whoever he is, won't bother you again.

HALL: He's got my money. (Pause) Listen, can you help me find him? (Pause) There would be a bonus.

Boldt said excitedly, "We can use this. It takes Ben out of the loop and just might give us our probable cause."

Daphne, eyes on Boldt, said into the walkie-talkie, "If you know where that money is, sweetheart, it's time for a vision. You tell him. We all want Ben out of this."

They held their breath as they awaited Emily's decision.

EMILY: I see a brown house. Small.

HALL: That's the boy's place!

EMILY: The money is there. (Pause) The boy's room. A box. A plastic box. Wait a second. (Pause) Rectangular.

HALL: A cigar box? Something like that?

EMILY: A lunchbox? (Pause) Ah! It's a box for a videotape.

HALL: (Excited; the sound of a chair moving) How much do I owe you?

Daphne said into the device, "Let him go."

EMILY: Ten for the reading.

HALL: I'm giving you twenty. (Pause) I'll try for sometime in the next three days. I'll be back to check with you.

Bobbie Gaynes asked, "Do we follow?"

Boldt answered, "No, we lead. We know exactly where he's going. He's going after that money."

JACKSON Street East was a dead end, up a steep hill. The Santori home backed up to Frink Park. The cream-colored van parked one block south of Jackson, a surveillance car one block north. ERT was deployed into the park, in case Hall fled on foot.

Dispatch confirmed that the blue-and-white vehicle came to a stop on Jackson, half a block from the Santori home. With the suspect effectively boxed in, Boldt checked his weapon and sat forward to leave the van.

"I'm coming with you," Daphne said, removing her weapon from her purse. Before Boldt could contradict this, she added, "Lou, I need to be reading this guy from the word go. If I'm there at the bust, it gives us a leg up."

Boldt did not argue. The more they understood about Hall, the better. "We partner on this, Daffy. And I'm the lead," he said.

Boldt secured a radio in his coat pocket and stuck the earpiece in his ear. The dispatcher's voice announced that ERT was in place and the truck had been spotted and was empty.

Boldt and Daphne hurried up the hill and cut in behind the house. They made for a decrepit gardening shack. Its doors were held closed by a piece of wood that spun on a nail. Boldt got the door open quietly and pulled Daphne inside.

It was dusty and dank—spiderwebs and mildew—but with the shed door open an inch, they had a good view of the house. A shadow moved in a window. "He's in there," Daphne said, sounding excited.

Hall could be heard hurrying down the steps inside the house. The back door cracked open.

Boldt drew his handgun. "Ready?" he whispered.

The suspect stepped out of the dark house and shut the door.

Boldt clicked the walkie-talkie button three times, then kicked open the shed door. "Police!" he shouted. "On the ground *now!*"

Hall dove to the earth, hands outstretched.

"One thing about those military boys," Daphne quipped. "They know how to follow orders."

CHAPTER EIGHT

NICHOLAS Hall was processed like a side of beef: his finger-prints inked, his clothes replaced with an orange jumpsuit. Boldt had ordered "full jewelry"—handcuffs and ankle manacles.

The prisoner had not yet requested a court-appointed attorney, a privilege offered him during three separate readings of the Miranda. They were taking no chances with Nicholas Hall. In homicide's eight-by-eight interrogation room A—the box—Boldt and Daphne took turns with him. Boldt took the first hour and the role of the heavy. Daphne took hour number two and played the friend. Boldt took hour three. By the fourth hour Daphne had begun to loosen him up by pitting Boldt against her and telling him how hard-liners like Boldt didn't like a woman doing their job.

"I put up with a lot around here," she informed Hall. "They think of me in terms of my sex, that's all. I'm different," she said, attempting to appeal to that hand of his, "so they don't trust me."

"I know all about that."

This was only the fourth full sentence that Hall had spoken. Daphne felt a tingle of excitement. "The hand," she said. "People think you're a freak."

"You got that right."

She nodded sympathetically. She reached up and scratched the back of her neck, signaling Boldt through the one-way glass.

The sergeant came charging angrily into the interrogation room. "It's my turn," he announced. "You're out of here."

"No way," Daphne said. "He doesn't want to talk to you."

"What do I care what he wants?" Boldt asked. "He killed a woman and left her in a crawl space—"

Hall said, "That's bull," his handcuffs dragging on the table.

"You're interrupting me, Sergeant," Daphne said. She glanced at her watch. "Nick and I aren't through."

"You're not going to get anything out of him," Boldt countered. "Let me have him."

"The door is that way. Out!" she told Boldt.

The sergeant glared at them and left the tiny room.

"I didn't kill no woman," Hall protested.

"They can place you in the house," she informed him. "What were you doing there if not trying to cover up your knowing her?"

"Never been in that house before!" he shouted at her. "You gotta believe me."

"The hand," she said, knowing this was a source of pain. "Tell me about that hand."

"No! We're not talking about my hand. We're talking about murder. I ain't never—"

"I'm talking about your hand," she interrupted. "What? You think I'm working against you here? Maybe we find out she was strangled *with bare hands*. That's all you need, you know."

"Is that true?" he asked.

"I said maybe. Now tell me about that hand. How long ago?"

"Three years," he said. "An accident. I was in the service."

"How?"

"An explosive device. Phosphorus. Detonator fired early."

She stared at his hand a moment, long enough to know that he too was engrossed in it. Then she asked, "Why were you in that house?"

He looked away. "A kid stole some money from me." Daphne felt ebullient. *More*, she pushed silently. "I got a tip it was in the house. You found it on me. That's *my* money."

She asked, "You know what they found when they found the body—the lab guys? Down in the crawl space, I'm talking about." She took a deep breath. "They found your fingerprints, Nick. Where they found the dead woman."

He wore a paralyzed expression, part shock, part realization. He said hurriedly, "No, listen. You don't understand. You got this wrong. I *had* been there. Last week."

"You're saying you just happened to be in the crawl space last week? Oh, well," she said sarcastically, "*that* explains it! Certainly fills in all the blanks for me." She fixed her eyes on him. "What were you doing there, Nick? Did you kill that woman?"

"No, no, no," the suspect said, shaking his head violently.

"Talk to me."

"I was at the airport," he stated. "I was doing some business, you know? Some punk kid ripped me for five bills. Drops his wallet in my truck. First time I went there, he hid from me in the crawl space. Second time—tonight—I took the money."

Daphne's pulse quickened. "What kind of business?" she asked.

"A phone call now and then. The guy knew more about my base

than I did. I swear. I never met him. I don't know what he looks like." Her skin crawled. A second person.

Hall placed his pink paddle on the table. "A hundred and twenty a month. That's the disability pay our fine country sees fit to give me for this. What kind of job am I supposed to get? A typist?" He twisted his lips into a grin that caused her to shiver.

"What was it?" she asked.

"It wasn't drugs," he declared.

"Something available on the base," she replied.

"I had access that he didn't have. Let's just leave it at that."

"Leave it? I don't think so. Have you been listening? We're trying to build a credible story here. I don't know what you were selling, but it's not going to bring you death row. The murder charge will."

His eyes hardened. "I want me a lawyer. I'm not answering any more questions."

"Then I won't ask any more questions," she informed him. She stood. "You want death row, it's all yours."

His chains rattled, but he did not speak up. Hall had the look of terror. Better to let Boldt go at him for a while.

"OKAY, here's the story," John LaMoia said, approaching Boldt, who stood behind the one-way glass, watching Daphne.

Boldt didn't like being interrupted, not even by LaMoia. "I'm busy here, Detective," he said sternly.

"The rocket fuel," LaMoia said slowly. "The suspect . . ."

Boldt's mind wandered from fatigue. He spoke to Liz each night. Though grateful for his efforts to protect his family, she was increasingly angry about her isolation at the cabin. She had spent nine days up there. The sheriff's department had two men assigned to her twenty-four hours a day. She felt captive.

He told her little of the investigation. They ended up discussing social engagements, seeking the comfort of familiarity. There was a dinner party being thrown by one of her vice presidents that she felt they were obligated to attend. Boldt hated these bank dinners, having little in common with the country club set.

He softened and reluctantly agreed to go, at which point she dropped the bombshell. "I have to be back in the city on Tuesday. No questions asked. I *have* to be." Jealousy welled up within him, and he nearly confronted her, yet he didn't want to know.

LaMoia's voice brought him back. "What I've found out is this: The air force, in all its wisdom, decommissioned the Titan missile program in phases. The rocket fuel back then was two liquids that when combined self-ignited. Part A meets part B and *kablaam!*— fire, controlled burn. The chemical reaction produced its own oxygen, perfect for burns that continued up into space. The term is *hypergolic:* binary self-igniting rocket fuel. The point is, it takes the two parts to tango. They moved the two parts to separate locations, keeping them as far from each other as possible. There was evidently talk of disposing of the two parts, but some genius decided we might be able to sell the stuff abroad. So they stored it. Part A went to Idaho, part B to California. Part A went to Texas, part B to Nevada. And then the base closures began. Base inventories were moved around like chess pieces. Things get a little fuzzy at this point, but it appears that by just plain old stupidity, parts A and B ended up on the same base: Chief Joseph Air Force Base."

Boldt said, "Which was closed down."

"But not fully. They reduced it to something called maintenance status. They maintained inventory—a few administrators stayed on, a few MPs to watch the place. But for all purposes there was no one left."

"Vulnerable."

"Exactly. Especially to an inside job."

Boldt speculated, "Nicholas Hall was an MP at Chief Joseph."

"That he was. Mr. Paddle Paw in there skimmed off a little juice and cashed in his retirement plan."

Boldt exhaled loudly and said, "Good work, John."

"Damn right. I'd say it earns me ten minutes with him, right?"

Daphne stepped out of the interrogation room at that moment, overhearing the request. "Let's give him a rest. Please."

LaMoia had proved himself incredibly effective in past interrogations. A wild card. Boldt agreed, but warned his detective, "Don't touch him."

Daphne, knowing Boldt's mind was made up, advised LaMoia, "Don't ask any questions. Just statements, John."

LaMoia moved to the box with a swagger.

Through the speaker below the one-way glass Boldt and Daphne heard LaMoia say, "I bet you're a killer at handball, Nicky." He kicked the empty chair away from the desk and sat down in it. "You could always get a job as an inspector in a mitten factory."

LaMoia stared for a moment. "What was life like out at Chief Joseph once everybody left?" he asked, breaking Daphne's request immediately.

The suspect paled noticeably. No answer.

"What else?" LaMoia asked. "You could direct traffic! Hey, what about that? You could be a traffic cop, Nicky." Then he said, "You could sell out your country, I'll bet."

LaMoia slapped the table so loudly that the speaker went fuzzy. "You worked security at Chief Joseph. You decided to make a few bucks. Don't shake your head, pal. I know all about you. You want to nod, that's okay. But don't lie to me.

"Maybe I need a little introduction," LaMoia continued. "I'm the one that those guys"—he pointed to the glass—"can't control. I'm the one who does the dirty work around here. I'm the guy who knows everybody. Ask anyone. I'm the guy who tells the guard to put the roaches in the soup, and the cook does it. I make friends easily. Like with you, right, Nicky? Let's have a little nod, Nicky."

If Boldt hadn't seen it a dozen other times, he might have been shocked to see the suspect nod.

Daphne, clearly amazed, said, "I could study LaMoia for a decade and never write a comprehensible paper about how he does what he does. He's despicable and yet he's lovable."

"He called me," Hall said, the first break in his silence.

Suddenly quiet and a fellow conspirator, LaMoia said, "Give us what we need, Nicky, and you just might walk out of here. No promises. But the flip side is that we can make life hell for you. It's like a game show, Nicky. Choose the door. Go ahead and pick. The doors are right in front of you: Truth or Dare. Pick one, Nicky, and pick fast." LaMoia pounded the table again. "Buzzer's ringing, Nicky Hall. Come on down!"

Daphne said, "I can't believe this. It's going to work."

LaMoia pounded the table again. "Truth or Dare, Mr. Paddle Paw! You start talking or I start walking. What's it going to be?"

"He knew that both parts of the stuff were stored on the base," Hall explained.

"Brilliant." LaMoia kicked his feet up onto the table and leaned back. "I'm listening, Nicky. I'm listening."

"I was working MP duty. I'd driven by those buildings for years and never did know what was inside," Hall began.

LaMoia glanced back at the window and grinned widely.

"Sometimes I hate LaMoia," Daphne said.

"Yeah," Boldt answered. "I know what you mean."

THE arrest of Nicholas Hall was broken by KOMO television and within minutes was the subject of talk radio. Newspapers proclaimed Hall's arrest in front-page headlines. For Boldt the public euphoria was subdued by a memo from Lofgrin received the Monday morning after the arrest.

Lou: FYI, Nicholas Hall's weight and height do not agree with our assessment of ladder impressions dated Oct. 4 this year. The suspect is twenty to thirty pounds heavy and, by our estimates, three to five inches tall for whoever climbed that ladder. Furthermore, the individual that carved the trees was right-handed. Hall's disfigured right hand would suggest he was not a viable suspect. Any questions, I'm around.—Bernie

They had the wrong man. An accomplice perhaps, but not the man the papers had dubbed the Scholar. Boldt and Daphne had both sensed this throughout LaMoia's interrogation, in which Hall detailed the theft, transportation, and sale of the binary rocket fuel. Worse, a search of his Parkland mobile home revealed no notepaper, no ladder. One positive note of the follow-up investigation was Bernie Lofgrin's decision to run an analysis of the ballpoint ink used in the threats, in hopes of discovering a like pen in Hall's possession.

But Boldt knew the truth: The killer remained at large.

He experienced an overwhelming bout of depression and frustration. So close, only to fail. He wanted Liz home. The kids.

The investigation rolled on. Boldt wanted a shot at what the boy, Ben Santori, knew. Kids saw more than adults. Maybe a lead to the accomplice. Open him up with a lineup, jog his memory.

BEN missed Emily. He was shuttled back and forth between talks with Susan Prescott, school classes in detention, and evenings with Daphne. The only thing keeping him from running away was Daphne's threat to put Emily out of business.

When Daphne showed up in the middle of classes, Ben knew it meant trouble. She consulted with the teacher, and Ben was excused. Heart beating fast, he met up with Daphne in the hallway.

"We need to ask a favor of you, Ben. Boldt and I."

"I don't like him."

"You should," she said. "It's good to have him on your side."

He was loath to admit it, but he liked Daphne. He even felt sorry for her in a way, because all she seemed to do was work and talk on the phone. "What kind of favor?"

"Sergeant Boldt wants to ask you some questions. Show you some pictures. Maybe do a lineup."

"What if I don't want to?" he asked sarcastically.

"Then I talk you into it," she answered.

"And how are you going to do that?"

"Bribery, probably. Like how about seeing Emily?"

He felt like shouting "Yes!" but tried to hide his feelings, not give her too much leverage.

On their way to her car, Ben asked her, "Are you divorced?"

"No," she answered, surprised.

"My mom was divorced before she met *him*." He had not told her much about himself, though she seemed to know a lot. Initially he had feared the police were after him for the five hundred dollars. But that was no longer the case; he knew it had to do with Nick.

"A lot of people get divorced these days," she explained. "It doesn't make your mother any less a person."

"I thought she went away," Ben said, his voice catching. Daphne started the car but glanced over at him before shifting gears. "She did, sort of. Go away. You know?" Ben felt tears coming. "He told me she left me. And I believed him." He felt a tear run down his cheek and turned toward the window so she couldn't see.

"Ben, you're old enough to understand that people like Jack Santori do bad things. They hurt other people. Talking about things can help."

He thought of her lying down there in the cold and the damp. As Daphne reached over and hugged him, he felt her warmth, and he buried his face in her chest and fell apart, images surfacing, feelings that he had no idea were buried inside him. He saw himself as a child. He saw his mother, her bruised face, her swollen eye, and he remembered her frightened warning: "Don't you say a thing about this in front of him. You act no different, Benjamin. You're my best boy, right? You gotta do this for me." She'd been protecting him; he realized that.

"He killed her," Ben sobbed. Daphne squeezed him all the tighter, tears running down her own cheeks. "He killed my mom and put her down there."

Daphne said, "You're safe here, Ben. Emily, me, Susan—we're your friends. You can talk to us. It's safe."

"I'm afraid," he said, admitting aloud for the first time something he had lived with for what felt like forever.

"Me too," said Daphne. "And know what? It's okay to be afraid."

THE big man was Boldt. Ben knew that much. The other guy to visit the houseboat was Danny, and he was some sort of artist. He set up his drawing pad on the small countertop bar that separated Daphne's galley from the tiny sitting room.

Boldt brought a videocassette with him that Daphne put into the machine and set up for Ben to view. Boldt explained, "You'll see five men, all standing alongside one another—"

"I know what a lineup is," Ben interrupted.

Boldt glanced over at Daphne, who asked Ben politely not to interrupt, saying that Boldt and this other guy had a job to do and it had to be done in a certain way. Then they played the video for him, and it looked just as it did on TV, with a line of five guys who kept their hands behind their backs. There was a short guy with a beard, and next to him a taller blond guy, and then Nick, and another tall guy, and a guy who looked pretty much like Nick but not really.

"The guy in the middle," Ben said.

"You're absolutely sure?" Boldt asked.

"His name is Nick. He drives a light blue pickup with a white camper shell. There was a gun inside the camper shell."

"Did you see drugs in the camper?" Boldt asked.

"Stuff to make them, I think. Milky stuff. In plastic things, like for leftovers. And they had chemistry stuff written on them. You know? Letters and numbers."

Boldt said, "Let's talk about who was at the airport. When you called 911 you said it was a drug deal, didn't you, son?"

"I'm not your son."

"How many people were there, Ben?" Daphne encouraged.

Daphne's asking made it different. "Two," Ben answered. "Nick and this other guy."

"Sergeant Boldt needs a description," Daphne said.

"I didn't see his face. He was over by some cars. It was dark."

The artist, on a barstool alongside Ben, started sketching. Ben watched in amazement as the inside of the parking garage came to life on the page.

Boldt said, "Was he taller or shorter than the cars?"

"Taller." Ben nodded. "Yeah, taller."

"My size? Danny's size?" Boldt pointed to the artist, who was shading the cars, making the page look even more realistic.

"Not as tall as you," he told the sergeant. "Skinnier."

Daphne smiled, and Boldt looked at her disapprovingly.

The artist worked furiously. On the page the shape of a body formed between two of the cars. Ben instructed the man: "He was standing back farther . . . a little taller than that." He couldn't believe how seeing the artist's sketch made it all so real for him—he knew exactly what was wrong with the picture. He waited for the artist to get more of the guy on the page, then said, "His head was . . . I don't know . . . thinner, you know? Narrow. He had glasses. Big glasses." The artist corrected the head to where it was just right. "A hat. One of those stretchy ones."

"A knit cap," Boldt said.

"Yeah. And a turtleneck up over his chin."

It amazed Ben how quickly the artist adjusted to every comment, the image growing out of nothing.

"No, not like that. Not a turtleneck, I guess." The artist erased it, and a moment later the man's head changed completely. "Oh, wow! That's him." Danny had drawn a hooded sweatshirt, the strings pulled tightly under the man's chin so that, when combined with the glasses, almost nothing showed of his face. "That's it."

"Any markings on the clothes?" Boldt questioned. "A sports team? The name of a city or town?"

Ben tried shutting his eyes, and the image on the artist's page suddenly came to life. He could smell the car exhaust, hear the airplanes. The guy had moved his head, looking at the truck where Ben hid. Light sparked off his mouth. "His teeth are shiny."

"Braces?" Boldt asked.

"I don't know," Ben said, his eyes still squinted shut. "Can't see."

"What's the man doing?" Boldt asked.

Ben described the scene as the guy headed toward the truck, his sense of panic, of diving back under the seat, then hearing that lock click into place. His terror at being locked up a second time.

"As he walked toward the truck," Daphne said calmly, "maybe he stepped out of the shadows a little. Into the light. Try to picture that for me. Can you see it?" Her voice was soothing, the same voice that had comforted him in the car, and sure enough, for an instant Ben thought he could see part of the man's face.

"I don't know. . . ." he mumbled.

"Go ahead," she encouraged. "It's all right, Ben. You were scared. He was coming toward you. And there was more light."

"Headlights. A car's headlights." The image inside his head happened quickly. "He's wearing a mask, I think. Plastic. A white mask. Shiny. Like a hockey goalie, maybe."

"He wore a disguise," Boldt said in a voice of disappointment.

The artist held up the sketch. It was the guy's head and shoulders, the sweatshirt up over most of his face. He wore big dark glasses and had plastic-looking skin.

"That's him," Ben whispered. He didn't want to talk too loudly. The picture seemed real enough that the guy might hear.

CHAPTER NINE

WHEN Boldt reached his hotel after questioning Ben, the clerk handed him a brown paper bag. Boldt opened it in his room. Inside was a note from LaMoia and items from a hardware store—items purchased by Melissa Heifitz on the day of her fire.

Boldt examined the contents of the bag: a compressed air canister called E-Z Flush, rubber gloves, a sponge head to a mop.

He was in his second week in the hotel. The items from Enwright were in the dresser's bottom drawer. He took these out and compared. Common to both groups were sponges and gloves. A bottle of Drano in the Enwright group, E-Z Flush in the other—a bottle of compressed gas to be used as a plunger to clear a stubborn drain. In his mind's eye he recalled his own bathtub having trouble draining the night of his family's evacuation.

Clogged drains. A link between Enwright, Heifitz, and himself.

Boldt called Bernie Lofgrin at home. "What are the chances that the hypergolics, that the ignition system, is somehow related to plumbing? To clogged drains?" he asked the lab man.

After a long silence Lofgrin said, "I'm thinking. Plumbing?"

Boldt said, "One of the victims bought a toilet plunger on the day she died, the other some Drano."

"A plunger!" Lofgrin shouted excitedly. "Hang on. Just hang on a second." Boldt overheard him calling out to his wife. Then he came back on the line.

"Do-It-Yourself: The Visual Dictionary," Lofgrin said, "page two fifty-seven shows a cutaway illustration of a house, revealing the plumbing. Left of the page is a stack vent. Right of the page, a waste stack. Drains from the toilet, a sink, a tub, are all connected by a common pipe labeled Branch. On either end of the branch is a vertical riser that passes through roof flashing to the outside.

"Draining water or waste creates a vacuum in the pipe," Lofgrin continued. "The waste pipes need to be vented to allow draining. Think of a drinking straw with your finger over the top end. Keep your finger tight and the straw holds in the fluid. Vent the straw by lifting your finger, the fluid drains out. Same in a house. Only the drains have stinky stuff in them, so the vents go out the roof. Two of them, Lou. You get it?"

"You lost me," Boldt admitted.

"Two vent stacks: two parts to the hypergolics. Right? Seal the vent stacks with a thin membrane. Wax paper? Cling wrap? Place the two parts of the hypergolics above those seals. It might not take much—maybe just draining a bathtub or running the clothes washer—and those seals break and run down the vent stacks. The two hypergolics contact each other in the branch pipe. You open a bathtub drain or flush a toilet, and suddenly every plumbing fixture in the house is a rocket nozzle. *The porcelain melts.* That was the clue I missed! That should have jumped out at me. Porcelain does not melt easily; it would have to be near the source of the burn. Every piece of porcelain in the houses was involved in the actual burn. You've got the answer, Lou."

"A plunger?"

Lofgrin exclaimed, "He can set the explosives without ever entering the house! Do it all from the roof. Wash a few windows, climb up on the roof, set the vents. A matter of minutes is all." It only took Lofgrin a second to make the connection that Boldt also made. "Lou! Your house. Your vents could be set. We could have *proof* here." He sounded thrilled. Boldt felt terrified.

"Give me forty minutes," Lofgrin said. "I need a big crew."

THE first man to reach the roof ridge of the house wore a fireman's turnouts and a handsfree walkie-talkie that communicated with Lofgrin on the ground. Lofgrin and Boldt and the others stood behind a fire line on the sidewalk. The six adjacent houses had been evacuated, and patrol cars blocked the street from traffic.

Lofgrin looked over at Boldt and said, "I gotta warn you. We're gonna find hypergolics. Why else go up the tree and watch the place, right? He was waiting for the show."

"I'm a nervous wreck," Boldt admitted.

"Think how Rick feels," he said, pointing to the roof man. "That fuel goes, and he's got about twenty seconds to get off that roof before he's three thousand feet up." The roof man was equipped with a fiber-optic camera about the size of a pencil eraser on a flexible aluminum cable about the diameter of a shoelace. His job was to lower the cable into each vent stack and report what he saw.

Into the walkie-talkie Lofgrin said, "Let's try one of the back stacks, Rick. You copy that?"

"I copy," the roof man reported. Boldt looked on as the man gingerly crossed the roof between vent stacks.

"I'm at the northernmost stack on the back side," announced the roof man through Lofgrin's radio.

"The kitchen," Boldt explained.

Lofgrin said, "Go easy, Rick. This may be a live one."

Boldt could not see Rick, and this bothered him. He heard Rick announce that he was feeding the camera into the stack, and Boldt could picture the tiny camera sliding down the black vent.

"Slowly," Lofgrin cautioned.

"Copy that," answered the roof man. "Going down." He continued easing the camera into the vent stack. "Howdy hey," he said. "I'm showing a translucent membrane at the eighteen-inch mark."

"Hold it!" Lofgrin spat into the radio. He turned and waved one of his assistants over. She carried a gray plastic toolbox in her right hand. Lofgrin told her, "The kitchen. Use the back door. Take it exceptionally slowly. It will be in the vertical somewhere. Give me a distance readout from the bottom of the vertical."

"Yes, sir." She hurried away.

"Why send her inside?" Boldt questioned.

"We need to check the stack from below. Rick can't head down through that membrane, so we go from the bottom up. That should give us some idea how to neutralize."

"Meaning what?"

"I see two options. One is he trapped part A and part B in two different stacks. A thin membrane on the bottom, the other stacks sealed off. Someone uses a plunger, the membranes go simultaneously and the place goes up. The second option is both parts in the same stack, a membrane between. The advantage is you only have to break one membrane. We don't know what he's done, so we sure can't go popping membranes." He explained, "There's a remote chance he's done this a third way. Casterstein found a possible detonator. What if that detonator is a pressure switch?"

"What if it is?" Boldt asked.

"We know the guy was up a tree watching the place. From his tree he activates the pressure switch—he could retrofit any remote-control toy to do the trick. Deactivated, the drains don't work well, but the place doesn't blow. Activated, the first time a toilet flushes—*boom!* A plunger, same thing. If both parts of the hypergolic are in the same stack and we go messing around, we could make one hell of a Roman candle."

The next few minutes progressed painstakingly slowly. The woman technician finally announced, "Okay, I see an opening to a riser up ahead. I'm twenty inches to the right."

"Good. Let's follow it. But be careful. That membrane may be transparent."

Lofgrin began nervously stroking the stubble on his chin. "She's heading up the vent stack. If she breaks whatever barrier he has in place—" He didn't complete the sentence.

The woman's voice sounded strained as she reported, "Thirty-one inches. Condensation on the pipe walls has increased."

Lofgrin said to Boldt, "We're close. This is a little like aiming a pin at a balloon but not wanting it to pop."

Boldt felt overly warm. He wiped his brow.

The woman counted off in quarter-inch increments from thirty and one half. Boldt tensed with each report.

"Going to thirty-three and three quarters . . . thirty-four. I'm picking up a slightly reflective black image. Okay. This is a foreign object. Repeat. A foreign object obstructing the passage. Black plastic." Boldt felt his scalp prickle. She said, "Maybe send a bomb boy in to look at this. I've got a rubber O-ring holding it in place. It appears to be a detonator."

"I knew it!" Lofgrin exclaimed to Boldt. "They don't pay me big bucks for nothing."

The joke was not lost on Boldt. The pay was horrible. "What's next?" he asked.

"We send in the bomb man to have a look, then attempt to neutralize. We're looking at about eighteen feet of four-inch vent stack packed with hypergolics. We're talking Apollo Eleven here."

Boldt's knees felt weak. He whispered, "My family was in there."

Thirty minutes passed incredibly slowly. The bomb man confirmed the existence of a detonator. A wet-vac vacuum was sent to the roof. Tension filled the air as the top membrane was intentionally punctured and the vent stack's contents carefully removed.

One of Lofgrin's assistants approached and spoke to him. Lofgrin announced proudly to Boldt, "Silver-and-blue cotton."

"What?"

"We lifted some fibers from the windows we know he washed. You remember those fibers alongside the ladder impressions at

Enwright? They were a synthetic/cotton blend. Silver and blue. Mean anything to you?"

"The Seahawks," Boldt replied. Seattle's football team.

"Bingo," said Lofgrin. "Towels? A uniform? How do I know? That's your job. But we have fiber samples now, Sergeant. We can compare these to any evidence you might provide us. These fibers can put this boy away, Lou."

Boldt's eyes were trained on the roof of his house. "I'm with you, Bernie."

A decision was made to drill through Boldt's kitchen wall and drain the part B chemical from below. As this decision was being relayed, the night sky lit up with a thin column of purple flame that raced up through the clouds. It was less than four miles away, in Ballard. The distant sound resembled that of a jet taking off. Within minutes sirens screamed in the distance.

Lofgrin said, "We're okay here, Lou. You go see if your boy's up a tree with a carving knife."

Boldt didn't want to leave his own home, but he did. The crime scene work lasted until three in the morning, at which point he drove past his house and found it standing. Another woman was believed dead. There was word that all three television networks were sending New York crews to shoot the fire remains.

Boldt did not remember drifting off to sleep but was awakened at his desk at seven a.m. by an excited John LaMoia. "You remember Garman telling us his truck was stolen, his Werner ladder in the back?" He continued. "The truck was for real. But he never reported it stolen. More incredible, he never claimed the insurance."

Boldt focused on this a moment, allowed his head to clear. "Let's pick him up."

LaMoia beamed. "It's a beautiful morning, isn't it, Sarge?"

It was pouring rain outside.

ON THE way to Garman's house LaMoia and Boldt, accompanied by a patrol car following at a close distance, listened to the radio news. The latest victim was identified as Veronica DeLatario. Boldt could describe her before he ever saw her: dark hair, nice figure, mother of a boy between the ages of eight and ten. The radio shows blasted police for arresting the wrong man, Nicholas Hall, and chastised all city services for the huge display of manpower at a police sergeant's home—"one of their own"—while Veronica DeLatario was "being stalked" by a serial arsonist.

It came out that the police had received another poem earlier in the day, accompanied by a melted green piece of plastic, and "had done nothing about it."

LaMoia, unable to bear it any longer, switched to a jazz station.

Boldt's phone rang. It was Daphne. "Are you near a radio?"

"In the car."

"Well, fasten your seat belt and tune in to KOMO. Garman is in the process of confessing publicly to being our killer."

Boldt nearly drove the car into a sideswipe. "Garman just confessed," Boldt told LaMoia. Boldt punched the radio and located the station. Garman was well along in describing every last detail of his crimes.

Fifteen minutes later, when they pulled up in front of Garman's apartment, the man was still live on the radio. LaMoia tried the door, called out a warning, and then reared back and kicked the door open.

Steven Garman sat peacefully in a recliner, telephone in hand. He spoke into the receiver. "Looks like my ride has arrived."

LaMoia began reciting the Miranda. Boldt, charged with anger and rage, nonetheless walked calmly up to Garman, took the phone out of his hand, and cradled the receiver.

Garman said venomously, "If you had caught me sooner, fewer would have died. You have to live with that, Sergeant."

Boldt answered, "I may have to live with it, but you're going to die with it. I'd say I got the better deal."

WITHIN the hour the chief of police held a packed press conference declaring that Garman was in custody. There was a celebration on the fifth floor. Boldt did his best to appear cheerful for the sake of the troops, but when he spotted LaMoia and Matthews during the levity, their eyes showed the same reservations that he felt. Garman had called in one of the city's most notorious defense attorneys. There would be no interrogation. They had the radio confession on tape, but it was vague and lacked detail.

Bernie Lofgrin and his team of identification technicians missed the festivities because they were combing Garman's home for evidence. Boldt was deep in thought when Lofgrin phoned.

"I've got bad news, and then I've got bad news," Lofgrin began. "Which do you want first?"

"Garman's place is clean," Boldt said, guessing.

"No hypergolics, no Werner ladder, no window-washing gear, no blue-and-silver fibers," Lofgrin confirmed. "If we're looking for this guy's lab, we had better start looking somewhere else."

"Is that possible?" Boldt asked, looking up to see Daphne standing nearby. A group of photos in her hand raised Boldt's curiosity. She motioned toward the conference room and walked off.

"Frankly, Lou, I don't like it," Lofgrin continued. "It's *too* clean. We'd expect some kind of connective tissue: tree bark, a penknife."

"He's an investigator," Boldt reminded him. "If the lab is off-site, he's smart enough to change clothes—take precautions not to track evidence home. He confessed. Maybe he knew we couldn't find enough to make it stick. Maybe it's a game for him."

"Yeah? Well, he's winning. I'm thinking the most likely connection is still this ink. Connect a pen in the house to the threats."

"Leads to his lab, that's what I need, Bernie. Find me something pointing to his shop. You do that, I can go home and go to sleep."

"In that case, I'd start drinking coffee, I was you."

Boldt hung up, thinking about his wife. Amid all the eighteen-hour tours, Liz had come to town for the day and had, as far as Boldt knew, returned to the cabin, having never contacted him. He tried her cellular, got her voice mail, and told her, "The coast is clear, love. We're back in the house. I miss you all. Hurry home."

He walked slowly down the long hall to the conference room, attempting to collect his thoughts.

Daphne sat at the table alone under the unforgiving glare of fluo-rescent light. She directed him to the city map, into which she had stabbed several pushpins. "Dorothy Enwright, Melissa Heifitz, Veronica DeLatario. All in the same general area of town. Why?"

Boldt studied the map. "He lives there. He'd have a firm work-ing knowledge of the area."

Her lips pursed. "Listen, it's true that psychopaths often restrict their movements to an area a mile or two in radius from their resi-dences, but Garman is so far outside the profile of a psychopath that there's no reason to make the comparisons. I've listened to that so-called confession, and I've got to tell you, there's a clever mind at work here. You listen carefully, most of it is fluff. He's not confess-ing to anything. And does an intelligent man like Garman start killing women in his own backyard? I don't think so, Lou."

She stared at him through a long silence. "He's too big and heavy for your boy up the ladder, isn't he?" she asked rhetorically. "Same as with Hall. When do we face we have the wrong man?"

"Facing it and discussing it openly are two different issues," he answered. "Shoswitz will not want to hear it. Period. The brass is crowing all over the airwaves that we caught the big one."

"I understand that. But we can't go along with it. Neither of us believes Garman set those fires, and there's going to be another one, Lou," she said. "Let's say he's still out there. But now we have Gar-man trying to cover for him. Why?"

"Protecting someone," Boldt said.

"Look at this." She produced a photograph. "His ex-wife." She moved her hand out of the way, and Boldt saw a woman's face smil-ing back at him in the photograph.

"Peas in a pod," she said, producing a recent photograph of Enwright. The similarities between Enwright and the ex-wife were astounding. "And here's the photo of Heifitz." The similarity was there as well. "It's what triggers him, Lou—that particular look."

"So it might be Garman after all? You actually buy that?"

"Not for a minute," said Daphne. "There's a third participant. Someone we don't even know exists—didn't know until now."

DETECTIVE BOBBIE GAYNES hung up the phone in her office cubicle. "Lofgrin has confirmed that the silver fibers are a silver fabric paint," she told Boldt. "The underlying blue is the actual color of the fabric. Second, commercially available Seahawk jerseys are not a sixty/forty blend—they're twenty/eighty, polyester to cotton, so we can rule them out."

"And that leaves?" Boldt asked.

"Silk-screen printers who handle terry cloth," she answered. "These are a spiral-twisted cotton-blend fiber typically seen in a towel or a terry-cloth robe. We're down to determining what companies produce this particular color in this blend and, alternately, which silk-screen companies have purchased that fabric. The bad news is that there are six hundred ninety-seven printers in the Seattle area alone."

"With those numbers we're stewed," Boldt said. "But let's brainstorm it a minute and see where we get."

They took turns, Gaynes first. "Cotton fibers," she said.

"Silver paint, blue fabric."

"Seahawk colors."

"Silk-screen paint."

"Contract work."

He nodded slowly. *Contract work.* Why had that interrupted his thoughts? "Let's go on," he said, making note of it.

"Similar fibers were found on your windows and in the mud by the ladder at Enwright's," said Gaynes.

"Window washing," Boldt said.

"A rag maybe, a torn towel."

LaMoia arrived, clearly worked up.

"Brainstorming," Boldt said, holding up a hand to prevent LaMoia from interrupting.

The detective nodded. "I'm with you," he said.

Boldt retraced their steps, saying, "Fibers by the ladder."

Gaynes went next. "Window washing. Soapy water."

"Window washing," LaMoia said, his voice ominous.

"Glass," Boldt said.

"A squeegee."

"Glass," LaMoia echoed. "The cars!" he said. "The wheels!"

Boldt snapped his head up.

"The cars," LaMoia repeated. "My assignment, remember? Lab report placed an abundance of cotton fibers inside the *cars,*" he emphasized, his eyes wide. "Sarge, I need to check something out."

"Go," Boldt told him, and LaMoia took off.

IT WAS not such a long drive, but for Daphne it felt nearly interminable. Boldt had not been told about the meeting. It was the conspiracy between Ben and Daphne—the promise of seeing Emily—that had convinced Ben to cooperate with the police.

The meeting could not take place at Emily's, because Daphne remained concerned about the Scholar's whereabouts and media references to the participation of a local psychic and a twelve-year-old witness. Daphne was taking no chances.

Boldt would have been highly critical of her for arranging such a meeting, but her fears ran far beyond the tongue-lashing she might suffer. More important, she might lose her newly formed bond with Ben. She wondered if she was using the boy to soften the loss of a possible future with Owen Adler. In fact, she had barely thought about Owen over the past few days. She had rid herself of him, and it felt good on many levels. But if she lost Ben, the world was going to seem incredibly empty.

Daphne did not trust Emily. The woman played on superstitions, fears, and aspirations. She tricked people. Worst of all, Emily owned Ben's heart free and clear. Just the mention of her name drove the boy's eyes wide. Daphne realized that she was in many ways jealous of Emily.

Martin Luther King Boulevard was a four-lane road through a patchy neighborhood separated from Lake Washington's upscale enclaves by a steep ridge. Ben pointed out the park in the distance, where a row of cement obelisks loomed like support piers for a highway overpass. Daphne followed Ben's directions and pulled over where he indicated.

The sidewalk climbed a steady grade to reach a wide bike path that ran down the center of the park and served as its focus. Ben walked fast. "Stay close," Daphne called to him.

Ben's legs began to run underneath him before he managed to say to Daphne, "There she is!" He took off at lightning speed, his eyes welling with tears.

Perhaps it was the sound of his footsteps, perhaps Emily sensed his approach, as she could sense so much, but something caused her to spin around. As she did, her face lifted in a big moon of a smile, and she opened her arms.

Daphne let the boy have some distance. She owed the two of them a moment in private, given all she had put them through. She strolled the bike path, intrigued by a series of stone posts that rose to knee height on either side. She approached the nearest of these posts, admiring the tile work at its base.

The tile held an odd stick-figure drawing, evoking a Native American pictograph. Surrounding the tile's perimeter was a quotation: "Crooked is the path of eternity." Nietzsche. She walked to the next post: more primitive art and a quote. Heart pounding, she hurried to the next post, where she read words emblazoned on her memory: *Suddenly a flash of understanding, a spark that leaps across to the soul.* Plato. The same quote that had accompanied a melted piece of green plastic. She hurried from one post to the next. A dozen such quotations and pictographs. She stopped and stared: *He has half the deed done, who has made a beginning.*

The first of the threats: Dorothy Enwright. The Scholar! He had walked or ridden through this park. The Bible-thumping disturbed man in the trees had not lined up well for her with poetic intellect, but with this discovery the two melded into one: a plagiarist with little education and the need to appear smart; a sociopath intent on burning women.

And then came the most important thought of all: The arsonist lived somewhere in the area.

"Quick, Ben!" she shouted. "We have to go. Right now!"

BOLDT WAS AWAITING A MEETING with King County Medical Examiner Dr. Ronald Dixon in the basement of the Harborview Medical Center when Dr. Roy McClure, Liz's internist, approached him. The two men shook hands.

McClure perched on the edge of the couch. "How are you taking it?" he asked with great sympathy.

"It's unsettling," Boldt admitted.

"I should say it is. The real battle is psychological. Attitude is ninety percent of the game. How about the kids?"

"The kids? They're fine, I think," Boldt answered. "I haven't seen them in a while, quite honestly. Liz has had them."

"Well, I certainly understand that," McClure replied.

"You know, Roy, I get the feeling that we're having two different conversations here."

"You'll feel that way from time to time. The world won't make any sense. The temptation may be to bury yourself in work, but the prudent course is to talk it out. Give Liz all the support you can."

"I *was* talking about work," Boldt stated. He felt too tired for conversation. He wished McClure would go away.

"I'm talking about Elizabeth."

It wasn't the doctor's words that jolted Boldt so much as the ominous tone of voice. Boldt felt a sickening nausea twist his stomach. "Liz? Roy, what are you talking about?"

"I'm talking about your wife's lymphoma, Lou. Your wife's life. Your children. You. How you are all coping with this."

Boldt's ears rang as if someone had detonated an explosive in the room. Though he struggled to get out some words, nothing happened. He could not move. Tears gushed down his cheeks and he felt himself swoon.

McClure's strong grip upon his shoulders brought Boldt back. "She didn't tell you." It was a statement. Definitive.

Boldt felt himself shake his head. "Is it . . . ?" He couldn't say the word, but McClure's expression was enough. Boldt pictured Liz looking so sad in the bathtub, recalled her request to spend time alone with the children. The pieces suddenly came together.

"It metastasized quickly," McClure answered. "Stage four by the time we caught it."

Tears continued to cascade down Boldt's face. He felt trapped inside a small dark box. It was a dream, he convinced himself. A nightmare. He would awaken and find himself at Harborview, awaiting his meeting with Dixon. "The baths?" he mumbled.

"They help with the pain," McClure said. "She's in a tremendous amount of pain."

BOLDT drove straight home, his shoulders shaking, his lips trembling. Time had stopped, yet a clock ran inside his head and heart as never before. Guilt banged at his chest for distrusting her. He dragged his shirtsleeve over his eyes.

Every second, every moment seemed a lost opportunity. So many had passed while he took their life together for granted. It seemed so fast, so quick. They had drifted apart and back together, like boats riding the ebb and flow of the tides. He felt anger, love, terror all combine in an inescapable emotional avalanche, with him at the bottom, looking up. It wasn't fair.

They help with the pain. Boldt pressed his hands to his ears. He didn't want McClure's words circulating inside his head. He wanted to awaken, to wash the nightmare from him.

At the house, Marina, the sitter, opened the door, the smile on her face replaced with a look of concern. "Mr. Boldt?"

"She here?"

A shake of the head. "Work."

Was she back at work? He couldn't remember what day it was. "The kids?"

On cue, Miles rounded the corner, yelped, "Daddy!" and held his arms outstretched for his father, who scooped him up and broke into tears. Marina gasped, "Everything okay?"

Miles cuddled himself around Boldt's neck, clinging tightly. Boldt nodded, tears dripping from his chin. He felt exhausted. He didn't want a world without Liz. He wanted to take her away, as if by leaving she might leave the illness behind as well.

His pager sounded. Boldt moved his jacket aside and looked at the device. It seemed attached to someone else. The pager had a sobering effect on him. There he was, once again faced with his job versus his relationship, and despite all the reasoning, all the regret of the last hour, it wasn't as simple as dropping the pager into the trash. The Scholar was out there. He knew this to his core.

Boldt pulled the pager off his belt. An internal voice asked, How could you? And there was no immediate answer. He had responsibilities to his team, to the city, to the innocent, but none of that entered his mind. All he could think was that he knew he was going to call in the summons, and that whatever it was would take him away from there, racing off to the next emergency.

He felt his throat constrict with grief, and he forced out the words. "Tell her I came by. Tell her I'm on the cell phone."

He reached the office on the radio from the car. The dispatcher said, "Message is from Detective LaMoia. 'Must talk ASAP.' "

Boldt squeezed the talk button. "Tell him I'm on my way."

He felt like a traitor and a cheat. He stopped at a church on his way downtown. To his surprise he felt a lot better.

AS THE elevator doors slid open on the fifth floor of the Public Safety Building, the painful silence inside Boldt's shattered psyche was cracked open by the cacophony of reporters all shouting at once, boom microphones waving in the air. In the blinding glare of television lights Shoswitz fought a path through to Boldt and escorted his sergeant to homicide's door, shouting, "No comment."

As the door opened for the pair, Boldt's own people fell in around him: Gaynes, LaMoia, Lofgrin from the lab, and several uniformed officers.

"What is it?" Boldt asked as the group entered the conference room.

An exasperated Shoswitz proclaimed, "It's another poem."

Daphne informed Boldt, as if it hardly mattered, "A reporter found it in Garman's morning mail. Not us."

"The Scholar is still out there!" Shoswitz declared.

Boldt just looked at him and shook his head. "Everybody out," he told those gathered. He held Daphne by the elbow, detaining her. "John, you stay," he told LaMoia. When the room was empty, Boldt closed the door, and the three of them were finally alone.

"The content of the poem," Boldt asked. "Is it significant?"

Daphne answered with her back to him. "Significant? I fouled up. He's no scholar, Lou. The profile is off." Boldt was able to leave his own sorrows briefly and recognize how upset she was. "There's a park built on top of the I-90 tunnel coming in from the floating bridge, a bike path running through it." She described her discovery of the various quotations. She repeated reluctantly, "The profile is all wrong. He's uneducated. Sociopathic. I'd put money on there being a revenge issue with Garman."

"That fits with what we've found out," LaMoia said. "Garman's tax returns for the '70s show *two* dependents."

"Two?" Boldt echoed, marveling at the detective's contacts. "So Garman has a child. Does that fit?" he asked Daphne. "A father would certainly cover for his child."

"And a child would vent anger against the father," Daphne said. "Given the right circumstances, a child might symbolically kill the mother, repeatedly kill the mother's look-alikes. Send the father threats. Do the kills on the father's turf, using what the child learned from the father: fire."

Boldt felt a chill, not heat. "That's a lot of anger."

She nodded. "Perhaps Garman's only guilty of being a protective father. Probably thought the killings would stop if he took the fall, if he ended up in jail."

"Why?" Boldt asked.

LaMoia spoke. "It was something that happened in North Dakota," he said. "One hell of a fire."

"I DON'T see my attorney," Steven Garman said as Boldt and Daphne stepped through the cell door. LaMoia remained on the other side of the bars. "I've got nothing to say without my attorney present," Garman added.

Daphne and Boldt sat down on the bunk opposite. By agreement, Daphne would be the first to break the silence. They would take turns after that.

They remained perfectly still for the better part of five minutes, the arrested man looking increasingly nervous. Finally Daphne said, "We can't match the notes with your handwriting."

Boldt told him, "The individual committing these arsons weighs sixty pounds less than you do."

LaMoia chimed in. "All the quotes are collected in a single source. Maybe you might enlighten us what that source is."

Garman's eyes continued to tick between them.

"You never reported your pickup truck stolen," Boldt said.

LaMoia added, "How is it you lose a seven-thousand-dollar truck and don't apply for insurance?"

Perspiration appeared on Garman's skin. "My attorney."

"We've notified him. He'll be here eventually," Boldt said. "Tell us about the fire," he added, intentionally ambiguous.

"Which fire?" Garman smiled slightly. "I've seen a few."

"The North Dakota air force base," Daphne said.

"Your trailer," said LaMoia. "It burned to the ground, according to the reports. Listed as accidental. But Fidler—you know Sidney Fidler—spoke to a couple of folks who remembered that burn. It was extremely unusual in that the water hoses appeared to add fuel to the fire. The thing just got hotter and hotter. That's hypergolic rocket fuel, Garman. You understand our curiosity."

Garman's eyes flashed between them.

Daphne spoke. "Was Diana unfaithful? Was that it?"

The suspect's jaw slacked open. He said vehemently, "You don't know anything about it."

Daphne glanced at Boldt and offered him a faint nod. LaMoia had come through with the name of Garman's son only moments before the questioning. He had pulled it off of medical insurance records that painted an ugly picture.

Boldt said softly, "Jonathan Carlyle Garman. He was admitted to the hospital on the Grand Forks base, June 14, 1983. Third-degree burns to the face and upper body. Seven months of reconstructive surgery followed."

Daphne pleaded, "Tell me it was Diana you meant to harm. Tell me you didn't mean for the boy to be hurt."

"Mother of God!" Garman said, hanging his head in his huge hands, his back shaking violently as he cried. Then through his sobs he said, "She took him with her. Kidnapped him. And not out of love, but because of the things he knew, because of things she had done to him. . . ."

"We're not here to judge you," Daphne whispered. "Only to find Jonathan. It's the boy who needs our help."

Garman sobbed for five of the longest minutes in Boldt's life. The minutes ticked by, the evening drawing ever closer, and the promise of another arson along with it. Another victim.

The phone company had no record of a Jonathan Garman; there was no driver's license in motor vehicle's database. Other sources were being checked, but it appeared that the arsonist either existed outside of the paper shuffle or within an alias.

"I never meant it the way it happened," Garman finally gasped. "She had been selling herself. Made the boy a part of it."

Boldt released a huge sigh and sat back on the bunk. Sometimes he hated the truth.

Footsteps were coming down the hall, and all three police officers looked in that direction. The guard handed Boldt a message.

Boldt looked up from the note. "It's a car wash," he said.

IN THE same afternoon the lab techs had determined that the blue-and-silver cotton fibers collected inside the cars of two of the arson victims matched not only each other but the fibers found on Boldt's kitchen window and those collected at the Enwright fire. The FBI crime lab kept the chemical signatures of paints on file. They could ID the manufacturer. Lofgrin's assistants were tracing the sale of that particular silver to only five silk-screen printers in the Northwest.

The fifth printer contacted, in Coeur d'Alene, Idaho, recognized the order by its color combination: fifteen hundred hand towels ordered by Lux-Wash and Detailing, Inc., Seattle. The towels carried the Lux-Wash logo. On the reverse side was printed GO SEAHAWKS!

Back in the conference room, which was churning with activity, Boldt sat down heavily. He said to Bobbie Gaynes, "So it could be any one of fifteen hundred Lux-Wash customers."

"No, I don't think it's a customer," the detective corrected. "This is a yuppie scrub. Eleven bucks a wash. Customer goes inside and drinks espresso while the wheels go down the line. Total vacuum, and windows *inside* and out. And the drying crew uses these promo towels. We're pulling employment tax records."

"He may not be on the payroll," advised Daphne. "He'll work part-time, possibly for cash. He may have worked at several car washes. The car wash is his trolling phase."

"Do we have a list of full-service car washes?" Boldt asked.

"We do," called out a uniformed patrol officer. "Seven within our jurisdiction, including two Lux-Washes."

"He moves around?" Shoswitz asked.

Daphne spoke up. "Not by choice. He carries that face around with him. He's not comfortable meeting new people, establishing himself in a scene."

Boldt found her familiarity with the suspect unsettling. He told the gathering, "The plastic mask our young witness thought he saw was this guy's skin. He's badly disfigured."

"We initiate clandestine video surveillance of Lux-Washes immediately," Shoswitz stated.

The phones in the room rang regularly. Each time one purred, Boldt hoped it was Elizabeth but then realized he had not forwarded his calls to the conference room.

He noticed a woman from the prosecuting attorney's office as she spoke up for the first time. She said, "What evidence do we have against this man?" She looked at Boldt, then at Daphne. "Not these towels, I hope. If we're going to walk this guy to death row, we're going to need some serious evidence. You need him to lead you to this stolen fuel—something like that." She wasn't being antagonistic, but her questions were probing to the point where Boldt felt uncomfortable.

Daphne arched her eyebrows. Boldt knew her too well. He said to her, "You have a plan, don't you?"

Daphne nodded, straight-faced and serious. Dragging out a copy of the department's personnel directory, she opened it and produced a photograph of a patrolwoman named Marianne Martinelli. Alongside it she placed a photo of Steven Garman's wife, Diana. The similarity between the faces was impossible to miss.

Her voice confident, Daphne explained to Boldt, "Maybe we get lucky and we follow him right to his next victim. Officer Marianne Martinelli. She's a dead ringer for the mother. Once she comes through that car wash, we can take him by a nose ring and lead him right to the home of our choice. He lifts their addresses off the vehicle registration, right? That's what we're guessing. So we give him an address. He shows up with his window-washing gear, prepared to pretend he's got the wrong place, and we have him right where we want him, chemicals and all. We get our man."

"And Martinelli gets an ulcer," Gaynes said.

Boldt called out loudly, "Anybody here know Marianne Martinelli?" Every eye in the room fell immediately on John LaMoia.

LaMoia looked like the cat caught with the mouse. He shrugged innocently. "She and her husband were separated for a while. So we had a few dates. So what?"

"Work the charm, John," Boldt ordered. "We need a volunteer."

THE events of the next ninety minutes ran like a video in fast-forward. At one seventeen p.m. the radio room alerted Boldt that a suspect had been identified at the Lux-Wash in Greenwood. His description included a slight frame, one hundred and thirty to one hundred and fifty pounds, and a face hidden by a sweatshirt and sunglasses.

On the way up to the surveillance Boldt stopped at home to leave a note for Liz. As he entered the kitchen, he broke into tears. Everywhere he looked he saw Liz, everything he touched. He could recall their discussions, holidays, birthdays, lovemaking—somehow he couldn't remember the bad times, only the good. It was not only for Liz that he wept but, selfishly, for himself as well, both out of self-pity and fear. He begged God for some kind of explanation and apologized for the years he had failed to pray, wondering if prayers could be heard when absent for so long.

How would he tell her that he knew? He wondered if he had any right to know or if she needed time to face this for herself first before sharing it with him. He had no idea what knowledge of one's own imminent death would inflict upon a person.

He dried his eyes and stepped out into the harshness of sunlight. Marina and the kids were being dropped off by Marina's husband, not Liz. For a moment his sentence was commuted. He greeted Miles and Marina and kissed Sarah. When the tears flowed again, he walked directly to his car and drove off, his little boy waving good-bye with troubled eyes.

CHAPTER TEN

WHAT do you think?" Daphne asked Boldt. They stood in the far corner of a parking lot, behind an abandoned supermarket, four blocks from the Lux-Wash. The surveillance radio traffic ran in a stream through Boldt's earpiece.

Daphne was referring to the car. On the floor of the passenger's side were some of Ben's work sheets from school. On the dash was a Tonka toy dump truck and a G.I. Joe action figure. In the back seat was a pair of kid's beat-up running shoes and one of Ben's three backpacks, which she had borrowed without asking.

"It's convincing," Boldt stated.

"We need the connection to a child to be made. The boy must be a trigger," she said. "That and the similarity to his mother."

"You sold me," Boldt said. "Now all we have to do," he added, studying the car's exterior, "is get this thing nice and dirty."

At five minutes after three Officer Martinelli, dressed in jeans and a sweatshirt, driving a Ford Explorer, entered the Lux-Wash. Martinelli's arrival was timed to place her car in the proper order so that the suspect would be the worker to clean her car's interior.

In the SPD's maroon surveillance van the video monitor flashed. Martinelli's radio channel filled with static. "I'm inside," the detective said. The monitor displayed a fish-eye view of the inside of the car's front seat.

Dialogue from Martinelli's microphone came through clearly as a male voice told her, "We're not allowed to touch your personal stuff, ma'am. You'll have to pick it up some if we're gonna vacuum for ya."

Daphne instructed into Martinelli's earpiece, "Leave it."

"Do what you can," Martinelli said.

On-screen, those in the van watched a pair of workers vacuum the floors. Martinelli was reported heading toward the reception area.

Boldt never took his eyes off the monitor as a man started to climb into the front seat, rag in one hand, spray bottle of cleanser in the other. The fuzzy video signal was of the worker's shoulders and the back of his head. "Show us your face, pal," Boldt encouraged the window washer.

"Go," Daphne told Martinelli, picturing the patrolwoman hurrying back to the car as if she had forgotten something. "Remember, you're a bitter and overworked mother. And you're just about at wits' end."

Martinelli yanked the earpiece from her ear, as directed, and walked toward Jonathan Garman with the swagger of a stuck-up woman. "Young man," she said, raising her hand derisively, stepping up to him and looking into his sunglasses.

The skin was not something he had been born with but had been applied to a face ravaged by fire. His nose looked like something made of clay by a first-year art student. That nose and his upper cheeks were all he allowed to be visible. Martinelli could imagine the scar tissue around the hole of a mouth. He cowered, painfully shy. And then as he looked at Martinelli, his body seized as if jolted by an electrical shock.

In as condescending a tone as she could muster she said, "My little angel has spilled some pop all over the dashboard. It's in front of the passenger seat. Be a good boy and clean it off for me."

She stepped closer to Garman. "You're not going to make a problem for me, are you?" She fumbled in her purse, held up a dollar bill. She stuffed the dollar into his unwilling hand. According to Matthews, he would abhor any physical contact with her. He would despise her for it and for her condescending tone. She repeated, "The pop on the dash. Did you hear me?"

"Spilled pop on the dash," he uttered in a voice that sounded like coarse sandpaper on bare metal. Martinelli felt a chill.

"That's better," she said, and walked away with a haughty and arrogant gait. She did not glance back. That voice had terrified her.

Boldt and Daphne watched as Jonathan Garman climbed into the Explorer hurriedly. For a long count of three he stared at a photo of Ben taped to the visor. He cleaned the dash, working his way toward the glove box. Inside was the vehicle's registration with the address of a safe house—114 Lakewood Avenue South. Go for the glove box! Daphne mentally encouraged.

"We've got problems," Boldt said as the suspect climbed out of the front seat and into the back. His rag worked furiously against the glass. Garman pushed the far door open, backing out of the vehicle, still wiping as he went.

Daphne sat transfixed. They would have to wait to study the tape recorded inside the car. But as far as she could tell, Garman had never gone for the glove box. It seemed impossible that she had judged him incorrectly. She mumbled, "I can't believe it."

Boldt too seemed in a daze. He wouldn't look over at her; for Daphne that said enough. "We go ahead as planned," Boldt said.

"We watch and see what he does. We'll stay with him, Daffy. We can beat the odds."

"I'm sorry," she apologized in a hushed whisper. But not to him, as he believed. Her apology was to Jonathan Garman's targeted victim—the one for whom he had sent the poem. The one she feared was scheduled to die.

BEN waited with Susan in the houseboat for an hour before they both became restless. Daphne was late, and Susan would not leave him alone there.

She suggested they head down to the police department. "I can't stay with you, Ben. You'll have to wait for her there."

"I'll wait here," he suggested for about the fifth time.

"Don't test me, young man. It's downtown or the youth detention center. Your choice."

"Downtown," he answered, terrified at the thought of going to the center.

When Ben and Susan stepped through homicide's controlled door, the place was jumping, cops hurrying back and forth, some with their guns showing, which Ben thought was cool. Susan pointed to a chair pushed up against the wall and told Ben to take a seat. She headed down the hall to look for Daphne.

Ben was alone for the first time in ages. He couldn't get his mind off Emily. If he just got up and walked through that door . . .

He carefully checked his pocket to make sure he still had the five bucks Daphne had given him for emergencies. He slipped off the chair, glancing around. Susan remained out of sight. He walked casually toward the exit, a kid looking for the bathroom. The moment he rounded the corner, he broke into a run.

AT FOUR forty-three p.m. the telephone at 114 Lakewood Avenue South rang. Patrolwoman Marianne Martinelli answered tentatively.

It was Boldt. "The suspect is still at the car wash. We expect him to remain there until five p.m. After that he'll be under constant surveillance, and you'll be notified of his movement."

"I copy that," she said.

"We're sending you a UPS delivery," Boldt reported. "Some mace, a fire hood, a bottle of oxygen. If he does watch your place, we'll want you to leave the house, leaving it completely dark."

"Yes. I understand."

"We'll have the place covered," Boldt said. "He shows up, we nab him."

The UPS truck pulled up at four fifty-five, and John LaMoia, dressed in a brown uniform, knocked on the door. He made Martinelli sign for the package. The two of them went through a charade then, for the benefit of anyone who might be watching. Martinelli held up a backpack, as if she wanted to send it. LaMoia returned to the truck and brought her back a paper box. She filled out a label, and the backpack went into the box.

Inside Ben's backpack was a videotape recorded by the hidden camera inside the Explorer, which promised a good look at Garman's activities inside the vehicle. LaMoia took the package and left.

In the house again, Martinelli heard over her radio that Jonathan Garman had just left the car wash.

> SURVEILLANCE 1: We got a problem. Suspect is leaving by bicycle, not a car. He's heading east. He's wearing a blue sweatshirt, hood up, jeans, riding a gray mountain bike. Sunglasses.
>
> BOLDT: Copy. Stay with him, One.

Daphne and Boldt were still inside the maroon van two blocks away. The dispatcher barked orders, deploying various surveillance teams. But Garman rode fast, passing cars on the right, crossing on red lights at pedestrian crosswalks. Dispatch scrambled to keep up. Garman rode south across Montlake Bridge. The road grew steep and difficult, and twice all visual contact was lost. With no apparent intention on his part, Jonathan Garman was giving them hell.

When Boldt called for a helicopter, Daphne realized they were in trouble. But the order for the chopper came too late. Entering a short cul-de-sac, the suspect jumped the sidewalk through a series of posts installed to stop vehicular traffic. He shot down a hill and vanished amid a light drizzle that turned the air the same color gray as the sky.

A bead of cool sweat trickled down Daphne's rib cage as the radio reports confirmed the disappearance. Beside her, Boldt was frantic. "He spotted us. He made us," Boldt said.

"I don't think so," Daphne said. "Not one surveillance report indicated any paranoid behavior on his part. He was riding a route, that's all. To the truck? To his lab? Who knows? A route, is all."

Then came the final straw. As the van bumped along the Seattle streets, the dispatcher turned around in his chair and said to Daphne, "Matthews, a message from headquarters. Someone named Ben has escaped."

Daphne gasped. "Pull this thing over!" she shouted.

LOU Boldt was a knot of emotions. Since the videotape shot at the car wash did not show Garman going for the glove box, there was no apparent basis for a surveillance operation, which meant that when Shoswitz looked for a scapegoat, he did not have to look very far. Aside from a psychological profile, Boldt had only his twelve-year-old witness to connect Jonathan Garman to any crime whatsoever—and now he had lost both Garman *and* the witness.

Standing in Lieutenant Shoswitz's office, Boldt prepared to eat crow. They had a fire inspector in lockup who had confessed to the arsons. Under questioning, Steven Garman had also confessed to setting fire to his estranged wife's house trailer, a fire that had burned his son to disfigurement, proving in the eyes of many that he was capable of just about anything. With Garman's confessions firmly in hand, the top brass upstairs had put the Scholar's reign of terror to bed, assuring the public the fires were over. Shoswitz was pushing Boldt to drop the surveillance.

"I don't know what to believe," Shoswitz said. "I mean, we are way late with this Jonathan Garman stuff, and they," he said, pointing overhead, "are not going to buy it. We've got *nada*. Zilch. Zippo. A kid drying windows in a car wash."

"We've got the towels. The fibers," Boldt reminded him.

"A thousand lousy towels over a six-month period," Shoswitz said. "Look, the only way out of this is to drop it. We pull Martinelli and send her home, we say a few thank-yous to all those involved, and we bury it in the budget somewhere and hope no one asks any questions."

"I think we should keep the surveillance running for tonight."

"Did you watch the video?" the lieutenant asked. "He never picked up the ball. He never went for that glove box."

"Maybe he has access to computers and can run the tags or something," Boldt said. "Give me my team for another day. LaMoia, Gaynes, Bahan, and Fidler. One day. Martinelli too. Drop the vans, the techies, the overtime."

"No way!" Shoswitz bellowed. "Bahan and Fidler stay where they are, working up Garman senior into something we can take to court. You and the others? I turn my back. I don't see. But I don't hear about it either. As far as I'm concerned, you're working on evidence against Garman. You need his son as a possible witness. A witness. That's all. Someone who can provide the state with damning testimony about Steven Garman setting that arson in North Dakota."

"Jonathan Garman is the Scholar, Lieutenant. His father is covering for him, that's all."

"And doing a fine job of it." He looked Boldt directly in the eye. "Go find your witness. Bring him in, and we'll chat him up and maybe something changes. But until then, not a peep to anybody. No hysterical comments about the Scholar still being out there. Mess this up and you're all alone."

Boldt nodded. He felt the tears coming again. "All alone anyway," he mumbled, heading to the door, thinking of Liz. His ears were ringing, and his right hand had tensed into a solid fist.

"WHERE is he?" Daphne demanded.

Ben's eye was trained to the peephole in Emily's kitchen wall. He couldn't see the front door, but he recognized Daphne's voice. His heart sank. Why was it that no matter what he did he disappointed someone?

"Ben? He's not here," Emily said defiantly.

"I have enough probable cause to search this property," Daphne said, "and that is exactly what I intend to do."

That was enough for Ben. He used the bathroom window and hit the ground running, thinking ahead. They were sure to check his house as well. He could get the sleeping bag from his room and head up to the tree fort. He could come back to Emily's in the morning.

It was raining, but he barely felt it. He splashed along sidewalks, down alleys, and through familiar backyards. He ran as if his life depended on it. He ran for his freedom.

"WE'RE getting somewhere with this ink," Bernie Lofgrin informed Boldt, stopping him in the hallway. Boldt was on his way to the communications room to initiate the dismantling of the surveillance of 114 Lakewood, where Marianne Martinelli waited as a possible target. He intended to leave LaMoia on that surveillance and move Gaynes to the park where Daphne had found the quotations, his two best chances at picking up Garman's trail again.

"It's not a Bic, a Parker, a Paper Mate, or any of a dozen other pens commonly available," Lofgrin said. "That's good news, believe me. What we do is graph the ink's chemical components—"

"I appreciate it, Bernie. But Shoswitz has pulled the plug, okay?"

Lofgrin appeared crushed. "Listen, the Bureau has all this stuff on file, chromatographs of every ink manufactured: ballpoint, felt tips, you name it. You bring me this guy with a pen in his pocket, and I can tie him to every one of those poems."

"We lost him, Bernie."

"A bicycle. I heard." He checked his watch. "You going home?"

"Can't do it," Boldt said. He wanted to go home, yet he didn't want to confront Liz. He wanted to comfort her, but he wanted her to tell him about the illness, not the other way around.

The evening's twilight was quickly fading. It would be dark soon, which would make surveillance efforts more difficult. Daphne had jumped out of the van forty minutes earlier, and Boldt hadn't heard from her since.

He hurried on toward the communications room. He willed his pager not to sound, for he feared it would mean another fire, another victim. And though that might prove him right about the Scholar's still being at large, it was a price he was unwilling to pay.

DAPHNE pulled up a chair in the tech services room. She plugged in the car-wash surveillance tape from Ben's backpack and hit PLAY.

Jonathan Garman entered the vehicle, took one long look at the photo of Ben, then set about squirting the windows with his spray bottle and wiping the glass with that towel. He cleaned the inside of the windshield, both side windows, the dashboard. Garman climbed into the back, where he attacked the rear window. He leaned over, nearly vanishing from sight, and surfaced with an ashtray in his hand, the unseen contents of which he dumped into a plastic trash bag. He shuffled out backward and closed the door.

He never looked in the glove box.

Daphne rewound and replayed the tape. The only brief moment the suspect disappeared was when he was in the back seat, not the front—and that did her no good whatsoever.

She ejected the tape, the sense of failure a bitter taste in her mouth. A tech caught up to her in the hallway and handed her Ben's backpack, returning it, reminding her of the boy and further disappointment. She carried it to her car and tossed it onto the seat.

She drove with her headlights on through early evening rain, going a little too fast when a light changed to yellow. She braked hard, and the car lurched to a stop.

The backpack flew off the front seat and onto the floor mat. Daphne leaned forward and hoisted it back by one of its straps.

The light changed, but Daphne didn't see it. Her attention was fixed on the backpack—the same pack that had been in the back seat of the Explorer. There, slipped into a plastic window, was an identification tag listing Ben's name and Jackson Street address.

Jonathan Garman had not needed to open the glove box. The address was available to him in the back seat. If Garman was watching any house, it was the Santori house, not 114 Lakewood.

As she hung a U-turn, Daphne was thinking about Ben and the fact that she had not bothered to check *his* home, where he clearly might hide in a panic.

She parked a block short of the Santori house on Jackson. She reached for her cellular phone to call for backup but reconsidered. She wanted to avoid making a fool of herself for the second time in the same day. Prudence dictated that she investigate further before calling it in.

Gripping the handgun inside her purse, she took a deep breath and left her vehicle. Up the hill was a small park. Tall trees, she thought, believing Garman would be found there, but she would not look up into the overhead branches and risk giving herself away. She would go inside and hope to find Ben.

She walked to the back of the house. A sheet of plastic covered the hole of broken glass where Nicholas Hall had forced his way inside. She punched through the plastic and let herself in.

Daphne glanced around the worn kitchen, suddenly thinking of everything as a trigger—the faucets, the toilets. But if Lofgrin was right, not the wiring. She threw the light switch. Nothing happened. Would he have had time to set his charge? She doubted it. Watch the house for action tonight, wash the windows in the morning.

She called Ben's name, moving room to room. A shiver passed through her. Garman was watching the house—she could *feel* it.

BEN heard the back door of his house slam shut and immediately lifted his head to the open window of the crude tree house. Jack Santori was still under arrest, so who . . . ? The kitchen light came on and, a few seconds later, the living-room light.

Ben had been crashed out in the tree house, waiting for tomorrow. He'd return to Emily and present his plan: They'd run away together. A new beginning. He was too excited to sleep, so he just lay in the dark, biding his time. And then the back door.

A light went on in his bedroom. What was going on?

Ben crept out onto the main limb to see down into his bedroom. When a beam of white headlights spread through the treetops, he paused briefly, waiting for them to pass.

That was when he saw the man perched in a nearby tree.

He gasped, and his release of air brought him to the man's attention. The guy was right at the same height, maybe thirty feet off the ground, three trees away. Ben recognized him immediately. He wore a sweatshirt pulled up on his head, though he had ditched the sunglasses since Ben had seen him at the airport.

The headlights swept past. The darkness washed the man out of sight, and Ben moved faster than his legs had ever moved before. He swung, one limb to the next, down, down. Glancing left, he saw the other guy descending too, and making better time, checking on Ben the entire way.

The guy had that same look Jack Santori had on a bad night. He intended to hurt Ben. Down . . . down. The guy had only a couple of limbs to go; Ben had fifteen feet.

The decision was not so much a conscious thought as an act of survival. His instincts propelled him off that limb, threw him into an open-armed jump that began with a scream and ended with the solid impact of both legs striking the ground. He hit hard, but no bones broke. And had his glass eye not popped out with the contact, he might never have thought of what came next. But he had played this game too many times not to think of it. He played dead.

Ben held his breath, popped both eyes wide open, and made no attempt to wipe the trickle of blood from his nose. Holding his breath was the hardest but also the most important to the performance. His chest could not move at all.

The man from the tree was down by the time Ben hit, and he ran to get a look at the boy. He reached Ben's silent body just as Daphne's voice cut through the woods, calling, "Ben? Ben?" The man glanced hotly in the direction of the voice, bent over, and looked directly into Ben's face, wincing as he saw the hollow eye socket. He tested Ben with the toe of his running shoe, checking for life. The two locked eye to eye, Ben getting a perfectly clear look at the man, who saw a fallen boy, dead of a broken neck.

The faceless man with eyes like a Halloween pumpkin—carved and artificial—hurried off through the woods as the back door banged shut: Daphne giving up.

Ben heard the man work back toward the small park. He heard the distinctive sound of a bike chain. He sat up, the image of the man a silhouette through the woods as he pedaled away. Wiping his bloody nose on his sleeve, Ben hurried to the shed behind his house. His bike was there. He had to follow the guy.

He did it for Emily, he told himself, and their chance for a future. He did it to help Daphne. But the truth was, he did it to erase the guilt of his earlier crime of taking the money. To be a hero. This was his chance. Leaving his glass eye behind, he jumped onto the bike and went speeding out his driveway.

CHAPTER ELEVEN

THE man with the dead face rode fast. Ben was riding as hard as he could, and it was like trying to chase a ghost.

They rode under the highway and turned into the International District. The Face, as Ben thought of him, connected up with Airport Way and started pumping like he was in some kind of race, growing smaller and smaller in the distance.

Ben felt all hope ride away with the guy. And then he heard the truck coming up fast from behind.

It was a stunt he had wanted to do a hundred times but had never had the belly to try. He pedaled hard, rising up off his seat, glancing once over his left shoulder, twisting his head around so his right eye could see back there. A good-sized truck, bigger than a pickup but smaller than a dump truck. Gaining on Ben.

His legs pushed hard. He needed to match the truck's speed. Gaining . . . gaining. It had to be exact. If he timed it wrong . . . Ben reached out and took hold of the truck. He was launched down the road like a rocket.

The truck picked up speed. Ben held on for dear life. Up ahead the tiny image of the Face on the bike grew larger as the truck closed the distance. Ben felt the wind in his smiling face. He wanted to cheer, to shout, to show everybody what he'd done. He felt empowered. A hero.

Suddenly the Face turned right and the bike pulled to a stop and the guy jumped off. The truck, and Ben with it, went whizzing right by. Ben looked back quickly to mark the location: U-STOR-IT—SELF-STORAGE UNITS AVAILABLE.

He looked ahead then, the road conditions worsening, potholes everywhere. He dodged left and right. Then, dodging one last pothole, he pulled the bike too far to the right, breaking his grip. He snapped his other hand onto the handlebars, and as he squeezed the back brake, the front wheel vibrated and danced with a life of its own. The truck lumbered on. Ben hit the curb and was launched through the air onto a patch of grass. He came to a stop sitting up, facing backward, his head swimming.

He felt his arms and legs. Nothing broken, he decided, for the second time in the same night. He glanced around. U-Stor-It was only a half mile behind him.

"CHECK it out," Lofgrin said proudly, hoisting up a pair of graphs for Boldt to compare. "The one on the left was downloaded from the FBI database. The one on the right is the chromatograph of the ink used on the Scholar's threats." They matched.

Boldt said, in a voice that sounded more like a prayer, "Tell me that two hundred thousand people in Seattle don't own this pen."

"They don't. It's from a company that specializes in cheap custom pens—giveaways. The kind that advertises in the back of magazines, 'Your logo here!' Golf clubs, hardware stores, rental shops."

"How big a field, Bernie? How many Seattle clients?"

"How many? How should I know? I match the graphs. That's *my* job. It's your phone call to make, not mine."

"*You* make the call, Bernie. Tonight—right now!"

Boldt smiled for the first time in days.

BEN pressed his face closer to the chain-link fence outside the automated gate to the U-Stor-It facility. The Face had evidently used the keypad to open the gate. And although Ben was curious to find out where the guy had gone, his eye lit on the pay phone outside the door marked OFFICE.

That pay phone called to him. Up and over the fence, a quick run across the open pavement, call Daphne. Tell her the Face was here. A hero. Back over the fence. Ride like hell. Simple.

He checked for traffic and began to climb.

It surprised him how loudly the fence rattled. Scared the life out of him. The more noise, the faster he climbed; the faster he climbed, the more noise. Finally he reached the top and threw a leg over. The wire bit into his thigh, and he let out a shout that cut off halfway when his brain kicked in and told him to shut up. He clawed his way down the other side and dropped to the blacktop.

What a mess, he thought, sprinting for the phone. A person would have to be deaf not to have heard that. What a stupid jerk!

He punched in 911—a number he was getting kind of used to.

"Emergency services," a man's voice said.

"This is Ben . . . Ben Santori. You gotta get a message to Daphne Matthews. She's a cop."

"I'm sorry, fella, we don't—"

"Listen to me!" he hissed. "She's at my house. S-a-n-t-o-r-i." Ben spelled it. "Call her. Tell her I followed the guy with the face. The *face*—remember that. It's an emergency—" He broke off. It sounded like a garage door. There it was again, the door, closing maybe. He dumped the phone into the cradle. The Face had heard him come over that fence. He was checking it out.

The storage units were built in long rows. Ben was closest to the end, near the gate. He spied more fence at the far end of the units and wondered if it wouldn't be safer to try getting over down there, away from the entrance. He sneaked off along the side of the building. He paused, listening, his heart hurting in his chest.

And then he saw a man's long, thin shadow stretch across the pavement to his right. It was the Face.

Out looking for him.

BERNIE Lofgrin came through. The pen company's client list showed four Seattle-area customers as having ordered ballpoint pens: a golf course, a dry cleaner, a self-storage company, and a Japanese restaurant.

Without hesitation Boldt took the self-storage company.

He decided to place the facility under surveillance, though he didn't want to drive too close without a first look. He stopped three blocks short on Airport Way and turned off his cellular phone so it wouldn't suddenly ring while he was poking around.

He headed off on foot, the U-Stor-It sign dimly visible a hundred yards ahead. His sense of certainty increased with each step. Garman could keep his father's stolen pickup truck there, could have his lab there. Self-store units were the perfect anonymous address. That Garman might have an unknown quantity of rocket fuel stored there did little to settle Boldt's nerves.

He moved along fence lines. He couldn't rule out the possibility, however remote, that Garman was at the facility. Boldt believed that Daphne might have been right after all: Garman could have taken the bait at the car wash. That suggested that he might be preparing for another arson. And where better than at a self-storage facility late at night?

DAPHNE found herself wondering what she was doing there in the Santori home. Fifteen minutes had passed since she had heard one of the neighborhood boys scream from the woods. Kids! She had actually allowed herself to believe it had been Ben.

The telephone rang, filling Daphne with anxiety. "Hello?"

"Daphne Matthews, please."

She wasn't sure how to answer. She was playing the roll of Marianne Martinelli, and it occurred to her that Garman might verify his victims by placing a call.

"My name's Marianne," she answered. "May I help you?"

"This is Seattle Communications Center. I'm calling for—"

She cut him off. "This is Matthews."

"It is or it isn't?"

"Lieutenant Matthews, Seattle Police."

"Okay. I got a weird message from some kid," the dispatcher told her. He read Ben's exact words. "We've got it on tape."

"An address? Do you have an address?" she called out.

"Sure do." He read her the address.

She went out of the Santori home at a full run. She wouldn't request backup from a patrol car, wouldn't put the boy at risk until she knew what was going on.

BOLDT increased his pace, removed his weapon from its holster, checked its load, and returned it to the leather.

The inspection of the gun rattled him. With Liz's illness, the importance of his own health, for the sake of their children, suddenly loomed large. He understood clearly for the first time why Liz was urging him to drop fieldwork. How long had she known about the cancer? What was he doing on a deserted stretch of industrial roadway, alone, sneaking up on a storage facility that could be the laboratory of a serial arsonist? Seen in this light, his situation seemed an act of foolishness.

He pulled into shadow, flipped open his phone, and turned it on. He wanted two pairs of plainclothes backup in unmarked cars. If he was going to do this, he was going to do it right.

He closed the phone, feeling better about his decision. At that moment a red Honda blurred past, slowed, and pulled to a stop a quarter mile past the U-Stor-It. Daphne. What was she up to?

Boldt began to run toward her.

BEN HAD COWERED IN HIS hiding place while the Face walked over to the fence and shook it loudly. He glanced around, then patrolled the place like a soldier, walking along the first row of storage units, passing twenty feet from Ben, who held his breath. A few minutes later the Face rounded the far corner, and Ben guessed he was going to check every row—ten or fifteen total.

Ben didn't dare break for the fence. It wasn't until several minutes later, when he heard the same sound of a garage door, that he decided the man had gone back inside his unit. Ben waited. Nothing. But what if the door shutting was a trick? What if the man had done it to fool Ben into *thinking* it was safe to make for the fence?

The possibility froze Ben in place. It was only as Daphne's red Honda pulled past out front—missed the place!—that Ben realized it was time to do something. Where was the army of cop cars like in the movies? The helicopters? Daphne, alone? Had 911 screwed up his message?

And what if the Face saw her? What then?

There was only one thing to do, Ben decided. He had to make his move. He ran to his right, away from the gate, around the office, and straight into a pair of arms that gripped him like a vise. He looked up into the white, shiny skin and hollow eyes, and his world began to spin. As total darkness came, a dry wind issued from the man's throat. "You?" he gasped, as if he too had seen a ghost.

DAPHNE was hiding behind a U-Haul trailer near the corner of the storage lot. When Boldt crept up on her, he scared her half to death.

"I might have shot you," she hissed at him, recovering.

Boldt disregarded the comment, his attention on the facility. "I didn't use the radio," he said, "so you didn't pick it up there."

"It was Ben." She explained about Ben's 911 call.

"He's *in* there?" Boldt asked incredulously.

"He claimed that he followed Garman here," she whispered. She seemed ready to cry. "Lou, why would he do this?"

Boldt was staying focused. "If Garman is in there too, who knows what we've got going?"

"I'm going in."

"Ridiculous," Boldt snapped. "I've called for backup. We wait him out, put up a net, take him on neutral ground."

"Who cares about *him?*" Daphne asked. "I'm talking about Ben. We have to get him out of there. Anything less than that and we invite a hostage situation."

Boldt grabbed her arm. "We don't know for a fact that the boy is in there. We cannot confirm that Garman is. What Ben reported and what actually is the case are two different animals."

"If you're suggesting reconnaissance," she said, "I'm in."

"We found out he's under the name Babcock at a rooming house over on Washington," Boldt informed her. "If he used the same name here, it would be in the files in the office. We'd know which unit is his."

"Forget him," she repeated. "We get Ben out."

"No way," he said.

"I'm sorry to do this," Daphne said, turning her head slowly to face him. Their eyes met. All at once she shoved him, sending him off-balance.

She took several long strides and leaped up onto the chain-link fence like a cat, vaulting it easily. She stole into the dark and was gone.

"I NEVER had me a little brother," Garman said to Ben as the boy came awake from unconsciousness. "I'm Jonny."

Ben found himself on the storage unit's cement floor, sitting in a back corner. His wrists were stuck together, as were his sneakers, sole to sole. His lips wouldn't open.

"Super Glue," Jonny explained. "Now don't go fighting it. You'll tear your skin, and I'll have to reglue you. Just sit still."

The sweatshirt hood was hanging down his back. The skin on his face looked like smooth white clay, but his ear looked like a big scab, yellow-and-rust colored. It took Ben a few minutes to adjust to not breathing out of his mouth. Every time he became too scared, he got dizzy and things would go soft and fuzzy.

Jonny was soldering something. There was a Coleman lantern going, making a loud hissing sound and throwing off a bright light.

"I ain't going to hurt you," Jonny said, reading Ben's thoughts. "You shouldn'ta followed me here, you know that."

Ben nodded, as terrified as he'd ever been. It looked like the guy was making some kind of bomb, all those wires coming out of a piece of plastic tubing.

"Why did you follow me?" he asked. "My face?"

Ben shook his head violently no. He dared to look into those eyes and felt light-headed again. He heard the words, "And now, 'cause of you, I gotta pack up and leave. Leave you here. Never killed no kid."

Ben tried to keep his eyes off the man, because every time he looked at him, he felt queasy. The area was occupied by a pickup truck, a pair of oil drums marked USAF, and lots of black plastic pipe. Stacked along the wall were boxes. There were two pictures in the place, a postcard of Jesus and a slightly larger image of a woman being burned at the stake.

Ben thought about God. He prayed to Him. He made all sorts of promises about how he would live his life, how he would obey Emily or whoever ended up taking care of him. He promised to listen. To learn respect. The prayers gushed out of him.

In his mind's eye he saw Daphne's red car driving past. He wanted so badly to believe it had been her car. Ben hung his head. He didn't want the man to see him crying.

BOLDT climbed the chain-link fence and landed at a run, pursuing Daphne around the side of the office building.

Daphne was athletic, a daily runner, and she was fast. If she had chosen to outrun Boldt, it would have been no contest, but her focus was on locating Ben, and she moved slowly, checking the shadows. Boldt bumped her from behind and whispered, "Move, move!" as he herded her to the end of the building. She glared at him but allowed him to guide her. He drove them into a recessed brick corner that felt protected and hissed, "Stupid move."

"He's here, dammit. You may not believe that, but—"

"We'll find him." He scanned the area. "We'll check the rows together, side to side. Listen, it's like a giant supermarket, these rows. We'll miss him if we don't do it in an organized way."

She nodded faintly. Boldt could sense her about to make another break. If she went running through the facility, she might get them all killed. "May I remind you," he said, "that Garman has an undetermined amount of rocket fuel? Just consider that."

"Point taken. Let's get on with it."

"Okay," Boldt said, forming a plan, wishing for the backup. "Right up against this first row. Weapons at the ready. We walk quietly, slowly. Round the next corner and make eye contact. Cross to the next row and start over. We're listening—for voices, for movement. Watch for trip wires, sensors maybe, who knows? Expect anything."

They moved methodically through the rows. Beyond the third set of blue units all doubts about Garman's whereabouts were suspended. A wash of pale light illuminated the fronts of the units that Boldt and Daphne faced. The source of that light was to Boldt's right. At the far end of the row Daphne's face appeared. They moved toward each other, ducking from one doorway to the next. Less than a minute later they stood on opposite sides of the garage door that was leaking light, ten feet apart. Boldt's heart pounded as he tried to discern the sound coming from within. It sounded like a cat hissing or water beginning to boil. But it was neither of these, he realized; it was the voice of Jonathan Garman, coming from a throat burned in a North Dakota fire.

Step by step they pulled back to the far corners. Boldt motioned toward the office, where they met outside a few minutes later.

"We're going to assume it's Garman," Boldt whispered, "and work from there. If Ben isn't hiding—"

"Then he's inside that storage unit," she completed for him.

Boldt looked exhausted. He said, "We wait him out. It's the safe way. We will not corner Garman in a place where he may be storing a lot of firepower. If his father's truck is in the storage area—and

I'm betting it is—we've got big problems, because he's going to leave here sometime tomorrow morning, ready to do a little window washing and set up the Santori house, believing it to be Martinelli's. We need a way to separate him from his truck and materials. We cannot move on him until he's away from that fuel."

"You won't get him away from that truck," she said.

"No," Boldt agreed. "That's *your* job. You figure it out." He added, "Stay here. I'm going to check on the backup."

Boldt walked off into the darkness.

BY THE time the inspiration came to her, Daphne had settled down onto the blacktop, knees into her chest, hidden in shadow. Boldt walked right past her.

"Here," she whispered. He pulled her up and led her around to the far side of the office, where they could talk.

"We have two north," he said, pointing, "and one south—five of us on the ground."

"Garman's there for the night," she speculated.

"Yes," Boldt agreed. "Until morning."

She said, "The time to do this is now, Lou." She believed if coaxed properly, Garman would give up. "The wild card is his father," she explained. "The son is doing this to prove something to his father. They both hate the mother. If we believe the husband, she had sex with strangers on a regular basis, sometimes in the presence of her son. Jonathan Garman is trying to one-up his father, show he can do what the father failed to do—kill the mother. Burn her to death. If we get Steven Garman down here, put him in front of that storage unit, Jonathan will walk out."

"No one but the bomb squad is going anywhere near that storage unit until Jonathan Garman is a mile away from here. This isn't productive, Daffy," Boldt said. "We're supposed to be focusing on how to get him as far away from the truck as possible."

In the silence a corporate jet came in low and loud overhead. It felt to her as if the ground shook. She thought about raiding the storage unit, how they could use the cover of a jet landing to make their move. But then she considered the idea of Ben caught in an inferno of purple flame rising hundreds of feet into the air.

"I know how to get him out of the truck," Daphne announced. "Fire. The one thing irresistible to Jonathan Garman is a fire."

CHAPTER TWELVE

IN THE hours between two a.m. and five a.m., sixty-seven patrol officers and twenty-four firemen, along with four Marshal Fives, organized into an instant task force whose sole mission was to burn an abandoned machine shop to the ground and divert morning traffic south of the International District so that it was required to pass within a city block of the fire. The building was scheduled for demolition and had been offered to the city—in exchange for tax breaks—for fire training.

From the moment Boldt proposed the operation, Lieutenant Shoswitz objected, claiming Boldt had yet to confirm the identity of the individual inside the storage unit. This hurdle was overcome at two twenty a.m., when Boldt, under advisement of the facility's manager, entered the U-Stor-It offices, disabled the security device, and confirmed that Jonny Babcock—a.k.a. Garman—rented unit 311, the same unit from which the light had come and the voice had been heard. That same unit, 311, went dark at one fifteen a.m., but the door never opened and no one ever left the property. At that point five different sets of eyes and a video camera using infrared night-sight technology had the unit under surveillance.

Boldt never experienced a moment of feeling tired. To the contrary, he had to slow himself down on several occasions simply to be understood. The nearly one hundred participants engaged in

Operation Inferno were his orchestra; Lou Boldt was the conductor. Shoswitz, Bahan, Fidler, and three FBI special agents, along with two dispatchers, worked out of the Seattle field office of the FBI. Dozens of radios and cellular phones were tied in to a central dispatch.

By six a.m. there were police officers in place posing as telephone linemen, street people, construction workers, and garbage collectors. Every major intersection along Airport Way was covered.

At eight a.m. the U-Stor-It office was opened by an FBI special agent, who took his place behind the desk inside as if it were part of his daily routine. At eight twelve a.m. the first report of activity at unit 311 was verified and delivered to Boldt over a radio earpiece.

A white pickup truck pulled out of unit 311 and stopped. A man wearing a sweatshirt hood drawn tightly around his head, eyes covered by sunglasses, was seen climbing out to lock the unit's door. Then he got back behind the wheel and drove north into the city.

"This is Birdman," reported a voice in Boldt's ear from a traffic helicopter being used for surveillance. "Looking down through the windshield, I'm not showing a hostage. In the back of the truck there appear to be two fifty-five-gallon drums and a variety of boxes. No tarp in place."

Fifty-five-gallon drums, Boldt thought. Either Garman had packed up shop or was planning an enormous hit.

Traffic moved slowly, Garman's position reported every fifteen to thirty seconds. At the abandoned machine shop, three ladder trucks and two pumpers stood by, lights flashing, hoses ready. Inside, the incendiary charges and detonator wire were double-checked.

Dressed in coveralls, Lou Boldt threw a pickax into a dirt hole in a vacant lot across from the machine shop. The three men around him, including Detective John LaMoia, also wore coveralls but were working shovels.

"Dig," Boldt said. "He's a half mile and closing."

LaMoia jumped on the shovel and dug. Boldt's hands were wet on the pickax's handle, but it had little to do with the light rain. His weapon weighed down the coveralls' right pocket.

WHEN GARMAN'S VEHICLE WAS a mile from the U-Stor-It facility, two members of the SPD bomb squad moved into place outside unit 311. They were accompanied by tech service officer Danny Kotch and psychologist Daphne Matthews.

Kotch worked flawlessly, feeding the cable of a fiber-optic camera under the gap in the garage door. Images of the unit's contents were revealed on the technician's tiny screen.

Daphne gasped as she saw Ben tucked into a ball in the corner, bound by a single rope. There was no gag in place, and she wondered why he hadn't called out.

"Ben, can you hear me?" she shouted.

A single eye angled to look for her. She burst into tears. Through a blur she said, "Hurry it up, would you? I want him out of there."

A plainclothes detective ran toward them, a radio in his hand. He shouted, "Matthews, they need you for the count."

The decision of when to light the machine shop was hers alone. Boldt knew she understood the dynamics of the psychology best, and insisted the call be hers. Daphne grabbed the radio. "Is the suspect within full visual range of the structure?" she inquired.

"A half mile and closing," the dispatcher informed her.

"When he's got the building fully in sight," she instructed, "torch it. He has to see it ignite, to *participate* in it. If he sees it go off, he'll stay to see them fight it."

"Another hundred yards," the dispatcher told her. "He'll have full visual in another hundred yards."

"WE'RE thirty seconds to ignition," Boldt heard in his earpiece. "Suspect is a quarter mile off and closing." With each intersection, Garman's position had been carefully reported.

The four cars in front of Garman's truck were all being driven by undercover members of the operation. The same had been intended for the traffic following the suspect's vehicle, but the first glitch occurred when a Chevrolet ran a red light and cut into the line immediately behind the pickup.

The ensuing radio traffic was heated.

CAR 1: Dispatch, we have a visitor. Some idiot just cut in.

SHOSWITZ: We need him out of there. Now.

DISPATCH: Okay. It's a bump and run by you, One. Make it a good collision, one he has to stop for. Williamson, you assist at the moment of impact. Get the civilian to safe cover. Copy?

The plainclothes officer behind the Chevy was to ram the car at the moment of the fire's ignition. He would then rush the driver, apologizing over the accident, as one of the detectives in the work crew went over as a "witness."

Boldt glanced up from his digging. The white pickup was advancing slowly in the bumper-to-bumper traffic. "Ten seconds," Boldt said, relaying the timing into his radio. "Five . . ."

THREE miles south of Garman's pickup truck, outside storage unit 311, the bomb squad's remote-control robot used a bolt cutter to sever the padlock on the unit's garage door. The robot's remote claw removed the lock and lifted the door.

Despite the reassurances that the unit was not wired, a collective breath was held. But the door came open without an explosion.

A fully padded man rolled under the door opening and inside the storage unit. Against all rules, Daphne Matthews broke through the restraining tape, ran forward, and rolled under the door right behind the bomb man.

At the first sound of dull explosions to the north, she pulled Ben into her arms and cradled him while her tears spilled into his hair.

"Paramedics!" Daphne shouted. The boy's lips were glued shut, and he seemed on the verge of passing out.

THE charges went off in a string of five. Six, counting the crunch of metal and glass as the Chevy was struck from behind.

The flames were instantaneous: huge blue and orange tongues licking up toward the sky. The traffic braked in unison as a giant plume of heat reached over four hundred feet into the air, the resulting column of smoke over ten times that.

Boldt leaned on his pickax, his eyes on the driver of that pickup. *Stay and watch it*, Boldt encouraged silently. Get out of the truck and watch. The burning building was a block and a half from traffic, but firemen were allowing pedestrians a closer look, having roped off a spot only half a block away. Of the seven people standing there watching, all were from law enforcement.

As part of the ruse, one of the four cars preceding Garman pulled over, and the driver climbed out and hurried toward the fire for a better look. Lead by example, Boldt thought. But to his horror Garman did not get out, electing to watch the fire from the truck. Some cars farther behind launched into a protest of honking.

The truck's wheels crept forward, as if Garman was to drive on. Boldt could feel the man drawn to the fire but concerned over his cargo and the job at hand. Boldt pleaded silently for him to stay. The fire roared as firemen charged.

Jonathan Garman pulled his truck over to the shoulder—he was getting out! Garman stepped down onto the pavement and spun his head forward and back, assessing his situation. Worried about the parking? Boldt wondered. Feeling something wrong? The suspect pushed the door shut and walked toward the front of his truck, toward a better view of the burn.

LaMoia, carrying his shovel—a worker fascinated by the fire— ran past Boldt, as if going for a closer look. Garman took no notice. His neck craned back and his head lifted up in eerie slow motion, and he drank in the power of the fire. The magnificence. He stepped several feet in front of the truck. His synthetic face filled with a childish glee as he rocked back and forth in joy. The fire erupted into a shower of flame, spark, and ash, and Boldt thought he saw Garman's body convulse, his awkward mouth shaped into the curve of a laugh.

Garman's excited eyes swept briefly over the scene behind him, where, in a failed attempt to convince the driver of the Chevy to retreat, the undercover cop had resorted to dragging the bystander to the ground in anticipation of a fire fight. In the process the cop's coat flew open and his gun holster showed.

Garman's elation collapsed. Realization stung him. His eyes registered the fifteen people immediately in his vicinity, and he seemed to acknowledge that every one was law enforcement. He backed up two steps toward the truck and the fuel it contained.

Gripping his pistol, Boldt launched himself in the direction of the suspect. Over the radio-transmitter earpiece he heard a sharp-shooter announce a line-of-sight shot. Shoswitz's voice gave the order to take him.

The shot went straight through Garman's shoulder and sprayed blood onto the truck, but he never felt it. He swung open the truck door and jumped in behind the wheel.

The pickup lurched ahead, smashing into the car parked in front of it. Boldt was three strides from the truck as Garman cut the wheel and jumped the sidewalk. The driver's side window blew out from another sniper attempt. Boldt jumped for the truck, his toes catching the running board, his right hand losing his gun as he clawed to hold on.

Garman shoved down the accelerator. The back tires squealed as he drove through a weedy vacant lot toward the raging fire.

Boldt did not know that the fuel in the truck was enough to consume over three city blocks; he knew only that Miles and Sarah needed a father, now more than ever, and that their father was riding a pickup truck toward hell.

The suspect aimed his blank white face at the sergeant, brown eyes recessed behind sculpted plastic skin. For that instant something sparked between them. Boldt reached for the gearshift, but Garman struck him hard. The sergeant shoved himself deeper into the window. Pushing the driver across the seat, Boldt got his arm inside the steering wheel, making it impossible to turn the wheel. As they bounced through the lot, Boldt's head struck the ceiling, and the pickup altered course just far enough to crash into one of the pumpers. It was like hitting a brick wall. They careened off to the right, heading once again for the burning building. Boldt felt his arm snap. His head swam with the pain, and for an instant he couldn't catch his breath.

They were headed straight for the front door of the burning building. I don't belong here, Boldt thought. It's not my time.

Garman clawed at Boldt's face, trying to drive him back. Garman's foot found the accelerator, and the truck surged forward.

Overcoming the pain, Boldt heaved his broken arm farther through the wheel, fingers fishing for the key. Garman's attention was fixed on the white bucket on the floor. It registered in Boldt that rocket fuel was inside it. The driver craned to reach for it, but Boldt grabbed the sweatshirt hood, pulled hard, and swung the man's head on the end of the tether back and forth. The man's right ear pounded into the rear panel of glass. Garman cried out and grabbed for the pain.

Boldt heaved his broken arm forward. His fingers groped and found the key, and he twisted.

The engine died.

The truck grumbled to a stop fifteen yards from the burning building. The paint on the hood bubbled and blistered from the heat. Inside, the truck was instantly an oven.

Fire hoses trained hundreds of gallons of water on the truck, with a force so powerful that Boldt was lifted up and driven farther into the cab, fully atop Garman. Boldt felt his legs grabbed by strong hands. "Hold tight!" a voice called. The pickup rocked onto two wheels and slid sideways as a fire truck collided with it and drove it away from the fire, the man holding Boldt never letting go.

The truck stopped, now twenty yards from the inferno. Loud voices shouted orders in what sounded to Boldt like total chaos. He felt Garman dragged out from underneath him. "Hold him!" Boldt shouted. "Hold on to him!"

As Garman hit the ground, he left his rescuers with only his sweatshirt in their heavily gloved hands. He rolled twice, and Boldt would later swear to Daphne that he and the suspect locked glances in the midst of one of these revolutions. He would swear there was nothing in those eyes: no remorse, no fear, no life.

Jonny Garman came to his feet. He looked once at the wall of armed police rushing him, glanced toward Boldt, turned, and ran at a full sprint into the burning building. Already engulfed in flames before his screams ripped toward the sky, he disappeared into the pulsing orange light.

APPROPRIATELY, it was raining. Daphne was glad for that because it would disguise her tears.

"You don't need to come in or anything," Ben said.

"I'll just see you to the door," she said.

It hurt her to see him so excited to be reunited with Emily. How she wished he might change his mind and beg to stay with her. But the finest things pass through your life, she thought, like migratory birds. They leave you with a glimpse of beauty and pass on.

Reading her thoughts as they sat in the dull glare of a red light, the windshield wipers working like a metronome, he said, "It's not like we won't see each other."

She reached out and took his hand in hers. When the light changed, she pulled away from him and drove on, feeling his intense gaze fixed upon her. Perhaps he had felt it too. Perhaps.

"You know, Ben, sometimes a person comes along in your life, a special person, and without knowing it, they show you something about yourself, they point you in a direction that maybe you didn't see until they came along. You know?"

"I guess so," he answered.

"What I mean to say is, you are that person for me. You helped me in ways I can't explain, I guess. Good stuff," she said.

"I don't see what I did except screw everything up."

"Watch the language."

He bit away a grin. "You're okay, D. I know you did a ton of stuff for me—to make this happen with Emily and all. And, well, it's really cool, is all."

"If you ever, *ever*, need *anything*, you had better call me," she said, trying to avoid crying. "You have a lot of love in you, Ben. Don't be afraid to share it." She finally dared look at him, and he was crying too. Selfishly this made her happy.

She pulled to a stop in front of the purple house. He reached into the back seat for his backpack and books. "You and Susan are going to help me move, right?"

"Right." She saw Emily open the door and wave. "Maybe I won't get out," she said. She abandoned any effort to stop the tears now. The wipers sounded peaceful, their rhythm soothing.

"Well," Ben said. He leaned forward and kissed her on the cheek, his excitement over seeing Emily already winning out. Daphne nodded and sniffled. He popped open the door and jumped out.

"Ben!" she called out sharply, sounding like a wire breaking.

Out in the rain, Ben leaned his head down into the car.

"Tell her to paint the damn house," Daphne said. She found a smile at last.

"Watch your language," Ben replied. But his expression said it all. She would remember that look for a lifetime. Cherish it.

He pushed the door shut and hurried off through the rain.

THE Dahlia Lounge was crowded. Boldt and Liz sat on two stools up by the receptionist as they waited for a table. She was drinking fruit juice. Boldt, uncharacteristically, was drinking straight vodka. She looked like a million dollars. His cast itched.

"He had moved all his stuff out, probably because if the kid talked, we could locate him. He had no desire to hurt the kid."

"It was two weeks ago." She studied him. For two weeks he had lain awake petting her hair as she slept. For two weeks they had said things they had always wanted to say. They had talked about why it took something so severe to bring two people to such rich honesty. He believed it unfair. She believed it a blessing.

The pain was worse. They were taking an evening out while they still had one to take.

"What about the boy?" she asked.

"Daphne pushed hard. He gets to be with the psychic short term, maybe long term. It's a good thing."

"Yes," she agreed. They clinked glasses.

"What's this dinner about?" she asked.

"Can't we just go out to dinner?"

"No. Not here. Not like this. What's it about?"

He snorted and looked to the drink for courage. "I'm going to put in for lieutenant."

She leaned over and kissed his cheek. When she reached up to take off the lipstick, Boldt leaned away.

"No," he said. "I want to keep it."

"It looks kind of silly."

"Good," he said. He lifted his glass and ordered another vodka.

"I'm driving," she said.

"You're driving," he agreed.

They looked into each other's eyes. Liz eventually couldn't fight off the smile, and Boldt joined her.

"Crazy, huh?" she said.

"Yeah. Weird." Boldt felt tears at the back of his throat. He fought against them.

"We'll help each other through it." She reached down and took his hand in hers and squeezed hard, tears in both their eyes.

But Boldt managed the smile that time. He realized that was how it was going to be, trading back and forth, the both of them. "A lot of this lately," he confessed.

"Yeah. Good for the tear ducts," she offered, blinking.

"Scared?" he asked, his voice trembling.

"Yes," she answered. "You bet I am." Her lips quivered, and she looked to him for some answer that he didn't have.

"Me too," he whispered to the most beautiful wife in the world.

ABOUT THE AUTHORS

BARBARA DELINSKY

In 1979 Barbara Delinsky, the wife of a lawyer and the mother of three young sons, read an article in the Boston *Globe* about writers of romance novels. Intrigued, she read thirty in the next month, then sat down and wrote one of her own. It would become the first of more than sixty books she would publish in the ensuing years.

Delinsky's sons are now in their twenties, but they return often to the Massachusetts home where they grew up—their mother's very own woman's place.

DANIEL SILVA

A veteran journalist, Daniel Silva is the chief Washington producer for CNN, responsible for such popular programs as *Crossfire* and *Evans & Novak*. But he'd always wanted to write a novel, and in 1994 he began fishing around for a plot. "It was the fiftieth anniversary of D-day," he says. "The Washington *Post* did a big piece on Operation Mulberry. I found the seed for the novel there." Silva is married to NBC news correspondent Jamie Gangel. The couple have two children.

LILIAN JACKSON BRAUN

Since Lilian Jackson Braun began publishing her best-selling Cat Who . . . mysteries nineteen books ago, her fictional Moose County has become so familiar to her legions of fans that many are convinced these settings really exist. She tells of one reader from Germany who wrote asking for directions to Pickax so he could visit. As for her characters, Braun says, "There's a little bit of me in every one." And of course, like her debonair hero Qwilleran, she adores cats.

RIDLEY PEARSON

It's no accident that tree climbing plays a big role in *Beyond Recognition*—it's one of Ridley Pearson's favorite pastimes. But Pearson's talents are not limited to shinning up trees and writing best sellers. For years he played and wrote songs for a folk-rock band, and he also composed an orchestral score for a documentary film. Now, when he's not writing suspense novels, Pearson—who lives with his wife in Hailey, Idaho—still jams with a "garage" rock band. And climbs trees every chance he gets.

The volumes in this series are issued
every two to three months. The typical volume
contains four outstanding books in condensed
form. None of the selections in any volume has
appeared in *Reader's Digest* itself. Any reader
may receive this service by writing
The Reader's Digest Association, Inc.,
Pleasantville, N.Y. 10570
or by calling 800-234-9000.

ACKNOWLEDGMENTS

Pages 6–7: photo © Bill Binzen/The Stock Market.
Pages 150–151: illustration by Michael Dudash.
Pages 320–321: illustration by Liz Kenyon. Pages 323, 335, 345, 360, 373, 385, 396, 407:
illustrations by Cheryl Taub.
Pages 418–419: photo by Robert Milazzo.